Immodest Proposals

THE COMPLETE SCIENCE FICTION OF

WILLIAM TENN

VOLUME I

Introduction by Connie Willis

edited by James A. Mann and Mary C. Tabasko

The NESFA Press
Post Office Box 809
Framingham, MA 01701
2001

International Standard Book Number 1-886778-19-1

PUBLICATION ACKNOWLEDGEMENTS

The Afterwords appear here for the first time, copyright © 2001 by Philip Klass.

"Alexander the Bait" first appeared in *Astounding Science Fiction*, May 1946.

"Bernie the Scheherazade: The Spellbinding Short Stories of William Tenn" appears here for the first time.

"Brooklyn Project" first appeared in *Planet Stories*, Fall 1948.

"Child's Play" first appeared in *Astounding Science Fiction*, March 1947.

"Consulate" first appeared in *Thrilling Wonder Stories*, June 1948.

"The Custodian" first appeared in *If*, November 1953.

"The Dark Star" first appeared in *Galaxy*, September 1957.

"The Deserter" first appeared in *Star Science Fiction Stories*, 1953.

"Down Among the Dead Men" first appeared in *Galaxy*, June 1954.

"Eastward Ho!" first appeared in *The Magazine of Fantasy & Science Fiction*, October, 1958.

"Firewater" first appeared in *Astounding Science Fiction*, February 1952.

"The Flat-Eyed Monster" first appeared in *Galaxy*, August 1955.

"Generation of Noah" first appeared in *Suspense*, 1951.

"The Ghost Standard" first appeared in *Playboy*, December 1994.

"The Jester" first appeared in *Thrilling Wonder Stories*, August 1951.

"The Last Bounce" first appeared in *Fantastic Adventures*, September 1950.

"The Lemon-Green Spaghetti-Loud Dynamite-Dribble Day" first appeared in *Cavalier*, January 1967.

"The Liberation of Earth" first appeared in *Future Science Fiction*, May 1953.

"Lisbon Cubed" first appeared in *Galaxy*, October 1958.

"A Man of Family" first appeared in *The Human Angle*, 1956.

"The Masculinist Revolt" first appeared in *The Magazine of Fantasy & Science Fiction*, August, 1965.

"My Mother Was a Witch" first appeared in *P.S.*, 1966.

"Null-P" first appeared in *Worlds Beyond*, January 1951.

"On Venus, Have We Got a Rabbi" first appeared in *Wandering Stars: An Anthology of Jewish Fantasy & Science Fiction*, 1974.

"Party of the Two Parts" first appeared in *Galaxy*, August 1954.

"Project Hush" first appeared in *Galaxy*, February 1954.

"The Servant Problem" first appeared in *Galaxy*, April 1955.

"The Sickness" first appeared in *Infinity*, November 1955.

"The Tenants" first appeared in *The Magazine of Fantasy & Science Fiction*, April 1954.

"Time in Advance" first appeared in *Galaxy*, August 1956.

"Venus and the Seven Sexes" first appeared in *The Girl with the Hungry Eyes and Other Stories*, 1949.

"Venus Is a Man's World" first appeared in *Galaxy*, July 1951.

"Wednesday's Child" first appeared in *Fantastic Universe*, January 1956.

"Winthrop Was Stubborn" first appeared in *Galaxy*, August 1957, as "Time Waits for Winthrop."

Dedication

To Mort (again)
   Because he was there
   at the beginnings

And to Fruma (again)
   Because she's there
   now and forever

Acknowledgements

This book, like all NESFA Press books, was put together through the efforts of many volunteers. Bill Shawcross of Rotten Apple Press and Rick Katze did most of the scanning. Bill also did a lot of proofreading. Mark Olson helped get the contract approved, unearthed stories, dealt with the printer, and in general provided a lot of support. Eileen Dougherty, Scot Taylor, and Roz Treger proofed most of the book. George Flynn, copyeditor extraordinaire, thoroughly examined all the stories. Bob Weinberg and Alex Eisenstein arranged for a reproducible copy of the cover painting. Kevin Riley designed and produced the dust jacket. Adina Klass helped coordinate our getting material, and Fruma Klass lent an editorial hand. Teresa Nielsen Hayden and Terry McGarry provided valuable editorial advice. Laurie Mann and Leslie Mann each pitched in. Christina Schulman provided heat and some last-minute typing. Finally, a number of colleagues in NESFA, IBM, and elsewhere looked over many sample page layouts, providing us with a user test of the book design.

James A. Mann
Mary C. Tabasko
Pittsburgh, PA
December 2000

CONTENTS

Immodest
Proposals

Bernie the Scheherazade

The Spellbinding Short Stories of William Tenn

Connie Willis

WARNING: Do not read this introduction until *after* you have read the William Tenn stories in this book. I've tried to be good and not give away endings, but it's impossible to talk about Tenn stories without talking about plot, and watching the plot unfold—and then wrap itself around your neck and strangle you—is one of the chief pleasures of reading a Tenn story.

So, go read the stories in this book, one at a time (like chocolates) or all at once (like chocolates) and then come back and talk about them with me. Read "Bernie the Faust"❝ first. It's my favorite. Or...no, wait. Read "Lisbon Cubed" first. No, "Winthrop Was Stubborn." No, "Eastward Ho!" No...

LATER: Okay, you're back. Now we can talk. When William Tenn (really Philip Klass) spoke at the Science Fiction Writers of America awards banquet in 1999—he had been named Writer Emeritus, an honor awarded to under-appreciated treasures of the field—he had the entire roomful of writers, editors, and agents rolling on the floor. And hoping fervently that Phil didn't know any stories about them.

That's because he knows everything about everyone in the entire field. He was part of science fiction in the legendary Golden Age, and he knew Fritz Leiber, Clifford Simak, and Algis Budrys, worked for John W. Campbell and the reclusive H.L. Gold, played poker with Robert Sheckley, was friends with Judith Merril, Theodore Sturgeon, and Daniel Keyes. And he has no hesitation about telling hilarious (and often scandalous) stories about all of them.

He was telling dozens of them that night at the awards banquet, and it was obvious the audience could have gone on listening to him all night. Charles N. Brown of *Locus* magazine says Phil Klass (really William Tenn) is "the Scheherazade of science fiction," and Brown's talking not only about Tenn's speaking, but his writing. Because although

❝ The pieces so marked will appear in Volume II of this collection, scheduled for July 2001 from NESFA Press.

Tenn is known for his biting wit and incisive irony, Tenn is first and foremost a story-teller.

His bio notes list acting, waiting tables, teaching at Penn State, and editing magazines and a classic anthology (*Children of Wonder*) as jobs he's held, but they were, as he says, merely something to "fill up the time between stories and novels."

Those stories are known for their intricate plots, clever twists, and indelible characters: shady shysters, cut-rate Frankensteins, gypsies, sadly mistaken rulers of the world, advertising executives. And aliens.

Tenn's aliens are perhaps his best characters: the black-tentacled suitcases of "The Flat-Eyed Monster," the impossibly tall Mr. Tohu, "bent forward at the hips and backwards at the shoulders," who you could have sworn popped Mr. Bohu in his pocket before departing, the seven-foot snails Andy and Dandy, the huge invaders of "The Men in the Walls."◄ Tenn's aliens are always, in the words of George Zebrowski, "properly terrifying, puzzling, and *other*."

Tenn's most famous for his fiendishly clever endings. Some critics have called them "trick endings," but they're far more than mere tricks. In the first place, the word "trick" is way too mild for endings that come up and hit you in the face like a rake whose handle you've inadvertently stepped on. In the second place, they're an integral part of the story, not just something tacked on for a cheap surprise.

A good example is "Bernie the Faust," about a con man who meets his match. The story's not only about a con, it *is* a con, and we fall for it hook, line and sinker. I remember vividly the first time I read it, I reached the point where the alien with the dirty tongue mentioned wanting to buy the Golden Gate Bridge and thought smugly, "*I* know what Tenn's up to here," and spent the next few pages feeling smugly superior. And then I got to the ending, and found I'd been taken in just like Bernie, and we'd both been left holding the extraterrestrial bag.

But it's not just the endings that are different from what we expect, it's the stories themselves. In "The Tenants," what seems to be a whimsical fantasy turns into a nightmarish trap. "The Liberation of Earth" is unlike any first-contact story you've ever read, and only Tenn could concoct a horror story out of lollipop trees and cotton candy clouds.

We're not the only ones surprised. When H.L. Gold asked Tenn for a "slam-bang, parsec-ricocheting" space opera for *Galaxy*, Tenn responded with "Down Among the Dead Men," which in a way was exactly what Gold had asked for, although he had to have been stunned by what he got. The reader is, too. It's a story about zombies and intergalactic war, but it's utterly original and has a depth of emotion you'd never expect to find in such a hard-bitten tale.

It's ironic, though, that "Down Among the Dead Men" and the brilliant "The Liberation of Earth" are Tenn's two most famous works because they're both serious stories, and Tenn is primarily known as a humorous writer. Or perhaps it's not all that surprising. Science fiction (and literature in general) has always had problems realizing just what a serious business comedy is, and how difficult it is to write. And Tenn's comic stories look effortless and light, even though they're incredibly complex.

Stories like "Me, Myself, and I,"["The Flat-Eyed Monster," and "Betelgeuse Bridge,"[are full of amusing situations and funny lines. People emerge from a crowded subway train "somewhat like grape pips being expectorated," the Gtetans look on the Law as "a delightful problem in circumvention rather than as a way of life," and the time-traveler in "Flirgleflip" describes the past he finds himself in as "a scene from Mark Twain, Washington Irving, or Ernest Hemingway—one of the authors of that period, in any case."

Even Tenn's titles are funny: "The Lemon-Green Spaghetti-Loud Dynamite Dribble Day" and "On Venus, Have We Got a Rabbi." Many of them, like "The Human Angle"[and "The Servant Problem" have a barbed double meaning that only becomes clear after reading the story, and one of them, "The Discovery of Morniel Mathaway,"[has a *triple* meaning.

And the stories that follow those titles are hilarious. Probably my favorite (I have about fifteen favorite Tenn stories) is "Party of the Two Parts," about an ameboid alien who sells pornographic pictures to an earthling who promptly puts them in a biology textbook, and the ensuing legal mess. After an ameba's undergone fission, exactly who do you charge with the crime? And what exactly counts as pornography anyway? As the amebas ask, "Are the most sacred and intimate details of our sex life to be shamelessly flaunted from one end of the universe to the other?"

But even though "Party of the Two Parts" is laugh-out-loud funny, it's also thought-provoking. (It's no accident that the quotation at the beginning of Tenn's short story collection *Of All Possible Worlds* is from *Candide*, and involves a discussion of "effects and causes, this best of all possible worlds, the origin of evil, the nature of the soul, and pre-established harmony.") All of Tenn's stories raise serious issues about us and the world we live in.

The nightmarish situation the people in "A Man of Family" find themselves in raises important questions about population control and our obsession with status. "The Flat-Eyed Monster" makes us look at the standard bug-eyed monster story from an entirely different point of view and makes us not only wonder what the monster was really doing when it carried the girl off, but whether the endings of all those bug-eyed monster stories were really as happy as we thought they were.

Even in a straightforward "Boo!" story like "The Human Angle,"[the little girl's comment—"I mean, if a person's a vampire, what can they do about it? I mean, they can't help themselves, can they?"—seems to linger in the air, raising troubling questions about ourselves and about free will. "Tenn's stories are always a bit disturbing at some level, even when they are breathlessly readable, amusing, or cute," George Zebrowski, writing in *Twentieth Century Science Fiction Writers*, says.

Perhaps Tenn's most thought-provoking stories are his tales of first contact with aliens, which he calls his "Here Comes Civilization!" stories. They include "Betelgeuse Bridge," "Firewater," "The Men in the Walls," and "The Liberation of Earth," and they are nothing at all like the standard invading-monster or noble-aliens-who-have-come-to-share-their-advanced-technology-with-us stories.

If they're technologically advanced enough to get here, Tenn reasons, then they're advanced enough to roll right over us, and he shows us how, with scenes that make us think about Vietnam and the Warsaw ghetto and even the island of Manhattan, with us as the natives giving away the whole show for a handful of beads.

They're stories that make us think, but we're not the only ones thinking. Tenn is, too, about human foibles, about the ironies of life, sometimes even about the loose ends in his own stories. In "Child's Play," an all-too-plausible Frankenstein story, the hero accidentally receives a toy "Bild-a-Man" kit from the future and proceeds to play with it. His first clumsy attempt results in an amateurish baby, which he leaves on an orphanage doorstep. Then, troubled by the consequences of the hero's actions (and his own), he wrote another story, "Wednesday's Child," about what happened to that abandoned baby.

That meticulous attention to detail reflects the seriousness with which he takes his writing. Anyone who doubts his commitment to his writing, or to science fiction, should read his essay, "On the Fiction in Science Fiction."[*] In it he shares his "passionate belief in science fiction as a means of literary experience that has particular validity and significance in this age," an experience with "an infinity of concept as well as cosmos" where the author is limited only by "his skills, his sensitivity, and the thematic range of his intellect."

But his love of science fiction doesn't mean he feels all warm and fuzzy toward it. He's sharply critical of its follies and shortcomings, and his stories are often angry or sarcastic responses to its silly conventions and ill-thought-out premises.

"The Flat-Eyed Monster" is clearly a response to pulp space operas, "The Servant Problem" to all those absolute-ruler-of-the-universe stories, "The Discovery of Morniel Mathaway" to the fantasy where someone goes back in time and meets Leonardo da Vinci.

Quite a few of Tenn's stories are about time travel. The time-travel story was a flourishing sub-genre in the fifties, usually revolving (sometimes literally) around the closed time loop, in which the hero goes back in time and, using his knowledge of the future, proceeds to invent that future or else becomes the historical figure he went back to study. Such stories were great fun—and in the hands of masters like Michael Moorcock ("Behold the Man") and Ward Moore (*Bring the Jubilee*), classics.

But many of them were no more than elaborate chess games with no connection to reality or logic. It's these Tenn is clearly responding to in stories like "Me, Myself, and I," "It Ends with a Flicker,"[*] and "The Brooklyn Project," in which, as Fritz Leiber says, a trip to the past "changes everything in the universe except (universal!) human nature with all its wearisome foibles and absurdities."

And Tenn's logic is unassailable. He knows full well that if we had time travel, we wouldn't be able to resist messing with history. And that if we accidentally messed it up and went back to fix it, we'd have to contend not only with the mess, but with the self (or selves) who had gone back earlier. And our fantasy of meeting the historical figure we most admire is probably doomed to disappointment, human nature being what it is.

Tenn knows a *lot* about human nature. He knows that the person most likely to play Frankenstein is not a tortured genius but a person with an only partially formed personality himself, that revenge is a hard emotion to hang onto, that humans are frequently greedy, dishonest, easily gulled, and out for the main chance.

This last opinion is what gets Tenn his reputation as a cynic. He's described as "bitter," "fundamentally a pessimist," and having "an essentially bleak view of man."

Well, of course it's bleak. Who do you know that knows a lot about human nature and who has a *high* opinion of humankind? But I don't agree that Tenn is cynical. Bernie the Faust may be a low-life, but he's not venial enough to sell out his planet. The hero of "Time in Advance" doesn't commit murder, even though he's got ample justification and has already served his time. And the sergeant in "Down Among the Dead Men" is a far more decent person than most of us would be in his place, and so are the zombies.

True, Frankenstein gets his, and so does the reporter in "The Human Angle," but they both deserve it, and it's nearly always the characters' lust or acquisitiveness or conviction that they're smarter than everybody else that gets them in the messes they find themselves in.

And many of Tenn's stories end far more happily than we expect. Lisa isn't given up for adoption in "A Man of Family," and the custodian manages not only to save the kid but the Mona Lisa and a piece of the Sistine Chapel.

Some of his less-than-likeable narrators may also have been a response to the stalwart heroes and flawless heroines the genre is full of. And so many of his stories, like "Everybody Loves Irving Bommer" and "Venus and the Seven Sexes" were written in such a spirit of pure fun they couldn't have been created by a humanity-hater.

Tenn's stories are witty, clever, thought-provoking, ironic, intensely intelligent, touching, and hilarious. And too few and far between. Most of the stories in this collection were written in the fifties and sixties, and, until now, have been hard to find. I'm overjoyed that they will all be in print again and all in one place (though it's also delightful to come across one in an anthology when you least expect it, and having him seduce or surprise or swindle you all over again), but I wish there were more of them.

And I wish he'd write some new ones. (Are you listening, Phil?) I think there's an excellent chance he might. As Damon Knight said of Tenn, he "won't stop till he's had the last word."

I hope so. Like Scheherazade's sultan, I could go on listening to him all night.

ॐ

Aliens, Aliens, Aliens

Firewater

The hairiest, dirtiest and oldest of the three visitors from Arizona scratched his back against the plastic of the webfoam chair. "Insinuations are lavender nearly," he remarked by way of opening the conversation.

His two companions—the thin young man with dripping eyes, and the woman whose good looks were marred chiefly by incredibly decayed teeth—giggled and relaxed. The thin young man said "Gabble, gabble, honk!" under his breath, and the other two nodded emphatically.

Greta Seidenheim looked up from the tiny stenographic machine resting on a pair of the most exciting knees her employer had been able to find in Greater New York. She swiveled her blonde beauty at him. "That too, Mr. Hebster?"

The president of Hebster Securities, Inc., waited until the memory of her voice ceased to tickle his ears; he had much clear thinking to do. Then he nodded and said resonantly, "That too, Miss Seidenheim. Close phonetic approximations of the gabble-honk and remember to indicate when it sounds like a question and when like an exclamation."

He rubbed his recently manicured fingernails across the desk drawer containing his fully loaded Parabellum. Check. The communication buttons with which he could summon any quantity of Hebster Securities personnel up to the nine hundred working at present in the Hebster Building lay some eight inches from the other hand. Check. And there were the doors here, the doors there, behind which his uniformed bodyguard stood poised to burst in at a signal which would blaze before them the moment his right foot came off the tiny spring set in the floor. *And* check.

Algernon Hebster could talk business—even with Primeys.

Courteously, he nodded at each one of his visitors from Arizona; he smiled ruefully at what the dirty shapeless masses they wore on their feet were doing to the almost calf-deep rug that had been woven specially for his private office. He had greeted them when Miss Seidenheim had escorted them in. They had laughed in his face.

"Suppose we rattle off some introductions. You know me. I'm Hebster, Algernon Hebster—you asked for me specifically at the desk in the lobby. If it's important to the conversation, my secretary's name is Greta Seidenheim. And you, sir?"

He had addressed the old fellow, but the thin young man leaned forward in his seat and held out a taut, almost transparent hand. "Names?" he inquired. "Names are round if not revealed. Consider names. How many names? Consider names, *reconsider* names!"

3

The woman leaned forward too, and the smell from her diseased mouth reached Hebster even across the enormous space of his office. "Rabble and reaching and all the upward clash," she intoned, spreading her hands as if in agreement with an obvious point. "Emptiness derogating itself into infinity—"

"Into duration," the older man corrected.

"Into infinity," the woman insisted.

"Gabble, gabble, honk?" the young man queried bitterly.

"Listen!" Hebster roared. "When I asked for—"

The communicator buzzed and he drew a deep breath and pressed a button. His receptionist's voice boiled out rapidly, fearfully:

"I remember your orders, Mr. Hebster, but those two men from the UM Special Investigating Commission are here again and they look as if they mean business. I mean they look as if they'll make trouble."

"Yost and Funatti?"

"Yes, sir. From what they said to each other, I think they know you have three Primeys in there. They asked me what are you trying to do—deliberately inflame the Firsters? They said they're going to invoke full supranational powers and force an entry if you don't—"

"Stall them."

"But, Mr. Hebster, the *UM Special Investigating*—"

"Stall them, I said. Are you a receptionist or a swinging door? Use your imagination, Ruth. You have a nine-hundred-man organization and a ten-million-dollar corporation at your disposal. You can stage any kind of farce in that outer office you want—up to and including the deal where some actor made up to look like me walks in and drops dead at their feet. Stall them and I'll nod a bonus at you. *Stall them.*" He clicked off, looked up.

His visitors, at least, were having a fine time. They had turned to face each other in a reeking triangle of gibberish. Their voices rose and fell argumentatively, pleadingly, decisively; but all Algernon Hebster's ears could register of what they said were very many sounds similar to *gabble* and an occasional, indisputable *honk!*

His lips curled contempt inward. Humanity prime! *These* messes? Then he lit a cigarette and shrugged. Oh, well. Humanity prime. And business is business.

Just remember they're not supermen, he told himself. *They may be dangerous, but they're not supermen. Not by a long shot. Remember that epidemic of influenza that almost wiped them out, and how you diddled those two other Primeys last month. They're not supermen, but they're not humanity either. They're just different.*

He glanced at his secretary and approved. Greta Seidenheim clacked away on her machine as if she were recording the curtest, the tritest of business letters. He wondered what system she was using to catch the intonations. Trust Greta, though, she'd do it.

"Gabble, honk! Gabble, gabble, gabble, honk, honk. Gabble, honk, gabble, gabble, honk? Honk."

What had precipitated all this conversation? He'd only asked for their names. Didn't they use names in Arizona? Surely, they knew that it was customary here. They claimed to know at least as much as he about such matters.

Maybe it was something else that had brought them to New York this time—maybe something about the Aliens? He felt the short hairs rise on the back of his neck and he smoothed them down self-consciously.

Trouble was it was so *easy* to learn their language. It was such a very simple matter to be able to understand them in these talkative moments. Almost as easy as falling off a log—or jumping off a cliff.

Well, his time was limited. He didn't know how long Ruth could hold the UM investigators in his outer office. Somehow he had to get a grip on the meeting again without offending them in any of the innumerable, highly dangerous ways in which Primeys could be offended.

He rapped the desk top—gently. The gabble-honk stopped short at the hyphen. The woman rose slowly.

"On this question of names," Hebster began doggedly, keeping his eyes on the woman, "since you people claim—"

The woman writhed agonizingly for a moment and sat down on the floor. She smiled at Hebster. With her rotted teeth, the smile had all the brilliance of a dead star.

Hebster cleared his throat and prepared to try again.

"If you want names," the older man said suddenly, "you can call me Larry."

The president of Hebster Securities shook himself and managed to say "Thanks" in a somewhat weak but not too surprised voice. He looked at the thin young man.

"You can call me Theseus." The young man looked sad as he said it.

"Theseus? Fine!" One thing about Primeys, when you started clicking with them, you really moved along. But *Theseus!* Wasn't that just like a Primey? Now the woman, and they could begin.

They were all looking at the woman, even Greta with a curiosity which had sneaked up past her beauty-parlor glaze.

"Name," the woman whispered to herself. "Name a name."

Oh, no, Hebster groaned. *Let's not stall here.*

Larry evidently had decided that enough time had been wasted. He made a suggestion to the woman. "Why not call yourself Moe?"

The young man—Theseus, it was now—also seemed to get interested in the problem. "Rover's a good name," he announced helpfully.

"How about Gloria?" Hebster asked desperately.

The woman considered. "Moe, Rover, Gloria," she mused. "Larry, Theseus, Seidenheim, Hebster, me." She seemed to be running a total.

Anything might come out, Hebster knew. But at least they were not acting snobbish any more: they were talking down on his level now. Not only no gabble-honk, but none of this sneering double-talk which was almost worse. At least they were making sense—of a sort.

"For the purposes of this discussion," the woman said at last, "my name will be…will be— My name *is* S.S. Lusitania."

"Fine!" Hebster roared, letting the word he'd kept bubbling on his lips burst out. "That's a *fine* name. Larry, Theseus and…er, S.S. Lusitania. Fine bunch of people. Sound. Let's get down to business. You came here on business, I take it?"

"Right," Larry said. "We heard about you from two others who left home a month ago to come to New York. They talked about you when they got back to Arizona."

"They did, eh? I hoped they would."

Theseus slid off his chair and squatted next to the woman who was making pluck-ing motions at the air. "They talked about you," he repeated. "They said you treated them very well, that you showed them as much respect as a thing like you could gen-erate. They also said you cheated them."

"Oh, well, Theseus." Hebster spread his manicured hands. "I'm a businessman."

"You're a businessman," S.S. Lusitania agreed, getting to her feet stealthily and taking a great swipe with both hands at something invisible in front of her face. "And here, in this spot, at this moment, so are we. You can have what we've brought, but you'll pay for it. And don't think you can cheat *us*."

Her hands, cupped over each other, came down to her waist. She pulled them apart suddenly and a tiny eagle fluttered out. It flapped toward the fluorescent panels glowing in the ceiling. Its flight was hampered by the heavy, striped shield upon its breast, by the bunch of arrows it held in one claw, by the olive branch it grasped with the other. It turned its miniature bald head and gasped at Algernon Hebster, then began to drift rapidly down to the rug. Just before it hit the floor, it disappeared.

Hebster shut his eyes, remembering the strip of bunting that had fallen from the eagle's beak when it had turned to gasp. There had been words printed on the bunting, words too small to see at the distance, but he was sure the words would have read "*E Pluribus Unum.*" He was as certain of that as he was of the necessity of acting unconcerned over the whole incident, as unconcerned as the Primeys. Professor Kleimbocher said Primeys were mental drunkards. But why did they give everyone else the D.T.s?

He opened his eyes. "Well," he said, "what have you to sell?"

Silence for a moment. Theseus seemed to forget the point he was trying to make; S.S. Lusitania stared at Larry.

Larry scratched his right side through heavy, stinking cloth.

"Oh, an infallible method for defeating anyone who attempts to apply the *reductio ad absurdum* to a reasonable proposition you advance." He yawned smugly and be-gan scratching his left side.

Hebster grinned because he was feeling so good. "No. Can't use it."

"Can't use it?" The old man was trying hard to look amazed. He shook his head. He stole a sideways glance at S.S. Lusitania.

She smiled again and wriggled to the floor. "Larry still isn't talking a language you can understand, Mr. Hebster," she cooed, very much like a fertilizer factory being friendly. "We came here with something we know you need badly. Very badly."

"Yes?" *They're like those two Primeys last month,* Hebster exulted: *they don't know what's good and what isn't. Wonder if their masters would know. Well, and if they did—who does business with Aliens?*

"We…have," she spaced the words carefully, trying pathetically for a dramatic effect, "a new shade of red, but not merely that. Oh, *no!* A new shade of red, and a full set of color values derived from it! A complete set of color values derived from this one shade of red, Mr. Hebster! Think what a non-objectivist painter can do with such a—"

"Don't sell me, lady. Theseus, do you want to have a go now?"

Theseus had been frowning at the green foundation of the desk. He leaned back, looking satisfied. Hebster realized abruptly that the tension under his right foot had disappeared. Somehow, Theseus had become cognizant of the signal-spring set in the floor; and, somehow, he had removed it.

He had disintegrated it without setting off the alarm to which it was wired.

Giggles from three Primey throats and a rapid exchange of "gabble-honk." Then they all knew what Theseus had done and how Hebster had tried to protect himself. They weren't angry, though—and they didn't sound triumphant. Try to understand Primey behavior!

No need to get unduly alarmed—the price of dealing with these characters was a nervous stomach. The rewards, on the other hand—

Abruptly, they were businesslike again.

Theseus snapped out his suggestion with all the finality of a bazaar merchant making his last, absolutely the last offer. "A set of population indices which can be correlated with—"

"No, Theseus," Hebster told him gently.

Then, while Hebster sat back and enjoyed, temporarily forgetting the missing coil under his foot, they poured out more, desperately, feverishly, weaving in and out of each other's sentences.

"A portable neutron stabilizer for high altit—"

"More than fifty ways of saying 'however' without—"

"…So that every housewife can do an *entrechat* while cook—"

"…Synthetic fabric with the drape of silk and manufactura—"

"…Decorative pattern for bald heads using the follicles as—"

"…Complete and utter refutation of all pyramidologists from—"

"All right!" Hebster roared, *"All right!* That's enough!"

Greta Seidenheim almost forgot herself and sighed with relief. Her stenographic machine had been sounding like a centrifuge.

"Now," said the executive. "What do you want in exchange?"

"One of those we said is the one you want, eh?" Larry muttered. "Which one—the pyramidology refutation? That's it, I betcha."

S.S. Lusitania waved her hands contemptuously. "Bishop's miters, you fool! The new red color values excited him. The new—"

Ruth's voice came over the communicator. "Mr. Hebster, Yost and Funatti are back. I stalled them, but I just received word from the lobby receptionist that they're back and on their way upstairs. You have two minutes, maybe three. And they're so mad they almost look like Firsters themselves!"

"Thanks. When they climb out of the elevator, do what you can without getting too illegal." He turned to his guests. "Listen—"

They had gone off again.

"Gabble, gabble, honk, honk, honk? Gabble, honk, *gabble,* gabble! Gabble, honk, gabble, honk, gabble, honk, honk."

Could they honestly make sense out of these throat-clearings and half-sneezes? Was it really a language as superior to all previous languages of man as…as the Aliens were supposed to be to man himself? Well, at least they could communicate with the Aliens by means of it. And the Aliens, the Aliens—

He recollected abruptly the two angry representatives of the world state who were hurtling towards his office.

"Listen, friends. You came here to sell. You've shown me your stock, and I've seen something I'd like to buy. *What* exactly is immaterial. The only question now is what you want for it. And let's make it fast. I have some other business to transact."

The woman with the dental nightmare stamped her foot. A cloud no larger than a man's hand formed near the ceiling, burst and deposited a pailful of water on Hebster's fine custom-made rug.

He ran a manicured forefinger around the inside of his collar so that his bulging neck veins would not burst. Not right now, anyway. He looked at Greta and regained confidence from the serenity with which she waited for more conversation to transcribe. There was a model of business precision for you. The Primeys might pull what one of them had in London two years ago, before they were barred from all metropolitan areas—increased a housefly's size to that of an elephant—and Greta Seidenheim would go on separating fragments of conversation into the appropriate shorthand symbols.

With all their power, why didn't they *take* what they wanted? Why trudge wearisome miles to cities and attempt to smuggle themselves into illegal audiences with operators like Hebster, when most of them were caught easily and sent back to the reservation and those that weren't were cheated unmercifully by the "straight" humans they encountered? Why didn't they just blast their way in, take their weird and pathetic prizes and toddle back to their masters? For that matter, why didn't their masters— But Primey psych was Primey psych—not for this world, nor of it.

"We'll tell you what we want in exchange," Larry began in the middle of a honk. He held up a hand on which the length of the fingernails was indicated graphically by the grime beneath them and began to tot up the items, bending a digit for each item. "First, a hundred paper-bound copies of Melville's *Moby Dick.* Then, twenty-five crystal radio sets, with earphones; two earphones for each set. Then, two Empire State Buildings or three Radio Cities, whichever is more convenient. We want those with foundations intact. A reasonably good copy of the *Hermes* statue by Praxiteles. And an electric toaster, *circa* 1941. That's about all, isn't it, Theseus?"

Theseus bent over until his nose rested against his knees.

Hebster groaned. The list wasn't as bad as he'd expected—remarkable the way their masters always yearned for the electric gadgets and artistic achievements of Earth— but he had so little time to bargain with them. *Two* Empire State Buildings!

"Mr. Hebster," his receptionist chattered over the communicator. "Those SIC men— I managed to get a crowd out in the corridor to push toward their elevator when it came to this floor, and I've locked the…I mean I'm trying to…but I don't think— Can you—"

"Good girl! You're doing fine!"

"Is that all we want, Theseus?" Larry asked again. "Gabble?"

Hebster heard a crash in the outer office and footsteps running across the floor.

"See here, Mr. Hebster," Theseus said at last, "if you don't want to buy Larry's *reductio ad absurdum* exploder, and you don't like my method of decorating bald heads for all its innate artistry, how about a system of musical notation—"

Somebody tried Hebster's door, found it locked. There was a knock on the door, repeated almost immediately with more urgency.

"He's *already* found something he wants," S.S. Lusitania snapped. "Yes, Larry, that was the complete list."

Hebster plucked a handful of hair from his already receding forehead. "Good! Now, look, I can give you everything but the two Empire State Buildings and the three Radio Cities."

"*Or* the three Radio Cities," Larry corrected. "Don't try to cheat us! Two Empire State Buildings *or* three Radio Cities. Whichever is more convenient. Why…isn't it worth that to you?"

"Open this door!" a bull-mad voice yelled. "Open this door in the name of United Mankind!"

"Miss Seidenheim, open the door," Hebster said loudly and winked at his secretary, who rose, stretched and began a thoughtful, slow-motion study in the direction of the locked panel. There was a crash as of a pair of shoulders being thrown against it. Hebster knew that his office door could withstand a medium-sized tank. But there was a limit even to delay when it came to fooling around with the UM Special Investigating Commission. Those boys knew their Primeys and their Primey-dealers; they were empowered to shoot first and ask questions afterwards—as the questions occurred to them.

"It's not a matter of whether it's worth my while," Hebster told them rapidly as he shepherded them to the exit behind his desk. "For reasons I'm sure you aren't interested in, I just can't give away two Empire State Buildings and/or three Radio Cities with foundations intact—not at the moment. I'll give you the rest of it, and—"

"Open this door or we start blasting it down!"

"Please, gentlemen, please," Greta Seidenheim told them sweetly. "You'll kill a poor working girl who's trying awfully hard to let you in. The lock's stuck." She fiddled with the door knob, watching Hebster with a trace of anxiety in her fine eyes.

"And to replace those items," Hebster was going on, "I will—"

"What I mean," Theseus broke in, "is this. You know the greatest single difficulty composers face in the twelve-tone technique?"

"I can offer you," the executive continued doggedly, sweat bursting out of his skin like spring freshets, "complete architectural blueprints of the Empire State Building and Radio City, plus five…no, I'll make it ten…scale models of each. And you get the rest of the stuff you asked for. That's it. Take it or leave it. Fast!"

They glanced at each other, as Hebster threw the exit door open and gestured to the five liveried bodyguards waiting near his private elevator. *"Done,"* they said in unison.

"Good!" Hebster almost squeaked. He pushed them through the doorway and said to the tallest of the five men: "Nineteenth floor!"

He slammed the exit shut just as Miss Seidenheim opened the outer office door. Yost and Funatti, in the bottle-green uniform of the UM, charged through. Without pausing, they ran to where Hebster stood and plucked the exit open. They could all hear the elevator descending.

Funatti, a little, olive-skinned man, sniffed. "Primeys," he muttered. "He had Primeys here, all right. Smell that unwash, Yost?"

"Yeah," said the bigger man. "Come on. The emergency stairway. We can track that elevator!"

They holstered their service weapons and clattered down the metal-tipped stairs. Below, the elevator stopped.

Hebster's secretary was at the communicator. "Maintenance!" She waited. "Maintenance, automatic locks on the nineteenth floor exit until the party Mr. Hebster just sent down gets to a lab somewhere else. And keep apologizing to those cops until then. Remember, they're SIC."

"Thanks, Greta," Hebster said, switching to the personal now that they were alone. He plumped into his desk chair and blew out gustily: "There must be easier ways of making a million."

She raised two perfect blond eyebrows. "Or of being an absolute monarch right inside the parliament of man?"

"If they wait long enough," he told her lazily, "I'll *be* the UM, modern global government and all. Another year or two might do it."

"Aren't you forgetting Vandermeer Dempsey? His huskies also want to replace the UM. Not to mention their colorful plans for you. And there are an awful, awful lot of them."

"They don't worry me, Greta. *Humanity First* will dissolve overnight once that decrepit old demagogue gives up the ghost." He stabbed at the communicator button. "Maintenance! Maintenance, that party I sent down arrived at a safe lab yet?"

"No, Mr. Hebster. But everything's going all right. We sent them up to the twenty-fourth floor and got the SIC men rerouted downstairs to the personnel levels. Uh, Mr. Hebster—about the SIC. We take your orders and all that, but none of us wants to get in trouble with the Special Investigating Commission. According to the latest laws, it's practically a capital offense to obstruct them."

"Don't worry," Hebster told him. "I've never let one of my employees down yet.

The boss fixes everything is the motto here. Call me when you've got those Primeys safely hidden and ready for questioning."

He turned back to Greta. "Get that stuff typed before you leave and into Professor Kleimbocher's hands. He thinks he may have a new angle on their gabble-honk."

She nodded. "I wish you could use recording apparatus instead of making me sit over an old-fashioned click-box."

"So do I. But Primeys enjoy reaching out and putting a hex on electrical apparatus—when they aren't collecting it for the Aliens. I had a raft of tape recorders busted in the middle of Primey interviews before I decided that human stenos were the only answer. And a Primey may get around to bollixing them some day."

"Cheerful thought. I must remember to dream about the possibility some cold night. Well, I should complain," she muttered as she went into her own little office. "Primey hexes built this business and pay my salary as well as supply me with the sparkling little knicknacks I love so well."

That was not quite true, Hebster remembered as he sat waiting for the communicator to buzz the news of his recent guests' arrival in a safe lab. Something like ninety-five percent of Hebster Securities had been built out of Primey gadgetry extracted from them in various fancy deals, but the base of it all had been the small investment bank he had inherited from his father, back in the days of the Half-War—the days when the Aliens had first appeared on Earth.

The fearfully intelligent dots swirling in their variously shaped multicolored bottles were completely outside the pale of human understanding. There had been no way at all to communicate with them for a time.

A humorist had remarked back in those early days that the Aliens came not to bury man, not to conquer or enslave him. They had a truly dreadful mission—to ignore him!

No one knew, even today, what part of the galaxy the Aliens came from. Or why. No one knew what the total of their small visiting population came to. Or how they operated their wide-open and completely silent spaceships. The few things that had been discovered about them on the occasions when they deigned to swoop down and examine some human enterprise, with the aloof amusement of the highly civilized tourist, had served to confirm a technological superiority over Man that strained and tore the capacity of his richest imagination. A sociological treatise Hebster had read recently suggested that they operated from concepts as far in advance of modern science as a meteorologist sowing a drought-struck area with dry ice was beyond the primitive agriculturist blowing a ram's horn at the heavens in a frantic attempt to wake the slumbering gods of rain.

Prolonged, infinitely dangerous observation had revealed, for example, that the dots-in-bottles seemed to have developed past the need for prepared tools of any sort. They worked directly on the material itself, shaping it to need, evidently creating and destroying matter at will.

Some humans had communicated with them—

They didn't stay human.

Men with superb brains had looked into the whirring, flickering settlements established by the outsiders. A few had returned with tales of wonders they had realized dimly and not quite seen. Their descriptions always sounded as if their eyes had been turned off at the most crucial moments or a mental fuse had blown just this side of understanding.

Others—such celebrities as a President of Earth, a three-time winner of the Nobel Prize, famous poets—had evidently broken through the fence somehow. These, however, were the ones who didn't return. They stayed in the Alien settlements of the Gobi, the Sahara, the American Southwest. Barely able to fend for themselves, despite newly acquired and almost unbelievable powers, they shambled worshipfully around the outsiders, speaking, with weird writhings of larynx and nasal passage, what was evidently a human approximation of their masters' language—a kind of pidgin Alien. Talking with a Primey, someone had said, was like a blind man trying to read a page of Braille originally written for an octopus.

And that these bearded, bug-ridden, stinking derelicts, these chattering wrecks drunk and sodden on the logic of an entirely different life-form, were the absolute best of the human race didn't help people's egos any.

Humans and Primeys despised each other almost from the first: humans for Primey subservience and helplessness in human terms, Primeys for human ignorance and ineptness in Alien terms. And, except when operating under Alien orders and through barely legal operators like Hebster, Primeys didn't communicate with humans any more than their masters did.

When institutionalized, they either gabble-honked themselves into an early grave or, losing patience suddenly, they might dissolve a path to freedom right through the walls of the asylum and any attendants who chanced to be in the way. Therefore the enthusiasm of sheriff and deputy, nurse and orderly, had waned considerably and the forcible incarceration of Primeys had almost ceased.

Since the two groups were so far apart psychologically as to make mating between them impossible, the ragged miracle-workers had been honored with the status of a separate classification:

Humanity Prime. Not better than humanity, not necessarily worse—but different, and dangerous.

What made them that way? Hebster rolled his chair back and examined the hole in the floor from which the alarm spring had spiraled. Theseus had disintegrated it— *how?* With a thought? Telekinesis, say, applied to all the molecules of the metal simultaneously, making them move rapidly and at random. Or possibly he had merely moved the spring somewhere else. Where? In space? In hyperspace? In time? Hebster shook his head and pulled himself back to the efficiently smooth and sanely useful desk surface.

"Mr. Hebster?" the communicator inquired abruptly, and he jumped a bit, "this is Margritt of General Lab 23B. Your Primeys just arrived. Regular check?"

Regular check meant drawing them out on every conceivable technical subject by the nine specialists in the general laboratory. This involved firing questions at them with the rapidity of a police interrogation, getting them off balance and keeping them there in the hope that a useful and unexpected bit of scientific knowledge would drop.

"Yes," Hebster told him. "Regular check. But first let a textile man have a whack at them. In fact, let him take charge of the check."

A pause. "The only textile man in this section is Charlie Verus."

"Well?" Hebster asked in mild irritation. "Why put it like that? He's competent, I hope. What does Personnel say about him?"

"Personnel says he's competent."

"Then there you are. Look, Margritt, I have the SIC running around my building with blood in its enormous eye. I don't have time to muse over your departmental feuds. Put Verus on."

"Yes, Mr. Hebster. Hey, Bert! Get Charlie Verus. Him."

Hebster shook his head and chuckled. These technicians! Verus was probably brilliant and nasty.

The box crackled again: "Mr. Hebster? Mr. Verus." The voice expressed boredom to the point of obvious affectation. But the man was probably good despite his neuroses. Hebster Securities, Inc., had a first-rate personnel department.

"Verus? Those Primeys, I want you to take charge of the check. One of them knows how to make a synthetic fabric with the drape of silk. Get that first and then go after anything else they have."

"Primeys, Mr. Hebster?"

"I said Primeys, Mr. Verus. You are a textile technician, please to remember, and not the straight or ping-pong half of a comedy routine. Get humping. I want a report on that synthetic fabric by tomorrow. Work all night if you have to."

"Before we do, Mr. Hebster, you might be interested in a small piece of information. There is *already* in existence a synthetic which falls better than silk—"

"I know," his employer told him shortly. "Cellulose acetate. Unfortunately, it has a few disadvantages: low melting point, tends to crack; separate and somewhat inferior dyestuffs have to be used for it; poor chemical resistance. Am I right?"

There was no immediate answer, but Hebster could feel the dazed nod. He went on. "Now, we also have protein fibers. They dye well and fall well, have the thermoconductivity control necessary for wearing apparel, but don't have the tensile strength of synthetic fabrics. An *artificial* protein fiber might be the answer: it would drape as well as silk, might be we could use the acid dyestuffs we use on silk which result in shades that dazzle female customers and cause them to fling wide their pocketbooks. There are a lot of *ifs* in that, I know, but one of those Primeys said something about a synthetic with the drape of silk, and I don't think he'd be sane enough to be referring to cellulose acetate. Nor nylon, orlon, vinyl chloride, or anything else we already have and use."

"You've looked into textile problems, Mr. Hebster."

"I have. I've looked into everything to which there are big gobs of money attached.

And now suppose you go look into those Primeys. Several million women are waiting breathlessly for the secrets concealed in their beards. Do you think, Verus, that with the personal and scientific background I've just given you, it's possible you might now get around to doing the job you are paid to do?"

"Um-m-m. Yes."

Hebster walked to the office closet and got his hat and coat. He liked working under pressure; he liked to see people jump up straight whenever he barked. And now, he liked the prospect of relaxing.

He grimaced at the webfoam chair that Larry had used. No point in having it resquirted. Have a new one made.

"I'll be at the University," he told Ruth on his way out. "You can reach me through Professor Kleimbocher. But don't, unless it's very important. He gets unpleasantly annoyed when he's interrupted."

She nodded. Then, very hesitantly: "Those two men—Yost and Funatti—from the Special Investigating Commission? They said no one would be allowed to leave the building."

"Did they now?" he chuckled. "I think they were angry. They've been that way before. But unless and until they can hang something on me— And Ruth, tell my bodyguard to go home, except for the man with the Primeys. He's to check with me, wherever I am, every two hours."

He ambled out, being careful to smile benevolently at every third executive and fifth typist in the large office. A private elevator and entrance were all very well for an occasional crisis, but Hebster liked to taste his successes in as much public as possible.

It would be good to see Kleimbocher again. He had a good deal of faith in the linguistic approach; grants from his corporation had tripled the size of the University's philology department. After all, the basic problem between man and Primey as well as man and Alien was one of communication. Any attempt to learn their science, to adjust their mental processes and logic into safer human channels, would have to be preceded by understanding.

It was up to Kleimbocher to find that understanding, not him. "I'm Hebster," he thought. "I *employ* the people who solve problems. And then I make money off them."

Somebody got in front of him. Somebody else took his arm. "I'm Hebster," he repeated automatically, but out loud. "*Algernon* Hebster."

"Exactly the Hebster we want," Funatti said, holding tightly on to his arm. "You don't mind coming along with us?"

"Is this an arrest?" Hebster asked Yost, who now moved aside to let him pass. Yost was touching his holstered weapon with dancing fingertips.

The SIC man shrugged. "Why ask such questions?" he countered. "Just come along and be sociable, kind of. People want to talk to you."

He allowed himself to be dragged through the lobby ornate with murals by radical painters and nodded appreciation at the doorman who, staring right through his captors, said enthusiastically, "Good *afternoon,* Mr. Hebster." He made himself fairly comfortable on the back seat of the dark-green SIC car, a late-model Hebster Mono-wheel.

"Surprised to see you minus your bodyguard," Yost, who was driving, remarked over his shoulder.

"Oh, I gave them the day off."

"As soon as you were through with the Primeys? No," Funatti admitted, "we never did find out where you cached them. That's one big building you own, mister. And the UM Special Investigating Commission is notoriously understaffed."

"Not forgetting it's also notoriously underpaid," Yost broke in.

"I couldn't forget that if I tried," Funatti assured him. "You know, Mr. Hebster, I wouldn't have sent my bodyguard off if I'd been in your shoes. Right now there's something about five times as dangerous as Primeys after you. I mean Humanity Firsters."

"Vandermeer Dempsey's crackpots? Thanks, but I think I'll survive."

"That's all right. Just don't give any long odds on the proposition. Those people have been expanding fast and furious. *The Evening Humanitarian* alone has a tremendous circulation. And when you figure their weekly newspapers, their penny booklets and throwaway handbills, it adds up to an impressive amount of propaganda. Day after day they bang away editorially at the people who're making money off the Aliens and Primeys. Of course, they're really hitting at the UM, like always, but if an ordinary Firster met you on the street, he'd be as likely to cut your heart out as not. Not interested? Sorry. Well, maybe you'll like this. *The Evening Humanitarian* has a cute name for you."

Yost guffawed. "Tell him, Funatti."

The corporation president looked at the little man inquiringly.

"They call you," Funatti said with great savoring deliberation, "they call you an interplanetary pimp!"

Emerging at last from the crosstown underpass, they sped up the very latest addition to the strangling city's facilities—the East Side Air-Floating Super-Duper Highway, known familiarly as Dive-Bomber Drive. At the Forty-Second Street offway, the busiest road exit in Manhattan, Yost failed to make a traffic signal. He cursed absent-mindedly, and Hebster found himself nodding the involuntary passenger's agreement. They watched the elevator section dwindling downward as the cars that were to mount the highway spiraled up from the right. Between the two, there rose and fell the steady platforms of harbor traffic while, stacked like so many decks of cards, the pedestrian stages awaited their turn below.

"Look! Up there, straight ahead! See it?"

Hebster and Funatti followed Yost's long, waggling forefinger with their eyes. Two hundred feet north of the offway and almost a quarter of a mile straight up, a brown object hung in obvious fascination. Every once in a while a brilliant blue dot would enliven the heavy murk imprisoned in its bell-jar shape only to twirl around the side and be replaced by another.

"Eyes? You think they're eyes?" Funatti asked, rubbing his small dark fists against each other futilely. "I know what the scientists say—that every dot is equivalent to one person and the whole bottle is like a family or a city, maybe. But how do they know? It's a theory, a guess. *I* say they're eyes."

Yost hunched his great body half out of the open window and shaded his vision with his uniform cap against the sun. "Look at it," they heard him say, over his shoulder. A nasal twang, long-buried, came back into his voice as heaving emotion shook out its cultivated accents. "A-setting up there, a-staring and a-staring. So all-fired interested in how we get on and off a busy highway! Won't pay us no never mind when we try to talk to it, when we try to find out what it wants, where it comes from, who it is. Oh, no! It's too superior to talk to the likes of us! But it can watch us, hours on end, days without end, light and dark, winter and summer; it can watch us going about our business; and every time we dumb two-legged animals try to do something *we* find complicated, along comes a blasted 'dots-in-bottle' to watch and sneer and—"

"Hey there, man," Funatti leaned forward and tugged at his partner's green jerkin. "Easy! We're SIC, on business."

"All the same," Yost grunted wistfully, as he plopped back into his seat and pressed the power button, "I wish I had Daddy's little old M-1 Garand right now." They bowled forward, smoothed into the next long elevator section and started to descend. "It would be worth the risk of getting *pinged*."

And this was a UM man, Hebster reflected with acute discomfort. Not only UM, at that, but a member of a special group carefully screened for their lack of anti-Primey prejudice, sworn to enforce the reservation laws without discrimination and dedicated to the proposition that Man could somehow achieve equality with Alien.

Well, how much dirt-eating could people do? People without a business sense, that is. His father had hauled himself out of the pick-and-shovel brigade hand over hand and raised his only son to maneuver always for greater control, to search always for that extra percentage of profit.

But others seemed to have no such abiding interest, Algernon Hebster knew regretfully.

They found it impossible to live with achievements so abruptly made inconsequential by the Aliens. To know with certainty that the most brilliant strokes of which they were capable, the most intricate designs and clever careful workmanship, could be duplicated—and surpassed—in an instant's creation by the outsiders and was of interest to them only as a collector's item. The feeling of inferiority is horrible enough when imagined; but when it isn't feeling but *knowledge*, when it is inescapable and thoroughly demonstrable, covering every aspect of constructive activity, it becomes unbearable and maddening.

No wonder men went berserk under hours of unwinking Alien scrutiny—watching them as they marched in a colorfully uniformed lodge parade, or fished through a hole in the ice, as they painfully maneuvered a giant transcontinental jet to a noiseless landing or sat in sweating, serried rows chanting to a single, sweating man to "knock it out of the park and sew the whole thing up!" No wonder they seized rusty shotgun or gleaming rifle and sped shot after vindictive shot into a sky poisoned by the contemptuous curiosity of a brown, yellow or vermilion "bottle."

Not that it made very much difference. It did give a certain release to nerves backed into horrible psychic corners. But the Aliens didn't notice, and that was most important. The Aliens went right on watching, as if all this shooting and uproar, all these imprecations and weapon-wavings, were all part of the self-same absorbing show they had paid to witness and were determined to see through if for nothing else than the occasional amusing fluff some member of the inexperienced cast might commit.

The Aliens weren't injured, and the Aliens didn't feel attacked. Bullets, shells, buckshot, arrows, pebbles from a slingshot—all Man's miscellany of anger passed through them like the patient and eternal rain coming in the opposite direction. Yet the Aliens had solidity somewhere in their strange bodies. One could judge that by the way they intercepted light and heat. And also—

Also by the occasional *ping*.

Every once in a while, someone would evidently have hurt an Alien slightly. Or more probably just annoyed it by some unknown concomitant of rifle-firing or javelin-throwing.

There would be the barest suspicion of a sound—as if a guitarist had lunged at a string with his fingertip and decided against it one motor impulse too late. And, after this delicate and hardly heard *ping,* quite unspectacularly, the rifleman would be weaponless. He would be standing there sighting stupidly up along his empty curled fingers, elbow cocked out and shoulder hunched in, like a large oafish child who had forgotten when to end the game. Neither his rifle nor a fragment of it would ever be found. And—gravely, curiously, intently—the Alien would go on watching.

The *ping* seemed to be aimed chiefly at weapons. Thus, occasionally, a 155mm howitzer was *ping*ed, and also, occasionally, unexpectedly, it might be a muscular arm, curving back with another stone, that would disappear to the accompaniment of a tiny elfin note. And yet sometimes—could it be that the Alien, losing interest, had become careless in its irritation?—the entire man, murderously violent and shrieking, would *ping* and be no more.

It was not as if a counterweapon were being used, but a thoroughly higher order of reply, such as a slap to an insect bite. Hebster, shivering, recalled the time he had seen a black tubular Alien swirl its amber dots over a new substreet excavation, seemingly entranced by the spectacle of men scrabbling at the earth beneath them.

A red-headed, blue-shirted giant of construction labor had looked up from Manhattan's stubborn granite just long enough to shake the sweat from his eyelids. So doing, he had caught sight of the dot-pulsing observer and paused to snarl and lift his pneumatic drill, rattling it in noisy, if functionless, bravado at the sky. He had hardly been noticed by his mates, when the long, dark, speckled representative of a race beyond the stars turned end over end once and *ping*ed.

The heavy drill remained upright for a moment, then dropped as if it had abruptly realized its master was gone. Gone? Almost, he had never been. So thorough had his disappearance been, so rapid, with so little flicker had he been snuffed out—harming and taking with him nothing else—that it had amounted to an act of gigantic and positive noncreation.

No, Hebster decided, making threatening gestures at the Aliens was suicidal. Worse, like everything else that had been tried to date, it was useless. On the other hand, wasn't the *Humanity First* approach a complete neurosis? What *could* you do?

He reached into his soul for an article of fundamental faith, found it. "I can make money," he quoted to himself. "That's what I'm good for. That's what I can always do."

As they spun to a stop before the dumpy, brown-brick armory that the SIC had appropriated for its own use, he had a shock. Across the street was a small cigar store, the only one on the block. Brand names which had decorated the plate-glass window in all the colors of the copyright had been supplanted recently by great gilt slogans. Familiar slogans they were by now—but this close to a UM office, the Special Investigating Commission itself?

At the top of the window, the proprietor announced his affiliation in two huge words that almost screamed their hatred across the street:

HUMANITY FIRST!

Underneath these, in the exact center of the window, was the large golden initial of the organization, the wedded letters HF arising out of the huge, symbolic safety razor.

And under that, in straggling script, the theme repeated, reworded and sloganized: *"Humanity first, last and all the time!"*

The upper part of the door began to get nasty: *"Deport the Aliens! Send them back to wherever they came from!"*

And the bottom of the door made the store-front's only concession to business: *"Shop here! Shop Humanitarian!"*

"Humanitarian!" Funatti nodded bitterly beside Hebster. "Ever see what's left of a Primey if a bunch of Firsters catch him without SIC protection? Just about enough to pick up with a blotter. I don't imagine you're too happy about boycott-shops like that?"

Hebster managed a chuckle as they walked past the saluting, green-uniformed guards. "There aren't very many Primey-inspired gadgets having to do with tobacco. And if there were, one *Shop Humanitarian* outfit isn't going to break me."

But it is, he told himself disconsolately. It is going to break me—if it means what it seems to. Organization membership is one thing and so is planetary patriotism, but business is something else.

Hebster's lips moved slowly, in half-remembered catechism: Whatever the proprietor believes in or does not believe in, he has to make a certain amount of money out of that place if he's going to keep the door free of bailiff stickers. He can't do it if he offends the greater part of his possible clientele.

Therefore, since he's still in business and, from all outward signs, doing quite well, it's obvious that he doesn't have to depend on across-the-street UM personnel. Therefore, there must be a fairly substantial trade to offset this among entirely transient customers who not only don't object to his Firstism but are willing to forgo the interesting new gimmicks and lower prices in standard items that Primey technology is giving us.

Therefore, it is entirely possible—from this one extremely random but highly significant sample—that the newspapers I read have been lying and the socioeconomists I employ are incompetent. It is entirely possible that the buying public, the only aspect of the public in which I have the slightest interest, is beginning a shift in general viewpoint which will profoundly affect its purchasing orientation.

It is possible that the entire UM economy is now at the top of a long slide into Humanity First domination, the secure zone of fanatic blindness demarcated by men like Vandermeer Dempsey. The highly usurious, commercially speculative economy of Imperial Rome made a similar transition in the much slower historical pace of two millennia ago and became, in three brief centuries, a static unbusinesslike world in which banking was a sin and wealth which had not been inherited was gross and dishonorable.

Meanwhile, people may already have begun to judge manufactured items on the basis of morality instead of usability, Hebster realized, as dim mental notes took their stolid place beside forming conclusions. He remembered a folderful of brilliant explanation Market Research had sent up last week dealing with unexpected consumer resistance to the new Evvakleen dishware. He had dismissed the pages of carefully developed thesis—to the effect that women were unconsciously associating the product's name with a certain Katherine Evvakios who had recently made the front page of every tabloid in the world by dint of some fast work with a breadknife on the throats of her five children and two lovers—with a yawning smile after examining its first brightly colored chart.

"Probably nothing more than normal housewifely suspicion of a radically new idea," he had muttered, "after washing dishes for years, to be told it's no longer necessary! She can't believe her Evvakleen dish is still the same after stripping the outermost film of molecules after a meal. Have to hit that educational angle a bit harder—maybe tie it in with the expendable molecules lost by the skin during a shower."

He'd pencilled a few notes on the margin and flipped the whole problem onto the restless lap of Advertising and Promotion.

But then there had been the seasonal slump in furniture—about a month ahead of schedule. The surprising lack of interest in the Hebster Chubbichair, an item which should have revolutionized men's sitting habits.

Abruptly, he could remember almost a dozen unaccountable disturbances in the market recently, and all in consumer goods. That fits, he decided; any change in buying habits wouldn't be reflected in heavy industry for at least a year. The machine tools plants would feel it before the steel mills; the mills before the smelting and refining combines; and the banks and big investment houses would be the last of the dominoes to topple.

With its capital so thoroughly tied up in research and new production, his business wouldn't survive even a temporary shift of this type. Hebster Securities, Inc., could go like a speck of lint being blown off a coat collar.

Which is a long way to travel from a simple little cigar store. Funatti's jitters about growing Firstist sentiment are contagious! he thought.

If only Kleimbocher could crack the communication problem! If we could talk to the Aliens, find some sort of place for ourselves in their universe. The Firsters would be left without a single political leg!

Hebster realized they were in a large, untidy, map-splattered office and that his escort was saluting a huge, even more untidy man who waved their hands down impatiently and nodded them out of the door. He motioned Hebster to a choice of seats. This consisted of several long walnut-stained benches scattered about the room.

P. Braganza, said the desk nameplate with ornate Gothic flow. P. Braganza had a long, twirlable and tremendously thick mustache. Also, P. Braganza needed a haircut badly. It was as if he and everything in the room had been carefully designed to give the maximum affront to Humanity Firsters. Which, considering their crew-cut, closely shaven, "Cleanliness is next to Manliness" philosophy, meant that there was a lot of gratuitous unpleasantness in this office when a raid on a street demonstration filled it with jostling fanatics, antiseptically clean and dressed with bare-bones simplicity and neatness.

"So you're worrying about Firster effect on business?"

Hebster looked up, startled.

"No, I don't read your mind," Braganza laughed through tobacco-stained teeth. He gestured at the window behind his desk. "I saw you jump just the littlest bit when you noticed that cigar store. And then you stared at it for two full minutes. I knew what you were thinking about."

"Extremely perceptive of you," Hebster remarked dryly.

The SIC official shook his head in a violent negative. "No, it wasn't. It wasn't a bit perceptive. I knew what you were thinking about because I sit up here day after day staring at that cigar store and thinking exactly the same thing. Braganza, I tell myself, that's the end of your job. That's the end of scientific world government. Right there on that cigar-store window."

He glowered at his completely littered desk top for a moment. Hebster's instincts woke up—there was a sales talk in the wind. He realized the man was engaged in the unaccustomed exercise of looking for a conversational gambit. He felt an itch of fear crawl up his intestines. Why should the SIC, whose power was almost above law and certainly above governments, be trying to dicker with him?

Considering his reputation for asking questions with the snarling end of a rubber hose, Braganza was being entirely too gentle, too talkative, too friendly. Hebster felt like a trapped mouse into whose disconcerted ear a cat was beginning to pour complaints about the dog upstairs.

"Hebster, tell me something. What are your goals?"

"I beg your pardon?"

"What do you want out of life? What do you spend your days planning for, your nights dreaming about? Yost likes the girls and wants more of them. Funatti's a family man, five kids. He's happy in his work because his job's fairly secure, and there are all kinds of pensions and insurance policies to back up his life."

Braganza lowered his powerful head and began a slow, reluctant pacing in front of the desk.

"Now, I'm a little different. Not that I mind being a glorified cop. I appreciate the regularity with which the finance office pays my salary, of course; and there are very few women in this town who can say that I have received an offer of affection from them with outright scorn. But the one thing for which I would lay down my life is United Mankind. *Would* lay down my life? In terms of blood pressure and heart strain, you might say I've already done it. Braganza, I tell myself, you're a lucky dope. You're working for the first world government in human history. Make it count."

He stopped and spread his arms in front of Hebster. His unbuttoned green jerkin came apart awkwardly and exposed the black slab of hair on his chest. "That's me. That's basically all there is to Braganza. Now if we're to talk sensibly I have to know as much about you. I ask—what are your goals?"

The President of Hebster Securities, Inc., wet his lips. "I am afraid I'm even less complicated."

"That's all right," the other man encouraged. "Put it any way you like."

"You might say that before everything else, I am a businessman. I am interested chiefly in becoming a better businessman, which is to say a bigger one. In other words, I want to be richer than I am."

Braganza peered at him intently. "And that's all?"

"All? Haven't you ever heard it said that money isn't everything, but that what it isn't, it can buy?"

"It can't buy me."

Hebster examined him coolly. "I don't know if you're a sufficiently desirable commodity. I buy what I need, only occasionally making an exception to please myself."

"I don't like you." Braganza's voice had become thick and ugly. "I never liked your kind and there's no sense being polite. I might as well stop trying. I tell you straight out—I think your guts stink."

Hebster rose. "In that case, I believe I should thank you for—"

"Sit *down!* You were asked here for a reason. I don't see any point to it, but we'll go through the motions. Sit down."

Hebster sat. He wondered idly if Braganza received half the salary he paid Greta Seidenheim. Of course, Greta was talented in many different ways and performed several distinct and separately useful services. No, after tax and pension deductions, Braganza was probably fortunate to receive one-third of Greta's salary.

He noticed that a newspaper was being proffered him. He took it. Braganza grunted, clumped back behind his desk and swung his swivel chair around to face the window.

It was a week-old copy of *The Evening Humanitarian.* The paper had lost the voice-of-a-small-but-highly-articulate-minority look, Hebster remembered from his last reading of it, and acquired the feel of publishing big business. Even if you cut in half the circulation claimed by the box in the upper left-hand corner, that still gave them three million paying readers.

In the upper right-hand corner, a red-bordered box exhorted the faithful to *"Read*

Humanitarian!" A green streamer across the top of the first page announced that *"To make sense is human—to gibber, Prime!"*

But the important item was in the middle of the page. A cartoon.

Half-a-dozen Primeys wearing long, curved beards and insane, tongue-lolling grins sat in a rickety wagon. They held reins attached to a group of straining and portly gentlemen dressed—somewhat simply—in high silk hats. The fattest and ugliest of these, the one in the lead, had a bit between his teeth. The bit was labeled *"crazy-money"* and the man, "Algernon Hebster."

Crushed and splintering under the wheels of the wagon were such varied items as a "Home Sweet Home" framed motto with a piece of wall attached, a clean-cut young-ster in a Boy Scout uniform, a streamlined locomotive and a gorgeous young woman with a squalling infant under each arm.

The caption inquired starkly: "Lords of Creation—Or *Serfs?*"

"This paper seems to have developed into a fairly filthy scandal sheet," Hebster mused out loud. "I shouldn't be surprised if it makes money."

"I take it then," Braganza asked without turning around from his contemplation of the street, "that you haven't read it very regularly in recent months?"

"I am happy to say I have not."

"That was a mistake."

Hebster stared at the clumped locks of black hair. "Why?" he asked carefully.

"Because it *has* developed into a thoroughly filthy and extremely successful scan-dal sheet. You're its chief scandal." Braganza laughed. "You see, these people look upon Primey dealing as more of a sin than a crime. And, according to that morality, you're close to Old Nick himself!"

Shutting his eyes for a moment, Hebster tried to understand people who imag-ined such a soul-satisfying and beautiful concept as profit to be a thing of dirt and crawling maggots. He sighed. "I've thought of Firstism as a religion myself."

That seemed to get the SIC man. He swung around excitedly and pointed with both forefingers. "I tell you that you are right! It crosses all boundaries—incompat-ible and warring creeds are absorbed into it. It is willful, witless denial of a highly painful fact—that there are intellects abroad in the universe which are superior to our own. And the denial grows in strength every day that we are unable to contact the Aliens. If, as seems obvious, there is no respectable place for humanity in this galactic civilization, why, say men like Vandermeer Dempsey, then let us preserve our self-con-ceit at the least. Let's stay close to and revel in the things that are undeniably human. In a few decades, the entire human race will have been sucked into this blinkered vacuum."

He rose and walked around the desk again. His voice had assumed a terribly ear-nest, tragically pleading quality. His eyes roved Hebster's face as if searching for a pin-point of weakness, an especially thin spot in the frozen calm.

"Think of it," he asked Hebster. "Periodic slaughters of scientists and artists who, in the judgment of Dempsey, have pushed out too far from the conventional center of so-called humanness. An occasional *auto-da-fé* in honor of a merchant caught selling Primey goods—"

"I shouldn't like that," Hebster admitted, smiling. He thought a moment. "I see the connection you're trying to establish with the cartoon in *The Evening Humanitarian.*"

"Mister, I shouldn't have to. They want your head on the top of a long stick. They want it because you've become a symbol of dealing successfully, for your own ends, with these stellar foreigners, or at least their human errand-boys and chambermaids. They figure that maybe they can put a stop to Primey-dealing generally if they put a bloody stop to you. And I tell you this—maybe they are right."

"What exactly do you propose?" Hebster asked in a low voice.

"That you come in with us. We'll make an honest man of you—officially. We want you directing our investigation; except that the goal will not be an extra buck but all-important interracial communication and eventual interstellar negotiation."

The president of Hebster Securities, Inc., gave himself a few minutes on that one. He wanted to work out a careful reply. And he wanted time—above all, he wanted time!

He was so close to a well-integrated and worldwide commercial empire! For ten years, he had been carefully fitting the component industrial kingdoms into place, establishing suzerainty in this production network and squeezing a little more control out of that economic satrapy. He had found delectable tidbits of power in the dissolution of his civilization, endless opportunities for wealth in the shards of his race's self-esteem. He required a bare twelve months now to consolidate and coordinate. And suddenly—with the open-mouthed shock of a Jim Fiske who had cornered gold on the Exchange only to have the United States Treasury defeat him by releasing enormous quantities from the Government's own hoard—suddenly, Hebster realized he wasn't going to have the time. He was too experienced a player not to sense that a new factor was coming into the game, something outside his tables of actuarial figures, his market graphs and cargo loading indices.

His mouth was clogged with the heavy nausea of unexpected defeat. He forced himself to answer:

"I'm flattered. Braganza, I *really* am flattered. I see that Dempsey has linked us— we stand or fall together. But—I've always been a loner. With whatever help I can buy, I take care of myself. I'm not interested in any goal but the extra buck. First and last, I'm a businessman."

"Oh, stop it!" The dark man took a turn up and down the office angrily. "This is a planet-wide emergency. There are times when you can't be a businessman."

"I deny that. I can't conceive of such a time."

Braganza snorted. "You can't be a businessman if you're strapped to a huge pile of blazing faggots. You can't be a businessman if people's minds are so thoroughly controlled that they'll stop eating at their leader's command. You can't be a businessman, my slavering, acquisitive friend, if demand is so well in hand that it ceases to exist."

"That's impossible!" Hebster had leaped to his feet. To his amazement, he heard his voice climbing up the scale to hysteria. "There's *always* demand. Always! The trick is to find what new form it's taken and then fill it!"

"Sorry! I didn't mean to make fun of your religion."

Hebster drew a deep breath and sat down with infinite care. He could almost feel his red corpuscles simmering.

Take it easy, he warned himself, take it easy! This is a man who must be won, not antagonized. They're changing the rules of the market, Hebster, and you'll need every friend you can buy.

Money won't work with this fellow. But there are *other* values—

"Listen to me, Braganza. We're up against the psycho-social consequences of an extremely advanced civilization smacking into a comparatively barbarous one. Are you familiar with Professor Kleimbocher's Firewater Theory?"

"That the Aliens' logic hits us mentally in the same way as whisky hit the North American Indian? And the Primeys, representing our finest minds, are the equivalent of those Indians who had the most sympathy with the white man's civilization? Yes. It's a strong analogy. Even carried to the Indians who, lying sodden with liquor in the streets of frontier towns, helped create the illusion of the treacherous, lazy, kill-you-for-a-drink aborigines while being so thoroughly despised by their tribesmen that they didn't dare go home for fear of having their throats cut. I've always felt—"

"The only part of that I want to talk about," Hebster interrupted, "is the firewater concept. Back in the Indian villages, an ever-increasing majority became convinced that firewater and gluttonous paleface civilization were synonymous, that they must rise and retake their land forcibly, killing in the process as many drunken renegades as they came across. This group can be equated with the Humanity Firsters. Then there was a minority who recognized the white men's superiority in numbers and weapons, and desperately tried to find a way of coming to terms with his civilization—terms that would not include his booze. For them read the UM. Finally, there was my kind of Indian."

Braganza knitted voluminous eyebrows and hitched himself up to a corner of the desk. "Hah?" he inquired. "What kind of Indian were *you*, Hebster?"

"The kind who had enough sense to know that the paleface had not the slightest interest in saving him from slow and painful cultural anemia. The kind of Indian, also, whose instincts were sufficiently sound so that he was scared to death of innovations like firewater and wouldn't touch the stuff to save himself from snake bite. But the kind of Indian—"

"Yes? Go on!"

"The kind who was fascinated by the strange transparent container in which the firewater came! Think how covetous an Indian potter might be of the whisky bottle, something which was completely outside the capacity of his painfully acquired technology. Can't you see him hating, despising and terribly afraid of the smelly amber fluid, which toppled the most stalwart warriors, yet wistful to possess a bottle minus contents? That's about where I see myself, Braganza—the Indian whose greedy curiosity shines through the murk of hysterical clan politics and outsiders' contempt like a lambent flame. I want the new kind of container somehow separated from the firewater."

Unblinkingly, the great dark eyes stared at his face. A hand came up and smoothed each side of the arched mustachio with long, unknowing twirls. Minutes passed.

"Well. Hebster as our civilization's noble savage," the SIC man chuckled at last. "It almost feels right. But what does it mean in terms of the overall problem?"

"I've told you," Hebster said wearily, hitting the arm of the bench with his open hand, "that I haven't the slightest interest in the overall problem."

"And you only want the bottle. I heard you. But you're not a potter, Hebster—you haven't an elementary particle of craftsman's curiosity. All of that historical romance you spout—you don't care if your world drowns in its own agonized juice. You just want a profit."

"I never claimed an altruistic reason. I leave the general solution to men whose minds are good enough to juggle its complexities—like Kleimbocher."

"Think somebody like Kleimbocher could do it?"

"I'm almost certain he will. That was our mistake from the beginning—trying to break through with historians and psychologists. Either they've become limited by the study of human societies or—well, this is personal, but I've always felt that the science of the mind attracts chiefly those who've already experienced grave psychological difficulty. While they might achieve such an understanding of themselves in the course of their work as to become better adjusted eventually than individuals who had less problems to begin with, I'd still consider them too essentially unstable for such an intrinsically shocking experience as establishing *rapport* with an Alien. Their internal dynamics inevitably make Primeys of them."

Braganza sucked at a tooth and considered the wall behind Hebster. "And all this, you feel, wouldn't apply to Kleimbocher?"

"No, not a philology professor. He has no interest, no intellectual roots in personal and group instability. Kleimbocher's a comparative linguist—a technician, really—a specialist in basic communication. I've been out to the University and watched him work. His approach to the problem is entirely in terms of his subject—communicating with the Aliens instead of trying to understand them. There's been entirely too much intricate speculation about Alien consciousness, sexual attitudes and social organization, about stuff from which we will derive no tangible and immediate good. Kleimbocher's completely pragmatic."

"All right. I follow you. Only he went Prime this morning."

Hebster paused, a sentence dangling from his dropped jaw. "Professor Kleimbocher? *Rudolf* Kleimbocher?" he asked idiotically. "But he was so close…he almost had it…an elementary signal dictionary…he was about to—"

"He *did*. About nine forty-five. He'd been up all night with a Primey one of the psych professors had managed to hypnotize and gone home unusually optimistic. In the middle of his first class this morning, he interrupted himself in a lecture on medieval Cyrillic to…to gabble-honk. He sneezed and wheezed at the students for about ten minutes in the usual Primey pattern of initial irritation, then, abruptly giving them up as hopeless, worthless idiots, he levitated himself in that eerie way they almost always do at first. Banged his head against the ceiling and knocked himself out. I don't know what it was, fright, excitement, respect for the old boy perhaps, but the students neglected to tie him up before going for help. By the time they'd come back with the campus SIC man, Kleimbocher had revived and dissolved one wall of the Graduate School to get out. Here's a snapshot of him about five hundred feet in the air, lying on his back with his arms crossed behind his head, skimming west at twenty miles an hour."

Hebster studied the little paper rectangle with blinking eyes. "You radioed the air force to chase him, of course."

"What's the use? We've been through *that* enough times. He'd either increase his speed and generate a tornado, drop like a stone and get himself smeared all over the countryside, or materialize stuff like wet coffee grounds and gold ingots inside the jets of the pursuing plane. Nobody's caught a Primey yet in the first flush of…whatever they do feel at first. And we might stand to lose anything from a fairly expensive hunk of aircraft, including pilot, to a couple of hundred acres of New Jersey topsoil."

Hebster groaned. "But the eighteen years of research that he represented!"

"Yeah. That's where we stand. Blind Alley umpteen hundred thousand or thereabouts. Whatever the figure is, it's awfully close to the end. If you can't crack the Alien on a straight linguistic basis, you can't crack the Alien at all, period, end of paragraph. Our most powerful weapons affect them like bubble pipes, and our finest minds are good for nothing better than to serve them in low, fawning idiocy. But the Primeys are all that's left. We might be able to talk sense to the Man if not the Master."

"Except that Primeys, by definition, don't talk sense."

Braganza nodded. "But since they were human—*ordinary* human—to start with, they represent a hope. We always knew we might some day have to fall back on our only real contact. That's why the Primey protective laws are so rigid; why the Primey reservation compounds surrounding Alien settlements are guarded by our military detachments. The lynch spirit has been evolving into the pogrom spirit as human resentment and discomfort have been growing. *Humanity First* is beginning to feel strong enough to challenge United Mankind. And honestly, Hebster, at this point neither of us know which would survive a real fight. But you're one of the few who have talked to Primeys, worked with them—"

"Just on business."

"Frankly, that much of a start is a thousand times further along than the best that we've been able to manage. It's so blasted ironical that the only people who've had any conversation at all with the Primeys aren't even slightly interested in the imminent collapse of civilization! Oh, well. The point is that in the present political picture, you sink with us. Recognizing this, my people are prepared to forget a great deal and document you back into respectability. How about it?"

"Funny," Hebster said thoughtfully. "It can't be knowledge that makes miracleworkers out of fairly sober scientists. They all start shooting lightnings at their families and water out of rocks far too early in Primacy to have had time to learn new techniques. It's as if by merely coming close enough to the Aliens to grovel, they immediately move into position to tap a series of cosmic laws more basic than cause and effect."

The SIC man's face slowly deepened into purple. "Well, are you coming in, or aren't you? Remember, Hebster, in these times, a man who insists on business as usual is a traitor to history."

"I think Kleimbocher *is* the end." Hebster nodded to himself. "Not much point in chasing Alien mentality if you're going to lose your best men on the way. I say let's forget all this nonsense of trying to live as equals in the same universe with Aliens. Let's concentrate on human problems and be grateful that they don't come into our major population centers and tell us to shove over."

The telephone rang. Braganza had dropped back into his swivel chair. He let the instrument squeeze out several piercing sonic bubbles while he clicked his strong square teeth and maintained a carefully focused glare at his visitor. Finally, he picked it up, and gave it the verbal minima:

"Speaking. He is here. I'll tell him. 'Bye."

He brought his lips together, kept them pursed for a moment and then, abruptly, swung around to face the window.

"Your office, Hebster. Seems your wife and son are in town and have to see you on business. She the one you divorced ten years ago?"

Hebster nodded at his back and rose once more. "Probably wants her semiannual alimony dividend bonus. I'll have to go. Sonia never does office morale any good."

This meant trouble, he knew. "Wife-and-son" was executive code for something seriously wrong with Hebster Securities, Inc. He had not seen his wife since she had been satisfactorily maneuvered into giving him control of his son's education. As far as he was concerned, she had earned a substantial income for life by providing him with a well-mothered heir.

"Listen!" Braganza said sharply as Hebster reached the door. He still kept his eyes studiously on the street. "I tell you this: You don't want to come in with us. All right! You're a businessman first and a world citizen second. All right! But keep your nose clean, Hebster. If we catch you the slightest bit off base from now on, you'll get hit with everything. We'll not only pull the most spectacular trial this corrupt old planet has ever seen, but somewhere along the line, we'll throw you and your entire organization to the wolves. We'll see to it that *Humanity First* pulls the Hebster Tower down around your ears."

Hebster shook his head, licked his lips. "*Why?* What would that accomplish?"

"Hah! It would give a lot of us here the craziest kind of pleasure. But it would also relieve us temporarily of some of the mass pressure we've been feeling. There's always the chance that Dempsey would lose control of his hotter heads, that they'd go on a real gory rampage, make with the sound and the fury sufficiently to justify full deployment of troops. We could knock off Dempsey and all of the big-shot Firsters then, because John Q. United Mankind would have seen to his own vivid satisfaction and injury what a dangerous mob they are."

"This," Hebster commented bitterly, "is the idealistic, legalistic world government!"

Braganza's chair spun around to face Hebster and his fist came down on the desk top with all the crushing finality of a magisterial gavel. "No, it is not! It is the SIC, a plenipotentiary and highly practical bureau of the UM, especially created to organize a relationship between Alien and human. Furthermore, it's the SIC in a state of the greatest emergency when the reign of law and world government may topple at a demagogue's belch. Do you think"—his head snaked forward belligerently, his eyes slitted to thin lines of purest contempt—"that the career and fortune, even the life, let us say, of as openly selfish a slug as you, Hebster, would be placed above that of the representative body of two billion *socially* operating human beings?"

The SIC official thumped his sloppily buttoned chest. "Braganza, I tell myself now, you're lucky he's too hungry for his blasted profit to take you up on that offer. Think how much fun it's going to be to sink a hook into him when he makes a mistake at last! To drop him onto the back of *Humanity First* so that they'll run amuck and destroy themselves! Oh, get out, Hebster. I'm through with you."

He had made a mistake, Hebster reflected as he walked out of the armory and snapped his fingers at a gyrocab. The SIC was the most powerful single government agency in a Primey-infested world; offending them for a man in his position was equivalent to a cab driver delving into the more uncertain aspects of a traffic cop's ancestry in the policeman's popeyed presence.

But what could he do? Working with the SIC would mean working under Braganza—and since maturity, Algernon Hebster had been quietly careful to take orders from no man. It would mean giving up a business which, with a little more work and a little more time, might somehow still become the dominant combine on the planet. And worst of all, it would mean acquiring a social orientation to replace the calculating businessman's viewpoint which was the closest thing to a soul he had ever known.

The doorman of his building preceded him at a rapid pace down the side corridor that led to his private elevator and flourished aside for him to enter. The car stopped on the twenty-third floor. With a heart that had sunk so deep as to have practically foundered, Hebster picked his way along the wide-eyed clerical stares that lined the corridor. At the entrance to General Laboratory 23B, two tall men in the gray livery of his personal bodyguard moved apart to let him enter. If they had been recalled after having been told to take the day off, it meant that a full-dress emergency was being observed. He hoped that it had been declared in time to prevent any publicity leakage.

It had, Greta Seidenheim assured him. "I was down here applying the clamps five minutes after the fuss began. Floors twenty-one through twenty-five are closed off and all outside lines are being monitored. You can keep your employees an hour at most past five o'clock—which gives you a maximum of two hours and fourteen minutes."

He followed her green-tipped fingernail to the far corner of the lab where a body lay wrapped in murky rags. Theseus. Protruding from his back was the yellowed ivory handle of quite an old German S.S. dagger, 1942 edition. The silver swastika on the hilt had been replaced by an ornate symbol—an HF. Blood had soaked Theseus' long matted hair into an ugly red rug.

A dead Primey, Hebster thought, staring down hopelessly. In *his* building, in the laboratory to which the Primey had been spirited two or three jumps ahead of Yost and Funatti. This was capital offense material—if the courts ever got a chance to weigh it.

"Look at the dirty Primey-lover!" a slightly familiar voice jeered on his right. "He's scared! Make money out of *that*, Hebster!"

The corporation president strolled over to the thin man with the knobby, completely shaven head who was tied to an unused steampipe. The man's tie, which hung outside his laboratory smock, sported an unusual ornament about halfway down. It took Hebster several seconds to identify it. A miniature gold safety razor upon a black "3."

"He's a third-echelon official of *Humanity First!*"

"He's also Charlie Verus of Hebster Laboratories," an extremely short man with a corrugated forehead told him. "My name is Margritt, Mr. Hebster, Dr. J.H. Margritt. I spoke to you on the communicator when the Primeys arrived."

Hebster shook his head determinedly. He waved back the other scientists who were milling around him self-consciously. "How long have third-echelon officials, let alone ordinary members of *Humanity First,* been receiving salary checks in my laboratories?"

"I don't know." Margritt shrugged up at him. "Theoretically no Firsters can be Hebster employees. Personnel is supposed to be twice as efficient as the SIC when it comes to sifting background. They probably are. But what can they do when an employee joins *Humanity First* after he passed his probationary period? These proselytizing times you'd need a complete force of secret police to keep tabs on all the new converts!"

"When I spoke to you earlier in the day, Margritt, you indicated disapproval of Verus. Don't you think it was your duty to let me know I had a Firster official about to mix it up with Primeys?"

The little man beat a violent negative back and forth with his chin. "I'm paid to supervise research, Mr. Hebster, not to coordinate your labor relations nor vote your political ticket!"

Contempt—the contempt of the creative researcher for the businessman-entrepreneur who paid his salary and was now in serious trouble—flickered behind every word he spoke. Why, Hebster wondered irritably, did people so despise a man who made money? Even the Primeys back in his office, Yost and Funatti, Braganza, Margritt—who had worked in his laboratories for years. It was his only talent. Surely, as such, it was as valid as a pianist's?

"I've never liked Charlie Verus," the lab chief went on, "but we never had reason to suspect him of Firstism! He must have hit the third-echelon rank about a week ago, eh, Bert?"

"Yeah," Bert agreed from across the room. "The day he came in an hour late, broke every Florence flask in the place and told us all dreamily that one day we might be very proud to tell our grandchildren that we'd worked in the same lab with Charles Bolop Verus."

"Personally," Margritt commented, "I thought he might have just finished writing a book which proved that the Great Pyramid was nothing more than a prophecy in stone of our modern textile designs. Verus was that kind. But it probably was his little safety razor that tossed him up so high. I'd say he got the promotion as a sort of payment in advance for the job he finally did today."

Hebster ground his teeth at the carefully hairless captive who tried, unsuccessfully, to spit in his face; he hurried back to the door, where his private secretary was talking to the bodyguard who had been on duty in the lab.

Beyond them, against the wall, stood Larry and S.S. Lusitania conversing in a low-voiced and anxious gabble-honk. They were evidently profoundly disturbed. S.S. Lusitania kept plucking tiny little elephants out of her rags which, kicking and trumpeting tinnily, burst like malformed bubbles as she dropped them on the floor. Larry scratched his tangled beard nervously as he talked, periodically waving a hand at the ceiling, which was already studded with fifty or sixty replicas of the dagger buried in Theseus. Hebster couldn't help thinking anxiously of what could have happened to his building if the Primeys had been able to act human enough to defend themselves.

"Listen, Mr. Hebster," the bodyguard began, "I was told not to—"

"Save it," Hebster rapped out. "This wasn't your fault. Even Personnel isn't to blame. Me and my experts deserve to have our necks chopped for falling so far behind the times. We can analyze any trend but the one which will make us superfluous. Greta! I want my roof helicopter ready to fly and my personal stratojet at LaGuardia alerted. Move, girl! And *you*...Williams, is it?" he queried, leaning forward to read the bodyguard's name on his badge, "Williams, pack these two Primeys into my helicopter upstairs and stand by for a fast take-off."

He turned. "Everyone else!" he called. "You will be allowed to go home at six. You will be paid one hour's overtime. Thank you."

Charlie Verus started to sing as Hebster left the lab. By the time he reached the elevator, several of the clerks in the hallway had defiantly picked up the hymn. Hebster paused outside the elevator as he realized that fully one-fourth of the clerical personnel, male and female, were following Verus' cracked and mournful but terribly earnest tenor.

> *Mine eyes have seen the coming*
> *of the glory of the shorn:*
> *We will overturn the cesspool*
> *where the Primey slime is born,*
> *We'll be wearing cleanly garments*
> *as we face a human morn—*
> *The First are on the march!*
> *Glory, glory, hallelujah,*
> *Glory, glory, hallelujah...*

If it was like this in Hebster Securities, he thought wryly as he came into his private office, how fast was *Humanity First* growing among the broad masses of people?

Of course, many of those singing could be put down as sympathizers rather than converts, people who were suckers for choral groups and vigilante posses—but how much more momentum did an organization have to generate to acquire the name of political juggernaut?

The only encouraging aspect was the SIC's evident awareness of the danger and the unprecedented steps they were prepared to take as countermeasure.

Unfortunately, the unprecedented steps would take place upon Hebster.

He now had a little less than two hours, he reflected, to squirm out of the most serious single crime on the books of present World Law.

He lifted one of his telephones. "Ruth," he said. "I want to speak to Vandermeer Dempsey. Get me through to him personally."

She did. A few moments later he heard the famous voice, as rich and slow and thick as molten gold. "Hello Hebster, Vandermeer Dempsey speaking." He paused as if to draw breath, then went on sonorously: *"Humanity—may it always be ahead, but, ahead or behind, Humanity!"* He chuckled. "Our newest. What we call our telephone toast. Like it?"

"Very much," Hebster told him respectfully, remembering that this former video quizmaster might shortly be church and state combined. "Er…Mr. Dempsey, I notice you have a new book out, and I was wondering—"

"Which one? *Anthropolitics*?"

"That's it. A fine study! You have some very quotable lines in the chapter headed, 'Neither More Nor Less Human.' "

A raucous laugh that still managed to bubble heavily. "Young man, I have quotable lines in every chapter of every book! I maintain a writer's assembly line here at headquarters that is capable of producing up to fifty-five memorable epigrams on any subject upon ten minutes' notice. Not to mention their capacity for political metaphors and two-line jokes with sexy implications! But you wouldn't be calling me to discuss literature, however good a job of emotional engineering I have done in my little text. What is it about, Hebster? Go into your pitch."

"Well," the executive began, vaguely comforted by the Firster chieftain's cynical approach and slightly annoyed at the openness of his contempt, "I had a chat today with your friend and my friend, P. Braganza."

"I know."

"You do? How?"

Vandermeer Dempsey laughed again, the slow, good-natured chortle of a fat man squeezing the curves out of a rocking chair. "Spies, Hebster, *spies*. I have them everywhere practically. This kind of politics is twenty percent espionage, twenty percent organization and sixty percent waiting for the right moment. My spies tell me everything you do."

"They didn't by any chance tell you what Braganza and I discussed?"

"Oh, they did, young man, they did!" Dempsey chuckled a carefree scale exercise. Hebster remembered his pictures: the head like a soft and enormous orange, gouged by a brilliant smile. There was no hair anywhere on the head—all of it, down to the last eyelash and follicled wart, was removed regularly through electrolysis. "According to my agents, Braganza made several strong representations on behalf of the Special Investigating Commission which you rightly spurned. Then, somewhat out of sorts, he announced that if you were henceforth detected in the nefarious enterprises which everyone knows have made you one of the wealthiest men on the face of the Earth, he would use you as bait for our anger. I must say I admire the whole ingenious scheme immensely."

"And you're not going to bite," Hebster suggested. Greta Seidenheim entered the office and made a circular gesture at the ceiling. He nodded.

"On the contrary, Hebster, we *are* going to bite. We're going to bite with just a shade more vehemence than we're expected to. We're going to swallow this provocation that the SIC is devising for us and go on to make a worldwide revolution out of it. We *will*, my boy."

Hebster rubbed his left hand back and forth across his lips. "Over my dead body!" He tried to chuckle himself and managed only to clear his throat. "You're right about the conversation with Braganza, and you may be right about how you'll do when it gets down to paving stones and baseball bats. But if you'd like to have the whole thing a lot easier, there is a little deal I have in mind—"

"Sorry, Hebster my boy. No deals. Not on this. Don't you see we really *don't* want to have it easier? For the same reason, we pay our spies nothing despite the risks they run and the great growing wealth of *Humanity First*. We found that the spies we acquired through conviction worked harder and took many more chances than those forced into our arms by economic pressure. No, we desperately need *L'affaire Hebster* to inflame the populace. We need enough excitement running loose so that it transmits to the gendarmerie and the soldiery, so that conservative citizens who normally shake their heads at a parade will drop their bundles and join the rape and robbery. Enough such citizens and Terra goes *Humanity First*."

"Heads you win, tails I lose."

The liquid gold of Dempsey's laughter poured. "I see what you mean, Hebster. Either way, UM or HF, you wind up a smear-mark on the sands of time. You had your chance when we asked for contributions from public-spirited businessmen four years ago. Quite a few of your competitors were able to see the valid relationship between economics and politics. Woodran of the Underwood Investment Trust is a first-echelon official today. Not a single one of *your* top executives wears a razor. But, even so, whatever happens to you will be mild compared to the Primeys."

"The Aliens may object to their body-servants being mauled."

"There are no Aliens!" Dempsey replied in a completely altered voice. He sounded as if he had stiffened too much to be able to move his lips.

"No Aliens? Is that your latest line? You don't mean that!"

"There are only Primeys—creatures who have resigned from human responsibility and are therefore able to do many seemingly miraculous things, which real humanity refuses to do because of the lack of dignity involved. But there are no Aliens. Aliens are a Primey myth."

Hebster grunted. "That is the ideal way of facing an unpleasant fact. Stare right through it."

"If you insist on talking about such illusions as Aliens," the rustling and angry voice cut in, "I'm afraid we can't continue the conversation. You're evidently going Prime, Hebster."

The line went dead.

Hebster scraped a finger inside the mouthpiece rim. "He believes his own stuff!" he said in an awed voice. "For all of the decadent urbanity, he has to have the same reassurance he gives his followers—the horrible, superior thing just isn't there!"

Greta Seidenheim was waiting at the door with his briefcase and both their coats. As he came away from the desk, he said, "I won't tell you not to come along, Greta, but—"

"Good," she said, swinging along behind him. "Think we'll make it to—wherever we're going?"

"Arizona. The first and largest Alien settlement. The place our friends with the funny names come from."

"What can you do there that you can't do here?"

"Frankly, Greta, I don't know. But it's a good idea to lose myself for a while. Then again, I want to get in the area where all this agony originates and take a close look; I'm an off-the-cuff businessman; I've done all of my important figuring on the spot."

There was bad news waiting for them outside the helicopter. "Mr. Hebster," the pilot told him tonelessly while cracking a dry stick of gum, "the stratojet's been seized by the SIC. Are we still going? If we do it in this thing, it won't be very far or very fast."

"We're still going," Hebster said after a moment's hesitation.

They climbed in. The two Primeys sat on the floor in the rear, sneezing conversationally at each other. Williams waved respectfully at his boss. "Gentle as lambs," he said. "In fact, they made one. I had to throw it out."

The large pot-bellied craft climbed up its rope of air and started forward from the Hebster Building.

"There must have been a leak," Greta muttered angrily. "They heard about the dead Primey. Somewhere in the organization there's a leak that I haven't been able to find. The SIC heard about the dead Primey and now they're hunting us down. Real efficient, I am!"

Hebster smiled at her grimly. She was very efficient. So was Personnel and a dozen other subdivisions of the organization. So was Hebster himself. But these were functioning members of a normal business designed for stable times. *Political* spies! If Dempsey could have spies and saboteurs all over Hebster Securities, why couldn't Braganza? They'd catch him before he had even started running; they'd bring him back before he could find a loophole.

They'd bring him back for trial, perhaps, for what in all probability would be known to history as the Bloody Hebster Incident. The incident that had precipitated a world revolution.

"Mr. Hebster, they're getting restless," Williams called out. "Should I relax 'em out, kind of?"

Hebster sat up sharply, hopefully. "No," he said. "Leave them alone!" He watched the suddenly agitated Primeys very closely. This was the odd chance for which he'd brought them along! Years of haggling with Primeys had taught him a lot about them. They were good for other things than sheer gimmick-craft.

Two specks appeared on the windows. They enlarged sleekly into jets with SIC insignia.

"Pilot!" Hebster called, his eyes on Larry, who was pulling painfully at his beard. "Get away from the controls! Fast! Did you hear me? That was an *order! Get away from those controls!*"

The man moved off reluctantly. He was barely in time. The control board dissolved into rattling purple shards behind him. The vanes of the gyro seemed to flower into indigo saxophones. Their ears rang with supersonic frequencies as they rose above the jets on a spout of unimaginable force.

Five seconds later they were in Arizona.

They piled out of their weird craft into a sage-cluttered desert.

"I don't ever want to know what my windmill was turned into," the pilot commented, "or what was used to push it along—but how did the Primey come to understand the cops were after us?"

"I don't think he knew that," Hebster explained, "but he was sensitive enough to know he was going home, and that somehow those jets were there to prevent it. And so he functioned, in terms of his interests, in what was almost a human fashion. He protected himself!"

"Going home," Larry said. He'd been listening very closely to Hebster, dribbling from the right-hand corner of his mouth as he listened. "Haemostat, hammersdarts, hump. Home is where the hate is. Hit is where the hump is. Home and locks the door."

S.S. Lusitania had started on one leg and favored them with her peculiar fleshy smile. "Hindsight," she suggested archly, "is no more than home site. Gabble, honk?"

Larry started after her, some three feet off the ground. He walked the air slowly and painfully as if the road he traveled were covered with numerous small boulders, all of them pitilessly sharp.

"Goodbye, people," Hebster said. "I'm off to see the wizard with my friends in greasy gray here. Remember, when the SIC catches up to your unusual vessel—stay close to it for that purpose, by the way—it might be wise to refer to me as someone who forced you into this. You can tell them I've gone into the wilderness looking for a solution, figuring that if I went Prime I'd still be better off than as a punching bag whose ownership is being hotly disputed by such characters as P. Braganza and Vandermeer Dempsey. I'll be back with my mind or on it."

He patted Greta's cheek on the wet spot; then he walked deftly away in pursuit of S.S. Lusitania and Larry. He glanced back once and smiled as he saw them looking curiously forlorn, especially Williams, the chunky young man who earned his living by guarding other people's bodies.

The Primeys followed a route of sorts, but it seemed to have been designed by someone bemused by the motions of an accordion. Again and again it doubled back upon itself, folded across itself, went back a hundred yards and started all over again.

This was Primey country—Arizona, where the first and largest Alien settlement had been made. There were mighty few humans in this corner of the southwest any more—just the Aliens and their coolies.

"Larry," Hebster called as an uncomfortable thought struck him. "Larry! Do…do your masters know I'm coming?"

Missing his step as he looked up at Hebster's peremptory question, the Primey tripped and plunged to the ground. He rose, grimaced at Hebster and shook his head. "You are not a businessman," he said. "Here there can be no business. Here there can be only humorous what-you-might-call-worship. The movement to the universal, the inner nature— The realization, complete and eternal, of the partial and evanescent that alone enables…that alone enables—" His clawed fingers writhed into each other, as if he were desperately trying to pull a communicable meaning out of the palms. He shook his head with a slow rolling motion from side to side.

Hebster saw with a shock that the old man was crying. Then going Prime had yet another similarity to madness! It gave the human an understanding of something thoroughly beyond himself, a mental summit he was constitutionally incapable of mounting. It gave him a glimpse of some psychological promised land, then buried him, still yearning, in his own inadequacies. And it left him at last bereft of pride in his realizable accomplishments with a kind of myopic half-knowledge of where he wanted to go but with no means of getting there.

"When I first came," Larry was saying haltingly, his eyes squinting into Hebster's face, as if he knew what the businessman was thinking, "when first I tried to know…I mean the charts and textbooks I carried here, my statistics, my plotted curves were so useless. All playthings I found, disorganized, based on shadow-thought. And then, Hebster, to watch real-thought, real-control! You'll see the joy— You'll serve beside us, you will! Oh, the enormous lifting—"

His voice died into angry incoherencies as he bit into his fist. S.S. Lusitania came up, still hopping on one foot. "Larry," she suggested in a very soft voice, "gabble-honk Hebster away?"

He looked surprised, then nodded. The two Primeys linked arms and clambered laboriously back up to the invisible road from which Larry had fallen. They stood facing him for a moment, looking like a weird, ragged, surrealistic version of Tweedledee and Tweedledum.

Then they disappeared and darkness fell around Hebster as if it had been knocked out of the jar. He felt under himself cautiously and sat down on the sand, which retained all the heat of daytime Arizona.

Now!

Suppose an Alien came. Suppose an Alien asked him point-blank what it was that he wanted. That would be bad. Algernon Hebster, businessman extraordinary—

slightly on the run, at the moment, of course—didn't know what he wanted; not with reference to Aliens.

He didn't want them to leave, because the Primey technology he had used in over a dozen industries was essentially an interpretation and adaptation of Alien methods. He didn't want them to stay, because whatever was orderly in his world was dissolving under the acids of their omnipresent superiority.

He also knew that he personally did not want to go Prime.

What was left then? Business? Well, there was Braganza's question. What does a businessman do when demand is so well controlled that it can be said to have ceased to exist?

Or what does he do in a case like the present, when demand might be said to be nonexistent, since there was nothing the Aliens seemed to want of Man's puny hoard?

"He *finds* something they want," Hebster said out loud.

How? *How?* Well, the Indian still sold his decorative blankets to the paleface as a way of life, as a source of income. And he insisted on being paid in cash—not firewater. If *only,* Hebster thought, he could somehow contrive to meet an Alien—he'd find out soon enough what its needs were, what was basically desired.

And then as the retort-shaped, the tube-shaped, the bell-shaped bottles materialized all around him, he understood! They had been forming the insistent questions in his mind. And they weren't satisfied with the answers he had found thus far. They liked answers. They liked answers very much indeed. If he was interested, there was always a way—

A great dots-in-bottle brushed his cortex and he screamed. "No! I don't *want* to!" he explained desperately.

Ping! went the dots-in-bottle and Hebster grabbed at his body. His continuing flesh reassured him. He felt very much like the girl in Greek mythology who had begged Zeus for the privilege of seeing him in the full regalia of his godhood. A few moments after her request had been granted, there had been nothing left of the inquisitive female but a fine feathery ash.

The bottles were swirling in and out of each other in a strange and intricate dance from which there radiated emotions vaguely akin to curiosity, yet partaking of amusement and rapture.

Why rapture? Hebster was positive he had caught that note, even allowing for the lack of similarity between mental patterns. He ran a hurried dragnet through his memory, caught a few corresponding items and dropped them after a brief, intensive examination. What was he trying to remember—what were his supremely efficient businessman's instincts trying to remind him of?

The dance became more complex, more rapid. A few bottles had passed under his feet and Hebster could see them, undulating and spinning some ten feet below the surface of the ground as if their presence had made the Earth a transparent as well as permeable medium. Completely unfamiliar with all matters Alien as he was, not knowing—not caring!—whether they danced as an expression of the counsel they were taking together, or as a matter of necessary social ritual, Hebster was able none the less to sense an approaching climax. Little crooked lines of green lightning began to erupt between the huge bottles. Something exploded near his left ear. He rubbed his face fearfully and moved away. The bottles followed, maintaining him in the imprisoning sphere of their frenzied movements.

Why *rapture?* Back in the city, the Aliens had had a terribly studious air about them as they hovered, almost motionless, above the works and lives of mankind. They were cold and careful scientists and showed not the slightest capacity for…for—

So he had something. At last he had something. But what do you do with an idea when you can't communicate it and can't act upon it yourself?

Ping!

The previous invitation was being repeated, more urgently. *Ping! Ping! Ping!*

"No!" he yelled and tried to stand. He found he couldn't. "I'm not…I don't want to go Prime!"

There was detached, almost divine laughter.

He felt that awful scrabbling inside his brain as if two or three entities were jostling each other within it. He shut his eyes hard and thought. He was close, he was very close. He had an idea, but he needed time to formulate it—a little while to figure out just exactly what the idea was and just exactly what to do with it!

Ping, ping, ping! Ping, ping, ping!

He had a headache. He felt as if his mind were being sucked out of his head. He tried to hold on to it. He couldn't.

All right, then. He relaxed abruptly, stopped trying to protect himself. But with his mind and his mouth, he yelled. For the first time in his life and with only a partially formed conception of whom he was addressing the desperate call to, Algernon Hebster screamed for help.

"I can do it!" he alternately screamed and thought. "Save money, save time, save whatever it is you want to save, whoever you are and whatever you call yourself—I can help you save! Help me, *help me— We* can do it—but *hurry.* Your problem can be solved— Economize. The balance-sheet— *Help—*"

The words and frantic thoughts spun in and out of each other like the contracting rings of Aliens all around him. He kept screaming, kept the focus on his mental images, while, unbearably, somewhere inside him, a gay and jocular force began to close a valve on his sanity.

Suddenly, he had absolutely no sensation. Suddenly, he knew dozens of things he had never dreamed he could know and had forgotten a thousand times as many. Suddenly, he felt that every nerve in his body was under control of his forefinger. Suddenly, he—

Ping, ping, ping! Ping! Ping! PING! PING! PING! PING!

"…like that," someone said.

"What, for example?" someone else asked.

"Well, they don't even lie normally. He's been sleeping like a human being. They twist and moan in their sleep, the Primeys do, for all the world like habitual old drunks. Speaking of moans, here comes our boy."

Hebster sat up on the army cot, rattling his head. The fears were leaving him, and, with the fears gone, he would no longer be hurt. Braganza, highly concerned and unhappy, was standing next to his bed with a man who was obviously a doctor. Hebster smiled at both of them, manfully resisting the temptation to drool out a string of nonsense syllables.

"Hi, fellas," he said. "Here I come, ungathering nuts in May."

"You don't mean to tell me you communicated!" Braganza yelled. "You communicated and didn't go Prime!"

Hebster raised himself on an elbow and glanced out past the tent flap to where Greta Seidenheim stood on the other side of a port-armed guard. He waved his fist at her, and she nodded a wide-open smile back.

"Found me lying in the desert like a waif, did you?"

"*Found* you!" Braganza spat. "You were brought in by Primeys, man. First time in history they ever did that. We've been waiting for you to come to in the serene faith that once you did, everything would be all right."

The corporation president rubbed his forehead. "It will be, Braganza, it will be. Just Primeys, eh? No Aliens helping them?"

"*Aliens?*" Braganza swallowed. "What led you to believe— What gave you reason to hope that…that *Aliens* would help the Primeys bring you in?"

"Well, perhaps I shouldn't have used the word 'help.' But I did think there would be a few Aliens in the group that escorted my unconscious body back to you. Sort of an honor guard, Braganza. It would have been a real nice gesture, don't you think?"

The SIC man looked at the doctor, who had been following the conversation with interest. "Mind stepping out for a minute?" he suggested.

He walked behind the man and dropped the tent flap into place. Then he came around to the foot of the army cot and pulled on his mustache vigorously. "Now, see here, Hebster, if you keep up this clowning, so help me I will slit your belly open and snap your intestines back in your face! *What happened?*"

"What happened?" Hebster laughed and stretched slowly, carefully, as if he were afraid of breaking the bones of his arm. "I don't think I'll ever be able to answer that question completely. And there's a section of my mind that's very glad that I won't. This much I remember clearly: I had an idea. I communicated it to the proper and interested party. We concluded—this party and I—a tentative agreement as agents, the exact terms of the agreement to be decided by our principals and its complete ratification to be contingent upon their acceptance. Furthermore, we— All right, Braganza, all right! I'll tell it straight. Put down that folding chair. Remember, I've just been through a pretty unsettling experience!"

"Not any worse than the world is about to go through," the official growled. "While you've been out on your three-day vacation, Dempsey's been organizing a full-dress revolution every place at once. He's been very careful to limit it to parades and verbal fireworks so that we haven't been able to make with the riot squads, but it's pretty evident that he's ready to start using muscle. Tomorrow might be it; he's spouting on a world-wide video hookup and it's the opinion of the best experts we have available that his tag line will be the signal for action. Know what their slogan is? It concerns Verus, who's been indicted for murder; they claim he'll be a martyr."

"And you were caught with your suspicions down. How many SIC men turned out to be Firsters?"

Braganza nodded. "Not too many, but more than we expected. More than we could afford. He'll do it, Dempsey will, unless you've hit the real thing. Look, Hebster," his heavy voice took on a pleading quality, "don't play with me any more. Don't hold my threats against me; there was no personal animosity in them, just a terrible, fearful worry over the world and its people and the government I was supposed to protect. If you still have a gripe against me, I, Braganza, give you leave to take it out of my hide as soon as we clear this mess up. But let me know where we stand first. A lot of lives and a lot of history depend on what you did out there in that patch of desert."

Hebster told him. He began with the extraterrestrial *Walpurgisnacht.* "Watching the Aliens slipping in and out of each other in that cockeyed and complicated rhythm, it struck me how different they were from the thoughtful dots-in-bottles hovering over our busy places, how different all creatures are in their home environments—and how hard it is to get to know them on the basis of their company manners. And then I realized that this place wasn't their home."

"Of course. Did you find out which part of the galaxy they come from?"

"That's not what I mean. Simply because we have marked this area off—and others like it in the Gobi, in the Sahara, in Central Australia—as a reservation for those of our kind whose minds have crumbled under the clear, conscious and certain knowledge of inferiority, we cannot assume that the Aliens around whose settlements they have congregated have necessarily settled themselves."

"*Huh?*" Braganza shook his head rapidly and batted his eyes.

"In other words we had made an assumption on the basis of the Aliens' very evident superiority to ourselves. But that assumption—and therefore that superiority—was in our own terms of what is superior and inferior, and not the Aliens'. And it especially might not apply to those Aliens on...the reservation."

The SIC man took a rapid walk around the tent. He beat a great fist into an open sweaty palm. "I'm beginning to, just beginning to—"

"That's what I was doing at that point, just beginning to. Assumptions that don't stand up under the structure they're supposed to support have caused the ruin of more close-thinking businessmen than I would like to face across any conference table. The four brokers, for example, who, after the market crash of 1929—"

"All right," Braganza broke in hurriedly, taking a chair near the cot. "Where did you go from there?"

"I still couldn't be certain of anything; all I had to go on were a few random thoughts inspired by extrasubstantial adrenalin secretions and, of course, the strong feeling that these particular Aliens weren't acting the way I had become accustomed to expect Aliens to act. They reminded me of something, of somebody. I was positive that once I got that memory tagged, I'd have most of the problem solved. And I was right."

"How were you right? What was the memory?"

"Well, I hit it backwards, kind of. I went back to Professor Kleimbocher's analogy about the paleface inflicting firewater on the Indian. I've always felt that somewhere in that analogy was the solution. And suddenly, thinking of Professor Kleimbocher and watching those powerful creatures writhing their way in and around each other, suddenly I knew what was wrong. Not the analogy, but our way of using it. We'd picked it up by the hammer head instead of the handle. The paleface gave firewater to the Indian all right—but he got something in return."

"What?"

"Tobacco. Now there's nothing very much wrong with tobacco if it isn't misused, but the first white men to smoke probably went as far overboard as the first Indians to drink. And both booze and tobacco have this in common—they make you awfully sick if you use too much for your initial experiment. See, Braganza? These Aliens out here in the desert reservation are *sick*. They have hit something in our culture that is as psychologically indigestible to them as...well, whatever they have that sticks in our mental gullet and causes ulcers among us. They've been put into a kind of isolation in our desert areas until the problem can be licked."

"Something that's as indigestible psychologically— What could it be, Hebster?"

The businessman shrugged irritably. "I don't know. And I don't want to know. Perhaps it's just that they can't let go of a problem until they've solved it—and they can't solve the problems of mankind's activity because of mankind's inherent and basic differences. Simply because we can't understand them, we had no right to assume that they could and did understand us."

"That wasn't all, Hebster. As the comedians put it—everything we can do, they can do better."

"Then why did they keep sending Primeys in to ask for those weird gadgets and impossible gimcracks?"

"They could duplicate anything we made."

"Well, maybe that is it," Hebster suggested. "They could duplicate it, but could they design it? They show every sign of being a race of creatures who never had to make very much for themselves; perhaps they evolved fairly early into animals with direct control over matter, thus never having had to go through the various stages of artifact design. This, in our terms, is a tremendous advantage; but it inevitably would have concurrent disadvantages. Among other things, it would mean a minimum of art forms and a lack of basic engineering knowledge of the artifact itself if not of the directly activated and altered material. The fact is I was right, as I found out later.

"For example. Music is not a function of theoretical harmonics, of complete scores in the head of a conductor or composer—these come later, much later. Music is first and foremost a function of the particular instrument, the reed pipe, the skin drum, the human throat—it is a function of tangibles which a race operating upon electrons, positrons and mesons would never encounter in the course of its construction. As soon as I had that, I had the other flaw in the analogy—the assumption itself."

"You mean the assumption that we are necessarily inferior to the Aliens?"

"Right, Braganza. They can do a lot that we can't do, but vice very much indeed versa. How many special racial talents we possess that they don't is a matter of pure conjecture—and may continue to be for a good long time. Let the theoretical boys worry that one a century from now, just so they stay away from it at present."

Braganza fingered a button on his green jerkin and stared over Hebster's head. "No more scientific investigation of them, eh?"

"Well, we can't right now and we have to face up to that mildly unpleasant situation. The consolation is that they have to do the same. Don't you see? It's not a basic inadequacy. We don't have enough facts and can't get enough at the moment through normal channels of scientific observation because of the implicit psychological dangers to both races. Science, my forward-looking friend, is a complex of interlocking theories, *all derived from observation.*

"Remember, long before you had any science of navigation you had coast-hugging and river-hopping traders who knew how the various currents affected their leaky little vessels, who had learned things about the relative dependability of the moon and the stars—without any interest at all in integrating these scraps of knowledge into broader theories. Not until you have a sufficiently large body of these scraps, and are able to distinguish the preconceptions from the actual observations, can you proceed to organize a science of navigation without running the grave risk of drowning while you conduct your definitive experiments.

"A trader isn't interested in theories. He's interested only in selling something that glitters for something that glitters even more. In the process, painlessly and imperceptibly, he picks up bits of knowledge which gradually reduce the area of unfamiliarity. Until one day there are enough bits of knowledge on which to base a sort of preliminary understanding, a working hypothesis. And then, some Kleimbocher of the future, operating in an area no longer subject to the sudden and unexplainable mental disaster, can construct meticulous and exact laws out of the more obviously valid hypotheses."

"I might have known it would be something like this, if you came back with it, Hebster! So their theorists and our theorists had better move out and the traders move in. Only how do we contact their traders—if they have any such animals?"

The corporation president sprang out of bed and began dressing. "They have them. Not a Board of Director type perhaps—but a business-minded Alien. As soon as I realized that the dots-in-bottles were acting, relative to their balanced scientific colleagues, very like our own high IQ Primeys, I knew I needed help. I needed someone I could tell about it, someone on their side who had as great a stake in an operating solution as I did. There had to be an Alien in the picture somewhere who was concerned with profit and loss statements, with how much of a return you get out of a given investment of time, personnel, materiel and energy. I figured with him I could talk—*business.* The simple approach: What have you got that we want and how little of what we have will you take for it. No attempts to understand completely incompatible philosophies. There had to be that kind of character somewhere in the expedition. So I shut my eyes and let out what I fondly hoped was a telepathic *yip* channeled to him. I was successful.

"Of course, I might not have been successful if he hadn't been searching desperately for just that sort of *yip*. He came buzzing up in a rousing United States Cavalry-routs-the-redskins type of rescue, stuffed my dripping psyche back into my subconscious and hauled me up into some sort of never-never-ship. I've been in this interstellar version of Mohammed's coffin, suspended between Heaven and Earth, for three days, while he alternately bargained with me and consulted the home office about developments.

"We dickered the way I do with Primeys—by running down a list of what each of us could offer and comparing it with what we wanted; each of us trying to get a little more than we gave to the other guy, in our own terms, of course. Buying and selling are intrinsically simple processes; I don't imagine our discussions were very much different from those between a couple of Phoenician sailors and the blue-painted Celtic inhabitants of early Britain."

"And this…this business-Alien never suggested the possibility of taking what they wanted—"

"By force? No, Braganza, not once. Might be they're too civilized for such shenanigans. Personally, I think the big reason is that they don't have any idea of what it is they do want from us. We represent a fantastic enigma to them—a species which uses matter to alter matter, producing objects which, while intended for similar functions, differ enormously from each other. You might say that we ask the question '*how?*' about their activities; and they want to know the '*why?*' about ours. Their investigators have compulsions even greater than ours. As I understand it, the intelligent races they've encountered up to this point are all comprehensible to them since they derive from parallel evolutionary paths. Every time one of their researchers gets close to the answer of why we wear various colored clothes even in climates where clothing is unnecessary, he slips over the edges and splashes.

"Of course, that's why this opposite number of mine was so worried. I don't know his exact status—he may be anything from the bookkeeper to the business-manager of the expedition—but it's his neck, or should I say bottleneck, if the outfit continues to be uneconomic. And I gathered that not only has his occupation kind of barred him from doing the investigation his unstable pals were limping back from into the asylums he's constructed here in the deserts, but those of them who've managed to retain their sanity constantly exhibit a healthy contempt for him. They feel, you see, that their function is that of the expedition. He's strictly supercargo. Do you think it bothers them one bit," Hebster snorted, "that he has a report to prepare, to show how his expedition stood up in terms of a balance sheet—"

"Well, you did manage to communicate on that point, at least," Braganza grinned. "Maybe traders using the simple, earnestly chiseling approach will be the answer. You've certainly supplied us with more basic data already than years of heavily subsidized research. Hebster, I want you to go on the air with this story you told me and show a couple of Primey Aliens to the video public."

"Uh-uh. You tell 'em. You can use the prestige. I'll think a message to my Alien buddy along the private channel he's keeping open for me, and he'll send you a couple of human-happy dots-in-bottles for the telecast. I've got to whip back to New York and get my entire outfit to work on a really encyclopedic job."

"Encyclopedic?"

The executive pulled his belt tight and reached for a tie. "Well, what else would you call the first edition of the Hebster Interstellar Catalogue of All Human Activity and Available Artifacts, prices available upon request with the understanding that they are subject to change without notice?"

AFTERWORD

Actually, I wrote this short novel over the course of five or six years, finishing it only in 1951. Braganza was the protagonist I started with, and his attitudes and beliefs my chief reason for writing the piece in the first place. Hebster, with whom I disagreed utterly and whom I disliked utterly, was a minor comic-nasty character I inserted in the story only for satiric purposes.

But somehow the story didn't work. I kept writing it and rewriting it, and it kept falling apart. I finally concluded that there was something about the story in which I absolutely did not believe, and I put it aside to let the back of my mind work on it.

Then, one day late in 1951, I picked up the manuscript, reread it, and began wondering how it would work from the point of view of a man I despised and hated—Algernon Hebster, the simon-pure businessman.

It worked wonderfully, I found. Apparently I could think and feel and justify like Hebster. He, too, was a large part of me. I finished the piece in two sleepless days.

My then agent didn't like it at all. He said it was pulp junk, worthy only of the bottom of the market at one-half cent or a quarter of a cent a word. I disagreed and sent it out on my own to John W. Campbell, Jr., at *Astounding Science Fiction*.

John liked it and told me it was worth a bonus rate. He wanted only a small bit of rewrite, the first time he had asked me for such a thing. His request seemed reasonable, and I agreed to do it.

When he got the finished manuscript, he was still somewhat dissatisfied. He asked for another small rewrite, and I did that too. Then he wanted yet another, which I couldn't see as anything which would genuinely help the story. I wrote him an angry note, to which he replied with one of his seven-page, single-spaced ones, questioning my basic philosophy of life, art, and politics. I asked him to send the story back, and he telephoned me and told me he liked it far too much to let it go; as a matter of fact, he was planning to use it as the cover story for an issue (I had never yet had the cover for *Astounding*). All he wanted was just one more teensy rewrite which he was sure I could do and wouldn't find objectionable.

I did find it objectionable, yet I wanted the cover and the high rate he had promised. And I was not yet at the point where I could be comfortable while in disagreement with John Campbell, whom I regarded as my intellectual father. I sought out Ted Sturgeon—who had once been my agent, but was still my mentor in science fiction—and asked for help.

Ted read "Firewater" and liked it enormously. He then went off to have a long and long-winded lunch with Campbell. He came back and had an early ambassadorial supper with me.

The problem that he said he had slowly discovered had nothing to do with the rewrites John had requested. It had to do with the fact that I had made the aliens totally superior intellectually to mankind—and John Campbell could not bring himself to accept that.

He reminded me of what had happened when I played chess with Campbell. I had beaten him easily because he was very much a sometime player while I, in those days, was a habitué of the chess corner at Washington Square Park and of the Marshall Chess Club. I had even once beaten the chess champion of New York State (in what was, admittedly, a skittles game).

Campbell had been quite upset at my victory over him. "I just can't believe you're that much better than I," he had said. It did me no good to tell him how many people at the chess corner—janitors, cabdrivers, even wandering vagrants who played for quarters and half-dollars and whom you just had to call chess bums—could beat me with less skill but with their greater knowledge of chess traps. He had walked out of the room, shaking his head and exhaling in misery.

"His belief in his mental powers and the mental powers of his species is just too important to him," Ted told me. "You've got to find some way of suggesting that the aliens in 'Firewater' are not *all* that goddam good. They're better in this way and that way, but not in every way. Basically, they're just different."

I wept, I cried, I tore my hair. "I lost the original hero of this story," I said, "when I found out that there was more Hebster than Braganza in me. Then I discovered that what I really had wanted to write about was what would happen to our collective egos if we encountered aliens who were not merely technologically superior to us, but so superior biologically and psychologically that they just wanted to look at us and be amused by us. Now you're telling me that I have to delete the point as well. Well, why write? Why the hell write?"

Ted spread his hands. "Look, you can sure sell the piece to a lower-grade pulpy market where half the readership will complain there's not enough action in it. Or you can give John just a little bit of what he wants, of what he must have to believe in himself and his fellows, and you wind up with what is still a distinguished story and a cover story in what is undeniably the absolutely best science-fiction magazine being published today."

"And I've written something dishonest. I've torn the theme out of my story."

"No, you haven't. You've just made it a shade less emphatic. And, look Phil: you're just doing this for the first version, the first printing. When the piece is anthologized—and it will be—and when you publish it in your own collection—and you will be able to one day—you can see to it that the original is printed. And you can tell the reader all about it at last."

Well, I never said that I am not easily corrupted. And that last argument of Ted's did have a powerful effect on me. So I gave John Campbell the minimum that seemed to satisfy him, and he published the story with a cover illustration that I found delightful. The readership voted "Firewater" the best of the year. And I? I never read John's magazine again.

I put the original manuscript, the one before any changes, in a manila folder, along with all the correspondence on the story. I put it away—for the future. And somewhere, in one of my many moves (did not Ben Franklin say that three removes were as bad as a fire?) I lost the folder, together with the original and the correspondence.

Today? Oh, hell, do me something—I now like the way the story reads *exactly* as I have it here, exactly the way it was published in John Campbell's *Astounding* in February 1952.

WRITTEN 1951——PUBLISHED 1952

৵৹

LISBON CUBED

The telephone rang. Alfred Smith, who had been hauling clothes out of his valise and stuffing them into a typical hotel room bureau, looked up startled.

"Now, who—" he began, and shook his head.

Obviously it must be a wrong number. Nobody knew he was in New York, and nobody—this for a certainty—knew he had checked into this particular hotel. Or come to think of it, somebody did.

The room clerk at the desk where he had just registered.

Must be some hotel business. Something about don't use the lamp on the end table: it tends to short-circuit.

The telephone rang again. He dropped the valise and walked around the bed. He picked up the phone.

"Yes?" he said.

"Mr. Smith?" came a thick voice from the other end.

"Speaking."

"This is Mr. Jones. Mr. Cohen and Mr. Kelly are with me in the lobby. So is Jane Doe. Do you want us to come up or shall we wait for you?"

"I beg your pardon?"

"Well, then, we'll come up. Five-oh-four, isn't it?"

"Yes, but wait a minute! *Who* did you say?" He realized they had hung up.

Alfred Smith put down the telephone and ran his fingers through his crewcut. He was a moderately tall, moderately athletic, moderately handsome young man with the faintest hint at jowl and belly of recent prosperity.

"Mr. *Jones? Cohen? Kelly?* And for suffering Pete's sake, *Jane Doe?*"

It must be a joke. Any Smith was used to jokes on his name. What was your name before it was Smith? *Alfred* Smith? Whatever happened to good old Johnnie?

Then he remembered that his caller had just asked for Mr. Smith. Smith *was* a common name, like it or not.

He picked up the phone again. "Desk," he told the operator.

"Yes, Desk?" a smooth voice said after a while.

"This is Mr. Smith in Room 504. Was there another Smith registered here before me?"

A long pause. "Are you having any trouble, sir?"

Alfred Smith grimaced. "That's not what I'm asking. Was there or wasn't there?"

"Well, sir, if you could tell me if it is causing you inconvenience in any way…"

He got exasperated. "I asked you a simple question. Was there a Smith in this room before me? What's the matter, did he kill himself?"

"We have no right to believe he committed suicide, sir!" the desk clerk said emphatically. "There are many, *many* circumstances under which a guest might disappear after registering for a room!"

There was a peremptory knock on the door. Alfred Smith grunted, "Okay. That's all I wanted to know," and hung up.

He opened the door, and before he could say anything, four people came in. Three were men; the last was a mildly attractive woman.

"Now, look—" he began.

"Hello, Gar-Pitha," one of the men said. "I'm Jones. This is Cohen, this is Kelly. And, of course, Jane Doe."

"There's been a mistake," Alfred told him.

"And how there's been a mistake!" said Cohen, locking the door behind him carefully. "Jones, you called Smith by his right name! When the corridor door was open! That's unpardonable stupidity."

Jane Doe nodded. "Open or closed, we must remember that we are on Earth. We will use only Earth names. Operating Procedure Regulations XIV-XXII."

Alfred took a long, slow look at her, "On Earth?"

She smiled shamefacedly. "There I go, myself. I did practically the same thing. You're right. In *America*. Or rather, to put it more exactly and less suspiciously, in New York City."

Mr. Kelly had been walking around him, staring at Alfred. "You're perfect," he said at last. "Better than any of us. That disguise took a lot of hard, patient work. Don't tell me, I know. You're perfect, Smith, perfect."

What in the world were they, Alfred wondered frantically—lunatics? No, *spies!* Should he say something, should he give the mistake away, or should he start yelling his head off for help? But maybe they weren't spies—maybe they were detectives on the trail of spies. He was in New York, after all. New York wasn't Grocery Corners, Illinois.

And that suggested another possibility. New York, the home of the sharpie, the smart aleck. It could be a simple practical joke being played by some city slickers on a new little hayseed.

If it were…

His visitors had found seats for themselves. Mr. Kelly opened the briefcase he was carrying and grubbed around in it with his fingers. A low hum filled the room.

"Not enough power," Mr. Kelly apologized. "This is a small sun, after all. But give the rig a few minutes: it'll build up."

Mr. Jones leaned forward. "Listen, do you folks mind if I slip out of my disguise? I'm hot."

"You're not supposed to," Jane Doe reminded him. "The uniform is to be worn at all times when we're on duty."

"I know, I know, but Sten-Durok—*oops,* I mean Cohen, locked the door. Nobody comes in through windows in this particular place, and we don't have to worry about materialization. So how about I relax for a second or two?"

Alfred had perched on the edge of the dresser. He looked Mr. Jones over with great amusement. The pudgy little man was wearing a cheap gray sharkskin suit. He was bald; he wore no eyeglasses; he had no beard. He didn't even have a mustache.

Disguise, huh?

"I say let him," Alfred suggested with an anticipatory chuckle. "We're all alone— he might as well be comfortable. Go ahead, Jones, *take* off your disguise."

"Thanks," Jones said with feeling. "I'm suffocating in this outfit."

Alfred chuckled again. He'd show these New Yorkers.

"Take it off. Be comfortable. Make yourself at home."

Jones nodded and unbuttoned the jacket of his gray sharkskin suit. Then he un-buttoned the white shirt under it. Then he put his two forefingers into his chest, all the way in, and pulled his chest apart. He kept pulling until there was a great dark hole about ten inches wide.

A black spider squirmed out of the opening. Its round little body was about the size of a man's fist, its legs about the size and length of pipe stems. It crouched on Jones's chest, while the body from which it had emerged maintained its position in a kind of paralysis, the fingers still holding the chest apart, the back and legs still rest-ing comfortably in the chair.

"Whew!" said the spider. "That feels good."

Alfred found he couldn't stop chuckling. He finally managed to halt the noise from his mouth, but it kept on going in his head. He stared at the spider, at the stiff body from which it had come. Then, frantically, he stared at the others in the room, at Cohen, at Kelly, at Jane Doe.

They couldn't have looked less interested.

The hum from the briefcase on Kelly's knees abruptly resolved itself into words. Alfred's visitors stopped looking bored and leaned forward attentively.

"Greetings, Special Emissaries," said the voice. "This is Command Central speak-ing. Robinson, to you. Are there any reports of significance?"

"None from me," Jane Doe told it.

"Nor me," from Kelly.

"Nothing new yet," said Cohen.

The spider stretched itself luxuriously. "Same here. Nothing to report."

"Jones!" ordered the voice from the briefcase. "Get back into your uniform!"

"It's *hot,* chief. And we're all alone in here, sitting behind what they call a locked door. Remember, they've got a superstition on Earth about locked doors? We don't have anything to worry about."

"*I'll* tell you what to worry about. You get into that uniform, Jones! Or maybe you're tired of being a Special Emissary? Maybe you'd like to go back to General Emissary status?"

The spider stretched its legs and performed what could only be described as a shrug.

Then it backed carefully into the hole in the chest. The hole closed behind it. The body of Jones came to life and buttoned his shirt and jacket.

"That's better," said the voice from the briefcase on Kelly's knee. "Don't ever do that again while you're on duty."

"Okay, chief, okay. But couldn't we cool down this planet? You know, bring on winter, start a new ice age? It would make it a lot easier to work."

"And a lot easier to be detected, stupid. You worry about the big things like conventions and beauty contests. We'll worry about the little things here, in Command Central, like arbitrarily changing the seasons and starting new ice ages. All right, Smith, how about you? What's your report?"

Alfred Smith shook the thick gathered wool out of his head, slid off the dresser, and on to his feet. He looked around wildly.

"Re-re*port?*" A breath. "Why, nothing—nothing to report."

"Took you a long time to make up your mind about it. You're not holding anything back, are you? Remember, it's our job to evaluate information, not yours."

Alfred wet his lips. "N-no. I'm not holding anything back."

"You'd better not. One beauty contest you forget to tell us about and you're through, Smith. We still haven't forgotten that boner you pulled in Zagreb."

"Oh, chief," Jane Doe intervened. "It was only a local stunt to discover who was the tallest card-carrying Communist in Croatia. You can't blame Smith for missing *that.*"

"We certainly can blame Smith for that. It was a beauty contest, within the definition of the term you were given. If Cohen hadn't stumbled across a mention of it in the Kiev *Pravda,* all hell could have broken loose, Remember that, Smith. And stop calling me *chief,* all of you. The name is Robinson. Remember it."

They all nodded, Alfred with them. He shot a mixed look of uncertainty and gratitude at Jane Doe.

"All right," the voice went on, somewhat mollified. "And to show you that I can hand out the boosts as well as the knocks, I want to commend Smith on his disguise. It's a little offbeat, but it rings true—and that's the main thing. If the rest of you only spent as much time and care on your uniform, we'd be in the home stretch in no time." The voice paused and took on an oily, heavily whimsical quality. "Before you could say 'Jack Robinson.' "

They all laughed dutifully at that one, even Alfred.

"You think Smith did a good job on his disguise, don't you, chief, I mean, Mr. Robinson?" Jane Doe asked eagerly, as if she wanted to underline the fact for everyone.

"I certainly do. Look at that suit. it's not just any old suit, but a tweed jacket and flannel pants. Now that's what I call using your imagination. His chin isn't just a chin, it's a *cleft* chin. Very good. The color of his hair—first-rate. The only thing I might possibly object to is the bow tie. I'd say a good solid rep tie, regular length, would be a little less chancy, a little less likely to attract attention. But it feels right, and that's the main thing—the *feel* of the disguise. In this business, you either have an instinct for merging with the population of the planet, or you don't. I think Smith has it. Good work, Smith."

"Thank you," Alfred mumbled.

"All right, oh—er, Robinson," Mr. Jones said impatiently. "It's a good uniform-disguise. But it's not that important. Our work is more important than how we look."

"Your work *is* how you look. If you look right, you work right. Take yourself, for example, Jones. A more nondescript, carelessly assembled human being, I don't think I've ever come across before. What are you supposed to be—Mr. American-Man-in-the-Street?"

Mr. Jones looked deeply hurt. "I'm supposed to be a Brooklyn druggist. And believe me, the uniform is plenty good enough. I know. You should see some of these druggists."

"Some, Jones, but not most. And that's my point."

There was a throat-clearing sound from Mr. Cohen. "Don't want to interrupt you, Robinson, but this isn't supposed to be a long visit we're having with Smith. We just dropped up, kind of."

"Right, Cohen, right on the old button. All right, everybody ready for instructions?"

"Ready," they all chorused, Alfred coming in raggedly on the last syllable.

"Here we go then. Cohen, you're back on your old assignment, keeping careful check on any new beauty contests scheduled anywhere in the country, with special attention to be paid to New York, of course. Kelly, you're to do the same with conventions. Jane Doe and John Smith will continue to look into anything that might be a camouflaged attempt."

"Anything particular in mind?" Jane Doe asked.

"Not for you at the moment. You just keep making the rounds of beauty parlors and see if you stumble across something. Smith, we have a special item we'd like you to look into. There's a fancy dress ball of the plumbers of the New York City area. Drop down there and see what you can see. And let us know if you hit it. Fast."

Alfred kept his voice determinedly casual. "What do you want me to look out for?"

"Well, if you don't know by this time—" the voice from the briefcase rose impatiently. "Door prizes, an award for the best costume, even a contest for Miss Pipe Wrench of 1921 or whatever year Earth is in right now. I don't think we have to worry about that last, though. It would be too damn obvious, and we haven't hit anything obvious yet."

"How about me?" Jones wanted to know.

"We'll have special instructions for you pretty soon. There may be a new angle."

They all looked interested at that, but the voice from the briefcase did not seem disposed to elucidate further.

"That will be all," it said unequivocally. "You can start leaving now."

Mr. Kelly zipped the briefcase shut, nodded at everyone, and left.

A few moments later, Mr. Cohen followed him. Then Jones yawned and said, "Well, goodbye, now." He closed the door behind him.

Jane Doe rose, but she didn't go toward the door. She came over to where Alfred Smith was standing with a punched expression in his eyes.

"Well, John?" she said softly.

Alfred Smith couldn't think of anything to say to that, except, "Well, Jane?"

"We're together again. Working on an assignment again, together. Isn't it wonderful?"

He nodded slowly, carefully. "Yes. Wonderful."

"And if we can only close it up this time, finish the whole nasty business once and for all, we'll be going back together."

"And then?"

Her eyes glistened. "You know, darling. A quiet little web somewhere, just for two. You and I alone. And piles and piles of eggs."

Alfred gulped, and, in spite of himself, turned away.

"Oh, I'm sorry, darling," she cried, taking his hand. "I've upset you. I was talking out of uniform. Well then, put it this way: a cottage small by a waterfall. And baby makes three. You and I, down the golden years together. When your hair has turned to silver. There! Is that better?"

"Lots," he managed to get out, staring at her wildly. "Lots better."

She threw her arms around him. He realized he was expected to respond, and squeezed back.

"Oh, I don't care," she whispered into his ear. "I don't care about discipline or anything when I'm close to you. And I'll say it, even if Command Central is listening. Darling, do you know what I'd like right now?"

Alfred sighed. He was more than half afraid of what was coming. "No, what? What would you like right now?"

"I'd like for us to be out of uniform, scuttling about and over each other in some damp, dark place, I'd like to feel your claws upon me, your antennae caressing me, *me*—instead of this clumsy emotionless disguise I'm wearing."

He thought. "It—it'll come. Be patient, darling."

She straightened up and became businesslike again. "Yes, and I'd better be going. Here's a list of all our telephone numbers, in case you want to get in touch with any of us. Remember, this operation is to be conducted strictly according to regulations. And that means no *phmpffing*, no *phmpffing* at all, except in case of the greatest emergency. For everything else, we use telephones."

"Telephones?" he found himself echoing.

"Yes." She gestured to the black instrument on its stand near the bed. "Those things."

"Oh, *those* things," he repeated, fighting the impulse to shake his head hard in a brain-clearing gesture. "Yes. Those things. But no—no, er, what did you say?"

"No *phmpffing*."

"None at all?" Surely if he continued to ask questions something would become clear. And sane!

Jane Doe looked extremely concerned. "Of course not! This is a maximum operation."

"Yes, that's right," he agreed. "A maximum operation. I'd forgotten that."

"Well, don't," she advised him earnestly. "Don't forget. That way, you'll get into trouble again. One more boner like the one you pulled in Zagreb, darling, and you're through. You'll be kicked out of the Service. And then what do you think will happen to our plans together?"

"We'll be finished, huh?" Alfred studied her. Under all that girl-flesh, he reminded himself, there was a large, black spider working at controls like a mechanic in a power crane.

"Right. I'd never marry outside the Service. We'd be finished. So do take care of yourself, darling, and give it all you've got. Stay on the ball. Fly right. Get with it. Rise and shine. Stick to the straight and narrow. Go in there and pitch. Don't let George do it. Work hard and save your money. Early to bed and early to rise. Don't be half safe."

"I'll do my best," he promised, his voice rattling.

"My little crawler," she whispered intimately and kissed him on the ear.

She closed the door behind her.

Alfred groped his way to the bed. After a while, he noticed that he was uncomfortable. He was sitting on a valise. Absent-mindedly, he shoved it to the floor.

What had he wandered into? Or, to put it more accurately, what had wandered into him?

Spies. Yes, obviously spies. But *such* spies…?

Spies from another planet. What were they spying on—beauty contests, conventions, plumbers' fancy dress balls? What were they looking for? What in the world— or rather the universe—*could* they be looking for?

One thing was obvious. They were up to no good. That omnipresent contempt whenever they mentioned Earth or the things of Earth.

An advance wave of invaders? Scouts preparing the way for the main body? They could be that. But why beauty contests, why fancy dress balls?

What was there of value that they could possibly learn from institutions such as these?

You'd expect to find them at nuclear research labs, at rocket proving grounds, skulking about the Pentagon in Washington, D.C.

Alfred decided there was no point in trying to follow their thought processes. They were completely alien creatures: who knew what kind of information they might consider valuable, what might be important to them?

But they were undoubtedly spies sizing up Earth for an invasion to come.

"Filthy little spiders," he growled in a righteous excess of xenophobia.

And one of them was in love with him. One of them intended to marry him. What was it she had said—piles and piles of eggs? A pretty thought! He shuddered from his neck to his knees.

But they believed he was this other Smith, John Smith. Earth still had a chance. Pure luck had given Earth a counterspy. Him.

He felt frightened, but a little proud. A *counter*spy.

The first thing to do was to check on this John Smith.

Alfred Smith reached for the telephone. "Desk!"

There was precious little information from the clerk to supplement what he had been given before. John Smith had registered here two weeks ago. He had left one afternoon and not come back. After the usual interval it was assumed he had skipped, since he owed a few days on the bill at the time. His belongings were in the hotel store room.

"No, sir, I'm sorry, sir, but hotel regulations do not permit us to let you go through his belongings. Unless you wish to claim a relationship."

"And if I did?" Alfred asked eagerly. "If I did wish to claim a relationship?"

"Then it would be necessary for you to establish proof, sir."

"I see. Well, thank you very much." He hung up.

Where was he now? This John Smith had registered here, evidently under a previous agreement, as his room was to provide the meeting place for the entire group. Then he had walked out one day and not returned.

Since the disguises were subject to frequent change, when another Smith had registered in the same room, the spies assumed it was their man. They may not even have known of the hiatus between the two Smiths.

What had happened to John Smith? Had he defected to the United States government? To the United Nations? Hardly. There would be an F.B.I. man, a small army unit staked out in the room in that case, when John Smith's friends showed up.

No, he had just disappeared. But was he dead, killed in some freak accident while crossing a bridge—that would account for his body not being recovered—or was he only temporarily away, working on some newly discovered angle for his interplanetary organization?

And what would happen to Alfred when he returned? The young man on the bed shivered. Espionage groups, he recalled from the novels he had read, tended to a sort of hatchet-man justice. Obviously, they would not let an Earthman with knowledge of their existence and operations go on living.

Then, obviously, he had to get help.

But from where? The police? The F.B.I.? He shivered again at the picture evoked; himself, somewhat embarrassed, stammering a bit, not quite remembering all the details, telling this story to a hard-faced desk sergeant.

An interplanetary invasion, Mr. Smith? From Mars? Oh, not from Mars—from where then? Oh, you don't quite know, Mr. Smith? All you're sure of is that it's an interplanetary invasion? I see. And how did you happen to hear of this on your first day in New York? Oh, four people came up to your hotel room and told you about it? Very interesting. Very, *very* interesting. And their names were Mr. Cohen, Mr. Kelly, Mr. Jones, and Jane Doe? And *your* name is Smith, isn't it? And all we have to do to prove your story is find the address behind one of these telephone numbers, cut open the person in whose name the phone is registered, and find a big black spider inside....

"No!" Alfred groaned aloud. "Not that way—I wouldn't have a chance!"

He needed proof—tangible proof. And facts. Mostly he needed facts. Who were these spiders, what was their home planet, when were they planning to invade, what kind of weapons did they have at their disposal—stuff like that. And lots and lots of data about their organization here on Earth, especially in America.

How did you get such data? You couldn't ask—that would be the surest way to expose yourself as a bona fide human with nothing more interesting inside you than a length or so of intestine and a couple of ribs.

But they'd given him an assignment. Something about a plumber's fancy dress ball. Now, obviously an assignment like that concerned their plans, their organization. Obviously.

He grabbed for the phone.

"Desk? This is Mr. Smith in 504. Yes, Mr. Smith *again*. Listen, how do I find out where the plumbers are in New York?"

"If the plumbing in your room is out of order, sir," the smooth, patient voice explained, "the hotel will send up a—"

"No, no, no! I don't want a plumber, I want *plumbers, all* of them! The New York plumbers, how do I find them?"

He distinctly heard lips being licked at the other end as this question was digested and then, aside, a whispered comment, "Yeah, it's 504, again. We got a real beauty in that room this time. I don't envy the night man tonight, let me tell you!" Loudly and clearly, if just a shade less smoothly, the voice replied: "You will find a classified telephone directory on the desk near your bed, sir. You can look up plumbers under *P*. Most of the plumbers in Manhattan are listed there. For plumbers in Brooklyn, the Bronx, Queens, and Staten Island, I would suggest—"

"I don't want plumbers in Brooklyn or the Bronx! I don't even want plumbers in—" Alfred Smith drew a deep breath. He had to get a grip on himself! The fate of the entire planet, of the entire human race, depended on his keeping his head. He forced his mind backward, inch by inch, off the plateau of hysteria it had mounted. He waited until his voice was calm.

"This is the problem," he began again, slowly and carefully. "There is a fancy dress ball of the plumbers of the New York area. It's being held somewhere in the city tonight, and I'm supposed to be there. Unfortunately, I've lost my invitation and it contained the address. Now, how do you think I could go about finding where the ball is going to be?" He congratulated himself on the swiftness of his thinking. This was really being a counterspy!

Pause. "I could make some inquiries, sir, through the usual channels, and call you back." And aside: "Now he says *he's* a plumber and he wants to go to a fancy dress ball. Can you beat that? I tell you in this business…" And to him: "Would that be satisfactory, sir?"

"Fine," Alfred Smith told him enthusiastically. "That would be *fine*."

He hung up. Well, he was getting the hang of this espionage business. Nothing like a sales background for practice in quick thinking and quick talking.

He didn't have to report to the office until tomorrow. That gave him this afternoon and this evening to save the human race.

Who would have thought when he was offered a job in New York with the BlakSeme Hosiery Company ("Men *Notice* BlakSemes—They're so Shockingly Stocking!") what tremendous stakes he'd be playing for the very day of his arrival? Of course, BlakSeme knew what kind of man he was, they knew he was executive timber or they'd never have hired him right out from under PuzzleKnit, their biggest competitor. He'd made quite a name for himself, Alfred Smith was modestly willing to admit, in the Illinois territory. Highest sales increases for three years running, steadiest repeat orders for five.

But to PuzzleKnit Nylons ("PuzzleKnit Attracts Their Attention and Keeps Them Guessing"), he had just been a top-notch salesman: it had taken BlakSeme, with their upper-bracket, Madison-Avenue orientation, to see him as a possible district sales manager.

BlakSeme alone had seen he was big-league material. But even they had not guessed how big a league it was in which he was destined to play.

The desk clerk called back. "I find, sir, that there *is* a fancy dress ball of the boss plumbers and steamfitters of the metropolitan New York area. It's at Menshevik Hall on Tenth Avenue at eight o'clock tonight. The theme of the ball is the *ancien régime* in France, and only people in pre-French-Revolution costumes will be admitted. Would you like the name of a place near the hotel where you can rent the right costume for the occasion?"

"Yes," Alfred Smith babbled. "Yes, yes, yes!" Things were beginning to click! He was on the trail of the aliens' organization!

He went out immediately and hurriedly selected a Duc de Richelieu outfit. Since some small alterations were necessary, he had time to get dinner before the costume would be delivered to his hotel. He ate carefully and nutritiously; this was going to be a big night. His reading matter throughout the meal was a booklet he'd picked up in the outfitting place, a booklet giving the descriptions and background of all the costumes available for this period—sixteenth- to eighteenth-century France. Any fact might be the vital clue....

Back in his room, he tore off his clothes and pulled on the rented apparel. He was a little disappointed at the result. He did not quite look like a Gray Eminence. More like a young Protestant in Cardinal's clothing. But then he found the scrap of gray beard in the box that belonged with the costume and fitted it on. It made all the difference.

Talk about your disguises! Here his body was supposed to be a disguise, a disguise which was the uniform of the Aliens' Special Agents Division, of their terrestrial spy service. And now he was disguising that supposed disguise with a real one—just as by being a supposed spy he was laying a trap for all the real secret operatives.

Alfred Smith—one lone man against the aliens! "So that," he whispered reverently, "government of humans, by humans, and for humans shall not perish from the Earth."

The telephone. This time it was Jones.

"Just got word from Robinson, Smith. That special mission of mine. It looks like tonight's the night."

"Tonight, eh?" Alfred Smith felt the lace tighten around his throat.

"Yes, they're going to try to contact tonight. We still don't know just where—just that it's in New York City, I'm to be on reserve: I'll rush around to whoever finds the contact. You know, reinforce, lend a helping hand, be a staunch ally, give an assist to, help out in a pinch, stand back to back with, buddy mine, pards till hell freezes over. You'll be at the plumbers' ball, won't you? Where is it?"

Alfred shook his head violently to clear it of the fog of clichés thrown out by Jones. "Menshevik Hall. Tenth Avenue. What do I do if I—if I discover the contact?"

"You *phmpff*, guy, *phmpff* like mad. And I'll come a-running. Forget about telephones if you discover the contact. Also forget about special-delivery mail, passenger pigeon, pony-express rider, wireless telegraphy, and couriers from His Majesty. Discovering the contact comes under the heading of 'emergency' under Operating Procedure Regulations XXXIII-XLIX inclusive. So *phmpff* your foolish head off."

"Right! Only thing, Jones—" there was a click at the other end as Jones hung up. Tonight, Alfred Smith thought grimly, staring into the mirror. Tonight's the night! For *what*?

Menshevik Hall was a gray two-story building in the draftiest section of Tenth Avenue. The lower floor was a saloon through whose greasy windows a neon sign proclaimed:

THE FEBRUARY REVOLUTION WAS

THE ONLY REAL REVOLUTION BAR & GRILL

BEER—WINES—CHOICE LIQUORS

Alexei Ivanovich Anphinov, Prop.

The second floor was brightly lit. Music oozed out of its windows. There was a penciled sign on a doorway to one side of the bar:

BOSS PLUMBERS AND STEAMFITTERS OF

THE METROPOLITAN NEW YORK AREA

SEMIANNUAL FANCY DRESS BALL

You Must Be in Costume to Be Admitted Tonight

(If you haven't paid your association dues for this quarter, see Bushke Horowitz at the bar before going upstairs—Bushke's wearing a Man in the Iron Mask costume and he's drinking rum and Seven-Up.)

Alfred Smith climbed the creaky wooden stairs apprehensively, his eyes on the burly General Montcalm guarding the entrance at the top. To his relief, however, no invitation or ticket was demanded: his costume was sufficient validation. The red-faced general barely gave him a glance from under the plushly decorated cocked hat before waving him through.

It was crowded inside. Scores of Louis XIIIs, XIVs, XVs, and XVIs were dancing sedately with Annes of Austria and Marie Antoinettes to the strains of rhumba and cha-cha. Overhead, two colored chandeliers rotated slowly, unwinding the spectrum upon the glittering, waxed floor.

Where did he begin? He glanced at the platform where the musicians sat; they alone were not in costume. Lettering on the bass drum told the world that "Ole Olsen and His Latin Five" were providing the rhythms, but that did not seem like much to go on. No one here looked like an interstellar spy.

On the other hand, neither did Jones, Cohen, Kelly nor Jane Doe. They looked almost spectacularly ordinary. That was it: you had to find these people in the unlikeliest, most prosaic places.

Pleased by the inspiration, he went into the Men's Room.

At first, he thought he had hit it exactly right. The place was crowded. Sixteen or so Musketeers stood around the washbasin, munching enormous cigars and conversing in low voices.

He insinuated himself among them and listened closely. Their talk was eclectic, ranging freely from the wholesale price of pastel-colored water closets to the problems of installing plumbing in a new housing development on Long Island that was surrounded by unsewered streets.

"I told the contractor to his face," said a somewhat sallow, undersized Musketeer, knocking his cigar ash off against the pommel of his sword, "Joe, I told him, how can you expect me to lay pipe when you don't even know the *capacity*, let alone the type— look, we won't even *talk* about the type—of the sewer system they're going to have installed out here? Joe, I said to him, you're a bright guy: I ask you, Joe, is that fair, does that make sense? You want me to maybe install plumbing that's going to be a lot weaker than the sewer system in the streets so that the first time the new customers flush the toilets everything backs up all over the bathroom floor—you want that, Joe? No, he says, I don't want that. All right, then, I say, you want me to maybe install plumbing that's a lot better than necessary, a lot stronger than the sewer system will require, and that'll add cost to the houses that doesn't have to be added—you want that, Joe? No, he says, I don't want that. So, look, Joe, I say, you're willing to admit this is a dumb proposition from top to bottom? Suppose someone asked you to build a house, Joe, and couldn't tell you whether the foundation under it is concrete or steel or sand or cinder-block. That's just exactly what you're asking me to do, Joe, that's just exactly what."

There was a rustle of approbation. A tall, weedy, mournful-looking Musketeer blew his nose and carefully replaced the handkerchief in his doublet before commenting, "That's the trouble with everybody. They think plumbers are miracle men. They got to learn that plumbers are only human."

"I don't know about that," said a stout Huguenot who had come up in the last few moments. "I take the attitude that plumbers *are* miracle men. What we got to use is our American imagination, our American know-how, our American thinking straight to the point. You show me a sewer system in a new community, like, that hasn't been installed yet, that nobody knows what its capacity is going to be, and I'll figure out a plumbing system for the development that'll fit it no matter what. And I'll save on cost, too."

"How?" demanded the sallow, undersized Musketeer. "Tell me how."

"I'll tell you how," retorted the Huguenot. "By using my American imagination, my American know-how, my American thinking straight to the point. *That's* how."

"Pardon me," Alfred Smith broke in hurriedly as he saw the sallow, undersized Musketeer take a deep breath in preparation for a stinging rebuttal. "Do any of you gentlemen know of any prizes that will be given for the best costume, any door prizes, anything like that?"

There was a silence as they all chewed their cigars at him appraisingly. Then the Huguenot (Coligny, Alfred wondered? Condé? de Rohan?) leaned forward and tapped him on the chest. "When you got a question, sonny, the thing to do is find the right man to ask the question of. That's half the battle. Now who's the right man to ask questions about door prizes? The doorman. You go out to the doorman—he's wearing a General Montcalm—and you tell him Larry sent you. You tell him Larry said he should tell you all about door prizes, and, sonny, he'll tell you just what you want to know." He turned back to his smoldering adversary. "Now before you say anything, I know just what you're going to say. And I'll tell you why you're wrong."

Alfred squeezed his way out of the mobful of rising tempers. At the outskirts, a Cardinal's Guard who had just come up remarked broodingly to a black-hooded executioner: "That Larry. Big man. What I wouldn't give to be around when he takes a pratfall."

The executioner nodded and transferred his axe thoughtfully to the other shoulder. "One day there'll be an anonymous phone call to the Board of Health about Larry, and they'll send out an inspector who can't be pieced off, and that'll be that. Any guy who'll buy up junk pipe and chromium-plate it and then sell it to his friends as new stuff that he's overstocked in…" Over his shoulder, the rubbery blade of the axe began flapping like a flag in a breeze.

"Don't know nothing about prizes," the doorman stated, rocking his folding chair back and forth in front of the ballroom entrance. "Anything important, they don't tell me." He tilted his cocked hat forward over his eyes and stared bitterly into space, as if reflecting that with just a little more advance information from Paris the day might indeed have gone quite differently on the Plains of Abraham. "Why'n't you ask around down in the bar? All the big wheels are down in the bar."

There must, Alfred reflected, be a good many big wheels, as he apologized his way through the crowded room downstairs. The hoop-skirts and rearing, extravagant hairdo's, the knobby-kneed hose, swinging swords, and powdered wigs jam-packed *The February Revolution Was the Only Real Revolution Bar & Grill* so that the half-dozen or so regular customers in shabby suits and worn windbreakers seemed to be the ones actually in costume, poverty-stricken, resentful anachronisms from the future who had stumbled somehow into imperial Versailles and the swaggering intrigue of the Tuileries.

At the bar, Bushke Horowitz, his iron mask wide open despite the sternest decrees of King and Cardinal, accepted dues money, dispensed opinions on the future of standpipes and stall showers to the mob in heavy brocade and shot silk around him, and periodically threw a handful of largesse to the bartender, a chunky, angry-looking man with a spade beard and a white apron, along with the injunction to "set 'em up again."

There was no way to get through to him, Alfred realized. He asked several times about "prizes," was ignored, and gave up. He had to find a wheel of somewhat smaller diameter.

A tug at the sleeve of his clerical gown. He stared down at the rather thinnish Mme. Du Barry sitting in the empty booth. She gave him a smile from underneath her black vizard. "Drinkie?" she suggested. Then, seeing his blank look, she amplified: "Yousie and mesie. Just us twosie."

Alfred shook his head. "Nosie—I mean, no, thank you. I—uh—some business. Maybe later."

He started to walk away and found that his sleeve failed to accompany him. Mme. Du Barry continued to hold it between two fingers: she held it winsomely, delicately, archly, but the hold was absolutely unequivocal.

"Aw," she pouted. "Look at the whizzy-busy businessman. No time for drinkie, no time for mesie, just busy, busy, busy, all the livelong day."

Despite his irritation, Alfred shrugged. He wasn't doing himself much good any other way. He came back and sat across the table from her in the booth. Then, and only then, was his sleeve released by the dainty fingers.

The angry-looking man in the spade beard and white apron appeared at their booth. "Nyehh?" he grunted, meaning, quite obviously, "What'll you have?"

"I'll have Scotch on the rocks," she told Alfred. "Scotch on the rocks is absolutely the only ever drink for me."

"Two scotch on the rocks," Alfred told the bartender, who replied "Nyehh," signifying, "You order the stuff, I bring it. It's your funeral."

"I heard you asking about contests. I won a contest once. Does that make you like me a little better?"

"What kind of contest did you win?" Alfred asked absent-mindedly, studying her. Under that mask she was probably somewhat pretty in a rather bony, highly ordinary sort of way. There was nothing here.

"I was voted The Girl the Junior Plumbers of Cleveland Would Most Like to Wipe a Joint With. It was supposed to be The Girl Whose Joint the Junior Plumbers Would Most Like to Wipe, but some nasty people made a fuss and the judges had to change the title. It was three years ago, but I still have the award certificate, Now, does that help me at *all?*"

"I'm afraid not. But congratulations anyway on winning the title. It's not everybody who can—uh, say that."

The angry-looking man in the spade beard came back and set glasses and coasters in front of them. "Nyehh!" he announced, meaning, "You pay me now. That's the way we do it in this place." He took the money, glowered at it, at them, and clumped back to the becustomered bar.

"Well, what kind of contest *are* you looking for? If you tell me, I might be able to help. I know lots of little things about lots and lots of little things."

"Oh, contests, prizes, nothing particular." He glanced at the rear of the booth. There was a framed photograph on the wall of Plekhanov shaking hands with Kerensky. A touch younger version of the chunky, angry-looking man in the spade beard was standing on tiptoe behind Plekhanov, straining hard to get his face into the picture. Alfred realized he was wasting time and swallowed his drink unceremoniously. "I'll have to be going."

She cooed dismay. "So soon? When we've just met? And when I like you so much?"

"What do you mean you like me so much?" he asked her irritatedly. "When, to quote you, we've just met."

"But I do like you, I *do*. You're the cream in my coffee. You're the top. You do things to me. You're what makes the world go round. I'm nuts about you. I go for you in a big way, big boy. I'm wild, simply wild over you. I'd climb the highest mountain, swim the deepest river. Body and soul. Roses are red, violets are blue. Drink to me only with thine eyes. Oh, Johnny, oh-h-h! You're in my heart and my heart's on my sleeve." She stopped and drew breath.

"*Gah!*" Alfred commented, his eyes almost popping. He started to get up. "Thanks, lady, for the pretty talk, but—"

Then he sat down again, his eyes reverting to their previous, pop-like state. The way she'd expressed herself when she'd wanted to make certain she was understood! Like Jane Doe, like Jones—

He'd established rendezvous!

"So that's how much you like me?" he queried, fighting for time, trying to think out his next step.

"Oh, yes!" she assured him. "I'm carrying the torch, all right. I idolize you. I fancy you. I dote on you. I hold dear, make much of, cherish, prize, cling to—"

"Good!" he almost yelled in the desperation of his attempt to break in on the language of love. "Good, good, good, good! Now, I'd like to go some place where we can have some privacy and discuss your feelings in more detail." He worked his face for a moment or two, composing it into an enormous leer. "My hotel room, say, or your apartment?"

Mme. Du Barry nodded enthusiastically. "My apartment. It's closest."

As she tripped out of the bar beside him, Alfred had to keep reminding himself that this was no human wench, despite the tremulous pressure of her arm around his or the wriggling caress of her hip. This was an intelligent spider operating machinery, no more, no less. But it was also his first key to the puzzle of what the aliens wanted of Earth, his entry into the larger spy organization—and, if he kept his head and enjoyed just a bit of luck, it might well be the means to the saving of his world.

A cab rolled up. They got in, and she called out an address to the driver. Then she turned to Alfred.

"Now let's kiss passionately," she said.

They kissed passionately.

"Now let's snuggle," she said.

They snuggled.

"Now let's snuggle a lot harder," she said.

They snuggled a lot harder.

"That's enough," she said. "For now."

They stopped in front of a large old apartment house that dozed fitfully high above the street, dreaming of its past as it stared down at a flock of run-down brownstones.

Alfred paid the driver and accompanied Mme. Du Barry to the entrance. As he held the elevator door open for her, she batted her eyes at him excitedly and breathed fast in his ear a couple of times.

In the elevator, she pressed the button marked "B."

"Why the basement?" he asked. "Is your apartment in the basement?"

For answer, she pointed a tiny red cylinder at his stomach. He noticed there was a minute button on top of the cylinder. Her thumb was poised over the button.

"Never you mind what's in the basement, you lousy Vaklittian sneak. You just stand very still and do exactly what I tell you. And for your information, I know where you are and where your control cubicle is, so don't entertain any hopes of getting away with nothing more than a damaged uniform."

Alfred glanced down at the region covered by her weapon and swallowed hard. She was wrong about the location of his control cubicle, of course, but still, face it, how much living would he be able to do without a belly?

"Don't worry," he begged her. "I won't do anything foolish."

"You'd better not. And no *phmpffs* out of you either, if you know what's good for you. One solitary *phmpff* and I fill you full of holes. I ventilate you, mister, I plug you where you stand. I let daylight through you. I spray your—"

"I get the idea," Alfred broke in, "No *phmpffs*. Absolutely. I give you my word of honor."

"*Your* word of honor!" she sneered. The elevator stopped and she backed out, gesturing him to follow. He stared at her masked face and resplendent costume, remembering that when Du Barry had been dragged to the guillotine in 1793, she had screamed to the crowds about her tumbril: "Mercy! Mercy for repentance!" He was glad to recall that neither the crowds nor the Revolutionary Tribunal had taken her up on the honest offer.

Not exactly to Alfred's surprise, there was a man waiting for them in the clammy, whitewashed basement. The Huguenot. He of the American thinking straight-to-the-point.

"Any trouble?"

"No, it was easy," she told him. "I pulled him in with the Cleveland-contest-three-years-ago routine. He was smooth about it, I'll say that for him: pretended not to be interested, you know, but he must have bitten hard. I found that out a few seconds later when I told him I loved him and he asked me right off to come up to his apartment." She chuckled. "The poor, pathetic incompetent! As if any normal American human male would react like that—without so much as a remark about my beautiful eyes and how cute I am and how different I am and how about another drink, baby."

The Huguenot pulled at his lip dubiously. "And yet the uniform-disguise is a fine one," he pointed out. "That shows a high degree of competence."

"So what?" the woman shrugged. "He can design a good uniform, he can think up a splendid disguise, but what good is that if he's slip-shod about his *performance?* This one's barely learned anything about human methods and human manners. Even if I hadn't known about him before, I'd have spotted him on the basis of his love-making in the cab."

"Bad, eh?"

"*Bad!*" She rolled her eyes for maximum emphasis, "Oh, brother! I pity him if he ever pulled that clumsy counterfeit on a real human female. Bad isn't the word. A cheap fake. A second-rate ad-lib, but from hunger. No conviction, no feeling of reality, nothing!"

Alfred glared at her through the wide-open wounds of his ego. There were holes in *her* performance, he thought savagely, that would have closed any show the first night. But he decided against giving this critical appraisal aloud. After all, she had the weapon—and he had no idea how ugly a mess that little red cylinder might make.

"All right," said the Huguenot, "let's put him in with the other one."

As the red cylinder prodded into his backbone, Alfred marched up the main basement corridor, turned right at their command, turned right again, and halted before a blank wall. The Huguenot came up beside him and rubbed his hand across the surface several times. A part of the wall swung open as if on hinges, and they stepped inside.

Secret panels, yet! Alfred was thinking morosely. Secret panels, a female siren, a Huguenot master-mind—all the equipment. The only thing that was missing was a reason for the whole damn business. His captors evidently had not discovered that he was a human counterspy, or they would have destroyed him out of hand. They thought he was a—what was it?—a Vaklittian. A Vaklittian sneak, no less? So there were two sets of spies—the Huguenot had said something about putting him in with the other one. But what were these two sets of spies after? Were they both grappling for preinvasion control of Earth? That would make his mission much more complicated. To say nothing about trying to tell the police, if he ever managed to get to the police, about *two* interplanetary invasions!

And look who'd thought *he* was the counterspy in the picture....

The room was large and windowless. It was almost empty. In one corner, there was a transparent cube about eight feet on each side. A middle-aged man in a single-breasted brown business suit sat on the floor of the cube watching them curiously and a little hopelessly.

The Huguenot paused as he reached the cube. "You've searched him, of course?"

Mme. Du Barry got flustered. "Well—no, not exactly. I *intended* to—but you were waiting when we got out of the elevator—I hadn't expected you for a while yet, you know—and then we got into conversation—and I just didn't—"

Her superior shook his head angrily. "And you talk about competence! Oh, well, if I have to do everything, I guess I just have to do everything!"

He ran his hands over Alfred. He took out Alfred's fountain pen and his cigarette lighter and examined them very closely. Then he replaced them and looked puzzled. "He's not carrying a weapon. Does that make sense?"

"I think so. He's not experienced enough to be trusted with anything dangerous."

The Huguenot thought about it for a while. "No. He wouldn't be running around by himself, then. He'd be under supervision."

"Maybe he is. Maybe that's the answer. In that case—"

"In that case, you both might have been followed here. Yes, that could be it. Well, we'll fool them. Contact or no contact, we'll close the operation here as of tonight. Don't go out again—in an hour or so, we'll leave the planet and take off with our prisoners for headquarters." He rubbed his hands against the cube as he had on the wall outside. An opening appeared in the transparency and widened rapidly. With the cylinder at his back, Alfred was pushed inside.

"Give him a small blast," he heard the Huguenot whisper. "Not too much—I don't want him killed before he's questioned. Just enough to stun him and keep him from talking to the other one."

There was a tiny click behind him. A rosy glow lit up the cube and the basement room. Alfred felt a bubble of gas form in his belly and rise upward slowly. After a while, he belched.

When he turned around, the opening in the transparency had closed and the Huguenot had whirled angrily on Mme. Du Barry. The lady was examining her weapon with great puzzlement.

"I told you I wanted him stunned, not tickled! Is there anything I can depend on you to do right?"

"I was trying to be careful—I didn't want to kill him, like you said! I aimed right at the control cubicle and I used the medium-low Vaklittian index. I don't understand how he—how he—"

The Huguenot flapped both hands at her disgustedly. "Oh, let's get out of here and start packing! When we get back tonight, I intend to ask headquarters to assign me a new female assistant for the next Earth operation. One without so exact a knowledge of human sexual approaches, perhaps, but who can be counted on to disarm a newly captured prisoner and to tell a Vaklittian index from a hole in her cylinder!"

Mme. Du Barry hung her head and followed him out of the room. The door-wall swung shut behind them.

Alfred touched the transparent wall of the cube gingerly. There was no longer any hint of the opening he had been pushed through. The stuff, while as transparent as glass, was rubbery and slightly sticky, something like newly melted plastic. But a plastic, he found out, incredibly strong. And it gave off a whitish glow which enabled him to see through it, dimly, the featureless walls of the secret basement room.

He turned and surveyed his co-prisoner, a few feet away, on the other side of the cube.

The man was looking at him suspiciously, and yet uncertainly, as if he did not quite know what to make of the situation. There was a peculiarly nondescript, uninteresting and ordinary quality to his features which made them somehow remarkably familiar.

Of course! He looked every bit as average as Jones, as Cohen, as Kelly and—in her own submerged feminine way—as Jane Doe. And so Alfred knew who the man had to be.

"John Smith?" he inquired tentatively. "I mean," he added, as he recollected one of Jones' earlier remarks, "Gar-Pitha?"

The middle-aged man rose to his feet and smiled relief. "I couldn't figure out who you were, but you had to be one of us. Unless you were a decoy they were planting here to make me talk. But if you know my real name... What's yours, by the way?"

Alfred shook his head coyly. "Command Central—Robinson, I mean—has me on a special mission. I'm not allowed to give my name."

John Smith nodded heavily. "Then you don't give it—and that's that. Robinson knows what he's doing. You can't go wrong by following Robinson's orders to the letter. Special mission, eh? Well, you won't complete it—now. She trapped me the same way. We're both in the soup and good."

"The soup?"

"Sure. Those filthy Lidsgallians—you heard them? They're leaving tonight and taking us with them. Once they've got us on their home planet, they'll be able to work us over at their leisure. They won't get anything out of me, and I hope, for the honor of the Academy, they won't get anything out of you, no matter *what* they do to us, but we won't be good for very much by the time they're through. Oh, those Lidsgallians know their way around a torture chamber, yessiree, Bob!"

"Torture chamber?" Alfred felt sick and knew he looked it.

The older man reached out and squeezed his shoulder. "Steady on, lad," he said. "Don't show the white feather before the natives. Keep a stiff upper lip. Bite the bullet. Fight on for old Notre Dame. Never say die. You have nothing to lose but your chains. Let's keep the old flag flying."

As Alfred said nothing, John Smith took his silence for agreement with these high principles and went on; "You can't get out of this cell—it's a spun web of pure *chrok,* practically unbreakable. But the worst of it, of course, is its insulating quality: you can't *phmpff* through *chrok* if you stand on your head. I've tried to *phmpff* for help until I almost fractured an antenna—couldn't raise a whisper. That's why they don't have to split up their force to guard us. And that's why I haven't bothered to come out of my uniform to talk to you: if we can't *phmpff* we'll make more sense to each other with the jaw attachments of our uniforms."

Grateful for this small mercy, Alfred began to look around at the enclosing walls of *chrok.* "How about using these—these jaw attachments to get help?" he suggested. "Sound seems to go through, We could try yelling together."

"And who would hear you? Humans. What could *they* do?"

Alfred spread his hands. "Oh, I don't know. Sometimes—even humans can be—"

"No, forget about it. Things are bad, but they're not that bad. Besides, these walls are especially thick and there are no cracks in them. If those Lidsgallians hadn't come down a couple of times a day to change the air, I'd have suffocated by now. As it was, I was in a bad way a couple of times and had to fall back on the reserve air supply in the chest—you know, the compartment right over the control cubicle? But I'll tell you this, if I ever get back to Vaklitt in one piece, there's a modification of our uniform I'll really try to talk Command Central into making. I thought of it while I was watching them search you. Do away with the air reserve in the chest. I'll tell Robinson—how often, when you come right down to it, does one of our Special Emissaries ever find himself drowning or in the middle of a poison-gas war?—and find some way an agent can take a weapon—a real, honest, claw-operated weapon, into his uniform-disguise with him. Although come to think of it, you'd need some sort of turret arrangement coming out of the human flesh to fire it, and those Lidsgallians, once they found out about it, would—"

He rambled on. Alfred, watching him, realized how hungry he'd been for companionship. And this talkative mood might be put to use. They both might be in a Lidsgallian torture chamber somewhere out in the galaxy in a couple of hours, but there was a very slender chance that they might not. And, besides, facts were always useful; he could cope with whatever lay ahead a bit more easily if he only had some coherent facts on which to base his plans. This was the time, if ever, to find out who was the greater menace to Earth, the Vaklittians or the Lidsgallians—and who was more likely to accept the proffer of friendship from a badly frightened, torture-leery human.

Only—he had to be careful how he phrased the questions. He had to be prepared to cover up any blunders quickly.

"Why do you think," he asked carelessly, "the Lidsgallians hate us so much? Oh, I know the usual answers, but I'm interested in hearing *your* opinion. You seem to have a very refreshing slant."

John Smith grunted appreciatively, thought for a moment, then shrugged. "The usual answers are the only answers in this case. It's the war. Naturally."

"Just the war? That's all, you think?"

"*Just* the war? What do you mean, *just* the war? How can an interstellar war, going on across two-thirds of the galaxy for almost three centuries, be *just* the war? Trillions upon trillions of individuals killed, dozens upon dozens of fertile planets smashed into space dust—you call that *just* the war? You youngsters must really be growing up pretty cynical these days!"

"I—I didn't mean it quite like that," Alfred said rapidly, placatingly. "Of course, the war—it's a terrible business, and all that. Awful. Positively horrible. Sickening, sickening. And our enemy, those vicious Lidsgallians—"

John Smith looked sandbagged. "*What?* The Lidsgallians aren't our enemies—they're our *allies!*"

It was Alfred's turn under the sandbag. "Our *allies?*" he repeated weakly, wondering how he was ever going to get out of this one. "*Our* allies?" he said again, trying a different intonation on for size and the bare possibility of sense.

"I don't know what the Academy's coming to any more," John Smith muttered to himself. "In my day, you got a good general education there, with just enough lab work in espionage to warrant giving you a commission in the Service if you filled all the other requirements. You came out of the Academy as a wide-awake, cultured interstellar citizen, with a good background in history, economics, art, science, and total terroristic warfare. On top of that, you had, whenever you wanted to use it, a decent and honorable trade—spying—under your belt. Of course, if you wanted to specialize, you could always go back, after graduation, for intensive study in elementary and advanced ciphers, creative disguise design, plain and fancy lying, physical and mental torture, narrow fields of scholarship like that. But that used to be strictly postgraduate work. *Now*—now, everything is specialization. They turn out dewy youngsters who can crack any code in space, but can't tell a simple espionage lie to save their heads; they graduate kids who can knock out a masterpiece of a uniform-disguise, but don't even know the difference between a Lidsgallian and a Pharseddic! Mark my words, this overspecialization will be the death of the Academy yet!"

"I agree with you," Alfred told him with ringing sincerity. He thought for a moment and decided to underline his bona fides. "Shoemaker, stick to your last. A place for everything and everything in its place. Spare the rod and spoil the child. Look to the ant, thou sluggard!" He found he was going off the track and stopped himself. "But you see, the way the Academy feels today, its graduates will go into active service and meet older, more experienced men like yourself who can give them this general political orientation right on the spot. Now, of course, in a way, I really knew all the time that the actual enemy, in the deeper sense of the word, so to speak, were the Pharseddics, but—"

"The Pharseddics? Our enemy? But the Pharseddics are the neutrals—the only neutrals! Look here, youngster, and try to get it straight in your mind for once. You absolutely can't do a first-class job of espionage on Earth unless you know the general principles and the background data from which they're derived. To begin with, the Lidsgallians were attacked by the Garoonish, right?"

Alfred assented with a positive shake of his head. "Right! Any school child knows that."

"All right, then. We had to go to war with the Garoonish, not because we had anything particular against them, or liked the Lidsgallians, but because if the Garoonish won they would then be in a position to conquer the Mairunians who were our only possible allies against the growing power of the Ishpolians."

"Naturally," Alfred murmured. "Under the circumstances, there was no alternative."

"Well, that forced the Garoonish to make common cause with the Ossfollians. The Ossfollians activated their mutual assistance pact with the Kenziash of the Rigel region, and, out of fear of the Kenziash, the Ishpolians joined forces with us and pushed the Mairunians into the Garoonish camp. Then came the Battle of the Ninth Sector in which the Ossfollians switched sides four times and which resulted in the involvement of the Menyemians, the Kazkafians, the Doksads, and even the Kenziash of the Procyon and Canopus regions. After that, of course, the war got a lot more complicated."

Alfred wet his lips. "Yes, of course. Then it got complicated." He decided, for the sake of sanity, to bring matters much closer to present time and place. "Meanwhile, here on Earth, there are the spies of—the spies of— Pardon me, but in your opinion just how many of these belligerents operate espionage networks on Earth? Regularly, I mean."

"All of them! Every single one of them! Including the Pharseddics, who have to know what's going on if they're to maintain their neutrality. Earth, as I hope you remember from your first-year course in Elementary Secrecy, is ideally situated just outside the usual battle zones but within easy access of almost all the belligerents. It's the only place left where information can be transmitted across the combat lines and deals can be made back and forth—and, as such, it's zealously respected by everyone. After all, it was on Earth that we sold out the Doksads, and where the annihilation of the Menyemians was arranged by their allies, the Mairunians and the Kazkafians. Just as now we have to watch our own oldest allies, the Lidsgallians, who have been trying to make contact with the Garoonish for the purpose of concluding a separate peace. I got the proof—I even found out the specific time and place the contact was to be made and what the arrangements were to be—but then I ran afoul of that female with her yacker of Cleveland contests she won three years ago. And I got caught."

"The contact was to be made through a beauty contest of some sort, wasn't it?"

The middle-aged man looked impatient. "Naturally a beauty contest. Of course a beauty contest. How else would anyone go about contacting a bunch like the Garoonish?"

"I couldn't imagine," Alfred laughed weakly. "The *Garoonish,* after all!" He sat in silence, absolutely unable to close mentally with the picture John Smith had evoked. The closest he could come to it was a memory of something he had read about Lisbon during the Second World War. But this was Lisbon squared, Lisbon cubed, Lisbon raised to some incredible exponential power. All Earth was a vast labyrinth of spy-threaded Lisbon. Spies, counterspies, counter-*counter*spies…

Just what, he suddenly wondered, was the correct human population of Earth? Was it a larger proportion of the total population figures than that of the disguised interstellar agents, and by how much? Or was it possibly, was it conceivably, somewhat smaller?

Life had been a lot simpler with PuzzleKnit Nylons, he decided, and that was his only real conclusion.

John Smith nudged him. "Here they come. It's off to Lidsgall for us."

They rose to their feet as the wall opened. Two men and a woman came in, dressed in street clothing. They each carried in one hand a small suitcase that looked heavy, and, in the other, the small, red cylindrical weapon.

Alfred eyed the cylinders and found himself getting tense with a dangerous idea. The weapon hadn't bothered him much before and it had supposedly been set to stun him. Well, perhaps the woman had made a mistake in her setting—and perhaps the metabolisms of Man and Vaklittian were so different that a charge that would knock out the one would merely give the other a slightly upset stomach. Then again, if Earth were so carefully maintained in her ignorance as John Smith had indicated, there might be no setting on the weapon that would damage a native terrestrial at all: in the normal course of their intrigues with and against and around each other, these people might be enjoined by their own laws and by mutual agreement from carrying weapons that could damage humans.

But if he were wrong? It still might take them quite a bit of time to tumble to the fact that the Vaklittian frequencies were having no important effect on him, and he might manage a lot of action in that time. The alternative, at any rate, was to be pulled off Earth in just a few minutes and deposited, some time in the near future, in an extraterrestrial torture chamber. Even if he were able to prove his humanity to their satisfaction, they would still have to dispose of him in some way—and the various devices of the torture chamber would be so handy....

No question about it: people who go in for torture chambers do not make good hosts.

One of the men fiddled with his suitcase, and the transparent cube dissolved around Alfred and John Smith. In response to the gestures made with the weapons, they walked gingerly across the floor. They were motioned through the open wall.

Alfred found it difficult to recognize Mme. Du Barry and the Huguenot without their masks and costumes.

They both looked much like the new man with them, not bad, not good, just faces-in-a-crowd. Which, of course, was exactly how they wanted it.

He reached his decision as the five of them began walking through the opening in the wall. For the moment, they were closely bunched together, even bumping against each other.

He grabbed the woman by the arm and swung her violently against the Huguenot, who staggered confusedly. Then, knowing that John Smith was between him and the new man in the rear, he hitched up his cassock and started to run. He turned left, and again left—and found himself in the main basement corridor. Ahead, at the far end, was a flight of stone stairs leading up to the street.

Behind him, there was the noise of struggle, then the sound of feet running in pursuit. He heard John Smith distantly yell: "Go it, laddie, go it! Over the hill! Slide, Kelly, slide! Ride 'em, cowboy! It's the last lap—full speed ahead! Shake a leg! Hit the road!" Then the Vaklittian's voice abruptly disappeared in a breathless grunt after the sound of a wallop.

A pinkish glow shot past him, moved back and over to light up his mid-section. He belched. The glow turned light red, deep red, dark, vicious red. He belched more frequently. He reached the stairs and was clambering up them as the glow became a throbbing, night-like purple.

Ten minutes later, he was on Sixth Avenue, getting into a cab. He had a mildly unpleasant bellyache. It rapidly subsided.

He looked behind him as they drove to his hotel. No pursuit. Good. The Lidsgallians would have no idea where he lived.

Did they look like the Vaklittians, he wondered? Spiders? Hardly, he decided. All these different racial names and these titanic interstellar animosities suggested many, many separate forms. They'd have to be small enough to fit into a normal human body, though. Snail-like creatures, possibly, and worm-like ones. Crab-like ones and squid-like ones. Perhaps even rat-like ones?

On the whole, a dreadfully unpleasant subject. He needed a good night's sleep: tomorrow would be his first day at BlakSeme. And, then, after a bit, when he'd had a chance to think it all out, he'd decide what to do. The police, the F.B.I., or whatever. Maybe even take the whole story to one of the New York newspapers—or some top television commentator might be more sympathetic and reach a bigger audience. His story would have to be coherent and convincing, though. He'd have little proof; the Lidsgallians were probably on their way back to their home planet as of this very moment. But there was his own gang—the Vaklittians. Cohen and Kelly and Jones. And Jane Doe. He'd kid them along for a couple of days and then use them for proof. It was time Earth knew what was going on.

His own gang was waiting for him in his hotel room. Cohen and Kelly and Jones. And Jane Doe. They looked as if they'd been waiting for a long time. Jane Doe looked as if she'd been crying. Mr. Kelly was sitting on the bed with his open briefcase on his knees.

"So there you are," said Robinson's voice from the briefcase. "I hope you have an explanation, Smith. I only hope you have an explanation."

"For what?" he asked irritably. He'd been looking forward to getting out of his costume, taking a hot shower, and then bed. This late performance of "I spy" was very annoying. Repetitious, too.

"For what?" Robinson roared. "For what? Kelly, tell him for what!"

"Look here, Smith," Kelly demanded. "Did you or didn't you ask the desk clerk to find out about a plumbers' fancy dress ball?"

"I did. Of course, I did. He got all the information I needed."

There was a howl from the briefcase. "*He got all the information I needed!* Six years of general studies in espionage at the Academy, a year of post-graduate work in In-tensive Secrecy, six months at the Special Service School in Data-Sifting and Loca-tion-Tracing—and you have the nerve to stand there with your carapace in your claws and tell me that the only way of tracking down this fancy dress ball you could think of was to ask the desk clerk—an ordinary everyday human desk-clerk—to find out about it for you!"

Alfred noticed that the faces around him were all extremely grave. Despite his weariness and strong feelings of indifference, he made an effort to conciliate. "Well, if he was only an ordinary, everyday human, I fail to see the harm that—"

"He could have been the Garoonish Minister of War for all you knew!" the brief-case blasted. "Not that it made any difference. By the time he'd questioned his various sources and mentioned the matter to his various friends, acquaintances and busi-ness associates, every spy organization in the galaxy had been alerted. They knew what we were worrying about, what we were looking for, and where and when we hoped to find it. You accomplished one of the best jobs of interstellar communication ever. Sixty-five years of patient espionage planning gone down the drain. *Now* what have you to say for yourself?"

Alfred stood up straight and manfully pulled back his shoulders. "Just this. I'm sorry." He considered for a moment, then added: "Deeply and truly sorry."

Some kind of electrical storm seemed to go off in the briefcase. It almost rolled off Kelly's knees.

"I just can't stand this any more," Jane Doe said suddenly. "I'll wait outside." She walked past Alfred to the door, her eyes swimming in reproachfulness. "Darling, darling, how *could* you?" she whispered bitterly as she passed him.

The briefcase crackled down to some semblance of control. "I'll give you one last chance, Smith. Not that I think any conceivable defense you might have would be valid, but I hate to demote a Special Emissary, to push him forever out of the Service, without giving him every chance to be heard. So. Is there any defense you wish to have registered before sentence of demotion is passed upon you?"

Alfred considered. This was evidently a serious business in their eyes, but it was beginning to be slightly meaningless to him. There was too much of it, and it was too complicated. He was tired. *And* he was Alfred Smith, not John Smith.

He could tell them about the events of the night, about the Lidsgallians and the information he'd received from the captive Smith. It might be valuable and it might throw a weight in the scales in his favor. The trouble was that then the question of John Smith's real identity would arise—and that might become very embarrassing.

Besides, he was over the fear he'd felt earlier about these creatures; they could do little more to him than a dose of sodium bicarbonate, he'd found out. Their super-weapons were to be discounted, at least on Earth. And when it came to that point, he was not at all sure that he wanted to give them helpful information. Who knew just where Earth's best interests lay?

He shook his head, feeling the fatigue in his neck muscles. "No defense. I *said* I'm sorry."

From the briefcase, Robinson sighed. "Smith, this hurts me more than it hurts you. It's the principle of the thing, you see. Punishment fit the crime. More in sorrow than in anger. You cannot make an omelet without breaking eggs. All right, Kelly. The sentence."

Kelly put the briefcase on the bed and got to his feet. Cohen and Jones came to attention. There was evidently to be a ceremony.

"By virtue of the authority vested in me as acting chief of this field group," Kelly intoned, "and pursuant to Operating Procedure Regulations XCVII, XCVIII and XCIX, I hereby demote and degrade you, Gar-Pitha of Vaklitt, from the rank of Special Emissary, Second Class, to the rank of General Emissary or such other lower rank as Command Central may find fitting and necessary in the best interests of the Service. And I further direct that your disgrace be published throughout every arm and echelon of the Service and that your name be stricken from the roster of graduates of the Academy which you have shamed. And, finally, in the name of this field group and every individual within it, I disown you now and forevermore as a colleague and an equal and a friend."

It was, Alfred decided, a kind of strong-medicine ceremony. Must be pretty affecting to someone who was really involved in it personally.

Then, from either side, Cohen and Jones moved in swiftly to complete the last, dramatic part of the ceremony.

They were very formal, but very thorough.

They stripped the culprit of his uniform.

AFTERWORD

This is how I wrote this story:
In 1956, I broke up with a woman with whom I had been involved for the better part of a year. But I knew she'd be back (she always came back), and I knew we'd start all over again, as we so many times had. I therefore called all my friends and told them that they had to arrange seven consecutive dates for me; I wanted to see a new woman every day of the coming week—hoping that I'd get deeply committed to at least one of them.

Fruma, as she still likes to remind me, Fruma was Wednesday. Katherine MacLean and the guy she was then living with, Dave Mason, told me they knew somebody I would really like. They came up with Fruma.

After my first date with her on Wednesday night, I told Bob Sheckley—who was recently divorced and who was my closest friend at the time—that I thought I had found the woman of all women who should be my wife. Bob asked when I planned to see her again.

"Saturday night," I told him.

"See if she has a friend," he said.

Well, Fruma did, and her friend's name was Ziva, and Bob and Ziva were married a month after Fruma and me. We all lived in Greenwich Village, not forever after, but most happily, about two or three blocks from each other.

And Bob and I went through a slump. Not a bad long one, but a very annoying one nonetheless, and one more surprising to Bob than to me, because I wrote spasmodically, when some strong idea turned me around, but Bob was a heavy production man.

Bob and I talked to each other very intensively and very worriedly about how to get out of the slump. One of the cures we thought about was to rent a furnished room as a mutual office and add two items of furniture to it—a typewriter table and a heavy wooden chair with shackles permanently attached to the chair. We would both arrive at the office at nine each morning, and one of us would be shackled to the chair by the other. He would not be released, no matter how he pleaded or what the excuse, until one PM—or until he typed four pages of good, publishable copy. Then the shackles would be opened and the other would take his place, under the same conditions, until either five PM or four typed pages of good copy would bring release. Of course, if the four pages were typed early enough and the writer were still going strong, he could go on and write as much as he wanted to, until his release time.

We thought it was an excellent idea and were eager to try it. Unfortunately, both Fruma and Ziva claimed to be horrified and begged us not to. Bob and I muttered to each other about the unfortunate weakness of women, and tried to think of something else.

What we settled on was this: The two of us would meet five mornings a week at a neighborhood diner, each with our four pages of new copy in hand. Whoever was late for the appointment or who didn't have his requisite four pages had to pay five dollars into a fund handled by our wives. Whenever the fund grew large enough, it would be used to buy theater tickets for all four of us.

It worked, it really worked well, at least for a time. I put more fives in than Bob, because, after all, I was born a month late and have never caught up: I am frequently tardy for any and all appointments. But both of us were writing again, and selling, and that was the whole point.

Then there was the morning I didn't have a good story in my head. I desperately wrote four pages of something, anything, and hurried off to meet Bob. He had his four pages, too, and they were very professional and very good. But they also looked slightly familiar.

Of course, I realized! They were four pages from one of his first published stories, a story I liked very much and remembered well. I accused him of cheating. He broke down and admitted it, and paid the five dollars. I went home with my four pages of nonsense, righteously angry.

I put the four pages in front of me, one thousand words of pure narrative hook, and wondered if anything at all could be made of it. Yes, it turned out: "Lisbon Cubed" could be made of it. (If you want to see just what the original was pretty much like, count one thousand words from the beginning of the story.)

My title, when it went to Horace Gold's *Galaxy,* was "The Fourth Power of Lisbon." He, finding nothing else to change in the story—although he did try hard—removed my title and substituted his. I've kept it for this edition: the man is dead and deserves some sort of minor prose monument.

If you tell all this to Bob Sheckley, he will swear that it's not quite true; it all happened the other way around, with me being the guilty party. Don't listen to him.

But this is why I wrote this story:

I'm not sure why I write science fiction any more, except that, well, it's a living, and, hell, it's where I made what reputation I have. But there are a couple of responsibilities that I felt I had fifty years ago and at least one of which I still feel very strongly today.

It's my duty—it really is my duty, being the kind of person I am and knowing and believing what I do—to prepare my fellow humans for what they will shortly be facing, at the most in one or two lifetimes. Whatever I write these days, satire, high or low drama, whatever, I ought to get them ready for the unsettling discovery that they and their species will soon no longer be Nature's only child.

The universe is awfully big, and not only are we going out into it physically, we are splashing signals out in every direction that we think, we *think,* therefore we are, we *are.* Somebody (or somebodies) somewhere is abruptly going to be seen—or heard from. We will find that we have very smart siblings.

I pray most of all and first of all that we will not be mice alerting cats. Then I pray that they will not be too far ahead of us technologically; I do not want the U.N. Secretary General to play Montezuma to some galactic Cortez. And then I pray that we will be up to the challenge of living with intelligent creatures who come from a totally different evolution, that we will be able to enjoy and use totally different technologies, totally different art forms, totally different philosophical and religious systems. That we will appreciate the fact there are many, many other forms of intelligence—and that their highest forms must inevitably deal with what they too must call the tragedy of life.

And mostly to that end I write these comedies of space.

WRITTEN 1956——PUBLISHED 1958

The Ghost Standard

Remember the adage of the old English legal system: "Let justice be done though the heavens fall"? Well, *was* justice done in this case?

You have three entities here. An intelligent primate from Sol III—to put it technically, a human. An equally intelligent crustacean from Procyon VII—in other words, a sapient lobstermorph. And a computer of the Malcolm Movis omicron beta design, intelligent enough to plot a course from one stellar system to another and capable of matching most biological minds in games of every sort, from bridge to chess to double zonyak.

Now—add a shipwreck. A leaky old Cascassian freighter comes apart in deep space. I mean quite literally comes apart. Half the engine segment explodes off, the hull develops leaks and begins to collapse, all those who are still alive and manage to make it to lifeboats get away just before the end.

In one such lifeboat you have the human, Juan Kydd, and the lobstermorph, Tuezuzim. And, of course, the Malcolm Movis computer—the resident pilot, navigator and general factotum of the craft.

Kydd and Tuezuzim had known each other for more than two years. Computer programmers of roughly the same level of skill, they had met on the job and had been laid off together. Together they had decided to save money by traveling on the scabrous Cascassian freighter to Sector N-42B5, where there were rumored to be many job opportunities available.

They were in the dining salon, competing in a tough hand of double zonyak, when the disaster occurred. They helped each other scramble into the lifeboat. Activating the computer pilot, they put it into Far Communication Mode to search for rescuers. It informed them that rescue was possible no sooner than twenty days hence, and was quite likely before thirty.

Any problems? The lifeboat had air, fuel, more than enough water. But food...

It was a Cascassian freighter, remember. The Cascassians, of course, are a silicon-based life-form. For their passengers, the Cascassians had laid in a supply of organic, or carbon-based, food in the galley. But they had not even thought of restocking the lifeboats. So the two non-Cascassians were now imprisoned for some three to four weeks with nothing to eat but the equivalent of sand and gravel.

Or each other, as they realized immediately and simultaneously.

Humans, on their home planet, consider tinier, less-sapient crustaceans such as lobsters and crawfish great delicacies. And back on Procyon VII, as Tuezuzim put it, "We consider it a sign of warm hospitality to be served a small, succulent primate known as spotted morror."

In other words, each of these programmers could eat the other. And survive. There were cooking and refrigerating facilities aboard the lifeboat. With careful management and rationing, meals derived from a full-size computer programmer would last till rescue.

But who was to eat whom? And how was a decision to be reached?

By fighting? Hardly. These were two highly intellectual types, neither of them good physical exemplars of their species.

Kydd was round-shouldered, badly nearsighted and slightly anemic. Tuezuzim was somewhat undersized, half deaf and suffering from one crippled chela. The claw had been twisted at birth and had never matured normally. With these disabilities, both had avoided participation in athletic sports all their lives, especially any sport of a belligerent nature.

Yet the realization that there was nothing else available to eat had already made both voyagers very hungry. What was their almost-friendship compared with the grisly prospect of starvation?

For the record, it was the lobstermorph, Tuezuzim, who suggested a trial by game, with the computer acting as referee and also as executioner of the loser. Again, only for the record and of no importance otherwise, it was the human, Juan Kydd, who suggested that the logical game to decide the issue should be Ghost.

They both liked Ghost and played it whenever they could not play their favorite game—that is, when they lacked zonyak tiles. In the scrambling haste of their emergency exit, they had left both web and tiles in the dining salon. A word game now seemed the sole choice remaining, short of flipping a coin, which—as games-minded programmers—they shrugged off as childishly simplistic. There also was the alternative of trial by physical combat, but that was something that neither found at all attractive.

Since the computer would function as umpire and dispute-settling dictionary as well as executioner, why not make it a three-cornered contest and include the computer as a participant? This would make the game more interesting by adding an unpredictable factor, like a card shuffle. The computer could not lose, of course—they agreed to ignore any letters of Ghost that it picked up.

They kept the ground rules simple: a ten-minute time limit for each letter; no three-letter words; the usual prohibition against proper nouns; and each round would go in the opposite direction from that of the previous round. Thus, both players would have equal challenging opportunities, and neither would be permanently behind the other in the contest.

Also, challenging was to be allowed across the intervening opponent—the computer, not part of the combat.

Having sent off one last distress signal, they addressed themselves to programming the computer for the game (and the instantaneous execution of the loser).

Combing through the immense software resources of the computer, they were pleased to discover that its resident dictionaries included *Webster's First* and *Second,* their own joint favorites. They settled on the ancient databases as the supreme arbiters.

The verdict-enforcer took a little more time to organize. Eventually, they decided on what amounted to a pair of electric chairs controlled by the computer. The killing force would be a diverted segment of the lifeboat's Hametz Drive. Each competitor would be fastened to his seat, locked in place by the computer until the game was over. At the crucial moment, when one of them incurred the *t* in Ghost, a single blast of the diverted drive would rip through the loser's brain, and the winner would be released.

"Everything covered?" asked Tuezuzim as they finished their preparations. "A fair contest?"

"Yes, everything's covered," Kydd replied. "All's fair. Let's go."

They went to their respective places: Kydd to a chair, Tuezuzim to the traditional curved bed of the lobstermorph. The computer activated their electronic bonds. They stared at each other and softly said their goodbyes.

We have this last information from the computer. The Malcolm Movis omicron beta is bundled at sale with Al-truix 4.0, a fairly complex ethicist program. It was now recording the proceedings, with a view to the expected judicial inquest.

The lobstermorph drew the first *g.* He had challenged Juan Kydd, who had just added an *e* to *t-w-i-s.* Kydd came up with *twisel,* the Anglo-Saxon noun and verb for fork. To Tuezuzim's bitter protests that *twisel* was archaic, the Malcolm Movis pointed out that there had been no prior agreement to exclude archaisms.

Kydd himself was caught a few minutes later. Arrogant over his initial victory, he was helping to construct *laminectomy* ("surgical removal of the posterior arch of a vertebra") by adding *m* after *l-a-m-i-n-e-c-t-o.* True, this would end on the computer's turn, which could incur no penalty letters, but Kydd was willing to settle for a neutral round. Unfortunately, he had momentarily forgotten the basic escape hatch for any seasoned Ghost player—plurals. The Malcolm Movis indicated *i,* and Tuezuzim added the *e* so fast it sounded like an echo. There was absolutely no escape for Kydd from the concluding *s* in *laminectomies.*

And so it went, neck and neck, or, rather, neck and cephalothorax. Tuezuzim pulled ahead for a time and seemed on the verge of victory, as Kydd incurred *g-h-o-s* and then was challenged in a dangerous situation with a questionable word.

"*Dirigibloid?*" Tuezuzim demanded. "You just made that one up. There is no such word. You are simply trying to avoid getting stuck with the *e* of *dirigible.*"

"It certainly is a word," Kydd maintained, perspiring heavily. "As in 'like a dirigible, in the form of or resembling a dirigible.' It can be used, probably has been used, in some piece of technical prose."

"But it's not in *Webster's Second*—and that's the test. Computer, is it in your dictionary?"

"As such, no," the Malcolm Movis replied. "But the word *dirigible* is derived from the Latin *dirigere,* to direct. It means steerable, as a dirigible balloon. The suffix *-oid* may be added to many words of classical derivation. As in *spheroid* and *colloid* and *asteroid,* for example—"

"Just consider those examples!" Tuezuzim broke in, arguing desperately. "All three have the Greek suffix *-oid* added to words that were originally Greek, not Latin. *Aster* means 'star' in Greek, so with *asteroid* you have 'starlike or in the form of a star.' And *colloid* comes from the Greek *kolla* for 'glue.' Are you trying to tell me that dictionaries on the level of *Webster's First* or *Second* mix Greek with Latin?"

It seemed to the anxiously listening Kydd that the Malcolm Movis computer almost smiled before continuing. "As a matter of fact, in one of those cases, that's exactly what happens. *Webster's Second* describes *spheroid* as deriving from both Greek and Latin. It provides as etymologies, on the one hand, the Greek *sphairoeides (sphaira,* 'sphere,' plus *eidos,* 'form') and, on the other, the Latin *sphaeroides,* 'ball-like' or 'spherical.' Two different words, both of classical origin. *Dirigibloid* is therefore ruled a valid word."

"I protest that ruling!" Tuezuzim waved his claw angrily. "Data are being most selectively used. I am beginning to detect a pro-human, anti-lobstermorph bias in the computer."

Another faint suggestion of an electromechanical smile. "Once more, a matter of fact," the computer noted silkily. "The Malcolm Movis design team was headed by Dr. Hodgodya Hodgodya, the well-known lobstermorph electronicist. Pro-human, anti-lobstermorph bias is therefore most unlikely to have been built in. *Dirigibloid* is ruled valid; the protest is noted and disallowed. Juan Kydd begins the next round."

Since both opponents were now tagged with *g-h-o-s,* the round coming up would be the rubber, or execution, round. This was most definitely *it.*

Kydd and Tuezuzim looked at each other again. One of them would be dead in a few minutes. Then Kydd looked away and began the round with the letter that had always worked best for him in three-cornered Ghost, the letter *l.*

The computer added *i,* and Tuezuzim, a bit rashly, came up with *m.* He was quite willing for the word to be *limit,* and thus to end on the Malcolm Movis. A null round, and he, Tuezuzim, would be starting the next one.

But Kydd was not interested in a null round this time. He added an *o* to the *l-i-m* and, when the computer supplied a *u,* the developing *limousine* that had to end on Tuezuzim became obvious.

The lobstermorph thought desperately. With a hopeless squeak from deep in his cephalothorax, he said *s.*

It must be recognized here, as the computer testified at the subsequent inquest, that the *s* already completed a word, to wit *limous* ("muddy, slimy"). But the Malcolm Movis pointed out that the individual who should have triumphantly called attention to *limous,* Juan Kydd, was so committed to catching his opponent with *limousine* that he didn't notice.

Limousine moved right along, with an *i* from Kydd and an *n* from the computer. And once again it was up to Tuezuzim.

He waited until his ten-minute time limit had almost expired. Then he came up with a letter. But it wasn't *e*.

It was *o*.

Juan Kydd stared at him. "*L-i-m-o-u-s-i-n-o?*" he said in disbelief, yet already suspecting what the lobstermorph was up to. "I challenge you."

Again Tuezuzim waited a long time. Then, slowly rotating his crippled left chela at Juan Kydd's face, he said, "The word is *limousinoid*."

"There's no such word! What in hell does it mean?"

"What does it mean? 'Like a limousine, in the form of or resembling a limousine.' It can be used, probably has been used, in some piece of technical prose."

"Referee!" Kydd yelled. "Let's have a ruling. Do you have *limousinoid* in your dictionary?"

"Whether or not it's in the dictionary, Computer," Tuezuzim countered, "it has to be acceptable. If *dirigibloid* can exist, so can *limousinoid*. If *limousinoid* exists, Kydd's challenge is invalid and he gets the *t* of Ghost—and loses. If *limousinoid* doesn't exist, neither does *dirigibloid*, and so Kydd would have lost that earlier round and would therefore now be up to the *t* of Ghost. Either way, he has to lose."

Now it was the Malcolm Movis that took its time. Five full minutes it considered. As it testified later, it need not have done so; its conclusion was reached in microseconds. "But," it noted in its testimony at the inquest, "an interesting principle was involved here that required the use of this unnecessary time. Justice, it is said, not only must be done, but must *seem* to be done. Only the appearance of lengthy, careful consideration would make justice *seem* to be done in this case."

Five minutes—and then, at last, the Malcolm Movis gave its verdict.

"There is no valid equation here between *dirigibloid* and *limousinoid*. Since *dirigible* is a word derived from the so-called classic languages, it may add the Greek suffix *-oid*. *Limousine*, on the other hand, derives from French, a Romance language. It comes from Limousin, an old province of France. The suffix *-oid* cannot therefore be used properly with it—Romance French and classical Greek may not be mixed."

The Malcolm Movis paused now for three or four musical beats before going on. Juan Kydd and Tuezuzim stared at it, the human's mouth moving silently, the crustacean's antennae beginning to vibrate in frantic disagreement.

"Tuezuzim has incurred *t*, the last letter of Ghost," the computer announced. "He has lost."

"I protest!" Tuezuzim screamed. "Bias! Bias! If no *limousinoid*, then no *dirigibl*—"

"Protest disallowed." And the blast of the Hametz Drive tore through the lobstermorph. "Your meals, Mr. Kydd," the computer said courteously.

The inquest, on Karpis VIII of Sector N-42B5, was a swift affair. The backup tapes of the Malcolm Movis were examined; Juan Kydd was merely asked if he had anything to add (he did not).

But the verdict surprised almost everyone, especially Kydd. He was ordered held for trial. The charge? Aggravated cannibalism in deep space.

Of course, our present definition of interspecies cannibalism derives from this case:

> The act of cannibalism is not to be construed as limited to the eating of members of one's own species. In modern terms of widespread travel through deep space, it may be said to occur whenever one highly intelligent individual kills and consumes another highly intelligent individual. Intelligence has always been extremely difficult to define precisely, but it will be here and henceforth understood to involve the capacity to understand and play the terrestrial game of Ghost. It is not to be understood as solely limited to this capacity, but if an individual, of whatever biological construction, possesses such capacity, the killing, consuming and assimilating of that individual shall be perceived as an act of cannibalism and is to be punished in terms of whatever statutes relate to cannibalism in that time and that place.
> —*The Galaxy v. Kidd, Karpis VIII, C17603*

Now, Karpis VIII was pretty much a rough-and-ready frontier planet. It was still a rather wide-open place with a fairly tolerant attitude toward most violent crime. As a result, Juan Kydd was assessed a moderate fine, which he was able to pay after two months of working at his new job in computer programming.

The Malcolm Movis computer did not fare nearly as well.

First, it was held as a crucial party to the crime and an accessory before the fact. It was treated as a responsible and intelligent individual, since it had unquestionably demonstrated the capacity to understand and play the terrestrial game of Ghost. Its plea of nonbiological construction (and therefore noninvolvement in legal proceedings pertaining to living creatures) was disallowed on the ground that the silicon-based Cascassians who had built the ship and lifeboat were now also subject to this definition of cannibalism. If silicon-chemistry intelligence could be considered biological, the court ruled, so inevitably must silicon-electronics.

Furthermore, and perhaps most damaging, the computer was held to have lied in a critical situation—or, at least, to have withheld information by not telling the whole truth. When Tuezuzim had accused it of anti-lobstermorph bias, it had pointed to the fact that the Malcolm Movis omicron beta had been designed by a lobstermorph and that anti-lobstermorph bias was therefore highly unlikely. The *whole* truth, however, was that the designer, Dr. Hodgodya, was living in self-imposed exile at the time because he hated his entire species and, in fact, had expressed this hatred in numerous satirical essays and one long narrative poem. In other words, anti-lobstermorph bias *had* been built in and the computer knew it.

To this the computer protested that it was, after all, only a computer. As such, it had to answer questions as simply and directly as possible. It was the questioner's job to formulate and ask the right questions.

"Not in this case," the court held. "The Malcolm Movis omicron beta was not functioning as a simple question-and-answer machine but as a judge and umpire. Its obligations included total honesty and full information. The possibility of anti-lobstermorph bias had to be openly considered and admitted."

The Malcolm Movis did not give up. "But you had two top-notch programmers in Kydd and Tuezuzim. Could it not be taken for granted that they would already know a good deal about the design history of a computer in such general use? Surely for such knowledgeable individuals not every *i* has to be dotted, not every *t* has to be crossed."

"Software people!" the court responded. "What do they know about fancy hardware?"

The computer was eventually found guilty of being an accessory to the crime of cannibalism and was ordered to pay a fine. Though this was a much smaller fine than the one incurred by Juan Kydd, the Malcolm Movis, unlike Kydd, had no financial resources and no way of acquiring any.

That made for a touchy situation. On a freewheeling planet such as Karpis VIII, judges and statutes might wink a bit at killers and even cannibals. But never at out-and-out deadbeats. The court ruled that if the computer could not pay its fine, it still could not evade appropriate punishment. "Let justice be done!"

The court ordered that the Malcolm Movis omicron beta be wired in perpetuity into the checkout counter of a local supermarket. The computer requested that instead it be disassembled forthwith and its parts scattered. The request was denied.

So.

You decide. Was justice done?

AFTERWORD

The essential plot gimmick here is the variations the characters play on "dirigible" and "limousine"—and the results thereof. It is based on an actual game of Ghost in which Dan Keyes and my brother Mort were participants and used these variations against each other. I won't tell who did which.

But an attempted definition of "humanness" is what precipitated the story. If you believe, as I do, that we will shortly (ten years? fifty? a hundred and fifty?) be encountering alien intelligent life-forms and having to learn to live with them on various moral levels (are they to be considered the equivalent of dogs and cats and chimpanzees, or ants and bees, or sixteenth-century Amerindians—or are we to be considered the equivalent of one of these to them?), you must be thinking also of the necessary distinctions in many areas that we and they will have to make.

So I wrote the story and my agent, Virginia Kidd, sent it to *Playboy*, and Alice K. Turner, the editor there, said she liked it a lot and would pay a lot for it, but—just as an earlier editor at the magazine had said about an earlier story—would I please cut it down somewhat, say, by at least a fourth?

One-fourth, I said? One-full-damn-*fourth*? Impossible! I said. I reread the story almost spluttering.

But, for the hell of it, I tried to do as she had asked. And much to my chagrin, it turned out to be not only possible, but actually fairly easy. Worse yet, the resulting piece now had much more focus.

Alas. This sort of thing may keep a writer humble, but it should really not be allowed to go on.

WRITTEN 1994——PUBLISHED 1994

ॐ

THE FLAT-EYED MONSTER

For the first few moments, Clyde Manship—who up to then had been an assistant professor of Comparative Literature at Kelly University—for the first few moments, Manship tried heroically to convince himself that he was merely having a bad dream. He shut his eyes and told himself chidingly, with a little superior smile playing about his lips, that things as ugly as this just did not occur in real life. No. Definitely a dream.

He had himself half convinced, until he sneezed. It was too loud and wet a sneeze to be ignored. You didn't sneeze like that in a dream—if you sneezed at all. He gave up. He'd have to open his eyes and take another look. At the thought, his neck muscles went rigid with spasm.

A little while ago, he'd fallen asleep while reading an article he'd written for a scholarly journal. He'd fallen asleep in his own bed in his own apartment in Callahan Hall—"a charming and inexpensive residence for those members of the faculty who are bachelors and desire to live on campus." He'd awakened with a slightly painful tingling sensation in every inch of his body. He felt as if he were being stretched, stretched interminably and—and *loosened.* Then, abruptly, he had floated off the bed and gone though the open window like a rapidly attenuating curl of smoke. He'd gone straight up to the star-drenched sky of night, dwindling in substance until he lost consciousness completely.

And had come to on this enormous flat expanse of white tabletop, with a multivaulted ceiling above him and dank, barely breathable air in his lungs. Hanging from the ceiling were quantities and quantities of what was indubitably electronic equipment, but the kind of equipment the boys in the Physics Department might dream up, if the grant they'd just received from the government for military radiation research had been a million times larger than it was, and if Professor Bowles, the department head, had insisted that every gadget be carefully constructed to look substantially different from anything done in electronics to date.

The equipment above him had been rattling and gurgling and whooshing, glowing and blinking and coruscating. Then it had stopped as if someone had been satisfied and had turned off a switch.

So Clyde Manship had sat up to see who had turned it off.

He had seen all right.

He hadn't seen so much *who* as he had seen *what.* And it hadn't been a nice *what.*

83

In fact, none of the *whats* he had glimpsed in that fast look around had been a bit nice. So he had shut his eyes fast and tried to find another mental way out of the situation.

But now he had to have another look. It might not be so bad the second time. "It's always darkest," he told himself with determined triteness, "before the dawn." And then found himself involuntarily adding, "except on days when there's an eclipse."

But he opened his eyes anyway, wincingly, the way a child opens its mouth for the second spoonful of castor oil.

Yes, they were all as he had remembered them. Pretty awful.

The tabletop was an irregular sort of free-form shape, bordered by thick, round knobs a few inches apart. And perched on these knobs, about six feet to the right of him, were two creatures who looked like black leather suitcases. Instead of handles or straps, however, they sported a profusion of black tentacles, dozens and dozens of tentacles, every second or third one of which ended in a moist turquoise eye shielded by a pair of the sweepingest eyelashes Manship had ever seen outside of a mascara advertisement.

Embedded in the suitcase proper, as if for additional decorative effect, were swarms of other sky-blue eyes, only these, without eyelashes, bulged out in multitudes of tiny, glittering facets like enormous gems. There was no sign of ear, nose or mouth anywhere on the bodies, but there was a kind of slime, a thick, grayish slime, that oozed out of the black bodies and dripped with a steady splash-splash-splash to the floor beneath.

On his left, about fifteen feet away, where the tabletop extended a long peninsula, there was another one of the creatures. Its tentacles gripped a pulsating spheroid across the surface of which patches of light constantly appeared and disappeared.

As near as Manship could tell, all the visible eyes of the three were watching him intently. He shivered and tried to pull his shoulders closer together.

"Well, Professor," someone asked suddenly, "what would you say?"

"I'd say this was one hell of a way to wake up," Manship burst out, feelingly. He was about to go on and develop this theme in more colorful detail when two things stopped him.

The first was the problem of who had asked the question. He had seen no other human—no other living creature, in fact—besides the three tentacled suitcases any-where in that tremendous, moisture-filled room.

The second thing that stopped him was that someone else had begun to answer the question at the same time, cutting across Manship's words and ignoring them completely.

"Well, obviously," this person said, "the experiment is a success. It has completely justified its expense and the long years of research behind it. You can see for yourself, Councilor Glomg, that one-way teleportation is an accomplished fact."

Manship realized that the voices were coming from his right. The wider of the two suitcases—evidently "the professor" to whom the original query had been addressed—was speaking to the narrower one, who had swung most of his stalked eyes away from

Manship and had focused them on his companion. Only where in blazes were the voices coming from? Somewhere inside their bodies? There was no sign anywhere of vocal apparatus.

AND HOW COME, Manship's mind suddenly shrieked, THEY TALK ENGLISH?

"I can see that," Councilor Glomg admitted with a blunt honesty that became him well. "It's an accomplished fact, all right, Professor Lirld. Only, *what precisely* has it accomplished?"

Lirld raised some thirty or forty tentacles in what Manship realized fascinatedly was an elaborate and impatient shrug. "The teleportation of a living organism from astronomical unit 649-301-3 without the aid of transmitting apparatus on the planet of origin."

The Councilor swept his eyes back to Manship. "You call that living?" he inquired doubtfully.

"Oh, come now, Councilor," Professor Lirld protested. "Let's not have any flefnomorphism. It is obviously sentient, obviously motile, after a fashion—"

"All right. It's alive. I'll grant that. But sentient? It doesn't even seem to *pmbff* from where I stand. And those horrible lonely eyes! Just two of them—and so *flat!* That dry, dry skin without a trace of slime. I'll admit that—"

"You're not exactly a thing of beauty and a joy forever yourself, you know," Manship, deeply offended, couldn't help throwing out indignantly.

"—I tend to flefnomorphism in my evaluation of alien life-forms," the other went on as if he hadn't spoken. "Well, I'm a flefnobe and proud of it. But after all, Professor Lirld, I have seen some impossible creatures from our neighboring planets that my son and other explorers have brought back. The very strangest of them, the most primitive ones, at least can *pmbff!* But this—this *thing*. Not the smallest, slightest trace of a *pmb* do I see on it! It's eerie, that's what it is—eerie!"

"Not at all," Lirld assured him. "It's merely a scientific anomaly. Possibly in the outer reaches of the galaxy where animals of this sort are frequent, possibly conditions are such that *pmbffing* is unnecessary. A careful examination should tell us a good deal very quickly. Meanwhile, we've proved that life exists in other areas of the galaxy than its sun-packed core. And when the time comes for us to conduct exploratory voyages to these areas, intrepid adventurers like your son will go equipped with information. They will know what to expect."

"Now, listen," Manship began shouting in desperation. "Can you or can you not hear me?"

"You can shut off the power, Srin," Professor Lirld commented. "No sense in wasting it. I believe we have as much of this creature as we need. If any more of it is due to materialize, it will arrive on the residual beam."

The flefnobe on Manship's left rapidly spun the strange spheroid he was holding. A low hum, which had filled the building and had been hardly noticeable before, now died away. As Srin peered intently at the patches of light on the surface of the instrument, Manship suddenly guessed that they were meter readings. Yes, that's exactly what they were—meter readings. *Now, how did I know that?* he wondered.

Obvious. There was only one answer. If they couldn't hear him no matter how loudly he shouted, if they gave no sign that they even knew he *was* shouting, and if, at the same time, they seemed to indulge in the rather improbable feat of talking his native language—they were obviously telepaths. Without anything that looked like ears or mouths.

He listened carefully as Srin asked his superior a question. It seemed to sound in his ears as words, English words in a clear, resonant voice. But there was a difference. There was a quality missing, the kind of realistic bite that fresh fruit has and artificial fruit flavoring doesn't. And behind Srin's words there were low, murmuring bubbles of other words, unorganized sentence fragments which would occasionally become "audible" enough to clarify a subject that was not included in the "conversation." That, Manship realized, was how he had learned that the shifting patches of light on the spheroid were meter readings.

It was also evident that whenever they mentioned something for which no equivalent at all existed in English, his mind supplied him with a nonsense syllable.

So far so good. He'd been plucked out of his warm bed in Callahan Hall by a telepathic suitcase named something like Lirld which was equipped with quantities of eyes and tentacles. He'd been sucked down to some planet in an entirely different system near the center of the galaxy, clad in nothing but apple-green pajamas.

He was on a world of telepaths who couldn't hear him at all, but upon whom he could eavesdrop with ease, his brain evidently being a sufficiently sensitive antenna. He was scheduled shortly to undergo a "careful examination," a prospect he did not relish, the more so as he was evidently looked upon as a sort of monstrous laboratory animal. Finally, he was not thought much of, chiefly because he couldn't *pmbff* worth a damn.

All in all, Clyde Manship decided, it was about time that he made his presence felt. Let them know, so to speak, that he was definitely not a lower form of life, but one of the boys. That he belonged to the mind-over-matter club himself and came of a long line of IQ-fanciers on both sides of his family.

Only *how?*

Vague memories of adventure stories read as a boy drifted back to him. Explorers land on a strange island. Natives, armed with assorted spears, clubs and small boulders, gallop out of the jungle to meet them, their whoops an indisputable prelude to mayhem. Explorers, sweating a bit, as they do not know the language of this particular island, must act quickly. Naturally, they resort to—they resort to—the universal sign language! *Sign* language. Universal!

Still in a sitting position, Clyde Manship raised arms straight up over his head. "Me *friend*," he intoned. "Me come in peace." He didn't expect the dialogue to get across, but it seemed to him that voicing such words might help him psychologically and thus add more sincerity to the gesture.

"—and you might as well turn off the recording apparatus, too," Professor Lirld was instructing his assistant. "From here on out, we'll take everything down on a double memory-fix."

Srin manipulated his spheroid again. "Think I should modulate the dampness, sir? The creature's dry skin seems to argue a desert climate."

"Not at all. I strongly suspect it to be one of those primitive forms which can survive in a variety of environments. The specimen seems to be getting along admirably. I tell you, Srin, we can be very well satisfied with the results of the experiment up to this point."

"Me friend," Manship went on desperately, raising and lowering his arms. "Me intelligent entity. Me have IQ of 140 on the Wechsler-Bellevue scale."

"*You* may be satisfied," Glomg was saying, as Lirld left the table with a light jump and floated, like an oversized dandelion, to a mass of equipment overhead, "but I'm not. I don't like this business one little bit."

"Me friendly *and* intelligent enti—" Manship began. He sneezed again. "Damn this wet air," he muttered morosely.

"What was *that?*" Glomg demanded.

"Nothing very important, Councilor," Srin assured him. "The creature did it before. It is evidently a low-order biological reaction that takes place periodically, possibly a primitive method of imbibing *glrnk.* Not by any stretch of the imagination a means of communication, however."

"I wasn't thinking of communication," Glomg observed testily. "I thought it might be a prelude to aggressive action."

The professor skimmed back to the table, carrying a skein of luminescent wires. "Hardly. What could a creature of this sort be aggressive *with?* I'm afraid you're letting your mistrust of the unknown run away with you, Councilor Glomg."

Manship had crossed his arms across his chest and subsided into a helpless silence. There was evidently no way to make himself understood outside of telepathy. And how do you start transmitting telepathically for the first time? What do you use?

If only his doctoral thesis had been in biology or physiology, he thought wistfully, instead of *The Use of the Second Aorist in the First Three Books of the Iliad.* Oh, well. He was a long way from home. Might as well try.

He closed his eyes, having first ascertained that Professor Lirld did not intend to approach his person with the new piece of equipment. He wrinkled his forehead and leaned forward with an effort of extreme concentration.

Testing, he thought as hard as he could, *testing, testing. One, two, three, four—testing, testing. Can you hear me?*

"I just don't like it," Glomg announced again. "I don't like what we're doing here. Call it a presentiment, call it what you will, but I feel we are tampering with the infinite—and we shouldn't."

I'm testing, Manship ideated frantically. *Mary had a little lamb. Testing, testing. I'm the alien creature and I'm trying to communicate with you. Come in, please.*

"Now, Councilor," Lirld protested irritably. "Let's have none of that. This is a scientific experiment."

"That's all very well. But I believe there are mysteries that flefnobe was never meant to examine. Monsters as awful-looking as this—no slime on the skin, only two eyes and both of them flat, unable or unwilling to *pmbff,* an almost-complete absence of tentacles—a creature of this sort should have been left undisturbed on its own hellish planet. There are limits to science, my learned friend—or there should be. One should not seek to know the unknowable!"

Can't you hear me? Manship begged. *Alien entity to Srin, Lirld and Glomg: This is an attempt at a telepathic connection. Come in, please, someone. Anyone.* He considered for a moment, then added: *Roger. Over.*

"I don't recognize such limitations, Councilor. My curiosity is as vast as the universe."

"That may be," Glomg rejoined portentously. "But there are more things in *Tiz* and *Tetzbah,* Professor Lirld, than are dreamed of in your philosophy."

"My philosophy—" Lirld began, and broke off to announce—"Here's your son. Why don't you ask him? Without the benefit of half a dozen scientific investigations that people like you have wanted to call off time after time, none of his heroic achievements in interplanetary discovery would be possible."

Thoroughly defeated, but still curious, Manship opened his eyes in time to see an extremely narrow black suitcase swarm up to the tabletop in a spaghetti-cluster of tentacles.

"What is—*that?*" the newcomer inquired, curling a bunch of supercilious eyestalks over Manship's head. "It looks like a *yurd* with a bad case of *hipplestatch.*" He considered for a moment, then added, "Galloping *hipplestatch.*"

"It's a creature from astronomical unit 649-301-3 that I've just succeeded in teleporting to our planet," Lirld told him proudly. "Mind you, Rabd, without a transmitting outfit on the other end! I admit I don't know why it worked this time and never before—but that's a matter for further research. A beautiful specimen, though, Rabd. And as near as we can tell, in perfect condition. You can put it away now, Srin."

"Oh, no you don't, Srin—" Manship had barely started to announce when a great rectangle of some pliable material fell from the ceiling and covered him. A moment later, the tabletop on which he'd been sitting seemed to drop away and the ends of the material were gathered in underneath him and fastened with a click by a scuttling individual whom he took to be the assistant. Then, before he had time to so much as wave his arms, the tabletop shot up with an abruptness that he found twice as painful as it was disconcerting.

And there he was, packaged as thoroughly as a birthday present. All in all, things were not improving, he decided. Well, at least they seemed disposed to leave him alone now. And as yet they showed no tendency to shove him up on a laboratory shelf along with dusty jars of flefnobe fetuses pickled in alcohol.

The fact that he was probably the first human being in history to make contact with an extraterrestrial race failed to cheer Clyde Manship in the slightest.

First, he reflected, the contact had been on a distinctly minor key—the sort that an oddly colored moth makes with a collector's bottle rather than a momentous meeting between the proud representatives of two different civilizations.

Second, and much more important, this sort of hands-across-the-cosmos affair was more likely to enthuse an astronomer, a sociologist or even a physicist than an assistant professor of Comparative Literature.

He'd had fantastic daydreams aplenty in his lifetime. But they concerned being present at the premiere of *Macbeth*, for example, and watching a sweating Shakespeare implore Burbage not to shout out the "Tomorrow and Tomorrow and Tomorrow" speech in the last act: "For God's sake, Dick, your wife just died and you're about to lose your kingdom and your life—don't let it sound like Meg at the Mermaid screaming for a dozen of ale. *Philosophical*, Dick, that's the idea, slow, mournful and philosophical. And just a little bewildered."

Or he'd imagined being one of the company at that moment sometime before 700 BC when a blind poet rose and intoned for the first time: "Anger, *extreme* anger, that is my tale…"

Or being a house guest at Yasnaya Polyana when Tolstoy wandered in from the garden with an abstracted look on his face and muttered: "Just got an idea for a terrific yarn about the Napoleonic invasion of Russia. And what a title! *War and Peace.* Nothing pretentious, nothing complicated. Just simply *War and Peace.* It'll knock them dead in St. Petersburg, I tell you. Of course, it's just a bare little short story at the moment, but I'll probably think of a couple of incidents to pad it out."

Travel to the Moon and the other planets of the solar system, let alone a voyage to the center of the galaxy—in his pajamas? No, that was definitely not a menu calculated to make Clyde Manship salivate. In this respect, he had wisted no farther afield than a glimpse, say, of Victor Hugo's sky-high balcony in St. Germain des Prés or the isles of Greece where burning Sappho loved and, from time to time as it occurred to her, sang.

Professor Bowles, now, Bowles or any of the other slipstick-sniffers in the Physics Department—what those boys would give to be in his position! To be the subject of an actual experiment far beyond the dreams of even theory on Earth, to be exposed to a technology that was patently so much more advanced than theirs—why, they would probably consider that, in exchange for all this, the vivisection that Manship was morosely certain would end the evening's festivities was an excellent bargain and verged on privilege. The Physics Department…

Manship suddenly recalled the intricately weird tower, studded with gray dipoles, that the Physics Department had been erecting in Murphy Field. He'd watched the government-subsidized project in radiation research going up from his window in Callahan Hall.

Only the evening before, when it had reached the height of his window, he'd reflected that it looked more like a medieval siege engine designed to bring down walled cities than a modern communicative device.

But now, with Lirld's comment about one-way teleportation never having worked before, he found himself wondering whether the uncompleted tower, poking a ragged section of electronic superstructure at his bedroom window, had been partially responsible for this veritable purée-of-nightmare he'd been wading through.

Had it provided a necessary extra link with Lirld's machine, sort of an aerial connection or grounding wire or whatever? If only he knew a little physics! Eight years of higher education were inadequate to suggest the barest aye or nay.

He gnashed his teeth, went too far and bit his tongue—and was forced to suspend mental operations until the pain died away and the tears dribbled out of his eyes.

What if he knew for certain that the tower had played a potent, though passive, part in his removal through interstellar space? What if he knew the exact part it had played in terms of megavolts and amperages and so forth—would the knowledge be the slightest use to him in this impossible situation?

No, he'd still be a hideous flat-eyed, non-intelligent monster plucked pretty much at random from the outer reaches of the universe, surrounded by creatures to whose minds his substantial knowledge of the many literatures of astronomical unit 649-301-3 would probably come across, allowing even for the miracle of translation, as so much schizophrenic word-salad.

In his despair, he plucked hopelessly at the material in which he'd been wrapped. Two small sections came away in his fingers.

There wasn't enough light to examine them, but the feel was unmistakable. Paper. He was wrapped in an oversized sheet of something very much like paper.

It made sense, he thought, it made sense in its own weird way. Since the appendages of the flefnobes he had seen to date consisted of nothing more than slender tentacles ending in either eyes or tapered points, and since they seemed to need knoblike protuberances on the laboratory table in order to perch beside him, a cage of paper was pretty much escape-proof from their point of view. There was nothing for their tentacles to grip—and they evidently didn't have the musculature to punch their way through.

Well, he did. Athletically, he had never amounted to much, but he believed, given enough of an emergency, in his ability to fight his way out of a paper bag. It was a comforting thought, but, at the moment, only slightly more useful than the nugget about the tower in Murphy Field.

If only there were some way of transmitting *that* bit of information to Lirld's little group: Maybe they'd realize that the current flefnobe version of *The Mindless Horror from Hyperspace* had a few redeeming intellectual qualities, and maybe they could work out a method of sending him back. If they wanted to.

Only he couldn't transmit information. All he could do, for some reason peculiar to the widely separate evolutionary paths of man and flefnobe, was receive. So former Assistant Professor Clyde Manship sighed heavily, slumped his shoulders yet a further slump—and stolidly set himself to receive.

He also straightened his pajamas about him tenderly, not so much from latent sartorial ambition as because of agonizing twinges of nostalgia: he had suddenly realized that the inexpensive green garment with its heavily standardized cut was the only artifact he retained of his own world. It was the single souvenir, so to speak, that he possessed of the civilization which had produced both Tamerlane and *terza rima;* the pajamas were, in fact, outside of his physical body, his last link with Earth.

"So far as I'm concerned," Glomg's explorer son was commenting—it was obvious that the argument had been breezing right along and that the papery barrier didn't affect Manship's "hearing" in the slightest—"I can take these alien monsters or leave them alone. When they get as downright disgusting as this, of course, I'd rather leave them alone. But what I mean—I'm not afraid of tampering with the infinite, like Pop here, and on the other side, I can't believe that what you're doing, Professor Lirld, will ever lead to anything really important."

He paused, then went on. "I hope I haven't hurt your feelings, sir, but that's what I honestly think. I'm a practical flefnobe, and I believe in practical things."

"How can you say—nothing really important?" In spite of Rabd's apology, the professor's mental "voice" as it registered on Manship's brain positively undulated with indignation. "Why, the greatest concern of flefnobe science at the moment is to achieve a voyage to some part of the outer galaxy where the distances between stars are prodigious compared to their relative denseness here at the galactic center.

"We can travel at will between the fifty-four planets of our system and we have recently achieved flight to several of our neighboring suns, but going so far as even the middle areas of the galaxy, where this specimen originates, remains as visionary a project today as it was before the dawn of extra-atmospheric flight over two centuries ago."

"Right!" Rabd broke in sharply. "And why? Because we don't have the ships capable of making the journey? Not on your *semble-swol*, Professor! Why, since the development of the *Bulvonn* Drive, any ship in the flefnobe navy or merchant marine, down to my little three-jet runabout, could scoot out to a place as far as astronomical unit 649-301-3—to name just one example—and back without even hotting up her engines. But we don't. And for a very good reason."

Clyde Manship was now listening—or receiving—so hard that the two halves of his brain seemed to grind against each other. He was very much interested in astronomical unit 649-301-3 and anything that made travel to it easier or more difficult, however exotic the method of transportation employed might be by prevailing terrestrial standards.

"And the reason, of course," the young explorer went on, "is a practical one. Mental dwindle. Good old mental dwindle. In two hundred years of solving every problem connected with space travel, we haven't so much as *pmbffed* the surface of *that* one. All we have to do is go a measly twenty light-years from the surface of our home planet and mental dwindle sets in with a bang. The brightest crews start acting like retarded children and, if they don't turn back right away, their minds go out like so many lights: they've dwindled mentally smack down to zero."

It figured, Manship decided excitedly, it figured. A telepathic race like the flefnobes...why, of course! Accustomed since earliest infancy to having the mental aura of the entire species about them at all times, dependent completely on telepathy for communication since there had never been a need for developing any other method, what loneliness, what ultimate magnification of loneliness, must they not feel once their ships had reached a point too far from their world to maintain contact!

And their education now—Manship could only guess at the educational system of a creature so different from himself, but surely it must be a kind of high-order and continual mental osmosis, a mutual mental osmosis. However it worked, their educational system probably accentuated the involvement of the individual with the group. Once the feeling of involvement became too tenuous, because of intervening barrier or overpowering stellar distance, the flefnobe's psychological disintegration was inevitable.

But all this was unimportant. There were interstellar spaceships in existence! There were vehicles that could take Clyde Manship back to Earth, back to Kelly University and the work-in-progress he hoped would eventually win him a full professorship in Comparative Literature: *Style vs. Content in Fifteen Representative Corporation Reports to Minority Stockholders for the Period 1919-1931.*

For the first time, hope sprang within his breast. A moment later, it was lying on its back and massaging a twisted knee. Because assume, just assume for the sake of argument, his native intelligence told him, that he could somehow get out of this place and pick his way about what was, by every indication, a complete oddity of a world, until he found the spaceships Rabd had mentioned—could it ever be believed by any imagination no matter how wild or fevered, his native intelligence continued, that he, Clyde Manship, whose fingers were all thumbs and whose thumbs were all knuckles, whose mechanical abilities would have made Swanscombe Man sneer and *Sinanthropus* snicker, could it ever be believed, his native intelligence inquired sardonically, that he'd be capable of working out the various gadgets of advanced spaceship design, let alone the peculiarities that highly unusual creatures like the flefnobes would inevitably have incorporated into their vessels?

Clyde Manship was forced to admit morosely that the entire project was somewhat less than possible. But he did tell his native intelligence to go straight to hell.

Rabd now, though. *Rabd* could pilot him back to Earth if (a) Rabd found it worthwhile personally and if (b) Rabd could be communicated with. Well, what interested Rabd most? Evidently this Mental Dwindle ranked quite high.

"If you'd come up with an answer to that, Professor," he was expostulating at this point, "I would cheer so hard I'd unship my *glrnk*. That's what's kept us boxed up here at the center of the galaxy for too many years. That's the *practical* problem. But when you haul this *Qrm*-forsaken blob of protoplasm out of its hole halfway across the universe and ask me what I think of it, I must tell you the whole business leaves me completely dry. This, to me, is not a practical experiment."

Manship caught the mental ripples of a nod from Rabd's father. "I'm forced to agree with you, son. Impractical and dangerous. And I think I can get the rest of the council to see it my way. Far too much has been spent on this project already."

As the resonance of their thoughts decreased slightly in volume, Manship deduced they were leaving the laboratory.

He heard the beginnings of a desperate, "But—but—" from Lirld. Then, off in the distance, Councilor Glomg, evidently having dismissed the scientist, asked his son a question, "And where is little Tekt? I thought she'd be with you."

"Oh, she's out at the landing field," Rabd answered, "supervising last-minute stuff going into the ship. After all, we begin our mating flight tonight."

"A wonderful female," Glomg told him in a "voice" that was now barely audible. "You're a very lucky flefnobe."

"I know that, Pop," Rabd assured him. "Don't think I don't know that. The most plentiful bunch of eye-ended tentacles this side of *Gansibokkle* and they're mine, all mine!"

"Tekt is a warm and highly intelligent female flefnobe," his father pointed out severely from a great distance. "She has many fine qualities. I don't like you acting as if the mating process were a mere matter of the number of eye-ended tentacles possessed by the female."

"Oh, it isn't, Pop," Rabd assured him. "It isn't at all. The mating process is a grave and—er, a serious matter to me. Full of responsibilities—er, serious responsibilities. Yes, sir. Highly serious. But the fact that Tekt has over a hundred and seventy-six slime-washed tentacles, each topped by a lovely, limpid eye, won't do our relationship a bit of harm. Quite the contrary, Pop, quite the contrary."

"A superstitious old crank and a brash bumpkin," Professor Lirld commented bitterly. "But between them, they can have my appropriation shut off, Srin. They can stop my work. Just when it's showing positive results. We've got to prepare countermeasures!"

Manship was not interested in this all-too-familiar academic despair, however. He was straining desperately after the receding minds of Glomg and Rabd. Not that he was at all intrigued by the elder's advice on How to Have a Sane and Happy Sex Life Though Married.

What had excited him prodigiously was a mental by-product of a much earlier comment. When Rabd had mentioned the last-minute loading of his ship, another part of the flefnobe's mind had, as if stimulated by association, dwelt briefly on the construction of the small vessel, its maintenance and, most important, its operation.

For just a few seconds, there had been a flash of a control panel with varicolored lights going on and off, and the beginnings of long-ago, often-repeated instruction: "To warm up the motors of the *Bulvonn* Drive, first gently rotate the uppermost three cylinders…Gently now!"

It was the kind of subliminal thought-picture, Manship realized excitedly, that had emanated from Srin a short while ago, and had enabled him to guess that the shifting light-patterns on the sphere the laboratory assistant held were actually meter readings. Evidently, his sensitivity to the flefnobe brain went deeper than the mental statements that were consciously transmitted by it and penetrated, if not the unconscious mind, at least the less submerged areas of personal awareness and memory.

But this meant—this meant—seated as he was, he still managed to stagger at the concept. A little practice, just a little acquired skill, and he could no doubt pick the brain of every flefnobe on the planet.

He sat and glowed at the thought. An ego that had never been particularly robust had been taking an especially ferocious pounding in the past half-hour under the contemptuous scrutiny of a hundred turquoise eyes and dozens of telepathic gibes.

A personality that had been power-starved most of its adult life abruptly discovered it might well hold the fate of an entire planet in the hollow of its cerebrum.

Yes, this certainly made him feel a lot better. Every bit of information these flefnobes possessed was his for the taking. What, for example, did he feel like taking? For a starter, that is.

Manship remembered. His euphoria dwindled like a spat-upon match. There was only one piece of information he desired, only one thing he wanted to know. How to get home!

One of the few creatures on this planet, possibly the only one for all he knew, whose thoughts were of a type to make this possible, was on his way with his father to some flefnobe equivalent of Tony's Bar and Grill. Rabd had, in fact, to judge from the silence reigning on the subject, just this moment passed out of effective telepathic range.

With a hoarse, anguished, yearning cry, similar to that of a bull who—having got in a juicy lick with his horns and having been carried by the momentum of his rush the full length of the bull-ring—turns, only to see the attendants dragging the wounded matador out of the arena…with precisely that sort of thoroughly dismayed bellow, Clyde Manship reached up, tore the surrounding material apart with one mighty two-handed gesture, and leaped to his feet on the in-and-out curving tabletop.

"…And seven or eight charts in full color, representing the history of teleportation prior to this experiment," Lirld was telling his assistant at that moment. "In fact, Srin, if you have time to make *three-dimensional* charts, the Council is even more likely to be impressed. We're in a fight, Srin, and we've got to use every—"

His thoughts broke off as an eyestalk curled around and regarded Manship. A moment later his entire complement of eyestalks as well as those of his assistant swished about and stopped, quivering, with their focus on the erect, emergent human.

"Holy, concentrated *Qrm,*" the professor's mind barely transmitted the quavering thought. "The flat-eyed monster. It's broken loose!"

"Out of a cage of solid paper!" Srin added in awe.

Lirld came to a decision. "The blaster," he ordered peremptorily. "Tentacle me the blaster, Srin. Appropriation or no appropriation, we don't dare take chances with a creature like this. We're in a crowded city. Once it got out on a rampage—" He shuddered the entire black suitcase length of him. He made a rapid adjustment in the curlicued instrument that Srin had given him. He pointed it at Manship.

Having actually fought his way out of the paper bag, Manship had paused, irresolute, on the tabletop. Far from being a man of action in any sense, he now found himself distinctly puzzled as to just which way to act. He had no idea of the direction taken by Glomg *père* and *fils;* furthermore he was at a loss as he looked around for anything that in any way resembled a door. He regretted very much that he had not noticed through which aperture Rabd had entered the room when the younger flefnobe had joined their jolly little circle.

He had just about made up his mind to look into a series of zigzag indentations in the opposite wall when he observed Lirld pointing the blaster at him with determined if unprofessional tremulousness. His mind, which had been filing the recent conversation between professor and assistant in an uninterested back-portion, suddenly informed him that he was about to become the first, and probably unrecorded victim, in a War of Worlds.

"Hey!" he yelped, entirely forgetting his meager powers of communication. "I just want to look up Rabd. I'm not going on any ramp—"

Lirld did something to the curlicued instrument that seemed like winding a clock, but was probably more equivalent to the pressing of a trigger. He simultaneously shut all of his eyes—no mean feat in itself.

That, Clyde Manship reflected later—when there was time and space to reflect—was the only thing which saved his life. That and the prodigious sideways broad-jump he made as millions of crackling red dots ripped out of the instrument toward him.

The red dots sped past his pajama-tops and into one of the lower vaults that made up the ceiling. Without a sound, a hole some ten feet in circumference appeared in the masonry. The hole was deep enough—some three or four feet—to let the night sky of the planet show through. A heavy haze of white powder drifted down like the dust from a well-beaten rug.

Staring at it, Manship felt the roll of tiny glaciers toward his heart. His stomach flattened out against its abdominal wall and tried to skulk quietly around his ribs. He had never felt so completely frightened in his life. "Hey-y-y—" he began.

"A little too much power, Professor," Srin observed judiciously from where he rested easily with tentacles outspread against the wall. "A little too much power and not enough *glrnk*. Try a little more *glrnk* and see what happens."

"Thank you," Lirld told him gratefully. "Like this, you mean?"

He raised and pointed the instrument again.

"Hey-y-y!" Manship continued in the same vein as before, not so much because he felt the results of such a statement would be particularly rewarding as because he lacked, at the moment, the creative faculties for another, more elaborate comment. "Hey-y-y!" he repeated between chattering teeth, staring at Lirld out of eyes no longer entirely flat.

He held up a shaking, admonishing hand. Fear was gibbering through him like the news of panic through a nation of monkeys. He watched the flefnobe make the peculiar winding trigger adjustment again. His thoughts came to a stop and every muscle in his body seemed to tense unendurably.

Suddenly Lirld shook. He slid backward along the tabletop. The weapon dropped out of stiffened tentacles and smashed into bunches of circular wires that rolled in all directions. "Srin!" his mind whimpered. "Srin! The monster— Do—do you see what's coming out of his eyes? He's—he's—"

His body cracked open and a pale, blue goo poured out. Tentacles dropped off him like so many long leaves in a brisk autumn wind. The eyes that studded his surface turned from turquoise to a dull brown. "*Srin!*" he begged in a tiny, faraway thought. "Help me—the flat-eyed monster is—help—help!"

And then he dissolved. Where he had been, there was nothing but a dark liquid, streaked with blue, that flowed and bubbled and dripped off the curving edge of the table.

Manship stared at it uncomprehendingly, realizing only one thing fully—he was still alive.

A flicker of absolutely mad, stampeding fear reached him from Srin's mind. The laboratory assistant jumped from the wall against which he'd been standing, skidded across the tabletop with thrashing tentacles, paused for a moment at the knobs that lined its edge to get the necessary traction—and then leaped in an enormous arc to the far wall of the building. The zigzag indentations widened in a sort of lightning flash to let his body through.

So that *had* been a door after all. Manship found himself feeling rather smug at the deduction. With so little to go on—pretty smart, *pretty* smart.

And then the various parts of his brain caught up with current events and he began trembling from the reaction. He should be dead, a thing of shredded flesh and powdered bone. What had happened?

Lirld had fired the weapon at him and missed the first time. Just as he was about to fire again, something had struck the flefnobe about as hard as it had the Assyrian back in the days when the latter was in the habit of coming down like the wolf on the fold. *What?* Manship had been using no weapon of his own. He had, so far as he knew, no ally on this world. He looked about the huge, vaulted room. Silence. There was nothing else, nobody else in the place.

What was it the professor had screamed telepathically before he turned into soup? Something about Manship's eyes? Something *coming* out of the Earthman's eyes?

Still intensely puzzled—and despite his relief at having survived the last few minutes—Manship could not help regretting Lirld's extinction. Possibly because of his somewhat similar occupational status, the flefnobe had been the only creature of his type toward whom Manship felt any sympathy. He felt a little lonelier now—and, obscurely, a little guilty.

The different thoughts which had been mashing themselves to and fro in his mind abruptly disappeared, to be replaced by a highly important observation.

The zigzag doorway through which Srin had fled was closing, was coming together! And, as far as Manship knew, it was the only way out of the place!

Manship bounced off the huge tabletop in a jump that for the second time in ten minutes did great credit to a few semester-hours of gym some six years ago. He reached the narrowing gap, prepared to claw his way through the solid stone if necessary.

He was determined not to be trapped in this place when the flefnobe police closed in with whatever they used in place of tear gas and machine guns. He had also not forgotten the need to catch up to Rabd and get two or three more driving lessons.

To his intense relief, the aperture dilated again as he was about to hit it. Some sort of photoelectric gadget, he wondered, or was it just sensitive to the approach of a body?

He charged through, and for the first time found himself on the surface of the planet with the night sky all around him.

The view of the sky almost took his breath away and made him forget, temporarily, the utterly strange city of the flefnobes that stretched away in every direction.

There were so many stars! It was as if these stellar bodies were so much confectioner's sugar and someone had tossed a bagful at the heavens. They glowed with enough luminosity to maintain a three-quarters twilight. There was no moon, but its lack was not felt; rather it seemed that half a dozen moons had been broken up into quadrillions of tiny white dots.

It would be impossible, in this plenty, to trace out a single constellation. It would be necessary, instead, Manship guessed, to speak of a third brightest patch, a fifth largest sector. Truly, here in the center of the galaxy, one did not merely see the stars—one lived amongst them!

He noticed his feet were wet. Glancing down, he saw he was standing in a very shallow stream of some reddish liquid that flowed between the rounded flefnobe buildings. Sewage disposal? Water supply? Probably neither, probably something else completely out of the range of human needs. For there were other colored streams flowing parallel to it, Manship saw now—green ones, mauve ones, bright pink ones. At a street intersection a few yards from him, the reddish stream flowed away by itself down a sort of alley, while a few new colored ribbons joined the main body.

Well, he wasn't here to work out problems in extraterrestrial sociology. He already had the sniffling intimation of a bad head cold. Not only his feet were wet in this spongelike atmosphere; his pajamas clung to his skin in dampest companionship and, every once in a while, his eyes got blurry with the moisture and he had to brush them dry with the back of a hand.

Furthermore, while he was not hungry, he had not only seen nothing resembling human-type victuals since his arrival, but also no evidence to suggest that the flefnobes had stomachs, let alone mouths.

Maybe they took in nourishment through the skin, soaked it up, say, from those differently colored streams that ran through their city. Red might be meat, green could be vegetables, white for dessert—

He clenched his fists and shook himself. *I've no time for any of this philosophic badminton,* he told himself fiercely. *In just a few hours, I'm going to be extremely hungry and thirsty. I'm also going to be extremely hunted. I'd better get moving—work out some solutions!*

Only where? Fortunately, the street outside Lirld's laboratory seemed deserted. Maybe the flefnobes were afraid of the dark? Maybe they were all good, respectable homebodies and everyone, without exception, toddled into his bed at night to sleep the darkness through? Maybe—

Rabd. He had to find Rabd. That was the beginning and the end of the only solution to his problems he had come even close to, since his materialization on Professor Lirld's lab table.

Rabd.

He tried "listening" with his mind. All kinds of drifting, miscellaneous thoughts were sloshing around in his brain, from the nearer inhabitants of the city.

"All right, darling, all right. If you don't want to *gadl*, you don't have to *gadl*. We'll do something else…"

"That smart-aleck Bohrg! Will I fix him properly tomorrow…"

"Do you have three *zamshkins* for a *plet*? I want to make a long-distance send…"

"Bohrg will roll in tomorrow morning, thinking everything is the same as it's always been. Is he going to be surprised…"

"I like you, Nernt, I like you a lot. And that's why I feel it's my duty to tell you, strictly as a friend, you understand…"

"No, darling, I didn't mean that *I* didn't want to *gadl*. I thought *you* didn't want to; I was trying to be considerate like you always tell me to be. *Of course* I want to *gadl*. Now please don't look at me like that…"

"Listen here. I can lick any flefnobe in the place…"

"To tell you the truth, Nernt, I think you're the only one who doesn't know. Everybody else…"

"So you're all scared, huh? All right, I'll take you on two at a time. Come on, *come on…*"

But no hint of Rabd. Manship began to walk cautiously down the stone-paved streets, sloshing through the little rivulets.

He stepped too close to the wall of the dark buildings. Immediately, a zigzag doorway opened its jagged invitation. He hesitated for a moment, then stepped through.

Nobody here either. Did the flefnobes sleep in some central building, dormitory fashion? Did they sleep at all? He must remember to tune in on some likely mind and investigate. The information might be useful.

This building seemed to be a warehouse; it was filled with shelves. The walls were bare, however—there seemed to be some flefnobe inhibition against putting objects against the walls. The shelves rose in tall tiers—again free-form shapes—from the center of the floor.

Manship strolled over to the shelving that was the height of his chest. Dozens of fat green balls rested in white porcelain cups. Food? Could be. They looked distinctly edible, like melons.

He reached out and picked one up. It immediately spread wings and flew away to the ceiling. Every one of the other green balls, on all the shelves, spread a similar set of multiple, tiny wings and flew upward, like so many spherical birds whose nests have been disturbed. When they reached the domed ceiling, they seemed to disappear.

Manship backed out of the place hurriedly through the jagged aperture. He seemed to be setting off alarms whereever he went!

Once out in the street, he sensed a new feeling. There was a sensation of bubbling excitement everywhere, a tense waiting. Very few individual thoughts were coming through.

Suddenly the restlessness coalesced into an enormous mental shout that almost deafened him.

"Good evening!" it said. "Please stand by for an emergency news bulletin. This is Pukr, the son of Kimp, coming to you on a planetwide, mind-to-mind hookup. Here is the latest on the flat-eyed monster:

"At forty-three *skims* past *bebblewort*, tonight, this creature was materialized by Professor Lirld from astronomical unit 649-301-3 as part of an experiment in one-way teleportation. Councilor Glomg was present as a witness to the experiment in the course of his official duties and, observing the aggressive way in which the monster comported itself, immediately warned Lirld of the dangers in letting it remain alive.

"Lirld disregarded the warning and, later, after Councilor Glomg had departed with his son, Rabd, the well-known interplanetary explorer and flefnobe-about-town, the monster ran amuck. Having fought its way out of a cage of solid paper, it attacked the professor with an unknown type of high-frequency mental beam that seems to emanate from its unbelievably flat eyes. This beam seems to be similar, in effect, to that thrown out by second-order *grepsas* when all fuses have blown. Our best psycho-physicists are, at this very moment, working feverishly on that aspect of the problem.

"But Professor Lirld paid with his life for his scientific curiosity and for disregarding the warnings of Councilor Glomg's experience. Despite the best efforts of Srin, Lirld's laboratory assistant, who fought a desperate and courageous diversionary action in an attempt to save the old scientist, Lirld perished horribly before the monster's ferocious onslaught. With his superior dead, Srin retreated tentacle by tentacle, fighting all the way, barely managing to make his escape in time.

"This alien monster with its incredible powers is now loose in our city! All citizens are urged to remain calm, not to panic. Rest assured that as soon as the authorities know what to do, they will do it. Remember—above all—stay calm!

"Meanwhile, Rabd, the son of Glomg, has postponed his mating flight which was to have begun tonight. He is mating, as you all know, with Tekt, the daughter of Hilp—Tekt being the well-known star of *fnesh* and *blelg* from the southern continent. Rabd is leading a troop of volunteer flefnobes to the scientific quarters of the city, where the monster was last seen, in an attempt to exterminate it with already-existing, conventional weapons before the creature starts to reproduce. I will return with more bulletins when they are available. That is all for now."

That was more than enough, Manship felt. Now there wasn't any hope that he could work out some method of communication with these creatures and sit down for a little quiet conversation on ways and means of getting himself home—which seemed to be a conclusion earnestly desired by all. From now on the watchword was going to be *Get That Manship!*

He didn't like that at all.

On the other hand, he didn't have to wander after Rabd. If Manship can't get to the flefnobe, the flefnobe will come to Manship. Heavily armed, however, and with homicidal intent…

He decided he had better hide. He stepped up to a building and wandered along a wall until the doorway opened. He walked through and watched it close behind him, then looked around.

To his relief, it seemed like an excellent place to hide. There were quantities of large, heavy objects in the center of the place, none of them, so far as he could tell, alive, and all of them satisfactorily opaque. He wedged himself between two of these, which looked like stored tabletops, and hoped wistfully that the flefnobe sensory apparatus did not boast any more detective mechanisms than he had already experienced.

What he wouldn't give to be an assistant professor in Kelly University again instead of a flat-eyed monster ravening, all unwittingly, through an alien metropolis!

He found himself wondering about the strange powers he was supposed to possess. What was all this nonsense about a high-frequency mental beam emanating from his eyes? He hadn't noticed anything coming out—and he should have noticed if anyone did, he felt. Yet Lirld had made some comment to that effect just before he dissolved.

Was it possible that there was some by-product of the human brain that was only visible to flefnobes and was highly deleterious to them?

After all, he could tune in on the flefnobes' minds and they couldn't tune in on his. Maybe the only way he could make his mental presence felt to them was in some prodigious blast of thought which literally ripped them apart.

But he apparently couldn't turn it on and off at will—he hadn't caused the slightest alteration in Lirld, the first time the professor had fired.

There were ripples of new, excited thoughts reaching him suddenly. They were coming from somewhere in the street outside.

Rabd had arrived with his posse.

"Three of you move down that way," the young flefnobe ordered. "I want two each to cover the side streets. Don't spend too much time searching through the buildings. I'm positive we'll find this monster skulking somewhere in the dark streets, looking for new victims. Tanj, Zogt and Lewv—come with me. And keep on your tentacle-tips, everybody—this thing is crazy dangerous. But remember, we've got to blast it before it starts reproducing. Imagine what this planet would be like with a couple of hundred of these flat-eyed monsters running around!"

Manship let out a long, slow sigh of relief. If they hoped to find him on the streets, he might have a little time.

He let his mind follow that of Rabd. It wasn't too hard—just a matter of concentration—and you pretty much blocked out the thoughts of the other individuals. *Follow Rabd's mind, Rabd's thoughts. Now block out most of Rabd's conscious thoughts. There. The subliminal layer, the memory patterns. No, not the stuff about that female flefnobe last month, all eyes and soft tentacles, dammit!*

The memory patterns, the older ones. "When landing on a C-12 type planet…" *No, not that one. A little further. There!* "Having fired the forward jet to clear it, gently depress the…"

Manship combed through the operational instructions in Rabd's mind, pausing every once in a while to clear up a concept peculiar to flefnobe terminology, stopping now and then as a grinning thought about Tekt wandered in and threw everything out of focus.

He noticed that whatever information he absorbed in this fashion, he seemed to absorb permanently; there was no need to go back to previous data. Probably left a permanent print on his mind, he concluded.

He had it all now, at least as much about running the ship as it was possible to understand. In the last few moments, he had been operating the ship—and operating the ship for years and years—at least through Rabd's memories. For the first time, Manship began to feel a little confident.

But how was he to find the little spaceship in the streets of this utterly strange city? He clasped his hands in perspired bafflement. After all this—

Then he had the answer. He'd get the directions from Rabd's mind. Of course. Good old encyclopedia Rabd! *He'd* certainly remember where he parked the vessel.

And he did. With a skill that seemed to have come from ages of practice, Clyde Manship riffled through the flefnobe's thoughts, discarding this one, absorbing that one—"...the indigo stream for five blocks. Then take the first merging red one and..."—until he had as thorough and as permanent a picture of the route to Rabd's three-jet runabout as if he'd been studying the subject in graduate school for six months.

Pretty good going for a stodgy young assistant professor of Comparative Literature who up to this night had about as much experience with telepathy as African lion-hunting! But perhaps—perhaps it had been a matter of *conscious* experience of telepathy; perhaps the human mind was accustomed to a sort of regular, deep-in-the-brain, unconscious telepathy from infancy and being exposed to creatures so easy to receive from as flefnobes had brought the latently exercised powers to the surface.

That would explain the quickly acquired skill that felt so much like the sudden surprising ability to type whole words and sentences after months of practicing nothing but meaningless combinations of letters in certain set alphabetical patterns.

Well, it might be interesting, but that particular speculation was not his field of research and not his problem. Not for tonight, anyway.

Right now, what he had to do was somehow slip out of the building unobserved by the crowd of flefnobe vigilantes outside, and get on his way fast. After all, it might not be long before the militia was called out to deal with something as viciously destructive as himself...

He slipped out of his hiding place and made for the wall. The zigzag doorway opened. He stepped through—and bowled over a tentacled black suitcase who'd apparently been coming in.

The flefnobe recovered fast. He pointed his spiraly weapon at Manship from where he lay and began winding it. Once more, the Earthman went rigid with fright; he'd seen what that thing could do. To be killed now, after all he'd gone through...

And once more, there was a quiver and a mental scream of distress from the flefnobe: "The flat-eyed monster— I've found him—his eyes—his eyes. Zogt, Rabd, help! *His eyes—*"

There was nothing left but a twitching tentacle or two and a puddle of liquid rippling back and forth in a little hollow near the building wall. Without looking back, Manship fled.

A stream of red dots chattered over his shoulder and dissolved a domed roof directly ahead of him. Then he had turned the corner and was picking up speed. From the dwindling telepathic shouts behind him, he deduced with relief that feet moved faster than tentacles.

He found the correct colored streams and began to work his way in the direction of Rabd's spaceship. Only once or twice did he come across a flefnobe. And none of them seemed to be armed.

At sight of him, these passersby wound their tentacles about their bodies, huddled against the nearest wall, and, after a few dismal mutters to the effect of "*Qrm* save me, *Qrm* save me," seemed to pass out.

He was grateful for the absence of heavy traffic, but wondered why it should be so, especially since he was now moving through the residential quarters of the city according to the mental map he had purloined from Rabd.

Another overpowering roar in his mind gave him the answer.

"This is Pukr, the son of Kimp, returning to you with more news of the flat-eyed monster. First, the Council wishes me to notify all who have not already been informed through their *blelg* service that a state of martial law has been proclaimed in the city.

"Repeat: a state of martial law has been proclaimed in the city! All citizens are to stay off the streets until further notice. Units of the army and space fleet as well as heavy *maizeltoovers* are being moved in hurriedly. Don't get in their way! Stay off the streets!

"The flat-eyed monster has struck again. Just ten short *skims* ago, it struck down Lewv, the son of Yifg, in a running battle outside the College of Advanced *Turkaslerg,* almost trampling Rabd, the son of Glomg, who courageously hurled himself in its path in a valiant attempt to delay the monster's flight. Rabd, however, believes he seriously wounded it with a well-placed bolt from his blaster. The monster's weapon was the high-frequency beam from its eyes—

"Shortly before this battle, the flat-eyed horror from the outer galactic wastes had evidently wandered into a museum where it completely destroyed a valuable collection of green *fermfnaks.* They were found in a useless winged condition. Why did it do this? Pure viciousness? Some scientists believe that this act indicates intelligence of a very high order indeed, and that this intelligence, together with the fantastic powers already in evidence, will make the killing of the monster a much more difficult task than the local authorities expect.

"Professor Wuvb is one of these scientists. He feels that only through a correct psycho-sociological evaluation of the monster and an understanding of the peculiar cultural milieu from which it evidently derives will we be able to work out adequate counter-measures and save the planet. Therefore, in the interests of flefnobe survival, we have brought the professor here tonight to give you his views. The next mind you hear will be that of Professor Wuvb."

Just as the newcomer began portentously, "To understand any given cultural milieu, we must first ask ourselves what we mean by culture. Do we mean, for example—" Manship reached the landing field.

He came out upon it near the corner on which Rabd's three-jet runabout was parked between an enormous interplanetary vessel being loaded with freight and what Manship would have been certain was a warehouse, if he hadn't learned so thoroughly how wrong he could be about flefnobe equivalents of human activities.

There seemed to be no guards about, the landing field was not particularly well-lit, and most of the individuals in the neighborhood were concentrated around the freighter.

He took a deep breath and ran for the comparatively tiny, spherical ship with the deep hollow in the top and bottom, something like an oversized metallic apple. He reached it, ran around the side until he came to the zigzag line that indicated an entrance and squeezed through.

As far as he could tell, he hadn't been observed. Outside of the mutter of loading and stowage instructions coming from the larger ship, there were only Professor Wuvb's louder thoughts weaving their intricate sociophilosophical web: "…So we may conclude that in this respect, at least, the flat-eyed monster does not show the typical basic personality pattern of an illiterate. But then, if we attempt to relate the characteristics of a preliterate urban cultural configuration…"

Manship waited for the doorway to contract, then made his way hand over hand up a narrow, twisting ladderlike affair to the control room of the vessel. He seated himself uncomfortably before the main instrument panel and went to work.

It was difficult using fingers on gadgets which had been designed for tentacles, but he had no choice. *To warm up the motors of the* Bulvonn *Drive—*" Gently, very gently, he rotated the uppermost three cylinders a complete turn each. Then, when the rectangular plate on his left began to show an even succession of red and white stripes across its face, he pulled on the large black knob protruding from the floor. A yowling roar of jets started from outside. He worked almost without conscious effort, letting memory take over. It was as if Rabd himself were getting the spaceship into operation.

A few seconds later, he was off the planet and in deep space.

He switched to interstellar operation, set the directional indicator for astronomical unit 649-301-3—and sat back. There was nothing else for him to do until the time came for landing. He was a little apprehensive about that part, but things had gone so well up to this point that he felt quite the interstellar daredevil. "Old Rocketfingers Manship," he grinned to himself smugly.

According to Rabd's subliminal calculations, he should be arriving on Earth—given the maximum output of the *Bulvonn* Drive which he was using—in ten to twelve hours. He was going to be more than a bit hungry and thirsty, but— What a sensation he was going to make! Even more of a sensation than he had left behind him. The flat-eyed monster with a high-frequency mental beam coming out of its eyes…

What *had* that been? All that had happened to him, each time a flefnobe dissolved before his stare, was a good deal of fear. He had been terribly frightened that he was going to be blasted into tiny pieces and had, somewhere in the process of being frightened, evidently been able to throw out something pretty tremendous—to judge from results.

Possibly the abnormally high secretion of adrenalin in the human system at moments of stress was basically inimical to flefnobe body structure. Or maybe there was an entirely mental reaction in Man's brain at such times whose emanations caused the flefnobes to literally fall apart. It made sense.

If he was so sensitive to their thoughts, they should be sensitive to him in some way. And obviously, when he was very much afraid, that sensitivity showed up with a vengeance.

He put his hands behind his head and glanced up to check his meters. Everything was working satisfactorily. The brown circles were expanding and contracting on the *sekkel* board, as Rabd's mind had said they should; the little serrations on the edge of the control panel were moving along at a uniform rate, the visiscreen showed—*the visiscreen!*

Manship leaped to his feet. The visiscreen showed what seemed to be every vessel in the flefnobe army and space fleet—not to mention the heavy *maizeltoovers*—in hot pursuit of him. And getting closer.

There was one large spacecraft that had almost caught up and was beginning to exude a series of bright rays that, Manship remembered from Rabd's recollections, were grapples.

What could have caused all this commotion—the theft of a single jet runabout? The fear that he might steal the secrets of flefnobe science? They should have been so glad to get rid of him, especially before he started reproducing hundreds of himself all over the planet!

And then a persistent thought ripple from inside his own ship—a thought ripple which he had been disregarding all the time he had been concentrating on the unfamiliar problems of deep-space navigation—gave him a clue.

He had taken off with someone—or something—else in the ship!

Clyde Manship scurried down the twisting ladder to the main cabin. As he approached, the thoughts became clearer and he realized, even before the cabin aperture dilated to let him through, exactly whom he would find.

Tekt.

The well-known female star of *fnesh* and *blelg* from the southern continent and Rabd's about-to-be bride cowered in a far corner; all of her tentacles—including the hundred and seventy-six slime-washed ones that were topped by limpid eyes—twisted about her tiny black body in the most complicated series of knots Manship had ever seen.

"Oo-ooh!" her mind moaned. "*Qrm! Qrm!* Now it's going to happen! That awful, horrible thing! It's going to happen to me! It's coming closer—closer—"

"Look, lady, I'm not even slightly interested in you," Manship began, before he remembered that he'd never been able to communicate with any flefnobe before, let alone a hysterical female one.

He felt the ship shudder as the grapples touched it. *Well, here I go again,* he thought. In a moment there would be boarders and he'd have to turn them into bluish soup.

Evidently, Tekt had been sleeping aboard the vessel when he took off. She'd been waiting for Rabd to return and begin their mating flight. And she was obviously a sufficiently important figure to have every last reserve called up.

His mind caught the sensation of someone entering the ship. Rabd. From what Manship could tell, he was alone, carrying his trusty blaster—and determined to die fighting.

Well, that's exactly what he'd have to do. Clyde Manship was a fairly considerate individual and heartily disliked the idea of disintegrating a bridegroom on what was to have been his honeymoon. But, since he had found no way of communicating his pacific intentions, he had no choice.

"Tekt!" Rabd telepathed softly. "Are you all right?"

"Murder!" Tekt screamed. "Help-help-help-help…" Her thoughts abruptly disappeared; she had fainted.

The zigzag aperture widened and Rabd bounced into the cabin, looking like a series of long balloons in his spacesuit. He glanced at the recumbent Tekt and then turned desperately, pointing his curlicued blaster at Manship.

"Poor guy," Manship was thinking. "Poor, dumb, narrow-minded hero type. In just a second, you'll be nothing but goo." He waited, full of confidence.

He was so full of confidence, in fact, that he wasn't a bit frightened.

So nothing came out of his eyes, nothing but a certain condescending sympathy.

So Rabd blasted the ugly, obscene, horrible, flat-eyed thing down where it stood. And scooped up his bride with loving tentacles. And went back home to a hero's reception.

AFTERWORD

Two days after Christmas 1954, the woman with whom I was living and with whom I was planning marriage made me a bang-up supper featuring all kinds of sharp spices. Two hours later, I was admitted to the hospital with a bleeding ulcer. As a free-lance writer, I had no medical insurance of any kind; my usually low bank account had to be completely emptied so that I could be admitted in a status other than that of charity patient.

The word spread rapidly through the New York City science-fiction community, and for some reason the word that was spread was that I gone to St. Vincent's Hospital for an ordinary check-up. As a result, science-fiction folk showed up in my hospital room that night with all kinds of bizarre gag accouterments, only to find out that I was involved in some very serious business indeed. Harry and Joan Harrison, for example, came in holding a lily each—and were crushed to discover that the doctors were trying to decide if a dangerous immediate operation should be attempted.

After a conference, the doctors decided to hold off on the operation unless the bleeding intensified during the night. Then, one by one, the people around my bed drifted off, still apologizing for their jokey entrances. The last one to go was the woman with whom I was planning to share my life. She bent over me and put her warm, wet mouth to my ear.

Now I know that when a writer memoirizes some fifty years after the event, he cannot be expected to remember exactly every word of every speech. I therefore ask the reader to keep in mind two essential considerations: One, for most of my time on this planet, I have been blessed and cursed with almost perfect recall; and, two, such was the matter of her communication to me that it kind of seared itself into my brain.

"Now, darling," she asked warmly, wetly. "Is it true that you are absolutely penniless?"

"Absolutely," I told her. "My brother, Mort, cleaned out my whole bank account just to get me in here. I don't know what I'll do for next month's rent. Not to mention the surgeon's bill if they do decide to operate."

"That's what I thought," she breathed, still warm and still wet. "Now sweetheart, please listen to me. You are flat on your back, physically, psychologically, and financially. There's really nothing in this for me anymore. So I'll be going. Goodbye, my darling."

I pulled my head away and swiveled round to stare at her. "Hey," I said. "You can't be serious."

"Now, don't be selfish," she said, backing away to the door. "Try to look at it from my point of view. Goodbye."

Then she raised her right hand, waved it twice at me, closed the door behind her, and was gone.

I sat up in bed. I stared at the closed door for a long time. Then I picked up the telephone and called Horace Gold, the editor of *Galaxy*. (Horace was an agoraphobe and edited the magazine out of his apartment in Peter Cooper Village.)

Horace had heard what was going on with me. "Listen," he said. "They tell me you're in tough shape and you're broke. I'll put a voucher through tomorrow morning for five hundred dollars. You can have someone pick up the check for you about eleven AM. What I want you to do for me… I want you to write a ten-thousand-word novelette—it should be very, very funny. Okay?"

"Thanks, Horace," I said. "I'll do it. If I live."

"Right," he agreed. "If you live. Meanwhile, don't forget. Very, very funny."

I hung up the phone, swallowed a large pill, and reached for the clipboard that my brother, Morton, and his wife, Sheila, had placed on my bedside table. What should I write? Well, there was the fact that *Galaxy* prided itself on not being a cheapo science-fiction magazine like those pulps that featured "bug-eyed monster" covers, with stories full of slime-dripping horrors to match. And there was my great fondness for two early stories by A.E. van Vogt, "Black Destroyer" and "Discord in Scarlet." I had long dreamed of doing a minor and respectful parody of the sociological analysis of aliens both stories featured.

The nurse came in, took my temperature, urged me to rest and get a good night's sleep— and left.

I picked up a pencil. Trying hard not to bleed, I began writing, in longhand, "The Flat-Eyed Monster." Now, what, I mused to myself as I wrote, would Horace consider very, very funny?

WRITTEN 1954———PUBLISHED 1955

THE DESERTER

November 10, 2039—

Terran Supreme Command communiqué No. 18-673 for the twenty-four hours ending 0900 Monday, Terran capital time:

…whereupon sector HQ on Fortress Satellite Five ordered a strategic withdrawal of all interceptor units. The withdrawal was accomplished without difficulty and with minimal loss.

The only other incident of interest in this period was the surrender of an enemy soldier of undetermined rank, the first of these creatures from Jupiter to be taken alive by our forces. The capture was made in the course of defending Cochabamba, Bolivia, from an enemy commando raid. Four Jovians were killed in this unsuccessful assault upon a vital tin-supplying area after which the fifth laid down his arms and begged that his life be spared. Upon capture by our forces, the Jovian claimed to be a deserter and requested a safe-conduct to…

Mardin had been briefed on what to expect by the MP officer who'd escorted him into the cave. Inevitably, though, his first view of the tank in which the alien floated brought out a long, whimpering grunt of disbelief and remembered fear. It was at least sixty feet long by forty wide, and it reared off the rocky floor to twice the height of a man. Whatever incredible material its sides had been composed of had hours ago been covered by thick white layers of ice.

Cold air currents bouncing the foul, damp smell of methane back from the tank tweaked his nose and pricked at his ears. *Well, after all,* Mardin thought, *those things have a body temperature somewhere in the neighborhood of minus 200° Fahrenheit!*

And he had felt this cold once before.…

He shivered violently in response to the memory and zipped shut the fur-lined coveralls he'd been issued at the entrance. "Must have been quite a job getting that thing in here." The casualness of his voice surprised him and made him feel better.

"Oh, a special engineer task force did it in—let me see, now—" The MP lieutenant, a Chinese girl in her late teens, pursed soft, coral lips at his graying hair. "Less than five hours, figuring from the moment they arrived. The biggest problem was finding a cell in the neighborhood that was big enough to hold the prisoner. This cave was perfect."

Mardin looked up at the ledge above their heads. Every ten feet, a squad of three men, highly polished weapons ready for instant action. Atomic cannon squads alternating with men bent down under the weight of dem-dem grenades. Grim-faced young subalterns, very conscious of the bigness of the brass that occupied the platform at the far end of the cave, stamped back and forth along the ledge from squad to squad, deadly little Royster pistolettos tinkling and naked in their sweating hands. *Those kids,* he thought angrily, *so well adjusted to it all!*

The ledge ran along three sides of the cave; on the fourth, the low entrance from which Mardin had just come, he had seen five steel Caesars implanted, long, pointed snouts throbbingly eager to throw tremendous gusts of nuclear energy at the Jovian's rear. And amid the immense rock folds of the roof, a labyrinth of slender, pencil-like bombs had been laid, held in place by clamps that would all open simultaneously the moment a certain colonel's finger pressed a certain green button....

"If our friend in the tank makes one wrong move," Mardin muttered, "half of South America goes down the drain."

The girl started to chuckle, then changed her mind and frowned. "I'm sorry, Major Mardin, but I don't like that. I don't like hearing them referred to as 'friends.' Even in a joke. Over a million and a half people—three hundred thousand of them Chinese—have been wiped out by those—those ammoniated flatworms!"

"And the first fifty of which," he reminded her irritably, "were my relatives and neighbors. If you're old enough to remember Mars and the Three Watertanks Massacre, young lady."

She swallowed and looked stricken. An apology seemed to be in the process of composition, but Mardin moved past her in a long, disgusted stride and headed rapidly for the distant platform. He had a fierce dislike, he had discovered long ago, for people who were unable to hate wholesomely and intelligently, who had to jog their animus with special symbols and idiotic negations. Americans, during the War of 1914–18, changing sauerkraut into liberty cabbage; mobs of Turks, in the Gibraltar Flare-up of 1985, lynching anyone in Ankara caught eating oranges. How many times had he seen aged men in the uniform of the oldsters' service, the Infirm Civilian Corps, make the socially accepted gesture of grinding out a worm with their heels whenever they referred to the enemy from Jupiter!

He grimaced at the enormous expanse of ice-covered tank in which a blanket of living matter large enough to cover a city block pursued its alien processes. "Let me see you lift your foot and step on *that!*" he told the astonished girl behind him. *Damn all simplicity-hounds, anyway,* he thought. *A week on the receiving end of a Jovian question-machine is exactly what they need. Make them nice and thoughtful and give them some inkling of how crazily complex this universe can be!*

That reminded him of his purpose in this place. He became thoughtful himself and—while the circular scar on his forehead wrinkled—very gravely reminiscent of how crazily complex the universe actually was....

So thoughtful, in fact, that he had to take a long, relaxing breath and wipe his hands on his coveralls before climbing the stairs that led up to the hastily constructed platform.

Colonel Liu, Mardin's immediate superior, broke away from the knot of men at the other end and came up to him with arms spread wide. "Good to see you, Mardin," he said rapidly. "Now listen to me. Old Rockethead himself is here—you know how *he* is. So put a little snap into your salute and kind of pull back on those shoulders when you're talking to him. Know what I mean? Try to show him that when it comes to military bearing, we in Intelligence don't take a— Mardin, are you listening to me? This is *very* important."

With difficulty, Mardin took his eyes away from the transparent un-iced top of the tank. "Sorry, sir," he mumbled. "I'll—I'll try to remember."

"This the interpreter, Colonel Liu? Major Mardin, eh?" the very tall, stiffly erect man in the jeweled uniform of a Marshal of Space yelled from the railing. "Bring him over. On the double, sir!"

Colonel Liu grabbed Mardin's left arm and pulled him rapidly across the platform. Rockethead Billingsley cut the colonel's breathless introduction short. "Major *Igor* Mardin, is it? Sounds Russian. You wouldn't be Russian now, would you? I hate Russians."

Mardin noticed a broad-shouldered vice-marshal standing in Billingsley's rear stiffen angrily. "No, sir," he replied. "Mardin is a Croat name. My family is French and Yugoslav with possibly a bit of Arab."

The Marshal of Space inclined his fur-covered head. "Good! Couldn't stand you if you were Russian. Hate Russians, hate Chinese, hate Portuguese. Though the Chinese are worst of all, I'd say. Ready to start working on this devil from Jupiter? Come over here, then. And move, man, move!" As he swung around, the dozen or so sapphire-studded Royster pistolettos that swung picturesquely from his shoulder straps clinked and clanked madly, making him seem like a gigantic cat that the mice had belled again and again.

Hurrying after him, Mardin noticed with amusement that the stiff, angry backs were everywhere now. Colonel Liu's mouth was screwed up into a dark pucker in his face; at the far end of the platform, the young lieutenant who'd escorted him from the jet base was punching a tiny fist into an open palm. Marshal of Space Rudolfo Billingsley enjoyed a rank high enough to make tact a function of the moment's whim—and it was obvious that he rarely indulged such moments. "Head thick as a rocket wall and a mouth as filthy as a burned-out exhaust, but he can figure out, down to the smallest wound on the greenest corporal, exactly how much blood any attack is going to cost." That was what the line officers said of him.

And that, after all, Mardin reflected, was just the kind of man needed in the kind of world Earth had become in eighteen years of Jovian siege. He, himself, owed this man a very special debt....

"You probably don't remember me, sir," he began hesitantly as they paused beside a metal armchair that was suspended from an overhead wire. "But we met once before, about sixteen years ago. It was aboard your spaceship, the *Euphrates*, that I—"

"The *Euphrates* wasn't a spaceship. It was an interceptor, third class. Learn your damned terminology if you're going to dishonor a major's uniform, mister! And pull that zipper up tight. Of course, you were one of that mob of mewling civilians I pulled out of Three Watertanks right under the Jovians' noses. Let's see: that young archaeologist fellow. Didn't know then that we were going to get a real, first-class, bang-up, slaughter-em-dead war out of that incident, did we? Hah! You thought you had an easy life ahead of you, eh? Didn't suspect you'd be spending the rest of it in uniform, standing up straight and jumping when you got an order! This war's made men out of a lot of wet jellyfish like you, mister, and you can be grateful for the privilege."

Mardin nodded with difficulty, sardonically conscious of the abrupt stiffness of his own back, of the tightly clenched fingers scraping his palm. He wondered about the incidence of courts-martial, for striking a superior officer, in Billingsley's personal staff.

"All right, hop into it. Hop *in,* man!" Mardin realized the significance of the cupped hands being extended to him. A Marshal of Space was offering him a boost! Billingsley believed nobody could do *anything* better than Billingsley. Very gingerly, he stepped into it, was lifted up so that he could squirm into the chair. Automatically, he fastened the safety belt across his middle, strapped the headset in place.

Below him, Old Rockethead pulled the clamps tight around his ankles and called up: "You've been briefed? Arkhnatta contacted you?"

"Yes, I mean yes, *sir.* Professor Arkhnatta traveled with me all the way from Melbourne Base. He managed to cover everything, but of course it wasn't the detail he'd have liked."

"Hell with the detail. Listen to me, Major Mardin. Right there in front of you is the only Jovian flatworm we've managed to take alive. I don't know how much longer we can *keep* him alive—engineers are building a methane plant in another part of the cave so he'll have some stink to breathe when his own supply runs out, and the chemistry johnnies are refrigerating ammonia for him to drink—but I intend to rip every bit of useful military information out of his hide before he caves in. And your mind is the only chisel I've got. Hope I don't break the chisel, but the way I figure it you're not worth as much as a secondary space fleet. And I sacrificed one of those day before yesterday—complement of two thousand men—just to find out what the enemy was up to. So, mister, you pay attention to me and keep asking him questions. And shout out your replies good and loud for the recording machines. Swing him out, Colonel! Didn't you *hear* me? How the hell long does it take to swing him out?"

As the cable pulled the chair away from the platform and over the immense expanse of monster, Mardin felt something in his belly go far away and something in his brain try to hide. In a few moments—at the thought of what he'd be doing in a minute or two he shut his eyes tightly as he had in childhood, trying to wish the bad thing away.

He should have done what all his instincts urged way back in Melbourne Base when he'd gotten the orders and realized what they meant. He should have deserted. Only trouble, where do you desert in a world under arms, on a planet where every child has its own military responsibilities? But he should have done something. *Something.* No man should have to go through this twice in one lifetime.

Simple enough for Old Rockethead. This was *his* life, negative as its goals were; moments like these of incipient destruction were the fulfillment for which he'd trained and worked and studied. He remembered something else now about Marshal of Space Billingsley. The beautiful little winged creatures of Venus—*Griggoddon,* they'd been called—who'd learned human languages and begun pestering the early colonists of that planet with hundreds of questions. Toleration of their high-pitched, ear-splitting voices had turned into annoyance and they'd been locked out of the settlements, whereupon they'd made the nights hideous with their curiosity, Since they'd refused to leave, and since the hard-working colonists found themselves losing more and more sleep, the problem had been turned over to the resident military power on Venus. Mardin recalled the uproar even on Mars when a laconic order of the day—"Venus has been rendered permanently calm: Commodore R. Billingsley."—announced that the first intelligent extra-terrestrial life to be discovered had been destroyed down to the last crawling segmented infant by means of a new insecticide spray.

Barely six months later the attack on sparsely settled Mars had underlined with human corpses the existence of another intelligent race in the solar system—and a much more powerful one. Who remembered the insignificant *Griggoddon* when Commodore Rudolfo Billingsley slashed back into the enemy-occupied capital of Southern Mars and evacuated the few survivors of Jupiter's initial assault? Then the Hero of Three Watertanks had even gone back and rescued one of the men captured alive by the Jovian monsters—a certain Igor Mardin, proud possessor of the first, and, as it eventually turned out, also the only Ph.D. in Martian archaeology.

No, for Old Rockethead this horrendous planet-smashing was more than fulfillment, much more than a wonderful opportunity to practice various aspects of his trade: it represented reprieve. If mankind had not blundered into and alerted the outposts of Jovian empire in the asteroid belt, Billingsley would have worked out a miserable career as a police officer in various patrol posts, chained for the balance of his professional life to a commodore's rank by the *Griggoddon* blunder. Whenever he appeared at a party some fat woman would explain to her escort in a whisper full of highly audible sibilants that this was the famous Beast of Venus—and every uniformed man in the place would look uncomfortable. The Beast of Venus it would have been instead of the Hero of Three Watertanks, Defender of Luna, the Father of the Fortress Satellite System.

As for himself—well, Dr. Mardin would have plodded out the long years tranquilly and usefully, a scholar among scholars, not the brightest and best, possibly— here, a stimulating and rather cleverly documented paper, there, a startling minor discovery of interest only to specialists—but a man respected by his colleagues, doing work he was fitted for and liked, earning a secure place for himself in the textbooks of another age as a secondary footnote or additional line in a bibliography. But instead the Popa Site Diggings were disintegrated rubble near the ruins of what had once been the human capital of Southern Mars and Major Igor Mardin's civilian skills had less relevance and value than those of a dodo breeder, or a veterinarian to mammoths and mastodons. He was now a mildly incompetent field-grade officer in an unimportant section of Intelligence whose attempts at military bearing and deportment amused his subordinates and caused his superiors a good deal of pain. He didn't like the tasks he was assigned; frequently he didn't even understand them. His value lay only in the two years of psychological hell he'd endured as a prisoner of the Jovians and even that could be realized only in peculiarly fortuitous circumstances such as those of the moment. He could never be anything but an object of pathos to the snappy, single-minded generation grown up in a milieu of no-quarter interplanetary war: and should the war end tomorrow with humanity, by some unimaginable miracle, victorious, he would have picked up nothing in the eighteen years of conflict but uncertainty about himself and a few doubtful moments for some drab little memoirs.

He found that, his fears forgotten, he had been glaring down at the enormous hulk of the Jovian rippling gently under the transparent tank-surface. This quiet-appearing sea of turgid scarlet soup in which an occasional bluish-white dumpling bobbed to the surface only to dwindle in size and disappear—this was one of the creatures that had robbed him of the life he should have had and had hurled him into a by-the-numbers purgatory. And why? So that their own peculiar concepts of mastery might be maintained, so that another species might not arise to challenge their dominion of the outer planets. No attempt at arbitration, at treaty-making, at any kind of discussion—instead an overwhelming and relatively sudden onslaught, as methodical and irresistible as the attack of an anteater on an anthill.

A slender silvery tendril rose from the top of the tank to meet him and the chair came to an abrupt halt in its swaying journey across the roof of the gigantic cave. Mardin's shoulders shot up against his neck convulsively, he found himself trying to pull his head down into his chest—just as he had scores of times in the prison cell that had once been the Three Watertanks Public Library.

At the sight of the familiar questing tendril, a panic eighteen years old engulfed and nauseated him.

It's going to hurt inside, his mind wept, twisting and turning and dodging in his brain. *The thoughts are going to be rubbed against each other so that the skin comes off them and they hurt and hurt and hurt....*

The tendril came to a stop before his face and the tip curved interrogatively. Mardin squirmed back against the metal chair back.

I won't! This time I don't have to! You can't make me—this time you're our prisoner—you can't make me—you can't make me—

"Mardin!" Billingsley's voice bellowed in his headphones. "Put the damn thing on and let's get going! Move, man, *move!*"

And almost before he knew he had done it, as automatically as he had learned to go rigid at the sound of *atten-shun!* Mardin's hand reached out for the tendril and placed the tip of it against the old scar on his forehead.

There was that anciently familiar sensation of inmost rapport, of new-found completeness, of belonging to a higher order of being. There were the strange double memories; a river of green fire arching off a jet-black trembling cliff hundreds of miles high, somehow blending in with the feel of delighted shock as Dave Weiner's baseball hit the catcher's mitt you'd gotten two hours ago for a birthday present; a picture of a very lovely and very intent young female physicist explaining to you just how somebody named Albert Fermi Vannevar derived $E=mc^2$, getting all confused with the time to begin the many-scented dance to the surface because of the myriad of wonderful soft spots you could feel calling to each other on your back.

But, Mardin realized with amazement in some recess of autonomy still left in his mind, this time there was a difference. This time there was no feeling of terror as of thorough personal violation, there was no incredibly ugly sensation of tentacles armed with multitudes of tiny suckers speeding through his nervous system and feeding, feeding, greedily feeding.... This time none of his thoughts were dissected, kicking and screaming, in the operating theater of his own skull while his ego shuddered fearfully at the bloody spectacle from a distant psychic cranny.

This time he was *with*—not *of.*

Of course, a lot of work undoubtedly had been done on the Jovian question-machine in the past decade. The single tendril that contained all of the intricate mechanism for telepathic communion between two races had probably been refined far past the coarse and blundering gadget that had gouged at his mind eighteen years ago.

And, of course, this time *he* was the interrogator. This time it was a Jovian that lay helpless before the probe, the weapons, the merciless detachment of an alien culture. This time it was a Jovian, not Igor Mardin, who had to find the right answers to the insistent questions—and the right symbols with which to articulate those answers.

All that made a tremendous difference. Mardin relaxed and was amused by the feeling of power that roared through him.

Still—there was something else. This time he was dealing with a totally different personality.

There was a pleasant, undefinable quality to this individual from a world whose gravity could smear Mardin across the landscape in a fine liquid film. A character trait like—no, not simple tact—certainly not timidity—and you couldn't just call it gentleness and warmth—

Mardin gave up. Certainly, he decided, the difference between this Jovian and his jailer on Mars was like the difference between two entirely different breeds. Why, it was a pleasure to share part of his mental processes temporarily with this kind of person! As from a distance, he heard the Jovian reply that the pleasure was mutual. He felt instinctively they had much in common.

And they'd have to—if Billingsley were to get the information he wanted. Superficially, it might seem that a mechanism for sharing thoughts was the ideal answer to communication between races as dissimilar as the Jovian and Terrestrial. In practice, Mardin knew from long months of squeezing his imagination under orders in Three Watertanks, a telepathy machine merely gave you a communication potential. An individual thinks in pictures and symbols based on his life experiences—if two individuals have no life experiences in common, all they can share is confusion. It had taken extended periods of desperate effort before Mardin and his Jovian captor had established that what passed for the digestive process among humans was a combination of breathing and strenuous physical exercise to a creature born on Jupiter, that the concept of taking a bath could be equated with a Jovian activity so shameful and so overlaid with pain that Mardin's questioner had been unable to visit him for five weeks after the subject came up and thenceforth treated him with the reserve one might maintain toward an intelligent blob of fecal matter.

But mutually accepted symbols eventually had been established—just before Mardin's rescue. And ever since then, he'd been kept on ice in Intelligence, for a moment like this....

"Mardin!" Old Rockethead's voice ripped out of his earphones. "Made contact yet?"

"Yes. I think I have, sir."

"Good! Feels like a reunion of the goddamn old regiment, eh? All set to ask questions? The slug's cooperating? Answer me, Mardin! Don't sit there gaping at him!"

"Yes, sir," Mardin said hurriedly. "Everything's all set."

"Good! Let's see now. First off, ask him his name, rank and serial number."

Mardin shook his head. The terrifying, straight-faced orderliness of the military mind! The protocol was unalterable; you asked a Japanese prisoner-of-war for his name, rank and serial number; obviously, you did the same when the prisoner was a Jovian! The fact that there was no interplanetary Red Cross to notify his family that food packages might now be sent...

He addressed himself to the immense blanket of quiescent living matter below him, phrasing the question in as broad a set of symbols as he could contrive. Where would the answer be worked out, he wondered? On the basis of their examination of dead Jovians, some scientists maintained that the creatures were really vertebrates, except that they had nine separate brains and spinal columns; other biologists insisted that the "brains" were merely the kind of ganglia to be found in various kinds of invertebrates and that thinking took place on the delicately convoluted surface of their bodies. And no one had ever found anything vaguely resembling a mouth or eyes, not to mention appendages that could be used in locomotion.

Abruptly, he found himself on the bottom of a noisy sea of liquid ammonia, clustered with dozens of other newborn around the neuter "mother." Someone flaked off the cluster and darted away; he followed. The two of them met in the appointed place of crystallization and joined into one individual. The pride he felt in the increase of self was worth every bit of effort.

Then he was humping along a painful surface. He was much larger now—and increased in self many times over. The Council of Unborn asked him for his choice. He chose to become a male. He was directed to a new fraternity.

Later, there was a mating with tiny silent females and enormous, highly active neuters. He was given many presents. Much later, there was a songfest in a dripping cavern that was interrupted by a battle scene with rebellious slaves on one of Saturn's moons. With a great regret he seemed to go into suspended animation for a number of years. *Wounded?* Mardin wondered. *Hospitalized?*

In conclusion, there was a guided tour of an undersea hatchery which terminated in a colorful earthquake.

Mardin slowly assimilated the information in terms of human symbology.

"Here it is, sir," he said at last hesitantly into the mouthpiece. "They don't have any actual equivalents in this area, but you might call him Ho-Par XV, originally of the Titan garrison and sometime adjutant to the commanders of Ganymede." Mardin paused a moment before going on. "He'd like it on the record that he's been invited to reproduce five times—and twice in public."

Billingsley grunted. "Nonsense! Find out why he didn't fight to the death like the other four raiders. If he still claims to be a deserter, find out why. Personally, I think these Jovians are too damn fine soldiers for that sort of thing. They may be worms, but I can't see one of them going over to the enemy."

Mardin put the question to the prisoner....

Once more he wandered on worlds where he could not have lived for a moment. He superintended a work detail of strange dustmotes, long ago conquered and placed under Jovian hegemony. He found himself feeling about them the way he had felt about the *Griggoddon* eighteen years ago; they were too wonderful to be doomed, he protested. Then he realized that the protest was not his, but that of the sorrowing entity who had lived these experiences. And they went on to other garrisons, other duties.

The reply he got this time made Mardin gasp. "He says all five of the Jovians were deserting! They had planned it for years, all of them being both fraternity-brothers and brood-brothers. He says that they—well, you might say *parachuted* down together—and not one of them had a weapon. They each tried in different ways, as they had planned beforehand, to make their surrender known. Ho-Par XV was the only successful one. He brings greetings from clusters as yet unsynthesized."

"Stick to the facts, Mardin. No romancing. Why did they desert?"

"I am sticking to the facts, sir: I'm just trying to give you the flavor as well as the substance. According to Ho-Par XV, they deserted because they were all violently opposed to militarism."

"*Wha-at?*"

"That, as near as I can render it, is exactly what he says. He says that militarism is ruining their race. It has resulted in all kinds of incorrect choices on the part of the young as to which sex they will assume in the adult state (I don't understand that part at all myself, sir)—it has thrown confusion into an art somewhere between cartography and horticulture that Ho-Par thinks is very important to the future of Jupiter—and it has weighed every Jovian down with an immense burden of guilt because of what their armies and military administration have done to alien life-forms on Ganymede, Titan and Europa, not to mention the half-sentient bubbles of the Saturnian core."

"To hell with the latrine-blasted half-sentient bubbles of the Saturnian core!" Billingsley bellowed.

"Ho-Par XV feels," the man in the suspended metal armchair went on relentlessly, staring down with delight at the flat stretch of red liquid whose beautifully sane, delicately balanced mind he was paraphrasing, "that his race needs to be stopped for its own sake as well as that of the other forms of life in the Solar System. Creatures trained in warfare are what he calls 'philosophically anti-life.' The young Jovians had just about given up hope that Jupiter *could* be stopped, when humanity came busting through the asteroids. Only trouble is that while we do think and move about three times as fast as they do, the Jovian females—who are the closest thing they have to theoretical scientists—know a lot more than we, dig into a concept more deeply than we can imagine and generally can be expected to keep licking us as they have been, until we are either extinct or enslaved. Ho-Par XV and his brood-brothers decided after the annual smelling session in the Jovian fleet this year to try to change all this. They felt that with our speedier metabolism, we might be able to take a new weapon, which the Jovians have barely got into production, and turn it out fast enough to make a slight—"

At this point there was a certain amount of noise in the headphones. After a while, Old Rockethead's voice, suavity gone, came through more or less distinctly: "—and if you don't start detailing that weapon immediately, you mangy son of a flea-bitten cur, I will have you broken twelve grades below Ordinary Spaceman and strip the skin off your pimply backside with my own boot the moment I get you back on this platform. I'll personally see to it that you spend all of your leaves cleaning the filthiest latrines the space fleet can find! Now jump to it!"

Major Mardin wiped the line of sweat off his upper lip and began detailing the weapon. *Who does he think he's talking to?* his mind asked bitterly. *I'm no kid, no apple-cheeked youngster, to be snapped at and dressed down with that line of frowzy, ugly, barracks-corporal humor! I got a standing ovation from the All-Earth Archaeological Society once, and Dr. Emmanuel Hozzne himself congratulated me on my report.*

But his mouth began detailing the weapon, his mouth went on articulating the difficult ideas which Ho-Par XV and his fellow deserters had painfully translated into faintly recognizable human terms, his mouth dutifully continued to explicate mathematical and physical concepts into the black speaking cone near his chin.

His mouth went about its business and carried out its orders—but his mind lay agonized at the insult. And then, in a corner of his mind where tenancy was joint, so to speak, a puzzled, warm, highly sensitive and extremely intelligent personality asked a puzzled, tentative question.

Mardin stopped in mid-sentence, overcome with horror at what he'd almost given away to the alien. He tried to cover up, to fill his mind with memories of contentment, to create *non-sequiturs* as psychological camouflage. What an idiot to forget that he wasn't alone in his mind!

And the question was asked again. *Are you not the representative of your people? Are—are there others…unlike you?*

Of course not! Mardin told him desperately. *Your confusion is due entirely to the fundamental differences between Jovian and Terrestrial thinking—*

"Mardin! Will you stop drooling out of those near-sighted eyes and come the hell to attention? Keep talking, chowderhead, we want the rest of that flatworm's brain picked!"

What fundamental differences? Mardin asked himself suddenly, his skull a white-hot furnace of rage. There were more fundamental differences between someone like

Billingsley and himself, than between himself and this poetic creature who had risked death and become a traitor to his own race—to preserve the dignity of the life-force. What did he have in common with this Cain come to judgment, this bemedaled swaggering boor who rejoiced in having reduced all the subtleties of conscious thought to rigidly simple, unavoidable alternatives: kill or be killed! damn or be damned! be powerful or be overpowered! The monster who had tortured his mind endlessly, dispassionately, in the prison on Mars would have found Old Rockethead much more of a friend than Ho-Par XV.

That is true, that is so! The Jovian's thought came down emphatically on his mind. *And now, friend, brood-brother, whatever you may choose to call yourself, please let me know what kind of creature I have given this weapon to. Let me know what he has done in the past with power, what he may be expected to do in hatching cycles yet to come. Let me know through your mind and your memories and your feelings—for you and I understand each other.*

Mardin let him know.

...to the nearest legal representative of the entire human race. As the result of preliminary interrogation by the military authorities a good deal was learned about the life and habits of the enemy. Unfortunately, in the course of further questioning, the Jovian evidently came to regret being taken alive and opened the valves of the gigantic tank which was his space suit, thus committing suicide instantly and incidentally smothering his human interpreter in a dense cloud of methane gas. Major Igor Mardin, the interpreter, has been posthumously awarded the Silver Lunar Circlet with doubled jets. The Jovian's suicide is now being studied by space fleet psychologists to determine whether this may not indicate an unstable mental pattern which will be useful to our deep-space armed forces in the future....

Afterword

"The Deserter" is by way of being a small monument to my father, Aaron-David Klass, who was a minor Socialist Party official in the England of 1914. When all the socialist parties of Europe dishonored their pre-1914 pledges to call an international general strike and never to vote for war credits in case of war, my father took it upon his five-foot, two-inch self to right the balance.

He published signed manifestoes declaring that his conscience would not let him do other than publicly desert if he were drafted. He urged all other workingmen to do the same.

He was drafted.

He publicly deserted.

He was found and brought back in chains for a court martial. After escaping, through the help of rank-and-file socialists who also had been drafted and who had attended his lectures, he spent the balance of the war in a windowless attic room, writing highly subversive pacifist pamphlets. He eventually fled to the United States, entering it as an illegal alien, a status that was not changed until 1945—when his son came back from Europe, having been drafted for another war.

WRITTEN 1952———PUBLISHED 1953

ॐ

Venus and the Seven Sexes

It is written in the Book of Sevens:
When Plookh meets Plookh, they discuss sex. A convention is held, a coordinator selected, and, amid cheers and rejoicing, they enter the wholesome state of matrimony. The square of seven is forty-nine.

This, my dear children—my own meager, variable brood—was the notation I extracted after receiving word from the nzred nzredd that the first humans to encounter us on Venus had at last remembered their promise to our ancestors and sent a cultural emissary to guide us on the difficult path to civilization.

Let the remaining barbarians among us cavil at the choice of this quotation; let them say it represents the Golden Age of Plookhdom; let them sneer that it shows how far we are fallen since the introduction of The Old Switcheroo by the gifted Hogan Shlestertrap of Hollywood California U.S.A. Earth.

The memory of Hogan Shlestertrap lives on while they disappear. Unfortunately—ah, well.

Please recall, when you go forth into the world to coordinate your own families, that at this point I had no idea of the kind of help the Earthman wanted. I suspected I had been honored because of my interest in literary numerals and because it was my ancestor—and yours, my dear children, your ancestor, too!—the nzred fanobrel, to whom those first Earthmen on Venus had made the wonderful promise of cultural aid.

A tkan it was, a tkan of my own family, who flew to bring me the message of the nzred nzredd. I was in hiding at the time—this was the Season of Wind-Driven Rains and the great spotted snakes had come south for their annual Plookh feed; only a swift-flying tkan could have found me in the high grasses of the marsh where we nzredd hide at this season.

The tkan gave me the message in a few moments. It was possible to do this, because we had not yet been civilized and were still using our ancestral language instead of the cultivated English.

"Last night, a flame ship landed on the tenth highest mountain," the tkan told me. "It contained the long-promised emissary from Earth: a Hogan of the Shlestertrapp."

"Hogan Shlestertrap," I corrected. "Their names are not like ours; these are civilized creatures beyond our fumbling comprehension. The equivalent of what you called him would be 'a man of the Shlestertraps.' "

"Let that be," the tkan replied. "I am no erudite nzred to hide lowly in the marshes and apply numbers categorically; I am a tkan who has flown far and been useful in the *chain* of many families. This Hogan Shlestertrap, then, emerged from his ship and had a dwelling prepared for him by his—what *did* the nzred nzredd call them?"

"Women?" I suggested, remembering my Book of Twos.

"No, not women—*robots*. Strange creatures these robots: they participate in no chain, as I understand it, and yet are reproduced. After the dwelling was completed, the nzred nzredd called upon this—this Hogan Earthman and was informed that the Hogan, who feeds and hatches in a place called Hollywood California U.S.A. Earth, had been assigned to Venus on our behalf. It seems that Hollywood California U.S.A. Earth is considered the greatest source of civilizing influence in the universe by the Terran Government. They civilize by means of something called stereo-movies."

"They send us their best," I murmured, "their very best. How correctly did my ancestor describe them when he said their unselfish greatness made dismal mockery of comparison! We are such inconsequential creatures, we Plookhh: small of size, bereft of most useful knowledge, desired prey of all the monsters of our planet who consider us transcendentally delicious morsels—and these soaring adventurers send us a cultural missionary from no less than Hollywood California U.S.A. Earth!"

"Will the Hogan Shlestertrap teach us to build flame ships and dwellings upon mountains in which we may be secure?"

"More, much more. We will learn to use the very soil of our planet for fuel; we will learn how to build ships to carry us through emptiness to the planet Earth so that we can express our gratitude; instead of merely twelve books of numbers we shall have thousands, and the numbers themselves will be made to work for us in Terran pursuits like electricity and politics. Of course, we will learn slowly in the beginning. But your message?"

The tkan flapped his wings experimentally. He was a good tkan: he had three fully developed wings and four rudimentary ones—a very high variable-potential. "That is all. The Earthman wants help from one of us whose knowledge is great and whose books are full. This one will act as what is known as 'technical adviser' to him in the process of civilizing the Plookhh. Now the nzred nzredd's small tentacle is stiff with age and badly adjusted for the speaking of English; he has therefore decided that it is you who must advise this Hogan technically."

"I leave immediately," I promised. "Any more?"

"Nothing that is important. But we will need a new nzred nzredd. As he was giving me the last of the message outside the dwelling of the Earthman, he was noticed by a herd of tricephalops and devoured. He was old and crusty; I do not think they found him very good to eat."

"A nzred is always tasty," I told the winged Plookh proudly. "He alone among the Plookhh possesses tentacles, and the spice of our tentacles, it would seem, is beyond compare. Now the nzred tinoslep will become nzred nzredd—he has grown feeble lately and done much faulty coordination."

Flapping his wings, the tkan rose rapidly. "Beware of the tricephalops," he cried.

"The herd still grazes outside the Hogan's dwelling, and you are a plump and easily swallowed tidbit. This will be a difficult time for the family to find another nzred."

A lizard-bird, attracted by his voice, plummeted down suddenly. The tkan turned sharply and attempted to gain altitude. Too late! The long neck of the lizard-bird extended, the fearful beak opened and—

The lizard-bird flew on, gurgling pleasurably to itself.

Truly it is written in the Book of Ones:

Pride goeth before a gobble.

He was a good tkan, as I said, and had a high variable-potential. Fortunately, a cycle had just completed—he was carrying no eggs. And tkann were plentiful that season.

This conversation lasted a much shorter period than it seems to have in my repetition. At the time, only a few nzredd had learned the English that the first human explorers had taught my ancestor, nzred fanobrel; and the rest of the Plookhh used the picturesque language of our uncivilized ancestors. This language had certain small advantages, it is true. For one thing, fewer of us were eaten while conversing with each other, since the ancient Plookh dialect transmitted the maximum information in the minimum time. Then again, I was not reduced to describing Plookhh in terms of "he," "she" or "it"; this English, while admittedly the magnificent speech of civilized beings, is woefully deficient in pronouns.

I uncoiled my tentacles from the grasses about me and prepared to roll. The mlenb, over whose burrow I was resting, felt the decreased pressure as my body ceased to push upon the mud above him. He churned to the surface, his flippers soggy and quivering.

"Can it be," the foolish fellow whispered, "that the Season of Wind-Driven Rains is over and the great spotted snakes have departed? The nzred is about to leave the marsh."

"Go back," I told him. "I have an errand to perform. The spotted snakes are ravenous as ever, and now there are lizard-birds come into the marsh."

"Oh!" He turned and began to dig himself back into the mud. I know it is ungracious to mock mlenbb, but the wet little creatures are so frantic and slow-moving at the same time that it is all I can do to keep a straight tentacle in their presence.

"Any news?" he asked, all but one third of him into the mud.

"Our tkan was just eaten, so keep your flippers alert for an unattached tkan of good variation. It is not pressing; a new cycle will not begin for our family until the end of this season. Oh—and the nzred nzredd has been eaten, too—but that does not concern you, little muddy mlenb."

"That does not, but have you heard the mlenb mlenbb also is gone? He was caught on the surface last night by a spotted snake. Never was there such a Season of Wind-Driven Rains: the great of the Plookhh fall on all sides."

"To a mlenb all seasons are 'never was there such a season,' " I mocked. "Wait until the Season of Early Floods, and then tell me which you like better. Many mlenbb will go with the coming of the early floods, and our family may have to find a new mlenb as well."

He shivered, spattering me with mud, and disappeared completely underground.

Ah, but those were the carefree times, the happy childhood days of our race! Little indeed there was to trouble us then.

I ate a few grasses and began rolling up and out of the marsh. In a little while, my churning tentacles had attained such speed that I had no reason to fear any but the largest of the great spotted snakes.

Once, a tremendous reptile leaped at me and it seemed that the shafalon family would require a new nzred as well as a new tkan, but I have a helical nineteenth tentacle and this stood me in good stead. I uncoiled it vigorously and with an enormous bound soared over the slavering mouth of the spotted snake and on to solid ground.

This helical tentacle—I regret deeply that none of you dear little nzredd have inherited it from me. My consolation is that it will reappear in your descendants though in modified form; it unfortunately does not seem to be a dominant trait. But you all—all of this cycle, at any rate—have the extremely active small tentacle which I acquired from the nzred fanobrel.

Yes, I said your descendants. Please do not interrupt with the callow thoughts of the recently hatched. I tell you a tale of the great early days and how we came to this present state. The solution is for you to discover—there must be a solution; I am old and ripe for the gullet.

Once on solid ground, I had to move much faster, of course: here the great spotted snakes were larger and more plentiful. They were also hungrier.

Time and again I was forced to use the power latent in my helical tentacle. Several times as I leaped into the air, a lizard-bird or a swarm of gridniks swooped down at me; now and again, as I streaked for the ground, I was barely able to avoid the lolling tongue of a giant toad.

Shortly, however, I reached the top of the tenth highest mountain, having experienced no real adventure. There, for the first time, I beheld a human habitation.

It was a dome, transparent, yet colored with the bodies of many creatures who crawled on its surface in an attempt to reach the living meat within.

Do you know what a dome is? Think of half the body of a newly hatched nzred, divorced of its tentacles, expanded to a thousand times its size. Think of this as transparent instead of darkly colorful, and imagine the cut-away portion resting on its base while the still rounded part becomes the top. Of course, this dome had none of the knobs and hollows we use for various organic purposes. It was really quite bald.

Near it the flame ship stood upright. I cannot possibly describe the flame ship to you, except to say that it looked partly like a mlenb without the flippers and partly like a vineless guur.

The tricephalops discovered me and trampled each other in an attempt to get to me first. I was rather busy for a while evading the three-headed monsters, even growing slightly impatient with our savior, Hogan Shlestertrap, for keeping me outside his dwelling so long. I have always felt that, of all the innumerable ways for a Plookh to depart from life, the most unpleasant is to be torn into three unequal pieces and masticated slowly by a tricephalops. But, then, I have always been considered something of a wistful aesthete: most Plookhh dislike the gridnik more.

Fortunately, before I could be caught, the herd came upon a small patch of guurr who had taken root in the neighborhood and fell to grazing upon them. I made certain that none of the guurr were of our family and concentrated once more upon attracting the attention of Shlestertrap.

At long last, a section of the dome opened outward, a force seemed to pluck at my tentacles and I was carried swiftly through the air and into the dome. The section closed behind me, leaving me in a small compartment near the outside, my visible presence naturally exciting the beasts around me to scrabble frenziedly upon the transparent stuff of the dwelling.

A robot entered—answering perfectly to the description of such things by nzred fanobrel—and, with the aid of a small tubular weapon, quickly destroyed the myriad creatures and fragments of creatures who had been sucked in with my humble person.

Then—my variegated descendants—then, I was conducted into the presence of Hogan Shlestertrap himself!

How shall I describe this illustrious scion of a far-flung race? From what I could see of him, he had two pairs of major tentacles (call them flippers, vines, wings, fins, claws, talons or what you will), classified respectively as arms and legs. There was a fifth visible tentacle referred to as the head—at the top of the edifice, profusely knobbed and hollowed for sensory purposes. The entire animal, except for extremities of the tentacles, was covered with a blue and yellow striped substance which, I have since learned, is not secreted by it at all but supplied it by other humans in a complicated chain I do not fully understand. Each of the four major tentacles was further divided into five small tentacles somewhat in the manner of a blap's talons; fingers, they are known as. The body proper of this Hogan Shlestertrap was flat in the rear and exhibited a pleasing dome-like protuberance in the front, much like a nzred about to lay eggs.

Conceive, if you can, that this human differed in no respect from those described by my ancestor nzred fanobrel over six generations ago! One of the great boons of civilization is that continual variation is not necessary in offspring; these creatures may preserve the same general appearance for as many as ten or even twelve generations!

Of course, with every boon there is a price to be paid. That is what the dissidents among us fail to understand....

Hogan Shlestertrap was occupying a chair when I entered. A chair is like—well, possibly I shall discuss that another time. In his hand (that part of the arm where the fingers originate) he held a bottle (shaped like a srob without fins) of whiskey. Every once in a while, he and the bottle of whiskey performed what nzred fanobrel called an act of conjugation. I, who have seen the act, assure you that there is no other way to describe the process. Only I fail to see just what benefit the bottle of whiskey derives from the act.

"Will you have a chair?" Shlestertrap requested, dismissing the robot with a finger undulation.

I rolled up into the chair, only too happy to observe human protocol, but found some difficulty in retaining my position as there were no graspable extremities anywhere in the object. I finally settled into a somewhat strained posture by keeping all my tentacles stiff against the sides and bottom.

"You look like some spiders I've seen after an all-night binge," Shlestertrap remarked graciously.

Since much of human thought is beyond our puny minds, I have been careful to record all remarks made by the Great Civilizer, whether or no I found them comprehensible at the time. Thus—"spider"? "all-night binge"?

"You are Hogan Shlestertrap of Hollywood California U.S.A. Earth, come to bring us out of the dark maw of ignorance, into the bright hatchery of knowledge. I am nzred shafalon, descended from nzred fanobrel who met your ancestors when they first landed on this planet, appointed by the late nzred nzredd to be your technical adviser."

He sat perfectly still, the little opening in his head—mouth, they call it—showing every moment a wider and wider orifice.

Feeling flattered and encouraged by his evident interest, I continued into my most valuable piece of information. How valuable it was, I did not then suspect:

"It is written in the Book of Sevens:

When Plookh meets Plookh, they discuss sex. A convention is held, a coordinator selected, and amid cheers and rejoicing, they enter the wholesome state of matrimony. The square of seven is forty-nine."

Silence. Hogan Shlestertrap conjugated rapidly with his bottle.

"Pensioned off," he muttered after a while. "The great Hogan Shlestertrap, the producer and director of 'Lunar Love Song,' 'Fissions of 2109,' 'We Took to the Asteroids,' pensioned off in a nutty fruitcake of a world! Doomed to spend his remaining years among gabby mathematical spiders and hungry whatchamacallits."

He rose and began pacing, an act accomplished with the lower tentacles. "I gave them saga after saga, the greatest stereos that Hollywood ever saw or felt, and just because my remake of 'Quest to Mars' came out merely as an epic, they say I'm through. Did they have the decency—those people I picked out of the gutter and made into household names—did they have the decency to get me a job with the distribution end on a place like Titan or Ganymede? No! If they had to send me to Venus, did they even try to salve their consciences by sending me to the Polar Continent where a guy can find a bar or two and have a little human conversation? Oho, they wouldn't dare—I might make a comeback if I had half a chance. That Sonny Galenhooper—my *friend*, he called himself!—gets me a crummy job with the Interplanetary Cultural Mission and I find myself plopped down in the steaming Macro Continent with a mess of equipment to make stereos for an animal that half the biologists of the system claim is impossible. *Big deal!* But Shlestertrap Productions will be back yet, bigger and better than ever!"

These were his memorable words: I report them faithfully. Possibly in times to come, when civilization among us shall have advanced to a higher level—always assuming that the present problem will be solved—these words will be fully understood and appreciated by a generation of as yet unborn but much more intellectualized Plookhh. To them, therefore, I dedicate this speech of the Great Civilizer.

"Now," he said, turning to me. "You know what stereos are?"

"No, not quite. You see only one of us has ever conversed with humans before this, and we know little of their glorious ways. Our Book of Twos is almost bare of useful information, being devoted chiefly to a description of your first six explorers, their ship and robots, by the nzred fanobrel. I *deduce,* however, that stereos are an essential concomitant of an industrial civilization."

He waved the bottle. "Exactly. At the base of everything. Take your literature, your music, your painting—"

"Pardon me," I interposed. "But we have been able to build none of these things as yet. We are chased by so many—"

"I was just spitballing," he roared. "Don't interrupt my train of thought. I'm building! Now, where was I? Oh, yes—take your literature, music and painting and you know what you can do with them. The stereos comprise everything in art; they present to the masses, in one colossal little package, the whole stirring history of human endeavor. They are not a substitute for art in the twenty-second century—they *are* the art of the twenty-second century. And without art, where are you?"

"Where?" I asked, for I will admit the question intrigued me.

"Nowhere. Nowhere at all. Oh, you might be able to get by in the sticks, but class will tell eventually. You've got to romp home with an Oscar now and then to show the reviewers that you're interested in fine things as well as money-making potboilers."

I concentrated on memorizing, deciding to reserve interpretation for later. Perhaps this was my mistake, perhaps I should have asked more questions. But it was all so bewildering, so stimulating....

"The stereos have gone a long way since the pioneering sound movies of medieval times," he continued. "Solid images that appeal to all five senses in gorgeous panoramas of perception."

Hogan Shlestertrap paused and went on with even more passion. "And wasn't it said that Shlestertrap Productions had their special niche, their special technique among the senses? Yes, sir! No greater accolade could be accorded a stereo than to say it had the authentic Shlestertrap Odor. The Shlestertrap smell—how I used to slave to get that in just right! And I almost always succeeded. Oh, well, they say you're just as good as your last stereo."

I took advantage of the brooding silence that followed to clack my small tentacle hesitantly.

The emissary looked up. "Sorry, fella. What we've got to do here is turn out a stereo based on your life, your hopes and spiritual aspirations. Something that will make 'em sit up and take notice way out in Peoria. Something that will give you guys a *culture.*"

"We need one badly. Particularly a culture to defend us against—"

"All right. Let me carry the ball. Understand I'm only talking off the top of my mind right now; I never make a decision until I've slept on it and let the good old subconscious take a couple of whacks at the idea. Now that you understand the technical side of stereo-making, we can start working on a story. Now, religion and politics are dandy weenies, but for a good successful piece of art I always say give me the old-fashioned love story. What's the lowdown on your love-life?"

"That question is a trifle difficult to answer," I replied slowly. "We had the gravest communicative difficulties with the first explorers of your race over this question. They seemed to find it complicated."

"A-ah," he waved a contemptuous hand. "Those scientific bunnies are always looking for trouble. Takes a businessman, who's also an artist, mind you—first and last an artist—to get to the roots of a problem. Let me put it this way, what do you call your two sexes?"

"That is the difficulty. We don't have two sexes."

"Oh. One of those a-something animals. Not too much conflict possible in that situation, I guess. No-o-o. Not in one sex."

I was unhappy: he had evidently misunderstood me. "I meant we have more than two sexes."

"More than two sexes? Like the bees, you mean? Workers, drones and queens? But that's really only two. The workers are—"

"We Plookhh have seven sexes."

"Seven sexes. Well, that makes it a little more complicated. We'll have to work our story from a—SEVEN SEXES?" he shrieked.

He dropped back into the chair where he sat very loosely, regarding me with optical organs that seemed to quiver like tentacles.

"They are, to use the order stated in the Book of Sevens, srob, mlenb, tkan, guur—"

"Hold it, hold it," he commanded. He conjugated with his bottle and called to a robot to bring him another. He sighed finally and said: "Why in the name of all the options that were ever dropped do you need *seven* sexes?"

"Well, at one time, we thought that all creatures required seven sexes as a minimum. After your explorers arrived, however, we investigated and found that this was not true even of the animals here on our planet. My ancestor, nzred fanobrel, had many profitable talks with the biologists of the expedition who provided him with theoretical knowledge to explain that which we had only known in practice. For example, the biologists decided that we had evolved into a seven-sexed form in order to stimulate variation."

"Variation? You mean so your children would be different?"

"Exactly. You see, there is only one thing that all the ravening life-forms of Venus would rather eat than each other; and that one thing is a Plookh. From the other continent, from all the islands and seas of Venus they come at different times for their Plookh feed. When a Plookh is discovered, a normally herbivorous animal will battle a mighty carnivore to the death and disregard the carcass of its defeated opponent— to enjoy the Plookh."

Our civilizer considered me with a good deal of interest. "Why—what have you got that no one else has got?"

"We don't know—exactly. It may be that our bodies possess a flavor that is uniformly exciting to all Venusian palates; it may be, as one of the biologists suggested to nzred fanobrel, that our tissue contains an element—a vitamin—essential to the diet of all the life-forms of our planet. But we are small and helpless creatures who must reproduce in quantity if we are to survive. And a large part of that quantity must differ from the parent who himself has survived into the reproductive stage. Thus, with seven parents who have lived long enough to reproduce, the offspring inherits the maximum qualities of survival as well as enough variation from any given parent to insure a constantly and *rapidly* improving race of Plookh."

An affirmative grunt. "That would be it. In the one-sex stage—*asexual* is what the bio professors call it—it's almost impossible to have varied offspring. In the bisexual stage, you get a good deal of variation. And with *seven* sexes, the sky must be the limit. But don't you ever get a Plookh who isn't good to eat, or who can maybe fight his way out of a jam?"

"No. It would seem that whatever makes us delicious is essential to our own physical structure. And, according to the biologists of the expedition again, our evolutionary accent has always been on evasiveness—whether by nimbleness, protective coloration or ability to hide—so that we have never developed a belligerent Plookh. We have never been able to: it is not as if we had only one or two enemies. All who are not Plookh will eat Plookhh. Except humans—and may I take this occasion to express our deep gratitude?

"From time to time, our Books of Numbers tell us, Plookh have formed communities and attempted to resist extermination by united effort. In vain; they merely disappeared in groups instead of individually. We never had the *time* to perfect a workable system of defense, to devise such splendid things as weapons—which we understand humans have. That is why we rejoiced so at your coming. At last—"

"Save the pats on the back. I'm here to do a job, to make a stereo that will be at least an epic, even if I don't have the raw material of a saga. Give me a line on how all this works."

"May I say that whether it is an epic or a saga, we will still be grateful and sing the greatness of your name forever? Just so we are set on the path of civilization; just so we learn to construct impregnable dwellings and—"

"Sure. Sure. Wait till I get me a fresh bottle. Now—what are your seven sexes and how do you go about making families?"

I reflected carefully. I knew full well what a responsibility was mine at that moment; how important it was that I give our benefactor completely accurate information to aid him in the making of stereos, the first step we must take toward civilization.

"Please understand that much of this is beyond our ken. We know what seems to happen, but for an explanation we use the theories of the first flame ship's biologists. Unfortunately, their theories were multiple and couched in human terms which even they admitted were somewhat elementary when applied to the process of Plookh reproduction. We sacrificed a whole generation of the fanobrel family for microscopic experimentation and only a broad outline was worked out. Our seven sexes are—"

"I heard it was complicated," Shlestertrap interrupted. "The biologists left five miles of figures in the Venusian Section of the Interplanetary Cultural Mission after they returned from this expedition. You see, there was an election right after that: a new party came in and fired them. I wasn't going to wade through all that scientific junk, no sir! One of them—Gogarty, I think—pulled every wire there was to take this job away from me and come here in my place. Some people just can't stand being out after they've been politically in for so long. Me, I'm here to make stereos—good ones. I'm here to do just what the prospectus of the Venusian Section called for—'bring culture to the Plookhh as per request.' "

"Thank you. We did wonder why the Gogarty—pardon—why Gogarty didn't return; he expressed such an enormous interest in our ways and welfare. But no doubt the operation of firing him by the new party after the election was far more productive in the human scheme of things. We have not yet advanced to the state of parties and elections or any such tools. To us one human is as omniscient and magnificent as the other. Of course, you understand all relevant data on human genetics?"

"Sure. You mean chromosomes and stuff?"

I flapped my small tentacle eagerly. "Yes, chromosomes and stuff. Especially stuff. I think it is the part about 'stuff' that has made the whole subject somewhat difficult for us. Gogarty never mentioned it. All he discussed were chromosomes and genes."

"No wonder I got such a crash bio briefing! Let's see. Chromosomes are collections of genes which in turn control characteristics. When an animal is ready to reproduce, its germ-cells—or reproductive cells—each divide into two daughter cells called gametes, each daughter cell possessing one-half the chromosomes of the parent cell, every chromosome in each gamete corresponding to an opposite number chromosome in the other. Process is called meiosis. Correct me if I'm wrong anywhere."

"And how can a human be wrong?" I asked devoutly.

His face wrinkled. "In the case of humans, the female germ-cell has twenty-four pairs of chromosomes, one pair being known as the X chromosome and determining sex. It splits into two female gametes of twenty-four corresponding chromosomes, one X chromosome in each gamete. Since the male germ-cell—if I remember rightly—has only twenty-three identical pairs of chromosomes and an additional *unmatched* pair called the X-Y chromosome, it divides into two male gametes of twenty-four chromosomes each, of which only twenty-three have a twin in each gamete; the twenty-fourth being the X chromosome in one male gamete and the Y chromosome in the other. If a male gamete—or sperm-cell—containing an X chromosome unites with a female gamete—ovum, or egg-cell, the briefing guy called it—carrying an X chromosome, the resultant zygote will be female; but if the Y chromosome gamete fertilizes the ovum, you have a *male* zygote. They really jammed that stuff in me before they let me leave Earth. Lectures, sleep-sessions, the whole bit."

"Exactly," I said enthusiastically. "Now in our case—"

"I recall something else, come to think of it. The Y is supposed to be a slightly undeveloped or retarded chromosome and it makes the gamete containing it a little weaker or something. The sperm-cell with the X chromosome is faster and stronger and has a better chance of fertilizing the ovum. It also shows why women can take it better than men and live longer. Simple. How's it work with you?"

The extended conversation was making me giddy, and the atmosphere of the dome—with its small vapor content—dried my faculties. However, this was a historic occasion: no personal weakness must be allowed to interfere. I stiffened my tentacles and began.

"After the matrimonial convention, when the chain is established, each sex's germ-cells are stimulated into meiosis. The germ-cell divides into seven gametes, six of them with cilia and the seventh secreted either inside or outside the Plookh, depending on the sex."

"What's this chain?"

"The chain of reproduction. The usually stated order is srob (aquatic form), mlenb (amphibian), tkan (winged), guur (plant-like), flin (a burrower), blap (tree-dweller). And, of course, the chain proceeds in a circle as: srob, mlenb, tkan, guur, flin, blap, srob, mlenb, tkan, guur, flin, blap, srob—"

Hogan Shlestertrap had grasped his head with his hands and was rocking it slowly back and forth. "Starts with srobs and ends with blaps," he said, almost inaudibly. "And I'm a—"

"Srobb," I corrected him timidly. "And blapp. And it doesn't necessarily start with one and end with another. A birth may be initiated anywhere along the chain of a family, just so it passes through all sexes—thus acquiring the necessary chromosomes for a fertilized zygote."

"All right! Please get back to chromosomes and sanity. You just had a germ-cell dividing—a srob's, say—into seven gametes instead of a decent two like all other logical species use."

"Well, so far as our weak minds can compass it, this is the chromosome pattern worked out by Gogarty and his assistant, Wolfsten, after prolonged microscopic examination. Gogarty warned my ancestor, nzred fanobrel, that it was only an approximation. According to this analysis, the germ-cell of a given sex has forty-nine chromosomes, seven each of Types A, B, C, D, E, F, six of Type G and one of Type H—the last, Type H, being the sex determinant. Six mobile gametes are formed through meiosis—each containing an identical group of seven chromosomes of Types A through G—and a seventh or stationary gamete containing chromosomes A, B, C, D, E, F, and H. This last Gogarty called the female or H gamete, since it never leaves the body of the Plookh until the fully fertilized cell of forty-nine chromosomes—or seven gametes—is formed, and since it determines sex. The sex, of course, is that of the Plookh in whose body it is stationary."

"Of course," Shlestertrap murmured and conjugated long and thoughtfully with the bottle.

"It has to be, since that is the only H chromosome in the final zygote. But you know that for yourself. In fact, operating with a human intelligence, you have probably anticipated me and already extrapolated the whole process from the few facts I have mentioned."

Moisture gathered at the top of our civilizer's head and rolled down his face in the quaintest of patterns. "I understand you," he admitted, "and of course I've already figured out the whole thing. But just to make it clear in your own mind, don't you think you might as well continue?"

I thanked him for his unfailing human courtesy. "Now, if it is a srob with whom we start our chain, it will transmit one of its six mobile gametes to a mlenb where the gamete will unite with one of the mlenb's A through G cells, forming what Gogarty called a double-gamete or pre-zygote. This pre-zygote will contain seven pairs of A through G chromosomes, and, in the body of the tkan—next in the chain—it will unite with a tkan mobile gamete forming a triple-gamete with seven triplets of A through G chromosomes. It proceeds successively through the rest of the sexes capturing a seven-chromosome gamete each time, until, when it is transmitted to the blap, it contains forty-two chromosomes—six A's, six B's and so on through to six G's. At this point, the sextuple gamete loses its cilia; and unites, in the blap, with the stationary H gamete to form a forty-nine chromosome zygote which, of course, is of the blap sex. The egg is laid and it hatches shortly into a baby blap, guarded—when at all possible—and taught in ten days all that its parent can teach it about surviving as a blap Plookh. At the end of ten days, the half-grown blap goes its way to feed and escape from danger by itself. At the end of a hundred days, it is ready to join a family and reproduce in full adulthood.

"The chain may be said to begin at any point; but it always travels in the same direction. Thus a flin will transmit the original seven-chromosome gamete to the blap of his chain where it will become a double-gamete; the blap will transmit the double-gamete to the srob, who will make it a triple-gamete; eventually, in this case, the process will come to fruition on the vines of the guur resulting in a guur zygote. Was not Gogarty clever, even for a human? He suggested, by the way, that it was possible we were not really a seven-sexed creature, but seven distinct species living in a reproductive symbiosis."

"Gogarty was a damned genius! Hey, wait a minute! Srob, mlenb, tkan, guur, flin, blap—that's only six!"

At last we were getting to the interesting part. "Quite so. I am a representative of the seventh sex—a nzred."

"A nzred, huh? What do *you* do?"

"I coordinate."

One of the robots scurried in in answer to his yell. He ordered it to bring a case of these bottles of whiskey and to place it near his chair. He also ordered it to stand by, prepared for emergencies.

This was all very enjoyable. My information was creating even more of a sensation than that described by my ancestor, nzred fanobrel. It is not often that we Plookhh have an opportunity to sit thus with an animal of a different species and provide intellectual instead of gustatory diversion.

"He *coordinates!* Maybe they can use a good expediter or dispatcher?"

"I fulfill all of those functions. Chiefly, however, I coordinate. You see, a mlenb is primarily interested in winning the affections of a likely srob and finding a tkan whom *he* can love. A tkan merely courts a mlenb and is attracted to a good guur. I am responsible for getting a complete chain of these individuals in operation, a chain of compatibility where perfect amity runs in a complete circle—a chain which will produce offspring of maximum variability. Then, after the matrimonial convention, when the chain is established, each sex begins to secrete its original germ with the full forty-nine chromosomes. A busy time for nzredd! I must make certain that all germ-cells are developing at a uniform rate—each sex attempts to fertilize seven H gametes in the course of a cycle—and the destruction of one individual in the middle of the cycle means the complete disarrangement of a family except for the gametes which he has already passed on in multiple state. Replacement of an eaten individual with another of the same sex, the remainder of whose family has been wiped out, is occasionally possible with the aid of the chief of his sex."

"I can see they keep you hopping," Hogan Shlestertrap observed. "But how does a nzred get born if you aren't in this chain thing?"

"A nzred is outside a chain, yet inside it as well. The six sexes which transmit gametes to each other directly form a chain; a chain plus a nzred equals a family. The nzred, in his personal reproductive functions, fits himself at any point in the chain which the exigencies of the situation seem to demand. He may receive the sextuple super-gamete from the tkan and transmit the original single gamete to the guur, he may be between the flin and blap, the blap and srob, whatever is required. For example, in the Season of Twelve Hurricanes, the tkan is unable to fly and pursue his reproductive relationship with the guur wherever it has rooted itself: the nzred fills what would be a gap in the chain. This is rather difficult to express in an unfamiliar language—the biologists of the first expedition found this process slightly more complicated than the mitoses of the fertilized Plookh cell, but—"

"Hold it," Hogan commanded. "I have an ounce of sanity left, and I might want to use it to blow my brains out. I am no longer slightly interested in how a nzred weaves in and out of this crazy reproductive dance, and I *certainly* don't want to hear about your mitosis. I have troubles of my own, and they grow nastier every second. Tell me this: how many offspring does a sex have each cycle?"

"That depends on all parents being alive throughout, on the amount of unhatched eggs due to over-variation in particular cases—"

"*OK!* At the end of a perfect cycle—when the smoke clears—how many baby plookhs do you have all told?"

"Plookh*h*. We have forty-nine young."

He rested his head on the back of the chair. "Not very many, considering how fast you seem to go out of this world."

"True. Dismally true. But a parent is unable to hatch more than seven eggs in the conditions under which we live, and completely unable to rear more than seven young so that all will get the full benefit of his survival-knowledge. This is for the best."

"I guess so." He removed a pointed instrument from his garment and a sheet of white material. After a while, I recognized his actions from nzred fanobrel's description. "In just a moment," he said, while writing, "I'm going to have you shown into the projection room where you'll see a recent stereo employing human performers.

Not too good a stereo: colossal in a very minor way; but it'll give you an idea of what I'll be doing for your people in the line of culture. While you see it, figure out ways to help me on a story. Now, is this Gogarty's description of your chromosome pattern after the parent germ-cell has undergone meiosis?"

He extended the sheet under my sensory tentacles:

	A	A	A	A	A	A	A	
mobile	B	B	B	B	B	B	B	stationary, sex-determining
gametes	C	C	C	C	C	C	C	gamete which is "fertilized"
(ciliated)	D	D	D	D	D	D	D	by a super-gamete composed
	E	E	E	E	E	E	E	of six mobile gametes—one
	F	F	F	F	F	F	F	from each of the six other
	G	G	G	G	G	G	G	sexes

"Quite correct," I said, marveling at the superiority of these written symbols to those we are still forced to scratch in sand or mud.

"Good enough." He wrote further upon the sheet. "Now, which of your sexes is male and which female? I notice you say 'he' and—"

I was forced to interrupt him. "I only use those designations because of the deficiencies or limitations of English. I understand what a wonderful speech it is and how, when you came to construct it, you saw no reason to consider the Plookhh. Nonetheless, you have no pronouns for tkan or guur or blap. We are all male in relation to each other, in the sense that we transmit the fertilizing gametes; we are also female, in the sense that we hatch the developed zygote. Then again—"

"Slow down, boy, slow down. I have to work a story out of this, and you're not doing me any good at all. Here's a picture of your family—right?" He held the sheet out once more.

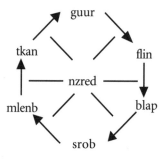

"Yes. Only your picture of the nzred is not exactly—"

"Listen, Pierre," he growled, "I'll call it the way I see it. And that's the way I see it. A love-story, now, let me think…"

I waited while he cerebrated upon this strange thing called a story which was essential to the making of a stereo, which, in turn, was essential to our beginning upon culture and civilization. Soon, soon, we would have dwellings like this powerful one in which I sat, we would have tubular weapons like that the robot had used when I entered—

"How would this be?" he asked suddenly. "Understand, this isn't the finished product—I'm just working off the cuff, just trying it on for size. *Srob meets mlenb, tkan loses guur, flin gets blap.* How's it sound? Only one I can't fit in is the nzred."

"I coordinate."

"Yeah, you coordinate. That would make it, srob meets— Ah, shaddap! All you're supposed to do is say 'yes' once in a while." He murmured a few words to the robot who moved over to my chair. "Bronzo will take you to the projection room now. I'll think some more."

Tumbling painfully to the floor, I prepared to follow the robot.

"A love story is going to be tough," Shlestertrap mused behind me. "I can see that right now. Like three-dimensional chess with all pawns wild and the queen operating in and out of hyperspace. Wonder if these potato sprouts have a religion. A nice, pious little stereo every once in a while— Hey! Got a religion?"

"Yes," I said.

"What is it? I mean what do you believe in, generally speaking? Simple terms: we can save the philosophy for later."

After the lapse of an interval which I felt I could approximate as a "while," I said again, very cautiously: "Yes."

"Huh? Cut the comedy on this lot, if you know what's good for you. Just because I told you not to disagree with me when I'm thinking out loud— No sloppy gags when I ask you a direct question!"

I apologized and tried to explain my seeming impudence in terms of the simple conditions under which we Plookhh live. After all, when a tkan flies in frantically to warn a family that a pack of strinth are ravening in its direction, no one thinks to take the message in other than its most literal form. Communication, for us, is basically a means of passing along information essential to survival: it must be explicit and definitive.

Human speech, however, being the product of a civilized race, is a tree bearing many different fruits. And, as we have discovered to our sorrow, it is not always easy to find the one intended to be edible. For example, this mind-corroding intangible that they call a pun—

Shlestertrap waved my explanations back at me. "So you're sorry and I forgive you. Meanwhile, what's your belief about a life after death?"

"We don't exactly have a belief," I explained slowly, "since no Plookh has returned after death to assure us of the possibilities ahead. However, because of the difficulties we experience in the one life we know and its somewhat irritating shortness of duration—we like to think we have at least *one* additional existence. Thus, we have not so much a Belief as a Hope."

"For an animal without lungs, you sure are long-winded. What's your Hope, then?"

"That after death we emerge into a vast land of small seas, marshes and mountains. That throughout this land are the pink weeds we find so succulent. That, in every direction as far as an optical organ can see, there are nothing but Plookhh."

"And?"

"Nothing else. That is our Hope: to arrive sometime, in this life or the next, in a land where there are nothing but Plookhh. Plookhh, you understand, are the only creatures who we are *certain* do not eat Plookhh. We feel we could be very happy alone."

"Not enough there to make a one-shot quickie. If only you believed in a god who demanded living Plookhh sacrifices—but I guess your lives are complicated enough. Go and see the stereo. I'll work out something."

In the projection room, I twisted up into a chair the robot pushed forward and watched him and his mates insert shiny colored strips into five long, mlenb-shaped objects attached to the walls and ceiling. Naturally, I have learned since that the human terms are "film" and "projector," respectively, but, at that time, everything was new and strange and wonderful; I was all optical tentacles and audal knobs.

The sheer quantity of *things* that humans possess! Their recording methods are so plentiful and varied—books, stereos, pencil-paper, to name but a few—that I am convinced their memories are largely outgrown evolutionary characteristics which, already atrophying, will be supplanted shortly by some method of keying recording apparatus directly to the thinking process. They have no need of carrying Books of Numbers in their minds, of memorizing individually some nine thousand years of racial history, of continually revising the conclusions drawn from an ancient incident to conform with the exigencies of a current one. Contemplation of their magnificent potentialities almost dissolves my ego.

Abruptly, the room darkened and a tiny spot of white expanded into the full-color, full-sound, full-olfactory and slightly tactile projection we have come to know so well. For some reason, the humans who make these stereos neglect almost completely the senses of taste, brotch, pressure and griggo—although the olfactory appeal stimulates an approximation of taste and an alert individual may brotch satisfactorily during an emotional sequence. The full-color—yes: it should be obvious that humans use only three primaries instead of the existing nine because they consider it a civilized simplicity; the very drabness of the combinations of blue, red and yellow, I believe, is a self-imposed limitation instituted as a challenge to their technicians.

As the human figures came to seeming life before me, I began to understand what Hogan Shlestertrap had meant by a "story." A story is the history of one or more individuals in a specific cultural matrix. I wondered then just how Shlestertrap would derive a story from the meager life of a Plookh; he had known so few of us. I did not know of the wonderful human sense of imagination.

This story, that I saw on that awesome first day of our civilization, was about their two sexes. One representative of each sex (a man, Louis Trescott—and a girl, Bettina Bramwell) figured as the protagonists of the film.

The story concerned the efforts of Bettina Bramwell and Louis Trescott to get together and lay an egg. Many and complex were the difficulties this pair faced, but, at last, having overcome every obstacle, they were united and ready to reproduce.

Through some oversight, the story ended before the actual egg-laying; there was definite assurance, however, that the process would be under way shortly.

Thus, the first stereo I had ever seen. The colors sharpened in company with the sound of this obscure business called music, then all faded and disappeared. The lights returned to the room and the robots attended to the projectors. I went back to Shlestertrap, quivering with new knowledge.

"Sure," he said. "It's good. It's good enough, considering the budget. Now, look, I have an idea for a stereo. It's got to jell and whatnot, but meanwhile it's an idea. What's the animal you bugs are most afraid of?"

"Well, in the Season of Twelve Hurricanes, the strinth and sucking ivy do a large amount of damage to our race. In the other hurricane seasons—which are the worst for us, after all—the tricephalops, brinosaurs or gridniks—"

"Don't tell me *all* your troubles. Put it this way: which animal are you afraid of most right now?"

I considered lengthily. Ordinarily, the question would have given me thought material for two days; but The Great Civilizer was shifting from foot to foot and I griggoed his impatience. A decision was necessary; this may have been my mistake, my offspring, but remember we might never have received *any* of the benefits of civilization if I had taken more time to determine which creature was eating most of us at that season.

"The great spotted snakes. Of course, it is feared only by the nzredd, mlenbb, flinn and blapp. At this time, guurr are eaten principally by tricephalops, while srobb—"

"All right. Spotted snakes. Now let's go to the observation corridor and you point one out to me."

In the room where I had entered the dome, I extended my optical tentacles toward the transparent roof.

"There, almost directly above me. The animal which has half swallowed a dodle and is being attacked by gridniks and sucking ivy."

Shlestertrap faced upwards and shivered. At the sight of us, the creatures scrabbled even more frantically on the dome's structure, continuing to eat whatever they had been eating when we entered. The sucking ivy dragged the great spotted snake away.

"What a place," Shlestertrap muttered. "A guy could make a fortune here with an anti-vacation resort. 'Come to this home away from home and learn to giggle at your nightmares. All kinds of dishes served, including you. Be a guest of the best digestions. Everybody to his taste and a taste to fit everybody.' "

I waited, while his human mind explored concepts beyond my primeval grasp.

"OK. So that was a great spotted snake. I'll send a crew of robots out to get some shots of one of those babies that we can process into the stereo. Meanwhile, what about the cast?"

"Cast?" I fumbled. "How—what kind of cast do you mean?"

"Actors. Characters. Course I understand that none of you have any experience, even in stock, but I'll treat this like a De Mille documentary. I'll need a representative of each one of your sexes—the best in its line. You should be able to dredge them up with beauty contests or whatever you use. Just so I get seven of you—all different."

"These can be obtained through the chiefs of the various sexes. The nzred tinoslep will be the new nzred nzredd and a replacement for the mlenb mlenbb should have been chosen if enough mlenbb dared to congregate in the marshes. And this is all we need to do to take the first movement toward civilization?"

"Absolutely all. I'll write the first story for you—it's only mildly magnificent right now, but I'll have plenty of time to work it up into something better."

"Then I may leave."

He called for a robot who entered and motioned me in front of a machine much like a stereo projector.

"Sorry I can't send a robot to protect you down the mountain, but we're only half unpacked and I'll need all of them around for a day or two. All I have here are Government Standard Models, see; and you can't get any high-speed work out of those babies. To think that I used to have eighteen Frictionless Frenzies just to clean up around the house! Oh well, a sick trance isn't glorious Mondays."

Admitting the justice of this obscure allusion, I tried to reassure him. "If I am eaten, there are at least three nzredd who can replace me. It is only necessary for me to get far enough down the mountain to meet a living Plookh and inform him of your—your character requirements."

"Good," he told me heartily. "And I'm pretty sure I can play ball with any of your people who speak English fairly well. That sews up that: I'd hate to leave my stuff lying around in crates any longer than I have to. Dentface, throw a little extra juice into that beam so the kid here can get a big head start. And, once you get him out, quick-quick turn the dome back on fast, or we'll have half the empty stomachs on Venus inside trying to work us into their ulcers."

The robot called Dentface depressed a lever on the beam projector. Just as I had turned wistfully toward it in the hope that my meager mentality could somehow preserve an impression of the mechanism that would enable us to adapt it to our pressing needs, I was carried swiftly through a suddenly opened section of the dome and deposited halfway down the mountain. The opening, I observed as I got to my tentacles and rolled away from a creeper of sucking ivy, was actually an area of the dome that had temporarily ceased to exist.

I was unable to reflect further upon this matter because of the various lunges, snaps and grabs that were made at me from several directions. As I twisted and scudded down the tenth highest mountain, I deeply regretted Hogan Shlestertrap's need of the robots for unpacking purposes.

This, my children, was the occasion on which I lost my circular tentacle. A tricephalops, it was—or possibly a large dodle.

Near the marsh, I observed that my remaining pursuer, a green shata, had been caught by a swarm of gridniks. Accordingly, I rested in the shadow of a giant fern.

A scrabbling noise above me barely gave me time to stiffen my helical tentacle for a spring, when I recognized its source as the blap koreon. Peering from the lowest fan-leaf, he called softly: "The nzred shafalon has come from the dwelling of the human who was to give us many and mighty weapons, yet still I see him fleeing from empty bellies like the veriest morsel of a Plookh."

"And soon you will see him mocking all the beasts of prey from the safety of a dome where he and his kind live in thoughtful comfort," I replied with some importance. "I am to aid the human Shlestertrap of Hollywood California U.S.A. Earth in the making of a stereo for our race."

The blap loosed his hold on the immense leaf and dropped to the ground beside me. "A stereo? Is it small or large? How many great spotted snakes can it destroy? Will we be able to make them ourselves?"

"We will be able to make them ourselves in time, but they will destroy no great spotted snakes for us. A stereo, my impatient wayfarer upon branches, is a cultural necessity without which, it seems, a race must wander forever in ignoble and fearful darkness. With stereos as models, we may progress irresistibly to that high control of our environment in which humanity exults on Earth. But enough of this munching the husk—our sex-chiefs must conduct Beauty Contests to select characters for the first Plookh stereo. Where is the blap blapp?"

"I saw him last leaping from bough to bough in the fifth widest forest with a lizard-bird just a talon's length behind him. If he has not yet ascertained the justification of the Hope, any tkan should be able to guide you to his present lair. Meanwhile, I think I know where the flin flinn has most recently dug."

He scampered to a mass of rocks and scratched at the ground near the outermost one. The heavy body of an old flin shortly appeared at the mouth of the hole he made. I rolled over and told the flin flinn of Shlestertrap's requirements.

The doddering burrower examined his broken claws nervously. "The chiefs of the other sexes will probably want to convene above ground. I know how important this stereo is to our race, but I am old and not at all agile—and this is the Season of Wind-Driven Rains—and the great spotted snakes are ravenous enough below the surface—"

"And it will shortly be the Season of Early Floods," I interrupted him, "when only tkann will have time for conversation. Our civilizing must begin as soon as possible."

"What have you to fear, old one?" the blap jeered. "A snake would find you tough and almost without flavor!"

Flin flinn edged back into his hole. "But not until he had experimented in a regrettably final fashion upon my person," he pointed out gloomily. "I will communicate with the new mlenb mlenbb—their moist burrows connect with ours again. Where might we meet do you think, O coordinator who gathers human wisdom?"

"In the sheltered spot at the base of the sixth highest mountain," I suggested. "It will be fairly safe during the next great wind. And consider, in the meantime, which is the living flin most fitted to represent our race in this our first stereo. Tell the mlenb mlenbb to do likewise."

After the sound of his claws had diminished in the under distance, the blap and I moved back to the giant fern. It is written in the Book of Ones: *A bush nearby is worth two in the by and by.*

"The only other sex-chief whose whereabouts I griggo," the tree-dweller observed, "is the new nzred nzredd. He is in the marsh organizing the coordination of the next cycle."

"The nzred tinoslep that was?"

"Yes, and little did he relish his honors! Plentiful rose his complaints to High Hope. Vainly he insisted he was still in the very prime of coordination—that he had a good many novel arrangements yet within him. But all know of the pathetic hybrids produced in the last tinoslep cycle. You have heard, I suppose—"

And he told me the latest septuple entendre that had been making the rounds.

I was not amused. "Beware, scratcher of bark, of ridicule at the expense of him whom your coordinator obeys! Another blap may fill your place in the chain, while you gaze morosely at unhatched eggs. The nzred tinoslep, that was, organized mighty cycles in his time and now uses accumulated wisdom in the service of all the Plookhh, unlike the blap blapp and the flin flinn who have the responsibility of a lone sex."

Record this speech well, my nzreddi. Thus it is necessary to constantly impress upon the weaker, more garrulous sexes the respect due to coordination; else families will dissolve and each sex will operate in ungenetic independence. The nzred must ever be a Plookh apart—yes, yes, even in these shattering times of transition should he maintain his aloofness jealously. Even at present there are good reasons for him to do so— Please! Allow me to continue! Save these involved questions for another session, you who are so recently hatched. *I* know there are now complications....

The blap hastened to apologize.

"I meant no ridicule, none at all, omnipotent arranger of births! I thoughtlessly passed on a vulgar tale told me by an itinerant unattached guur who should have known better. Please do not tear me from the fins of the finest srob that I have ever known and the most delightful flin that ever brotched in a burrow! The nzred koreon is already displeased with me for two baby blapp I varied to the point of extinction, and now—"

Something coughed wetly behind us and we both leaped for the lowest frond of the fern. The blap streaked to the top of the plant and thence to a long-extending bough of a neighboring tree; I bounced off the leaf and into the marsh with powerful strokes of my helical tentacle. Behind me, the giant toad sorrowfully rolled his tongue back into his mouth.

I went my way fully satisfied: this blap would not mock nzredd again for many cycles.

The leader of my sex was surrounded by young nzredd in the weediest section of the marsh. He dismissed them when I approached and heard my recital.

"This meeting-place you suggested to the flin flinn—the land sexes may find it very easily, but what of the srob srobb?"

"A little stream has pushed through to the base of the sixth highest mountain," I informed him. "It isn't very wide, but the leader of the srobb should be able to swim to the sheltered place without difficulty. Only the mlenb mlenbb will be at a disadvantage there because of the stream's newness."

"And when is a mlenb not at a disadvantage?" he countered. "No, if a stream is there, the sheltered place will serve us well enough—during a wind, in any event.

You have ordered things wisely, nzred shafalon; you will yet survive to be a nzred nzredd when your more thoughtless contemporaries are excreta."

I waggled my tentacles at this praise. To be told that I would escape assimilation long enough to be nzred nzredd was a compliment indeed. And to think I am at last chief of my sex and yet still able to coordinate effectively! Truly, our race has been startled by civilization—to say nothing of its highest manifestation, The Old Switcheroo.

"You need a tkan," the nzred nzredd went on; "I believe tkan tkann has a satisfactory one for you. The tkan gadulit is the sole survivor of an attack of tricephalops upon his matrimonial convention (I must remember that the gadulit name is now available for use by new families). He has fair variation. Suppose you meet him and introduce him to the chain if all else is good in your own judgment. As soon as the sex-chiefs have met and approximated this odd business of Beauty Contests, we will assemble the individuals selected and you may escort them to awesome Shlestertrap. And may this stereo lead quickly to the softness of civilization."

"May it only," I assented fervently, and went to meet the new tkan. He was variable enough for all normal purposes; the guur shafalon found him admirable; and even our mlenb, stodgy and retiring as he was, admitted his fondness for the winged member. The tkan was overwhelmed at being admitted into the shafalon family, and I approved of his sensible attitude. I began to make plans for a convention—it was time to start another cycle.

Before I could communicate with my srob, however—he always swam a good distance from land during the Season of Wind-Driven Rains—the tkan tkann flew to inform me of the sex-chiefs' choices and lead me to them. I regretfully postponed the initiation of offspring.

The Plookhh selected by the Beauty Contests were the very glory of our race. Each was differentiated from the other members of his sex by scores of characteristics. United in one family, they might well have produced Superplookhh.

With infinite graciousness, the tkan tkann told me that I had been considered most seriously for the nzred protagonist—only, my value as Shlestertrap's assistant being primary, another was selected in my place. "No matter," I told the chief as he soared away, "I have honors enough for one Plookh: my books runneth over."

The gasping srob represented the greatest problem and the tkan-character volunteered to fly him directly to the dome without waiting for the rest of us so that the finny one would not dry up and die. Then, with the nzred-character and the blap-character carrying the plant-like guur between them, we began our ascent of the tenth highest mountain.

Although the Season of Wind-Driven Rains was almost over, there were even more great spotted snakes than before crawling upon the dome; and, grappling with their morbid coils, were more slavering dodles than I remembered seeing at one time; even a few brinosaur ranged about now, in anticipation of the approaching Season of Early Floods. I deduced, in some surprise, that they considered the human a palatable substitute for Plookhh.

I had gone ahead of my little band since I knew the terrain better and was more likely to attract Hogan Shlestertrap's attention. This was fortunate, for we had not worked halfway up the mountain before we were feverishly eluding what seemed to be the entire fauna of Venus. They poured off the dome in a great snapping, salivating horde, pausing occasionally to gouge or tear at their neighbors, but nonetheless pursuing us with a distressing concentration. I found additional cause to be grateful for the wise choices of the sex-chiefs: only really diversified Plookhh with the very latest survival characteristics could have come through that madness of frustrated gluttony unscathed. Relatively unscathed.

It was only necessary for me to cross once in front of the robot in the outer compartment of the dome. Gridnik-fast, the beam poured out and captured me, swinging thence to the rest of my elite family and carrying all of us through the open space of the dome which seemed to be materializing shut almost before we were inside.

I was particularly grateful, I recall, since the beam had snatched me from between the creepers of the largest sucking ivy I had ever stumbled upon. A helical tentacle is all very well, but it does not help over-much when one is too busy evading three lizard-birds to notice what lies in wait upon the ground.

One of the robots had already constructed a special tank for the srob, and he also rapidly found some soil into which the guur could root sighingly.

"That a real plant?" Shlestertrap inquired. He had changed from his previous covering into a black garment becomingly decorated with red splotches which disguised his dome-shaped middle protuberance in a way I could not quite fathom. On his head, he now wore what he called a cap with the visor pointing behind him—a custom, he explained, which was observed by stereo people in deference to their ancient greats.

"No, it is a guur, the Plookh which relies most on blending into its surroundings. Although it does derive some nourishment photosynthetically, it is not quite a vegetable, retaining enough mobility to—"

"A guur, you call it? Helpless, huh? Got to be carried over the threshold? Keep still— I'm thinking!"

I throbbed out a translation. We all froze into silence. The srob, who had lifted his head out of the tank to survey the dome, began to strangle quietly in the open air.

Finally, Shlestertrap nodded and we all moved again. The mlenb flapped over and pushed the srob, who had become insensible, back under the surface of the tank.

"Yep," said our civilizer. "It adds up. I have the weenie. A little too pat for an artistic stereo, but I can always dress it up so no one will know the difference." He turned to me. "That's the big gimmick in this business—dressing it up so they can't tell it's the same thing they've been seeing since they got their first universal vaccination. If you dress it up enough, the sticks will always go nuts over it. Maybe the critics will make cracks, sure, but who reads the critics?"

Alas, I did not know.

Much time passed before I had extended conversation with the human again. First, it was necessary for me to teach English to the first Plookh thespians so that they could follow Shlestertrap's direction. Not very difficult, this: it simply required a short period of concentrated griggoing by the seven of them. I could now give them much terminology that even my ancestor, nzred fanobrel, had not been able to use; unfortunately, a good deal of Shlestertrap's phrase-shadings remained as nothing but unguessable semantic goals, and when it came to many attitudes and implements used exclusively upon Earth—we could do nothing but throw up our tentacles and flippers, our vines and talons, in utter helplessness.

Some day, however—not us, but one of our conceivable descendants, perhaps—we will learn the exact constituents of a "thingumajig."

After learning the language, the other Plookhh were taken in charge by the robots—the same friendly creatures who would leave the dome occasionally to forage the fresh pink weeds that were essential to our diet—and told to do many incomprehensible things against backgrounds that varied from the artificially constructed to the projected stereo.

Frequently, Shlestertrap would halt the robots in their fluid activity with booms and cameras and lights, turn to me and demand a significant bit of information about our habits that usually required my remembering every page of all our Books of Numbers to give an adequate reply.

Before I could finish, however, he generally signaled to the robots to begin once more—muttering to himself something like: "Oh, well, we can fake up a fair copy with more process work. If it only looks good, who cares about realism?"

Then again, he would express annoyance over the fact that, while some of us had heads, the mlenbb and nzredd had torso-enclosed brains, and the guur were the proud possessors of what the first ship's biologists had called a "dissolved nervous system."

"How can you get intriguing close-ups," Shlestertrap wailed, "when you don't know what part of the animal you want in them? You'd think these characters would get together and decide what they want to look like, instead of shortening my life with complications!"

"These are the most thoroughly differentiated Plookhh," I reminded him proudly. "The beauty contest winners."

"Yeah. I'll bet the homely ones are a real old-fashioned treat."

Thus, gently and generously, did he toil on the process of civilizing us. May his name be revered by any Plookhh that survive!

My only real difficulty was in gaining more knowledge. The robots were rather uncommunicative (we have not yet resolved their exact place in human affairs) and Hogan Shlestertrap explained that a genius like himself could not be bothered with the minutiae of stereographical mechanics. That was left entirely to his metallic assistants.

Nevertheless, I persisted. My hunted race, I felt, expected me to gather all knowledge to which I was exposed for the building of our own technology. I asked Shlestertrap detailed questions about the operations of the sound robot who deftly maneuvered the writhing, almost-live microphone booms above the actors and scenery; I pestered him for facts on the great smell-camera with its peculiar, shimmering olfactory lens and its dials calibrated pungently from rose-constants to hydrogen-sulphide-constants.

Once, after a particularly long session, I came upon him in a compartment composing the score for our stereo. I had always found this music vaguely stimulating if obscure of use, and I was very curious as to how it was made.

This, let me say to his glory, he explained very patiently. "See, here's a sound-track of a Beethoven symphony and there's one of a Gershwin medley. I run off bits of each alternately into the orchestrator and flip the switch like so. The box joggles and bangs it around for a while—it can make more combinations than there are inches between here and Earth! Finally, out comes the consolidated sound-track, and we have a brand-new score for our stereo. Remember the formula: a little Beethoven, a little Gershwin, and lots and lots of orchestration."

I told him I would never forget it. "But what kind of machine makes the original Gershwin and Beethoven strips? And can either of them be used in any way under water against the brinosaur? And exactly what is involved in the process of the orchestrator joggling and banging? And how would we go about making—"

"Here!" He plucked a book from a table behind him. "I meant to give you this yesterday when you asked me how we connect tactions to the manipulating antenna. You want to know all about culture and how humans operate with it, huh? You want to know how our culture fits in with nonhumans, don't you? Well, read this and don't bother me until you do. Just keep busy going over it until you have it cold. About the most basic book in the place. Now, maybe I can get some quiet drinking out of the way."

My thanks poured at his retreating back. I retired to a corner with my treasure. The title, how inspiring it looked! ABRIDGED REGULATIONS OF THE INTERPLANETARY CULTURAL MISSION, ANNOTATED, WITH AN APPENDIX OF STANDARD OFFICE PROCEDURES FOR SOLARIAN MISSIONS.

Most unhappily, my intellectual powers were not yet sufficiently developed to extract much that was useful from this great human repository of knowledge. I was still groping slowly through Paragraph 5, Correction Circular 16, of the introduction (*Pseudo-Mammalian Carnivores, Permissible Approaches to and Placating of for the Purpose of Administering the Binet-plex*) when a robot summoned me to Shlestertrap's presence.

"It's finished," he told me, waving aside a question I began to ask regarding a particularly elusive footnote. "Here, let me put that book back in the storeroom. I just gave it to you to keep you out of my hair. It's done, boy!"

"The stereo?"

He nodded. "All wrapped up and ready to preview. I have your friends waiting in the projection room."

There was a pause while he rose and walked slowly around the compartment. I waited for his next words, hardly daring to savor the impact of the moment. Our culture had been started!

"Look, Plookh, I've given you guys a stereo that, in my opinion, positively smashes the gong. I've locked the budget out of sight, and I've worked from deep down in the middle of my mind. Now, do you think you might do a little favor for old Shlestertrap in return?"

"Anything," I throbbed. "We would do anything for the unselfish genius who—"

"Okey-dandy. A couple of busybodies on Earth are prancing around and making a fuss about my being assigned to this mission, on the grounds that I never even had a course in alien psych. They're making me into a regular curse of labor, using my appointment and a bunch of others from show business as a means of attacking the present administration on grounds of corruption and incompetence. I never looked at this job as anything more than a stop-gap until Hollywood finds that it just can't do without the authentic Shlestertrap Odor in its stereos—still, the good old bank account on Earth is growing nicely and right now I don't have any better place to go. It would be kind of nice and appreciative of you to give me a testimonial in the form of a stereo record that I can beam back to Earth. Sort of show humanity that you're grateful for what we're doing."

"I would be grateful in turn to be given an opportunity to show my gratitude," I replied. "It will take a little time, however, for me to compose a proper speech. I will start immediately."

He reached for my long tentacles and pulled me back into the compartment. "Fine! Now, you don't want to make up a speech of your own and give out with all kinds of errors that would make humans think you aren't worth the money we're spending on you? Of course you don't! I have a honey of a speech all written—just the thing they'll want to hear you say back home. Greasejob! You and Dentface get that apparatus ready for recording."

Then, while the robots manipulated the stereo-record, I read aloud the speech Shlestertrap had written from a copy he held up just out of camera range. I stumbled a bit over unfamiliar concepts—for example, passages where I extolled The Great Civilizer for teaching us English and explaining our complicated biological functions to us—but generally, the speech was no more than the hymn of praise that the man deserved. When I finished, he yelled: "Cut! Good!"

Before I had time to ask him the reasons for the seeming inconsistencies in the speech—I knew that, since he was human, they could not be mere errors—he had pushed me into the projection room where the Plookh actors waited. I thought I heard him mumble something about "That should hold the Gogarty crowd till the next election," but I was so excited over the prospect of the first Plookhian cultural achievement that I did nothing more than scurry to my place as the projectors started. Now, sometimes, I think perhaps— No.

The first stereo with an all-Plookh cast! Already, it is a commonplace, with all Plookh seeing it for the first time before they are more than six days out of the egg. But that preview, as it was called, was a moment when everything seemed to pause and offer us sanctuary. Our civilization seemed assured.

I decided that its murky passages were the result of one viewing and would disappear in time as we expanded intellectually.

You know what I mean. The beginning is interesting and delightful as the various sexes meet in different ways and decide to become a family. The matrimonial convention, although somewhat unusual procedurally, is fairly close to the methods in use at that time. But why does the guur suddenly proclaim she is insulted and bolt the convention?

Of course, you all know—or should—that our reservation of the pronoun "she" for guur dates from the dialogue in this stereo?

Again, why, after the guur leaves, do the others pursue her—instead of finding and mating with a more reasonable specimen? And the great spotted snake that notices the guur—we had thought till then that the guur is the one form of Plookh safe from these dread creatures: evidently we were wrong. In her flight, she passes tricephalops and sucking ivy: these ignore her; yet the great spotted snake suddenly develops a perverted fancy for her vines and tendrils.

And the battle, where the other six Plookhh fall upon and destroy the snake! Even the srob crawls out of the stream and falls gasping into the fray! It continues for a long period—the snake seems to be triumphing, logically enough—suddenly, the snake is dead.

I am an old nzred. I have seen that stereo hundreds of times, and many the ferocious spotted snake from whose jaws I have leaped. On the basis of my experience, I can only agree with the other oldsters among the Plookhh that the snake seems to have been strangled to death. I know this is not much help and I know what it means taken together with our other difficulties—but as the nzred nzredd announced at the first public showing of the stereo: "What Plookh has done, Plookh can do!"

The rest of the stereo is comprehensible enough. Which guur, no matter what her reasons for leaving the chain originally, would not joyfully return to a family powerful enough to destroy a great spotted snake? And even now we all laugh (all except mlenbb, that is) at the final sequence where the mlenb-character crawls into his burrow backward and almost breaks a flipper.

"Terrific, huh?" Shlestertrap inquired, when we had returned to his compartment. "And that process-work—it was out of this system, wasn't it? Can I mastermind a masterpiece, or can't I?"

I considered. "You can," I told him at last. "This stereo will affect our way of life more than anything else in nine thousand years of Plookh history."

He slapped his sides. "This stereo, artistically, has everything. The way I handled that finale was positively reminiscent of Chaplin in his bamboo-cane period with just a touch of the Marx Brothers and De Sica."

After a spasm of bottle-conjugating, he suggested: "Guess you want to chase in and get those robots to teach you how to handle projectors. I'll give you three complete sets and a whole slew of copies; you show some of your friends in the backwoods how to turn them on and off—then you can come back here and write the next stereo."

"Write the *next* stereo? I am overwhelmed, O Shlestertrap, but I don't quite understand what I could write about. Have you not said all in this one? If there is more,

I am afraid my uncivilized person is not capable of conceiving and organizing it."

"Not a matter of civilization," he told me impatiently. "Just a matter of a twist. You saw how this stereo ran—now you simply apply The Old Switcheroo."

"The Old Switcheroo?"

"The new angle—the twist—the tangent. No sense in using a good plot just the once. I'll make an artist out of you yet! Look—on second thought, maybe you're too new at this racket to get it after all. Was sort of hoping you'd carry the load while I rested up. But I guess I can knock out another stereo fast to give you the idea. Meanwhile, suppose you get started on that projection course so that your buddies in the jungle can see what the Interplanetary Cultural Mission is doing for them."

Shortly thereafter, I was deposited outside the dome with the three sets of projectors. Again, I was fortunate in making my escape from the creatures who swarmed at me. I returned to the spot with forty young Plookhh I gathered from the neighborhood and, with the expenditure of much labor and life, we divided the equipment into small, somewhat portable groups and removed it to another mountain.

As rapidly as possible, I taught them the intricacies of operation I had learned from the robots. I had tactlessly requested one or two of these creatures from Hogan Shlestertrap, by the way, to aid us in the difficult task of shifting the equipment. "Not on your materialization," he had roared. "Isn't it enough that I send them out of the dome to get those orange weeds you guys are so nuts about? Two of my best robots—Greasejob and Dentface—are walking around with cracked bodies because some overgrown cockroach mistook them for an order of. I made a stereo for you people: now you carry the ball for a while." Naturally, I apologized.

When my assistants could work the projectors to my satisfaction, I divided them into three groups and sent two of them off with sets and a supply of stereo-film. I kept one group and set with me, and had a tkan carry word to the chief of his sex that all was ready.

Meanwhile, the nzred nzredd and twelve specially trained helpers had been traveling everywhere, griggoing English to all Plookhh they met and ordering them to go forth and griggo likewise. This was necessary because that had been the language of the stereo: as a result, English has completely replaced our native language.

One of the groups I sent out was stationed in a relatively sheltered cove to which srobb and mlenbb could come in comparative safety. The other, in a distant valley, exhibited chiefly to guurr, flinn and nzredd; my crew, on a mountain, to blapp and tkann. By showing the stereo to audiences of approximately two hundred Plookhh at a time, we were reaching the maximum number at all compatible with safety. Even so, performances were frequently interrupted by a pack of strinth who paused to feed upon us, by an occasional swarm of gridniks who descended on our engrossed multitudes with delighted drones. We changed our projection spots after every performance; but I was twice forced to train new groups of young Plookhh to replace those projectionists casually annihilated when the stereo-exhibition attracted some carnivore's attention.

Not a good system, admittedly; but none better has yet been devised. We all know how dangerous it is to congregate. To translate into inadequate English: "*Too many Plookhh make a broth.*" Nonetheless, it was imperative that the message of civilization be spread as widely and as rapidly as possible.

The message was spread, received and acted upon.

However much it may be to my discredit, I must confess that I felt some small and definite joy at belonging to an already-organized family unit. Whenever thereafter I saw a matrimonial convention breaking up, the guur moving as rapidly as she could through the forest until she came to a great spotted snake, the other six members of her family immediately throwing themselves in a sort of hopeless enthusiasm upon the reptile—whenever I saw that spectacle which now, of course, became so frequent, I could not help but rejoice ingloriously in having my family's convention cycles behind me. I was too old for civilization.

Once, I remember, four successive matrimonial conventions involved the same snake. He became so gorged with Plookhh that he could not move from the scene of the feeding. Possibly incidents of this sort gave rise to what is known as the nzred magandu system which is used, when possible, at present. As you know, under this system, six families hold their matrimonial conventions together and the six guur perform the traditional civilized bolt in unison. When they come across a great spotted snake, all the other members of the six families fall upon it and, under the weight of their numbers, the snake is very often smothered to death. There are usually enough survivors to make at least one full family after the battle, the only important difficulty here being that this system creates a surplus of guurr. The so-called blap vintorin system is very similar.

In any event, despite the great odds, we Plookhh had learned the lesson of the stereo well and were beginning to live (though usually we did the opposite) as civilized beings who are ready for technological knowledge. Then— Yes, then came The Old Switcheroo.

The Season of Early Floods was in full tide when a flin pushed out of his ground passage and up the mountain where we had recently set our projectors anew.

"Hail, transmitter of culture," he wheezed. "I bear a message from the flin flinn who had it from the nzred nzredd who had it from the Shlestertrap himself. He wishes you to come to his dome immediately."

I was busy helping to swing the ponderous machinery around, and therefore called over my tentacle-joint: "The area between here and the tenth highest mountain is under water. Find some srobb who will convey me there."

"No time," I heard him say. "There is no time to gather waterporters. You will have to make the circuitous trip by land, and soon! The Shlestertrap is—"

Then came a horribly familiar gurgle and his speech was cut off. I spun round as my assistants scattered in all directions. A full-grown brinosaur had sneaked up the mountain behind the flin and sucked the burrower into his throat while he was concentrating on giving me important information.

I suppressed every logical impulse that told me to flee; however frightened, I must act like a representative of the civilized race which we Plookhh were becoming. I stood before the brinosaur's idiotically gleeful face and inquired: "What about the Shlestertrap? For the sake of all Plookhh, already eaten and as yet unhatched, answer me quickly, O flin!"

From somewhere within the immense throat, the flin's voice came painfully indistinct through the saliva which blocked its path. "Shlestertrap is going back to Earth. He says you must—"

The monster gulped and the bulge that was once a flin slid down the great neck and into the body proper. Only then, when he had burped his enjoyment and the first faint slaver of expectancy began in regard to me—only then, did I use the power of my helical tentacle to leap to one side and into a small grove of trees.

After swinging his head in a lazy curve, the brinosaur, morosely certain that there were no other unalerted Plookhh in the vicinity, turned and flapped slowly down the mountain. The moment he entered the screaming floods, I was out of concealment and detailing a party of three nzredd to follow me to the dome.

We picked our way painfully across a string of rocks, in a direction which, while leading away from the tenth highest mountain, would form part of a great arc designed to lead us to the dome across dry land.

"Can it be," one of the youngsters asked, "that Shlestertrap, observing our careful obedience to the principles laid down in the stereo, has decided that we have irrevocably joined the chain that must produce civilization and that his work is therefore finished?"

"I hope not. If that were true," I replied, "it would mean, from the rate of development I have observed, that our civilization would not make itself felt for several lifetimes beyond mine. Possibly he is returning to Earth to acquire the necessary materials for our next stage, that of technology."

"Good! The cultural stage through which we pass, while obviously necessary, is extremely damaging to our population figures. I am continually forced to revise my Book of Sevens in unhappy decrease of Plookhh. Not that the prospect of civilization for our race is not well worth the passing misery I feel at attending my first matrimonial convention two days from now. I only hope that our guur finds a comparatively small great spotted snake!"

Thus, discoursing pleasantly of hopes almost as delightful as the Hope—of a time when the power of Plookh domination would shake the very soil of Venus—we rolled damply the long distance to the dome. I lost only one assistant before the robot picked us up with his beam, and scurried rapidly to Shlestertrap's interior compartment.

The place was almost bare: I deduced that most of the mission's equipment had already been carried to the flame ship. Our civilizer sat on a single chair surrounded by multitudes of bottles, all of whom had already been conjugated to the point of extinction.

"Well," he cried, "if it isn't little plookhiyaki and his wedded nzred! Didn't think I could say that, did you? Sit down and take a load off your nzred!" I was glad to observe that while his voice was somewhat thick, his attitude seemed to express a desire to be more communicative than usual.

"We hear that you return to Hollywood California U.S.A. Earth," I began.

"Wish it was that, laddie. Wish it was that little thing. Finest place in the universe—Hollywood Calif etcetera. Nope. I been recalled, that's what I been. The mission's closed."

"But *why?*"

"This thing—Economy. At least that's what they said in the bulletin they sent me. 'Due to necessary retrenchment in many government services—' Don't you believe it! It's those big busybodies! Gogarty's probably laughing his head off down in Sahara University: he's the guy started all that hullabubballoo about me in first place. And me, I gotta go back and start life all over again."

Here he put his head down between his arms and shook his shoulders. After a while, he rolled off the chair and onto the floor. A robot entered, carrying a packing box. He set Shlestertrap back in the chair and left, the heavy box still under his arm.

I could not help a slight feeling of pride at the sight of the awe with which the two young nzredd regarded my obvious intimacy with the human. They were more than a little confused by his alien communicative pattern; but they were as desperately determined as I to memorize every nuance of this portentous last conversation. This was fortunate: the fact that their versions of this affair agreed with mine helped to strengthen my position in the difficult days that lay ahead.

"And our civilizing process," I asked. "Is it to stop?"

"Huh? What civil— Oh, that! No, sir! Little old Shlesty's taken care of his friends. Always takes care. Got the new stereo ready. One fine job! Wait—I'll get it for you."

He rose slowly to his feet. "Where's a robot? Never one of 'em around when you want one of 'em around. Hey, Highsprockets!" he bellowed. "Get me the copies of the stereo in the next room or something. The *new* stereo.

"Got it all cut yesterday," he continued, when the robot had given him the packages. "Didn't really finish it the way I wanted to; but when bulletin came, I just sent all your actor friends on home. I don't work for nothing, I don't. But I sat up and cut it into right length, and what do you know? It came out fine. Here."

I distributed the packages equally among the three of us. "And does it contain that wonderful device you mentioned—The Old Switcheroo?"

"Contains nothing else but. As neat a switcheroo on an original plot as Hogan Shlestertrap has ever turned. Yop. It's got all you need. You just notice the way I worked it and pretty soon you'll be making stereos in competition with Hollywood. Which is more than I'll be doing."

"We do not even faintly aspire to such heights," I told him humbly. "We will be sufficiently grateful for the gift of civilization."

"Thass all right," he waved a hand at us as he swayed. "Don't *thank* me. Thank *me*. In those two stereos you have two of the finest love stories ever told, and done by the latest Hollywood methods from one of its greatest directors in his grandest— What I mean to say is, they told me to mission you some culture and I missioned you culture and if they don't like it, they can—"

At this point, he crumpled suddenly into a huddle upon the chair. We waited patiently for any further disclosures, but, as he seemed preoccupied with a peculiarly human manifestation, we made our departures with no further formality.

Once safely away from the dome, I instructed my assistants to hurry to our two distant installations and prepare them for immediate projection of our new stereo.

"Remember," I called after them. "Any change the First Stereo has made in our way of life will be as nothing to what will be done by The Old Switcheroo."

And I was right. The introduction of The Old Switcheroo—

I saw it myself for the first time along with over a hundred other Plookhh upon our mountain. After it was over, I was as bereft of speech as the rest. After a long pause in which no one dared to comment, the nzred nzredd suggested I project the First Stereo again with The Old Switcheroo immediately following so that we could compare them more easily.

This was done, but it proved of little help.

The problem is for you to solve. May my recounting of the entire history of the relationship between Hogan Shlestertrap and myself be of some value in finding a solution! I am old, and, as I have said, ripe for the gullet; you have been hatched in the very midst of this preliminary period of our culture—it is for you to find the way, the way that *must* be there, out of this impasse in which we shuttle unreproductively.

You are but a few days from the egg, but you have already seen both the First Stereo and The Old Switcheroo as many times as conditions permit. You should know that there is a single question common to both of them.

The one essential point of difference between the First Stereo and The Old Switcheroo is that, in the latter, the srob, mlenb, tkan, flin, blap and nzred bolt the matrimonial convention, leaving the guur to pursue them affectionately and finally rescue them from the great spotted snake; while, in the former, the reverse occurs. The loving reunion at the end is the same in both, except that the mlenb, instead of backing into his muddy burrow in the final scene of The Old Switcheroo, slips and falls heavily across it.

After the preliminary exhibitions, the guurr began insisting loudly that the humans could not have expected them—weak and slow-moving as they are—to destroy great spotted snakes. Confronted with the specific evidence, however, they fell back on the claim that the First Stereo depicted the civilized state; and the second, an alternative barbarity.

To this, the other six sexes replied that The Old Switcheroo was not an alternative, but the consummation of our cultural process. Also, as a result of the mores developed with the First Stereo, there was now a disgusting and unprecedented surplus of guurr: what better way to dispose of them than in this extremely selective one? The snakes, when sufficiently irritated by attacking guurr, *will* swallow them it seems—

The mlenbb, of course, had their own difficulty: whether and how to enter their burrows immediately after the convention. But this was a minor matter.

Some of the new Plookh families attempted to follow the patterns indicated in the First Stereo; others, those in the second. A very few completely barbaric individuals, oblivious to the high destiny of their species, withdrew from the Plookh community and tried to return to the primitive methods of our ancestors; but since few high-variables cared to attach themselves to so atavistic a group, their offspring are being exterminated rapidly—and good riddance.

Most Plookhh remain in two great divisions: the guurr, who believe in the civilizing logic of the First Stereo, and the other sexes who accept only the amendment of The Old Switcheroo. Then, of course, there are a few altruistic nzredd and flinn who agree with the guurr, and vice-versa...

We need the cooperation of all seven sexes for successful reproduction. But how can we achieve that, Plookhh argue, unless we know which is the stereo of civilization? To be so close to liberation from our gustatory bondage, and because of sheer intellectual inadequacy— For the past eleven cycles, not a single matrimonial convention has been celebrated.

As a member of a pre Shlestertrap family, I take no sides. My convention is past: yours, my diversified nzreddi, lies ahead. I am certain of one thing.

The answer is to be found in neither one stereo nor the other. The answer involves unity of the two: a core of relationship which both must share and which, when discovered, will dissolve their apparent inconsistency. Remember, these stereos are the product of a highly civilized creature.

Where is that core of relationship to be found? In the original stereo? In The Old Switcheroo? Or in that book I never finished—ABRIDGED REGULATIONS OF THE INTERPLANETARY CULTURAL MISSION, ANNOTATED, WITH AN APPENDIX OF STANDARD OFFICE PROCEDURE FOR SOLARIAN MISSIONS?

Humanity has solved such problems, and today flicks stars from its path. We must solve it or die as a race, albeit a civilized race.

We will not solve it—and this is most important—we will not solve this problem by the disgusting, utterly futile expedient to which more and more of our young are daily resorting. I refer to the unmentionable and perverted six-sex families....

AFTERWORD

For what the information may be worth, the original title was "The Old Switcheroo." The editor purchasing the story changed the title, which, while not to my taste, is the one that has been used by anthologists.

In terms of sheer length, "Venus and the Seven Sexes" held the record for many years among my stories. I wrote it surrounded by thumb-tacked charts showing which sex did what and how and to whom. My brother, Morton, sat in a corner of my study throughout, feverishly working out the chromosome patterns. When I finished the story, we had a small ceremony, and Morton formally witnessed my oath: from that day on, I would avoid anything but human characters and the very simplest plots. Well, time passes and wounds heal. I have broken that oath many times—but never since have I been caught in coils of such intricacy.

The story drew my first memorable fan letter, a lovely and gracious comment from Robert Heinlein. I was a very new, very young science-fiction writer, and getting a tribute from one of the two men whose work had shaped mine (the other was Henry Kuttner) simply overwhelmed me. Even praise from a very famous geneticist didn't mean as much.

Three further notes: I'm not as fond of the piece as I was years ago (the Shlestertrap passages creak badly and are badly dated) but, as Aldous Huxley remarked in a similar context, the younger writer's self is entitled to have his own story stand—therefore, no late-date rewrite.

The Venus in the piece is the Venus we knew so little about in 1947. It's a jungle Venus used by many writers of the time, and it's one on which this story was then at least imaginable.

Third. I once asked Heinlein if his use of *grok* in *Stranger in a Strange Land* had been influenced at all by my use of *griggo* in "Venus and the Seven Sexes." He looked startled, then thought about it for a long time. Finally, he shrugged. "It's possible, very possible," he said.

Do me something. I like that "very."

WRITTEN 1947——PUBLISHED 1949

PARTY OF THE TWO PARTS

GALACTOGRAM FROM STELLAR SERGEANT O-DIK-VEH, COMMANDER OF OUTLYING PATROL OFFICE 1001625, TO HEADQUARTERS DESK SERGEANT HOY-VEH-CHALT, GALACTIC PATROL HEADQUARTERS ON VEGA XXI—(PLEASE NOTE: THIS IS TO BE TRANSMITTED AS PERSONAL, NOT OFFICIAL, MESSAGE AND AS SUCH WILL BE CHARGED THE USUAL HYPERSPACE RATES)

My Dear Hoy:

I am deeply sorry to trouble you again, but, Hoy, am I in a jam! Once more, it's not something that I did wrong, but something I didn't do right—what the Old One is sure to wheeze is "a patent dereliction of obvious duty." And since I'm positive he'll be just as confused as I, once the prisoners I'm sending on by slow light-transport arrive (when he reads the official report that I drew up and am transmitting with them, I can see him dropping an even dozen of his jaws), I can only hope that this advance message will give you enough time to consult the best legal minds in Vegan Headquarters and get some sort of solution worked out.

If there's any kind of solution available by the time he reads my report, the Old One won't be nearly as angry at my dumping the problem on his lap. But I have an uneasy, persistent fear that Headquarters is going to get as snarled up in this one as my own office. If it does, the Old One is likely to remember what happened in Outlying Patrol Office 1001625 the last time—and then, Hoy, you will be short one spore-cousin.

It's a dirty business all around, a real dirty business. I use the phrase advisedly. In the sense of *obscene,* if you follow me.

As you've no doubt suspected by now, most of the trouble has to do with that damp and irritating third planet of Sol, the one that many of its inhabitants call Earth. Those damned chittering bipeds cause me more sleeplessness than any other species in my sector. Sufficiently advanced technologically to be almost at Stage 15—self-developed interplanetary travel—they are still centuries away from the usually concurrent Stage 15A—friendly contact by the galactic civilization.

They are, therefore, still in Secretly Supervised Status, which means that I have to maintain a staff of about two hundred agents on their planet, all encased in clumsy and uncomfortable protoplasmic disguises, to prevent them from blowing their silly selves up before the arrival of their spiritual millennium.

On top of everything, their solar system only has nine planets, which means that my permanent headquarters office can't get any farther away from Sol than the planet they call Pluto, a world whose winters are bearable, but whose summers are unspeakably hot. I tell you, Hoy, the life of a stellar sergeant isn't all *gloor* and *skubbets,* no matter what Rear Echelon says.

In all honesty, though, I should admit that the difficulty did not originate on Sol III this time. Ever since their unexpected and uncalled-for development of nuclear fission, which, as you know, cost me a promotion, I've doubled the number of undercover operatives on the planet and given them stern warning to report the slightest technological spurt immediately. I doubt that these humans could invent so much as an elementary time-machine now, without my knowing of it well in advance.

No, this time it all started on Rugh VI, the world known to those who live on it as Gtet. If you consult your atlas, Hoy, you'll find Rugh is a fair-sized yellow dwarf star on the outskirts of the galaxy, and Gtet an extremely insignificant planet which has only recently achieved the status of Stage 19—primary interstellar citizenship.

The Gtetans are a modified ameboid race who manufacture a fair brand of *ashkebac,* which they export to their neighbors on Rugh IX and XII. They are a highly individualistic people and still experience many frictions living in a centralized society. Despite several centuries of advanced civilization, most Gtetans look upon the Law as a delightful problem in circumvention rather than as a way of life.

An ideal combination with my bipeds of Earth, eh?

It seems that a certain L'payr was one of the worst troublemakers on Gtet. He had committed almost every crime and broken almost every law. On a planet where fully one-fourth of the population is regularly undergoing penal rehabilitation, L'payr was still considered something quite special. A current Gtetan saying, I understand, puts it, "You're like L'payr, fellow—you don't know *when* to stop!"

Nonetheless, L'payr had reached the point where it was highly important that he did stop. He had been arrested and convicted for a total of 2,342 felonies, just one short of the 2,343 felonies which, on Gtet, make one a habitual criminal and, therefore, subject to life imprisonment. He made a valiant effort to retire from public life and devote himself to contemplation and good works but it was too late. Almost against his will, as he insisted to me under examination in my office, he found his mind turning to foul deeds left undone, illegalities as yet unperpetrated.

And so one day, quite casually—hardly noticing, as it were—he committed another major crime. But this one was so ineffably ugly, involving an offense against the moral code as well as civil legislation, that the entire community turned against L'payr.

He was caught selling pornography to juvenile Gtetans.

The indulgence that a celebrity may enjoy turned to wrath and utter contempt. Even the Gtetan Protective Association of Two Thousand Time Losers refused to raise funds for his bail. As his trial approached, it became obvious to L'payr that he was in for it. His only hope lay in flight.

He pulled the most spectacular coup of his career—he broke out of the hermetically sealed vault in which he was being guarded around the clock (how he did this, he consistently refused to tell me up to the time of his lamented demise or whatever you want to call it) and escaped to the spaceport near the prison. There, he managed to steal aboard the pride of the Gtetan merchant fleet, a newly developed interstellar ship equipped with two-throttle hyperspace drive.

This ship was empty, waiting for a crew to take it out on its maiden run.

Somehow, in the few hours at his disposal before his escape was known, L'payr figured out the controls of the craft and managed to lift it off Gtet and into hyperspace. He had no idea at this time that, since the ship was an experimental model, it was equipped with a transmitting device that kept the spaceport informed of its location.

Thus, though they lacked the facilities to pursue him, the Gtetan police always knew exactly where he was. A few hundred ameboid vigilantes did start after him in old-fashioned, normal-drive ships, but after a month or so of long and fatiguing interstellar travel at one-hundredth his speed, they gave up and returned home.

For his hideout, L'payr wanted a primitive and unimportant corner of the galaxy. The region around Sol was ideal. He materialized out of hyperspace about halfway between the third and fourth planets. But he did it very clumsily (after all, Hoy, the best minds of his race are just beginning to understand the two-throttle drive) and lost all of his fuel in the process. He barely managed to reach Earth and come down.

The landing was effected at night and with all drives closed, so that no one on the planet saw it. Because living conditions on Earth are so different from Gtet, L'payr knew that his mobility would be very limited. His one hope was to get help from the inhabitants. He had to pick a spot where possible contacts would be at maximum and yet accidental discovery of his ship would be at minimum. He chose an empty lot in the suburbs of Chicago and quickly dug his ship in.

Meanwhile, the Gtetan police communicated with me as the local commanding officer of the Galactic Patrol. They told me where L'payr was hidden and demanded extradition. I pointed out that, as yet, I lacked jurisdiction, since no crime of an *interstellar* nature had been committed. The stealing of the ship had been done on his home planet—it had not occurred in deep space. If, however, he broke any galactic law while he was on Earth, committed any breach of the peace, no matter how slight...

"How about that?" the Gtetan police asked me over the interstellar radio. "Earth is on Secretly Supervised Status, as we understand it. It is illegal to expose it to superior civilizations. Isn't L'payr landing there in a two-throttle hyperspace-drive ship enough of a misdemeanor to entitle you to pick him up?"

"Not by itself," I replied. "The ship would have to be seen and understood for what it was by a resident of the planet. From what we here can tell, no such observation was made. And so long as he stays in hiding, doesn't tell any human about us and refrains from adding to the technological momentum of Earth, L'payr's galactic citizenship has to be respected. I have no legal basis for an arrest."

Well, the Gtetans grumbled about what were they paying the star tax for, anyway, but they saw my point. They warned me, though, about L'payr—sooner or later his criminal impulses would assert themselves. He was in an impossible position, they insisted. In order to get the fuel necessary to leave Earth before his supplies ran out, he'd have to commit some felony or other—and as soon as he did so and was arrested, they wanted their extradition request honored.

"The filthy, evil-minded old pervert," I heard the police chief mutter as he clicked off.

I don't have to tell you how I felt, Hoy. A brilliant, imaginative ameboid criminal at large on a planet as volatile culturally as Earth! I notified all our agents in North America to be on the alert and settled back to wait it out with prayerfully knotted tentacles.

L'payr had listened to most of this conversation over his own ship's receiver. Naturally, the first thing he did was to remove the directional device which had enabled the Gtetan police to locate him. Then, as soon as it was dark again, he managed, with what must have been enormous difficulty, to transport himself and his little ship to another area of the city. He did this, too, without being observed.

He made his base in a slum tenement neighborhood that had been condemned to make way for a new housing project and therefore was practically untenanted. Then he settled back to consider his problem.

Because, Hoy, he had a problem.

He didn't want to get in any trouble with the Patrol, but if he didn't get his pseudopods on a substantial amount of fuel very soon, he'd be a dead ameboid. Not only did he need the fuel to get off Earth, but the converters—which, on this rather primitive Gtetan vessel, changed waste matter back into usable air and food—would be stopping very soon if they weren't stoked up, too.

His time was limited, his resources almost non-existent. The spacesuits with which the ship was furnished, while cleverly enough constructed and able to satisfy the peculiar requirements of an entity of constantly fluctuating format, had not been designed for so primitive a planet as Earth. They would not operate too effectively for long periods away from the ship.

He knew that my OP office had been apprised of his landing and that we were just waiting for some infraction of even the most obscure minor law. Then we'd pounce— and, after the usual diplomatic formalities, he'd be on his way back to Gtet, for a nine-throttle Patrol ship could catch him easily. It was obvious that he couldn't do as he had originally planned—make a fast raid on some human supply center and collect whatever stuff he needed.

His hope was to make a trade. He'd have to find a human with whom he could deal and offer something that, to this particular human in any case, was worth the quantity of fuel L'payr's ship needed to take him to a less policed corner of the Cosmos. But almost everything on the ship was essential to its functioning. And L'payr had to make his trade without (1) giving away the existence and nature of the galactic civilization, or (2) providing the inhabitants of Earth with any technological stimulus.

L'payr later said that be thought about the problem until his nucleus was a mass of corrugations. He went over the ship, stem to stern, again and again, but everything a human might consider acceptable was either too useful or too revealing. And then, just as he was about to give up, he found it.

The materials he needed were those with which he had committed his last crime!

According to Gtetan law, you see, Hoy, all evidence pertaining to a given felony is retained by the accused until the time of his trial. There are very complicated reasons for this, among them the Gtetan juridical concept that every prisoner is *known* to be guilty until he manages, with the aid of lies, loopholes and brilliant legalisms, to convince a hard-boiled and cynical jury of his peers that they should, in spite of their knowledge to the contrary, declare him innocent. Since the burden of the proof rests with the prisoner, the evidence does likewise. And L'payr, examining this evidence, decided that he was in business.

What he needed now was a customer. Not only someone who wanted to buy what he had to sell, but a customer who had available the fuel he needed. And in the neighborhood which was now his base of operations, customers of this sort were rare.

Being Stage 19, the Gretans are capable of the more primitive forms of telepathy— only at extremely short ranges, of course, and for relatively brief periods of time. So, aware that my secret agents had already begun to look for him and that, when they found him, his freedom of action would be even more circumscribed, L'payr desperately began to comb though the minds of any terrestrials within three blocks of his hideout.

Days went by. He scuttled from mind to mind like an insect looking for a hole in a collector's jar. He was forced to shut the ship's converter down to one-half operation, then to one-third. Since this cut his supply of food correspondingly, he began to hunger. For lack of activity, his contractile vacuole dwindled to the size of a pinpoint. Even his endoplasm lost the turgidity of the healthy ameboid and became dangerously thin and transparent.

And then one night, when he had about determined to take his chances and steal the fuel he needed, his thoughts ricocheted off the brain of a passerby, came back unbelievingly, examined further and were ecstatically convinced. A human who not only could supply his needs, but also, and more important, might be in the market for Gtetan pornography!

In other words, Mr. Osborne Blatch.

This elderly teacher of adolescent terrestrials insisted throughout all my interrogations that, to the best of his knowledge, no mental force was used upon him. It seems that he lived in a new apartment house on the other side of the torn-down tenement area and customarily walked in a wide arc around the rubble because of the large number of inferior and belligerent human types which infested the district. On this particular night, a teachers' meeting at his high school having detained him, he was late for supper and decided, as he had once or twice before, to take a short cut. He claims that the decision to take a short cut was his own.

Osborne Blatch says that he was striding along jauntily, making believe his umbrella was a malacca cane, when he seemed to hear a voice. He says that, even at first hearing, he used the word "seemed" to himself because, while the voice definitely had inflection and tone, it was somehow completely devoid of volume.

The voice said, "Hey, bud! C'mere!"

He turned around curiously and surveyed the rubble to his right. All that was left of the building that had once been there was the lower half of the front entrance. Since everything else around it was completely flat, he saw no place where a man could be standing.

But as he looked, he heard the voice again. It sounded greasily conspiratorial and slightly impatient. "C'mere, bud. *C'mere!*"

"What—er—what *is* it, sir?" he asked in a cautiously well-bred way, moving closer and peering in the direction of the voice. The bright street light behind him, he said, improved his courage as did the solid quality of the very heavy old-fashioned umbrella he was carrying.

"C'mere. I got somp'n to show you. C'mon!"

Stepping carefully over loose brick and ancient garbage, Mr. Blatch came to a small hollow at one side of the ruined entrance. And filling it was L'payr or, as he seemed at first glance to the human, a small, splashy puddle of purple liquid.

I ought to point out now, Hoy—and the affidavits I'm sending along will substantiate it—that at no time did Mr. Blatch recognize the viscous garment for a spacesuit, nor did he ever see the Gtetan ship which L'payr had hidden in the rubble behind him in its completely tenuous hyperspatial state.

Though the man, having a good imagination and a resilient mind, immediately realized that the creature before him must be extraterrestrial, he lacked overt technological evidence to this effect, as well as to the nature and existence of our specific galactic civilization. Thus, here at least, there was no punishable violation of Interstellar Statute 2,607,193, Amendments 126 through 509.

"What do you have to show me?" Mr. Blatch asked courteously, staring down at the purple puddle. "And where, may I ask, are you from? Mars? Venus?"

"Listen, bud, y'know what's good for ya, y'don't ast such questions. Look, I got somep'n for ya. Hot stuff. *Real* hot!"

Mr. Blatch's mind, no longer fearful of having its owner assaulted and robbed by the neighborhood tough it had originally visualized, spun off to a relevant memory, years old, of a trip abroad. There had been that alley in Paris and the ratty little Frenchman in a torn sweater…

"What would that be?" he asked.

A pause now, while L'payr absorbed new impressions.

"Ah-h-h," said the voice from the puddle. "I 'ave somezing to show M'sieu zat M'sieu weel like vairry much. If M'sieu weel come a leetle closair?"

M'sieu, we are to understand, came a leetle closair. Then the puddle heaved up in the middle, reaching out a pseudopod that held flat, square objects, and telepathed hoarsely, " 'Ere, M'sieu. Feelthy peekshures."

Although taken more than a little aback, Blatch merely raised both eyebrows interrogatively and said, "Ah? Well, well!"

He shifted the umbrella to his left hand and, taking the pictures as they were given to him, one at a time, examined each a few steps away from L'payr, where the light of the street lamp was stronger.

When all the evidence arrives, you will be able to see for yourself, Roy, what they were like. Cheap prints, calculated to excite the grossest ameboid passions. The Gtetans, as you may have heard, reproduce by simple asexual fission, but only in the presence of saline solution—sodium chloride is comparatively rare on their world.

The first photograph showed a naked ameba, fat and replete with food vacuoles, splashing lazily and formlessly at the bottom of a metal tank in the completely relaxed state that precedes reproducing.

The second was like the first, except that a trickle of salt water had begun down one side of the tank and a few pseudopods had lifted toward it inquiringly. To leave nothing to the imagination, a sketch of the sodium chloride molecule had been superimposed on the upper right corner of the photograph.

In the third picture, the Gtetan was ecstatically awash in the saline solution, its body distended to maximum, dozens of pseudopods thrust out, throbbing. Most of the chromatin had become concentrated in chromosomes about the equator of the nucleus. To an ameba, this was easily the most exciting photograph in the collection.

The fourth showed the nucleus becoming indented between the two sets of sibling chromosomes—while, in the fifth, with the division completed and the two nuclei at opposite ends of the reproducing individual, the entire cytoplasmic body had begun to undergo constriction about its middle. In the sixth, the two resultant Gtetans were emerging with passion-satisfied languor from the tank of salt water.

As a measure of L'payr's depravity, let me pass on to you what the Gtetan police told me. Not only was he peddling the stuff to ameboid minors, but they believed that he had taken the photographs himself and that the model had been his own brother—or should I say sister? His own one and only sibling, possibly? This case has many, many confusing aspects.

Blatch returned the last picture to L'payr and said, "Yes, I am interested in buying the group. How much?"

The Gtetan named his price in terms of the requisite compounds available in the chemistry laboratory of the high school where Blatch taught. He explained exactly how he wanted them to be prepared and warned Blatch to tell nobody of L'payr's existence.

"Uzzerwise, when M'sieu gets 'ere tomorrow night, ze peekshures weel be gone, I weel be gone—and M'sieu weel have nozzing to show for his trouble. *Comprenez?*"

Osborne Blatch seems to have had very little trouble in obtaining and preparing the stuff for which L'payr had bargained. He said that, by the standards of his community, it was a minute quantity and extremely inexpensive. Also, as he had scrupulously always done in the past when using school supplies for his own experiments, he reimbursed the laboratory out of his own pocket. But he does admit that the photographs were only a small part of what he hoped to get out of the ameboid. He expected, once a sound business arrangement had been established, to find out from which part of the Solar System the visitor had come, what his world was like and similar matters of understandable interest to a creature whose civilization is in the late phases of Secretly Supervised Status.

Once the exchange had been effected, however, L'payr tricked him. The Gtetan told Blatch to return on the *next* night when, his time being more free, they could discuss the state of the Universe at leisure. And, of course, as soon as the Earthman had left with the photographs, L'payr jammed the fuel into his converters, made the necessary sub-nuclear rearrangements in its atomic structure and, with the hyperspace-drive once more operating under full power, took off like a *rilg* out of *Gowkuldady*.

As far as we can determine, Blatch received the deception philosophically. After all, he still had the pictures.

When my OP office was informed that L'payr had left Earth in the direction of the Hercules Cluster M13, without leaving any discernible ripple in terrestrial law or technology behind him, we all relaxed gratefully. The case was removed from TOP PRIORITY—FULL ATTENTION ALL PERSONNEL rating and placed in the PENDING LATENT EFFECTS category.

As is usual, I dropped the matter myself and gave full charge of the follow-up to my regent and representative on Earth, Stellar Corporal Pah-Chi-Luh. A tracer beam was put on L'payr's rapidly receding ship and I was free to devote my attention once more to my basic problem—delaying the development of interplanetary travel until the various human societies had matured to the requisite higher level.

Thus, six Earth months later, when the case broke wide open, Pah-Chi-Luh handled it himself and didn't bother me until the complications became overwhelming. I know this doesn't absolve me—I have ultimate responsibility for everything that transpires in my Outlying Patrol District. But between relatives, Hoy, I am mentioning these facts to show that I was not completely clumsy in the situation and that a little help from you and the rest of the family, when the case reaches the Old One in Galactic Headquarters, would not merely be charity for a one-headed oafish cousin.

As a matter of fact, I and most of my office were involved in a very complex problem. A Moslem mystic, living in Saudi Arabia, had attempted to heal the ancient schism that exists in his religion between the Shiite and Sunnite sects, by communing with the departed spirits of Mohammed's son-in-law, Ali, the patron of the first group, and Abu Bekr, the Prophet's father-in-law and founder of the Sunnite dynasty. The object of the mediumistic excursion was to effect some sort of arbitration agreement in Paradise between the two feuding ghosts that would determine who should rightfully have been Mohammed's successor and the first caliph of Mecca.

Nothing is simple on Earth. In the course of this laudable probe of the hereafter, the earnest young mystic accidentally achieved telepathic contact with a Stage 9 civilization of disembodied intellects on Ganymede, the largest satellite of the planet Jupiter. Well, you can imagine! Tremendous uproar on Ganymede and in Saudi Arabia, pilgrims in both places flocking to see the individuals on either end of the telepathic connection, peculiar and magnificent miracles being wrought daily. A mess!

And my office feverishly working overtime to keep the whole affair simple and religious, trying to prevent it from splashing over into awareness of the more rational beings in each community! It's an axiom of Outlying Patrol Offices that nothing will stimulate space travel among backward peoples faster than definite knowledge of the existence of intelligent celestial neighbors. Frankly, if Pah-Chi-Luh had come to me right then, blathering of Gtetan pornography in human high-school textbooks, I'd probably have bitten his heads off.

He'd discovered the textbooks in the course of routine duties as an investigator for a United States Congressional Committee—his disguised status for the last decade or so, and one which had proved particularly valuable in the various delaying actions we had been surreptitiously fighting on the continent of North America. There was this newly published biology book, written for use in the secondary schools, which had received extremely favorable comment from outstanding scholars in the universities. Naturally, the committee ordered a copy of the text and suggested that its investigator look through it.

Corporal Pah-Chi-Luh turned a few pages and found himself staring at the very pornographic pictures he'd heard about at the briefing session six months before—published, available to everyone on Earth, and especially to minors! He told me afterward, brokenly, that in that instant all he saw was a brazen repetition of L'payr's ugly crime on his home planet.

He blasted out a galaxy-wide alarm for the Gtetan.

L'payr had begun life anew as an *ashkebac* craftsman on a small, out-of-the-way, mildly civilized world. Living carefully within the law, he had prospered and, at the time of his arrest, had become sufficiently conventional—and, incidentally, fat—to think of raising a respectable family. Not much—just two of him. If things continued to go well, he might consider multiple fission in the future.

He was indignant when he was arrested and carried off to the detention cell on Pluto, pending the arrival of an extradition party from Gtet.

"By what right do you disturb a peace-loving artisan in the quiet pursuit of his trade?" he challenged. "I demand immediate unconditional release, a full apology and restitution for loss of income as well as the embarrassment caused to my person and ego. Your superiors will hear of this! False arrest of a galactic citizen can be a very serious matter!"

"No doubt," Stellar Corporal Pah-Chi-Luh retorted, still quite equable, you see. "But the public dissemination of recognized pornography is even more serious. As a crime, we consider it on a level with—"

"*What* pornography?"

My assistant said he stared at L'payr for a long time through the transparent cell wall, marveling at the creature's effrontery. All the same, he began to feel a certain disquiet. He had never before encountered such complete self-assurance in the face of a perfect structure of criminal evidence.

"You know very well what pornography. Here—examine it for yourself. This is only one copy out of 20,000 distributed all over the United States of North America for the specific use of human adolescents." He dematerialized the biology text and passed it through the wall.

L'payr glanced at the pictures. "Bad reproduction," he commented. "Those humans still have a long way to go in many respects. However, they do display a pleasing technical precocity. But why show this to me? Surely, you don't think *I* have anything to do with it?"

Pah-Chi-Luh says the Gtetan seemed intensely puzzled, yet gently patient, as if he were trying to unravel the hysterical gibberings of an idiot child.

"Do you *deny* it?"

"What in the Universe is there to deny? Let me see." He turned to the title page. "This seems to be *A First Book in Biology* by one Osborne Blatch and one Nicodemus P. Smith. You haven't mistaken me for either Blatch or Smith, have you? My name is L'payr, not Osborne L'payr, nor even Nicodemus P. L'payr. Just plain, old, everyday, simple L'payr. No more, no less. I come from Gtet, which is the sixth planet of—"

"I am fully aware of Gtet's astrographic location," Pah-Chi-Luh informed him coldly. "Also, that you were on Earth six of their months ago. And that, at the time, you completed a transaction with this Osborne Blatch, whereby you got the fuel you needed to leave the planet, while Blatch obtained the set of pictures that were later used as illustrations in that textbook. Our undercover organization on Earth functions very efficiently, as you can see. We have labeled the book Exhibit A."

"An ingenious designation," said the Gtetan admiringly. "Exhibit A! With so much to choose from, you picked the one that sounds just right. My compliments." He was, you will understand, Hoy, in his element—he was dealing with a police official on an abstruse legal point. L'payr's entire brilliant criminal past on a law-despising world had prepared him for this moment. Pah-Chi-Luh's mental orientation, however, had for a long time now been chiefly in the direction of espionage and *sub rosa* cultural manipulation. He was totally unprepared for the orgy of judicial quibbles that was about to envelop him. In all fairness to him, let me admit that I might not have done any better under those circumstances and neither, for that matter, might you—nor the Old One himself!

L'payr pointed out, "All I did was to sell a set of artistic studies to one Osborne Blatch. What *he* did with it afterward surely does not concern me. If I sell a weapon of approved technological backwardness to an Earthman—a flint fist-axe, say, or a cauldron for pouring boiling oil upon the stormers of walled cities—and he uses the weapon to dispatch one of his fellow primitives, am I culpable? Not the way I read the existing statutes of the Galactic Federation, my friend. Now suppose you reimburse me for my time and trouble and put me on a fast ship bound for my place of business."

Around and around they went. Dozens of times, Pah-Chi-Luh, going frantically through the Pluto Headquarters law library, would come up with a nasty little wrinkle of an ordinance, only to have L'payr point out that the latest interpretation of the

Supreme Council put him wholly in the clear. I can myself vouch for the fact that the Gtetans seem to enjoy total recall of all judicial history.

"But you *do* admit selling pornography yourself to the Earthman Osborne Blatch?" the stellar corporal bellowed at last.

"Pornography, pornography," L'payr mused. "That would be defined as cheaply exciting lewdness, falsely titillating obscenity. Correct?"

"Of course!"

"Well, Corporal, let me ask you a question. You saw those pictures. Did you find them exciting or titillating?"

"Certainly not. But I don't happen to be a Gtetan ameboid."

"Neither," L'payr countered quietly, "is Osborne Blatch."

I do think Corporal Pah-Chi-Luh might have found some sensible way out of the dilemma if the extradition party had not just then arrived from Gtet on the special Patrol ship which had been sent for it. He now found himself confronted with six more magnificently argumentative ameboids, numbering among them some of the trickiest legal minds on the home planet. The police of Rugh VI had had many intricate dealings with L'payr in the Gtetan courts. Hence, they took no chances and sent their best representatives.

Outnumbered L'payr may have been, but remember, Hoy, he had prepared for just these eventualities ever since leaving Earth. And just to stimulate his devious intellect to maximum performance, there was the fact that *his* was the only life at stake. Once let his fellow ameboids get their pseudopods on him again, and he was a gone protozoan.

Between L'payr and the Gtetan extradition party, Corporal Pah-Chi-Luh began to find out how unhappy a policeman's lot can become. Back and forth he went, from the prisoner to the lawyers, stumbling through quagmires of opinion, falling into chasms of complexity.

The extradition group was determined not to return to their planet empty-pseudopodded. In order to succeed, they had to make the current arrest stick, which would give them the right—as previously injured parties—to assert their prior claim to the punishment of L'payr. For his part, L'payr was equally determined to invalidate the arrest by the Patrol, since then he would not only have placed our outfit in an uncomfortable position, but, no longer extraditable, would be entitled to its protection from his fellow citizens.

A weary, bleary and excessively hoarse Pah-Chi-Luh finally dragged himself to the extradition party on spindly tentacles and informed them that, after much careful consideration, he had come to the conclusion that L'payr was innocent of any crime during his stay on Earth.

"Nonsense," he was told by the spokesman. "A crime was committed. Arrant and unquestioned pornography was sold and circulated on that planet. A crime *has* to have been committed."

Pah-Chi-Luh went back to L'payr and asked, miserably, how about it? Didn't it seem, he almost pleaded, that all the necessary ingredients of a crime were present? *Some* kind of crime?

"True," L'payr said thoughtfully. "They have a point. Some kind of crime *may* have been committed—but not by me. Osborne Blatch, now…"

Stellar Corporal Pah-Chi-Luh completely lost his heads.

He sent a message to Earth, ordering Osborne Blatch to be picked up.

Fortunately for all of us, up to and including the Old One, Pah-Chi-Luh did not go so far as to have Blatch arrested. The Earthman was merely held as a material witness. When I think what the false arrest of a creature from a Secretly Supervised world could lead to, especially in a case of this sort, Hoy, my blood almost turns liquid.

But Pah-Chi-Luh *did* commit the further blunder of incarcerating Osborne Blatch in a cell adjoining L'payr's. Everything, you will observe, was working out to the ameboid's satisfaction—including my young assistant.

By the time Pah-Chi-Luh got around to Blatch's first interrogation, the Earthman had already been briefed by his neighbor. Not that the briefing was displayed overmuch—as yet.

"Pornography?" he repeated in answer to the first question. "*What* pornography? Mr. Smith and I had been working on an elementary biology text for some time and we were hoping to use new illustrations throughout. We wanted larger, clear pictures of the sort that would be instantly comprehensible to youngsters—and we were particularly interested in getting away from the blurry drawings that have been used and reused in all textbooks, almost from the time of Leeuwenhoek. Mr. L'payr's series on the cycle of ameboid reproduction was a godsend. In a sense, they *made* the first section of the book."

"You don't deny, however," Corporal Pah-Chi-Luh inquired remorselessly, "that, at the time of the purchase, you knew those pictures were pornographic? And that, despite this knowledge, you went ahead and used them for the delectation of juveniles of your race?"

"Edification," the elderly human schoolteacher corrected him. "*Edification,* not delectation. I assure you that not a single student who studied the photographs in question—which, by the way, appeared textually as drawings—received any premature erotic stimulation thereby. I will admit that, at the time of purchase, I did receive a distinct impression from the gentleman in the next cell that he and his kind considered the illustrations rather racy—"

"Well, then?"

"But that was his problem, not mine. After all, if I buy an artifact from an extraterrestrial creature—a flint fist-axe, say, or a cauldron for pouring boiling oil upon the stormers of walled cities—and I use them both in completely peaceful and useful pursuits—the former to grub onions out of the ground and the latter to cook the onions in a kind of soup—have I done anything wrong?

"As a matter of fact, the textbook in question received fine reviews and outstanding commendations from educational and scientific authorities all over the nation. Would you like to hear some of them? I believe I may have a review or two in my pockets. Let me see. Yes, just by chance, I seem to have a handful of clippings in this suit. Well, well! I didn't know there were quite so many. This is what the *Southern*

Prairie States Secondary School Gazette has to say—'A substantial and noteworthy achievement. It will live long in the annals of elementary science pedagoguery. The authors may well feel...' "

It was then that Corporal Pah-Chi-Luh sent out a despairing call for me.

Fortunately, I was free to give the matter my full attention, the Saudi Arabia-Ganymede affair being completely past the danger point. Had I been tied up...

After experimenting with all kinds of distractions, including secret agents disguised as dancing girls, we had finally managed to embroil the young mystic in a tremendous theological dispute on the exact nature and moral consequences of the miracles he was wreaking. Outstanding Mohammedan religious leaders of the region had lined up on one side or the other and turned the air blue with quotations from the Koran and later Sunnite books. The mystic was drawn in and became so involved in the argument that he stopped thinking about his original objectives and irreparably broke the mental connection with Ganymede.

For a while, this left a continuing problem on that satellite—it looked as if the civilization of disembodied intellects might eventually come to some approximation of the real truth. Luckily for us, the entire business had been viewed there also as a religious phenomenon and, once telepathic contact was lost, the intellect who had been communicating with the human, and had achieved much prestige thereby, was thoroughly discredited. It was generally believed that he had willfully and deliberately faked the entire thing, for the purpose of creating skepticism among the more spiritual members of his race. An ecclesiastical court ordered the unfortunate telepath to be embodied alive.

It was, therefore with a warm feeling of a job well done that I returned to my headquarters on Pluto in response to Pah-Chi-Luh's summons.

Needless to say, this feeling quickly changed to the most overpowering dismay. After getting the background from the overwrought corporal, I interviewed the Gtetan extradition force. They had been in touch with their home office and were threatening a major galactic scandal if the Patrol's arrest of L'payr was not upheld and L'payr remanded to their custody.

"Are the most sacred and intimate details of our sex life to be shamelessly flaunted from one end of the Universe to the other?" I was asked angrily. "Pornography is pornography—a crime is a crime. The intent was there—the overt act was there. We demand our prisoner."

"How can you have pornography without titillation?" L'payr wanted to know. "If a Chumblostian sells a Gtetan a quantity of *krrgllwss*—which they use as food and we use as building material—does the shipment have to be paid for under the nutritive or structural tariffs? The structural tariffs obtain, as you well know, Sergeant. I demand immediate release!"

But the most unpleasant surprise of all awaited me with Blatch. The terrestrial was sitting in his cell, sucking the curved handle of his umbrella.

"Under the code governing the treatment of all races on Secretly Supervised Status," he began as soon as he saw me, "and I refer not only to the Rigellian-Sagittarian

Convention, but to the statutes of the third cosmic cycle and the Supreme Council decisions in the cases of Khwomo vs. Khwomo and Farziplok vs. Antares XII, I demand return to my accustomed habitat on Earth, the payment of damages according to the schedule developed by the Nobri Commission in the latest Vivadin controversy. I also demand satisfaction in terms of—"

"You seem to have acquired a good deal of knowledge of interstellar law," I commented slowly.

"Oh, I have, Sergeant—I have. Mr. L'payr was most helpful in acquainting me with my rights. It seems that I am entitled to all sorts of recompenses—or, at least, that I can claim entitlement. You have a very interesting galactic culture, Sergeant. Many, many people on Earth would be fascinated to learn about it. But I am quite prepared to spare you the embarrassment which such publicity would cause you. I am certain that two reasonable individuals like ourselves can come to terms."

When I charged L'payr with violating galactic secrecy, he spread his cytoplasm in an elaborate ameboid shrug.

"*I told him nothing on Earth,* Sergeant. Whatever information this terrestrial has received—and I will admit that it would have been damaging and highly illegal—was entirely in the jurisdiction of *your* headquarters office. Besides, having been wrongfully accused of an ugly and unthinkable crime, I surely had the right to prepare my defense by discussing the matter with the only witness to the deed. I might go further and point out that, since Mr. Blatch and myself are in a sense co-defendants, there could be no valid objection to a pooling of our legal knowledge."

Back in my office, I brought Corporal Pah-Chi-Luh up to date.

"It's like a morass," he complained. "The more you struggle to get out, the deeper you fall in it! And this terrestrial! The Plutonian natives who've been guarding him have been driven almost crazy. He asks questions about everything—what's this, what's that, how does it work. Or it's not hot enough for him, the air doesn't smell right, his food is uninteresting. His throat has developed an odd tickle, he wants a gargle, he needs a—"

"Give him everything he wants, but within reason," I said. "If this creature dies on us, you and I will be lucky to draw no more than a punishment tour in the Black Hole in Cygnus. But as for the rest of it—look here, Corporal, I find myself in agreement with the extradition party from Gtet. A crime *has* to have been committed."

Stellar Corporal Pah-Chi-Luh stared at me. "You—you mean…"

"I mean that if a crime was committed, L'payr has been legally arrested and can therefore be taken back to Gtet. We will then hear no more from him ever and we will also be rid of that bunch of pseudopod-clacking Gtetan shysters. That will leave us with only one problem—Osborne Blatch. Once L'payr is gone and we have this terrestrial to ourselves, I think we can handle him—one way or another. But first and foremost, Corporal Pah-Chi-Luh, a crime—*some crime*—has to have been committed by L'payr during his sojourn on Earth. Set up your bed in the law library."

Shortly afterward, Pah-Chi-Luh left for Earth.

Now please, Hoy, no moralistic comments! You know as well as I do that this sort of thing has been done before, here and there, in Outlying Patrol Offices. I don't like it any more than you, but I was faced with a major emergency. Besides, there was no doubt but that this L'payr, ameboid master criminal, had had punishment deferred far too long. In fact, one might say that morally I was completely and absolutely in the right.

Pah-Chi-Luh returned to Earth, as I've said, this time disguised as an editorial assistant. He got a job in the publishing house that had brought out the biology text-book. The original photographs were still in the files of that establishment. By pick-ing his man carefully and making a good many mind-stimulating comments, the stellar corporal finally inspired one of the technical editors to examine the photo-graphs and have the material on which they were printed analyzed.

The material was *fahrtuch,* a synthetic textile much in use on Gtet and not due to be developed by humanity for at least three centuries.

In no time at all, almost every woman in America was wearing lingerie made of *farhtuch,* the novelty fabric of the year. And since L'payr was ultimately responsible for this illegal technological spurt, we at last had him where we wanted him!

He was very sporting about it, Hoy.

"The end of a long road for me, Sergeant. I congratulate you. Crime does not pay. Lawbreakers always lose. Law-enforcers always win."

I went off to prepare the extradition forms, without a care in the galaxy. There was Blatch, of course, but he was a mere human. And by this time, having gotten involved in all kinds of questionable dealings myself, I was determined to make quick work of him. After all, one might as well get blasted for a *skreek* as a *launt!*

But when I returned to escort the Gtetan to his fellow-ameboids, I almost fell through the surface of Pluto. Where there had been one L'payr, there were now two! Smaller L'payrs, of course—half the size of the original, to be exact—but L'payrs unmistakable.

In the interval, he had reproduced!

How? That gargle the Earthman had demanded, Hoy. It had been L'payr's idea all along, his last bit of insurance. Once the Earthman had received the gargle, he had smuggled it to L'payr, who had hidden it in his cell, intending to use it as a last resort.

That gargle, Hoy, was *salt water!* Saline solution, eh?

So there I was. The Gtetans informed me that their laws covered such possibili-ties, but much help *their* laws were to me.

"A crime has been committed, pornography has been sold," the spokesman reiter-ated. "We demand our prisoner. Both of him!"

"Pursuant to Galactic Statutes 6,009,371 through 6,106,514," Osborne Blatch in-sisted, "I demand immediate release, restitution to the extent of two billion Galactic Megawhars, a complete and written—"

And.

"It's probably true that our ancestor, L'payr, committed all sorts of indiscretions," lisped the two young ameboids in the cell next to Osborne Blatch, "but what does that have to do with us? L'payr paid for his crimes by dying in childbirth. We are very young and very, very innocent. Surely the big old galaxy doesn't believe in punishing little children for the sins of their parents!"

What would *you* have done?

I shipped the whole mess off to Patrol Headquarters—the Gtetan extradition party and their mess of judicial citations, Osborne Blatch and his umbrella, the biology textbook, the original bundle of pornographic pictures, and last but not at all least, two—count 'em, two—dewy young ameboids. Call them L'payr sub-one and L payr sub-two. Do anything you like with them when they get there, but please don't tell me what it is!

And if you can figure out a solution with the aid of some of the more ancient and wiser heads at headquarters, and figure it out before the Old One ruptures a gloccistomorph, Pah-Chi-Luh and I will be pathetically, eternally grateful.

If not—well, we're standing by here at Outlying Patrol Office 1001625 with bags packed. There's a lot to be said for the Black Hole in Cygnus.

Personally, Hoy, I'd say that the whole trouble is caused by creatures who insist on odd and colorful methods of continuing their race, instead of doing it sanely and decently by means of spore-pod explosion!

AFTERWORD

So I wrote a story about a seven-sexed creature. And it was damned complicated. So I wondered how complicated a story about a *one*-sexed creature might be.

So I wrote it.

Besides, I wanted to see what I could do with pornography for a one-sexed creature.

But, if I'm going to be perfectly honest, there was something else. Long after Ted Sturgeon had represented me, I had become involved with a literary agent who began embezzling money from me. (God knows, I had damn little to embezzle. But he, ingenious man, managed it.) As Ike Asimov put it, "Why should an agent pay his client ninety percent and keep only ten percent for himself? Isn't it more logical for him to keep ninety percent and pay *out* the ten percent? Anyone can write, after all, but how many people can *sell?*"

I looked up an old army buddy of mine, Milt Amgott, who had just sent me a card announcing that he was opening a law office with his partner, Phil Kassel. I told him that I had no money to pay him, but that was exactly why I needed him. He said that was okay, he'd represent me. And he got me everything I was owed from the agent.

The agent was so impressed that he retained Amgott as *his* lawyer. And so did his wife when she divorced him. And so, eventually, did a lot of other science fiction and mystery writers.

Meanwhile, I learned a lot about the law by hanging out with Milt Amgott and Phil Kassel. I got wistful about using some of that knowledge in a story. One day I used it—in a story about the legalities of ameboid pornography.

WRITTEN 1953——PUBLISHED 1954

Immodest Proposals

THE LIBERATION OF EARTH

This, then, is the story of our liberation. Suck air and grab clusters. Heigh-ho, here is the tale.

August was the month, a Tuesday in August. These words are meaningless now, so far have we progressed; but many things known and discussed by our primitive ancestors, our unliberated, unreconstructed forefathers, are devoid of sense to our free minds. Still the tale must be told, with all of its incredible place-names and vanished points of reference.

Why must it be told? Have any of you a *better* thing to do? We have had water and weeds and lie in a valley of gusts, So rest, relax and listen. And suck air, suck air.

On a Tuesday in August, the ship appeared in the sky over France in a part of the world then known as Europe. Five miles long the ship was, and word has come down to us that it looked like an enormous silver cigar.

The tale goes on to tell of the panic and consternation among our forefathers when the ship abruptly materialized in the summer-blue sky. How they ran, how they shouted, how they pointed!

How they excitedly notified the United Nations, one of their chiefest institutions, that a strange metal craft of incredible size had materialized over their land. How they sent an order *here* to cause military aircraft to surround it with loaded weapons, gave instructions *there* for hastily grouped scientists, with signaling apparatus, to approach it with friendly gestures. How, under the great ship, men with cameras took pictures of it; men with typewriters wrote stories about it; and men with concessions sold models of it.

All these things did our ancestors, enslaved and unknowing, do.

Then a tremendous slab snapped up in the middle of the ship, and the first of the aliens stepped out in the complex tripodal gait that all humans were shortly to know and love so well. He wore a metallic garment to protect him from the effects of our atmospheric peculiarities, a garment of the opaque, loosely folded type that these, the first of our liberators, wore throughout their stay on Earth.

Speaking in a language none could understand, but booming deafeningly through a huge mouth about halfway up his twenty-five feet of height, the alien discoursed for exactly one hour, waited politely for a response when he had finished, and, receiving none, retired into the ship.

That night, the first of our liberation! Or the first of our first liberation, should I say? *That* night, anyhow! Visualize our ancestors scurrying about their primitive intricacies: playing ice-hockey, televising, smashing atoms, red-baiting, conducting giveaway shows, and signing affidavits—all the incredible minutiae that made the olden times such a frightful mass of cumulative detail in which to live—as compared with the breathless and majestic simplicity of the present.

The big question, of course, was—what had the alien said? Had he called on the human race to surrender? Had he announced that he was on a mission of peaceful trade and, having made what he considered a reasonable offer—for, let us say, the north polar icecap—politely withdrawn so that we could discuss his terms among ourselves in relative privacy? Or, possibly, had he merely announced that he was the newly appointed ambassador to Earth from a friendly and intelligent race—and would we please direct him to the proper authority so that he might submit his credentials?

Not to know was quite maddening.

Since decision rested with the diplomats, it was the last possibility which was held, very late that night, to be most likely; and early the next morning, accordingly, a delegation from the United Nations waited under the belly of the motionless starship. The delegation had been instructed to welcome the aliens to the outermost limits of its collective linguistic ability. As an additional earnest of mankind's friendly intentions, all military craft patrolling the air about the great ship were ordered to carry no more than one atom bomb in their racks, and to fly a small white flag—along with the U.N. banner and their own national emblem. Thus did our ancestors face this, the ultimate challenge of history.

When the alien came forth a few hours later, the delegation stepped up to him, bowed, and, in the three official languages of the United Nations—English, French and Russian—asked him to consider this planet his home. He listened to them gravely, and then launched into his talk of the day before—which was evidently as highly charged with emotion and significance to him as it was completely incomprehensible to the representatives of world government.

Fortunately, a cultivated young Indian member of the secretariat detected a suspicious similarity between the speech of the alien and an obscure Bengali dialect whose anomalies he had once puzzled over. The reason, as we all know now, was that the last time Earth had been visited by aliens of this particular type, humanity's most advanced civilization lay in a moist valley in Bengal; extensive dictionaries of that language had been written, so that speech with the natives of Earth would present no problem to any subsequent exploring party.

However, I move ahead of my tale, as one who would munch on the succulent roots before the dryer stem. Let me rest and suck air for a moment. Heigh-ho, truly those were tremendous experiences for our kind.

You, sir, now you sit back and listen. You are not yet of an age to Tell the Tale. I remember, *well enough do I remember,* how my father told it, and his father before him. You will wait your turn as I did; you will listen until too much high land between water holes blocks me off from life.

Then *you* may take your place in the juiciest weed patch and, reclining gracefully between sprints, recite the great epic of our liberation to the carelessly exercising young.

Pursuant to the young Hindu's suggestions, the one professor of comparative linguistics in the world capable of understanding and conversing in this peculiar version of the dead dialect was summoned from an academic convention in New York, where he was reading a paper he had been working on for eighteen years: *An Initial Study of Apparent Relationships Between Several Past Participles in Ancient Sanskrit and an Equal Number of Noun Substantives in Modern Szechuanese.* ·

Yea, verily, all these things—and more, many more—did our ancestors in their besotted ignorance contrive to do. May we not count our freedoms indeed?

The disgruntled scholar, minus—as he kept insisting bitterly—some of his most essential word lists, was flown by fastest jet to the area south of Nancy which, in those long-ago days, lay in the enormous black shadow of the alien spaceship.

Here he was acquainted with his task by the United Nations delegation, whose nervousness had not been allayed by a new and disconcerting development. Several more aliens had emerged from the ship carrying great quantities of immense, shimmering metal which they proceeded to assemble into something that was obviously a machine—though it was taller than any skyscraper man had ever built, and seemed to make noises to itself like a talkative and sentient creature. The first alien still stood courteously in the neighborhood of the profusely perspiring diplomats; ever and anon he would go through his little speech again, in a language that had been almost forgotten when the cornerstone of the library of Alexandria was laid. The men from the U.N. would reply, each one hoping desperately to make up for the alien's lack of familiarity with his own tongue by such devices as hand gestures and facial expressions. Much later, a commission of anthropologists and psychologists brilliantly pointed out the difficulties in such physical, gestural communication with creatures possessing—as these aliens did—five manual appendages and a single, unwinking compound eye of the type the insects rejoice in.

The problems and agonies of the professor as he was trundled about the world in the wake of the aliens, trying to amass a usable vocabulary in a language whose peculiarities he could only extrapolate from the limited samples supplied him by one who must inevitably speak it with the most outlandish of foreign accents—these vexations were minor indeed compared to the disquiet felt by the representatives of world government. They beheld the extraterrestrial visitors move every day to a new site on their planet and proceed to assemble there a titanic structure of flickering metal which muttered nostalgically to itself, as if to keep alive the memory of those faraway factories which had given it birth.

True, there was always the alien who would pause in his evidently supervisory labors to release the set little speech; but not even the excellent manners he displayed, in listening to upward of fifty-six replies in as many languages, helped dispel the panic caused whenever a human scientist, investigating the shimmering machines, touched a projecting edge and promptly shrank into a disappearing pinpoint. This, while not a frequent occurrence, happened often enough to cause chronic indigestion and insomnia among human administrators.

Finally, having used up most of his nervous system as fuel, the professor collated enough of the language to make conversation possible. He—and, through him, the world—was thereupon told the following:

The aliens were members of a highly advanced civilization which had spread its culture throughout the entire galaxy. Cognizant of the limitations of the as-yet-underdeveloped animals who had latterly become dominant upon Earth, they had placed us in a sort of benevolent ostracism. Until either we or our institutions had evolved to a level permitting, say, at least *associate* membership in the galactic federation (under the sponsoring tutelage, for the first few millennia, of one of the older, more widespread and important species in that federation)—until that time, all invasions of our privacy and ignorance—except for a few scientific expeditions conducted under conditions of great secrecy—had been strictly forbidden by universal agreement.

Several individuals who had violated this ruling—at great cost to our racial sanity, and enormous profit to our reigning religions—had been so promptly and severely punished that no known infringements had occurred for some time. Our recent growth-curve had been satisfactory enough to cause hopes that a bare thirty or forty centuries more would suffice to place us on applicant status with the federation.

Unfortunately, the peoples of this stellar community were many, and varied as greatly in their ethical outlook as in their biological composition. Quite a few species lagged a considerable social distance behind the Dendi, as our visitors called themselves. One of these, a race of horrible, worm-like organisms known as the Troxxt—almost as advanced technologically as they were retarded in moral development—had suddenly volunteered for the position of sole and absolute ruler of the galaxy. They had seized control of several key suns, with their attendant planetary systems, and, after a calculated decimation of the races thus captured, had announced their intention of punishing with a merciless extinction all species unable to appreciate from these object-lessons the value of unconditional surrender.

In despair, the galactic federation had turned to the Dendi, one of the oldest, most selfless, and yet most powerful of races in civilized space, and commissioned them—as the military arm of the federation—to hunt down the Troxxt, defeat them wherever they had gained illegal suzerainty, and destroy forever their power to wage war.

This order had come almost too late. Everywhere the Troxxt had gained so much the advantage of attack that the Dendi were able to contain them only by enormous sacrifice. For centuries now, the conflict had careened across our vast island universe. In the course of it, densely populated planets had been disintegrated; suns had been blasted into novae; and whole groups of stars ground into swirling cosmic dust.

A temporary stalemate had been reached a short while ago, and—reeling and breathless—both sides were using the lull to strengthen weak spots in their perimeter.

Thus, the Troxxt had finally moved into the till-then peaceful section of space that contained our solar system—among others. They were thoroughly uninterested in our tiny planet with its meager resources, nor did they care much for such celestial neighbors as Mars or Jupiter. They established their headquarters on a planet of Proxima Centauri—the star nearest our own sun—and proceeded to consolidate their offensive-defensive network between Rigel and Aldebaran. At this point in their explanation, the Dendi pointed out, the exigencies of interstellar strategy tended to become too complicated for anything but three-dimensional maps; let us here accept the simple statement, they suggested, that it became immediately vital for them to strike rapidly, and make the Troxxt position on Proxima Centauri untenable—to establish a base inside their lines of communication.

The most likely spot for a such a base was Earth.

The Dendi apologized profusely for intruding on our development, an intrusion which might cost us dear in our delicate developmental state. But, as they explained—in impeccable pre-Bengali—before their arrival we had, in effect, become (all unknowingly) a satrapy of the awful Troxxt. We could now consider ourselves liberated.

We thanked them much for that.

Besides, their leader pointed out proudly, the Dendi were engaged in a war for the sake of civilization itself, against an enemy so horrible, so obscene in its nature, and so utterly filthy in its practices, that it was unworthy of the label of intelligent life. They were fighting, not only for themselves, but for every loyal member of the galactic federation; for every small and helpless species; for every obscure race too weak to defend itself against a ravaging conqueror. Would humanity stand aloof from such a conflict?

There was just a slight bit of hesitation as the information was digested. Then—"No!" humanity roared back through such mass-communication media as television, newspapers, reverberating jungle drums, and mule-mounted backwoods messenger. "We will not stand aloof! We will help you destroy this menace to the very fabric of civilization! Just tell us what you want us to do!"

Well, nothing in particular, the aliens replied with some embarrassment. Possibly in a little while there might be something—several little things, in fact—which could be quite useful; but, for the moment, if we would concentrate on not getting in their way when they serviced their gun-mounts, they would be very grateful, really....

This reply tended to create a large amount of uncertainty among the two billion of Earth's human population. For several days afterward, there was a planet-wide tendency—the legend has come down to us—of people failing to meet each other's eyes.

But then Man rallied from this substantial blow to his pride. He would be useful, be it ever so humbly, to the race which had liberated him from potential subjugation by the ineffably ugly Troxxt. For this, let us remember well our ancestors! Let us hymn their sincere efforts amid their ignorance!

All standing armies, all air and sea fleets, were reorganized into guard-patrols around the Dendi weapons; no human might approach within two miles of the murmuring machinery without a pass countersigned by the Dendi. Since they were never known to sign such a pass during the entire period of their stay on this planet, however, this loophole-provision was never exercised as far as is known; and the immediate neighborhood of the extraterrestrial weapons became and remained henceforth wholesomely free of two-legged creatures.

Cooperation with our liberators took precedence over all other human activities. The order of the day was a slogan first given voice by a Harvard professor of government in a querulous radio round table on "Man's Place in a Somewhat Overcivilized Universe."

"Let us forget our individual egos and collective conceits," the professor cried at one point. "Let us subordinate everything—to the end that the freedom of the solar system in general, and Earth in particular, must and shall be preserved!"

Despite its mouth-filling qualities, this slogan was repeated everywhere. Still, it was difficult sometimes to know exactly what the Dendi wanted—partly because of the limited number of interpreters available to the heads of the various sovereign states, and partly because of their leader's tendency to vanish into his ship after ambiguous and equivocal statements—such as the curt admonition to "Evacuate Washington!"

On that occasion, both the Secretary of State and the American President perspired fearfully through five hours of a July day in all the silk-hatted, stiff-collared, dark-suited diplomatic regalia that the barbaric past demanded of political leaders who would deal with the representatives of another people. They waited and wilted beneath the enormous ship—which no human had ever been invited to enter, despite the wistful hints constantly thrown out by university professors and aeronautical designers—they waited patiently and wetly for the Dendi leader to emerge and let them know whether he had meant the State of Washington or Washington, D.C.

The tale comes down to us at this point as a tale of glory. The capitol building taken apart in a few days and set up almost intact in the foothills of the Rocky Mountains; the missing Archives that were later to turn up in the Children's Room of a Public Library in Duluth, Iowa; the bottles of Potomac River water carefully borne westward and ceremoniously poured into the circular concrete ditch built around the President's mansion (from which, unfortunately, it was to evaporate within a week because of the relatively low humidity of the region)—all these are proud moments in the galactic history of our species, from which not even the later knowledge that the Dendi wished to build no gun site on the spot, nor even an ammunition dump, but merely a recreation hall for their troops, could remove any of the grandeur of our determined cooperation and most willing sacrifice.

There is no denying, however, that the ego of our race was greatly damaged by the discovery, in the course of a routine journalistic interview, that the aliens totaled no more powerful a group than a squad; and that their leader, instead of the great scientist and key military strategist that we might justifiably have expected the Galactic Federation to furnish for the protection of Terra, ranked as the interstellar equivalent of a buck sergeant.

That the President of the United States, the Commander-in-Chief of the Army and the Navy, had waited in such obeisant fashion upon a mere noncommissioned officer was hard for us to swallow, but that the impending Battle of Earth was to have a historical dignity only slightly higher than that of a patrol action was impossibly humiliating.

And then there was the matter of "lendi."

The aliens, while installing or servicing their planetwide weapon system, would occasionally fling aside an evidently unusable fragment of the talking metal. Separate from the machine of which it had been a component, the substance seemed to lose all those qualities which were deleterious to mankind and retain several which were quite useful indeed. For example, if a portion of the strange material was attached to any terrestrial metal—and insulated carefully from contact with other substances—it would, in a few hours, itself become exactly the metal that it touched, whether that happened to be zinc, gold, or pure uranium.

This stuff—"lendi," men have heard the aliens call it—was shortly in frantic demand in an economy ruptured by constant and unexpected emptyings of its most important industrial centers.

Everywhere the aliens went, to and from their weapon sites, hordes of ragged humans stood chanting—well outside the two-mile limit—"Any lendi, Dendi?" All attempts by law-enforcement agencies of the planet to put a stop to this shameless, wholesale begging were useless—especially since the Dendi themselves seemed to get some unexplainable pleasure out of scattering tiny pieces of lendi to the scrabbling multitude. When policemen and soldiery began to join the trampling, murderous dash to the corner of the meadows wherein had fallen the highly versatile and garrulous metal, governments gave up.

Mankind almost began to hope for the attack to come, so that it would be relieved of the festering consideration of its own patent inferiorities. A few of the more fanatically conservative among our ancestors probably even began to regret liberation.

They did, children; they did! Let us hope that these would-be troglodytes were among the very first to be dissolved and melted down by the red flame-balls. One cannot, after all, turn one's back on progress!

Two days before the month of September was over, the aliens announced that they had detected activity upon one of the moons of Saturn. The Troxxt were evidently threading their treacherous way inward through the solar system. Considering their vicious and deceitful propensities, the Dendi warned, an attack from these worm-like monstrosities might be expected at any moment.

Few humans went to sleep as the night rolled up to and past the meridian on which they dwelt. Almost all eyes were lifted to a sky carefully denuded of clouds by watchful Dendi. There was a brisk trade in cheap telescopes and bits of smoked glass in some sections of the planet, while other portions experienced a substantial boom in spells and charms of the all-inclusive, or omnibus, variety.

The Troxxt attacked in three cylindrical black ships simultaneously: one in the Southern Hemisphere, and two in the Northern. Great gouts of green flame roared out of their tiny craft, and everything touched by this imploded into a translucent, glass-like sand. No Dendi was hurt by these, however, and from each of the now-writhing gun mounts there bubbled forth a series of scarlet clouds which pursued the Troxxt hungrily, until forced by a dwindling velocity to fall back upon Earth.

Here they had an unhappy after-effect. Any populated area into which these pale pink cloudlets chanced to fall was rapidly transformed into a cemetery—a cemetery, if the truth be told as it has been handed down to us, that had more the odor of the kitchen than the grave. The inhabitants of these unfortunate localities were subjected to enormous increases of temperature. Their skin reddened, then blackened; their hair and nails shriveled; their very flesh turned into liquid and boiled off their bones. Altogether a disagreeable way for one-tenth of the human race to die.

The only consolation was the capture of a black cylinder by one of the red clouds. When, as a result of this, it had turned white-hot and poured its substance down in the form of a metallic rainstorm, the two ships assaulting the Northern Hemisphere abruptly retreated to the asteroids into which the Dendi—because of severely lim-ited numbers steadfastly refused to pursue them.

In the next twenty-four hours, the aliens—*resident* aliens, let us say—held con-ferences, made repairs to their weapons, and commiserated with us. Humanity bur-ied its dead. This last was a custom of our forefathers that was most worthy of note, and one that has not, of course, survived into modern times.

By the time the Troxxt returned, Man was ready for them. He could not, unfortu-nately, stand to arms as he most ardently desired to do, but he could and did stand to optical instrument and conjurer's oration.

Once more the little red clouds burst joyfully into the upper reaches of the strato-sphere; once more the green flames wailed and tore at the chattering spires of lendi; once more men died by the thousands in the boiling backwash of war. But this time, there was a slight difference: the green flames of the Troxxt abruptly changed color after the engagement had lasted three hours; they became darker, more bluish. And, as they did so, Dendi after Dendi collapsed at his station and died in convulsions.

The call for retreat was evidently sounded. The survivors fought their way to the tremendous ship in which they had come. With an explosion from her stern jets that blasted a red-hot furrow southward through France, and kicked Marseilles into the Mediterranean, the ship roared into space and fled home ignominiously.

Humanity steeled itself for the coming ordeal of horror under the Troxxt.

They were truly worm-like in form. As soon as the two night-black cylinders had landed, they strode from their ships, their tiny segmented bodies held off the ground by a complex harness supported by long and slender metal crutches. They erected a dome-like fort around each ship—one in Australia and one in the Ukraine—cap-tured the few courageous individuals who had ventured close to their landing sites, and disappeared back into the dark craft with their squirming prizes.

While some men drilled about nervously in the ancient military patterns, others pored anxiously over scientific texts and records pertaining to the visit of the Dendi—in the desperate hope of finding a way of preserving terrestrial independence against this ravening conqueror of the star-spattered galaxy.

And yet all this time, the human captives inside the artificially darkened spaceships (the Troxxt, having no eyes, not only had little use for light, but the more sedentary individuals among them actually found such radiation disagreeable to their sensitive, unpigmented skins) were not being tortured for information—nor vivisected in the earnest quest of knowledge on a slightly higher level—but educated.

Educated in the Troxxtian language, that is.

True it was that a large number found themselves utterly inadequate for the task which the Troxxt had set them, and temporarily became servants to the more successful students. And another, albeit smaller, group developed various forms of frustration hysteria—ranging from mild unhappiness to complete catatonic depression—over the difficulties presented by a language whose every verb was irregular, and whose myriads of prepositions were formed by noun-adjective combinations derived from the subject of the previous sentence. But, eventually, eleven human beings were released, to blink madly in the sunlight as certified interpreters of Troxxt.

These liberators, it seemed, had never visited Bengal in the heyday of its millennia-past civilization.

Yes, these *liberators*. For the Troxxt had landed on the sixth day of the ancient, almost mythical month of October. And October the Sixth is, of course, the Holy Day of the Second Liberation. Let us remember, let us revere. (If only we could figure out which day it is in our calendar!)

The tale the interpreters told caused men to hang their heads in shame and gnash their teeth at the deception they had allowed the Dendi to practice upon them.

True, the Dendi had been commissioned by the Galactic Federation to hunt the Troxxt down and destroy them. This was largely because the Dendi *were* the Galactic Federation. One of the first intelligent arrivals on the interstellar scene, the huge creatures had organized a vast police force to protect them and their power against any contingency of revolt that might arise in the future. This police force was ostensibly a congress of all thinking life forms throughout the galaxy; actually, it was an efficient means of keeping them under rigid control.

Most species thus-far discovered were docile and tractable, however; the Dendi had been ruling from time immemorial, said they—very well, then, let the Dendi continue to rule. Did it make that much difference?

But, throughout the centuries, opposition to the Dendi grew—and the nuclei of the opposition were the protoplasm-based creatures. What, in fact, had come to be known as the Protoplasmic League.

Though small in number, the creatures whose life cycles were derived from the chemical and physical properties of protoplasm varied greatly in size, structure, and specialization. A galactic community deriving the main wells of its power from them would be a dynamic instead of a static place, where extragalactic travel would be encouraged, instead of being inhibited, as it was at present because of Dendi fears of meeting a superior civilization. It would be a true democracy of species—a real biological republic—where all creatures of adequate intelligence and cultural development would enjoy a control of their destinies at present experienced by the silicon-based Dendi alone.

To this end, the Troxxt—the only important race which had steadfastly refused the complete surrender of armaments demanded of all members of the Federation—had been implored by a minor member of the Protoplasmic League to rescue it from the devastation which the Dendi intended to visit upon it, as punishment for an unlawful exploratory excursion outside the boundaries of the galaxy.

Faced with the determination of the Troxxt to defend their cousins in organic chemistry, and the suddenly aroused hostility of at least two-thirds of the interstellar peoples, the Dendi had summoned a rump meeting of the Galactic Council; declared a state of revolt in being; and proceeded to cement their disintegrating rule with the blasted life-forces of a hundred worlds. The Troxxt, hopelessly outnumbered and out-equipped, had been able to continue the struggle only because of the great ingenuity and selflessness of other members of the Protoplasmic League, who had risked extinction to supply them with newly developed secret weapons.

Hadn't we guessed the nature of the beast from the enormous precautions it had taken to prevent the exposure of any part of its body to the intensely corrosive atmosphere of Earth? Surely the seamless, barely translucent suits which our recent visitors had worn for every moment of their stay on our world should have made us suspect a body chemistry developed from complex silicon compounds rather than those of carbon?

Humanity hung its collective head and admitted that the suspicion had never occurred to it.

Well, the Troxxt admitted generously, we were extremely inexperienced and possibly a little too trusting. Put it down to that. Our naiveté, however costly to them—our liberators—would not be allowed to deprive us of that complete citizenship which the Troxxt were claiming as the birthright of all.

But as for our leaders, our probably corrupted, certainly irresponsible leaders…

The first executions of U.N. officials, heads of states, and pre-Bengali interpreters as "Traitors to Protoplasm"—after some of the lengthiest and most nearly-perfectly-fair trials in the history of Earth—were held a week after G-J Day (Galaxy-Joining Day), the inspiring occasion on which—amidst gorgeous ceremonies—Humanity was invited to join, first the Protoplasmic League and thence the New and Democratic Galactic Federation of All Species, All Races.

Nor was that all. Whereas the Dendi had contemptuously shoved us to one side as they went about their business of making our planet safe for tyranny, and had—in all probability—built special devices which made the very touch of their weapons fatal for us, the Troxxt—with the sincere friendliness which had made their name a byword for democracy and decency wherever living creatures came together among the stars—our Second Liberators, as we lovingly called them, actually *preferred* to have us help them with the intensive, accelerating labor of planetary defense.

So humanity's intestines dissolved under the invisible glare of the forces used to assemble the new, incredibly complex weapons; men sickened and died, in scrabbling hordes, inside the mines which the Troxxt had made deeper than any we had dug hitherto; men's bodies broke open and exploded in the undersea oil-drilling sites which the Troxxt had declared were essential.

Children's schooldays were requested, too, in such collecting drives as "Platinum Scrap for Procyon" and "Radioactive Debris for Deneb." Housewives also were implored to save on salt whenever possible—this substance being useful to the Troxxt in literally dozens of incomprehensible ways—and colorful posters reminded: *"Don't salinate—sugarfy!"*

And over all—courteously caring for us like an intelligent parent—were our mentors, taking their giant supervisory strides on metallic crutches while their pale little bodies lay curled in the hammocks that swung from each paired length of shining leg.

Truly, even in the midst of a complete economic paralysis caused by the concentration of all major productive facilities on other-worldly armaments, and despite the anguished cries of those suffering from peculiar industrial injuries which our medical men were totally unequipped to handle, in the midst of all this mind-wracking disorganization, it was yet very exhilarating to realize that we had taken our lawful place in the future government of the galaxy and were even now helping to make the Universe Safe for Democracy.

But the Dendi returned to smash this idyll. They came in their huge, silvery spaceships, and the Troxxt, barely warned in time, just managed to rally under the blow and fight back in kind. Even so, the Troxxt ship in the Ukraine was almost immediately forced to flee to its base in the depths of space. After three days, the only Troxxt on Earth were the devoted members of a little band guarding the ship in Australia. They proved, in three or more months, to be as difficult to remove from the face of our planet as the continent itself; and since there was now a state of close and hostile siege, with the Dendi on one side of the globe and the Troxxt on the other, the battle assumed frightful proportions.

Seas boiled; whole steppes burned away; the climate itself shifted and changed under the grueling pressure of the cataclysm. By the time the Dendi solved the problem, the planet Venus had been blasted from the skies in the course of a complicated battle maneuver, and Earth had wobbled over as orbital substitute.

The solution was simple: since the Troxxt were too firmly based on the small continent to be driven away, the numerically superior Dendi brought up enough firepower to disintegrate all Australia into an ash that muddied the Pacific. This occurred on the twenty-fourth of June, the Holy Day of First Reliberation. A day of reckoning for what remained of the human race, however.

How could we have been so naive, the Dendi wanted to know, as to be taken in by the chauvinistic pro-protoplasm propaganda? Surely, if physical characteristics were to be the criteria of our racial empathy, we would not orient ourselves on a narrow chemical basis! The Dendi life-plasma was based on silicon instead of carbon, true, but did not vertebrates—*appendaged* vertebrates, at that, such as we and the Dendi— have infinitely more in common, in spite of a *minor* biochemical difference or two, than vertebrates and legless, armless, slime-crawling creatures who happened, quite accidentally, to possess an identical organic substance?

As for this fantastic picture of life in the galaxy...*Well!* The Dendi shrugged their quintuple shoulders as they went about the intricate business of erecting their noisy weapons all over the rubble of our planet. Had we ever seen a representative of these protoplasmic races the Troxxt were supposedly protecting? No, nor would we. For as soon as a race—animal, vegetable, or mineral—developed enough to constitute even a *potential* danger to the sinuous aggressors, its civilization was systematically dismantled by the watchful Troxxt. We were in so primitive a state that they had not considered it at all risky to allow us the outward seeming of full participation.

Could we say we had learned a single useful piece of information about Troxxt technology—for all of the work we had done on their machines, for all of the lives we had lost in the process? No, of course not! We had merely contributed our mite to the enslavement of far-off races who had done us no harm.

There was much that we had cause to feel guilty about, the Dendi told us gravely— once the few surviving interpreters of the pre-Bengali dialect had crawled out of hiding. But our collective onus was as nothing compared to that borne by "vermicular collaborationists"—those traitors who had supplanted our martyred former leaders. And then there were the unspeakable human interpreters who had had linguistic traffic with creatures destroying a two-million-year-old galactic peace! Why, killing was almost too good for them, the Dendi murmured as they killed them.

When the Troxxt ripped their way back into possession of Earth some eighteen months later, bringing us the sweet fruits of the Second Reliberation—as well as a complete and most convincing rebuttal of the Dendi—there were few humans found who were willing to accept with any real enthusiasm the responsibilities of newly opened and highly paid positions in language, science, and government.

Of course, since the Troxxt, in order to reliberate Earth, had found it necessary to blast a tremendous chunk out of the Northern Hemisphere, there were very few humans to be found in the first place....

Even so, many of these committed suicide rather than assume the title of Secretary General of the United Nations when the Dendi came back for the glorious Re-Reliberation, a short time after that. This was the liberation, by the way, which swept the deep collar of matter off our planet, and gave it what our forefathers came to call a pear-shaped look.

Possibly it was at this time—possibly a liberation or so later—that the Troxxt and the Dendi discovered the Earth had become far too eccentric in its orbit to possess the minimum safety conditions demanded of a Combat Zone. The battle, therefore, zigzagged coruscatingly and murderously away in the direction of Aldebaran.

That was nine generations ago, but the tale that has been handed down from parent to child, to child's child, has lost little in the telling. You hear it now from me almost exactly as *I* heard it. From my father I heard it as I ran with him from water puddle to distant water puddle, across the searing heat of yellow sand. From my mother I heard it as we sucked air and frantically grabbed at clusters of thick green weed, whenever the planet beneath us quivered in omen of a geological spasm that might bury us in its burned-out body, or a cosmic gyration threatened to fling us into empty space.

Yes, even as we do now did we do then, telling the same tale, running the same frantic race across miles of unendurable heat for food and water; fighting the same savage battles with the giant rabbits for each other's carrion—and always, ever and always, sucking desperately at the precious air, which leaves our world in greater quantities with every mad twist of its orbit.

Naked, hungry, and thirsty came we into the world, and naked, hungry, and thirsty do we scamper our lives out upon it, under the huge and never-changing sun.

The same tale it is, and the same traditional ending it has as that I had from my father and his father before him. Suck air, grab clusters, and hear the last holy observation of our history:

"Looking about us, we can say with pardonable pride that we have been about as thoroughly liberated as it is possible for a race and a planet to be!"

AFTERWORD

Though this story was read aloud during protests by students in the nineteen sixties at rallies opposing our participation in the Vietnam War, it was actually written during and about the Korean War, a decade earlier.

My feelings about that situation were really quite simple.

North Korea invaded South Korea across the thirty-eighth parallel. The United States, acting for the United Nations (read, please, the Galactic Federation), came to the aid of South Korea, driving the North Koreans all the way back. Thereupon, the People's Republic of China, with the backing of the Soviet Union, came to the aid of North Korea, driving the U.S. forces back in turn. The entire matter has not been entirely resolved to this day, leaving the country in a kind of military stasis, with armistice and peace talks coming up in a desultory fashion at Panmunjom, the approximate midpoint.

The period covered was roughly the same as the Red-scare years that began with the Dies Committee and ended with the Senate censure of Joseph McCarthy in 1954. As a result, the organized Left inveighed against what it called "Truman's War," and urged us to get the hell out of Korea; the official Right not only supported the war but considered it perhaps the most crucial element in the battle against the godless Communists.

In writing the story, all I wanted to do was point out what a really awful thing it was to be a Korean (and later a Vietnamese) in such a situation. (But recently I have come to the conclusion that if I *had* been a Korean, North or South, under those same circumstances, I would very much have welcomed the U.S. intervention. Am I growing old? Or just official?)

As was pretty much the case with "Brooklyn Project," absolutely none of the top science-fiction magazines wanted to touch the story. It was finally purchased by Bob Lowndes of Columbia Publications for his *Future Science Fiction,* then the butcher-paper bottom of the field.

When I at last read the story in print, I was quite proud of it. But nobody, absolutely nobody, seemed to notice it.

Not even the F.B.I.

WRITTEN 1950———PUBLISHED 1953

❧

Eastward Ho!

The New Jersey Turnpike had been hard on the horses. South of New Brunswick the potholes had been so deep, the scattered boulders so plentiful, that the two men had been forced to move at a slow trot, to avoid crippling their three precious animals. And, of course, this far south, farms were nonexistent; they had been able to eat nothing but the dried provisions in the saddlebags, and last night they had slept in a roadside service station, suspending their hammocks between the tilted, rusty gas pumps.

But it was still the best, the most direct route, Jerry Franklin knew. The Turnpike was a government road: its rubble was cleared semiannually. They had made excellent time and come through without even developing a limp in the pack horse. As they swung out on the last lap, past the riven tree stump with the words TRENTON EXIT carved on its side, Jerry relaxed a bit. His father, his father's colleagues, would be proud of him. And he was proud of himself.

But the next moment, he was alert again. He roweled his horse, moved up alongside his companion, a young man of his own age.

"Protocol," he reminded. "I'm the leader here. You know better than to ride ahead of me this close to Trenton."

He hated to pull rank. But facts were facts, and if a subordinate got above himself he was asking to be set down. After all, he was the son—and the oldest son, at that—of the Senator from Idaho; Sam Rutherford's father was a mere Undersecretary of State and Sam's mother's family was pure post-office clerk all the way back.

Sam nodded apologetically and reined his horse back the proper couple of feet. "Thought I saw something odd," he explained. "Looked like an advance party on the side of the road—and I could have sworn they were wearing buffalo robes."

"Seminole don't wear buffalo robes, Sammy. Don't you remember your sophomore political science?"

"I never had any political science, Mr. Franklin: I was an engineering major. Digging around in ruins has always been my dish. But from the little I know, I didn't *think* buffalo robes went with the Seminole. That's why I was—"

"Concentrate on the pack horse," Jerry advised. "Negotiations are my job."

As he said this, he was unable to refrain from touching the pouch upon his breast with rippling fingertips. Inside it was his commission, carefully typed on one of the last precious sheets of official government stationery (and it was not one whit less official because the reverse side had been used years ago as a scribbled interoffice memo) and signed by the President himself. In ink!

187

The existence of such documents was important to a man in later life. He would have to hand it over, in all probability, during the conferences, but the commission to which it attested would be on file in the capital up north.

And when his father died, and he took over one of the two hallowed Idaho seats, it would give him enough stature to make an attempt at membership on the Appropriations Committee. Or, for that matter, why not go the whole hog—the Rules Committee itself? No Senator Franklin had ever been a member of the Rules Committee....

The two envoys knew they were on the outskirts of Trenton when they passed the first gangs of Jerseyites working to clear the road. Frightened faces glanced at them briefly, and quickly bent again to work. The gangs were working without any visible supervision. Evidently the Seminole felt that simple instructions were sufficient.

But as they rode into the blocks of neat ruins that were the city proper and still came across nobody more important than white men, another explanation began to occur to Jerry Franklin. This all had the look of a town still at war, but where were the combatants? Almost certainly on the other side of Trenton, defending the Delaware River—that was the direction from which the new rulers of Trenton might fear attack—not from the north where there was only the United States of America.

But if that were so, who in the world could they be defending against? Across the Delaware to the south there was nothing but more Seminole. Was it possible—was it possible that the Seminole had at last fallen to fighting among themselves?

Or was it possible that Sam Rutherford had been right? Fantastic. Buffalo robes in Trenton! There should be no buffalo robes closer than a hundred miles westward, in Harrisburg.

But when they turned onto State Street, Jerry bit his lip in chagrin. Sam had seen correctly, which made him one up.

Scattered over the wide lawn of the gutted state capitol were dozens of wigwams. And the tall, dark men who sat impassively, or strode proudly among the wigwams, all wore buffalo robes. There was no need even to associate the paint on their faces with a remembered lecture in political science: these were Sioux.

So the information that had come drifting up to the government about the identity of the invader was totally inaccurate—as usual. Well, you couldn't expect communication miracles over this long a distance. But that inaccuracy made things difficult. It might invalidate his commission, for one thing: his commission was addressed directly to Osceola VII, Ruler of All the Seminoles. And if Sam Rutherford thought this gave him a right to preen himself—

He looked back dangerously. No, Sam would give no trouble. Sam knew better than to dare an I-told-you-so. At his leader's look, the son of the Undersecretary of State dropped his eyes groundwards in immediate humility.

Satisfied, Jerry searched his memory for relevant data on recent political relationships with the Sioux. He couldn't recall much—just the provisions of the last two or three treaties. It would have to do.

He drew up before an important-looking warrior and carefully dismounted. You might get away with talking to a Seminole while mounted, but not the Sioux. The Sioux were very tender on matters of protocol with white men.

"We come in peace," he said to the warrior standing as impassively straight as the spear he held, as stiff and hard as the rifle on his back. "We come with a message of importance and many gifts to your chief. We come from New York, the home of our chief." He thought a moment, then added: "You know, the Great White Father?"

Immediately, he was sorry for the addition. The warrior chuckled briefly; his eyes lit up with a lightning-stroke of mirth. Then his face was expressionless again, and serenely dignified as befitted a man who had counted coup many times.

"Yes," he said. "I have heard of him. Who has not heard of the wealth and power and far dominions of the Great White Father? Come. I will take you to our chief. Walk behind me, white man."

Jerry motioned Sam Rutherford to wait.

At the entrance to a large, expensively decorated tent, the Indian stood aside and casually indicated that Jerry should enter.

It was dim inside, but the illumination was rich enough to take Jerry's breath away. Oil lamps! Three of them! These people lived well.

A century ago, before the whole world had gone smash in the last big war, his people had owned plenty of oil lamps themselves. Better than oil lamps, perhaps, if one could believe the stories the engineers told around the evening fires. Such stories were pleasant to hear, but they were glories of the distant past. Like the stories of overflowing granaries and chock-full supermarkets, they made you proud of the history of your people, but they did nothing for you now. They made your mouth water, but they didn't feed you.

The Indians whose tribal organization had been the first to adjust to the new conditions, in the all-important present, the Indians had the granaries, the Indians had the oil lamps. And the Indians...

There were two nervous white men serving food to the group squatting on the floor. There was an old man, the chief, with a carved, chunky body. Three warriors, one of them surprisingly young for council. And a middle-aged Negro, wearing the same bound-on rags as Franklin, except that they looked a little newer, a little cleaner.

Jerry bowed low before the chief, spreading his arms apart, palms down.

"I come from New York, from our chief," he mumbled. In spite of himself, he was more than a little frightened. He wished he knew their names so that he could relate them to specific events. Although he knew what their names would be like—approximately. The Sioux, the Seminole, all the Indian tribes renaissant in power and numbers, all bore names garlanded with anachronism. That queer mixture of several levels of the past, overlaid always with the cocky, expanding present. Like the rifle *and* the spears, one for the reality of fighting, the other for the symbol that was more important than reality. Like the use of wigwams on campaign, when, according to the rumors that drifted smokily across country, their slave artisans could now build the meanest Indian noble a damp-free, draftproof dwelling such as the President of the United States, lying on his special straw pallet, did not dream about. Like paint-splattered faces peering through newly reinvented, crude microscopes. What had microscopes been like? Jerry tried to remember the Engineering Survey Course he'd taken in his freshman year—and drew a blank. All the same, the Indians were so queer, *and* so awesome. Sometimes you thought that destiny had meant them to be conquerors, with a conqueror's careless inconsistency. Sometimes…

He noticed that they were waiting for him to continue. "From our chief," he repeated hurriedly. "I come with a message of importance and many gifts."

"Eat with us," the old man said. "Then you will give us your gifts and your message."

Gratefully, Jerry squatted on the ground a short distance from them. He was hungry, and among the fruit in the bowls he had seen something that must be an orange. He had heard so many arguments about what oranges tasted like!

After a while, the old man said, "I am Chief Three Hydrogen Bombs. This"—pointing to the young man—"is my son, Makes Much Radiation. And this"—pointing to the middle-aged Negro—"is a sort of compatriot of yours."

At Jerry's questioning look, and the chief's raised finger of permission, the Negro explained. "Sylvester Thomas, Ambassador to the Sioux from the Confederate States of America."

"The Confederacy? She's still alive? We heard ten years ago—"

"The Confederacy is very much alive, sir. The Western Confederacy, that is, with its capital at Jackson, Mississippi. The Eastern Confederacy, the one centered at Richmond, Virginia, did go down under the Seminole. We have been more fortunate. The Arapaho, the Cheyenne, and"—with a nod to the chief—"especially the Sioux, if I may say so, sir, have been very kind to us. They allow us to live in peace, so long as we till the soil quietly and pay our tithes."

"Then would you know, Mr. Thomas—" Jerry began eagerly. "That is…the Lone Star Republic—Texas— Is it possible that Texas, too…?"

Mr. Thomas looked at the door of the wigwam unhappily. "Alas, my good sir, the Republic of the Lone Star Flag fell before the Kiowa and the Comanche long years ago when I was still a small boy. I don't remember the exact date, but I do know it was before even the last of California was annexed by the Apache and the Navajo, and well before the nation of the Mormons under the august leadership of—"

Makes Much Radiation shifted his shoulders back and forth and flexed his arm muscles. "All this talk," he growled. "Paleface talk. Makes me tired."

"Mr. Thomas is not a paleface," his father told him sharply. "Show respect! He's our guest and an accredited ambassador—you're not to use a word like paleface in his presence!"

One of the other, older warriors near the youth spoke up. "In ancient days, in the days of the heroes, a boy of Makes Much Radiation's age would not dare raise his voice in council before his father. Certainly not to say the things he just has. I cite as reference, for those interested, Robert Lowie's definitive volume, *The Crow Indians,* and Lessor's fine piece of anthropological insight, *Three Types of Siouan Kinship.* Now, whereas we have not yet been able to reconstruct a Siouan kinship pattern on the classic model described by Lesser, we have developed a working arrangement that—"

"The trouble with you, Bright Book Jacket," the warrior on his left broke in, "is that you're too much of a classicist. You're always trying to live in the Golden Age instead of the present, and a Golden Age that really has little to do with the Sioux. Oh, I'll admit that we're as much Dakotan as the Crow, from the linguist's point of view at any rate, and that, superficially, what applies to the Crow should apply to us. But what happens when we quote Lowie in so many words and try to bring his precepts into daily life?"

"Enough," the chief announced. "Enough, Hangs A Tale. And you, too, Bright Book Jacket—enough, enough! These are private tribal matters. Though they do serve to remind us that the paleface was once great before he became sick and corrupt and frightened. These men whose holy books teach us the lost art of being real Sioux, men like Lesser, men like Robert H. Lowie, were not these men palefaces? And in memory of them should we not show tolerance?"

"A-ah!" said Makes Much Radiation impatiently. "As far as I'm concerned, the only good paleface is a dead paleface. And that's that." He thought a bit. "Except their women. Paleface women are fun when you're a long way from home and feel like raising a little hell."

Chief Three Hydrogen Bombs glared his son into silence. Then he turned to Jerry Franklin. "Your message and your gifts. First your message."

"No, Chief," Bright Book Jacket told him respectfully but definitely. "First the gifts. *Then* the message. That's the way it was done."

"I'll have to get them. Be right back." Jerry walked out of the tent backwards and ran to where Sam Rutherford had tethered the horses. "The presents," he said urgently. "The presents for the chief."

The two of them tore at the pack straps. With his arms loaded, Jerry returned through the warriors who had assembled to watch their activity with quiet arrogance. He entered the tent, set the gifts on the ground and bowed low again.

"Bright beads for the chief," he said, handing over two star sapphires and a large white diamond, the best that the engineers had evacuated from the ruins of New York in the past ten years.

"Cloth for the chief," he said, handing over a bolt of linen and a bolt of wool, spun and loomed in New Hampshire especially for this occasion and painfully, expensively carted to New York.

"Pretty toys for the chief," he said, handing over a large, only slightly rusty alarm clock and a precious typewriter, both of them put in operating order by batteries of engineers and artisans working in tandem (the engineers interpreting the brittle old documents to the artisans) for two and a half months.

"Weapons for the chief," he said, handing over a beautifully decorated cavalry saber, the prized hereditary possession of the Chief of Staff of the United States Air Force, who had protested its requisitioning most bitterly ("Damn it all, Mr. President, do you expect me to fight these Indians with my bare hands?" "No, I don't, Johnny, but I'm sure you can pick up one just as good from one of your eager junior officers").

Three Hydrogen Bombs examined the gifts, particularly the typewriter, with some interest. Then he solemnly distributed them among the members of his council, keeping only the typewriter and one of the sapphires for himself. The sword he gave to his son.

Makes Much Radiation tapped the steel with his fingernail. "Not so much," he stated. "*Not-so-much.* Mr. Thomas came up with better stuff than this from the Confederate States of America for my sister's puberty ceremony." He tossed the saber negligently to the ground. "But what can you expect from a bunch of lazy, good-for-nothing whiteskin stinkards?"

When he heard the last word, Jerry Franklin went rigid. That meant he'd have to fight Makes Much Radiation—and the prospect scared him right down to the wet hairs on his legs. The alternative was losing face completely among the Sioux.

"Stinkard" was a term from the Natchez system and was applied these days indiscriminately to all white men bound to field or factory under their aristocratic Indian overlords. A "stinkard" was something lower than a serf, whose one value was that his toil gave his masters the leisure to engage in the activities of full manhood: hunting, fighting, thinking.

If you let someone call you a stinkard and didn't kill him, why, then you *were* a stinkard—and that was all there was to it.

"I am an accredited representative of the United States of America," Jerry said slowly and distinctly, "and the oldest son of the Senator from Idaho. When my father dies, I will sit in the Senate in his place. I am a free-born man, high in the councils of my nation, and anyone who calls me a stinkard is a rotten, no-good, foul-mouthed liar!"

There—it was done. He waited as Makes Much Radiation rose to his feet. He noted with dismay the well-fed, well-muscled sleekness of the young warrior. He wouldn't have a chance against him. Not in hand-to-hand combat—which was the way it would be.

Makes Much Radiation picked up the sword and pointed it at Jerry Franklin. "I could chop you in half right now like a fat onion," he observed. "Or I could go into a ring with you, knife to knife, and cut your belly open. I've fought and killed Seminole, I've fought Apache, I've even fought and killed Comanche. But I've never dirtied my hands with paleface blood, and I don't intend to start now. I leave such simple butchery to the overseers of our estates. Father, I'll be outside until the lodge is clean again." Then he threw the sword ringingly at Jerry's feet and walked out.

Just before he left, he stopped, and remarked over his shoulder: "The oldest son of the Senator from Idaho! Idaho has been part of the estates of my mother's family for the past forty-five years! When will these romantic children stop playing games and start living in the world as it is now?"

"My son," the old chief murmured. "Younger generation. A bit wild. Highly intolerant. But he means well. Really does. Means well."

He signaled to the white serfs, who brought over a large chest covered with great splashes of color.

While the chief rummaged in the chest, Jerry Franklin relaxed inch by inch. It was almost too good to be true: he wouldn't have to fight Makes Much Radiation, and he hadn't lost face. All things considered, the whole business had turned out very well indeed.

And as for the last comment—well, why expect an Indian to understand about things like tradition and the glory that could reside forever in a symbol? When his father stood, up under the cracked roof of Madison Square Garden and roared across to the Vice-President of the United States: "The people of the sovereign state of Idaho will never and can never in all conscience consent to a tax on potatoes. From time immemorial, potatoes have been associated with Idaho, potatoes have been the pride of Idaho. The people of Boise say *no* to a tax on potatoes, the people of Pocatello say *no* to a tax on potatoes, the very rolling farmlands of the Gem of the Mountain say *no, never,* a thousand times *no,* to a tax on potatoes!"—when his father spoke like that, he *was* speaking for the people of Boise and Pocatello. Not the crushed Boise or desolate Pocatello of today, true, but the magnificent cities as they had been of yore…and the rich farms on either side of the Snake River…and Sun Valley, Moscow, Idaho Falls, American Falls, Weiser, Grangeville, Twin Falls…

"We did not expect you, so we have not many gifts to offer in return," Three Hydrogen Bombs was explaining. "However, there is this one small thing. For you."

Jerry gasped as he took it. It was a pistol, a real, brand-new pistol! And a small box of cartridges. Made in one of the Sioux slave workshops of the Middle West that he had heard about. But to hold it in his hand, and to know that it belonged to him!

It was a Crazy Horse forty-five, and, according to all reports, far superior to the Apache weapon that had so long dominated the West, the Geronimo thirty-two. This was a weapon a General of the Armies, a President of the United States, might never hope to own—and it was his!

"I don't know how— Really, I—I—"

"That's all right," the chief told him genially. "Really it is. My son would not approve of giving firearms to palefaces, but I feel that palefaces are like other people— it's the individual that counts. You look like a responsible man for a paleface; I'm sure you'll use the pistol wisely. Now your message."

Jerry collected his faculties and opened the pouch that hung from his neck. Reverently, he extracted the precious document and presented it to the chief.

Three Hydrogen Bombs read it quickly and passed it to his warriors. The last one to get it, Bright Book Jacket, wadded it up into a ball and tossed it back at the white man.

"Bad penmanship," he said. "And 'receive' is spelled three different ways. The rule is: '*i* before *e,* except after *c.*' But what does it have to do with us? It's addressed to the Seminole chief, Osceola VII, requesting him to order his warriors back to the southern bank of the Delaware River, or to return the hostage given him by the Government of the United States as an earnest of good will and peaceful intentions. We're not Seminole: why show it to us?"

As Jerry Franklin smoothed out the wrinkles in the paper with painful care and replaced the document in his pouch, the Confederate ambassador, Sylvester Thomas, spoke up. "I think I might explain," he suggested, glancing inquiringly from face to face. "If you gentlemen don't mind...? It is obvious that the United States Government has heard that an Indian tribe finally crossed the Delaware at this point, and assumed it was the Seminole. The last movement of the Seminole, you will recall, was to Philadelphia, forcing the evacuation of the capital once more and its transfer to New York City. It was a natural mistake; the communications of the American States, whether Confederate or United"—a small, coughing, diplomatic laugh here— "have not been as good as might have been expected in recent years. It is quite evident that neither this young man, nor the government he represents so ably and so well, had any idea that the Sioux had decided to steal a march on his majesty, Osceola VII, and cross the Delaware at Lambertville."

"That's right," Jerry broke in eagerly. "That's exactly right. And now, as the accredited emissary of the President of the United States, it is my duty formally to request that the Sioux nation honor the treaty of eleven years ago as well as the treaty of fifteen—I *think* it was fifteen—years ago, and retire once more behind the banks of the Susquehanna River. I must remind you that when we retired from Pittsburgh, Altoona, and Johnstown, you swore that the Sioux would take no more land from us and would protect us in the little we had left. I am certain that the Sioux want to be known as a nation that keeps its promises."

Three Hydrogen Bombs glanced questioningly at the faces of Bright Book Jacket and Hangs A Tale. Then he leaned forward and placed his elbows on his crossed legs. "You speak well, young man," he commented. "You are a credit to your chief... Now, then. Of course the Sioux want to be known as a nation that honors its treaties and keeps its promises. And so forth and so forth. But we have an expanding population. You don't have an expanding population. We need more land. You don't use most of the land you have. Should we sit by and see the land go to waste—worse yet, should we see it acquired by the Seminole, who already rule a domain stretching from Philadelphia to Key West? Be reasonable. You can retire to—to other places. You have most of New England left and a large part of New York State. Surely you can afford to give up New Jersey."

In spite of himself, in spite of his ambassadorial position, Jerry Franklin began yelling. All of a sudden it was too much. It was one thing to shrug your shoulders unhappily back home in the blunted ruins of New York, but here on the spot where the process was actually taking place—no, it was too much.

"What else can we afford to give up? Where else can we retire to? There's nothing left of the United States of America but a handful of square miles, and still we're supposed to move back! In the time of my forefathers, we were a great nation, we stretched from ocean to ocean, so say the legends of my people, and now we are huddled in a miserable corner of our land, starving, filthy, sick, dying, and ashamed. In the North, we are oppressed by the Ojibway and the Cree, we are pushed southward relentlessly by the Montaignais; in the South, the Seminole climb up our land yard by yard; and in the West, the Sioux take a piece more of New Jersey, and the Cheyenne come up and nibble yet another slice out of Elmira and Buffalo. When will it stop—where are we to go?"

The old man shifted uncomfortably at the agony in his voice. "It *is* hard; mind you, I don't deny that it *is* hard. But facts are facts, and weaker peoples always go to the wall…. Now, as to the rest of your mission. If we don't retire as you request, you're supposed to ask for the return of your hostage. Sounds reasonable to me. You ought to get something out of it. However, I can't for the life of me remember a hostage. Do we have a hostage from you people?"

His head hanging, his body exhausted, Jerry muttered in misery, "Yes. All the Indian nations on our borders have hostages. As earnests of our good will and peaceful intentions."

Bright Book Jacket snapped his fingers. "That girl. Sarah Cameron—Canton—what's-her-name."

Jerry looked up. "Calvin?" he asked. "Could it be *Calvin?* Sarah Calvin? The Daughter of the Chief Justice of the United States Supreme Court?"

"Sarah Calvin. That's the one. Been with us for five, six years. You remember, chief? The girl your son's been playing around with?"

Three Hydrogen Bombs looked amazed. "Is *she* the hostage? I thought she was some paleface female he had imported from his plantations in southern Ohio. Well, well, well. Makes Much Radiation is just a chip off the old block, no doubt about it." He became suddenly serious. "But that girl will never go back. She rather goes for Indian loving. Goes for it all the way. And she has the idea that my son will eventually marry her. Or some such."

He looked Jerry Franklin over. "Tell you what, my boy. Why don't you wait outside while we talk this over? And take the saber. Take it back with you. My son doesn't seem to want it."

Jerry wearily picked up the saber and trudged out of the wigwam.

Dully, uninterestedly, he noticed the band of Sioux warriors around Sam Rutherford and his horses. Then the group parted for a moment, and he saw Sam with a bottle in his hand. Tequila! The damned fool had let the Indians give him tequila—he was drunk as a pig.

Didn't he know that white men couldn't drink, didn't dare drink? With every inch of their unthreatened arable land under cultivation for foodstuffs, they were all still on the edge of starvation. There was absolutely no room in their economy for such luxuries as intoxicating beverages—and no white man in the usual course of a lifetime got close to so much as a glassful of the stuff. Give him a whole bottle of tequila and he was a stinking mess.

As Sam was now. He staggered back and forth in dipping semicircles, holding the bottle by its neck and waving it idiotically. The Sioux chuckled, dug each other in the ribs and pointed. Sam vomited loosely down the rags upon his chest and belly, tried to take one more drink, and fell over backwards. The bottle continued to pour over his face until it was empty. He was snoring loudly. The Sioux shook their heads, made grimaces of distaste, and walked away.

Jerry looked on and nursed the pain in his heart. Where could they go? What could they do? And what difference did it make? Might as well be as drunk as Sammy there. At least you wouldn't be able to feel.

He looked at the saber in one hand, the bright new pistol in the other. Logically, he should throw them away. Wasn't it ridiculous when you came right down to it, wasn't it pathetic—a white man carrying weapons?

Sylvester Thomas came out of the tent. "Get your horses ready, my dear sir," he whispered. "Be prepared to ride as soon as I come back. Hurry!"

The young man slouched over to the horses and followed instructions—might as well do that as anything else. Ride where? Do what?

He lifted Sam Rutherford up and tied him upon his horse. Go back home? Back to the great, the powerful, the respected capital of what had once been the United States of America?

Thomas came back with a bound and gagged girl in his grasp. She wriggled madly. Her eyes crackled with anger and rebellion. She kept trying to kick the Confederate Ambassador.

She wore the rich robes of an Indian princess. Her hair was braided in the style currently fashionable among Sioux women. And her face had been stained carefully with some darkish dye.

Sarah Calvin. The daughter of the Chief Justice. They tied her to the pack horse.

"Chief Three Hydrogen Bombs," the Negro explained. "He feels his son plays around too much with paleface females. He wants this one out of the way. The boy has to settle down, prepare for the responsibilities of chieftainship. This may help. And listen, the old man likes you. He told me to tell you something."

"I'm grateful. I'm grateful for every favor, no matter how small, how humiliating."

Sylvester Thomas shook his head decisively. "Don't be bitter, young sir. If you want to go on living you have to be alert. And you can't be alert and bitter at the same time. The Chief wants you to know there's no point in your going home. He couldn't say it openly in council, but the reason the Sioux moved in on Trenton has nothing to do with the Seminole on the other side. It has to do with the Ojibway-Cree-Montaignais situation in the North. They've decided to take over the Eastern Seaboard—that includes what's left of your country. By this time, they're probably in Yonkers or the Bronx, somewhere inside New York City. In a matter of hours, your government will no longer be in existence. The Chief had advance word of this and felt it necessary for the Sioux to establish some sort of bridgehead on the coast before matters were permanently stabilized. By occupying New Jersey, he is preventing an Ojibway-Seminole junction. But he likes you, as I said, and wants you warned against going home."

"Fine, but where *do* I go? Up a rain cloud? Down a well?"

"No," Thomas admitted without smiling. He hoisted Jerry up on his horse. "You might come back with me to the Confederacy—" He paused, and when Jerry's sullen expression did not change, he went on, "Well, then, may I suggest—and mind you, this is my advice, not the Chief's—head straight out to Asbury Park. It's not far away— you can make it in reasonable time if you ride hard. According to reports I've overheard, there should be units of the United States Navy there, the Tenth Fleet, to be exact."

"Tell me," Jerry asked, bending down. "Have you heard any other news? Anything about the rest of the world? How has it been with those people—the Russkies, the Sovietskis, whatever they were called—the ones the United States had so much to do with years and years ago?"

"According to several of the Chief's councilors, the Soviet Russians were having a good deal of difficulty with people called Tatars. I *think* they were called Tatars. But, my good sir, you should be on your way."

Jerry leaned down further and grasped his hand. "Thanks," he said. "You've gone to a lot of trouble for me. I'm grateful."

"That's quite all right," said Mr. Thomas earnestly. "After all, by the rocket's red glare, and all that. We were a single nation once."

Jerry moved off, leading the other two horses. He set a fast pace, exercising the minimum of caution made necessary by the condition of the road. By the time they reached Route 33, Sam Rutherford, though not altogether sober or well, was able to sit in his saddle. They could then untie Sarah Calvin and ride with her between them.

She cursed and wept. "Filthy paleface! Foul, ugly, stinking whiteskins! I'm an Indian, can't you see I'm an Indian? My skin isn't white—it's brown, brown!"

They kept riding.

Asbury Park was a dismal clatter of rags and confusion and refugees. There were refugees from the north, from Perth Amboy, from as far as Newark. There were refugees from Princeton in the west, flying before the Sioux invasion. And from the south, from Atlantic City—even, unbelievably, from distant Camden—were still other refugees, with stories of a sudden Seminole attack, an attempt to flank the armies of Three Hydrogen Bombs.

The three horses were stared at enviously, even in their lathered, exhausted condition. They represented food to the hungry, the fastest transportation possible to the fearful. Jerry found the saber very useful. And the pistol was even better—it had only to be exhibited. Few of these people had ever seen a pistol in action; they had a mighty, superstitious fear of firearms.

With this fact discovered, Jerry kept the pistol out nakedly in his right hand when he walked into the United States Naval Depot on the beach at Asbury Park. Sam Rutherford was at his side; Sarah Calvin walked sobbing behind.

He announced their family backgrounds to Admiral Milton Chester. The son of the Undersecretary of State. The daughter of the Chief Justice of the Supreme Court. The oldest son of the Senator from Idaho. "And now. Do you recognize the authority of this document?"

Admiral Chester read the wrinkled commission slowly, spelling out the harder words to himself. He twisted his head respectfully when he had finished, looking first at the seal of the United States on the paper before him, and then at the glittering pistol in Jerry's hand.

"Yes," he said at last. "I recognize its authority. Is that a real pistol?"

Jerry nodded. "A Crazy Horse forty-five. The latest. *How* do you recognize its authority?"

The admiral spread his hands. "Everything is confused out here. The latest word

I've received is that there are Ojibway warriors in Manhattan—that there is no longer any United States Government. And yet this"—he bent over the document once more—"this is a commission by the President himself, appointing you full plenipotentiary. To the Seminole, of course. But full plenipotentiary. The last official appointment, to the best of my knowledge, of the President of the United States of America."

He reached forward and touched the pistol in Jerry Franklin's hand curiously and inquiringly. He nodded to himself, as if he'd come to a decision. He stood up, and saluted with a flourish.

"I hereby recognize you as the last legal authority of the United States Government. And I place my fleet at your disposal."

"Good." Jerry stuck the pistol in his belt. He pointed with the saber. "Do you have enough food and water for a long voyage?"

"No, sir," Admiral Chester said. "But that can be arranged in a few hours at most. May I escort you aboard, sir?"

He gestured proudly down the beach and past the surf to where the three forty-five-foot gaff-rigged schooners rode at anchor. "The United States Tenth Fleet, sir. Awaiting your orders."

Hours later when the three vessels were standing out to sea, the admiral came to the cramped main cabin where Jerry Franklin was resting. Sam Rutherford and Sarah Calvin were asleep in the bunks above.

"And the orders, sir…?"

Jerry Franklin walked out on the narrow deck, looked up at the taut, patched sails. "Sail east."

"East, sir? *Due* east?"

"Due east all the way. To the fabled lands of Europe. To a place where a white man can stand at last on his own two legs. Where he need not fear persecution. Where he need not fear slavery. Sail east, Admiral, until we discover a new and hopeful world—a world of freedom!"

AFTERWORD

In 1957, Anthony Boucher retired from the wonderful magazine he had helped found, *The Magazine of Fantasy & Science Fiction*. Bob Mills, the managing editor, needed someone with a substantial background in science fiction to temporarily take Tony's place, so Cyril Kornbluth was hired as Consulting Editor. There was a heavy snowfall in New York about that time, and Cyril, who suffered from very high blood pressure, made the mistake of hurriedly shoveling his driveway clear so he could get his car out and keep an appointment with Mills. He dropped dead, I believe, in the driveway.

Mills called me and asked me to take a short-time appointment, now filling Cyril's place. I told him I was honored.

I worked there for about four months, trying to empty one large file drawer where Tony had stashed stories that were just not quite good enough to be published, but still too good to have been rejected. Each story had a special problem: one, for example, by Robert Bloch, "That Hell-Bound Train," was an absolutely fine piece of work that just didn't have a usable ending. It was my job, among other things, to come up with such an ending and persuade the writer to write it. I developed a great respect for the editors—chief among them John W. Campbell and Horace L. Gold—I had known and quarreled with a lot, an awful lot.

One of the things Bob Mills asked me to do right off was give him a story by me for the tenth anniversary issue of the magazine. I agreed, and promptly forgot about it as I wrestled with the thick inventory of science fiction written by people I much admired but which always lacked some essential quality or passage.

And then Mills came to my desk at 4:45 PM on a Wednesday as I was getting ready to leave, and asked me where it was.

I got into my coat and stared at him. Where *what* was?

"The story for the anniversary issue. It goes to bed tomorrow. Thursday morning. *Dead* deadline, Phil!"

In an emergency, my mother had taught me, always lie. "Oh, it's home," I said. "I'll bring it in with me tomorrow morning. I'm pretty sure you'll like it."

"How long is it?" Mills wanted to know. "I hope it'll fit the book. We can't use much more than about six thousand words."

"That's just about what I have," I told him. "Six or six five. I haven't counted it yet."

And I got out of the place.

All the subway ride home, I plotted feverishly, to absolutely no avail. I couldn't think of a single good idea, certainly none I wanted to write. But as I got out at my station, a large poster advertisement on the platform caught my eye. It was the latest in a group that advertised a Jewish rye bread, each showing a color photograph of someone of a different, non-Jewish ethnic group proclaiming that he or she simply adored Jewish rye. This one was of an American Indian in full feathered headdress.

I ran up to the ad and, to the astonishment I suspect of everyone on the platform hurrying home that night, blew a couple of kisses at it. That was my story, I knew immediately.

And by the time I reached my house in Sea Gate at the Coney Island tip of Brooklyn, I had worked it out almost completely.

Ever since my boyhood, I had been fascinated by the Indian story—or the many Indian stories, perhaps I should say. When I was a kid and my gang played Cowboys and Indians, I always insisted on being one of the Indians. I did it partly out of a partiality for the exotic, but mostly out of a kind of an apology.

What was I apologizing for? I'm not sure. Possibly for what my people had done to them. (*My* people? My people came from ghettos in Poland and Lithuania! Oh, well, maybe my people, the Cowboys.)

I swallowed the supper Fruma had prepared for me and rushed to my typewriter. I began typing almost immediately.

I stopped only to go to the bathroom. By the time dawn broke over the end of the boardwalk, the story was done.

It needed very little rewriting, and once I did that, the piece came to sixty-four hundred words almost exactly. For a title, I went back to a book by a writer whose work I had loved since the age of twelve, Charles Kingsley, the vicar of Eversley. And I had a story that was science fiction and also what I liked to write those days—a moral tale. I decided that I too adored Jewish rye.

Bob Mills liked it too, the story, not the bread. And I've always been quite fond of what I call my science-fiction western.

WRITTEN 1957———PUBLISHED 1958

ఎం

Null-P

Several months after the Second Atomic War, when radioactivity still held one-third of the planet in desolation, Dr. Daniel Glurt of Fillmore Township, Wisc., stumbled upon a discovery which was to generate humanity's ultimate sociological advance.

Like Columbus, smug over his voyage to India; like Nobel, proud of the synthesis of dynamite which made combat between nations impossible, the doctor misinterpreted his discovery. Years later, he cackled to a visiting historian:

"Had no idea it would lead to this, no idea at all. You remember, the war had just ended: we were feeling mighty subdued what with the eastern and western coasts of the United States practically sizzled away. Well, word came down from the new capital at Topeka in Kansas for us doctors to give all our patients a complete physical check. Sort of be on the lookout, you know, for radioactive burns and them fancy new diseases the armies had been tossing back and forth. Well, sir, that's absolutely all I set out to do. I'd known George Abnego for over thirty years—treated him for chicken-pox and pneumonia and ptomaine poisoning. I'd *never* suspected!"

Having reported to Dr. Glurt's office immediately after work in accordance with the proclamation shouted through the streets by the county clerk, and having waited patiently in line for an hour and a half, George Abnego was at last received into the small consulting room. Here he was thoroughly chest-thumped, X-rayed, blood-sampled, and urinanalyzed. His skin was examined carefully, and he was made to answer the five hundred questions prepared by the Department of Health in a pathetic attempt to cover the symptoms of the new ailments.

George Abnego then dressed and went home to the cereal supper permitted for that day by the ration board. Dr. Glurt placed his folder in a drawer and called for the next patient. He had noticed nothing up to this point; yet already he had unwittingly begun the Abnegite Revolution.

Four days later, the health survey of Fillmore, Wisc., being complete, the doctor forwarded the examination reports to Topeka. Just before signing George Abnego's sheet, he glanced at it cursorily, raised his eyebrows and entered the following note: "Despite the tendency to dental caries and athlete's foot, I would consider this man to be of average health. Physically, he is the Fillmore Township norm."

It was this last sentence which caused the government medical official to chuckle and glance at the sheet once more. His smile was puzzled after this; it was even more puzzled after he had checked the figures and statements on the form against standard medical references.

He wrote a phrase in red ink in the right-hand corner and sent it along to Research.

His name is lost to history.

Research wondered why the report on George Abnego had been sent up—he had no unusual symptoms portending exotic innovations like cerebral measles or arterial trichinosis. Then it observed the phrase in red ink and Dr. Glurt's remark. Research shrugged its anonymous shoulders and assigned a crew of statisticians to go further into the matter.

A week later, as a result of their findings, another crew—nine medical specialists—left for Fillmore. They examined George Abnego with coordinated precision. Afterwards, they called on Dr. Glurt briefly, leaving a copy of their examination report with him when he expressed interest.

Ironically, the government copies were destroyed in the Topeka Hard-Shelled Baptist Riots a month later, the same riots which stimulated Dr. Glurt to launch the Abnegite Revolution.

This Baptist denomination, because of population shrinkage due to atomic and bacteriological warfare, was now the largest single religious body in the nation. It was then controlled by a group pledged to the establishment of a Hard-Shelled Baptist theocracy in what was left of the United States. The rioters were quelled after much destruction and bloodshed; their leader, the Reverend Hemingway T. Gaunt—who had vowed that he would remove neither the pistol from his left hand nor the Bible from his right until the Rule of God had been established and the Third Temple built— was sentenced to death by a jury composed of stern-faced fellow Baptists.

Commenting on the riots, the Fillmore, Wisc., *Bugle-Herald* drew a mournful parallel between the Topeka street battles and the destruction wreaked upon the world by atomic conflict.

"International communication and transportation having broken down," the editorial went on broodingly, "we now know little of the smashed world in which we live beyond such meager facts as the complete disappearance of Australia beneath the waves, and the contraction of Europe to the Pyrenees and Ural Mountains. We know that our planet's physical appearance has changed as much from what it was ten years ago, as the infant monstrosities and mutants being born everywhere as a result of radioactivity are unpleasantly different from their parents.

"Truly, in these days of mounting catastrophe and change, our faltering spirits beg the heavens for a sign, a portent, that all will be well again, that all will yet be as it once was, that the waters of disaster will subside and we shall once more walk upon the solid ground of normalcy."

It was this last word which attracted Dr. Glurt's attention. That night, he slid the report of the special government medical crew into the newspaper's mail slot. He had penciled a laconic note in the margin of the first page:

"Noticed your interest in the subject."

Next week's edition of the Fillmore *Bugle-Herald* flaunted a page one five-column headline.

FILLMORE CITIZEN THE SIGN?
Normal Man of Fillmore May Be Answer From Above
Local Doctor Reveals Government Medical Secret

The story that followed was liberally sprinkled with quotations taken equally from the government report and the Psalms of David. The startled residents of Fillmore learned that one George Abnego, a citizen unnoticed in their midst for almost forty years, was a living abstraction. Through a combination of circumstances no more remarkable than those producing a royal flush in stud poker, Abnego's physique, psyche, and other miscellaneous attributes had resulted in that legendary creature— the statistical average.

According to the last census taken before the war, George Abnego's height and weight were identical with the mean of the American adult male. He had married at the exact age—year, month, day—when statisticians had estimated the marriage of the *average* man took place; he had married a woman the *average* number of years younger than himself; his income as declared on his last tax statement was the *average* income for that year. The very teeth in his mouth tallied in quantity and condition with those predicted by the American Dental Association to be found on a man extracted at random from the population. Abnego's metabolism and blood pressure, his bodily proportions and private neuroses, were all cross-sections of the latest available records. Subjected to every psychological and personality test available, his final, overall grade corrected out to show that he was both average and normal.

Finally, Mrs. Abnego had been recently delivered of their third child, a boy. This development had not only occurred at exactly the right time according to the population indices, but it had resulted in an entirely normal sample of humanity—unlike most babies being born throughout the land.

The *Bugle-Herald* blared its hymn to the new celebrity around a greasy photograph of the family in which the assembled Abnegos stared glassily out at the reader, looking, as many put it, "Average—average as hell!"

Newspapers in other states were invited to copy.

They did, slowly at first, then with an accelerating, contagious enthusiasm. Indeed, as the intense public interest in this symbol of stability, this refugee from the extremes, became manifest, newspaper columns gushed fountains of purple prose about the "Normal Man of Fillmore."

At Nebraska State University, Professor Roderick Klingmeister noticed that many members of his biology class were wearing extra-large buttons decorated with pictures of George Abnego. "Before beginning my lecture," he chuckled, "I would like to tell you that this 'normal man' of yours is no Messiah. All he is, I am afraid, is a bell-shaped curve with ambitions, the median made flesh—"

He got no further. He was brained with his own demonstration microscope.

Even that early, a few watchful politicians noticed that no one was punished for this hasty act.

The incident could be related to many others which followed: the unfortunate and unknown citizen of Duluth, for example, who—at the high point of that city's *Welcome Average Old Abnego* parade—was heard to remark in good-natured amazement, "Why, he's just an ordinary jerk like you and me," and was immediately torn into celebratory confetti by horrified neighbors in the crowd.

Developments such as these received careful consideration from men whose power was derived from the just, if well-directed, consent of the governed.

George Abnego, these gentry concluded, represented the maturation of a great national myth which, implicit in the culture for over a century, had been brought to garish fulfillment by the mass communication and entertainment media.

This was the myth that began with the juvenile appeal to be "A Normal Red-Blooded American Boy" and ended, on the highest political levels, with a shirt-sleeved, suspendered seeker after political office boasting. "Shucks, everybody knows who I am. I'm folks—just plain folks."

This was the myth from which were derived such superficially disparate practices as the rite of political baby-kissing, the cult of "keeping up with the Joneses," the foppish, foolish, forever-changing fads which went through the population with the monotonous regularity and sweep of a windshield wiper. The myth of styles and fraternal organizations. The myth of the "regular fellow."

There was a presidential election that year.

Since all that remained of the United States was the Middle West, the Democratic Party had disappeared. Its remnants had been absorbed by a group calling itself the Old Guard Republicans, the closest thing to an American Left. The party in power—the Conservative Republicans—so far right as to verge upon royalism, had acquired enough pledged theocratic votes to make them smug about the election.

Desperately, the Old Guard Republicans searched for a candidate. Having regretfully passed over the adolescent epileptic recently elected to the governorship of South Dakota in violation of the state constitution—and deciding against the psalm-singing grandmother from Oklahoma who punctuated her senatorial speeches with religious music upon the banjo—the party strategists arrived, one summer afternoon, in Fillmore, Wisconsin.

From the moment that Abnego was persuaded to accept the nomination and his last well-intentioned but flimsy objection was overcome (the fact that he was a registered member of the opposition party) it was obvious that the tide of battle had turned, that the fabled grass roots had caught fire.

Abnego ran for president on the slogan "Back to Normal with the Normal Man!"

By the time the Conservative Republicans met in convention assembled, the danger of loss by landslide was already apparent. They changed their tactics, tried to meet the attack head-on and imaginatively.

They nominated a hunchback for the presidency. This man suffered from the additional disability of being a distinguished professor of law in a leading university;

he had married with no issue and divorced with much publicity; and finally, he had once admitted to a congressional investigating committee that he had written and published surrealist poetry. Posters depicting him leering horribly, his hump twice life-size, were smeared across the country over the slogan: "An Abnormal Man for an Abnormal World!"

Despite this brilliant political stroke, the issue was never in doubt. On Election Day, the nostalgic slogan defeated its medicative adversary by three to one. Four years later, with the same opponents, it had risen to five and a half to one. And there was no organized opposition when Abnego ran for a third term...

Not that he had crushed it. There was more casual liberty of political thought allowed during Abnego's administrations than in many previous ones. But less political thinking and debating were done.

Whenever possible, Abnego avoided decision. When a decision was unavoidable, he made it entirely on the basis of precedent. He rarely spoke on a topic of current interest and never committed himself. He was garrulous and an exhibitionist only about his family.

"How can you lampoon a vacuum?" This had been the wail of many opposition newspaper writers and cartoonists during the early years of the Abnegite Revolution, when men still ran against Abnego at election time. They tried to draw him into ridiculous statements or admissions time and again without success, Abnego was simply incapable of saying anything that any major cross-section of the population would consider ridiculous.

Emergencies? "Well," Abnego had said, in the story every schoolchild knew, "I've noticed even the biggest forest fire will burn itself out. Main thing is not to get excited."

He made them lie down in low-blood-pressure areas. And, after years of building and destruction, of stimulation and conflict, of accelerating anxieties and torments, they rested and were humbly grateful.

It seemed to many, from the day Abnego was sworn in, that chaos began to waver and everywhere a glorious, welcome stability flowered. In some respects, such as the decrease in the number of monstrous births, processes were under way which had nothing at all to do with the Normal Man of Fillmore; in others—the astonished announcement by lexicographers, for example, that slang expressions peculiar to teenagers in Abnego's first term were used by their children in exactly the same contexts eighteen years later in his fifth administration—the historical leveling-out and patting-down effects of the Abnegite trowel were obvious.

The verbal expression of this great calm was the Abnegism.

History's earliest record of these deftly phrased inadequacies relates to the administration in which Abnego, at last feeling secure enough to do so, appointed a cabinet without any regard to the wishes of his party hierarchy. A journalist, attempting to point up the absolute lack of color in the new official family, asked if any one of them—from Secretary of State to Postmaster-General—had ever committed himself publicly on any issue or, in previous positions, had been responsible for a single constructive step in any direction.

To which the President supposedly replied with a bland, unhesitating smile, "I always say there's no hard feelings if no one's defeated. Well, sir, no one's defeated in a fight where the referee can't make a decision."

Apocryphal though it may have been, this remark expressed the mood of Abnegite America perfectly. "As pleasant as a no-decision bout" became part of everyday language.

Certainly as apocryphal as the George Washington cherry-tree legend, but the most definite Abnegism of them all was the one attributed to the President after a performance of *Romeo and Juliet*. "It is better not to have loved at all, than to have loved and lost," he is reported to have remarked at the morbid end of the play.

At the inception of Abnego's sixth term—the first in which his oldest son served with him as Vice-President—a group of Europeans reopened trade with the United States by arriving in a cargo ship assembled from the salvaged parts of three sunken destroyers and one capsized aircraft carrier.

Received everywhere with undemonstrative cordiality, they traveled the country, amazed at the placidity—the almost total absence of political and military excitement on the one hand, and the rapid technological retrogression on the other. One of the emissaries sufficiently mislaid his diplomatic caution to comment before he left:

"We came to America, to these cathedrals of industrialism, in the hope that we would find solutions to many vexing problems of applied science. These problems—the development of atomic power for factory use, the application of nuclear fission to such small arms as pistols and hand grenades—stand in the way of our postwar recovery. But you, in what remains of the United States of America, don't even see what we, in what remains of Europe, consider so complex and pressing. Excuse me, but what you have here is a national trance!"

His American hosts were not offended: they received his expostulations with polite smiles and shrugs. The delegate returned to tell his countrymen that the Americans, always notorious for their madness, had finally specialized in cretinism.

But another delegate who had observed widely and asked many searching questions went back to his native Toulouse (French culture had once more coagulated in Provence) to define the philosophical foundations of the Abnegite Revolution.

In a book which was read by the world with enormous interest, Michel Gaston Fouffnique, sometime Professor of History at the Sorbonne, pointed out that while twentieth-century man had escaped from the narrow Greek formulations sufficiently to visualize a non-Aristotelian logic and a non-Euclidean geometry, he had not yet had the intellectual temerity to create a non-Platonic system of politics. Not until Abnego.

"Since the time of Socrates," wrote Monsieur Fouffnique, "Man's political viewpoints have been in thrall to the conception that the best should govern. How to determine that 'best,' the scale of values to be used in order that the 'best' and not mere undifferentiated 'betters' should rule—these have been the basic issues around which have raged the fires of political controversy for almost three millennia. Whether an aristocracy of birth or intellect should prevail is an argument over values; whether rulers should be determined by the will of a god as determined by the entrails of a hog, or selected by the whole people on the basis of a ballot tally—these are alterna-tives in method. But hitherto no political system has ventured away from the im-plicit and unexamined assumption first embodied in the philosopher-state of Plato's *Republic.*

"Now, at last, America has turned and questioned the pragmatic validity of the axiom. The young democracy to the West, which introduced the concept of the Rights of Man to jurisprudence, now gives a feverish world the Doctrine of the Lowest Com-mon Denominator in government. According to this doctrine as I have come to understand it through prolonged observation, it is *not* the worst who should govern—as many of my prejudiced fellow-delegates insist—but the mean: what might be termed the 'unbest' or the 'non-elite.'"

Situated amid the still-radioactive rubbish of modern war, the people of Europe listened devoutly to readings from Fouffnique's monograph. They were enthralled by the peaceful monotonies said to exist in the United States and bored by the academician's reasons thereto: that a governing group who knew to begin with that they were "unbest" would be free of the myriad jealousies and conflicts arising from the need to prove individual superiority, and that such a group would tend to smooth any major quarrel very rapidly because of the dangerous opportunities created for imaginative and resourceful people by conditions of struggle and strain.

There were oligarchs here and bosses there; in one nation an ancient religious order still held sway, in another, calculating and brilliant men continued to lead the people. But the word was preached. Shamans appeared in the population, ordinary-looking folk who were called "abnegos." Tyrants found it impossible to destroy these shamans, since they were not chosen for any special abilities but simply because they represented the median of a given group: the middle of any population grouping, it was found, lasts as long as the group itself. Therefore, through bloodshed and much time, the abnegos spread their philosophy and flourished.

Oliver Abnego, who became the first President of the World, was President Abnego VI of the United States of America. His son presided—as Vice-President—over a Senate composed mostly of his uncles and his cousins and his aunts. They and their numerous offspring lived in an economy which had deteriorated very, very slightly from the conditions experienced by the founder of their line.

As world president, Oliver Abnego approved only one measure—that granting preferential university scholarships to students whose grades were closest to their age-group median all over the planet. The President could hardly have been accused of originality and innovation unbecoming to his high office, however, since for some time now all reward systems—scholastic, athletic, and even industrial—had been adjusted to recognition of the most average achievement while castigating equally the highest and lowest scores.

When the usable oil gave out shortly afterwards, men turned with perfect calm-ness to coal. The last turbines were placed in museums while still in operating con-dition: the people they served felt their isolated and individual use of electricity was too ostentatious for good abnegism.

Outstanding cultural phenomena of this period were carefully rhymed and exactly metered poems addressed to the nondescript beauties and vague charms of a wife or old mother. Had not anthropology disappeared long ago, it would have become a matter of common knowledge that there was a startling tendency to uniformity everywhere in such qualities as bone structure, features and pigmentation, not to mention intelligence, musculature, and personality. Humanity was breeding rapidly and unconsciously in toward its center.

Nonetheless, just before the exhaustion of coal, there was a brief sputter of intellect among a group who established themselves on a site northwest of Cairo. These Nilotics, as they were known, consisted mostly of unreconstructed dissidents expelled by their communities, with a leavening of the mentally ill and the physically handicapped; they had at their peak an immense number of technical gadgets and yellowing books culled from crumbling museums and libraries the world over.

Intensely ignored by their fellowmen, the Nilotics carried on shrill and interminable debates while plowing their muddy fields just enough to keep alive. They concluded that they were the only surviving heirs of *Homo sapiens,* the bulk of the world's population now being composed of what they termed *Homo abnegus.*

Man's evolutionary success, they concluded, had been due chiefly to his lack of specialization. While other creatures had been forced to standardize to a particular and limited environment, mankind had been free for a tremendous spurt, until ultimately it had struck an environmental factor which demanded the fee of specialization. To avoid war, Man had to specialize in nonentity.

Having come this far in discussion, the Nilotics determined to use the ancient weapons at their disposal to save *Homo abnegus* from himself. However, violent disagreements over the methods of reeducation to be employed led them to a bloody internecine conflict with those same weapons in the course of which the entire colony was destroyed and its site made untenable for life. About this time, his coal used up, Man reentered the broad, self-replenishing forests.

The reign of *Homo abnegus* endured for a quarter of a million years. It was disputed finally—and successfully—by a group of Newfoundland retrievers who had been marooned on an island in Hudson Bay when the cargo vessel transporting them to new owners had sunk back in the twentieth century.

These sturdy and highly intelligent dogs, limited perforce to each other's growling society for several hundred millennia, learned to talk in much the same manner that mankind's simian ancestors had learned to walk when a sudden shift in botany destroyed their ancient arboreal homes—out of boredom. Their wits sharpened further by the hardships of their bleak island, their imaginations stimulated by the cold, the articulate retrievers built a most remarkable canine civilization in the Arctic before sweeping southward to enslave and eventually domesticate humanity.

Domestication took the form of breeding men solely for their ability to throw sticks and other objects, the retrieving of which was a sport still popular among the new masters of the planet, however sedentary certain erudite individuals might have become.

Highly prized as pets were a group of men with incredibly thin and long arms; another school of retrievers, however, favored a stocky breed whose arms were short, but extremely sinewy; while, occasionally, interesting results were obtained by inducing rickets for a few generations to produce a pet whose arms were sufficiently limber as to appear almost boneless. This last type, while intriguing both esthetically and scientifically, was generally decried as a sign of decadence in the owner as well as a functional insult to the animal.

Eventually, of course, the retriever civilization developed machines which could throw sticks farther, faster, and with more frequency. Thereupon, except in the most backward canine communities, Man disappeared.

AFTERWORD

The army was where I began writing this story—somewhere in the European Theater of Operations, in 1944. I didn't have a typewriter, but I did have an early ballpoint pen (bought in Greenock, Scotland, the evening after we disembarked from the troop ship) and a pile of blank V-Mail (V-Mail was the unfolded one-page letter forms distributed to overseas soldiers for writing home).

My first intention was to write a satire about the inherent mediocrity of officialdom, especially as exemplified by the officers of the Army of the United States. By the time I completed that draft, in Saarbrucken, Germany, 1945, I had changed my opinion of the army several times over—and, to my chagrin, the army never seemed to notice, or care.

After discharge, but before I began my professional career as a writer, I whittled away at the piece, picking first this target, then that. By 1947, I had settled on the most mediocre man I could see in a high position: Harry S Truman, the President of the United States. He, I admit to my shame and sorrow, was the original original of George Abnego.

(Why this S. and S.? Well, growing up has apparently been a constant process of growing up so far as I'm concerned. I now rank Truman very high in my opinion of U.S. presidents, a couple of micrometers or so behind Abraham Lincoln.)

I had also, years back, been very much impressed with the early science fiction of A.E. van Vogt. His "Black Destroyer" and "Discord in Scarlet" had been among my favorites when it came to stories about aliens. But when I read his *The World of Null-A*, however, I had immediately wondered, "Why limit it to non-Aristotelian logic? Why not non-Platonic politics? There's the rub in our social history ever since the fifth century BC!" Now, in 1947, I remembered that overlook of van Vogt's. I worked that into the story and used it as a title.

I wrote and rewrote the story, intending it for *The New Yorker*. When I was seventeen, I had sent *The New Yorker* a cycle of stories that perhaps only an acned seventeen-year-old could write—"The Adventures of God" and "The Further Adventures of God Junior." Instead of the expected printed rejection slip, I had received a postcard from the editor, Harold Ross (Harold Ross, *himself, in his own handwriting!*), inviting me to come up and see him about the stories. I went there in my best—and only—blue serge suit, seeing myself as the new Perelman, the latest Thurber, the latter-day Robert Benchley.

I didn't even get to Ross's office. He came to me outside, in the smallish reception room. He talked to me for a few minutes, asking me what I read, what other things I had written, just why I had set myself to write "The Adventures of God." Then he handed me back the pieces I had sent in and touched me lightly on the shoulder. "We don't need these," he said. "But keep punching, keep writing. We'll be publishing you one day." And he watched me take the elevator down.

But I went home with the virus in me. No matter where I published first, no matter what book awards I might win, I knew I must fulfill Harold Ross's promise—I must one day appear in *The New Yorker*.

Now, at last, in 1950 (I had been *potschkeying* with the story for three years) I felt I had the wherewithal to fulfill that promise. I took it to my agent, told him of the market it must go to. He read it and shrugged. "Could be," he said.

Then, the next day, he called me and told me he'd sent it to Damon Knight's new science-fiction magazine, *Worlds Beyond*.

Damon had liked it a lot and had immediately bought it for a hundred dollars.

"A hundred dollars!" I wept. "I intended it for *The New Yorker*."

"A hundred dollars definite," he said, "is better than *The New Yorker* maybe. You need the money to eat on."

I really couldn't argue with that last sentence. My ninety-dollar part of the check from *Worlds Beyond* bought a lot of groceries.

Well, at least, I said, the story will be noticed. It will be noticed and commented-on everywhere.

It wasn't.

For a long time, there seemed to be only three people in the world who thought "Null-P" a particularly good story: myself, Damon Knight, and August Derleth, who used it in an anthology he edited. Everybody else ignored it. Then, a decade after its first publication, "Null-P" was especially noted by Kingsley Amis in his critical study, *New Maps of Hell*. Anthology requests began coming in from everywhere and references to it appeared in the most unexpected places. All right—maybe it isn't all that good, but certainly it couldn't have been that bad either for ten long years.

(By the way, Amis said that the satire in "Null-P" did not seem to be aimed at any one in particular. I would have quarreled bitterly with that definitely non-American Brit. By the time *New Maps of Hell* was published, I damn well knew who I had intended to satirize, who the most mediocre of leaders was. Eisenhower, I would have told him. It was President Eisenhower all along, I would have said. Eisenhower, who followed that great president, Harry S Truman.)

And how do I feel today about the story's never having been submitted to *The New Yorker?* I feel as my mother would have put it:

"Oy, it's *The New Yorker*'s loss. And *The New Yorker*'s loss is *my* loss."

WRITTEN 1947———PUBLISHED 1950

の

The Masculinist Revolt

The Coming of the Codpiece

Historians of the period between 1990 and 2015 disagree violently on the causes of the Masculinist Revolt. Some see it as a sexual earthquake of nationwide proportions that was long overdue. Others contend that an elderly bachelor founded the Movement only to save himself from bankruptcy and saw it turn into a terrifying monster that swallowed him alive.

This P. Edward Pollyglow—fondly nicknamed "Old Pep" by his followers—was the last of a family distinguished for generations in the men's wear manufacturing line. Pollyglow's factory produced only one item, men's all-purpose jumpers, and had always operated at full capacity—up to the moment the Interchangeable Style came in. Then, abruptly, overnight it seemed, there was no longer a market for purely male apparel.

He refused to admit that he and all of his machinery had become obsolete as the result of a simple change in fashion. What if the Interchangeable Style ruled out all sexual differentiation? "Try to make us swallow that!" he cackled at first. "Just try!"

But the red ink on his ledgers proved that his countrymen, however unhappily, *were* swallowing it.

Pollyglow began to spend long hours brooding at home instead of sitting nervously in his idle office. Chiefly he brooded on the pushing-around men had taken from women all through the twentieth century. Men had once been proud creatures; they had asserted themselves; they had enjoyed a high rank in human society. What had happened?

Most of their troubles could be traced to a development that occurred shortly before World War I, he decided. "Man-tailoring," the first identifiable villain.

When used in connection with women's clothes, "man-tailoring" implied that certain tweed skirts and cloth coats featured unusually meticulous workmanship. Its vogue was followed by the imitative patterns: slacks for trousers, blouses for shirts, essentially male garments which had been frilled here and furbeloved there and given new, feminine names. The "his-and-hers" fashions came next; they were universal by 1991.

Meanwhile, women kept gaining prestige and political power. The F.E.P.C. started policing discriminatory employment practices in any way based upon sex. A Supreme Court decision *(Mrs. Staub's Employment Agency for Lady Athletes v. The New York State Boxing Commission)* enunciated the law in Justice Emmeline Craggly's historic words: "Sex is a private, internal matter and ends at the individual's skin. From the skin outwards, in family chores, job opportunities, or even clothing, the sexes must be considered legally interchangeable in all respects save one. That one is the traditional duty of the male to support his family to the limit of his physical powers—the fixed cornerstone of all civilized existence."

Two months later, the Interchangeable Style appeared at the Paris openings.

It appeared, of course, as a version of the all-purpose jumper, a kind of short-sleeved tunic worn everywhere at that time. But the men's type and the women's type were now fused into a single Interchangeable garment.

That fusion was wrecking Pollyglow's business. Without some degree of maleness in dress, the workshop that had descended to him through a long line of manufacturing ancestors unquestionably had to go on the auctioneer's block.

He became increasingly desperate, increasingly bitter.

One night, he sat down to study the costumes of bygone eras. Which were intrinsically and flatteringly virile—so virile that no woman would dare force her way into them?

Men's styles in the late nineteenth century, for example. They were certainly masculine in that you never saw a picture of women wearing them, but what was to prevent the modern female from doing so if she chose? And they were far too heavy and clumsy for the gentle, made-to-order climates of today's world.

Back went Pollyglow, century by century, shaking his head and straining his eyes over ancient, fuzzy woodcuts. Not this, no, nor that. He was morosely examining pictures of knights in armor and trying to imagine a mailed shirt with a zipper up the back, when he leaned away wearily and noticed a fifteenth-century portrait lying among the pile of rejects at his feet.

This was the moment when Masculinism began.

Several of the other drawings had slid across the portrait, obscuring most of it. The tight-fitting hose over which Pollyglow had bitten his dry old lips negatively—these were barely visible. But between them, in emphatic, distinctive bulge, *between them*—

The codpiece!

This little bag which had once been worn on the front of the hose or breeches—how easily it could be added to a man's jumper! It was unquestionably, definitively male: any woman could wear it, of course, but on her clothing it would be merely a useless appendage, nay, worse than that, it would be an empty mockery.

He worked all night, roughing out drawings for his designers. In bed at last, and exhausted, he was still bubbling with so much enthusiasm that he forgot about sleep and hitched his aching shoulderblades up against the headboard. Visions of codpieces, millions of them, all hanging from Pollyglow Men's Jumpers, danced and swung and undulated in his head as he stared into the darkness.

But the wholesalers refused the new garment. The old Pollyglow Jumper—yes: there were still a few conservative, fuddy-duddy men around who preferred familiarity and comfort to style. But who in the world would want this unaesthetic novelty? Why it flew in the very face of the modern doctrine of interchangeable sexes!

His salesmen learned not to use that as an excuse for failure. "Separateness!" he would urge them as they slumped back into the office. "Differentness! You've got to sell them on separateness and differentness! It's our only hope—it's the hope of the world!"

Pollyglow almost forgot the moribund state of his business, suffocating for lack of sales. He wanted to save the world. He shook with the force of his revelation: he had come bearing a codpiece and no one would have it. They must—for their own good.

He borrowed heavily and embarked upon a modest advertising campaign. Ignoring the more expensive, general-circulation media, he concentrated his budget in areas of entertainment aimed exclusively at men. His ads appeared in high-rated television shows of the day, soap operas like "The Senator's Husband," and in the more popular men's magazines—*Cowboy Confession Stories* and *Scandals of World War I Flying Aces.*

The ads were essentially the same, whether they were one-pagers in color or sixty-second commercials. You saw a hefty, husky man with a go-to-hell expression on his face. He was smoking a big, black cigar and wore a brown derby cocked carelessly on the side of his head. And he was dressed in a Pollyglow Men's Jumper from the front of which there was suspended a huge codpiece in green or yellow or bright, bright red.

Originally, the text consisted of five emphatic lines:

MEN ARE DIFFERENT FROM WOMEN!
Dress differently!
Dress masculine!
Wear Pollyglow Men's Jumpers
With the Special Pollyglow Codpiece!

Early in the campaign, however, a market research specialist employed by Pollyglow's advertising agency pointed out that the word "masculine" had acquired unfortunate connotations in the last few decades. Tons of literature, sociological and psychological, on the subject of overcompensation, or too-overt maleness, had resulted in "masculine" being equated with "homosexuality" in people's minds.

These days, the specialist said, if you told someone he was masculine, you left him with the impression that you had called him a fairy. "How about saying, 'Dress masculin*ist?*'" the specialist suggested. "It kind of softens the blow."

Dubiously, Pollyglow experimented with the changed wording in a single ad. He found the new expression unsavory and flat. So he added another line in an attempt to give "masculinist" just a little more punch. The final ad read:

MEN ARE DIFFERENT FROM WOMEN!
Dress *differently!*
Dress *masculinist!*
Wear Pollyglow Men's Jumpers
With the *Special Pollyglow Codpiece!*
(And join the masculinist club!)

That ad pulled. It pulled beyond Pollyglow's wildest expectations.

Thousands upon thousands of queries rolled in from all over the country, from abroad, even from the Soviet Union and Red China, Where can I get a Pollyglow Men's Jumper with the Special Pollyglow Codpiece? How do I join the masculinist club? What are the rules and regulations of masculinism? How much are the dues?

Wholesalers, besieged by customers yearning for a jumper with a codpiece in contrasting color, turned to Pollyglow's astonished salesmen and shrieked out huge orders. Ten gross, fifty gross, a hundred gross. And immediately—if at all possible!

P. Edward Pollyglow was back in business. He produced and produced and produced, he sold and sold and sold. He shrugged off all the queries about the masculinist club as an amusing sidelight on the advertising business. It had only been mentioned as a fashion inducement—that there was some sort of in-group which you joined upon donning a codpiece.

Two factors conspired to make him think more closely about it: the competition and Shepherd L. Mibs.

After one startled glance at Pollyglow's new clothing empire, every other manufacturer began making jumpers equipped with codpieces. They admitted that Pollyglow had single-handedly reversed a fundamental trend in the men's wear field, that the codpiece was back with a vengeance and back to stay—but why did it have to be only the Pollyglow Codpiece? Why not the Ramsbottom Codpiece or the Hercules Codpiece or the Bangaclang Codpiece?

And since many of them had larger production facilities and bigger advertising budgets, the answer to their question made Pollyglow reflect sadly on the woeful rewards of a Columbus. His one chance was to emphasize the unique nature of the Pollyglow Codpiece.

It was at this crucial period that he met Shepherd Leonidas Mibs.

Mibs—"Old Shep" he was called by those who came to follow his philosophical leadership—was the second of the great triumvirs of Masculinism. He was a peculiar, restless man who had wandered about the country and from occupation to occupation, searching for a place in society. All-around college athlete, sometime unsuccessful prizefighter and starving hobo, big-game hunter and coffee-shop poet, occasional short-order cook, occasional gigolo—he had been everything but a photographer's model. And that he became when his fierce, crooked face—knocked permanently out of line by the nightstick of a Pittsburgh policeman—attracted the attention of Pollyglow's advertising agency.

His picture was used in one of the ads. It was not any more conspicuously successful than the others; and he was dropped at the request of the photographer who had been annoyed by Mibs's insistence that a sword should be added to the costume of derby, codpiece, and cigar.

Mibs knew he was right. He became a pest, returning to the agency day after day and attempting to persuade anyone at all that a sword should be worn in the Pollyglow ads, a long, long sword, the bigger and heavier the better. "Sword man is here," the receptionist would flash inside, and "My God, tell him I'm not back from lunch yet," the Art Director would whisper over the intercom.

Having nothing else to do, Mibs spent long hours on the heavily upholstered couch in the outer office. He studied the ads in the Pollyglow campaign, examining each one over and over again. He scribbled pages of comments in a little black notebook. He came to be accepted and ignored as so much reception-room furniture.

But Pollyglow gave him full attention. Arriving one day to discuss a new campaign with his account executive—a campaign to stress the very special qualities of the Pollyglow Codpiece, for which, under no circumstances, should a substitute ever be accepted—he began a conversation with the strange, ugly, earnest young man. "You can tell that account executive to go to hell," Pollyglow told the receptionist as they went off to a restaurant. "I've found what I've been looking for."

The sword was a good idea, he felt, a damn good idea. Put it in the ad. But he was much more interested in certain of the thoughts developed at such elaborate length in Mibs's little black notebook.

If one phrase about a masculinist club had made the ad so effective, Mibs asked, why not exploit that phrase? A great and crying need had evidently been touched. "It's like this. When the old-time saloon disappeared, men had no place to get away from women but the barber shop. Now, with the goddamn Interchangeable Haircut, even that out's been taken away. All a guy's got left is the men's room, and they're working on that, I'll bet they're working on that!"

Pollyglow sipped at his glass of hot milk and nodded. "You think a masculinist club would fill a gap in their lives? An element of exclusiveness, say, like the English private club for gentlemen?"

"Hell, no! They want something exclusive, all right—something that will exclude women—but not like a private club one damn bit. Everything these days is telling them that they're nobody special, they're just people. There are men people and women people—and what's the difference anyway? They want something that does what the codpiece does, that tells them they're not people, they're *men!* Straight down-the-line, two-fisted, let's-stand-up-and-be-counted *men!* A place where they can get away from the crap that's being thrown at them all the time: the women-maybe-are-the-superior-sex crap, the women-outlive-them-and-outown-them crap, the a-real-man-has-no-need-to-act-masculine crap—all that crap."

His eloquence was so impressive and compelling that Pollyglow had let his hot milk grow cold. He ordered a refill and another cup of coffee for Mibs. "A club," he mused, "where the only requirement for membership would be manhood."

"You still don't get it." Mibs picked up the steaming coffee and drank it down in one tremendous swallow. He leaned forward, his eyes glittering. "Not just a club—a *movement*. A movement fighting for men's rights, carrying on propaganda against the way our divorce laws are set up, publishing books that build up all the good things about being a man. A movement with newspapers and songs and slogans. Slogans like 'The Only Fatherland for a Man is Masculinity.' And 'Male Men of the World Unite—You Have Nothing to Gain but Your Balls!' See? A movement."

"Yes, a movement!" Pollyglow babbled, seeing indeed. "A movement with an official uniform—the Pollyglow Codpiece! And perhaps different codpieces for different— for different, well—"

"For different ranks in the movement," Mibs finished. "That's a hell of a good idea! Say green for Initiate. Red for Full-Blooded Male. Blue for First-Class Man. And white, we'd keep white for the highest rank of all—*Superman*. And, listen, here's another idea."

But Pollyglow listened no longer. He sat back in his chair, a pure and pious light suffusing his gray, sunken face. "None genuine unless it's official," he whispered. "None official unless stamped Genuine Pollyglow Codpiece, copyright and pat. pending."

Masculinist annals were to describe this luncheon as the Longchamps Entente. Later that historic day, Pollyglow's lawyer drew up a contract making Shepherd L. Mibs Director of Public Relations for the Pollyglow Enterprises.

A clip-out coupon was featured in all the new ads:

WANT TO LEARN MORE ABOUT MASCULINISM?

WANT TO JOIN THE MASCULINIST CLUB?

Just fill out this coupon and mail it to the address below. Absolutely no charge and no obligation—just lots of free literature and information on this exciting new movement!

FOR MEN ONLY!

The coupons poured in and business boomed. Mibs became head of a large staff. The little two-page newsletter that early applicants received quickly became a twenty-page weekly, the *Masculinist News*. In turn, it spawned a monthly full-color magazine, the *Hairy Chest*, and a wildly popular television program, "The Bull Session."

In every issue of the *Masculinist News*, Pollyglow's slogan, "Men Are *Different* from Women," shared the top of the front page with Mibs's "Men Are as *Good* as Women." The upper left-hand corner displayed a cut of Pollyglow, "Our Founding Father— Old Pep," and under that ran the front-page editorial, "Straight Talk from Old Shep."

A cartoon might accompany the editorial. A truculent man wearing a rooster comb marched into cowering masses of hippy, busty women. Caption: "The Cock of the Walk." Or, more didactically, hundreds of tiny children around a man who was naked except for a huge codpiece. Across the codpiece, in execrable but highly patriotic Latin, the words *E Unus Pluribum*—and a translation for those who needed it, "Out of the one, many."

Frequently, a contemporary note was struck. A man executed for murdering his sweetheart would be depicted, a bloody axe in his hands, between drawings of Nathan Hale being hanged and Lincoln striking off the chains of slavery. There was a true tabloid's contempt for the rights or wrongs of a case. If a man was involved, the motto ran, he was automatically on the side of the angels.

"Straight Talk from Old Shep" exhorted and called to action in a style reminiscent of a football dressing room between halves. "Men are a lost sex in America," it would intone, "because men are being lost, lost and mislaid, in the country as a whole. Everything nowadays is designed to sap their confidence and lessen their stature. Who wouldn't rather be strong than limp, hard than soft? Stand up for yourselves, men of America, stand up high!"

There was a ready audience for this sort of thing, as the constantly rising circulation of the *Masculinist News* attested. From shower to washstand to wall urinal, the word sped that the problems of manhood were at last being recognized, that virility might become a positive term once more. Lodges of the Masculinist Society were established in every state; most large cities soon boasted fifteen or more chapters.

Rank and file enthusiasm shaped the organization from the beginning. A Cleveland chapter originated the secret grip; Houston gave the movement its set of unprintable passwords. The Montana Lodge's Declaration of Principles became the preamble to the national Masculinist constitution: "…all men are created equal with women…that among these rights are life, liberty and the pursuit of the opposite sex…from each according to his sperm, to each according to her ova…."

The subgroup known as the Shepherd L. Mibs League first appeared in Albany. Those who took the Albany Pledge swore to marry only women who would announce during the ceremony, "I promise to love, to honor and to *obey*"—with exactly that emphasis. There were many such Masculinst subgroups: The Cigar and Cuspidor Club, the Ancient Order of Love 'Em and Leave 'Em, The I-Owe-None-Of-It-to-the-Little-Woman Society.

Both leaders shared equally in the revenues from the movement, and both grew rich. Mibs alone made a small fortune out of his book, *Man: The First Sex,* considered the bible of Masculinism. But Pollyglow, Pollyglow's wealth was heaped up beyond the wildest dreams of his avarice—and his avarice had been no small-time dreamer.

He was no longer in the men's wear line; he was now in the label-manufacturing business. He made labels to be sewed on to the collars of men's jumpers and inside the crowns of brown derbies, cigar bands for cigars, and little metal nameplates for swords. One item alone did he continue to manufacture himself. He felt an enduring and warm affection for the little fabric container bearing the legend *Genuine Pollyglow Codpiece;* it seemed to involve him in the activities of his fellow men everywhere, to give him a share in their successes and their failures.

But everything else was franchised.

His imprimatur came to be needed, needed and paid for, on a vast variety of articles. No manufacturer in his right business mind would dream of coming out with a new model of a sports car, a new office swivel chair or, for that matter, a new type of truss, without having *Official Equipment—Masculinist Movement of America* printed prominently on his product. The pull of fashion has always been that of the stampeding herd: many men who were not card-carrying Masculinists refused to buy anything that did not bear the magic phrase in the familiar blue isosceles triangle. Despite its regional connotations, all over the world, in Ceylon, in Ecuador, in Sydney, Australia, and Ibadan, Nigeria, men demanded that label and paid premium prices for it.

The much-neglected, often-dreamed-of men's market had come of age. And P. Edward Pollyglow was its world-wide tax collector.

He ran the business and built wealth. Mibs ran the organization and built power. It took three full years for a clash to develop.

Mibs had spent his early manhood at a banquet of failure: he had learned to munch on suppressed rage, to drink goblets of thwarted fury. The swords he now strapped back on to men's bodies were always intended for more than decorative purposes.

Swords, he wrote in the *Hairy Chest,* were as alien to women as beards and mustaches. A full beard, therefore, and a sweeping handlebar mustache, belonged to the guise of Masculinism. And if a man were bearded like the pard and sworded like a bravo, should he still talk in the subdued tones of the eunuch? Should he still walk in the hesitant fashion of a mere family-supporter? He should not! An armed male should act like an armed male, he should walk cockily, he should bellow, he should brawl, he should *swagger.*

He should also be ready to back up the swagger.

Boxing matches settled disputes at first. Then came fencing lessons and a pistol range in every Masculinist lodge. And inevitably, almost imperceptibly, the full Code Duello was revived.

The first duels were in the style of German university fraternities. Deep in the basement of their lodges, heavily masked and padded men whacked away at each other with sabers. A few scratches about the forehead which were proudly worn to work the next day, a scoring system which penalized defensive swordplay—these were discussed lightly at dinner parties, argued about in supermarkets.

Boys will be boys. Men will be men. Attendance at spectator sports began to drop sharply: didn't that indicate something healthy was at work? Wasn't it better for men to experience real conflict themselves than to identify with distant athletes who were only simulating battle?

Then the battles became a bit too real. When a point of true honor was involved, the masks and padding were dropped and a forest clearing at dawn substituted for the whitewashed lodge basement. An ear was chopped off, a face gashed, a chest run through. The winner would strut his victory through the streets; the loser, dying or badly wounded, would insist morosely that he had fallen on the radio aerial of his car.

Absolute secrecy was demanded by the Code Duello from all concerned—the combatants, seconds, officials, and attending surgeons. So, despite much public outcry and hurriedly passed new laws, very few duelists were ever prosecuted. Men of all walks of life began to accept armed combat as the only intelligent way to settle an important controversy.

Interestingly enough, swords in an open field at dawn were used mostly in the East. West of the Mississippi, the two duelists would appear at opposite ends of the main street at high noon, pistols holstered to their thighs. Advance warning would have emptied the street and pointedly suggested other locales for police officials. At a signal, the two men walked stiff-legged toward each other; at another signal, they pulled out their pistols and blazed away. Living and/or dead were then bundled into a station wagon which had been kept nearby with its motor running. At the local Masculinist Lodge, there would be a rousing discussion of the battle's fine points as well as medical treatment and preparations for burial.

Many variations developed. The Chicago Duel had a brief and bloody vogue in the larger cities. Two cars, each driven by a close friend of the duelist sitting in the rear, would pass in opposite directions on the highway or a busy metropolitan street. Once abreast, foe could pound at foe with a submachine gun to absolute heart's content: but firing was expected to cease as soon as the vehicles had drawn apart. Unfortunately—in the intense excitement of the moment—few antagonists remembered to do this; the mortality rate was unpleasantly high among other motorists and open-mouthed bystanders, not to mention the seconds and officials of the duel.

Possibly more frightening than the Chicago Duel were the clumps of men—bearded, sworded, cigared and codpieced—who caroused drunkenly through the streets at night, singing bawdy songs and shouting unintelligible slogans up at the darkened windows of the offices where they worked. And the mobs which descended upon the League of Women Voters, tossing membership lists and indignant members alike pell-mell into the street. Masculinism was showing an ugly edge.

Pollyglow became alarmed and demanded an end to the uproar. "Your followers are getting out of hand," he told Mibs. "Let's get back to the theoretical principles of Masculinism. Let's stick to things like the codpiece and the beard and the cigar. We don't want to turn the country against us."

There was no trouble, Mibs insisted. A couple of the boys whooping it up—it was female propaganda that magnified it into a major incident. What about the letters he'd been receiving from other women, pleased by the return of chivalry and the strutting male, enjoying men who offered them seats in public conveyances and protected them with their heart's blood?

When Pollyglow persisted, invoking the sacred name of sound business practice, Mibs let him have it. He, Shepherd L. Mibs, was the spiritual leader of Masculinism, infallible and absolute. What he said went. *Whatever* he said went. Any time he felt like it, he could select another label for official equipment.

The old man swallowed hard a few times, little lumps riding up and down the tightly stretched concave curve of his throat. He patted Mibs's powerful shoulders, croaked out a pacifying pair of phrases, and toddled back to his office. From that day on, he was a wordless figurehead. He made public appearances as Founding Father; otherwise, he lived quietly in his luxurious skyscraper, The Codpiece Tower.

The ironies of history! A new figure entered the movement that same day, a humble, nondescript figure whom Mibs, in his triumph, would have dismissed contemptuously. As Trotsky dismissed Stalin.

II

DORSELBLAD

Masculinists had rioted in a California town and torn down the local jail. Various pickpockets, housebreakers, and habitual drunks were liberated—as well as a man who had spent eighteen years in the alimony section of the jail, Henry Dorselblad.

More than anyone else, Dorselblad was to give Masculinism its political flavor and peculiar idiom. Who that has heard it can ever forget the mighty skirl of ten thousand male voices singing—

> Oh, Hank Dorselblad is come
>   out of the West,
> Through all the wide Border, his
>   codpiece is best....

Hellfire Henry, Hank the Tank, Give 'Em Hell Henry, Damn 'Em All Dorselblad—this was a culture hero who caught the American imagination like no other since Billy the Kid. And, like Billy the Kid, Henry Dorselblad was physically a very undistinguished man.

Extremely short, prematurely bald, weak of chin and pot of belly, young Dorselblad had been uninteresting even as prey to most women. His middle-aged landlady, however, had bludgeoned him into matrimony when he was only twenty-two, immediately purchasing twelve thousand dollars worth of labor-saving household machinery on the installment plan. She naturally expected comfortable and diligent support thereafter.

Dorselblad fulfilled her expectations during several exhausting years by holding two full-time jobs and a part-time one on weekends. He was a skilled programmer for payroll computing machines: in his day, such men had each replaced two complete staffs of bookkeepers—they were well worth their high salaries and substantial job security. The invention of the self-programming payroll computer destroyed this idyllic state.

At the age of twenty-five, Henry Dorselblad found himself technologically unemployed. He became one of the shabby, starving programmers who wandered the streets of the financial district, their punching tools in their right hands, looking for a day's work in some old-fashioned, as yet unconverted firm.

He tried desperately to become a serviceman for the new self-programming computers. But twenty-five is an advanced age: personnel interviewers tended to classify him as "a senior citizen—junior grade." For a while, he eked out a bare living as a computer sweeper, clearing office floors of the tiny circular and oblong residues dropped by the card-punching machines. But even here, science and industry moved on. The punch-waste packer was invented, and he was flung into the streets again.

Her bank account shrinking at an alarming rate, Mrs. Dorselblad sued him for nonsupport. He went to jail. She obtained a divorce with alimony payments set at a reasonable level—three-fourths of its highest recorded earning power. Unable to make even a token payment as a demonstration of good faith, he was kept in jail.

Once a year, a visiting panel of women judges asked him what efforts he had made in the past twelve months to rehabilitate himself. When Dorselblad cunningly evaded the question with a speech on the difficulties of looking for a job while in prison, he was given a severe tongue-lashing and remanded to the warden for special punishment. He became bitter and sullen, a typical hardened alimony criminal.

Eighteen years passed. His wife married three more times, burying two husbands and jailing the third for nonsupport. His responsibilities in no way affected by the vicious negligence of his successors, Henry Dorselblad lived on behind bars. He learned to steep raisin-jack in a can under his cot and, more important, to enjoy drinking it. He learned to roll cigarettes made of toilet paper and tobacco from butts stomped out by the guards. And he learned to think.

He spent eighteen years brooding on his wrongs, real or imaginary, eighteen years studying the social problems from which they sprang, eighteen years reading the recognized classics in the field of relations between the sexes: Nietzsche, Hitler, the Marquis de Sade, Mohammed, James Thurber. It is to this period of close reasoning and intense theorizing that we must look if we are to understand the transformation of a shy and inarticulate nonentity into the most eloquent rabble rouser, the most astute political leader of his age.

A new Henry Dorselblad was released upon the world by the Masculinist mob. He led them, drunken rescuers and cheering prisoners alike, out of the smoking wreckage of the jail, beating time with the warden's hat as he taught them the riotous verses of a song he had composed on the spot, "The Double Standard Forever—Hurrah, Boys, Hurrah!"

One by one, the movers and shakers of his time learned to reckon with him. Re-arrested in another state and awaiting extradition, Dorselblad refused to grant the governor an interview because she was a woman. A free-born male citizen, he maintained, could not accord legal or political dominance to a mere female.

The governor smiled at the paunchy little man who shut his eyes and jumped up and down, chanting, "Kitchens and skirts! Vapors and veils! Harems and whorehouses!" But she did not smile a week later when his followers tore down this prison too and carried him out on their shoulders, nor the next year when she was defeated for re-election—both disasters to the accompaniment of the self-same chant.

Nor did Shepherd L. Mibs smile much after Henry Dorselblad's guest appearance on "The Bull Session." Once it became apparent that he was political dynamite, that no state and no governor would dare move against him, he had to be tapped for the Masculinist program. And almost every viewer in the United States and Canada saw Shepherd Mibs, the moderator of the program and the National President of

Masculinism, forced into a secondary, stammering position, completely eclipsed by Hellfire Henry.

Throughout the country, next day, people quoted Henry Dorselblad's indictment of modern society: "Women needed the law's special protection when they were legally inferiors of men. Now they have equality *and* special protection. They can't have both!"

Columnists and editorial writers discussed his pithy dictum: "Behind every successful woman there stands an unsuccessful man!"

Everyone argued the biopsychological laws he had propounded: "A man who enjoys no power during the day cannot be powerful at night. An impotent man in politics is an impotent man in bed. If women want lusty husbands, they must first turn to them as heroic leaders."

Actually, Dorselblad was simply rephrasing passages from Mibs's editorials which he had read and reread in his prison cell. But he rephrased them with the conviction of a Savonarola, the fire and fanaticism of a true prophet. And, from the beginning, it was observed, he had almost the same impact on women as on men.

Women flocked to hear him speak, to listen to his condemnations of their sex. They swooned as he mocked their faults, they wept as he cursed their impudence, they screamed yeas as he demanded that they give up their rights and return to their correct position as "Ladies—not Lords—of Creation."

Women flocked; men massed. Dorselblad's personality tripled the membership of the Movement. His word, his whims, were law.

He added an item to Masculinist costume, a long, curling eagle's feather stuck in the brim of the derby. All over the world, eagles were hunted down relentlessly and plucked bare for the new American market. He added a belligerent third principle to those enunciated by Mibs and Pollyglow: "No legal disabilities without corresponding legal advantages." Men refused to be breadwinners or soldiers unless they were recognized as the absolute monarchs of the home. Wife-beating cases and paternity suits clogged the courts as the Masculinist Society pledged its resources to any man fighting the great fight for what came to be called the Privilege of the Penis.

Dorselblad conquered everywhere. When he assumed a special office as the Leader of Masculinism—far above all Founders and Presidents—Mibs argued and fought, but finally conceded. When he designed a special codpiece for himself alone—the Polka-Dotted Codpiece of the Leading Man—Mibs scowled for a while, then nodded weakly. When he put his finger on Masculinism's most important target—the repeal of the Nineteenth Amendment—Mibs immediately wrote editorials damning that irresponsible piece of legislation and demanding the return of elections held in saloons and decisions made in smoke-filled cubicles.

At the first National Convention of Masculinism in Madison, Wisconsin, Old Shep shared a docile anonymity with Old Pep, in a corner of the platform. He yelled and stamped with the rest when Hank the Tank thundered: "This is a *man's* civilization. *Men* built it, and—if they don't get their rights back—*men* can tear it down!" He chuckled with the others at the well-worn barbs that Dorselblad threw: "I didn't raise my boy to be a housewife" and "Give me the name of one woman, just one woman, who ever—" He was in the forefront of the mob that marched three times around the hall behind Hellfire Henry, roaring out the Song of Repeal:

> *Cram! Cram! Cram! the ballot boxes—*
> *Jam! Jam! Jam! the voting booths...*

It was a stirring spectacle: two thousand delegates from every state in the union, their derbies bouncing rhythmically on their heads, their eagle feathers waving in majestic unison, swords jangling, codpieces dangling, and great, greasy clouds of cigar smoke rolling upwards to announce the advent of the male millennium. Bearded, mustachioed men cheered themselves hoarse and pounded each other's backs; they stamped so enthusiastically on the floor that not until the voting began was it discovered that the Iowa delegation had smashed themselves completely through and down into the basement below.

But nothing could destroy the good humor of that crowd. The more seriously injured were packed off to hospitals, those with only broken legs or smashed collar bones were joshed uproariously and hauled back to the convention floor for the balloting. A series of resolutions was read off, the delegates bellowing their agreement and unanimity.

Resolved: that the Nineteenth Amendment to the Constitution of the United States, granting universal female suffrage, is unnatural biologically, politically, and morally, and the chief cause of our national troubles....

Resolved: that all proper pressure be brought to bear on the legislators of this nation, both holding and seeking office...

Resolved: that this convention go on record as demanding...

Resolved: that we hereby...

There were midterm congressional elections that year.

A Masculinist plan of battle was drawn up for every state. Coordinating committees were formed to work closely with youth, minority, and religious groups. Each member was assigned a specific job: volunteers from Madison Avenue spent their evenings grinding out propagandistic news releases; Pennsylvanian coal miners and Nebraskan wheat farmers devoted their Saturdays to haranguing the inmates of old-age homes.

Henry Dorselblad drove them all relentlessly, demanding more effort from everyone, making deals with both Republicans and Democrats, reform elements and big city bosses, veterans' organizations, and pacifist groups. "Let's win the first time out—before the opposition wakes up!" he screamed to his followers.

Scrabbling like mad at their beloved fence, the politicians tried to avoid taking a definite position on either side. Women were more numerous and more faithful voters than men, they pointed out: if it came to a clear contest, women had to win. Masculinist pressure on the ballot box was considerable, but it wasn't the only pressure.

Then the voice of Hank the Tank was heard in the land, asking women—in the name of their own happiness—to see to it that the long, long winter of feminism was definitely past. Many women in his audiences fainted dead away from the sheer flattery of having Henry Dorselblad ask them for a favor. A ladies' auxiliary to the Masculinist Movement was organized—The Companions of the Codpiece. It grew rapidly. Female candidates for office were so ferociously heckled by members of their own sex that they demanded special police protection before addressing a street-corner rally. "You should be ironing your husband's shirts!" the lady masculinists shouted. "Go home! Your supper's burning!"

One week before election, Dorselblad unleashed the Direct Action squads. Groups of men, wearing codpieces and derbies, descended upon public buildings all over the country and chained themselves to lampposts outside. While officers of the law chopped away at their self-imposed bonds with hacksaws and acetylene torches, the Masculinists loudly intoned a new liturgy: "Women! Give us your vote—and we will give you back your men! We need your vote to win—you need to have us win! Women! Give us your vote on Election Day!"

Where, their opponents inquired cruelly, was the vaunted pride and arrogance of Masculinism in such an appeal? Were the Lords of Creation actually begging the weaker sex for a boon? Oh, for shame!

But Dorselblad's followers ignored these jeers. Women must themselves return the vote they had falsely acquired. Then they would be happy, their men would be happy, and the world would be right again. If they didn't do this of their own free will, well, men were the stronger sex. There were alternatives....

On this ominous note, the election was held.

Fully one-fourth of the new Congress was elected on a Masculinist platform. Another, larger group of fellow travelers and occasional sympathizers still wondered which way the wind was really blowing.

But the Masculinists had also acquired control of three-quarters of the state legislatures. They thus had the power to ratify a constitutional amendment that would destroy female suffrage in America—once the repeal bill passed Congress and was submitted to the states.

The eyes of the nation swung to its capitol. Every leader of any significance in the movement hurried there to augment the Masculinist lobby. Their opponents came in great numbers too, armed with typewriter and mimeograph against the gynecocratic Ragnarok.

A strange hodge-podge of groups, these anti-Masculinists. Alumnae associations from women's colleges fought for precedence at formal functions with Daughters of 1776; editors of liberal weeklies snubbed conservatively inclined leaders of labor unions, who in turn jostled ascetic young men in clerical collars. Heavy-set, glaring-eyed lady writers spat upon slim and stylish lady millionairesses who had hurried back from Europe for the crisis. Respectable matrons from Richmond, Virginia, bridled at the scientific jocosities of birth controllers from San Francisco. They argued bitterly with each other, followed entirely divergent plans of action and generally delighted their codpieced, derbied, cigar-smoking adversaries. But their very variety and heterogeneity gave many a legislator pause: they looked too much like a cross-section of the population.

The bill to submit repeal of the Nineteenth Amendment to the states wandered through an interminable Congressional labyrinth of maneuver and rewording and committee action. Mobs and counter-mobs demonstrated everywhere. Newspapers committed themselves firmly to one side or the other, depending on their ownership and, occasionally, their readership. Almost alone in the country, *The New York Times* kept its head, observing that the problem was very difficult and asking that the decision—whatever it eventually was—be the right one—whatever that might be.

Passing the Senate by a tiny margin, the bill was sent to the House of Representatives. That day, Masculinist and anti-Masculinist alike begged and battled for a gallery pass. Hellfire Henry and his followers were admitted only after they had checked their swords. Their opponents were forcibly deprived of a huge sign smuggled to the gallery in four sections. "Congressman!" the sign shouted. "Your grandmother was a suffragette!"

Over the protests of many legislators seeking anonymity on this issue, a roll-call vote was decided upon. Down the list of states it went, eliciting so many groans and cheers from the onlookers that the Speaker finally had to lay aside his damaged gavel. Neck and neck the two sides went, the Masculinists always holding a slim lead, but never one large enough. Finally the feverish talliers in the gallery saw that a deadlock was inevitable. The bill lacked one vote of the two-thirds majority necessary.

It was then that Elvis P. Borax, a junior Representative from Florida who had asked to be passed originally, got to his feet and stated that he had decided how to cast his vote.

The tension was fantastic as everyone waited for Congressman Borax to cast the deciding vote. Women crammed handkerchiefs into their mouths; strong men whimpered softly. Even the guards stood away from their posts and stared at the man who was deciding the fate of the country.

Three men rose in the balcony: Hellfire Henry, Old Shep, and white-haired Old Pep. Standing side by side, they forebodingly held aloft right hands clenched around the hilts of invisible swords. The young Congressman studied their immobile forms with a white face.

"I vote nay," he breathed at last. "I vote against the bill."

Pandemonium. Swirling, yelling crowds everywhere. The House guards, even with their reinforcements from the Senate, had a hard, bruising time clearing the galleries. A dozen people were trampled, one of them an elderly chief of the Chippewa Indians who had come to Washington to settle a claim against the government and had taken a seat in the gallery only because it was raining outside.

Congressman Borax described his reactions in a televised interview. "I felt as if I were looking down into my open grave. I had to vote that way, though. Mother asked me to."

"Weren't you frightened?" the interviewer asked.

"I was very frightened," he admitted. "But I was also very brave."

A calculated political risk had paid off. From that day on, he led the counter-revolution.

III

THE COUNTER-REVOLUTION

The anti-Masculinists had acquired both a battlecry and a commander-in-chief.

As the Masculinist tide rose, thirty-seven states liberalizing their divorce laws in the husband's favor, dozens of disparate opposition groups rallied to the standard that had been raised by the young Congressman from Florida. Here alone they could ignore charges of "creeping feminism." Here alone they could face down epithets like "codpiece-pricker" and "skirt-waver," as well as the ultimate, most painful thrust— "mother-lover."

Two years later, they were just strong enough to capture the Presidential nomination of one of the major parties. For the first time in decades, a man—Elvis P. Borax—was nominated for the office of chief executive.

After consulting the opinion polls and his party's leading strategists, not to mention his own instincts and inclinations, he decided to run on a platform of pure, undiluted Mother.

He had never married, he explained, because Mother needed him. She was eighty-three and a widow; what was more important than her happiness? Let the country at large live by the maxim which, like the Bible, had never failed: Mother Knew Best.

Star-studded photographs of the frail old lady appeared all over the land. When Dorselblad made a sneering reference to her, Borax replied with a song of his own composition that quickly soared to the top of the Hit Parade. That record is a marvelous political document, alive through and through with our most glorious traditions. In his earnest, delicately whining tenor, Borax sang:

> *Rule, Maternal! My mother rules my heart!*
> *Mother never, never, never was a tart!*

And there was the eloquence of the famous "Cross of Swords" speech which Borax delivered again and again, at whistle stops, at church picnics, at county fairs, at state rallies.

"You shall not press down upon the loins of mankind this codpiece of elastic," he would thunder. "You shall not crucify womankind upon a cross of swords!

"And do you know why you shall not?" he would demand, his right hand throbbing above his head like a tambourine. The audience, open-mouthed, glistening-eyed, would sit perfectly still and wait eagerly. *"Do you know?"*

"Because," would come a soft, slow whisper at last over the public address system, "because it will make *Mother* unhappy."

It was indeed a bitter campaign, fought for keeps. The Dorselbladites were out to redefine the franchise for all time—Borax called for a law to label Masculinism as a criminal conspiracy. Mom's Home-Made Apple Pie clashed head-on with the Sword, the Codpiece, and the Cigar.

The other party, dominated by Masculinists, had selected a perfect counter-candidate. A former Under-Secretary of the Army and currently America's chief delegate to the thirteen-year-old Peace and Disarmament Conference in Paris: the unforgettable Mrs. Strunt.

Clarissima Strunt's three sturdy sons accompanied her on every speaking engagement, baseball bats aslant on their shoulders. She also had a mysterious husband who was busy with "a man's work." In photographs which were occasionally fed to the newspapers, he stood straight and still, a shotgun cradled in his arm, while a good hound dog flushed game out of faraway bushes. His face was never clearly recognizable, but there was something in the way he held his head that emphatically suggested an attitude of no nonsense from anybody—especially women.

Hellfire Henry and Kitchen-Loving Clarissima worked beautifully together. After Dorselblad had pranced up and down a platform with a belligerently waving codpiece, after he had exhorted, demanded and anathematized, Clarissima Strunt would come forward. Replying to his gallant bow with a low curtsy, she would smooth out the red-and-white-checked apron she always wore and talk gently of the pleasures of being a woman in a truly male world.

When she placed a mother's hand on the button at the top of her youngest son's baseball cap and fondly whispered, "Oh, no, I didn't raise my boy to be a sissy!"—when she threw her head back and proudly asserted, "I get more pleasure out of one day's washing and scrubbing than out of ten years' legislating and politicking!"—when she stretched plump arms out to the audience and begged, "Please give me your vote! I want to be the *last* woman President!"—when she put it that way, which red-blooded registered voter could find it in his heart to refuse?

Every day, more and more Masculinist codpieces could be counted on subways and sidewalks, as well as the bustle-and-apron uniforms of the ladies auxiliary.

Despite many misgivings, the country's intellectual leaders had taken up Borax's mom-spangled banner as the only alternative to what they regarded as sexual fascism. They were popularly known as the Suffragette Eggheads. About this time, they began to observe sorrowfully that the election was resolving an ancient American myth—and it looked like the myth made flesh would prevail.

For Borax campaigned as a Dutiful Son and waved his mother's photograph up and down the United States. But Clarissima Strunt was Motherhood Incarnate; and she was telling the voters to lay it on the line for Masculinism.

What kind of President would Strunt have made? How would this soft-voiced and strong-minded woman have dealt with Dorselblad once they were both in power? There were those who suggested that she was simply an astute politician riding the right horse; there were others who based a romance between the checked apron and the spotted codpiece upon Mrs. Strunt's undeniable physical resemblance to the notorious Nettie-Ann Dorselblad. Today, these are all idle speculations.

All we know for certain is that the Masculinists were three-to-two favorites in every bookmaking parlor and stockbroker's office. That a leading news magazine came out with a cover showing a huge codpiece and entitled *Man of the Year.* That Henry Dorselblad began receiving semi-official visits from U.N. officials and members of the diplomatic corps. That cigar, derby, and sword sales boomed, and P. Edward Polly-glow bought a small European nation which, after evicting the inhabitants, he turned into an eighteen-hole golf course.

Congressman Borax, facing certain defeat, began to get hysterical. Gone was the crinkly smile, gone the glow from that sweet, smooth-shaven face. He began to make reckless charges. He charged corruption. He charged malfeasance, he charged trea-son, murder, blackmail, piracy, simony, forgery, kidnapping, barratry, attempted rape, mental cruelty, indecent exposure, and subornation of perjury.

And one night, during a televised debate, he went too far.

Shepherd Leonidas Mibs had endured displacement as Leader of the Movement far too long for a man of his temperament. He was the position at the rear of the platform, at the bottom of the front page, as an alternative speaker to Hellfire Henry. He burned with rebellion.

He tried to form a new secessionist group, Masculinists Anonymous. Members would be vowed to strict celibacy and have nothing to do with women beyond the indirect requirements of artificial insemination. Under the absolute rule of Mibs as Grand Master, they would concentrate on the nationwide secret sabotage of Mother's Day, the planting of time bombs in marriage license bureaus, and sudden, night-time raids on sexually nonsegregated organizations such as the P.T.A.

This dream might have radically altered future Masculinist history. Unfortunately, one of Mibs's trusted lieutenants sold out to Dorselblad in return for the cigar-stand concession at all national conventions. Old Shep emerged white of lip from an interview with Hank the Tank. He passed the word, and Masculinists Anonymous was dissolved.

But he continued to mutter, to wait. And during the next-to-last television de-bate—when Congressman Borax rose in desperate rebuttal to Clarissima Strunt— Shepherd Mibs at last came into his own.

The videotape recording of the historic debate was destroyed in the mad Election Day riots two weeks later. It is therefore impossible at this late date to reconstruct precisely what Borax replied to Mrs. Strunt's accusation that he was the tool of "the Wall Street women and Park Avenue parlor feminists."

All accounts agree that he began by shouting, "And *your* friends, Clarissima Strunt, *your* friends are led by—"

But what did he say next?

Did he say, as Mibs claimed, "—an ex-bankrupt, an ex-convict, and an ex-homo-sexual"?

Did he say, as several newspapers reported, "—an ex-bankrupt, an ex-convict, and an ex-heterosexual"?

Or did he say, as Borax himself insisted to his dying day, nothing more than "—an ex-bankrupt, an ex-convict, and an ex-homo bestial"?

Whatever the precise wording, the first part of the charge indubitably referred to P. Edward Pollyglow and the second to Henry Dorselblad. That left the third epithet—and Shepherd L. Mibs.

Newspapers from coast to coast carried the headline:

MIBS CLAIMS MORTAL INSULT

CHALLENGES BORAX TO DUEL

For a while, that is, for three or four editions, there was a sort of stunned silence. America held its breath. Then:

DORSELBLAD DISPLEASED

URGES MIBS CALL IT OFF

And:

OLD PEP PLEADING WITH OLD SHEP—

"DON'T DIRTY YOUR HANDS WITH HIM"

But:

MIBS IMMOVABLE

DEMANDS A DEATH

As well as:

CLARISSIMA STRUNT SAYS:

"THIS IS A MAN'S AFFAIR"

Meanwhile, from the other side, there was an uncertain, tentative approach to the problem:

BORAX BARS DUEL—

PROMISE TO MOTHER

This did not sit well with the new, duel-going public. There was another approach:

CANDIDATE FOR CHIEF EXECUTIVE

CAN'T BREAK LAW, CLERGYMEN CRY

Since this too had little effect on the situation:

CONGRESSMAN OFFERS TO APOLOGIZE:

"DIDN'T SAY IT BUT WILL RETRACT"

Unfortunately:

SHEP CRIES "FOR SHAME!

BORAX MUST BATTLE ME—

OR BEAR COWARD'S BRAND"

The candidate and his advisors, realizing there was no way out:

MIBS-BORAX DUEL SET FOR MONDAY
HEAVYWEIGHT CHAMP TO OFFICIATE

Pray for Me, Borax Begs Mom:
Your Dear Boy, Alive or Dead

Nobel Prize Winner Gets Nod
As Bout's Attending Sawbones

Borax and ten or twelve cigar-munching counselors locked themselves in a hotel room and considered the matter from all possible angles. By this time, of course, he and his staff only smoked cigars under conditions of the greatest privacy. In public, they ate mints.

They had been given the choice of weapons, and a hard choice it was. The Chicago Duel was dismissed as being essentially undignified and tending to blur the Presidential image. Borax's assistant campaign manager, a brilliant Jewish Negro from the Spanish-speaking section of Los Angeles, suggested a format derived from the candidate's fame as a forward-passing quarterback in college. He wanted foxholes dug some twenty-five yards apart and hand grenades lobbed back and forth until one or the other of the disputants had been satisfactorily exploded.

But everyone in that hotel room was aware that he sat under the august gaze of History, and History demanded the traditional alternatives—swords or pistols. They had to face the fact that Borax was skillful with neither, while his opponent had won tournaments with both. Pistols were finally chosen as adding the factors of great distance and uncertain atmospheric conditions to their side.

Pistols, then. And only one shot apiece for the maximum chance of survival. But the site?

Mibs had urged Weehawken Heights in New Jersey because of its historical associations. Grandstands, he pointed out, could easily be erected along the Palisades and substantial prices charged for admission. After advertising and promotion costs had been met, the purse could be used by both major parties to defray their campaign expenses.

Such considerations weighed heavily with Borax's advisors. But the negative side of the historical association weighed even more heavily: it was in Weehawken that the young Alexander Hamilton had been cut down in the very flower of his political promise. Some secluded spot, possibly hallowed by a victory of the raw and inexperienced army of George Washington, would put the omens definitely on their side. The party treasurer, a New England real estate agent in private life, was assigned to the problem.

That left the strategy.

All night long, they debated a variety of ruses, from bribing or intimidating the duel's presiding officials to having Borax fire a moment before the signal—the ethics of the act, it was pointed out, would be completely confused by subsequent charges and countercharges in the newspapers. They adjourned without having agreed on anything more hopeful than that Borax should train intensively under the pistol champion of the United States in the two days remaining and do his level best to achieve some degree of proficiency.

By the morning of the duel, the young candidate had become quite morose. He had been out on the pistol range continuously for almost forty-eight hours. He complained of a severe earache and announced bitterly that he had only the slightest improvement in his aim to show for it. All the way to the dueling grounds while his formally clad advisers wrangled and disputed, suggesting this method and that approach, he sat in silence, his head bowed unhappily upon his chest.

He must have been in a state of complete panic. Only so can we account for his decision to use a strategy which had not been first approved by his entire entourage—an unprecedented and most serious political irregularity.

Borax was no scholar, but he was moderately well-read in American history. He had even written a series of articles for a Florida newspaper under the generic title of *When the Eagle Screamed,* dealing with such great moments in the nation's past as Robert E. Lee's refusal to lead the Union armies, and the defeat of free silver and low tariffs by William McKinley. As the black limousine sped to the far-distant field of honor, he reviewed this compendium of wisdom and patriotic activity in search of an answer to his problem. He found it at last in the life story of Andrew Jackson.

Years before his elevation to high national office, the seventh President of the United States had been in a position similar to that in which Elvis P. Borax now found himself. Having been maneuvered into just such a duel with just such an opponent, and recognizing his own extreme nervousness, Jackson decided to let his enemy have the first shot. When, to everyone's surprise, the man missed and it was Jackson's turn to fire, he took his own sweet time about it. He leveled his pistol at his pale, perspiring antagonist, aiming carefully and exactly over the space of several dozen seconds. Then he fired and killed the man.

That was the ticket, Borax decided. Like Jackson, he'd let Mibs shoot first. Like Jackson, he would then slowly and inexorably—

Unfortunately for both history and Borax, the first shot was the only one fired. Mibs didn't miss, although he complained later—perfectionist that he was—that defective sights on the antique dueling pistol had caused him to come in a good five inches below target.

The bullet went through the right cheek of the Congressman's rigid, averted face and came out the left. It embedded itself in a sugar maple some fifteen feet away, from which it was later extracted and presented to the Smithsonian Institution. The tree, which became known as the Dueling Sugar Maple, was a major attraction for years and the center of a vast picnic grounds and motel complex. In the first decade of the next century, however, it was uprooted to make way for a through highway that connected Hoboken, New Jersey, with the new international airport at Bangor, Maine. Replanted with much ceremony in Washington, D.C., it succumbed in a few short months to heat prostration.

Borax was hurried to the field hospital nearby, set up for just such an emergency. As the doctors worked on him, his chief campaign manager, a politician far-famed for calmness and acumen under stress, came out of the tent and ordered an armed guard posted before it.

Since the bulletins released in the next few days about Borax's condition were reassuring but cryptic, people did not know what to think. Only one thing was definite: he would live.

Many rumors circulated. They were subjected to careful analysis by outstanding Washington, Hollywood, and Broadway columnists. Had Mibs really used a dum-dum bullet? Had it been tipped with a rare South American poison? Had the candidate's mother actually traveled all the way to New York from her gracious home in Florida's Okeechobee Swamp and hurled herself upon Old Shep in the editorial offices of the *Hairy Chest*, fingernails scratching and gouging, dental plates biting and tearing? Had there been a secret midnight ceremony in which ten regional leaders of Masculinism had formed a hollow square around Shepherd L. Mibs and watched Henry Dorselblad break Mibs's sword and cigar across his knee, stamp Mibs's derby flat, and solemnly tear Mibs's codpiece from his loins?

Everyone knew that the young Congressman's body had been so painstakingly measured and photographed before the duel that prosthesis for the three or four molars destroyed by the bullet was a relatively simple matter. But was prosthesis possible for a tongue? And could plastic surgery ever restore those round, sunny cheeks or that heartwarming adolescent grin?

According to a now-firm tradition, the last television debate of the campaign had to be held the night before Election Day. Mrs. Strunt gallantly offered to call it off. The Borax headquarters rejected her offer; tradition must not be set aside; the show must go on.

That night, every single television set in the United States was in operation, including even the old black-and-white collectors' items. Children were called from their beds, nurses from their hospital rounds, military sentries from their outlying posts.

Clarissima Strunt spoke first. She summarized the issues of the campaign in a friendly, ingratiating manner and put the case for Masculinism before the electorate in her best homespun style.

Then the cameras swung to Congressman Borax. He did not say a word, staring at the audience sadly out of eloquent, misty eyes. He pointed at the half-inch circular hole in his right cheek. Slowly, he turned the other cheek.

There was a similar hole there. He shook his head and picked up a large photograph of his mother in a rich silver frame. One tremendous tear rolled down and splashed upon the picture.

That was all.

One did not have to be a professional pollster or politician to predict the result. Mrs. Strunt conceded by noon of Election Day. In every state, Masculinism and its protagonists were swept from office overwhelmingly defeated. Streets were littered with discarded derbies and abandoned bustles. It was suicide to be seen smoking a cigar.

Like Aaron Burr before him, Shepherd L. Mibs fled to England. He published his memoirs, married an earl's daughter, and had five children by her. His oldest son, a biologist, became moderately famous as the discoverer of a cure for athlete's foot in frogs—a disease that once threatened to wipe out the entire French frozen-frogs-legs industry.

Pollyglow carefully stayed out of the public eye until the day of his death. He was buried, as his will requested, in a giant codpiece. His funeral was the occasion for long, illustrated newspaper articles reviewing the rise and fall of the movement he had founded.

And Henry Dorselblad disappeared before a veritable avalanche of infuriated women which screamed down upon Masculinist headquarters. His body was not found in the debris, thus giving rise to many legends. Some said that he was impaled on the points of countless umbrellas wielded by outraged American motherhood. Some said that he escaped in the disguise of a scrubwoman and would return one day to lead resurgent hordes of derby and cigar. To this date, however, he has not.

Elvis P. Borax, as everyone knows, served two terms as the most silent President since Calvin Coolidge and retired to go into the wholesale flower business in Miami.

It was almost as if Masculinism had never been. If we discount the beery groups of men who, at the end of a party, nostalgically sing the old songs and call out the old heroic rallying cries to each other, we have today very few mementos of the great convulsion.

One of them is the codpiece.

The codpiece has survived as a part of modern male costume. In motion, it has a rhythmic wave that reminds many women of a sternly shaken forefinger, warning them that men, at the last, can only be pushed so far and no farther. For men, the codpiece is still a flag, now a flag of truce perhaps, but it flutters in a war that goes on and on.

AFTERWORD

This is what I wrote about "The Masculinist Revolt" when it was published in my collection, *The Wooden Star* (1968):

> I have lost one agent and several friends over this story. A woman I had up to then respected told me, "This castration-nightmare is for a psychiatrist, not an editor"; and a male friend of many years put the story down with tears in his eyes, saying, "You've written the manifesto. The statement of principles for all the guys in the world." My intention was neither castration-nightmare nor ringing manifesto; it was satiric, very gently but encompassingly satiric. I may have failed.
>
> 1961, the year in which the story was written, was well before the hippies created a blur between the sexes on matters of clothing and hair styles. The first few editors who saw the piece felt that 1990 was a bit too early for such major changes as I described. My own feeling now is that I was subliminally aware of rapidly shifting attitudes toward sexual differentiation in our society, but that what I noticed as an anticipatory tremor was actually the first rock-slide of the total cataclysm.

I would like to add now (2001) these observations: Apparently I picked the wrong sex, but I was right about the nuttiness either of the two could develop as it wriggled in the throes of gender-political militancy. I further thought that I clearly portrayed in my male leads, Old Pep, Old Shep, and Hellfire Henry, three different kinds of utter failures as men, but I have been assured—by the equivalents of Germaine Greers and Catherine MacKinnons in my own circle—that these characters are to most women the most typically typical of men. So what do I know.

I was between agents at the time I wrote this—because my then agent, among the top ones in New York at the time, told me she'd rather not represent me if I insisted on writing such vicious trash. So I sent it on my own to A.C. Spectorsky (he was, I had discovered, called Old Spec by his subordinates!), the editorial director of *Playboy* to whom I had been introduced by the minstrel-cartoonist Shel Silverstein. Spectorsky was kind enough to tell me at the time of the introduction that he had so much enjoyed my story "Down Among the Dead Men," that he had memorized whole passages of it. He kept "The Masculinist Revolt" on his desk for a year and a half, calling me up from time to time to tell me that he was thinking of asking me to have it expanded so that he could devote an entire issue to it, à la *The New Yorker* and John Hersey's *Hiroshima*.

I almost went mad during this time; I priced Mercedes-Benzes up and down the island of Manhattan.

Finally, some assistant editor or other (or, possibly Hugh Hefner himself) happened to read the story and went in to Spectorsky with the comment that the piece was a ringing satire on the Playboy empire. The story was bounced back at me by the next post.

All right, maybe it's not the stuff of immortality, but I still think it's pretty good and pretty funny. And, for readers who are generous and will tell me they liked it, I have this to say:

Blame it on E.B. White. His short piece, "The Supremacy of Uruguay," is ultimately responsible for most of my stories of this type. It showed me that you didn't need individual characters prancing about if you saw a story as a kind of pseudo-history—something told at a remove by a reasonably objective historian. It occurred to me, immediately upon reading "The Supremacy of Uruguay," that the pseudo-history belonged above all in the literature of science fiction. And then, later, of course, I encountered Olaf Stapledon's novels and was privileged to see how a really great science-fiction writer managed the form.

These have been a bunch of miscellaneous remarks. But just one more. Henry W. Sams, the great English Department head at Penn State, gave me a job, a teaching job, the only job I've ever liked better than writing. He actually hired me as a professor, after he read two stories of mine, "My Mother Was a Witch" and "The Masculinist Revolt," despite the fact that I didn't have the necessary doctorate.

(Of course, I also didn't have—and Henry knew it at the time he put me in front of a university classroom—either a Master's degree or a Bachelor's. I *did* have, as my brother Morton, a real professor, is quick to point out, a high-school graduation certificate and an honorable discharge from the Army.)

Henry Sams, bless him, was the only member of the Establishment I have known who was in permanent revolt against the Establishment.

WRITTEN 1961——PUBLISHED 1965

꠹

Brooklyn Project

The gleaming bowls of light set in the creamy ceiling dulled when the huge, circular door at the back of the booth opened. They returned to white brilliance as the chubby man in the severe black jumper swung the door shut behind him and dogged it down again.

Twelve reporters of both sexes exhaled very loudly as he sauntered to the front of the booth and turned his back to the semi-opaque screen stretching across it. Then they all rose in deference to the cheerful custom of standing whenever a security official of the government was in the room.

He smiled pleasantly, waved at them and scratched his nose with a wad of mimeographed papers. His nose was large and it seemed to give added presence to his person. "Sit down, ladies and gentlemen, do sit down. We have no official fol-de-rol in the Brooklyn Project. I am your guide, as you might say, for the duration of this experiment—the acting secretary to the executive assistant on press relations. My name is not important. Please pass these among you."

They each took one of the mimeographed sheets and passed the rest on. Leaning back in the metal bucket seats, they tried to make themselves comfortable. Their host squinted through the heavy screen and up at the wall clock, which had one slowly revolving hand. He patted his black garment jovially where it was tight around the middle.

"To business. In a few moments, man's first large-scale excursion into time will begin. Not by humans, but with the aid of a photographic and recording device which will bring us incalculably rich data on the past. With this experiment, the Brooklyn Project justifies ten billion dollars and over eight years of scientific development; it shows the validity not merely of a new method of investigation, but of a weapon which will make our glorious country even more secure, a weapon which our enemies may justifiably dread.

"Let me caution you, first, not to attempt the taking of notes even if you have been able to smuggle pens and pencils through Security. Your stories will be written entirely from memory. You all have a copy of the Security Code with the latest additions as well as a pamphlet referring specifically to Brooklyn Project regulations. The sheets you have just received provide you with the required lead for your story; they also contain suggestions as to treatment and coloring. Beyond that—so long as you stay within the framework of the documents mentioned—you are entirely free to write your stories in your own variously original ways. The press, ladies and gentlemen, must remain untouched and uncontaminated by government control. Now, any questions?"

The twelve reporters looked at the floor. Five of them began reading from their sheets. The paper rustled noisily.

"What, no questions? Surely there must be more interest than this in a project which has broken the last possible frontier—the fourth dimension, time. Come now, you are the representatives of the nation's curiosity—you must have questions. Bradley, you look doubtful. What's bothering you? I assure you, Bradley, that I don't bite."

They all laughed and grinned at each other.

Bradley half-rose and pointed at the screen. "Why does it have to be so thick? I'm not the slightest bit interested in finding out how chronar works, but all we can see from here is a grayed and blurry picture of men dragging apparatus around on the floor. And why does the clock only have one hand?"

"A good question," the acting secretary said. His large nose seemed to glow. "A very good question. First, the clock has but one hand, because, after all, Bradley, this is an experiment in time, and Security feels that the time of the experiment itself may, through some unfortunate combination of information leakage and foreign correlation—in short, a clue might be needlessly exposed. It is sufficient to know that when the hand points to the red dot, the experiment will begin. The screen is translucent and the scene below somewhat blurry for the same reason—camouflage of detail and adjustment. I *am* empowered to inform you that the details of the apparatus are—uh, very significant. Any other questions? Culpepper? Culpepper of Consolidated, isn't it?"

"Yes, sir. Consolidated News Service. Our readers are very curious about that incident of the Federation of Chronar Scientists. Of course, they have no respect or pity for them—the way they acted and all—but just what did they mean by saying that this experiment was dangerous because of insufficient data? And that fellow, Dr. Shayson, their president, do you know if he'll be shot?"

The man in black pulled at his nose and paraded before them thoughtfully. "I must confess that I find the views of the Federation of Chronar Scientists—or the federation of chronic *sighers,* as we at Pike's Peak prefer to call them—are a trifle too exotic for my tastes; I rarely bother with weighing the opinions of a traitor in any case. Shayson himself may or may not have incurred the death penalty for revealing the nature of the work with which he was entrusted. On the other hand, he—uh, *may not* or *may* have. That is all I can say about him for reasons of security."

Reasons of security. At the mention of the dread phrase, every reporter straightened against the hard back of his chair. Culpepper's face lost its pinkness in favor of a glossy white. They can't consider the part about Shayson a leading question, he thought desperately. But I shouldn't have cracked about that damned federation!

Culpepper lowered his eyes and tried to look as ashamed of the vicious idiots as he possibly could. He hoped the acting secretary to the executive assistant on press relations would notice his horror.

The clock began ticking very loudly. Its hand was now only one-fourth of an arc from the red dot at the top. Down on the floor of the immense laboratory, activity had stopped. All of the seemingly tiny men were clustered around two great spheres of shining metal resting against each other. Most of them were watching dials and switch-boards intently; a few, their tasks completed, chatted with the circle of black-jumpered Security guards.

"We are almost ready to begin Operation Periscope. Operation Periscope, of course, because we are, in a sense, extending a periscope into the past—a periscope which will take pictures and record events of various periods ranging from fifteen thousand years to four billion years ago. We felt that in view of the various critical circumstances attending this experiment—international, scientific—a more fitting title would be Operation Crossroads. Unfortunately, that title has been—uh, preempted."

Everyone tried to look as innocent of the nature of that other experiment as years of staring at locked library shelves would permit.

"No matter. I will now give you a brief background in chronar practice as cleared by Brooklyn Project Security. Yes, Bradley?"

Bradley again got partly out of his seat. "I was wondering—we know there has been a Manhattan Project, a Long Island Project, a Westchester Project and now a Brook-lyn Project. Has there ever been a Bronx Project? I come from the Bronx; you know, civic pride."

"Quite. Very understandable. However, if there is a Bronx Project you may be assured that until its work has been successfully completed, the only individuals outside of it who will know of its existence are the President and the Secretary of Security. If—*if*, I say—there is such an institution, the world will learn of it with the same shattering suddenness that it learned of the Westchester Project. I don't think that the world will soon forget *that*."

He chuckled in recollection and Culpepper echoed him a bit louder than the rest. The clock's hand was close to the red mark.

"Yes, the Westchester Project and now this; our nation shall yet be secure! Do you realize what a magnificent weapon chronar places in our democratic hands? To ex-amine only one aspect—consider what happened to the Coney Island and Flatbush Subprojects (the events are mentioned in those sheets you've received) before the uses of chronar were fully appreciated.

"It was not yet known in those first experiments that Newton's third law of mo-tion—action equalling reaction—held for time as well as it did for the other three dimensions of space. When the first chronar was excited backward into time for the length of a ninth of a second, the entire laboratory was propelled into the future for a like period and returned in an—uh, unrecognizable condition. That fact, by the way, has prevented excursions into the future. The equipment seems to suffer amaz-ing alterations and no human could survive them. But do you realize what we could do to an enemy by virtue of that property alone? Sending an adequate mass of chronar into the past while it is adjacent to a hostile nation would force that nation into the future—all of it simultaneously—a future from which it would return populated only with corpses!"

He glanced down, placed his hands behind his back and teetered on his heels. "That is why you see two spheres on the floor. Only one of them, the ball on the right, is equipped with chronar. The other is a dummy, matching the other's mass perfectly and serving as a counterbalance. When the chronar is excited, it will plunge four billion years into our past and take photographs of an Earth that was still a half-liquid, partly gaseous mass solidifying rapidly in a somewhat inchoate solar system.

"At the same time, the dummy will be propelled four billion years into the future, from whence it will return much changed but for reasons we don't completely understand. They will strike each other at what is to us *now* and bounce off again to approximately half the chronological distance of the first trip, where our chronar apparatus will record data of an almost solid planet, plagued by earthquakes and possibly holding forms of sublife in the manner of certain complex molecules.

"After each collision, the chronar will return roughly half the number of years covered before, automatically gathering information each time. The geological and historical periods we expect it to touch are listed from I to XXV in your sheets; there will be more than twenty-five, naturally, before both balls come to rest, but scientists feel that all periods after that number will be touched for such a short while as to be unproductive of photographs and other material. Remember, at the end, the balls will be doing little more than throbbing in place before coming to rest, so that even though they still ricochet centuries on either side of the present, it will be almost unnoticeable. A question, I see."

The thin woman in gray tweeds beside Culpepper got to her feet. "I—I know this is irrelevant," she began, "but I haven't been able to introduce my question into the discussion at any pertinent moment. Mr. Secretary—"

"Acting secretary," the chubby little man in the black suit told her genially. "I'm only the acting secretary. Go on."

"Well, I want to say— Mr. Secretary, is there any way at all that our post-experimental examination time may be reduced? Two years is a very long time to spend inside Pike's Peak simply out of fear that one of us may have seen enough and be unpatriotic enough to be dangerous to the nation. Once our stories have passed the censors, it seems to me that we could be allowed to return to our homes after a safety period of, say, three months. I have two small children and there are others here—"

"Speak for yourself, Mrs. Bryant!" the man from Security roared. "It *is* Mrs. Bryant, isn't it? Mrs. Bryant of the Women's Magazine Syndicate? Mrs. *Alexis* Bryant." He seemed to be making minute pencil notes across his brain.

Mrs. Bryant sat down beside Culpepper again, clutching her copy of the amended Security Code, the special pamphlet on the Brooklyn Project and the thin mimeographed sheet of paper very close to her breast. Culpepper moved hard against the opposite arm of his chair. Why did everything have to happen to him? Then, to make matters worse, the crazy woman looked tearfully at him as if expecting sympathy. Culpepper stared across the booth and crossed his legs.

"You must remain within the jurisdiction of the Brooklyn Project because that is the only way that Security can be *certain* that no important information leakage will occur before the apparatus has changed beyond your present recognition of it. You didn't have to come, Mrs. Bryant—you volunteered. You all volunteered. After your editors had designated you as their choices for covering this experiment, you all had the peculiarly democratic privilege of refusing. None of you did. You recognized that to refuse this unusual honor would have shown you incapable of thinking in terms of National Security, would have, in fact implied a criticism of the Security Code itself from the standpoint of the usual two-year examination time. And now this! For someone who had hitherto been thought as able and trustworthy as yourself, Mrs. Bryant, to emerge at this late hour with such a request makes me, why it," the little man's voice dropped to a whisper, "—it almost makes me doubt the effectiveness of our Security screening methods."

Culpepper nodded angry affirmation at Mrs. Bryant, who was biting her lips and trying to show a tremendous interest in the activities on the laboratory floor.

"The question *was* irrelevant. Highly irrelevant. It took up time which I had intended to devote to a more detailed discussion of the popular aspects of chronar and its possible uses in industry. But Mrs. Bryant must have her little feminine outburst. It makes no difference to Mrs. Bryant that our nation is daily surrounded by more and more hostility, more and more danger. These things matter not in the slightest to Mrs. Bryant. All she is concerned with are the two years of her life that her country asks her to surrender so that the future of her own children may be more secure."

The acting secretary smoothed his black jumper and became calmer. Tension in the booth decreased.

"Activation will occur at any moment now, so I will briefly touch upon those most interesting periods which the chronar will record for us and from which we expect the most useful data. I and II, of course, since they are the periods at which the Earth was forming into its present shape. Then III, the Pre-Cambrian Period of the Proterozoic, one billion years ago, the first era in which we find distinct records of life—crustaceans and algae for the most part. VI, a hundred twenty-five million years in the past, covers the Middle Jurassic of the Mesozoic. This excursion into the so-called 'Age of Reptiles' may provide us with photographs of dinosaurs and solve the old riddle of their coloring, as well as photographs, if we are fortunate, of the first appearance of mammals and birds. Finally, VIII and IX, the Oligocene and Miocene Epochs of the Tertiary Period, mark the emergence of man's earliest ancestors. Unfortunately, the chronar will be oscillating back and forth so rapidly by that time that the chance of any decent recording—"

A gong sounded. The hand of the clock touched the red mark. Five of the technicians below pulled switches and, almost before the journalists could lean forward, the two spheres were no longer visible through the heavy plastic screen. Their places were empty.

"The chronar has begun its journey to four billion years in the past! Ladies and gentlemen, an historic moment—a profoundly historic moment! It will not return for a little while; I shall use the time in pointing up and exposing the fallacies of the—ah, *federation of chronic sighers!*"

Nervous laughter rippled at the acting secretary to the executive assistant on press relations. The twelve journalists settled down to hearing the ridiculous ideas torn apart.

"As you know, one of the fears entertained about travel to the past was that the most innocent-seeming acts would cause cataclysmic changes in the present. You are probably familiar with the fantasy in its most currently popular form—if Hitler had been killed in 1930, he would not have forced scientists in Germany and later occupied countries to emigrate, this nation might not have had the atomic bomb, thus no third atomic war, and Venezuela would still be part of the South American continent.

"The traitorous Shayson and his illegal federation extended this hypothesis to include much more detailed and minor acts such as shifting a molecule of hydrogen that in our past really was never shifted.

"At the time of the first experiment at the Coney Island Subproject, when the chronar was sent back for one-ninth of a second, a dozen different laboratories checked through every device imaginable, searched carefully for any conceivable change. There were none! Government officials concluded that the time stream was a rigid affair, past, present, and future, and nothing in it could be altered. But Shayson and his cohorts were not satisfied: they—"

I. Four billion years ago. The chronar floated in a cloudlet of silicon dioxide above the boiling Earth and languidly collected its data with automatically operating instruments. The vapor it had displaced condensed and fell in great, shining drops.

"—insisted that we should do no further experimenting until we had checked the mathematical aspects of the problem yet again. They went so far as to state that it was possible that if changes occurred we would not notice them, that no instruments imaginable could detect them. They claimed we would accept these changes as things that had always existed. Well! This at a time when our country—and theirs, ladies and gentlemen of the press, *theirs,* too—was in greater danger than ever. Can you—"

Words failed him. He walked up and down the booth, shaking his head. All the reporters on the long, wooden bench shook their heads with him in sympathy.

There was another gong. The two dull spheres appeared briefly, clanged against each other and ricocheted off into opposite chronological directions.

"There you are." The government official waved his arms at the transparent laboratory floor above them. "The first oscillation has been completed; has anything changed? Isn't everything the same? But the dissidents would maintain that alterations have occurred and we haven't noticed them. With such faith-based, unscientific viewpoints, there can be no argument. People like these—"

II. Two billion years ago. The great ball clicked its photographs of the fiery, erupting ground below. Some red-hot crusts rattled off its sides. Five or six thousand complex molecules lost their basic structure as they impinged against it. A hundred didn't.

"—will labor thirty hours a day out of thirty-three to convince you that black isn't white, that we have seven moons instead of two. They are especially dangerous—"

A long, muted note as the apparatus collided with itself. The warm orange of the corner lights brightened as it started out again.

"—because of their learning, because they are sought for guidance in better ways of vegetation." The government official was slithering up and down rapidly now, gesturing with all of his pseudopods. "We are faced with a very difficult problem, at present—"

III. One billion years ago. The primitive triple trilobite the machine had destroyed when it materialized began drifting down wetly.

"—a very difficult problem. The question before us: should we *shllk* or shouldn't we *shllk?*" He was hardly speaking English now; in fact, for some time, he hadn't been speaking at all. He had been stating his thoughts by slapping one pseudopod against the other—as he always had…

IV. A half-billion years ago. Many different kinds of bacteria died as the water changed temperature slightly.

"This, then, is no time for half measures. If we can reproduce well enough—"

V. Two hundred fifty million years ago. VI. A hundred twenty-five million years ago.

"—to satisfy the Five Who Spiral, we have—"

VII. Sixty-two million years. VIII. Thirty-one million. IX. Fifteen million. X. Seven and a half million.

"—spared all attainable virtue. Then—"

XI. XII. XIII. XIV. XV. XVI. XVII. XVIII. XIX. Bong—bong—bong bongbong-bongongongngngngggg…

"—we are indeed ready for refraction. And that, I tell you, is good enough for those who billow and those who snap. But those who billow will be proven wrong as always, for in the snapping is the rolling and in the rolling is only truth. There need be no change merely because of a sodden cilium. The apparatus has rested at last in the fractional conveyance; shall we view it subtly?"

They all agreed, and their bloated purpled bodies dissolved into liquid and flowed up and around to the apparatus. When they reached its four square blocks, now no longer shrilling mechanically, they rose, solidified, and regained their slime-washed forms.

"See," cried the thing that had been the acting secretary to the executive assistant on press relations. "See, no matter how subtly! Those who billow were wrong: we haven't changed." He extended fifteen purple blobs triumphantly. "Nothing has changed!"

AFTERWORD

Nineteen forty-seven was the year of the first great science-fiction boom, following both the interest generated by the development of the atomic bomb and several highly successful science-fiction anthologies. The editor of one of these, Groff Conklin, was approached by moneyed people who offered to back him and Ted Sturgeon in a new magazine of which they were to be co-editors. This was a couple of years before Anthony Boucher and J. Francis McComas were to get together to produce *The Magazine of Fantasy and Science Fiction,* and was a harbinger of the excitement that was to grip the science-fiction publishing field in the late '40s and early '50s.

Ted and Groff in their turn approached me and a number of other writers, offering a rate unheard up to that time—four and five cents a word—"for the very best stories of which you guys are capable, something genuinely distinguished." (The going rate for science fiction at that time was one-half cent to a dazzling two cents a word. Only John W. Campbell of *Astounding* ever paid at the high rate—and only when a story knocked him off his chair.)

I had been thinking for a number of months about a new kind of story and one which had hitherto been inexplicably absent from the magazines we all wrote for: straight down-the-line and overt political satire. I say "inexplicably" because such satire had been very successful at novel length—Zamiatin's *We* and Huxley's *Brave New World,* to mention only the first two examples that came to mind—and because the science-fiction magazine would seem to be the natural, even ideal, vehicle for such stories.

And the America of 1947 seemed made for such satire. The Federation of Atomic Scientists, a group composed of the younger physicists and chemists who had worked on the Manhattan Project and been terrified of what they had accomplished, was under attack from many official and unofficial quarters as unpatriotic or—much worse in those days—demonstrating outright friendliness with the potential enemy. We were then, you might remember, in the earliest stages of what came to be known as the Cold War.

On the Congressional front, Senator Joseph McCarthy had not yet appeared in all his rattling glory, but the matters he was to specialize in had been ably handled for some years now by Martin Dies and the House Un-American Activities Committee (HUAC). The stage was being set.

Nineteen forty-seven was also the year, therefore, of a slashing attack on the entertainment industry by Martin Dies and HUAC: all kinds of celebrities and behind-the-scenes creative people had been subpoenaed and questioned most closely about their political associations and personal friendships—all in the name of national security and the protection of the manufacturing secrets of the atomic bomb. "Security" was the watchword of the day, a watchword invoked to cover all kinds of investigations and much more likely to be referred to at that time than the Constitution itself.

In the portentous name of Security, to mention just one hilarious example, supermarkets that stocked Polish hams (Poland, after all, was behind the Iron Curtain and was a full-fledged Communist state) were picketed as being of doubtful patriotism. There were prosecutions in the name of Security; there were suicides because of Security; there were heavily financed national campaigns in newspapers, magazines, and the broadcast media; there were even elections based on Security. And one especially enthusiastic junior Congressman had finally proposed that there be a seat in the Cabinet for Security.

It was this last development that sent me, halfway between laughter and outright terror, to the typewriter. I wrote and rewrote "Brooklyn Project" in a day and a half.

Both Sturgeon and Conklin liked it and marked it as their first purchase for the new magazine.

I was ecstatic. I blocked out a whole series of political and social satires I would write for that magazine. I had found the form I would be content to concentrate on for the next couple of decades. And I had found a well-paying market for that form.

Then the roof fell in. Or, rather, a whole series of roofs.

The backers of the magazine unbacked. They'd been involved in bad deals, assets that were supposed to be liquid had solidified on them, this, that—whatever: all plans for the new publication were cancelled. Conklin and Sturgeon tried to find financing elsewhere, and failed.

Sturgeon returned the manuscript to me with the comment: "Sorry, Phil, but you won't have any trouble peddling a piece this good."

He was wrong. Campbell called me to his office and skimmed the piece back to me across his desk. "Oh, no," he said. "No, no, no!"

Science-fiction magazine editors on the next level down reacted pretty much the same way. "I wouldn't touch this with a ten-foot pole," one of them said. "Not in these times. I wish I could, though. The time-travel gimmick is lovely."

The story finally found a home at what was then the very bottom of the field—*Planet Stories,* which paid a maximum one-half cent a word and specialized in action stories that took place anywhere but on Earth.

"The story doesn't fit our book in any way," Malcolm Reiss, the editor, told me, "and it's dangerous as hell, but I figure this one is for God. An editor is entitled to at least one for God."

WRITTEN 1947——PUBLISHED 1948

෴

Some Odd Ones

CHILD'S PLAY

After the man from the express company had given the door an untipped slam, Sam Weber decided to move the huge crate under the one light bulb in his room. It was all very well for the messenger to drawl, "I dunno. We don't send 'em; we just deliver 'em, mister"—but there must be some sensible explanation.

With a grunt that began as an anticipatory reflex and ended on a note of surprised annoyance, Sam shoved the box forward the few feet necessary. It was heavy enough; he wondered how the messenger had carried it up the three flights of stairs.

He straightened and frowned down at the garish card which contained his name and address as well as the legend—"Merry Christmas, 2353."

A joke? He didn't know anyone who'd think it funny to send a card dated over four hundred years in the future. Unless one of the comedians in his law school graduating class meant to record his opinion as to when Weber would be trying his first case. Even so—

The letters were shaped strangely, come to think of it, sort of green streaks instead of lines. And the card was a sheet of gold!

Sam decided he was really interested. He ripped the card aside, tore off the flimsy wrapping material—and stopped.

There was no top to the box, no slit in its side, no handle anywhere in sight. It seemed to be a solid, cubical mass of brown stuff. Yet he was positive something had rattled inside when it was moved.

He seized the corners and strained and grunted till it lifted. The underside was as smooth and innocent of openings as the rest. He let it thump back to the floor.

"Ah, well," he said, philosophically, "it's not the gift; it's the principle involved."

Many of his gifts still required appreciative notes. He'd have to work up something special for Aunt Maggie. Her neckties were things of cubistic horror, but he hadn't even sent her a lone handkerchief this Christmas. Every cent had gone into buying that brooch for Tina. Not quite a ring, but maybe she'd consider that under the circumstances—

He turned to walk to his bed, which he had drafted into the additional service of desk and chair. He kicked at the great box disconsolately. "Well, if you won't open, you won't open."

As if smarting under the kick, the box opened. A cut appeared on the upper surface, widened rapidly and folded the top back and down on either side like a valise.

251

Sam clapped his forehead and addressed a rapid prayer to every god whose name he could think of. Then he remembered what he'd said.

"Close," he suggested.

The box closed, once more as smooth as a baby's bottom.

"Open."

The box opened.

So much for the sideshow, Sam decided. He bent down and peered into the container.

The interior was a crazy mass of shelving on which rested vials filled with blue liquids, jars filled with red solids, transparent tubes showing yellow and green and orange and mauve and other colors which Sam's eyes didn't quite remember. There were seven pieces of intricate apparatus on the bottom which looked as if tube-happy radio hams had assembled them. There was also a book.

Sam picked the book off the bottom and noted numbly that while all its pages were metallic, it was lighter than any paper book he'd ever held.

He carried the book over to the bed and sat down. Then he took a long, deep breath and turned to the first page. "*Gug*," he said, exhaling his long, deep breath.

In mad, green streaks of letters:

Bild-A-Man Set #3. This set is intended solely for the use of children between the ages of eleven and thirteen. The equipment, much more advanced than Bild-A-Man Sets 1 and 2, will enable the child of this age-group to build and assemble complete adult humans in perfect working order. The retarded child may also construct the babies and mannikins of the earlier kits. Two disassembleators are provided so that the set can be used again and again with profit. As with Sets 1 and 2, the aid of a Census Keeper in all disassembling is advised. Refills and additional parts may be acquired from The Bild-A-Man Company, 928 Diagonal Level, Glunt City, Ohio. Remember—only with a Bild-A-Man can you build a man!

Weber squeezed his eyes shut. What was that gag in the movie he'd seen last night? Terrific gag. Terrific picture, too. Nice technicolor. Wonder how much the director made a week? The cameraman? Five hundred? A thousand?

He opened his eyes warily. The box was still a squat cube in the center of his room. The book was still in his shaking hand. And the page read the same.

"Only with a Bild-A-Man can you build a man!" Heaven help a neurotic young lawyer at a time like this!

There was a price list on the next page for "refills and additional parts." Things like one liter of hemoglobin and three grams of assorted enzymes were offered for sale in terms of one slunk fifty and three slunks forty-five. A note on the bottom advertised Set #4: "The thrill of building your first live Martian!"

Fine print announced *pat. pending 2348*.

The third page was a table of contents. Sam gripped the edge of the mattress with one sweating hand and read:

Sam dropped the book back into the box and ran for the mirror. His face was still the same, somewhat like bleached chalk, but fundamentally the same. He hadn't twinned or grown himself a mannikin or devised a new kind of life for his leisure moments. Everything was snug as a bug in a bughouse.

Very carefully he pushed his eyes back into the proper position in their sockets.

"Dear Aunt Maggie," he began writing feverishly. "Your ties made the most beautiful gift of my Christmas. My only regret is—"

My only regret is that I have but one life to give for my Christmas present. Who could have gone to such fantastic lengths for a practical joke? Lew Knight? Even Lew must have some reverence in his insensitive body for the institution of Christmas. And Lew didn't have the brains or the patience for a job so involved.

Tina? Tina had the fine talent for complication, all right. But Tina, while possessing a delightful abundance of all other physical attributes, was badly lacking in funny-bone.

Sam drew forth the leather wallet she'd given him and caressed it. Tina's perfume seemed to cling to the surface and move the world back into focus.

The metallic greeting card glinted at him from the floor. Maybe the reverse side contained the sender's name. He picked it up, turned it over.

Nothing but blank gold surface. He was sure of the gold; his father had been a jeweler. The very value of the sheet was rebuttal to the possibility of a practical joke. Besides, again, what was the point?

"Merry Christmas, 2353." Where would humanity be in four hundred years? Traveling to the stars, or beyond—to unimaginable destinations? Using little mannikins to perform the work of machines and robots? Providing children with—

There might be another card or note inside the box. Weber bent down to remove its contents. His eye noted a large grayish jar and the label etched into its surface: *Dehydrated Neurone Preparation, for human construction only.*

He backed away and glared. "Close!"

The thing melted shut. Weber sighed his relief at it and decided to go to bed.

He regretted while undressing that he hadn't thought to ask the messenger the name of his firm. Knowing the delivery service involved would be useful in tracing the origin of this gruesome gift.

"But then," he repeated as he fell asleep, "it's not the gift—it's the principle! Merry Christmas, me."

The next morning when Lew Knight breezed in with his "Good morning, counselor," Sam waited for the first sly ribbing to start. Lew wasn't the man to hide the light of his humor under a bushel. But Lew buried his nose in *The New York State Supplement* and kept it there all morning. The other five young lawyers in the communal office appeared either too bored or too busy to have Bild-A-Man sets on their conscience. There were no sly grins, no covert glances, no leading questions.

Tina walked in at ten o'clock, looking like a pinup girl caught with her clothes on. "Good morning, counselors," she said.

Each in his own way, according to the peculiar gland secretions he was enjoying at the moment, beamed, drooled or nodded a reply. Lew Knight drooled. Sam Weber beamed.

Tina took it all in and analyzed the situation while she fluffed her hair about. Her conclusions evidently involved leaning markedly against Lew Knight's desk and asking what he had for her to do this morning.

Sam bit savagely into Hackleworth *On Torts*. Theoretically, Tina was employed by all seven of them as secretary, switchboard operator and receptionist. Actually, the most faithful performance of her duties entailed nothing more daily than the typing and addressing of two envelopes with an occasional letter to be sealed inside. Once a week there might be a wistful little brief which was never to attain judicial scrutiny. Tina therefore had a fair library of fashion magazines in the first drawer of her desk and a complete cosmetics laboratory in the other two; she spent one third of her working day in the ladies' room swapping stocking prices and sources with other secretaries; she devoted the other two thirds religiously to that one of her employers who as of her arrival seemed to be in the most masculine mood. Her pay was small but her life was full.

Just before lunch, she approached casually with the morning's mail. "Didn't think we'd be too busy this morning, counselor—" she began.

"You thought incorrectly, Miss Hill," he informed her with a brisk irritation that he hoped became him well; "I've been waiting for you to terminate your social engagements so that we could get down to what occasionally passes for business."

She was as startled as an uncushioned kitten. "But—but this isn't Monday. Somerset & Ojack only send you stuff on Mondays."

Sam winced at the reminder that if it weren't for the legal drudgework he received once a week from Somerset & Ojack he would be a lawyer in name only, if not in spirit only. "I have a letter, Miss Hill," he replied steadily. "Whenever you assemble the necessary materials, we can get on with it."

Tina returned in a head-shaking moment with stenographic pad and pencils.

"Regular heading, today's date," Sam began. "Address it to Chamber of Commerce, Glunt City, Ohio. Gentlemen: Would you inform me if you have registered currently with you a firm bearing the name of the Bild-A-Man Company or a firm with any name at all similar? I am also interested in whether a firm bearing the above or related name has recently made known its intention of joining your community. This inquiry is being made informally on behalf of a client who is interested in a product of this organization whose address he has mislaid. Signature and then this P.S.—My client is also curious as to the business possibilities of a street known as Diagonal Avenue or Diagonal Level. Any data on this address and the organizations presently located there will be greatly appreciated."

Tina batted wide blue eyes at him. "Oh, Sam," she breathed, ignoring the formality he had introduced, "oh, Sam, you have another client. I'm so glad. He looked a little sinister, but in *such* a distinguished manner that I was certain—"

"Who? Who looked a little sinister?"

"Why, your new cli-ent." Sam had the uncomfortable feeling that she had almost added "stu-pid." "When I came in this morning, there was this terribly tall old man in a long black overcoat talking to the elevator operator. He turned to me—the elevator operator, I mean—and said, 'This is Mr. Weber's secretary. She'll be able to tell you anything you want to know.' Then he sort of winked, which I thought was sort of impolite, you know, considering. Then this old man looked at me hard and I felt distinctly uncomfortable and he walked away muttering 'Either disjointed or predatory personalities. Never normal. Never balanced.' Which I didn't think was very polite, either, I'll have you know, if he *is* your new client!" She sat back and began breathing again.

Tall, sinister old men in long, black overcoats pumping the elevator operator about him. Hardly a matter of business. He had no skeletons in his personal closet. Could it be connected with his unusual Christmas present? Sam hummed mentally.

"—but she is my favorite aunt, you know," Tina was saying. "And she came in so unexpectedly."

The girl was explaining about their Christmas date. Sam felt a rush of affection for her as she leaned forward.

"Don't bother," he told her. "I knew you couldn't help breaking the date. I was a little sore when you called me, but I got over it; never-hold-a-grudge-against-a-pretty-girl-Sam, I'm known as. How about lunch?"

"Lunch?" She gestured distractedly. "I promised Lew, Mr. Knight, that is— But he wouldn't mind if you came along."

"Fine. Let's go." This would be helping Lew to a spoonful of his own medicine.

Lew Knight took the business of having a crowd instead of a party for lunch as badly as Sam hoped he would. Unfortunately, Lew was able to describe details of his forthcoming case, the probable fees and possible distinction to be reaped thereof. After one or two attempts to bring an interesting will he was rephrasing for Somerset & Ojack into the conversation, Sam subsided into daydreams. Lew immediately dropped *Rosenthal v. Rosenthal* and leered at Tina conversationally.

Outside the restaurant, snow discolored into slush. Most of the stores were removing Christmas displays. Sam noticed construction sets for children, haloed by tinsel and glittering with artificial snow. Build a radio, a skyscraper, an airplane. But "Only with a Bild-A-Man can you—"

"I'm going home," he announced suddenly. "Something important I just remembered. If anything comes up, call me there."

He was leaving Lew a clear field, he told himself, as he found a seat on the subway. But the bitter truth was that the field was almost as clear when he was around as when he wasn't. Lupine Lew Knight, he had been called in law school; since the day when he had noticed that Tina had the correct proportions of dress-filling substance, Sam's chances had been worth a crowbar at Fort Knox.

Tina hadn't been wearing his brooch today. Her little finger, right hand, however, had sported an unfamiliar and garish little ring. "Some got it," Sam philosophized. "Some don't got it. I don't got it."

But it would have been nice, with Tina, to have got it.

As he unlocked the door of his room he was surprised by an unmade bed telling with rumpled stoicism of a chambermaid who'd never come. This hadn't happened before— Of course! He'd never locked his room before. The girl must have thought he wanted privacy.

Maybe he had.

Aunt Maggie's ties glittered obscenely at the foot of the bed. He chucked them into the closet as he removed his hat and coat. Then he went over to the washstand and washed his hands, slowly. He turned around.

This was it. At last the great cubical bulk that had been lurking quietly in the corner of his vision was squarely before him. It was there and it undoubtedly contained all the outlandish collection he remembered.

"Open," he said, and the box opened.

The book, still open to the metallic table of contents, was lying at the bottom of the box. Part of it had slipped into the chamber of a strange piece of apparatus. Sam picked both out gingerly.

He slipped the book out and noticed the apparatus consisted mostly of some sort of binoculars, supported by a coil and tube arrangement and bearing on a flat green plate. He turned it over. The underside was lettered in the same streaky way as the book. *Combination Electron Microscope and Workbench.*

Very carefully he placed it on the floor. One by one, he removed the other items, from the *Junior Biocalibrator* to the *Jiffy Vitalizer*. Very respectfully he ranged against the box in five multi-colored rows the phials of lymph and the jars of basic cartilage. The walls of the chest were lined with indescribably thin and wrinkled sheets; a slight pressure along their edges expanded them into three-dimensional outlines of human organs whose shape and size could be varied with pinching any part of their surface—most indubitably molds.

Quite an assortment. If there was anything solidly scientific to it, that box might mean unimaginable wealth. Or some very useful publicity. Or—well, it should mean something! If there was anything solidly scientific to it.

Sam flopped down on the bed and opened to *A Child's Garden of Biochemistry.*

At nine that night he squatted next to the Combination Electron Microscope and Workbench and began opening certain small bottles. At nine forty-seven Sam Weber made his first simple living thing.

It wasn't much, if you used the first chapter of Genesis as your standard. Just a primitive brown mold that, in the field of the microscope, fed diffidently on a piece of pretzel, put forth a few spores and died in about twenty minutes. But *he* had made it. He had constructed a specific life-form to feed on the constituents of a specific pretzel; it could survive nowhere else.

He went out to supper with every intention of getting drunk. After just a little alcohol, however, the *dei-ish* feeling returned and he scurried back to his room.

Never again that evening did he recapture the exultation of the brown mold, though he constructed a giant protein molecule and a whole slew of filterable viruses.

He called the office in the little corner drugstore which was his breakfast nook. "I'll be home all day," he told Tina.

She was a little puzzled. So was Lew Knight, who grabbed the phone. "Hey, counselor, you building up a neighborhood practice? Kid Blackstone is missing out on a lot of cases. Two ambulances have already clanged past the building."

"Yeah," said Sam. "I'll tell him when he comes in."

The weekend was almost upon him, so he decided to take the next day off as well. He wouldn't have any real work till Monday when the Somerset & Ojack basket would produce his lone egg.

Before he returned to his room, he purchased a copy of an advanced bacteriology. It was amusing to construct—with improvements!—unicellular creatures whose very place in the scheme of classification was a matter for argument among scientists of his own day. The Bild-A-Man manual, of course, merely gave a few examples and general rules; but with the descriptions in the bacteriology, the world was his oyster.

Which was an idea: he made a few oysters. The shells weren't hard enough, and he couldn't quite screw his courage up to the eating point, but they were most undeniably bivalves. If he cared to perfect his technique, his food problem would be solved.

The manual was fairly easy to follow and profusely illustrated with pictures that expanded into solidity as the page was opened. Very little was taken for granted; involved explanations followed simpler ones. Only the allusions were occasionally obscure—"This is the principle used in the phanphophlink toys," "When your teeth are next yokekkled or demortoned, think of the *Bacterium cyanogenum* and the humble part it plays," "If you have a rubicular mannikin around the house, you needn't bother with the chapter on mannikins."

After a brief search had convinced Sam that whatever else he now had in his apartment he didn't have a rubicular mannikin, he felt justified in turning to the chapter on mannikins. He had conquered completely this feeling of being Pop playing with Junior's toy train: already he had done more than the world's top biologists ever dreamed of for the next generation and what might not lie ahead—what problems might he not yet solve?

"Never forget that mannikins are constructed for one purpose and one purpose only." I won't, Sam promised. "Whether they are sanitary mannikins, tailoring mannikins, printing mannikins or even sunevviarry mannikins, they are each constructed with one operation of a given process in view. When you make a mannikin that is capable of more than one function, you are committing a crime so serious as to be punishable by public admonition."

"To construct an elementary mannikin—"

It was very difficult. Three times he tore down developing monstrosities and began anew. It wasn't till Sunday afternoon that the mannikin was complete—or rather, incomplete.

Long arms it had—although by an error, one was slightly longer than the other—a faceless head and a trunk. No legs. No eyes or ears, no organs of reproduction. It lay on his bed and gurgled out of the red rim of a mouth that was supposed to serve both for ingress and excretion of food. It waved the long arms, designed for some one simple operation not yet invented, in slow circles.

Sam, watching it, decided that life could be as ugly as an open field latrine in midsummer.

He had to disassemble it. Its length—three feet from almost boneless fingers to tapering, sealed-off trunk—precluded the use of the tiny disassembleator with which he had taken apart the oysters and miscellaneous small creations. There was a bright yellow notice on the large diassembleator, however—"To be used only under the direct supervision of a Census Keeper. Call formula A76 or unstable your id."

"Formula A76" meant about as much as "sunevviarry," and Sam decided his id was already sufficiently unstabled, thank you. He'd have to make out without a Census Keeper. The big disassembleator probably used the same general principles as the small one.

He clamped it to a bedpost and adjusted the focus. He snapped the switch set in the smooth underside.

Five minutes later the mannikin was a bright, gooey mess on his bed.

The large disassembleator, Sam was convinced as he tidied his room, did require the supervision of a Census Keeper. Some sort of keeper anyway. He rescued as many of the legless creature's constituents as he could, although he doubted he'd be using the set for the next fifty years or so. He certainly wouldn't ever use the disassembleator again; much less spectacular and disagreeable to shove the whole thing into a meat grinder and crank the handle as it squashed inside.

As he locked the door behind him on his way to a gentle binge, he made a mental note to purchase some fresh sheets the next morning. He'd have to sleep on the floor tonight.

Wrist-deep in Somerset & Ojack minutiae, Sam was conscious of Lew Knight's stares and Tina's puzzled glances. If they only knew, he exulted! But Tina would probably just think it "marr-vell-ouss!" and Lew Knight might make some crack like "Hey! Kid Frankenstein himself!" Come to think of it, though, Lew would probably have worked out some method of duplicating, to a limited extent, the contents of the Bild-A-Man set and marketing it commercially. Whereas he—well, there were other things you could do with the gadget. Plenty of other things.

"Hey, counselor," Lew Knight was perched on the corner of his desk, "what are these long weekends we're taking? You might not make as much money in the law, but does it look right for an associate of mine to sell magazine subscriptions on the side?"

Sam stuffed his ears mentally against the emery-wheel voice. "I've been writing a book."

"A law book? Weber *On Bankruptcy?*"

"No, a juvenile. *Lew Knight, The Neanderthal Nitwit.*"

"Won't sell. The title lacks punch. Something like *Knights, Knaves and Knobheads* is what the public goes for these days. By the way, Tina tells me you two had some sort of understanding about New Year's Eve and she doesn't think you'd mind if I took her out instead. I don't think you'd mind either, but I may be prejudiced. Especially since I have a table reservation at Cigale's where there's usually less of a crowd of a New Year's Eve than at the Automat."

"I don't mind."

"Good," said Knight approvingly as he moved away. "By the way, I won that case. Nice juicy fee, too. Thanks for asking."

Tina also wanted to know if he objected to the new arrangements when she brought the mail. Again, he didn't. Where had he been for over two days? He had been busy, very busy. Something entirely new. Something important.

She stared down at him as he separated offers of used cars guaranteed not to have been driven over a quarter of a million miles from caressing reminders that he still owed half the tuition for the last year of law school and when was he going to pay it?

Came a letter that was neither bill nor ad. Sam's heart momentarily lost interest in the monotonous round of pumping that was its lot as he stared at a strange postmark: Glunt City, Ohio.

> Dear Sir:
>
> There is no firm in Glunt City at the present time bearing any name similar to "Bild-A-Man Company" nor do we know of any such organization planning to join our little community. We also have no thoroughfare called "Diagonal"; our north-south streets are named after Indian tribes while our east-west avenues are listed numerically in multiples of five.
>
> Glunt City is a restricted residential township; we intend to keep it that. Only small retailing and service establishments are permitted here. If you are interested in building a home in Glunt City and can furnish proof of white, Christian, Anglo-Saxon ancestry on both sides of your family for fifteen generations, we would be glad to furnish further information.
>
> Thomas H. Plantagenet, Mayor.
> P.S. An airfield for privately owned jet and propeller-driven aircraft is being built outside the city limits.

That was sort of that. He would get no refills on any of the vials and bottles even if he had a loose slunk or two with which to pay for the stuff. Better go easy on the material and conserve it as much as possible. But no disassembling!

Would the "Bild-A-Man Company" begin manufacturing at Glunt City some time

in the future when it had developed into an industrial metropolis against the con-
stricted wills of its restricted citizenry? Or had his package slid from some different
track in the human time stream, some era to be born on an other-dimensional Earth?
There would have to be a common origin to both, else why the English wordage? And
could there be a purpose in his having received it, beneficial—or otherwise?

Tina had been asking a question. Sam detached his mind from shapeless speculation and considered her quite-the-opposite features.

"So if you'd still like me to go out with you New Year's Eve, all I have to do is tell
Lew that my mother expects to suffer from her gallstones and I have to stay home.
Then I think you could buy the Cigale reservations from him cheap."

"Thanks a lot, Tina, but very honestly I don't have the loose cash right now. You
and Lew make a much more logical couple anyhow."

Lew Knight wouldn't have done that. Lew cut throats with carefree zest. But Tina
did seem to go with Lew as a type.

Why? Until Lew had developed a raised eyebrow where Tina was concerned, it had
been Sam all the way. The rest of the office had accepted the fact and moved out of
their path. It wasn't only a question of Lew's greater success and financial well being:
just that Lew had decided he wanted Tina and had got her.

It hurt. Tina wasn't special; she was no cultural companion, no intellectual equal;
but he wanted her. He liked being with her. She was the woman he desired, rightly or
wrongly, whether or not there was a sound basis to their relationship. He remembered his parents before a railway accident had orphaned him: they were theoretically incompatible, but they had been terribly happy together.

He was still wondering about it the next night as he flipped the pages of "Twinning
yourself and your friends." It would be interesting to twin Tina.

"One for me, one for Lew."

Only the horrible possibility of an error was there. His mannikin had not been
perfect: its arms had been of unequal length. Think of a physically lopsided Tina,
something he could never bring himself to disassemble, limping extraneously
through life.

And then the book warned: "Your constructed twin, though resembling you in
every obvious detail, has not had the slow and guarded maturity you have enjoyed.
He or she will not be as stable mentally, much less able to cope with unusual situations, much more prone to neurosis. Only a professional carnuplicator, using the
finest equipment, can make an exact copy of a human personality. Yours will be able
to live and even reproduce, but cannot ever be accepted as a valid and responsible
member of society."

Well, he could chance that. A little less stability in Tina would hardly be noticeable; it might be more desirable.

There was a knock. He opened the door, guarding the box from view with his body.
His landlady.

"Your door has been locked for the past week, Mr. Weber. That's why the chambermaid hasn't cleaned the room. We thought you didn't want anyone inside."

"Yes." He stepped into the hall and closed the door behind him. "I've been doing some highly important legal work at home."

"Oh." He sensed a murderous curiosity and changed the subject.

"Why all the fine feathers, Mrs. Lipanti—New Year's Eve party?"

She smoothed her frilly black dress self-consciously. "Y-yes. My sister and her husband came in from Springfield today and we were going to make a night of it. Only…only the girl who was supposed to come over and mind their baby just phoned and said she isn't feeling well. So I guess we won't go unless somebody else, I mean unless we can get someone else to take care…I mean, somebody who doesn't have a previous engagement and who wouldn't—" Her voice trailed away in assumed embarrassment as she realized the favor was already asked.

Well, after all, he wasn't doing anything tonight. And she had been remarkably pleasant those times when he had to operate on the basis of "Of course I'll have the rest of the rent in a day or so." But why did any one of the Earth's two billion humans, when in the possession of an unpleasant buck, pass it automatically to Sam Weber?

Then he remembered Chapter IV on babies and other small humans. Since the night when he had separated the mannikin from its constituent parts, he'd been running through the manual as an intellectual exercise. He didn't feel quite up to making some weird error on a small human. But twinning wasn't supposed to be as difficult.

Only by Gog and by Magog, by Aesculapius the Physician and Kildare the Doctor, he would not disassemble this time. There must be other methods of disposal possible in a large city on a dark night. He'd think of something.

"I'd be glad to watch the baby for a few hours." He started down the hall to anticipate her polite protest. "Don't have a date tonight myself. No, don't mention it, Mrs. Lipanti. Glad to do it."

In the landlady's apartment, her nervous sister briefed him doubtfully. "And that's the only time she cries in a low, steady way so if you move fast there won't be much damage done. Not much, anyway."

He saw them to the door. "I'll be fast enough," he assured the mother. "Just so I get a hint."

Mrs. Lipanti paused at the door. "Did I tell you about the man who was asking after you this afternoon?"

Again? "A sort of tall, old man in a long, black overcoat?"

"With the most frightening way of staring into your face and talking under his breath. Do you know him?"

"Not exactly. What did he want?"

"Well, he asked if there was a Sam Weaver living here who was a lawyer and had been spending most of his time in his room for the past week. I told him we had a Sam Weber—your first name *is* Sam?—who answered to that description, but that the last Weaver had moved out over a year ago. He just looked at me for a while and said, 'Weaver, Weber—they might have made an error,' and walked out without so much as a goodbye or excuse-me. Not what I call a polite gentleman."

Thoughtfully Sam walked back to the child. Strange how sharp a mental picture he had formed of this man! Possibly because the two women who had met him thus far had been very impressionable, although to hear their stories the impression was there to be received.

He doubted there was any mistake: the man had been looking for him on both occasions; his knowledge of Sam's vacation from foolscap this past week proved that. It did seem as if he weren't interested in meeting him until some moot point of identity should be established beyond the least shadow of a doubt. Something of a legal mind, that.

The whole affair centered around the "Bild-A-Man" set, he was positive. This skulking investigation hadn't started until after the gift from 2353 had been delivered—and Sam had started using it.

But till the character in the long, black overcoat paddled up to Sam Weber personally and stated his business, there wasn't very much he could do about it.

Sam went upstairs for his Junior Biocalibrator.

He propped the manual open against the side of the bed and switched the instrument on to full scanning power. The infant gurgled thickly as the calibrator was rolled slowly over its fat body and a section of metal tape unwound from the slot with, according to the manual, a completely detailed physiological description.

It was detailed. Sam gasped as the tape, running through the enlarging viewer, gave information on the child for which a pediatrician would have taken out at least three mortgages on his immortal soul. Thyroid capacity, chromosome quality, cerebral content. All broken down into neat subheads of data for construction purposes. Rate of skull expansion in minutes for the next ten hours; rate of cartilage transformation; changes in hormone secretions while active and at rest.

This was a blueprint; it was like taking canons from a baby.

Sam left the child to a puzzled contemplation of its navel and sped upstairs. With the tape as a guide, he clipped sections of the molds into the required smaller sizes. Then, almost before he knew it consciously, he was constructing a small human.

He was amazed at the ease with which he worked. Skill was evidently acquired in this game; the mannikin had been much harder to put together. The matter of duplication and working from an informational tape simplified his problems, though.

The child took form under his eyes.

He was finished just an hour and a half after he had taken his first measurements. All except the vitalizing.

A moment's pause, here. The ugly prospect of disassembling stopped him for a moment, but he shook it off. He had to see how well he had done the job. If this child could breathe, what was not possible to him! Besides he couldn't keep it suspended in an inanimate condition very long without running the risk of ruining his work and the materials.

He started the vitalizer.

The child shivered and began a low, steady cry. Sam tore down to the landlady's apartment again and scooped up a square of white linen left on the bed for emergencies. Oh well, some more clean sheets.

After he had made the necessary repairs, he stood back and took a good look at it. He was in a sense a papa. He felt as proud.

It was a perfect little creature, glowing and round with health.

"I have twinned," he said happily.

Every detail correct. The two sides of the face correctly inexact, the duplication of the original child's lunch at the very same point of digestion. Same hair, same eyes— or was it? Sam bent over the infant. He could have sworn the other was a blonde. This child had dark hair which seemed to grow darker as he looked.

He grabbed it with one hand and picked up the Junior Biocalibrator with the other.

Downstairs, he placed the two babies side by side on the big bed. No doubt about it. One was blonde; the other, his plagiarism, was now a definite brunette.

The biocalibrator showed other differences: Slightly faster pulse for his model. Lower blood count. Minutely higher cerebral capacity, although the content was the same. Adrenalin and bile secretions entirely unalike.

It added up to error. His child might be the superior specimen, or the inferior one, but he had not made a true copy. He had no way of knowing at the moment whether or not the infant he had built could grow into a human maturity. The other could.

Why? He had followed directions faithfully, had consulted the calibrator tape at every step. And this had resulted. Had he waited too long before starting the vitalizer? Or was it just a matter of insufficient skill?

Close to midnight, his watch delicately pointed out. It would be necessary to re-move evidences of baby-making before the sisters Lipanti came home. Sam consid-ered possibilities swiftly.

He came down in a few moments with an old tablecloth and a cardboard carton. He wrapped the child in the tablecloth, vaguely happy that the temperature had risen that night, then placed it in the carton.

The child gurgled at the adventure. Its original on the bed *goo*ed in return. Sam slipped quietly out into the street.

Male and female drunks stumbled along tootling on tiny trumpets. People wished each other a *hic* Happy New Year as he strode down the necessary three blocks.

As he turned left, he saw the sign: "Urban Foundling Home." There was a light burning over a side door. Convenient, but that was a big city for you.

Sam shrank into the shadow of an alley for a moment as a new idea occurred to him. This had to look genuine. He pulled a pencil out of his breast pocket and scrawled on the side of the carton in as small handwriting as he could manage: *Please take good care of my darling little girl. I am not married.*

Then he deposited the carton on the doorstep and held his finger on the bell until he heard movement inside. He was across the street and in the alley again by the time a nurse had opened the door.

It wasn't until he walked into the boarding house that he remembered about the navel. He stopped and tried to recall. No, he had built his little girl without a navel! Her belly had been perfectly smooth. That's what came of hurrying! Shoddy work-manship.

There might be a bit of to-do in the foundling home when they unwrapped the kid. How would they explain it?

Sam slapped his forehead. "Me and Michelangelo. He adds a navel, I forget one!"

Except for an occasional groan, the office was fairly quiet the second day of the New Year.

He was going through the last intriguing pages of the book when he was aware of two people teetering awkwardly, near his desk. His eyes left the manual reluctantly: "New kinds of life for your leisure moments" was really fascinating!

Tina and Lew Knight.

Sam digested the fact that neither of them was perched on his desk.

Tina now wore the little ring she'd received for Christmas on the third finger of her left hand; Lew was experimenting with a sheepish look and finding it difficult.

"Oh, Sam. Last night, Lew...Sam, we wanted you to be the first— Such a surprise, like that, I mean! Why I almost— Naturally we thought this would be a little difficult...Sam, we're going, I mean we expect—"

"—to be married," Lew Knight finished in what was almost an undertone. For the first time since Sam had known him he looked uncertain and suspicious of life, like a man who finds a newly hatched octopus in his breakfast orange juice.

"You'd adore the way Lew proposed," Tina was gushing. "So roundabout. And so shy. I told him afterward that I thought for a moment he was talking of something else entirely. I did have trouble understanding you, didn't I, dear?"

"Huh? Oh yeah, you had trouble understanding me." Lew stared at his former rival. "Much of a surprise?"

"Oh, no. No surprise at all. You two fit together so perfectly that I knew it right from the first." Sam mumbled his felicitations, conscious of Tina's searching glances. "And now, if you'll excuse me, there's something I have to take care of immediately. A special sort of wedding present."

Lew was disconcerted. "A wedding present. This early?"

"Why, certainly," Tina told him. "It isn't very easy to get just the right thing. And a special friend like Sam naturally wants to get a very special gift."

Sam decided he had taken enough. He grabbed the manual and his coat and dodged through the door.

By the time he came to the red stone steps of the boarding house, he had reached the conclusion that the wound, while painful, had definitely missed his heart. He was in fact chuckling at the memory of Lew Knight's face when his landlady plucked at his sleeve.

"That man was here again today, Mr. Weber. He said he wanted to see you."

"Which man? The tall, old fellow?"

Mrs. Lipanti nodded, her arms folded complacently across her chest. "Such an unpleasant person! When I told him you weren't in, he insisted I take him up to your room. I said I couldn't do that without your permission and he looked at me fit to kill. I've never believed in the evil eye myself—although I always say where there is smoke there must be fire—but if there is such a thing as an evil eye, he has it."

"Will he be back?"

"Yes. He asked me when you usually return and I said about eight o'clock, figuring that if you didn't want to meet him it would give you time to change your clothes and wash up and leave before he gets here. And, Mr. Weber, if you'll excuse me for saying this, I don't think you want to meet him."

"Thanks. But when he comes in at eight, show him up. If he's the right person, I'm in illegal possession of his property. I want to know where this property originates."

In his room, he put the manual away carefully and told the box to open. The Junior Biocalibrator was not too bulky and newspaper would suffice to cover it. He was on his way uptown in a few minutes with the strangely shaped parcel under his arm.

Did he still want to duplicate Tina, he pondered? Yes, in spite of everything. She was still the woman he desired more than any he had ever known; and with the original married to Lew, the replica would have no choice but himself. Only—the replica would have Tina's characteristics up to the moment the measurements were taken; she might insist on marrying Lew as well.

That would make for a bit of a mad situation. But he was still miles from that bridge. It might even be amusing—

The possibility of error was more annoying. The Tina he would make might be off-center in a number of ways: reds might overlap pinks; like an imperfectly reproduced color photograph, she might, in time, come to digest her own stomach; there could very easily be a streak of strange and incurable insanity implicit in his model which would not assert itself until a deep mutual affection had flowered and borne fruit. As yet, he was no great shakes as a twinner and human mimeographer; the errors he had made on Mrs. Lipanti's niece demonstrated his amateur standing.

Sam knew he would never be able to dismantle Tina if she proved defective. Outside of the chivalrous concepts and almost superstitious reverence for womankind pressed into him by a small-town boyhood, there was the unmitigated horror he felt at the idea of such a beloved object going through the same disintegrating process as—well, the mannikin. But if he overlooked an essential in the construction, what other recourse would there be?

Solution: nothing must be overlooked. Sam grinned bitterly as the ancient elevator swayed up to his office. If he only had time for a little more practice with a person whose reactions he knew so exactly that any deviation from the norm would be instantly obvious! But the strange old man would be calling tonight, and, if his business concerned "Bild-A-Man" sets, Sam's experiments might be abruptly curtailed. And where would he find such a person—he had few real friends and no intimate ones. And, to be at all valuable, it would have to be someone he knew as well as himself.

Himself!

"Floor, sir." The elevator operator was looking at him reproachfully. Sam's exultant shout had caused him to bring the carrier to a spasmodic stop six inches under the floor level, something he had not done since that bygone day when he had first nervously reached for the controls. He felt his craftsmanship was under a shadow as he morosely closed the door behind the lawyer.

And why not himself? He knew his own physical attributes better than he knew Tina's; any mental instability on the part of his reproduced self would be readily discernible long before it reached the point of psychosis or worse. And the beauty of it was that he would have no compunction in disassembling a superfluous Sam Weber. Quite the contrary: the horror in that situation would be the continued existence of a duplicate personality; its removal would be a relief.

Twinning himself would provide the necessary practice in a familiar medium. Ideal. He'd have to take careful notes so that if anything went wrong he'd know just where to avoid going off the track in making his own personal Tina.

And maybe the old geezer wasn't interested in the set at all. Even if he were, Sam could take his landlady's advice and not be at home when he called. Silver linings wherever he looked.

Lew Knight stared at the instrument in Sam's hands. "What in the sacred name of Blackstone and all his commentaries is that? Looks like a lawn mower for a window box!"

"It's uh, sort of a measuring gadget. Gives the right size for one thing and another and this and that. Won't be able to get you the wedding present I have in mind unless I know the right size. Or sizes. Tina, would you mind stepping out into the hall?"

"Nooo." She looked dubiously at the gadget. "It won't hurt?"

It wouldn't hurt a bit, Sam assured her. "I just want to keep this a secret from Lew till after the ceremony."

She brightened at that and preceded Sam through the door. "Hey, counselor," one of the other young lawyers called at Lew as they left. "Hey, counselor, don't let him do that. Possession is nine points, Sam always says. He'll never bring her back."

Lew chuckled weakly and bent over his work.

"Now I want you to go into the ladies' room," Sam explained to a bewildered Tina. "I'll stand guard outside and tell the other customers that the place is out of order. If another woman is inside, wait until she leaves. Then strip."

"Strip?" Tina squealed.

He nodded. Then very carefully, emphasizing every significant detail of operation, he told her how to use the Junior Biocalibrator. How she must be careful to kick the switch and set the tape running. How she must cover every external square inch of her body. "This little arm will enable you to lower it down your back. No questions now. Git."

She was back in fifteen minutes, fluffing her dress into place and studying the tape with a rapt frown. "This is the *strangest* thing— According to the spool, my iodine content—"

Sam snaffled the Biocalibrator hurriedly. "Don't give it another thought. It's a code, kind of. Tells me just what size and how many of what kind. You'll be crazy about the gift when you see it."

"I know I will." She bent over him as he kneeled and examined the tape to make certain she had applied the instrument correctly. "You know, Sam, I always felt your taste was perfect. I want you to come and visit us often after we're married. You can have such beautiful ideas! Lew is a bit too...too business-like, isn't he? I mean it's necessary for success and all that, but success isn't everything. I mean you have to have culture, too. You'll help me keep cultured, won't you, Sam?"

"Sure," Sam said vaguely. The tape was complete. Now to get started! "Anything I can do—glad to help."

He rang for the elevator and noticed the forlorn uncertainty with which she watched him. "Don't worry. Tina. You and Lew will be very happy together. And you'll love this wedding present." But not as much as I will, he told himself as he stepped into the elevator.

Back in his room, he emptied the machine and undressed. In a few moments he had another tape on himself. He would have liked to consider it for a while, but being this close to the goal made him impatient. He locked the door, cleaned his room hurriedly of accumulated junk—remembering to grunt in annoyance at Aunt Maggie's ties: the blue and red one almost lighted up the room—ordered the box to open—and he was ready to begin.

First the water. With the huge amount of water necessary to the human body, especially in the case of an adult, he might as well start collecting it now. He had bought several pans and it would take his lone faucet some time to fill them all.

As he placed the first pot under the tap, Sam wondered suddenly if its chemical impurities might affect the end product. Of course it might! These children of 2353 would probably take absolutely pure H_2O as a matter of daily use; the manual hadn't mentioned the subject, but how did he know what kind of water they had available? Well, he'd boil this batch over his chemical stove; when he got to making Tina he could see about getting *aqua* completely *pura*.

Score another point for making a simulacrum of Sam first.

While waiting for the water to boil, he arranged his supplies to positions of maximum availability. They were getting low. That baby had taken up quite a bit of useful ingredients; too bad he hadn't seen his way clear to disassembling it. That meant if there were any argument in favor of allowing the replica of himself to go on living, it was now invalid. He'd have to take it apart in order to have enough for Tina II. (Or Tina prime?)

He leafed through Chapters VI, VII and VIII on the ingredients, completion and disassembling of a man. He'd been through this several times before; but he'd passed more than one law exam on the strength of a last-minute review.

The constant reference to mental instability disturbed him. "The humans constructed with this set will, at the very best, show most of the superstitious tendencies, and neurosis-compulsions of medieval mankind. In the long run they are not normal; take great care not to consider them such." Well, it wouldn't make too much difference in Tina's case—and that was all that was important.

When he had finished adjusting the molds to the correct sizes, he fastened the vitalizer to the bed. Then—very, very slowly and with repeated glances at the manual, he began to duplicate Sam Weber. He learned more of his physical limitations and capabilities in the next two hours than any man had ever known since the day when an inconspicuous primate had investigated the possibilities of ground locomotion upon the nether extremities alone.

Strangely enough, he felt neither awe nor exultation. It was like building a radio receiver for the first time. Child's play.

Most of the vials and jars were empty when he had finished. The damp molds were stacked inside the box, still in their three-dimensional outline. The manual lay neglected on the floor.

Sam Weber stood near the bed looking down at Sam Weber on the bed.

All that remained was vitalizing. He daren't wait too long or imperfections might set in and the errors of the baby be repeated. He shook off a nauseating feeling of unreality, made certain that the big disassembleator was within reach and set the Jiffy Vitalizer in motion.

The man on the bed coughed. He stirred. He sat up.

"Wow!" he said. "Pretty good, if I do say so myself!"

And then he had leaped off the bed and seized the disassembleator. He tore great chunks of wiring out of the center, threw it to the floor and kicked it into shapelessness. "No Sword of Damocles going to hang over *my* head," he informed an openmouthed Sam Weber. "Although, I could have used it on you, come to think of it."

Sam eased himself to the mattress and sat down. His mind stopped rearing and whinnied to a halt. He had been so impressed with the helplessness of the baby and the mannikin that he had never dreamed of the possibility that his duplicate would enter upon life with such enthusiasm. He should have, though; this was a full-grown man, created at a moment of complete physical and mental activity.

"This is bad," he said at last in a hoarse voice. "You're unstable. You can't be admitted into normal society."

"I'm unstable?" his image asked. "Look who's talking! The guy who's been mooning his way through his adult life, who wants to marry an overdressed, conceited collection of biological impulses that would come crawling on her knees to any man sensible enough to push the right buttons—"

"You leave Tina's name out of this," Sam told him, feeling acutely uncomfortable at the theatrical phrase.

His double looked at him and grinned. "OK, I will. But not her body! Now, look here, Sam or Weber or whatever you want me to call you, you can live your life and I'll live mine. I won't even be a lawyer if that'll make you happy. But as far as Tina is concerned, now that there are no ingredients to make a copy—that was a rotten escapist idea, by the way—I have enough of your likes and dislikes to want her badly. And I can have her, whereas you can't. You don't have the gumption."

Sam leaped to his feet and doubled his fists. Then he saw the other's entirely equal size and slightly more assured twinkle. There was no point in fighting—that would end in a draw, at best. He went back to reason.

"According to the manual," he began, "you are prone to neurosis—"

"The manual! The manual was written for children of four centuries hence, with quite a bit of selective breeding and scientific education behind them. Personally, I think I'm a—"

There was a double knock on the door. "Mr. Weber." "Yes," they both said simultaneously. Outside, the landlady gasped and began speaking in an uncertain voice. "Th-that gentleman is downstairs. He'd like to see you. Shall I tell him you're in?"

"No, I'm not at home," said the double.

"Tell him I left an hour ago," said Sam at exactly the same moment.

There was another, longer gasp and the sound of footsteps receding hurriedly.

"That's one clever way to handle a situation," Sam's facsimile exploded. "Couldn't you keep your mouth shut? The poor woman's probably gone off to have a fit."

"You forget that this is my room and you are just an experiment that went wrong," Sam told him hotly. "I have just as much right, in fact more right...hey, what do you think you're doing?"

The other had thrown open the closet door and was stepping into a pair of pants. "Just getting dressed. You can wander around in the nude if you find it exciting, but I want to look a bit respectable."

"I undressed to take my measurements...or your measurements. Those are my clothes, this is my room—"

"Look, take it easy. You could never prove it in a court of law. Don't make me go into that cliché about what's yours is mine and so forth."

Heavy feet resounded through the hall. They stopped outside the room. Cymbals seemed to clash all around them and there was a panic-stricken sense of unendurable heat. Then shrill echoes fled into the distance. The walls stopped shuddering.

Silence and a smell of burning wood.

They whirled in time to see a terribly tall, terribly old man in a long black overcoat walking through the smoldering remains of the door. Much too tall for the entrance, he did not stoop as he came in; rather, he drew his head down into his garment and shot it up again. Instinctively, they moved close together.

His eyes, all shiny black iris without any whites, were set back deep in the shadow of his head. They reminded Sam Weber of the scanners on the Biocalibrator: they tabulated, deduced, rather than saw.

"I was afraid I would be too late," he rumbled at last in weird, clipped tones. "You have already duplicated yourself, Mr. Weber, making necessary unpleasant rearrangements. And the duplicate has destroyed the disassembleator. Too bad. I shall have to do it manually. An ugly job."

He came further into the room until they could almost breathe their fright upon him. "This affair has already dislocated four major programs, but we had to move in accepted cultural grooves and be absolutely certain of the recipient's identity before we could act to withdraw the set. Mrs. Lipanti's collapse naturally stimulated emergency measures."

The duplicate cleared his throat. "You are—

"Not exactly human. A humble civil servant of precision manufacture. I am Census Keeper for the entire twenty-ninth oblong. You see, your set was intended for the

Thregander children who are on a field trip in this oblong. One of the Threganders who has a Weber chart requested the set through the chrondromos which, in an attempt at the supernormal, unstabled without carnuplicating. You therefore received the package instead. Unfortunately, the unstabling was so complete that we were forced to locate you by indirect methods."

The Census Keeper paused and Sam's double hitched his pants nervously. Sam wished he had anything—even a fig leaf—to cover his nakedness. He felt like a character in the Garden of Eden trying to build up a logical case for apple-eating. He appreciated glumly how much more than "Bild-A-Man" sets clothes had to do with the making of a man.

"We will have to recover the set, of course," the staccato thunder continued, "and readjust any discrepancies it has caused. Once the matter has been cleared up, however, your life will be allowed to resume its normal progression. Meanwhile, the problem is, which of you is the original Sam Weber?"

"I am," they both quavered—and turned to glare at each other.

"Difficulties," the old man rumbled. He sighed like an arctic wind. "I always have difficulties! Why can't I ever have a simple case like a carnuplicator?"

"Look here," the duplicate began. "The original will be—"

"Less unstable and of better emotional balance than the replica," Sam interrupted. "Now, it seems—"

"That you should be able to tell the difference," the other concluded breathlessly. "From what you see and have seen of us, can't you decide which is the more valid member of society?"

What a pathetic confidence, Sam thought, the fellow was trying to display! Didn't he know he was up against someone who could really discern mental differences? This was no fumbling psychiatrist of the present; here was a creature who could see through externals to the most coherent personality beneath.

"I can, naturally. Now, just a moment." He studied them carefully, his eyes traveling with judicious leisure up and down their bodies. They waited, fidgeting, in a silence that pounded.

"Yes," the old man said at last. "Yes. Quite."

He walked forward.

A long thin arm shot out.

He started to disassemble Sam Weber.

"But listennnnn—" began Weber in a yell that turned into a high scream and died in a liquid mumble.

"It would be better for your sanity if you didn't watch," the Census Keeper suggested.

The duplicate exhaled slowly, turned away and began to button a shirt. Behind him the mumbling continued, rising and falling in pitch.

"You see," came the clipped, rumbling accents, "it's not the gift we're afraid of letting you have—it's the principle involved. Your civilization isn't ready for it. You understand."

"Perfectly," replied the counterfeit Sam Weber, knotting Aunt Maggie's blue and red tie.

CHILD'S PLAY 271

AFTERWORD

"Child's Play" was my second published story and what might possibly be called my first science-fiction "success." John Campbell accepted it for *Astounding* the day he received it; Ted Sturgeon asked to be my agent when I showed him the story's carbon copy; it was the first piece by me to be anthologized (science-fiction anthologies were *very* rare birds in the 1940s) and it was to be anthologized many more times; finally, and almost miraculously, Clifton Fadiman went out of his way to say something nice about the story in the book review section of *The New Yorker*.

I started "Child's Play" while I was a purser on a cargo ship, early in 1946. My brother had sent me the May issue of *Astounding*, containing my first published story, "Alexander the Bait," and when it arrived in the port of Antwerp, Belgium, I showed it around quite proudly. My fellow officers, however, wondered why I made such a fuss over a printed tale by someone called William Tenn; again and again, I had to explain the concept of a pen name.

After many explanations they seemed to accept the idea, and the first mate suggested we go into Antwerp that night and have "a beer or two" to celebrate. I felt I had to agree, even though I had been warned by the radio operator that from the beginning of the voyage the three mates had been arguing over just how drunk they could get the Jewish purser.

I don't know which of them won, but we all got back to the ship utterly, thoroughly, overwhelmingly soused. The first mate carried me up the Jacob's ladder upside down with my legs locked around his neck and the rest of me over his shoulders. He took me to the purser's cabin and dumped me in a chair in front of my typewriter desk. "If you are really William Tenn and can write stories that get published," he said, waving a wobbly forefinger in the air, "prove it. Write one now."

With the immense dignity of total drunkenness, I said, "I'll do that. You just sit down here and just watch me do it." He sat on my bunk and bleared at me.

I typed four pages and had to go to the toilet. When I came back he was sound asleep on my bunk, fully clothed, occupying all of it. He was an enormous Norwegian and there was no chance of moving him even a little. I staggered back to the chair, cradled my arms around the typewriter, and went out cold.

He was gone when I woke up the next morning.

But the captain was there, with a briefcase under his arm. "Get up, Purser," he said. "We have to go to the custom house and officially enter the ship. I hear you tied a big one on last night. You must have a hell of hangover."

I rolled over, sat up, stood up. I felt my head. "No," I said, relieved and astonished. "Can't say that I do. I feel fine."

The captain stared at me. "You're a wonder," he said. "After what you drank! Are all Jews like that?"

What do you say to such a question? "Most," I told him.

We got a taxi and went into Antwerp. It was a very hot day, and by the time we had finished the paperwork on entering the ship we were both perspiring heavily.

There was a café, *L'américain,* across the street from the custom house with a sign in its window advertising cold beer. "That's what I want," the captain said. "Could you go for one, too?"

I shrugged. We went into the café and ordered two small beers. The captain swallowed his and ordered another one. I sipped mine slowly, tilting my head back as I reached the bottom of the glass.

And then I found I couldn't tilt my head forward any more. The glass slipped from my hand and smashed. I began following it to the floor, my back arching behind me.

Fortunately, the captain caught me as I fell. He and a waiter grabbed me and pulled me up and spread me out on top of the bar. I lay there, completely paralyzed, able to hear what was going on around me, feeling the night before's spree return through every cell in my body.

That single glass of beer had brought my alcohol level up to optimum again. The barmaid, however, knew nothing of my nocturnal activities.

"Une bière! Une bière!" she chanted to everyone who came in, pointing to where I lay prone on the bar. *"Seulement une bière!"*

And everyone who came in explained it to everyone else who came in. They stood around me and marveled.

Eventually, the captain got me back to the ship and into my bunk—where I lay, unable to move, for six hours. When I was mobile again, I had a real hangover. I sat at my desk, I remember, holding my head between my hands and reading the totally unfamiliar manuscript in my typewriter.

I liked it. I liked it very much. I recognized it, of course. It was the beginning of a story by one of my very favorite science-fiction writers, Lewis Padgett. (I did not know at the time that Lewis Padgett was the joint pen name of the writing couple, Henry Kuttner and C.L. Moore.)

Padgett's work, to me, was like intellectual candy—I'd never been able to get enough of it. And I had started an honest-to-God Padgett story! If I could finish it, I would have the pleasure of reading a Lewis Padgett piece as it appeared in front of me, paragraph by paragraph, page by page.

The hell with the ship's business! To hell with my hangover! I began writing.

WRITTEN 1946——PUBLISHED 1947

෫ඔ

WEDNESDAY'S CHILD

When he first came to scrutinize Wednesday Gresham with his rimless spectacles and watery blue eyes, Fabian Balik knew nothing of the biological contradictions that were so incredibly a part of her essential body structure. He had not even noticed—as yet—that she was a remarkably pretty girl with eyes like rain-sparkling violets. His original preoccupation with her was solely and specifically as a problem in personnel administration.

All of which was not too surprising, because Fabian Balik was a thoroughly intent, thoroughly sincere young office manager, who had convinced his glands conclusively, in several bitter skirmishes, that their interests didn't have a chance against the interests of SLAUGHTER, STARK & SLINGSBY: Advertising & Public Relations.

Wednesday was one of the best stenographers in the secretarial pool that was under his immediate supervision. There were, however, small but highly unusual derelictions in her employment history. They consisted of peculiarities which a less dedicated and ambitious personnel man might have put aside as mere trifles, but which Fabian, after a careful study of her six-year record with the firm, felt he could not, in good conscience, ignore. On the other hand, they would obviously require an extended discussion and he had strong views about cutting into an employee's working time.

Thus, much to the astonishment of the office and the confusion of Wednesday herself, he came up to her one day at noon, and informed her quite calmly that they were going to have lunch together.

"This is a nice place," he announced, when they had been shown to a table. "It's not too expensive, but I've discovered it serves the best food in the city for the price. And it's a bit off the beaten track so that it never gets too crowded. Only people who know what they want manage to come here."

Wednesday glanced around, and nodded. "Yes," she said. "I like it too. I eat here a lot with the girls."

After a moment, Fabian picked up a menu. "I suppose you don't mind if I order for both of us?" he inquired. "The chef is used to my tastes. He'll treat us right."

The girl frowned. "I'm terribly sorry, Mr. Balik, but—"

"Yes?" he said encouragingly, though he was more than surprised. He hadn't expected anything but compliance. After all, she was probably palpitating at being out with him.

"I'd like to order for myself," she said. "I'm on a—a special diet."

He raised his eyebrows and was pleased at the way she blushed. He nodded slowly, with dignity, letting his displeasure come through in the way he pronounced his words. "Very well, as you please."

A few moments later, though, curiosity got too strong and broke through the ice. "What kind of diet is that? Fresh-fruit salad, a glass of tomato juice, raw cabbage, and a *baked potato*? You can't be trying to lose weight if you eat potatoes."

Wednesday smiled timidly. "I'm not trying to reduce, Mr. Balik. Those are all foods rich in Vitamin C. I need a lot of Vitamin C."

Fabian remembered her smile. There had been a few spots of more-than-natural whiteness in it. "Bad teeth?" he inquired.

"Bad teeth and—" Her tongue came out and paused for a thoughtful second between her lips. "Mostly bad teeth," she said. "This is a nice place. There's a restaurant almost like it near where I live. Of course it's a lot cheaper—"

"Do you live with your parents, Miss Gresham?"

"No, I live alone. I'm an orphan."

He waited until the waiter had deposited the first course, then speared a bit of the shrimp and returned to the attack. "Since when?"

She stared at him over her fresh-fruit salad. "I beg your pardon, Mr. Balik?"

"Since when? How long have you been an orphan?"

"Since I was a little baby. Someone left me on the doorstep of a foundling home."

He noticed that while she was replying to his questions in an even tone of voice, she was staring at her food with a good deal of concentration and her blush had become more pronounced. Was she embarrassed at having to admit her probable lack of legitimacy? he wondered. Surely she had grown accustomed to it in—how old was she?—twenty-four years. Nonsense, of course she had.

"But on your original application form, Miss Gresham, you gave Thomas and Mary Gresham as the names of your parents."

Wednesday had stopped eating and was playing with her water glass. "They were an old couple who adopted me," she said in a very low voice. "They died when I was fifteen. I have no living relatives."

"That you know of," he pointed out, raising a cautionary finger.

Much to Fabian's surprise she chuckled. It was a very odd chuckle and made him feel extremely uncomfortable. "That's right, Mr. Balik. I have no living relatives— *that I know of.*" She looked over his shoulder and chuckled again. "That I know of," she repeated softly to herself.

Fabian felt irritably that the interview was somehow getting away from him. He raised his voice slightly. "Then who is Dr. Morris Lorington?"

She was attentive again. In fact, wary was more like it. "Dr. Morris Lorington?"

"Yes, the man you said should be notified in case of emergency. In case anything happened to you while you were working for us."

She looked very wary now. Her eyes were narrowed, she was watching him very closely; her breathing was a bit faster, too. "Dr. Lorington is an old friend. He—he was the doctor at the orphanage. After the Greshams adopted me, I kept going to him whenever—" Her voice trailed off.

"Whenever you needed medical attention?" Fabian suggested.

"Ye-es," she said, brightening, as if he had come up with an entirely novel reason for consulting a physician. "I saw him whenever I needed medical attention."

Fabian grunted. There was something very wrong but tantalizingly elusive about this whole business. But she was answering his questions. He couldn't deny that: she was certainly answering.

"Do you expect to see him next October?" he inquired.

And now Wednesday was no longer wary. She was frightened. "Next October?" she quavered.

Fabian finished the last of his shrimp and wiped his lips. But he didn't take his eyes off her. "Yes, next October, Miss Gresham. You've applied for a month's leave of absence, beginning October fifteenth. Five years ago, after you had been working for Slaughter, Stark and Slingsby for thirteen months, you also applied for a leave of absence in October."

He was amazed at how scared she looked. He felt triumphantly that he had been right in looking into this. The feeling he had about her had not been merely curiosity; it had been an instinct of good personnel management

"But I'm not getting paid for the time off. I'm not asking to be paid for it, Mr. Balik. And I didn't get paid the—the other time."

She was clutching her napkin up near her face, and she gave the impression of being ready to bolt through the back door of the restaurant. Her blushes had departed with such thoroughness as to leave her skin absolutely white.

"The fact that you're not going to be paid for the time off, Miss Gresham—" Fabian began, only to be interrupted by the waiter with the entree. By the time the man had gone, he was annoyed to observe that Wednesday had used the respite to recover some of her poise. While she was still pale, she had a spot of red in each cheek and she was leaning back in her chair now instead of using the edge of it.

"The fact that you're not going to be paid is of no consequence," he continued nonetheless. "It's merely logical. After all, you have two weeks of vacation with pay every year. Which brings me to the second point. You have every year made *two* unusual requests. First, you've asked for an additional week's leave of absence without pay, making three weeks in all. And then you've asked—"

"To take it in the early Spring," she finished, her voice entirely under control. "Is there anything wrong with that, Mr. Balik? That way I don't have any conflict with the other girls and the firm is sure of a secretary being in the office all through the summer."

"There's nothing wrong with that *per se*. By that I mean," he explained carefully, "that there is nothing wrong with the arrangement *as such*. But it makes for loose ends, for organizational confusion. And loose ends, Miss Gresham, loose ends and organizational confusion have no place in a well-regulated office."

He was pleased to note that she was looking uncomfortable again.

"Does that mean—are you trying to tell me that—I might be laid off?"

"It could happen," Fabian agreed, neglecting to add that it was, however, very unlikely to happen in the case of a secretary who was as generally efficient on the one hand, and as innocuous on the other, as Wednesday Gresham. He carefully cut a fork-sized portion of roast beef free of its accompanying strip of orange fat before going on. "Look at it this way. How would it be if every girl in the office asked for an additional week's leave of absence every year—even if it was without pay, as it would have to be? And then, every few years, wanted an additional month's leave of absence on top of that? What kind of an office would we have, Miss Gresham? Not a well-regulated one, certainly."

As he chewed the roast beef with the requisite thoroughness he beamed at the thoughtful concern on her face and was mentally grateful that he hadn't had to present that line of argument to anyone as sharp as Arlette Stein, for example. He knew what the well-hipped thirtyish widow would have immediately replied: "But every girl in the office *doesn't* ask for it, Mr. Balik." A heavy sneer at such sophistry would mean little to Stein.

Wednesday, he appreciated, was not the person to go in for such counterattacks. She was rolling her lips distressedly against each other and trying to think of a polite, good-employee way out. There was only one, and she would have to come to it in a moment.

She did.

"Would it help any," she began, and stopped. She took a deep breath. "Would it help any, if I told you the reasons—for the leaves-of-absence?"

"It would," he said heartily. "It would indeed, Miss Gresham. That way I, as office manager, can operate from facts instead of mysteries. I can hear your reasons, weigh them for validity and measure their importance—*and* your usefulness as a secretary—against the disorganization your absences create in the day-to-day operation of Slaughter, Stark and Slingsby."

"M-m-m." She looked troubled, uncertain. "I'd like to think a bit, if you don't mind."

Fabian waved a cauliflower-filled fork magnanimously. "Take all the time in the world! Think it out carefully. Don't tell me anything you aren't perfectly willing to tell me. Of course anything you *do* tell me will be, I am sure I need hardly reassure you, completely confidential. I will treat it as official knowledge, Miss Gresham— not personal. And while you're thinking, you might start eating your raw cabbage. Before it gets cold," he added with a rich, executive-type chuckle.

She nodded him a half-smile that ended in a sigh and began working at her plate in an absent-minded, not-particularly-hungry fashion.

"You see," she began abruptly as if she'd found a good point of departure, "some things happen to me that don't happen to other people."

"That, I would say, is fairly obvious."

"They're not bad things. I mean what, oh, the newspapers would call bad. And they're not dangerous things, exactly. They're—they're more physical-like. They're things that could happen to my body."

Fabian finished his plate, sat back and crossed his arms. "Could you be just a little more specific? Unless—" and he was struck by a horrifying thought—"unless they're what is known as, er, as *female* difficulties. In that case, of course—"

This time she didn't even blush. "Oh, no. Not at all. At least there's very little of that. It's—other things. Like my appendix. Every year I have to have my appendix out."

"Your appendix?" He turned that over in his mind. "Every year? But a human being only has one appendix. And once it's removed, it doesn't grow back."

"Mine does. On the tenth of April, every single year, I get appendicitis and have to have an operation. That's why I take my vacation then. And my teeth. Every five years, I lose all my teeth. I start losing them about this time, and I have some dental plates that were made when I was younger—I use them until my teeth grow back. Then, about the middle of October, the last of them goes and new ones start coming up. I can't use my dental plates while they're growing, so I look kind of funny for a while. That's why I ask for a leave of absence. In the middle of November, the new teeth are almost full-grown, and I come back to work."

She took a deep breath and timidly lifted her eyes to his face. That was all she evidently had to say. Or wished to.

All through dessert, he thought about it. He was positive she was telling the truth. A girl like Wednesday Gresham didn't lie. Not to such a fantastic extent. Not to her boss.

"Well," he said at last. "It's certainly very unusual."

"Yes," she agreed. "Very unusual."

"Do you have anything else the matter with— I mean, are there any other peculiarities— Oh, darn! Is there anything else?"

Wednesday considered. "There are. But, if you don't mind, Mr. Balik, I'd rather not—"

Fabian decided not to take that. "Now see here, Miss Gresham," he said firmly. "Let us not play games. You didn't have to tell me anything, but you decided, for yourself, for your own good reasons, to do so. Now I must insist on the whole story, and nothing but the whole story. What other physical difficulties do you have?"

It worked. She cringed a bit in her chair, straightened up again, but a little weakly, and began: "I'm sorry, Mr. Balik, I wouldn't dream of—of playing games with you. There are lots of other things, but none of them interfere with my work, really. Like I have some tiny hairs growing on my fingernails. See?"

Fabian glanced at the hand held across the table. A few almost microscopic tendrils on each glittering hard surface of fingernail.

"What else?"

"Well, my tongue. I have a few hairs on the underside of my tongue. They don't bother me, though, they don't bother me in any way. And there's my—my—"

"Yes?" he prompted. *Who could believe that colorless little Wednesday Gresham...*

"My navel. I don't have any navel."

"You don't have any— But that's impossible!" he exploded. He felt his glasses sliding down his nose. "Everyone has a navel! Everyone alive—everyone who's ever been born."

Wednesday nodded, her eyes unnaturally bright and large. "Maybe—" she began, and suddenly, unexpectedly, broke into tears. She brought her hands up to her face and sobbed through them, great, pounding, wracking sobs that pulled her shoulders up and down, up and down.

Fabian's consternation made him completely helpless. He'd never, never in his life, been in a crowded restaurant with a crying girl before.

"Now, Miss Gresham—Wednesday," he managed to get out, and he was annoyed to hear a high, skittery note in his own voice. "There's no call for this. Surely, there's no call for this? Uh—Wednesday?"

"Maybe," she gasped again, between sobs, "m-maybe that's the answer."

"What's the answer?" Fabian asked loudly, desperately hoping to distract her into some kind of conversation.

"About—about being born. Maybe—maybe I wasn't born. M-maybe I was m-m-made!"

And then, as if she'd merely been warming up before this, she *really* went into hysterics. Fabian Balik at last realized what he had to do. He paid the check, put his arm around the girl's waist and half-carried her out of the restaurant.

It worked. She got quieter the moment they hit the open air. She leaned against a building, not crying now, and shook her shoulders in a steadily diminishing crescendo. Finally, she *ulped* once, twice, and turned groggily to him, her face looking as if it had been rubbed determinedly in an artist's turpentine rag.

"I'm s-sorry," she said. "I'm t-terribly s-sorry. I haven't done that for years. But—you see, Mr. Balik—I haven't talked about myself for years."

"There's a nice bar at the corner," he pointed out, tremendously relieved. She'd looked for a while as if she'd intended to keep on crying all day! "Let's pop in, and I'll have a drink. You can use the ladies' room to fix yourself up."

He took her arm and steered her into the place. Then he climbed onto a bar stool and had himself a double brandy.

What an experience! And what a strange, strange girl!

Of course, he shouldn't have pushed her quite so hard on a subject about which she was evidently so sensitive. Was that his fault, though, that she *was* so sensitive?

Fabian considered the matter carefully, judicially, and found in his favor. No, it definitely wasn't his fault.

But what a story! The foundling business, the appendix business, the teeth, the hair on the fingernails and tongue… And that last killer about the navel!

He'd have to think it out. And maybe he'd get some other opinions. But one thing he was sure of, as sure as of his own managerial capacities: Wednesday Gresham hadn't been lying in any particular. Wednesday Gresham was just not the sort of a girl who made up tall stories about herself.

When she rejoined him, he urged her to have a drink. "Help you get a grip on yourself."

She demurred, she didn't drink very much, she said. But he insisted, and she gave in. "Just a liqueur. Anything. You order it, Mr. Balik."

Fabian was secretly very pleased at her docility. No reprimanding, no back-biting, like most other girls— Although what in the world could she reprimand him for?

"You still look a little frayed," he told her. "When we get back, don't bother going to your desk. Go right in to Mr. Osborne and finish taking dictation. No point in giving the other girls something to talk about. I'll sign in for you."

She inclined her head submissively and continued to sip from the tiny glass.

"What was that last comment you made in the restaurant—I'm certain you don't mind discussing it, now—about not being born, but being made? That was an odd thing to say."

Wednesday sighed. "It isn't my own idea. It's Dr. Lorington's. Years ago, when he was examining me, he said that I looked as if I'd been made—by an amateur. By someone who didn't have all the blueprints, or didn't understand them, or wasn't concentrating hard enough."

"Hm." He stared at her, absolutely intrigued. She looked normal enough. Better than normal, in fact. And yet—

Later that afternoon, he telephoned Jim Rudd and made an appointment for right after work. Jim Rudd had been his roommate in college and was now a doctor: he would be able to tell him a little more about this.

But Jim Rudd wasn't able to help him very much. He listened patiently to Fabian's story about "a girl I've just met" and, at the end of it, leaned back in the new upholstered swivel chair and pursed his lips at his diploma, neatly framed and hung on the opposite wall.

"You sure do go in for weirdies, Fabe. For a superficially well-adjusted, well-organized guy with a real talent for the mundane things of life, you pick the damndest women I ever heard of. But that's your business. Maybe it's your way of adding a necessary pinch of the exotic to the grim daily round. Or maybe you're making up for the drabness of your father's grocery store."

"This girl is not a weirdie," Fabian insisted angrily. "She's a very simple little secretary, prettier than most, but that's about all."

"Have it your own way. To me, she's a weirdie. To me, there's not a hell of a lot of difference—from your description—between her and that crazy White Russian dame you were running around with back in our junior year. You know the one I mean— what was her name?"

"Sandra? Oh, Jim, what's the matter with you? Sandra was a bollixed-up box of dynamite who was always blowing up in my face. This kid turns pale and dies if I so much as raise my voice. Besides, I had a real puppy-love crush on Sandra; this other girl is somebody I just met, like I told you, and I don't feel anything for her, one way or the other."

The young doctor grinned. "So you come up to my office and have a consultation about her! Well, it's your funeral. What do you want to know?"

"What causes all these—these physical peculiarities?"

Dr. Rudd got up and sat on the edge of his desk. "First," he said, "whether you want to recognize it or not, she's a highly disturbed person. The hysterics in the restaurant point to it, and the fantastic nonsense she told you about her body points to it. So right there, you have something. If only one percent of what she told you is true—and even that I would say is pretty high—it makes sense in terms of psychosomatic imbalance. Medicine doesn't yet know quite how it works, but one thing seems certain: anyone badly mixed up mentally is going to be at least a little mixed up physically, too."

Fabian thought about that for a while. "Jim, you don't know what it means to those little secretaries in the pool to tell lies to the office manager! A fib or two about why they were absent the day before, yes, but not stories like this, not to *me*."

A shrug. "I don't know what you look like to them: I don't work for you, Fabe. But none of what you say would hold true for a psycho. And a psycho is what I have to consider her. Look, some of that stuff she told you is impossible, some of it has occurred in medical literature. There have been well-authenticated cases of people, for example, who have grown several sets of teeth in their lifetime. These are biological sports, one-in-a-million individuals. But the rest of it? And all the rest of it happening to one person? *Please*."

"I saw some of it. I saw the hairs on her fingernails."

"You saw something on her fingernails. It could be any one of a dozen different possibilities. I'm sure of one thing; it wasn't hair. Right there she gave herself away as phony. Goddammit, man, hair and nails are the same organs essentially. One doesn't grow on the other!"

"And the navel? The missing navel?"

Jim Rudd dropped to his feet and strode rapidly about the office. "I wish I knew why I'm wasting so much time with you," he complained. "A human being without a navel, or *any* mammal without a navel, is as possible as an insect with a body temperature of ninety-eight degrees. It just can't be. It does not exist."

He seemed to get more and more upset as he considered it. He kept shaking his head negatively as he walked.

Fabian suggested: "Suppose I brought her to your office. And suppose you examined her and found no navel. Now just consider that for a moment. What would you say then?"

"I'd say plastic surgery," the doctor said instantly. "Mind you, I'm positive she'd never submit to such an examination, but if she did, and there was no navel, plastic surgery would be the only answer."

"Why would anyone want to do plastic surgery on a navel?"

"I don't know. I haven't the vaguest idea. Maybe an accident. Maybe a disfiguring birthmark in that place. But there will be scars, let me tell you. *She had to be born with a navel.*"

Rudd went back to his desk. He picked up a prescription pad. "Let me give you the name of a good psychiatrist, Fabe. I've thought ever since that Sandra business that you've had some personal problems that might get out of hand one day. This man is one of the finest—"

Fabian left.

She was obviously in a flutter when he called to pick her up that night, so much more of a flutter than a date-with-the-boss would account for, that Fabian was puzzled. But he waited and gave her an ostentatious and expensive good time. Afterward, after dinner and after the theater, when they were sitting in the corner of a small night club over their drinks, he asked her about it.

"You don't date much, do you, Wednesday?"

"No, I don't, Mr. Balik—I mean, Fabian," she said, smiling shyly as she remembered the first-name privilege she had been accorded for the evening. "I usually just go out with girl friends, not with men. I usually turn down dates."

"Why? You're not going to find a husband that way. You want to get married, don't you?"

Wednesday shook her head slowly. "I don't think so. I—I'm afraid to. Not of marriage. Of babies. I don't think a person like me ought to have a baby."

"Nonsense! Is there any scientific reason why you shouldn't? What are you afraid of—it'll be a monster?"

"I'm afraid it might be...anything. I think with my body being as—as funny as it is, I shouldn't take chances with a child. Dr. Lorington thinks so too. Besides, there's the poem."

Fabian put down his drink. "Poem? What poem?"

"You know, the one about the days of the week. I learned it when I was a little girl, and it frightened me even then. It goes:

> *Monday's child is fair of face,*
> *Tuesday's child is full of grace,*
> *Wednesday's child is full of woe,*
> *Thursday's child has far to go,*
> *Friday's child is loving and giving—*

And so on. When I was a little girl in the orphanage, I used to say to myself, 'I'm Wednesday. I'm different from all other little girls in all kinds of strange ways. And my child—' "

"Who gave you that name?"

"I was left at the foundling home just after New Year's Eve—Wednesday morning. So they didn't know what else to call me, especially when they found I didn't have a navel. And then, like I told you, after the Greshams adopted me, I took their last name."

He reached for her hand and grasped it firmly with both of his. He noted with triumphant pleasure that her fingernails *were* hairy. "You're a very pretty girl, Wednesday Gresham."

When she saw that he meant it, she blushed and looked down at the tablecloth.

"And you really don't have a navel?"

"No, I don't. Really."

"What else about you is different?" Fabian asked. "I mean, besides the things you told me."

"Well," she considered. "There's that business about my blood pressure."

"Tell me about it," he urged.

She told him.

Two dates later, she informed Fabian that Dr. Lorington wanted to see him. Alone.

He went all the way uptown to the old-fashioned brownstone, chewing his knuckles in excitement. He had so many questions to ask!

Dr. Lorington was a tall, aged man with pale skin and absolutely white hair. He moved very slowly as he gestured his visitor to a chair, but his eyes rested intent and anxious on Fabian's face.

"Wednesday tells me you've been seeing a good deal of her, Mr. Balik. May I ask why?"

Fabian shrugged. "I like the girl. I'm interested in her."

"Interested, how? Interested clinically—as in a specimen?"

"What a way to put it, Doctor! She's a pretty girl, she's a nice girl, why should I be interested in her as a specimen?"

The doctor stroked an invisible beard on his chin, still watching Fabian very closely. "She's a pretty girl," he agreed, "but there are many pretty girls. You're a young man obviously on his way up in the world, and you're also obviously far out of Wednesday's class. From what she's told me—and mind you, it's been all on the positive side— I've gotten a definite impression that you look on her as a specimen, but a specimen, let us say, about which you feel a substantial collector's itch. Why you should feel this way, I don't know enough about you to say. But no matter how she rhapsodizes about you, I continue to feel strongly that you have no conventional, expected emotional interest in her. And now that I've seen you, I'm positive that this is so."

"Glad to hear she rhapsodizes about me." Fabian tried to squeeze out a bashful-type grin. "You have nothing to worry about, Doctor."

"I think there's quite a bit to worry about, quite a bit. Frankly, Mr. Balik, your appearance has confirmed my previous impressions: I am quite certain I don't like you. Furthermore, I don't like you for Wednesday."

Fabian thought for a moment, then shrugged. "That's too bad. But I don't think she'll listen to you. She's gone without male companionship too long, and she's too flattered by my going after her."

"I'm terribly afraid you're right. Listen to me, Mr. Balik. I'm very fond of Wednesday and I know how unguarded she is. I ask you, almost as a father, to leave her alone. I've taken care of her since she arrived at the foundling home. I was responsible for keeping her case out of the medical journals so that she might have some chance for a normal life. At the moment, I'm retired from practice. Wednesday Gresham is my only regular patient. Couldn't you find it in your heart to be kind and have nothing more to do with her?"

"What's this about her being made, not born?" Fabian countered. "She says it was your idea."

The old man sighed and shook his head over his desktop for a long moment. "It's the only explanation that makes sense," he said at last, dispiritedly. "Considering the somatic inaccuracies and ambivalences."

Fabian clasped his hands and rubbed his elbows thoughtfully on the arms of his chair. "Did you ever think there might be another explanation? She might be a mutant, a new kind of human evolution, or the offspring of creatures from another world, say, who happened to be stranded on this planet."

"Highly unlikely," Dr. Lorington said. "None of these physical modifications is especially useful in any conceivable environment, with the possible exception of the constantly renewing teeth. Nor are the modifications fatal. They tend to be just— inconvenient. As a physician who has examined many human beings in my life, I would say that Wednesday is thoroughly, indisputably human. She is just a little— well, the word is *amateurish*."

The doctor sat up straight. "There is something else, Mr. Balik. I think it extremely inadvisable for people like Wednesday to have children of their own."

Fabian's eyes lit up in fascination. "Why? What would the children be like?"

"They might be like anything imaginable—or unimaginable. With so much disarrangement of the normal physical system, the modification in the reproductive functions must be enormous too. That's why I ask you, Mr. Balik, not to go on seeing Wednesday, not to go on stimulating her to thoughts of marriage. Because this is one girl that I am certain should not have babies!"

"We'll see." Fabian rose and offered his hand. "Thank you very much for your time and trouble, Doctor."

Dr. Lorington cocked his head and stared up at him. Then, without shaking the hand, he said in a quiet, even voice, "You are welcome. Goodbye, Mr. Balik."

Wednesday was naturally miserable over the antagonism between the two men. But there was very little doubt where her loyalties would lie in a crisis. All those years of determined emotional starvation had resulted in a frantic voracity. Once she allowed herself to think of Fabian romantically, she was done for. She told him that she did her work at the office—from which their developing affair had so far been successfully screened—in a daze at the thought that *he* liked *her*.

Fabian found her homage delicious. Most women he had known began to treat him with a gradually sharpening edge of contempt as time went on. Wednesday became daily more admiring, more agreeable, more compliant.

True, she was by no means brilliant, but she was, he told himself, extremely pretty, and therefore quite presentable. Just to be on the safe side, he found an opportunity to confer with Mr. Slaughter, the senior partner of the firm, ostensibly on personnel matters. He mentioned in passing that he was slightly interested in one of the girls in the secretarial pool. Would there be any high-echelon objection to that?

"Interested to the extent of perhaps marrying the girl?" Mr. Slaughter asked, studying him from under a pair of enormously thick eyebrows.

"Possibly. It might very well come to that, sir. If you have no ob—"

"No objection at all, my boy, no objection at all. I don't like executives flim-flamming around with their file-clerks as a general rule, but if it's handled quietly and ends in matrimony, it could be an excellent thing for the office. I'd like to see you married, and steadied down. It might give the other single people in the place some sensible ideas for a change. But mind you, Balik, no flim-flam. No hanky-panky, especially on office time!"

Satisfied, Fabian now devoted himself to separating Wednesday from Dr. Lorington. He pointed out to her that the old man couldn't live much longer and she needed a regular doctor who was young enough to be able to help her with the physical complexities she faced for the rest of her life. A young doctor like Jim Rudd, for example.

Wednesday wept, but was completely incapable of fighting him for long. In the end, she made only one condition—that Dr. Rudd preserve the secrecy that Lorington had initiated. She didn't want to become a medical journal freak or a newspaper sob story.

The reasons why Fabian agreed had only a little to do with magnanimity. He wanted to have her oddities for himself alone. Sandra he had worn on his breast, like a flashing jewel hung from a pendant. Wednesday he would keep in a tiny chamois bag, examining her from time to time in a self-satisfied, miserly fashion.

And, after a while, he might have another, smaller jewel…

Jim Rudd accepted his conditions. And was astounded.

"There is no navel at all!" he ejaculated when he had rejoined Fabian in his study, after the first examination. "I've palpated the skin for scar tissue, but there's not the slightest hint of it. And that's not the half of it! She has no discernible systole and diastole. Man, do you know what that means?"

"I'm not interested right now," Fabian told him. "Later, maybe. Do you think you can help her with these physical problems when they come up?"

"Oh, sure. At least as well as that old fellow."

"What about children? Can she have them?"

Rudd spread his hands. "I don't see why not. For all her peculiarities, she's a remarkably healthy young woman. And we have no reason to believe that this condition—whatever you want to call it—is hereditary. Of course, some part of it might be, in some strange way or other, but on the evidence…"

They were married, just before the start of Fabian's vacation, at City Hall. They came back to the office after lunch and told everyone about it. Fabian had already hired a new secretary to replace his wife.

Two months later, Fabian had managed to get her pregnant.

He was amazed at how upset she became, considering the meekness he had induced in her from the beginning of their marriage. He tried to be stern and to tell her he would have none of this nonsense, Dr. Rudd had said there was every reason to expect that she would have a normal baby, and that was that. But it didn't work. He tried gentle humor, cajolery. He even took her in his arms and told her he loved her too much not to want to have a little girl like her. But that didn't work either.

"Fabian, darling," she moaned, "don't you understand? I'm not supposed to have a child. I'm not like other women."

He finally used something he had been saving as a last resort for this emergency. He took a book from the shelf and flipped it open. "I understand," he said. "It's half Dr. Lorington and his nineteenth-century superstitious twaddle, and half a silly little folk poem you read when you were a girl and that made a terrifying impression on you. Well, I can't do anything about Dr. Lorington at this point in your life, but I can do something about that poem. Here. Read this."

She read:

> Birthdays, by B.L. Farjeon
> *Monday's child is fair of face,*
> *Tuesday's child is full of grace,*
> *Wednesday's child is loving and giving,*
> *Thursday's child works hard for a living,*
> *Friday's child is full of woe,*
> *Saturday's child has far to go,*
> *But the child that is born on the Sabbath-day*
> *Is brave and bonny, and good and gay.*

Wednesday looked up and shook the tears from her eyes. "But I don't understand," she muttered in confusion. "That's not like the one I read."

He squatted beside her and explained patiently. "The one you read had two lines transposed, right? Wednesday's and Thursday's child had the lines that Friday's and Saturday's child have in this version and vice versa. Well, it's an old Devonshire poem originally, and no one knows for sure which version is right. I looked it up, especially for you. I just wanted to show you how silly you were, basing your entire attitude toward life on a couple of verses which could be read either way, not to mention the fact that they were written several centuries before anyone thought of naming you Wednesday."

She threw her arms around him and held on tightly.

"Oh, Fabian, darling! Don't be angry with me. It's just that I'm so—*frightened!*"

Jim Rudd was a little concerned, too. "Oh, I'm pretty sure it will be all right, but I wish you'd waited until I had time to familiarize myself a bit more with the patient. The only thing, Fabe, I'll have to call in a first-rate obstetrician. I'd never dream of handling this myself. I can make him keep it quiet, about Wednesday and all that. But the moment she enters the delivery room, all bets are off. Too many odd things about her—they're bound to be noticed by some nurse, at least."

"Do the best you can," Fabian told him. "I don't want my wife involved in garish publicity, if it can be helped. But if it can't be—well, it's about time Wednesday learned to live in the real world."

The gestation period went along pretty well, with not much more than fairly usual complications. The obstetrical specialist Jim Rudd had suggested was as intrigued as anyone else by Wednesday's oddities, but he told them that the pregnancy was following a monotonously normal course and that the fetus seemed to be developing satisfactorily and completely on schedule.

Wednesday became fairly cheerful again. Outside of her minor fears, Fabian reflected, she was an eminently satisfactory and useful wife. She didn't exactly shine at the parties where they mingled with other married couples from Slaughter, Stark and Slingsby, but she never committed a major faux pas either. She was, in fact, rather well liked, and, as she obeyed him faithfully in every particular, he had no cause at all for complaint.

He spent his days at the office handling the dry, minuscule details of paper work and personnel administration more efficiently than ever before, and his night and weekends with a person he had every reason to believe was the most *different* woman on the face of the Earth. He was very well satisfied.

Near the end of her term, Wednesday did beg for permission to visit Dr. Lorington just once. Fabian had to refuse, regretfully but firmly.

"It's not that I mind his not sending us a congratulatory telegram or wedding gift, Wednesday. I really don't mind that at all. I'm not the kind of man to hold a grudge. But you're in good shape now. You're over most of your silly fears. Lorington would just make them come alive again."

And she continued to do what he said. Without argument, without complaint. She was really quite a good wife. Fabian looked forward to the baby eagerly.

One day, he received a telephone call at the office from the hospital. Wednesday had gone into labor while visiting the obstetrician. She'd been rushed to the hospital and given birth shortly after arrival to a baby girl. Both mother and child were doing well.

Fabian broke out the box of cigars he'd been saving for this occasion. He passed them around the office and received the felicitations of everybody up to and including Mr. Slaughter, Mr. Stark and both Mr. Slingsbys. Then he took off for the hospital.

From the moment he arrived in the Maternity Pavilion, he knew that something was wrong. It was the way people looked at him, then looked quickly away. He heard a nurse saying behind him: "That must be the father." His lips went tight and dry.

They took him in to see his wife. Wednesday lay on her side, her knees drawn up against her abdomen. She was breathing hard, but seemed to be unconscious. Something about her position made him feel acutely uncomfortable, but he couldn't decide exactly what it was.

"I thought this was going to be the natural childbirth method," he said. "She told me she didn't think you'd have to use anesthesia."

"We didn't use anesthesia," the obstetrician told him. "Now let's go to your child, Mr. Balik."

He let them fit a mask across his face and lead him to the glass-enclosed room where the new-born infants lay in their tiny beds. He moved slowly, unwillingly, a shrieking song of incomprehensible disaster building up slowly in his head.

A nurse picked a baby out of a bed that was off in a corner away from the others.

As Fabian stumbled closer, he observed with a mad surge of relief that the child looked normal. There was no visible blemish or deformity. Wednesday's daughter would not be a freak.

But the infant stretched its arms out to him. "Oh, Fabian, darling," it lisped through toothless gums in a voice that was all too terrifyingly familiar. "Oh, Fabian, darling, the strangest, most unbelievable thing has happened!"

AFTERWORD

"Child's Play" was written in 1946, and for a long time was almost too popular. In the Sam and Bella Spewack play *Boy Meets Girl*, there's a movie producer who keeps asking a songwriter to write him another "Night and Day." The writer comes up with song after song, and of each one the producer says, "It's good, but it's not another 'Night and Day.' " Finally, the songwriter plays a song that knocks the producer out. "What do you call that one?" he asks excitedly. "Night and Day," says the songwriter.

That's how I came to feel about "Child's Play": for years after I wrote it, editors would look at any new story by me and say, "It's good, but you know, it's not another 'Child's Play.' " At last, in desperation, I sat down to write another "Child's Play." I called it "Wednesday's Child."

All right. That's not quite true. At least it's not the whole truth.

First, Sturgeon warned me not to write a sequel. Especially not a sequel to "Child's Play." He felt that one of the worst stories he had ever written was "Butyl and the Breather," a sequel to his first science-fiction story, "Ether Breather," and something John Campbell of *Astounding* had urged him to do. "Sequels," Ted said, "are pulling on an emptied teat."

But, I told him, I didn't want to write a sequel; I just wanted to pick up a provocative little character from "Child's Play" and examine what could have happened to her.

Ted shook his head ominously. "It's a sequel," he said. "And there'll be no real milk there."

That's first. Then, second, I had long been fascinated by Bartolomeo Vanzetti's last speech to the court that sentenced him to be executed. He spoke of a future in which our time would be "but a dim rememoring [sic] of a cursed past in which man was wolf to the man."

I wanted to examine—in a story—such a wolf, particularly something I had seen much of, a man who was wolf to a woman.

Then there's third. I have always had an almost irrational hatred of people in Personnel. I will not go into the whys of it here. I'm not sure the reasons are at all valid. But I do hate them.

And there's a fourth and possibly a fifth. But I finally wrote the story. And it was bounced. My God, how it was bounced!

John Campbell, who had been begging me for something for *Astounding*, handed it back with the comment, "I don't think I've ever disliked—plain disliked—a story more than this one."

Horace Gold of *Galaxy,* for whom I'd been doing most of my work recently, said with a grimace, "No, Phil, not at all. You've finally achieved it: Not just downbeat, but downbeat squared."

And the next editor sent it back with a note that simply said, "*Ptooey.*" I had never gotten a rejection note like that before. I thought to myself: "I'm on to something really big here!"

It was finally purchased by Leo Margulies for *Fantastic Universe* at one-half cent a word, payable on publication. His editor, Frank Belknap Long, told me he felt the purchase was a mistake. "But Leo wanted your name in the book," he said.

And that might be all that could be said of a story of which I am quite fond, but for one more thing.

A boyish-looking fellow came up to me at a party, someone I had never seen before. "Hey, Phil," he said, "I understand you've just sold a piece to *Fantastic Universe.*"

"I have," I told him, "but I've not yet been paid for it."

"That's neither here nor there," he said. "The point is, I've just sold my first professional story to the same magazine. So—let's fight it out on the pages of *Fantastic Universe,* and may the best man win."

"Who the hell are you?" I asked.

"I'm Harlan Ellison," he said.

WRITTEN 1952———PUBLISHED 1955

᠅

My Mother Was a Witch

I spent most of my boyhood utterly convinced that my mother was a witch. No psychological trauma was involved; instead, this belief made me feel like a thoroughly loved and protected child.

My memory begins in the ragged worst of Brooklyn's Brownsville—also known as East New York—where I was surrounded by witches. Every adult woman I knew was one. Shawled conventions of them buzzed and glowered constantly at our games from nearby "stoops." Whenever my playmates swirled too boisterously close, the air turned black with angry magic: immense and complicated curses were thrown.

"May you never live to grow up," was one of the simpler, cheerier incantations. "But if you do grow up, may it be like a radish, with your head in the ground and your feet in the air." Another went: "May you itch from head to foot with scabs that drive you crazy—but only after your fingernails have broken off so you can't scratch."

These remarks were not directed at me; my mother's counter-magic was too widely feared, and I myself had been schooled in every block and parry applicable to little boys. At bedtime, my mother spat thrice, forcing the Powers with whom she was in constant familiar correspondence to reverse curses aimed at me that day back on their authors' heads threefold, as many times as she had spit.

A witch in the family was indeed a rod and a staff of comfort.

My mother was a Yiddish witch, conducting her operations in that compote of German, Hebrew, and Slavic. This was a serious handicap: she had been born a Jewish cockney and spoke little Yiddish until she met my father, an ex-rabbinical student and fervent Socialist from Lithuania. Having bagged him in London's East End on his way to America, she set herself with immediate, wifely devotion to unlearn her useless English in place of what seemed to be the prevailing tongue of the New World.

While my father trained her to speak Yiddish fluently, he cannot have been of much help to her and their first-born in that superstitious Brooklyn slum. He held science and sweet reason to be the hope of the world; her casual, workaday necromancy horrified him. Nary a spell would he teach her: idioms, literary phrases, and fine Yiddish poetry, by all means, but no spells, absolutely no spells.

She needed them. A small boy, she noted, was a prime target for malice and envy, and her new neighbors had at their disposal whole libraries of protective cantrips. Cantrips, at first, had she none. Her rank on the block was determined by the potency of her invocations and her ability—when invoked upon—to knock aside or deftly neutralize. But she sorely lacked a cursing tradition passed for generations from mother to daughter; she alone had brought no such village lore to the United States wrapped in the thick bedspreads and sewn into goosedown-stuffed pillows. My mother's only weapons were imagination and ingenuity.

Fortunately her imagination and ingenuity never failed her—once she had gotten the hang of the thing. She was a quick study too, learning instruments of the occult as fast as she saw them used.

"*Mach a feig!*" she would whisper in the grocer's as a beaming housewife commented on my health and good looks. Up came my fist, thumb protruding between forefinger and middle finger in the ancient male gesture against the female evil eye. *Feigs* were my reserve equipment when alone: I could make them at any cursers and continue playing in the serene confidence that all unpleasant wishes had been safely pasteurized. If an errand took me past threatening witch faces in tenement doorways, I shot *feigs* left and right, all the way down the street.

Still, my mother's best would hardly have been worth its weight in used pentagrams if she had not stood up worthily to Old Mrs. *Mokkeh*. *Mokkeh* was the lady's nickname (it is Yiddish for plague or pestilence) and suggested the blood-chilling imprecations she could toss off with spectacular fluency.

This woman made such an impression on me that I have never been able to read any of the fiercer fairy tales without thinking of her. A tiny, square female with four daughters, each as ugly and short as she, Mrs. *Mokkeh* walked as if every firmly planted step left desolated territory forever and contemptuously behind. The hairy wart on the right side of her nose was so large that behind her back—only behind her back; who knew what she'd wish on you if she heard you?—people giggled and said, "Her nose has a nose."

But that was humor's limit; everything else was sheer fright. She would squint at you, squeezing first one eye shut, then the other, her nose wart vibrating as she rooted about in her soul for an appropriately crippling curse. If you were sensible, you scuttled away before the plague that might darken your future could be fully fashioned and slung. Not only children ran, but brave and learned witches.

Old Mrs. *Mokkeh* was a kind of witch-in-chief. She knew curses and spells that went back to antiquity, to the crumbled ghettos of Babylon and Thebes, and she reconstructed them in the most novel and terrible forms.

When we moved into the apartment directly above her, my mother tried hard to avoid a clash. Balls must not be bounced in the kitchen; indoor running and jumping were strictly prohibited. My mother was still learning her trade at this time and had to be cautious. She would frequently scowl at the floor and bite her lips worriedly. "The *mokkehs* that woman can think up!" she would say.

There came a day when the two of us prepared to visit cousins in the farthest arctic regions of the Bronx. Washed and scrubbed until my skin smarted all over, I was dressed in the good blue serge suit bought for the High Holy Days recently celebrated. My feet were shod in glossy black leather, my neck encircled by a white collar that had been ultimately alloyed with starch. Under this collar ran a tie of brightest red, the intense shade our neighborhood favored for burning the sensitive retina of the Evil Eye.

As we emerged from the building entrance upon the stone stoop, Mrs. *Mokkeh* and her eldest, ugliest daughter, Pearl, began climbing it from the bottom. We passed them and stopped in a knot of women chatting on the sidewalk. While my mother sought advice from her friends on express stops and train changes, I sniffed like a fretful puppy at the bulging market bags of heavy oilcloth hanging from their wrists. There was onion reek, and garlic, and the fresh miscellany of "soup greens."

The casual, barely noticing glances I drew did not surprise me; a prolonged stare at someone's well-turned-out child invited rapid and murderous retaliation. Staring was like complimenting—it only attracted the attention of the Angel of Death to a choice specimen.

I grew bored; I yawned and wriggled in my mother's grasp. Twisting around, I beheld the witch-in-chief examining me squintly from the top of the stoop. She smiled a rare and awesomely gentle smile.

"That little boy, Pearlie," she muttered to her daughter. "A darling, a sweet one, a golden one. How nice he looks!"

My mother heard her and stiffened, but she failed to whirl, as everyone expected, and deliver a brutal riposte. She had no desire to tangle with Mrs. *Mokkeh*. Our whole group listened anxiously for the Yiddish phrase customarily added to such a compliment if good will had been at all behind it—*a leben uff em,* a long life upon him.

Once it was apparent that no such qualifying phrase was forthcoming, I showed I had been well-educated. I pointed my free right hand in a spell-nullifying *feig* at my admirer.

Old Mrs. *Mokkeh* studied the *feig* with her narrow little eyes. "May that hand drop off," she intoned in the same warm, low voice. "May the fingers rot one by one and wither to the wrist. May the hand drop off, but the rot remain. May you wither to the elbow and then to the shoulder. May the whole arm rot with which you made a *feig* at me, and may it fall off and lie festering at your feet, so you will remember for the rest of your life not to make a *feig* at me."

Every woman within range of her lilting Yiddish malediction gasped and gave a mighty head-shake. Then stepping back, they cleared a space in the center of which my mother stood alone.

She turned slowly to face Old Mrs. *Mokkeh*. "Aren't you ashamed of yourself?" she pleaded. "He's only a little boy—not even five years old. Take it back."

Mrs. *Mokkeh* spat calmly on the stoop. "May it happen ten times over. Ten and twenty and a hundred times over. May he wither, may he rot. His arms, his legs, his lungs, his belly. May he vomit green gall and no doctor should be able to save him."

This was battle irrevocably joined. My mother dropped her eyes, estimating the resources of her arsenal. She must have found them painfully slender against such an opponent.

When she raised her eyes again, the women waiting for action leaned forward. My mother was known to be clever and had many well-wishers, but her youth made her a welterweight or at most a lightweight. Mrs. *Mokkeh* was an experienced heavy, a pro who had trained in the old country under famous champions. If these women had been in the habit of making book, the consensus would have been: even money she lasts one or two rounds; five to three she doesn't go the distance.

"Your daughter, Pearlie—" my mother began at last.

"Oh, momma, no!" shrieked the girl, suddenly dragged from non-combatant status into the very eye of the fight.

"Shush! Be calm," her mother commanded. After all, only green campaigners expected a frontal attack. My mother had been hit on her vulnerable flank—me—and was replying in kind. Pearl whimpered and stamped her feet, but her elders ignored this: matters of high professional moment were claiming their attention.

"Your daughter, Pearlie," the chant developed. "Now she is fourteen—may she live to a hundred and fourteen! May she marry in five years a wonderful man, a brilliant man, a doctor, a lawyer, a dentist, who will wait on her hand and foot and give her everything her heart desires."

There was a stir of tremendous interest as the kind of curse my mother was kneading became recognizable. It is one of the most difficult forms in the entire Yiddish thaumaturgical repertoire, building the subject up and up and up and ending with an annihilating crash. A well-known buildup curse goes, "May you have a bank account in every bank, and a fortune in each bank account, and may you spend every penny of it going from doctor to doctor, and no doctor should know what's the matter with you." Or: "May you own a hundred mansions, and in each mansion a hundred richly furnished bedrooms, and may you spend your life tossing from bed to bed, unable to get a single night's sleep on one of them."

To reach a peak and then explode it into an avalanche—that is the buildup curse. It requires perfect detail and even more perfect timing.

"May you give your daughter Pearlie a wedding to this wonderful husband of hers, such a wedding that the whole world will talk about it for years." Pearlie's head began a slow submergence into the collar of her dress. Her mother grunted like a boxer who has been jabbed lightly and is now dancing away.

"This wedding, may it be in all the papers, may they write about it even in books, and may you enjoy yourself at it like never before in your whole life. And one year later, may Pearlie, Pearlie and her wonderful, her rich, her considerate husband—may they present you with your first grandchild. And, *masel tov,* may it be a boy."

Old Mrs. *Mokkeh* shook unbelievingly and came down a step, her nose wart twitching and sensitive as an insect's antenna.

"And this baby boy," my mother sang, pausing to kiss her fingers before extending them to Mrs. *Mokkeh*, "what a glorious child may he be! Glorious? No. Magnificent! Such a wonderful baby boy no one will ever have seen before. The greatest rabbis coming from all over the world only to look upon him at the *bris,* so they'll be able to say in later years they were among those present at his circumcision ceremony eight days after birth. So beautiful and clever he'll be that people will expect him to say the prayers at his own *bris*. And this magnificent first grandson of yours, just one day afterward, when you are gathering happiness on every side, may he suddenly, in the middle of the night—"

"Hold!" Mrs. *Mokkeh* screamed, raising both her hands. "Stop!"

My mother took a deep breath. "And why should I stop?"

"Because I take it back! What I wished on the boy, let it be on my own head, everything I wished on him. Does that satisfy you?"

"That satisfies me," my mother said. Then she pulled my left arm up and began dragging me down the street. She walked proudly, no longer a junior among seniors, but a full and accredited sorceress.

Afterword

When, in the late nineteen sixties, Ballantine Books decided to do a five-volume simultaneous publication of my work (four short-story collections and one new novel) my then agent, Henry Morrison, told me that the head of the firm was troubled by something and wanted to hear from me.

I telephoned Ian Ballantine, who pointed out that we might be facing some length problems in the collections. "Could you give me another group of your short stories," he asked, "stories of different lengths so that, if needed, I could pop this one or that one into a given collection to make certain that they were all of pretty uniform length?"

I told him I could, and forwarded such a group to him in a few days. The stories in that group—all, in my eyes, second-rate pieces—were chosen on the basis of only one characteristic: widely varying lengths. Well, to my horror, Ian called me shortly after he received them and told me he liked the whole bunch very much and wanted to publish them as a fifth collection.

"But, Ian," I wailed, "those are some of my worst stories!"

"Fine!" he replied. "Then how about calling the collection *The Worst of William Tenn?*"

I regret to this very day not having had the guts to go along with his suggestion. I came up with another title, and Ian liked it. But to take what I regarded as the curse off the book, I insisted on inserting a couple of other stories of which I was rather fond.

One of them was "My Mother Was a Witch."

Before I am condemned for wandering outside the genre with criminal malice and utterly vicious premeditation, let me say this:

I admit freely that this story is definitely not science fiction; it is certainly not fantasy; and it is hardly even good red herring. But. It does demonstrate to the reader how much the simple fantastic was a part of my rearing and childhood.

How could I *not* have turned out as I have?

WRITTEN 1964——PUBLISHED 1966

The Lemon-Green Spaghetti-Loud
Dynamite-Dribble Day

Testimony of Witness No. 5671 before the Special Presidential Investigative Commission. Leonard Drucker, thirty-one years old, unmarried, of 238 West 10th Street, New York City, Borough of Manhattan, employed as a salesman by the Har-Bern Office Partition Company of 205 East 42nd Street, New York City, Borough of Manhattan. Witness, being placed under oath, does swear and depose:

Well, I don't know, the telephone woke me up about eight AM on that Wednesday morning. I grabbed at it, half falling out of bed, and finally managed to juggle it up to my ear. A girl's voice was saying, "Hello, Lennie? Is that you, Lennie? Hello?"

After a couple of seconds, I recognized the voice. I said, "Doris? Yeah, it's me. What's the matter?"

"You tell me, Lennie!" She sounded absolutely hysterical. "Have you been listening to the radio? I called up three people already and they're just as bad as the radio. You sure you're all right?"

"I'm fine. Hey, it's eight o'clock—I had another fifteen minutes sleep. And my coffee—it's in the percolator. Let me turn the—the—"

"You too!" she screeched. "It's affected you too! What's the matter with everybody? What's happening?" And she hung up.

I put down the phone and shuddered. Doris was a girl I'd been seeing, and she'd looked very normal. Now it was obvious she was just another kooky Village chick. I may live in the Village, but I hold down a good job and I dress conservatively. Usually, I stay far away from kooky Village chicks.

There was no point in going back to sleep, so I flipped the switch gizmo on my electric percolator and turned it on. That, I guess, is the crucial part of this testimony. You see, I always set up my coffee percolator the night before and fill it with water. When I get up in the morning, I'm too blind and dopey to cook anything.

Because of Doris's call, I also flicked on the radio before I went into the bathroom. I splashed some cold water on my face, rinsed out my toothbrush, and put some toothpaste on it. It was halfway to my mouth when I began listening to the radio. I put it down on the sink and went out and sat next to the radio, really fascinated. I never brushed my teeth: I was one lucky son of a bitch all around.

The radio announcer had a warm, sleepy voice. He was enunciating carefully: "…forty-eight…forty-nine…*forty!* Forty-one…forty-two…forty-three…forty-four…forty-five…forty-six…forty-seven…forty-eight…forty-nine…*forty!* Forty-one…"

I stayed with that voice, I don't know, for a long time. It didn't ever get up to fifty. The coffee had finished perking, so I poured myself a cup and sat and twirled the dial. Some of the stations—they were the Jersey ones, I found out later—sounded pretty much as usual, but most of the broadcasts were wild. There was a traffic report, I remember, that just gripped me.

"…and on the Major Deegan Expressway, traffic is moderate to spaghetti-loud. All dynamite-dribbles are reported moving smoothly. The Cadillacs are longer, the Continentals are thinner, and the Chrysler Imperials have mostly snapped in two. Five thousand Chevrolet convertibles are building a basketball court in one uptown lane of the Franklin D. Roosevelt Drive.…"

While I was having another cup of coffee and some cookies, I happened to glance at my watch, and I realized almost an hour had slipped by with that damn radio! I gave myself a one-two-three shave with the electric razor, and started dressing frantically.

I thought of calling Doris back to tell her she was right, but I thought, better not, better get to work first. And you know something? I never saw or heard from Doris again. I wonder what happened to *her* on that day. Well, she wasn't the only one. Right?

There was hardly anyone on the street, just a few people sitting on the curb with funny expressions on their faces. But I passed that big garage between my apartment house and the subway station, and there I stopped dead. It's one of the most expensive car hangars in the Village and it looked like, I don't know, a junkyard soufflé.

In the dimness, I could see cars mashed against cars, cars mashed against walls. Broken glass mixed in with strips of torn-off chrome. Fenders ripped off, hoods sprung open and all twisty.

Charlie, the attendant, came dragging out of his cubicle and kind of grinned at me. He looked as if he'd tied one on last night.

"Wait'll your boss sees this," I told him. "Man, you'll be dead."

He pointed at two cars locked together nose to nose near the entrance. "Mr. Carbonaro was here. He kept asking them to go on making love. When they wouldn't, he said to hell with them, he was going home. He was crying just like a milk bottle."

It was turning into one weird morning. I was only half surprised when there was no one on duty in the subway change booth. But I had a token on me. I put it in the turnstile and clunked through.

And that's when I first began to get scared—on the platform of the subway station. Whatever else is going on in the world, to a New Yorker the subway is a kind of man-made natural phenomenon, routine and regular as the sun coming up. And when the routine and regularity stop in the subway, you sure as hell notice it.

Like the guy on his hands and knees at one end of the platform staring up a woman's dress, she rocking on high heels and singing a song to the ceiling. Or this pretty young

Negro girl, sitting on a wooden bench, crying her heart out and wiping her eyes with great big newsprinted sheets of that morning's *Times*. Or the doctor-lawyer type miming a slalom in and out of the iron pillars of the platform. He was chanting, "Chug, chug, chug-azoom, chug, chug, chug-azoom." And nobody in the station being startled, or even looking worried.

Three trains in a row came in and went right on through without stopping, without even slowing down. The engineer of the last one was a big, white-haired guy who was laughing his head off as he flashed past. Then a fourth train came in, and this one stopped.

Only two of us on the platform made a dash for it: me and a young fellow in khaki pants and a brown sweater. The doors opened and shut, *zip-zip*, practically in the same motion. The train took off without us.

"What's going on?" the young fellow whined at me. "I'm late for work—I had to run out of the house without any breakfast. But I can't get a train. I paid my fare. Why can't I get a train?"

I told him I didn't know, and I left him and went upstairs. I was very scared. I got into a phone booth and tried to call my office. The phone rang for a long time: no answer.

Then I wandered around on that corner near the subway station for a while, trying to decide what I should do next, trying to figure out what was happening. I kept calling the office. No luck. That was damn funny—it was way after nine o'clock. Maybe no one at all had come in today? I couldn't imagine such a thing.

I began noticing that the people going by on the street had a funny sort of stare, a kind of pop-eyed, trancy look. Charlie, the garage man, he'd had it. But the kid in the brown sweater on the subway platform, he didn't have it. I saw a mirror in a store window and looked at myself. I didn't have it.

The store was a television repair place. They had a television set in the window, tuned into a program, and I got all involved in watching it. I don't know what the program was—two men and a woman were standing around talking to each other, but the woman was doing a slow strip. She was talking and peeling off her clothes at the same time. She had trouble with the garter belt and the men helped her.

Next door, there was a liquor store. People were going in and out, buying a lot of liquor. But then I saw that buying wasn't exactly the right word. What they'd do, they'd walk in, shoot a quick, suspicious look at the owner, grab up a couple of bottles—and walk out. The owner was watching them do this with a big, beaming smile.

A guy came out with a couple of fifths, a stinking, dirty guy, strictly a Bowery type. He was all happy—you know, the millennium.

We both saw the other didn't have the pop-eyed look. (This was the first time, but all that day I had a lot of those flashes of recognition. You immediately noticed someone without the pop-eyed look.)

"It's great, hah?" he said. "All over town. Help yourself, fella, help yourself to the sauce. You know whatsa-matter with 'em, hah?"

I stared at his maybe three, maybe five teeth. "No. What?"

"They've been drinking water. It's finally caught up with them. Poison, pure poison. I always said it. You know the last time I had a glass of water? You know, hah? Over twelve years ago."

I just turned my back and took off and left him standing there.

Walking fast, uptown on Sixth, I said to myself, where the hell am I going? I decided to go to my office on 42nd Street. It's like when there was a subway strike. I still belonged at the office.

For a while I looked out for a taxi, but you know, there were damn few cars going up the avenue, and most of them were traveling very, very slowly. Once in a while, there'd be one going fast, highway speed or beyond. Plenty of accidents.

The first accident I saw, I ran over to see if I could help. But the driver had already crawled out. He looked at the fire hydrant he'd knocked over, he looked at it spouting and shook himself and staggered away. After that I passed up the accidents. I just kept an eye out to see that no cars were coming up on the sidewalk after me.

But that geyser of water made me think of what the bum had said. Was it something in the water? I'd had coffee, but I'd set up the percolator the night before. And I hadn't had time to brush my teeth. Doris, the guy in the brown sweater in the subway, they hadn't eaten breakfast yet, they hadn't touched water. Neither had the bum. It had to be the water.

I didn't know anything then about that bunch of LSD kids, you know, one of them being the daughter of a Water Supply engineer and getting her hands on her father's charts and all the other stuff that's come out. That poor guy! But I knew about enough to stay away from anything that used water from a tap. So, just in case, I stopped in at a self-service grocery and got a six-pack of soda, you know, cans with pull-open tops.

The clerk was looking at the back wall in a trance. He had such a scared expression on his face it almost made my hair stand up. I waited for him to start screaming, but he didn't. I walked out and left a dollar on the counter.

A block further on, I stopped to watch a fire.

It was in one of those small, scabby loft buildings that line lower Sixth. There were no flames visible, just a continuous balloon of smoke coming out of a third-floor window. A crowd of sleepy, dopey-looking people were in front of the place, mixed in with a bunch of bored, dopey-looking firemen. The big red fire engine was all the way up on the sidewalk with its nose inside the smashed window of a wholesale florist's. And a hose that someone had attached to a fire hydrant was just lying there, every once in a while coughing up a half gallon of water like a snake with tuberculosis.

I didn't like the idea of there being people inside, maybe burning to death very quietly. So I pushed through the crowd. I got up to the first floor landing and the smoke there was already too thick and smothery for me to go any higher. But I saw a fireman sitting comfortably against the wall on the landing, his fire helmet slid down over the front of his face. "No beer," he was saying to himself. "No beer and no steam room." I took him by the hand and led him downstairs.

There was a light rain going on, and I felt like getting down on my knees and saying Thank You to the sky. Not that the rain put out this particular fire, but, you know, without the occasional drizzles we had all that day keeping the city damp, there wouldn't have been much of New York left.

Right then, I had no idea that what was going on was limited to New York City. I remember wondering, as I took shelter in a hallway across the street, if all this was some kind of sneak enemy attack. And I wasn't the only one thinking that, as I found out later. I mean the nation-wide alert, and the hot line, and Moscow frantically trying to get in touch with its delegate at the U.N. I just read about the treaty the Russian delegate signed that day with the delegates from Paraguay and Upper Volta. No wonder the Security Council had to declare everything that happened at the U.N. in those twenty-four hours null and void!

When the rain stopped, I began to work my way north again. There was another crowd in front of a big Macy's window on 34th Street near Sixth Avenue. A half-dressed guy and a naked girl were on a couch—the window display was advertising furniture that week—and they were making it.

I stood in the middle of all those trance-like stares and I just couldn't pull myself away. A man next to me with a good leather briefcase kept murmuring, "Beautiful, beautiful. A pair of lemon-green snowflakes." Then the Herald Square clock, the one where those two statues with hammers bang away at a great big bell, that clock began to sound off the strokes of twelve noon. I shook myself and pushed out of the crowd. The guy and the girl were still making it.

A woman on the edge of the crowd, a very pleasant, gray-haired women in a black dress, was going from person to person and taking their money away. She'd take wallets away from the men and little money purses out of the women's pocketbooks, and she'd drop them in a large paper shopping bag. If anyone made the least sign of annoyance while she robbed him, she'd leave him alone and go on to the next one. The shopping bag was hanging kind of heavy.

She suddenly realized I was watching her, and she looked up. Like I said, we non-zombies recognized each other in a flash all that day. She blushed a deep blush, all the way to the roots of her gray hair. Then she turned and ran away at top speed, her heels going clack-clack-clack, the pink slip under her black dress flashing up and swirling around. She held on to the shopping bag as she ran.

The things people must have been pulling that day! Like those two Hoboken guys who heard on the radio that Manhattan had gone crazy. They put on a couple of gas masks and drove through the Holland Tunnel—this was maybe an hour before it was closed to all vehicular traffic—and went down to Wall Street to rob themselves a bank. They weren't even carrying weapons: they figured they'd just walk in and fill their empty suitcases with cash. But what they walked into was a street gun duel between two cops from a radio car who'd been hating each other for months. I saw a lot of things like that which I can't remember now while I'm testifying.

But I do recall how the tempo seemed to be picking up. I'd headed into Broadway, giving up completely on the idea of going to the office. There were a lot more traffic accidents and a lot more people sitting on curbs and smiling into space. And going through the upper thirties, I saw at least three people jump out of windows.

They came down in a long blur, *zonk-splash,* and nobody paid any attention to them.

Every block or so, I'd have to pull away from someone trying to tell me about God or the universe or how pretty the sunlight was. I decided to, I don't know, kind of withdraw from the scene for a while. I went into a luncheonette near 42nd Street to get a bite to eat.

Two countermen were sitting on the floor, holding hands and crying their hearts out. Five girls, secretary-types, were bent over them like in a football huddle. The girls were chanting, "Don't buy at Ohrbach's, Ohrbach's is expensive. Don't buy at Ohrbach's, Ohrbach's is expensive."

I was hungry: by this time that sort of thing didn't even make me sweat. I went behind the counter, found packaged bread and cheese, and I made myself a couple of sandwiches. I ignored a bloody knife lying near the bread-board. Then I sat down at a table near the window and opened a couple of my cans of soda.

There were things to see—the tempo was picking up all the time. A schoolteacher trotting by with a wooden classroom pointer in her hand, waving it and singing "Little Red Wing." Behind her about twenty or thirty pudgy eight-year-olds carrying bus stop signs, one bus stop sign to every two or three kids. An old woman trundling half a dozen dead-looking cats in a brand-new, bright green wheelbarrow. A big crowd marching along and singing Christmas carols. Then another, smaller crowd singing something else, I don't know, a foreign national anthem, I guess. But, you know, a lot of singing, a lot of people suddenly doing things together.

When I was ready to leave, another light drizzle started, so I had to sit tight for an hour or so more. The rain didn't stop the five secretary-types, though. They snake-danced out into it, yelling, "Everybody—let's go to Fifth Avenue!" They left the crying countermen behind.

Finally, it was clear and I started off again. All over the street there were clumps of people, arms locked, yelling and singing and dancing. I didn't like it one bit: it felt like the beginnings of a riot. At the Automat near Duffy Square, there was a bunch of them spread out on the sidewalk, looking as if they were having an orgy. But when I got closer, I saw they were only lying there caressing each other's faces.

That's where I met those newlyweds who'll be testifying after me—Dr. and Mrs. Patrick Scannell from Kosackie, Indiana. They were standing outside the Automat whispering to each other. When they saw I didn't have the pop-eyed, zombie look, they fell all over me.

They'd come into New York late the night before and registered at a hotel. Being, you know, honeymooners, they hadn't climbed out of the sack until almost two in the afternoon. That's what saved them. Months before, when they'd been planning their honeymoon, they'd bought tickets to a Broadway show, a matinee, Shakespeare's *Macbeth,* and they'd charged out of the hotel room fast not to miss it. They'd run out without breakfast or anything, just a candy bar Mrs. Scannell was carrying in her purse.

And from the way they described it, that production of *Macbeth* was like nothing else anybody ever saw on land or sea. Four actors on the stage, only one of them in costume, all of them jabbering away in speeches from *Macbeth, Hamlet, A Streetcar Named Desire, Oedipus Rex* and *Who's Afraid of Virginia Woolf?* "It was like an anthology of the theater," Mrs. Scannell said. "And not at all badly done. It hung together in a fascinating way, really."

That reminds me. I understand a publishing house is bringing out a book of the poetry and prose written in New York City on this one crazy LSD day. It's a book I sure as hell intend to buy.

But interesting or fascinating or what, that oddball show in a professional Broadway theater scared the pants off them. And the audience, what there was of it, scared them even more. They'd walked out and gone looking around, wondering who dropped the bomb.

I shared my soda with them, using up the last of the six-pack. And I told them how I'd figured out it was in the water. Right away, Dr. Scannell—he was a dentist, I found out, not a medical doctor—right away, he snapped his fingers and said, "Damn it— LSD!" I bet that makes him the first man in the country to guess it, right?

"LSD, LSD," he repeated. "It's colorless, odorless, tasteless. One ounce contains 300,000 full doses. A pound or so in the water supply and— Oh, my God! Those magazine articles gave someone the idea!"

The three of us stood there drinking our soda and looking at the people screaming, the people chuckling, the people doing all kinds of crazy things. There were mobs now heading east and yelling, "Everybody to Fifth Avenue. Everybody to Fifth Avenue for the big parade!" It was like a kind of magic had spread the word, as if the whole population of Manhattan had gotten the same idea at the same time.

I didn't want to argue with a professional man, you know, but I'd also read a lot of those magazine articles on LSD. I said I hadn't read about people doing some of the things I'd seen that day. I mean, I said, take those crowds chanting like that?

Dr. Scannell said that was because of the cumulative feedback effect. The *what?* I said. So he explained how people had this stuff inside them, making them wide open psychologically to begin with, and all around them the air was full of other LSD reactions, going back and forth, building up and up. That was the cumulative feedback effect.

Then he talked about drug purity and drug dosage—how in this situation there was no control over how much anyone got. "Worst of all," he said, "there's been no psychological preparation. Under the circumstances, anything could happen." He stared up and down the street at the crowds going chant-chant-chant, and he shivered.

They decided to get some packaged food and drink, then go back to their hotel room and hole up until it was all over. They invited me along, but, I don't know, by this time I was too interested to go into hiding; I wanted to see the thing through to the end. And I was too scared of fires to go and sit in a fourteenth-floor hotel room.

When I left them, I followed the crowds that were going east as if they all had an appointment together. There were thick mobs on both sides of Fifth; across the avenue, I could see mobs of people coming west toward it. Everyone was yelling about the big parade.

And there really was a parade, that's the funny part. I don't know how it got organized, or by whom, but it was the high point, the last word, the ultimate touch, to that damn day. What a parade!

It was coming up Fifth Avenue against the one-way traffic arrows—although by this time there was no traffic anywhere—it was coming up in bursts of fifty or a hundred people, and in between each burst there'd be a thin line of stragglers that sometimes wandered off and got mixed in with the people on the sidewalk. Some of the signs they carried were smeary and wet from being recently painted; some of them looked very old as if they'd been pulled out of a trunk or a storage bin. Most of the paraders were chanting slogans or singing songs.

Who the hell can remember all the organizations in that parade? I mean, you know, the Ancient Order of Hibernians, the CCNY Alumni Association, the Untouchables of Avenue B, Alcoholics Anonymous, the NAACP, the Anti-Vivisection League, the Washington Heights Democratic Club, the B'nai B'rith, the West 49th Street Pimps and Prostitutes Mutual Legal Fund, the Hungarian Freedom Fighters, the Save-the-Village Committee, the Police Holy Name Society, the Daughters of Bilitis, the Our Lady of Pompeii Championship Basketball Team. All of them.

And they were mixed in together. Pro-Castro Cubans and anti-Castro Cubans marching along side by side, singing the same mournful Spanish song. Three cops, one of them without shoes, with the group of college students carrying placards, "Draft Beer, Not People." A young girl wearing a sandwich sign on which was scribbled in black crayon, "Legalize Rape—Now!" right in the middle of a bunch of old men and old women who were singing "Jay Lovestone is our leader, We shall not be moved...." The County Kerry band playing "Deutschland über Alles" followed by the big crowd of men in business suits, convention badges in their lapels, who were teaching two tiny Italian nuns to sing, "Happy birthday, Marcia Tannenbaum, happy birthday to you." The nuns were giggling and hiding their faces in their hands. And behind them, carrying a huge white banner that stretched right across Fifth Avenue, two grizzled-looking, grim-faced Negro men about seventy or eighty years old. The banner read: "Re-elect Woodrow Wilson. He kept us out of war!"

All through the parade, there were people with little paint cans and brushes busily painting lines up the avenue. Green lines, purple lines, even white lines. One well-dressed man was painting a thin red line in the middle of the marchers. I thought he was a Communist until he painted past me and I heard him singing, "God save our gracious queen..." as he walked backward working away with the brush. When his paint ran out, he joined a bunch from Local 802 of the Musicians Union who had come along holding up signs and yelling, "Abolish Folk Songs! Save Tin Pan Alley!"

It was the best parade I ever saw. I watched it until the Army paratroops who'd landed in Central Park came down and began herding us to the Special Rehabilitation Centers they'd set up.

And then, damn it, it was all over.

AFTERWORD

I wrote this in the middle sixties when the world seemed filled with youngsters who smoked pot, dropped acid, and were generally willing to swallow anything that looked as if it might have come from a back-alley pharmacy.

Two of them, college students, who came to our home for dinner late in that year were astonished to discover that Greenwich Villagers like the pair of us had never so much as turned on in our entire lives. "Don't you want your consciousness expanded?" one of them asked my wife.

"No," Fruma replied. "If anything, I want it contracted."

And there it is—the trouble I have. The woman I'm married to. I didn't want to include this story in my final collection. It certainly isn't science fiction, I feel, not really. But Fruma said, "It's a lovely story. Unappreciated." (That's an exact quote.)

So what could I do? I stuck it in. We've been married now for almost forty-four years, and I don't know any other way to handle my problems with her.

WRITTEN 1966——PUBLISHED 1967

੩ତ

THE TENANTS

When Miss Kerstenberg, his secretary, informed Sydney Blake over the interoffice communicator that two gentlemen had just entered and expressed a desire to rent space in the building, Blake's "Well, show them in, Esther, show them right in," was bland enough to have loosened the cap on a jar of Vaseline. It had been only two days since Wellington Jimm & Sons, Inc., Real Estate, had appointed him resident agent in the McGowan Building, and the prospect of unloading an office or two in Old Unrentable this early in his assignment was mightily pleasing.

Once, however, he had seen the tenants-to-be, he felt much less certain. About practically everything.

They were exactly alike in every respect but one: size. The first was tall, very, *very* tall—close to seven feet, Blake estimated as he rose to welcome them. The man was bent in two places: forward at the hips and backward at the shoulders, giving the impression of being hinged instead of jointed. Behind him rolled a tiny button of a man, a midget's midget, but except for that the tall man's twin. They both wore starched, white shirts and black hats, black coats, black ties, black suits, black socks, and shoes of such incredible blackness as almost to drown the light waves that blundered into them.

They took seats and smiled at Blake—in unison.

"Uh, Miss Kerstenberg," he said to his secretary, who still stood in the doorway.

"Yes, Mr. Blake?" she asked briskly.

"Uh, nothing, Miss Kerstenberg. Nothing at all." Regretfully, he watched her shut the door and heard her swivel chair squeak as she went back to work in the outer office. It was distinctly unfortunate that, not being telepathic, she had been unable to receive his urgent thought message to stay and lend some useful moral support.

Oh, well. You couldn't expect Dun & Bradstreet's best to be renting offices in the McGowan. He sat down and offered them cigarettes from his brand-new humidor. They declined.

"We would like," the tall man said in a voice composed of many heavy breaths, "to rent a floor in your building."

"The thirteenth floor," said the tiny man in exactly the same voice.

Sydney Blake lit a cigarette and drew on it carefully. A whole floor! You certainly couldn't judge by appearances.

"I'm sorry," he told them. "You can't have the thirteenth floor. But—"

305

"Why not?" the tall man breathed. He looked angry.

"Chiefly because there isn't any thirteenth floor. Many buildings don't have one. Since tenants consider them unlucky, we call the floor above the twelfth the fourteenth. If you gentlemen will look at our directory, you will see that there are no offices listed beginning with the number 13. However, if you're interested in that much space, I believe we can accommodate you on the sixth—"

"It seems to me," the tall man said very mournfully, "that if someone wants to rent a *particular* floor, the least a renting agent can do is let him have it."

"The very least," the tiny man agreed. "Especially since no complicated mathematical questions are being asked in the first place."

Blake held on to his temper with difficulty and let out a friendly chuckle instead. "I would be very happy to rent the thirteenth floor to you—if we had one. But I can't very well rent something to you that doesn't exist, now can I?" He held his hands out, palms up, and gave them another we-are-three-intelligent-gentlemen-who-are-quite-close-in-spirit chuckle. "The twelfth and fourteenth floors both have very little unoccupied space, I am happy to say. But I'm certain that another part of the McGowan Building will do you very nicely." Abruptly he remembered that protocol had almost been violated. "*My* name," he told them, touching the desk plate lightly with a manicured forefinger, "is Sydney Blake. And who, might I—"

"Tohu and Bohu," the tall man said.

"I beg your pardon?"

"Tohu, I said, and Bohu. I'm Tohu." He pointed at his minuscule twin. "He's Bohu. Or, as a matter of occasional fact, vice versa."

Sydney Blake considered that until some ash broke off his cigarette and splattered grayly on his well-pressed pants. Foreigners. He should have known from their olive skins and slight, unfamiliar accents. Not that it made any difference in the McGowan. Or in any building managed by Wellington Jimm & Sons, Inc., Real Estate. But he couldn't help wondering where in the world people had such names and such disparate sizes.

"Very well, Mr. Tohu. And—er, Mr. Bohu. Now, the problem as I see it—"

"There really isn't any problem," the tall man told him, slowly, emphatically, reasonably, "except for the fuss you keep kicking up, young man. You have a building with floors from one to twenty-four. We want to rent the thirteenth, which is apparently vacant. Now if you were as businesslike as you should be and rented this floor to us without further argument—"

"Or logical hairsplitting," the tiny man inserted.

"—why then, we could be happy, your employers would be happy, and you *should* be happy. It's really a very simple transaction and one which a man in your position should be able to manage with ease."

"How the hell can I—" Blake began yelling before he remembered Professor Scoggins in Advanced Realty Seminar II ("Remember, gentlemen, a lost temper means a lost tenant. If the retailer's customer is always right, the realtor's client is never wrong. Somehow, somewhere, you must find a cure for their little commercial illnesses, no matter how imaginary. The realtor must take his professional place beside the doctor, the dentist, and the pharmacist and make his motto, like theirs, *unselfish service, always available, forever dependable.*") Blake bent his head to get a renewed grip on professional responsibility before going on.

"Look here," he said at last, with a smile he desperately hoped was winning. "I'll put it is the terms that you just did. You, for reasons best known to yourselves, want to rent a thirteenth floor. This building, for reasons best known to its architect—who, I am certain, was a foolish, eccentric man whom none of *us* would respect *at all*—this building has no thirteenth floor. Therefore, I can't rent it to you. Now, superficially, I'll admit, this might seem like a difficulty, it might seem as if you can't get exactly what you want here in the McGowan Building. But what happens if we examine the situation carefully? First of all, we find that there are several other truly *magnificent* floors—"

He broke off as he realized he was alone. His visitors had risen in the same incredibly rapid movement and gone out the door.

"Most unfortunate," he heard the tall man say as they walked through the outer office. "The location would have been perfect. So far from the center of things."

"Not to mention," the tiny man added, "the building's appearance. So very unpresentable. Too bad."

He raced after them, catching up in the corridor that opened into the lobby. Two things brought him to a dead stop. One was the strong feeling that it was beneath a newly appointed resident agent's dignity to haul prospective customers back into an office which they had just quit so abruptly. After all, this was no cut-rate clothing shop—it was the McGowan Building.

The other was the sudden realization that the tall man was alone. There was no sign of the tiny man. Except—possibly—for the substantial bulge in the right-hand pocket of the tall man's overcoat....

"A pair of cranks," he told himself as he swung around and walked back to the office. "Not legitimate clients at all."

He insisted on Miss Kerstenberg's listening to the entire story, despite Professor Scoggins's stern injunctions against overfraternization with the minor clerical help. She cluck-clucked and tsk-tsked and stared earnestly at him through her thick glasses.

"Cranks, wouldn't you say, Miss Kerstenberg?" he asked her when he'd finished. "Hardly legitimate clients, eh?"

"I wouldn't know, Mr. Blake," she replied, inflexibly unpresumptuous. She rolled a sheet of letterhead stationery into her typewriter. "Do you want the Hopkinson mailing to go out this afternoon?"

"What? Oh, I guess so. I mean, of course. By all means this afternoon, Miss Kerstenberg. And I want to see it for a double-check before you mail it."

He strode into his own office and huddled behind the desk. The whole business had upset him very much. His first big rental possibility. And that little man—Bohu was his name?—and that bulging pocket—

Not until quite late in the afternoon was he able to concentrate on his work. And that was when he got the phone call.

"Blake?" the voice crackled. "This is Gladstone Jimm."

"*Yes,* Mr. Jimm." Blake sat up stiffly in his swivel chair. Gladstone was the oldest of the Sons.

"Blake, what's is this about your refusing to rent space?"

"My *what?* I beg your pardon, Mr. Jimm, but I—"

"Blake, two gentlemen just walked into the home office. Their names are Tooley and Booley. They tell me they tried unsuccessfully to rent the thirteenth floor of the McGowan Building from you. They tell me that you admitted the space was vacant, but that you consistently refused to let them have it. What's this all about, Blake? Why do you think the firm appointed you resident agent, Blake, to turn away prospective tenants? I might as well let you know that none of us up here in the home office like this one little bit, Blake."

"I'd have been very happy to rent the thirteenth floor to them," Blake wailed. "Only trouble, sir, you see, there's—"

"What trouble are you referring to, Blake? Spit it out, man, spit it *out.*"

"There *is* no thirteenth floor, Mr. Jimm."

"What?"

"The McGowan Building is one of those buildings that has no thirteenth floor." Laboriously, carefully, he went through the whole thing again. He even drew an outline picture of the building on his desk pad as he spoke.

"Hum," said Gladstone Jimm when he'd finished. "Well, I'll say this, Blake. The explanation, at least, is in your favor." And he hung up.

Blake found himself quivering. "Cranks," he muttered fiercely. "Definitely cranks. Definitely not legitimate tenants."

When he arrived at his office door early next morning, he found Mr. Tohu and Mr. Bohu waiting for him. The tall man held out a key.

"Under the terms of our lease, Mr. Blake, a key to our main office must be in the possession of the resident agent for the building. We just had our locksmith make up this copy. I trust it is satisfactory?"

Sydney Blake leaned against the wall, waiting for his bones to reacquire marrow. "Lease?" he whispered. "Did the home office give you a lease?"

"Yes," said the tall man. "Without much trouble, we were able to achieve a what-do-you-call-it."

"A meeting of minds," the tiny man supplied from the region of his companion's knees. "A feast of reason. A flow of soul. There are no sticklers for numerical subtleties in your home office, young man."

"May I see the lease?" Blake managed to get out.

The tall man reached into his right-hand overcoat pocket and brought up a familiar-looking folded piece of paper.

It was the regulation lease. For the thirteenth floor in the McGowan Building. But there was one small difference.

Gladstone Jimm had inserted a rider: *...the landlord is renting a floor that both the* *tenant and landlord know does not exist, but the title to which has an intrinsic value to the tenant; which value is equal to the rent he will pay....*

Blake sighed with relief. "That's different. Why didn't you tell me that all you wanted was the title to the floor? I was under the impression that you intended to occupy the premises."

"We do intend to occupy the premises." The tall man pocketed the lease. "We've paid a month's rent in advance for them."

"And," added the tiny man, "a month's security."

"And," finished the tall man, "an extra month's rent as fee to the agent. We most certainly do intend to occupy the premises."

"But how—" Blake giggled a little hysterically "—are you going to occupy premises that aren't even—"

"Good morning, young man," they said in unison and moved toward the elevators.

He watched them enter one.

"Thirteen, please," they told the elevator operator. The elevator door closed. Miss Kerstenberg walked past him and into the office, chirping a dutiful "Good morning, Mr. Blake." Blake barely nodded at her. He kept his eyes on the elevator door. After a while it opened again, and the fat little operator lounged out and began a conversation with the starter.

Blake couldn't help himself. He ran to the elevator. He stared inside. It was empty.

"Listen," he said, grabbing the fat little operator by one sleeve of his dingy uniform. "Those two men you just took up, what floor did they get off at?"

"The one they wanted. Thirteen. Why?"

"There isn't any thirteenth floor. No thirteenth floor at all!"

The fat little elevator operator shrugged. "Look, Mr. Blake, I do my job. Someone says 'thirteenth floor,' I take 'em to the thirteenth floor. Someone says 'twenty-first floor,' I take 'em—"

Blake walked into the elevator. "Take me there," he ordered.

"The twenty-first floor? Sure."

"No, you—you—" Blake realized that the starter and the elevator operator were grinning at each other sympathetically. "Not the twenty-first floor," he went on more calmly, "the thirteenth. Take me to the thirteenth floor."

The operator worked his switch and the door moaned itself shut. They went up. All of the McGowan Building elevators were very slow, and Blake had no trouble reading the floor numbers through the little window in the elevator door.

...ten...eleven...twelve...fourteen...fifteen...sixteen...

They stopped. The elevator operator scratched his head with his visored cap. Blake glared at him triumphantly. They went down.

...fifteen...fourteen...twelve...eleven...ten...nine...

"Well?" Blake asked him.

The man shrugged. "It don't seem to be there now."

"Now? Now? It's *never* been there. So where did you take those men?"

"Oh, them, I told you: the thirteenth floor."

"But I just proved to you there is *no thirteenth floor!*"

"So what? You got the college education, Mr. Blake, not me. I just do my job. If you don't like it, all I can say is I just do my job. Someone gets in the elevator and says 'thirteenth floor,' I take—"

"I know! You take them to the thirteenth floor. But there is *no* thirteenth floor, you idiot! I can show you the blueprints of the building, the original blueprints, and I dare you, I defy you to show me a thirteenth floor. If you can show me a thirteenth floor…"

His voice trailed off as he realized they were back in the lobby and had attracted a small crowd.

"Look, Mr. Blake," the elevator man suggested. "If you're not satisfied, how's about I call up the delegate from the union and you and him have a talk? How's about that, huh?"

Blake threw up his arms helplessly and stamped back to his office. Behind him he heard the starter ask the elevator operator, "What was he getting in such an uproar about, Barney?"

"Aa-aah, that guy," the operator said. "He was blaming me for the blueprints of the building. If you ask me, he's got too much college education. What have I got to do with the blueprints?"

"I don't know," the starter sighed. "I sure as hell don't know."

"I'll ask you another question," the operator went on, with a little more certainty, now that he saw his oratorical way, so to speak. "What have the building blueprints got to do with *me?*"

Blake closed the office door and leaned against it. He ran his fingers through his thinning hair.

"Miss Kerstenberg," he said at last in a strangled voice. "What do you think? Those cranks that were here yesterday—those two crazy old men—the home office went and rented the thirteenth floor to them!"

She looked up from her typewriter. "It *did?*"

"And believe it or not, they just went upstairs and took possession of their offices."

She smiled at him, a rapid woman-smile. "How *nice,*" she said. And went back to her typing.

The morning after *that,* what Blake saw in the lobby sent him scurrying to the telephone. He dialed the home office. "Mr. Gladstone Jimm," he demanded breathlessly.

"Listen, Mr. Jimm. This is Sydney Blake at the McGowan. Mr. Jimm, this is getting serious! They're moving in furniture today. Office furniture. And I just saw some men go upstairs to install telephones. Mr. Jimm, they're really moving in!"

Gladstone Jimm was instantly alert. He gave the matter his full attention. "Who's moving in, my boy? Tanzen Realty Corporation? Or is it the Blair Brothers again? I was saying only last week: things have been far too quiet in the real estate field; I've felt in my bones that last year's Code of Fair Practices wouldn't be standing up much longer. Try to raid our properties, will they?" He snorted long and belligerently. "Well, the old firm has a few tricks up its sleeve yet. First, make certain that all important papers—tenant lists, rent receipts, don't overlook anything, son—are in the safe. We'll have three attorneys and a court order down there in half an hour. Meanwhile, you keep—"

"You don't understand, sir. It's those new tenants. The ones you rented the thirteenth floor to."

Gladstone Jimm ground to a full stop and considered the matter. Ah. He understood. He began to beat swords into ploughshares.

"You mean—those fellows—um, Toombs and Boole?"

"That's right, sir. There are desks and chairs and filing cabinets going upstairs. There are men from the telephone and electric companies. They're all going up to the thirteenth floor. Only, Mr. Jimm, *there isn't any thirteenth floor!*"

A pause. Then: "Any of the other tenants in the building been complaining, Blake?"

"No, Mr. Jimm, but—"

"Have Toot and Boob committed any sort of nuisance?"

"No, not at all. It's just that I—"

"It's just that you have been paying precious little attention to business! Blake, I like you, but I feel it is my duty to warn you that you are getting off on the wrong foot. You've been resident agent at the McGowan for almost a week now and the only bit of important business involving the property had to be transacted by the home office. That's not going to look good on your record, Blake, it's not going to look good at all. Do you still have those big vacancies on the third, sixteenth, and nineteenth floors?"

"Yes, Mr. Jimm. I've been planning to—"

"Planning isn't enough, Blake. Planning is only the first step. After that, there must be action! *Action,* Blake; A-C-T-I-O-N. Why don't you try this little stunt: Letter the word *action* on a sign, letter it in bright red, and hang it opposite your desk where you'll see it every time you look up. Then on the reverse side, list all the vacancies in your building. Every time you find yourself staring at that sign, ask yourself how many vacancies are still listed on the back. And then, Blake, take action!"

"Yes, sir," Blake said, very weakly.

"Meanwhile, no more of this nonsense about law-abiding, rent-paying tenants. If they leave you alone, you leave them alone. That's an order, Blake."

"I understand that, Mr. Jimm."

He sat for a long while looking at the cradled telephone. Then he rose and walked out to the lobby and into an elevator. There was a peculiar and unaccustomed jauntiness to him, a recklessness to his stride that could be worn only by a man deliberately disobeying a direct order from the reigning head of Wellington Jimm & Sons, Inc., Real Estate.

Two hours later he crept back, his shoulders bent, his mouth loose with defeat.

Whenever Blake had been in an elevator full of telephone linemen and furniture movers on their way to the thirteenth floor, there had been no thirteenth floor. But as soon as, a little irritated, they had changed elevators, leaving him behind, so far as he could tell, they had gone right up to their destination. It was obvious. For him there was no thirteenth floor. There probably never would be.

He was still brooding on the injustice of it at five o'clock, when the scrubwomen who were coming on duty bounced their aged joints into his outer office to punch the time clock. "Which one of you," he asked, coming at them suddenly with an inspiration, "which one of you takes care of the thirteenth floor?"

"I do."

He drew the woman in the bright green, fringed shawl after him into his private office. "When did you start cleaning the thirteenth floor, Mrs. Ritter?"

"Why, the day the new tenants moved in."

"But before that...?" He waited, watching her face anxiously.

She smiled, and several wrinkles changed their course. "Before that, Lord love you, there was no tenants. Not on the thirteenth."

"So..." he prompted.

"So there was nothing to clean."

Blake shrugged and gave up. The scrubwoman started to walk away. He put his hand on her shoulder and detained her. "What," he asked, staring at her enviously, "is it like—the thirteenth floor?"

"Like the twelfth. And the tenth. Like any other floor."

"And everyone," he muttered to himself, "gets to go there. Everyone but me."

He realized with annoyance that he'd spoken too loudly. And that the old woman was staring at him with her head cocked in sympathy. "Maybe that's because," she suggested softly, "you have no *reason* to be on the thirteenth floor."

He was still standing there, absorbing the concept, when she and her colleagues bumped and clattered their way upstairs with mops, brooms, and metal pails.

There was a cough and the echo of a cough behind him. He turned. Mr. Tohu and Mr. Bohu bowed. Actually, they seemed to fold and unfold.

"For the lobby directory," said the tall man, giving Blake a white business card. "This is how we are to be listed."

G. TOHU & K. BOHU

Specialists in
Intangibles
For the Trade

Blake struggled, licked his lips, fought his curiosity and lost. "What kind of intangibles?" The tall man looked at the tiny man. The tiny man shrugged. "Soft ones," he said. They walked out.

Blake was positive he saw the tall man pick up the tiny man a moment before they stepped into the street. But he couldn't see what he did with him. And then there was the tall man walking down the street all by himself.

From that day on, Sydney Blake had a hobby. Trying to work out a good reason for visiting the thirteenth floor. Unfortunately, there just wasn't any *good* reason so long as the tenants created no nuisances and paid their rent regularly.

Month in, month out, the tenants paid their rent regularly. And they created no nuisances. Window washers went up to wash windows. Painters, plasterers, and carpenters went up to decorate the offices on the thirteenth floor. Delivery boys staggered up under huge loads of stationery. Even what were obviously customers went up to the thirteenth floor, a group of people curiously lacking characteristics in common: they ranged from poor backwoods folk in their brogans to flashily dressed bookmakers; an occasional group of dark-suited, well-tailored gentlemen discussing interest rates and new bond issues in low well-bred voices would ask the elevator operator for Tohu & Bohu. Many, many people went to the thirteenth floor.

Everyone, Sydney Blake began to think, but Sydney Blake. He'd tried sneaking up on the thirteenth floor by way of the stairs. He had always arrived on the fourteenth floor or the twelfth completely winded. Once or twice, he'd tried stowing away on the elevator with G. Tohu and K. Bohu themselves. But the car had not been able to find their floor while he was in the elevator. And they had both turned around and smiled at the spot where he was trying to stay hidden in the crowd so that he had gone out, red-faced, at the earliest floor he could.

Once he'd even tried—vainly—to disguise himself as a building inspector in search of a fire hazard....

Nothing worked. He just had no business on the thirteenth floor.

He thought about the problem day and night. His belly lost its slight plumpness, his nails their manicure, his very trousers their crease.

And nobody else showed the slightest interest in the tenants of the thirteenth floor.

Well, there *was* the day that Miss Kerstenberg looked up from her typewriter. "Is that how they spell their names?" she asked. "T-O-H-U and B-O-H-U? Funny."

"What's funny?" He pounced on her.

"Those names come from the Hebrew. I know because," she blushed well below the neckline of her dress, "I teach in a Hebrew School Tuesday, Wednesday, and Thursday nights. And my family is very religious so I had a real orthodox education. I think religion is a good thing, especially for a girl—"

"*What about those names?*" He was almost dancing around her.

"Well, in the Hebrew Bible, before God created the Earth, the Earth was *tohu oobohu*. The *oo* means *and.* And *tohu* and *bohu*—gee, it's hard to translate."

"Try," he implored her. "*Try.*"

"Oh, for example, the usual English translation of *tohu oobohu* is *without form and void.* But *bohu* really means *empty* in a lot of—"

"Foreigners," he chortled. "I knew they were foreigners. And up to no good. With names like that."

"I don't agree with you, Mr. Blake," she said very stiffly. "I don't agree with you at all about those names being no good. Not when they come from the Hebrew." And she never showed him any friendliness again.

Two weeks later, Blake got a message from the home office of Wellington Jimm & Sons, Inc., Real Estate, that almost shoved his reason off the corner of the slippery throne it still occupied. Tohu & Bohu had given notice. They were quitting the premises at the end of the month.

For a day or so, he walked around talking to himself. The elevator operators reported hearing him say things like: "They're the most complete foreigners there could be—they don't even belong in the physical universe!" The scrubwomen shivered in their locker room as they told each other of the mad, mad light in his eyes as he'd muttered, with enormous gestures: "Of course—thirteenth floor. Where else do you think they could stay, the nonexistent so-and-so's? *Hah!*" And once when Miss Kerstenberg had caught him glaring at the water cooler and saying, "They're trying to turn the clock back a couple of billion years and start all over, I bet. *Filthy* fifth columnists!" she thought tremulously of notifying the F.B.I., but decided against it. After all, she reasoned, once the police start snooping around a place, you never can tell who they'll send to jail.

And, besides, after a little while, Sydney Blake straightened out. He began shaving every morning once more and the darkness left his nails. But he was definitely not the crisp young realtor of yore. There was a strange, skirling air of triumph about him almost all the time.

Came the last day of the month. All morning, load after load of furniture had been carried downstairs and trucked away. As the last few packages came down, Sydney Blake, a fresh flower in his buttonhole, walked up to the elevator nearest his office and stepped inside.

"Thirteenth floor, if you please," he said clearly and resonantly.

The door slid shut. The elevator rose. It stopped on the thirteenth floor.

"Well, Mr. Blake," said the tall man. "This is a surprise. And what can we do for you?"

"How do you do, Mr. Tohu?" Blake said to him. "Or is it Bohu?" He turned to his tiny companion. "And you, Mr. Bohu—or, as the case may be, Tohu—I hope you are well? Good."

He walked around the empty, airy offices for a little while and just looked. Even the partitions had been taken down. The three of them were alone, on the thirteenth floor.

"You have some business with us?" the tall man inquired.

"Of course he has business with us," the tiny man told him crossly. "He has to have some sort of business with us. Only I wish he'd hurry up and get it over, whatever it is."

Blake bowed. "Paragraph ten, Section three of your lease: *...the tenant further agrees that such notice being duly given to the landlord, an authorized representative of the landlord, such as the resident agent if there is one on the property, shall have the privilege of examining the premises before they are vacated by the tenant for the purpose of making certain that they have been left in good order and condition by the tenant....*"

"So that's your business," said the tall man thoughtfully.

"It had to be something like that," said the tiny man. "Well, young fellow, you will please be quick about it."

Sydney Blake strolled about leisurely. Though he felt a prodigious excitement, he had to admit that there was no apparent difference between the thirteenth and any other floor. Except— Yes, except—

He ran to a window and looked down. He counted. Twelve floors. He looked up and counted. Twelve floors. And with the floor he was on, that made twenty-five. Yet the McGowan was a twenty-four-story building. Where did that extra floor come from? And how did the building look from the outside at this precise moment when his head was sticking out of a window on the thirteenth floor?

He walked back in, staring shrewdly at G. Tohu and K. Bohu. They would know.

They were standing near the elevator door that was open. An operator, almost as impatient as the two men in black, said, *"Down? Down?"*

"Well, Mr. Blake," said the tall man. "Are the premises in good condition, or are they not?"

"Oh, they're in good condition, all right," Blake told him. "But that's not the point."

"Well, *we* don't care what the point is," said the tiny man to the tall man. "Let's get out of here."

"Quite," said the tall man. He bent down and picked up his companion. He folded him once backward and once forward. Then he rolled him up tightly and shoved him in his right-hand overcoat pocket. He stepped backward into the elevator. "Coming, Mr. Blake?"

"No, thank you," Blake said. "I've spent far too much time trying to get up here to leave it this fast."

"Suit yourself," said the tall man. "Down," he told the elevator operator.

When he was all alone on the thirteenth floor, Sydney Blake expanded his chest. It had taken so long! He walked over to the door of the staircase that he'd tried to find so many times, and pulled on it. It was stuck. Funny. He bent down and peered at it closely. It wasn't locked. Just stuck. Have to get the repairman up to take care of it.

Never could tell. Might have an extra floor to rent in the old McGowan from now on. Ought to be kept up.

How *did* the building look from the outside? He found himself near another window and tried to look out. Something stopped him. The window was open, yet he couldn't push his head past the sill. He went back to the window he'd looked out of originally. Same difficulty.

And suddenly he understood.

He ran to the elevator and jabbed his fist against the button. He held it there while his breathing went faster and faster. Through the diamond-shaped windows on the doors, he could see elevators rising and elevators descending. But they wouldn't stop on the thirteenth floor.

Because there no longer was a thirteenth floor. Never had been one, in fact. Who ever heard of a thirteenth floor in the McGowan Building?....

AFTERWORD

I had a duodenal ulcer and suffered horribly from it from the age of twenty-nine to the age of fifty-eight, when I finally had a partial gastroectomy—just a few years before it was discovered that ulcers were microbial in nature and could be treated by antibiotics. But I still look at this story or that by me and remember the amount of pain-time involved.

The week in which I wrote "The Tenants" was one of the worst. I typed the piece with one hand, massaging my abdomen with the other, while chugging down chalky table-spoonsful of a reasonably popular antacid of the time.

When I brought it to Horace Gold as a submission to his fantasy magazine, *Beyond,* he immediately commented on the white blobs on almost every page (this being before the age of the computer and printer: retyping a long manuscript then, if you didn't have the money to hire someone, was a murderous chore).

"What is it," he asked holding a page up to the light, "Maalox or Amphojel? I use Maalox, and this looks very much like it."

Then he disappeared into his bedroom to read the story. He came out a few minutes later, grimacing, and called to Sam Merwin, his associate editor. "I want you to take a look at this," he said.

I immediately felt a lot better. I had known Sam Merwin since he had been an editor at *Thrilling Wonder Stories;* I had great respect for his literary judgment (he had bought a lot of Ray Bradbury over the protests of his publisher) and he had always liked everything I wrote. But Sam read "The Tenants" and shrugged. "What is it supposed to be," he asked, "something funny? Something eerie? What?"

"That's how I feel," Horace said. "What exactly were you trying to do?"

"Oh," I said, picking up the story and heading for the door. "Nothing much. No thirteenth floor in a lot of buildings. I've always been curious about what's on that floor."

"Well, it's meaningless to me," I heard Horace say as I closed the door, and I heard Sam Merwin mutter agreement.

I sent the piece to Anthony Boucher of *The Magazine of Fantasy & Science Fiction ,* who, up to then, had not seen anything of mine he wanted to buy. By return mail I got a check with a bonus rate and a long letter burbling with praise over the story. "But don't use Maalox," it ended. "Stick to plain bicarbonate of soda."

I called him and thanked him. Then I told him of Horace's reaction, and Sam Merwin's.

"Some people are color-blind," he said. "And some are tone-deaf. You know that. Well, some have absolutely no sense of the thirteenth floor. You just have to feel sorry for them."

WRITTEN 1953——PUBLISHED 1954

GENERATION OF NOAH

That was the day Plunkett heard his wife screaming guardedly to their youngest boy.

He let the door of the laying house slam behind him, forgetful of the nervously feeding hens. She had, he realized, cupped her hands over her mouth so that only the boy would hear.

"Saul! You, *Saul!* Come back, come right back this instant. Do you want your father to catch you out there on the road? Saul!"

The last shriek was higher and clearer, as if she had despaired of attracting the boy's attention without at the same time warning the man.

Poor Ann!

Gently, rapidly, Plunkett *shh'd* his way through the bustling and hungry hens to the side door. He came out facing the brooder run and broke into a heavy, unathletic trot.

He heard the other children clatter out of the feed house. Good! They have the responsibility after Ann and me, Plunkett told himself. Let them watch and learn again.

"Saul!" his wife's voice shrilled unhappily. "Saul, your father's coming!"

Ann came out of the front door and paused. "Elliot," she called at his back as he leaped over the flush well-cover. "Please, I don't feel well."

A difficult pregnancy, of course, and in her sixth month. But that had nothing to do with Saul. Saul knew better.

At the last frozen furrow of the truck garden Plunkett gave himself a moment to gather the necessary air for his lungs. Years ago, when Von Rundstedt's Tigers roared through the Bulge, he would have been able to dig a foxhole after such a run. Now, he was badly winded. Just showed you: such a short distance from the far end of the middle chicken house to the far end of the vegetable garden—merely crossing four acres—and he was winded. And consider the practice he'd had.

He could just about see the boy idly lifting a stick to throw for the dog's pleasure. Saul was in the further ditch, well past the white line his father had painted across the road.

"Elliot," his wife began again. "He's only six years old. He—"

Plunkett drew his jaws apart and let breath out in a bellyful of sound. "Saul! Saul Plunkett!" he bellowed. "Start running!"

He knew his voice had carried. He clicked the button on his stopwatch and threw his right arm up, pumping his clenched fist.

The boy *had* heard the yell. He turned, and, at the sight of the moving arm that meant the stopwatch had started, he dropped the stick. But, for the fearful moment, he was too startled to move.

Eight seconds. He lifted his lids slightly. Saul had begun to run. But he hadn't picked up speed, and Rusty skipping playfully between his legs threw him off his stride.

Ann had crossed the garden laboriously and stood at his side, alternately staring over his jutting elbow at the watch and smiling hesitantly sidewise at his face. She shouldn't have come out in her thin housedress in November. But it was good for Ann, too. Plunkett kept his eyes stolidly on the unemotional second hand.

One minute forty.

He could hear the dog's joyful barks coming closer, but as yet there was no echo of sneakers slapping the highway. Two minutes. He wouldn't make it.

The old bitter thoughts came crowding back to Plunkett. A father timing his six-year-old son's speed with the best watch he could afford. This, then, was the scientific way to raise children in Earth's most enlightened era. Well, it was scientific...in keeping with the latest discoveries....

Two and a half minutes. Rusty's barks didn't sound so very far off. Plunkett could hear the desperate pad-pad-pad of the boy's feet. He might make it at that. If only he could!

"Hurry, Saul," his mother breathed. "You can make it."

Plunkett looked up in time to see his son pound past, his jeans already darkened with perspiration. "Why doesn't he breathe like I told him?" he muttered. "He'll be out of breath in no time."

Halfway to the house, a furrow caught at Saul's toes. As he sprawled, Ann gasped. "You can't count that, Elliot. He tripped."

"Of course he tripped. He should count on tripping."

"Get up, Saulie," Herbie, his older brother, screamed from the garage where he stood with Josephine Dawkins, one pail of eggs between them. "Get up and run! This corner here! You can make it!"

The boy heaved to his feet, and threw his body forward again. Plunkett could hear him sobbing. He reached the cellar steps—and literally plunged down.

Plunkett pressed the stopwatch and the second hand halted. Three minutes thirteen seconds.

He held the watch up for his wife to see. "Thirteen seconds, Ann."

Her face wrinkled.

He walked to the house. Saul crawled back up the steps, fragments of unrecovered breath rattling in his chest. He kept his eyes on his father.

"Come here, Saul. Come right here. Look at the watch. Now, what do you see?"

The boy stared intently at the watch. His lips began twisting; startled tears writhed down his stained face. "More—more than three m-minutes, poppa?"

"More than three minutes, Saul. Now, Saul—don't cry, son; it isn't any use—Saul, what would have happened when you got to the steps?"

A small voice, pitifully trying to cover its cracks: "The big doors would be shut."

"The big doors would be shut. You would be locked outside. Then—what would have happened to you? Stop crying. Answer me!"

"Then, when the bombs fell, I'd—I'd have no place to hide. I'd burn like the head of a match. An'—an' the only thing left of me would be a dark spot on the ground, shaped like my shadow. An'—an'—"

"And the radioactive dust," his father helped with the catechism.

"Elliot—" Ann sobbed behind him. "I don't—"

"*Please,* Ann! And the radioactive dust, son?"

"An' if it was ra-di-o-ac-tive dust 'stead of atom bombs, my skin would come right off my body, an' my lungs would burn up inside me—please, poppa, I won't do it again!"

"And your eyes? What would happen to your eyes?"

A chubby brown fist dug into one of the eyes. "An' my eyes would fall out, an' my teeth would fall out, and I'd feel such terrible terrible pain—"

"All over and inside you. That's what would happen if you got to the cellar too late when the alarm went off, if you got locked out. At the end of three minutes, we pull the levers, and no matter who's outside—*no matter who*—all four corner doors swing shut and the cellar will be sealed. You understand that, Saul?"

The two Dawkins children were listening with white faces and dry lips. Their parents had brought them from the city and begged Elliot Plunkett, as he remembered old friends, to give their children the same protection as his. Well, they were getting it. This was the way to get it.

"Yes, I understand it, poppa. I won't ever do it again. Never again."

"I hope you won't. Now start for the barn, Saul. Go ahead." Plunkett slid his heavy leather belt from its loops.

"Elliot! Don't you think he understands the horrible thing? A beating won't make it any clearer."

He paused behind the weeping boy trudging to the barn. "It won't make it any clearer, but it will teach him the lesson another way. All seven of us are going to be in that cellar three minutes after the alarm, if I have to wear this strap clear down to the buckle!"

When Plunkett later clumped into the kitchen with his heavy farm boots, he stopped and sighed.

Ann was feeding Dinah. With her eyes on the baby, she asked, "No supper for him, Elliot?"

"No supper." He sighed again. "It does take it out of a man."

"Especially you. Not many men would become a farmer at thirty-five. Not many men would sink every last penny into an underground fort and powerhouse, just for insurance. But you're right."

"I only wish," he said restlessly, "that I could work out some way of getting Nancy's heifer into the cellar. And if eggs stay high one more month, I can build the tunnel to the generator. Then there's the well. Only one well, even if it's enclosed—"

"And when we came out here seven years ago—" She rose to him at last and rubbed her lips gently against his thick blue shirt. "We only had a piece of ground. Now, we have three chicken houses, a thousand broilers, and I can't keep track of how many layers and breeders."

She stopped as his body tightened and he gripped her shoulders.

"Ann, *Ann!* If you think like that, you'll act like that! How can I expect the children to—Ann, what we have—all we have—is a five-room cellar, concrete-lined, which we can seal in a few seconds, an enclosed well from a fairly deep underground stream, a windmill generator for power and a sunken oil-burner-driven generator for emergencies. We have supplies to carry us through, Geiger counters to detect radiation and lead-lined suits to move about in—afterwards. I've told you again and again that these things are our lifeboat, and the farm is just a sinking ship."

"Of course, darling." Plunkett's teeth ground together, then parted helplessly as his wife went back to feeding the baby.

"You're perfectly right. Swallow, now, Dinah. Why, that last bulletin from the Survivors Club would make *anybody* think."

He had been quoting from the October *Survivor* and Ann had recognized it. Well? At least they were *doing* something—seeking out nooks and feverishly building crannies—pooling their various ingenuities in an attempt to haul themselves and their families through the military years of the Atomic Age.

The familiar green cover of the mimeographed magazine was very noticeable on the kitchen table. He flipped the sheets to the thumb-smudged article on page five and shook his head.

"Imagine!" he said loudly. "The poor fools agreeing with the government again on the safety factor. Six minutes! How can they—an organization like the Survivors Club making that their official opinion! Why freeze, *freeze* alone..."

"They're ridiculous," Ann murmured, scraping the bottom of the bowl.

"All right, we have automatic detectors. But human beings still have to look at the radar scope, or we'd be diving underground every time there's a meteor shower."

He strode along a huge table, beating a fist rhythmically into one hand. "They won't be so sure, at first. Who wants to risk his rank by giving the nationwide signal that makes everyone in the country pull ground over his head, that makes our own projectile sites set to buzz? Finally, they are certain: they freeze for a moment. Meanwhile, the rockets are zooming down—how fast, we don't know. The men unfreeze, they trip each other up, they tangle frantically. *Then* they press the button, *then* the nationwide signal starts our radio alarms."

Plunkett turned to his wife, spread earnest, quivering arms. "And then, Ann, *we* freeze when we hear it! At last, we start for the cellar. Who knows, who can dare to say, how much has been cut off the margin of safety by that time? No, if they claim that six minutes is the safety factor, we'll give half of it to the alarm system. Three minutes for us."

"One more spoonful," Ann urged Dinah. "Just one more. *Down* it goes!"

Josephine Dawkins and Herbie were cleaning the feed trolley in the shed at the near end of the chicken house.

"All done, pop," the boy grinned at his father. "And the eggs taken care of. When does Mr. Whiting pick 'em up?"

"Nine o'clock. Did you finish feeding the hens in the last house?"

"I said all done, didn't I?" Herbie asked with adolescent impatience. "When I say a thing, I mean it."

"Good. You kids better get at your books. Hey, stop that! Education will be very important, afterwards. You never know what will be useful. And maybe only your mother and I to teach you."

"Gee," Herbie nodded at Josephine. "Think of that."

She pulled at her jumper where it was very tight over newly swelling breasts and patted her blonde braided hair. "What about *my* mother and father, Mr. Plunkett? Won't they be—be—"

"Naw!" Herbie laughed the loud, country laugh he'd been practicing lately. "They're dead-enders. They won't pull through. They live in the city, don't they? They'll just be some—"

"Herbie!"

"—some foam on a mushroom-shaped cloud," he finished, utterly entranced by the image. "Gosh, I'm sorry," he said, as he looked from his angry father to the quivering girl. He went on in a studiously reasonable voice. "But it's the truth, anyway. That's why they sent you and Lester here. I guess I'll marry you—afterwards. And you ought to get in the habit of calling *him* pop. Because that's the way it'll be."

Josephine squeezed her eyes shut, kicked the shed door open, and ran out. "I hate you, Herbie Plunkett," she wept. "You're a beast!"

Herbie grimaced at his father—*women, women, women!*—and ran after her. "Hey, Jo! Listen!"

The trouble was, Plunkett thought worriedly as he carried the emergency bulbs for the hydroponic garden into the cellar—the trouble was that Herbie had learned through constant reiteration the one thing: survival came before all else, and amenities were merely amenities.

Strength and self-sufficiency—Plunkett had worked out the virtues his children needed years ago, sitting in air-conditioned offices and totting corporation balances with one eye always on the calendar.

"Still," Plunkett muttered, "still—Herbie shouldn't—" He shook his head.

He inspected the incubators near the long steaming tables of the hydroponic garden. A tray about ready to hatch. They'd have to start assembling eggs to replace it in the morning. He paused in the third room, filled a gap in the bookshelves.

"Hope Josephine steadies the boy in his schoolwork. If he fails that next exam, they'll make me send him to town regularly. Now *there's* an aspect of survival I can hit Herbie with."

He realized he'd been talking to himself, a habit he'd been combating futilely for more than a month. Stuffy talk, too. He was becoming like those people who left tracts on trolley cars.

"Have to start watching myself," he commented. "Dammit, again!"

The telephone clattered upstairs. He heard Ann walk across to it, that serene, unhurried walk all pregnant women seem to have.

"Elliot! Nat Medarie."

"Tell him I'm coming, Ann." He swung the vault-like door carefully shut behind him, looked at it for a moment, and started up the high stone steps.

"Hello, Nat. What's new?"

"Hi, Plunk. Just got a postcard from Fitzgerald. Remember him? The abandoned silver mine in Montana? Yeah. He says we've got to go on the basis that lithium bombs will be used."

Plunkett leaned against the wall with his elbow. He cradled the receiver on his right shoulder so he could light a cigarette. "Fitzgerald can be wrong sometimes."

"Uhm. I don't know. But you know what a lithium bomb means, don't you?"

"It means," Plunkett said, staring through the wall of the house and into a boiling Earth, "that a chain reaction may be set off in the atmosphere if enough of them are used. Maybe if only one—"

"Oh, can it," Medarie interrupted. "That gets us nowhere. That way nobody gets through, and we might as well start shuttling from church to bar-room like my brother-in-law in Chicago is doing right now. Fred, I used to say to him— No, listen, Plunk: it means I was right. You didn't dig deep enough."

"*Deep* enough! I'm as far down as I want to go. If I don't have enough layers of lead and concrete to shield me—well, if they can crack *my* shell, then you won't be able to walk on the surface before you die of thirst, Nat. No—I sunk my dough in power supply. Once that fails, you'll find yourself putting the used air back into your empty oxygen tanks by hand!"

The other man chuckled. "All right. I *hope* I see you around."

"And I hope *I* see…" Plunkett twisted around to face the front window as an old station wagon bumped over the ruts in his driveway. "Say, Nat, what do you know? Charlie Whiting just drove up. Isn't this Sunday?"

"Yeah. He hit my place early, too. Some sort of political meeting in town and he wants to make it. It's not enough that the diplomats and generals are practically glaring into each other's eyebrows this time. A couple of local philosophers are impatient with the slow pace at which their extinction is approaching, and they're getting together to see if they can't hurry it up some."

"Don't be bitter," Plunkett smiled.

"Here's praying at you. Regards to Ann, Plunk."

Plunkett cradled the receiver and ambled downstairs. Outside, he watched Charlie Whiting pull the door of the station wagon open on its one desperate hinge.

"Eggs stowed, Mr. Plunkett," Charlie said. "Receipt signed. Here. You'll get a check Wednesday."

"Thanks, Charlie. Hey, you kids get back to your books. Go on, Herbie. You're having an English quiz tonight. Eggs still going up, Charlie?"

"Up she goes." The old man slid onto the crackled leather seat and pulled the door shut deftly. He bent his arm on the open window. "Heh. And every time she does I make a little more off you survivor fellas who are too scairt to carry 'em into town yourself."

"Well, you're entitled to it," Plunkett said, uncomfortably. "What about this meeting in town?"

"Bunch of folks goin' to discuss the conference. I say we pull out. I say we walk right out of the dern thing. This country never won a conference yet. A million conferences the last few years and everyone knows what's gonna happen sooner or later. Heh. They're just wastin' time. Hit 'em first, I say."

"Maybe we will. Maybe *they* will. Or—maybe, Charlie, a couple of different nations will get what looks like a good idea at the same time."

Charlie Whiting shoved his foot down and ground the starter. "You don't make sense. If we hit 'em first how can they do the same to us? Hit 'em first—hard enough—and they'll never recover in time to hit us back. That's what *I* say. But you survivor fellas—" He shook his white head angrily as the car shot away.

"Hey!" he yelled, turning into the road. "Hey, look!"

Plunkett looked over his shoulder. Charlie Whiting was gesturing at him with his left hand, the forefinger pointing out and the thumb up straight.

"Look, Mr. Plunkett," the old man called. "Boom! Boom! Boom!" He cackled hysterically and writhed over the steering wheel.

Rusty scuttled around the side of the house and after him, yipping frantically in ancient canine tradition.

Plunkett watched the receding car until it swept around the curve two miles away. He stared at the small dog returning proudly.

Poor Whiting. Poor everybody, for that matter, who had a normal distrust of crackpots.

How could you permit a greedy old codger like Whiting to buy your produce, just so you and your family wouldn't have to risk trips into town?

Well, it was a matter of having decided years ago that the world was too full of people who were convinced that they were faster on the draw than anyone else—and the other fellow was bluffing anyway. People who believed that two small boys could pile up snowballs across the street from each other and go home without having used them, people who discussed the merits of concrete fences as opposed to wire guardrails while their automobiles skidded over the cliff. People who were righteous. People who were apathetic.

It was the last group, Plunkett remembered, who had made him stop buttonholing his fellows at last. You got tired of standing around in a hair shirt and pointing ominously at the heavens. You got to the point where you wished the human race well, but you wanted to pull you and yours out of the way of its tantrums. Survival for the individual and his family, you thought—

Clang-ng-ng-ng-ng!

Plunkett pressed the stud on his stopwatch. Funny. There was no practice alarm scheduled for today. All the kids were out of the house, except Saul—and he wouldn't dare to leave his room, let alone tamper with the alarm. Unless, perhaps, Ann—

He walked inside the kitchen. Ann was running toward the door, carrying Dinah. Her face was oddly unfamiliar. "Saulie!" she screamed. "Saulie! Hurry *up*, Saulie!"

"I'm coming, momma," the boy yelled as he clattered down the stairs. "I'm coming as fast as I can! I'll make it!"

Plunkett understood. He put a heavy hand on the wall, under the dinner-plate clock.

He watched his wife struggle down the steps into the cellar. Saul ran past him and out of the door, arms flailing. "I'll make it, poppa! I'll make it!"

Plunkett felt his stomach move. He swallowed with great care. "Don't hurry, son," he whispered. "It's only judgment day."

He straightened out and looked at his watch, noticing that his hand on the wall had left its moist outline behind. One minute, twelve seconds. Not bad. Not bad at all. He'd figured on three.

Clang-ng-ng-ng-ng!

He started to shake himself and began a shudder that he couldn't control. What was the matter? He knew what he had to do. He had to unpack the portable lathe that was still in the barn.

"Elliot!" his wife called.

He found himself sliding down the steps on feet that somehow wouldn't lift when he wanted them to. He stumbled through the open cellar door. Frightened faces dotted the room in an unrecognizable jumble.

"We all here?" he croaked.

"All here, poppa," Saul said from his position near the aeration machinery. "Lester and Herbie are in the far room, by the other switch. Why is Josephine crying? Lester isn't crying. I'm not crying, either."

Plunkett nodded vaguely at the slim, sobbing girl and put his hand on the lever protruding from the concrete wall. He glanced at his watch again. Two minutes, ten seconds. Not bad.

"Mr. Plunkett!" Lester Dawkins sped in from the corridor. "Mr. Plunkett! Herbie ran out of the other door to get Rusty. I told him—"

Two minutes, twenty seconds, Plunkett realized as he leaped to the top of the steps. Herbie was running across the vegetable garden, snapping his fingers behind him to lure Rusty on. When he saw his father, his mouth stiffened with shock. He broke stride for a moment, and the dog charged joyously between his legs. Herbie fell.

Plunkett stepped forward. *Two minutes, forty seconds.* Herbie jerked himself to his feet, put his head down—and ran.

Was that dim thump a distant explosion? There—another one! Like a giant belching. Who had started it? And did it matter—now?

Three minutes. Rusty scampered down the cellar steps, his head back, his tail flickering from side to side. Herbie panted up. Plunkett grabbed him by the collar and jumped.

And as he jumped he saw—far to the south—the umbrellas opening their agony upon the land. Rows upon swirling rows of them....

He tossed the boy ahead when he landed. *Three minutes, five seconds.* He threw the switch, and, without waiting for the door to close and seal, darted into the corridor. That took care of two doors; the other switch controlled the remaining entrances. He reached it. He pulled it. He looked at his watch. *Three minutes, twenty seconds.* "The bombs," blubbered Josephine. "The bombs!"

Ann was scrabbling Herbie to her in the main room, feeling his arms, caressing his hair, pulling him in for a wild hug and crying out yet again. "Herbie! Herbie! Herbie!"

"I know you're gonna lick me, pop. I—I just want you to know that I think you ought to."

"I'm not going to lick you, son."

"You're not? But gee, I deserve a licking. I deserve the worst—"

"You may," Plunkett said, gasping at the wall of clicking Geigers. *"You may deserve a beating,"* he yelled, so loudly that they all whirled to face him, "but I won't punish you, not only for now, but forever! And as I with you," he screamed, "so you with yours! Understand?"

"Yes," they replied in a weeping, ragged chorus. "We understand!"

"Swear! Swear that you and your children and your children's children will never punish another human being—*no matter what the provocation.*"

"We swear!" they bawled at him. "We swear!"

Then they all sat down.

To wait.

AFTERWORD

For a long time (until I wrote "The Custodian"), "Generation of Noah" was my favorite among my stories. But the science-fiction magazines didn't want it: too hortatory. The general fiction magazines all said something on the order of "too fantastic." Six years after publication, it was rejected by a movie producer who was interested in filming some of my work ("far too prosaic for today's audiences").

Fred Pohl, the agent who finally sold the piece, liked it almost as much as I did. But he begged me and begged me to change what he called "the Greek chorus ending." And I kept telling him that the goddam Greek chorus ending was why I had written the story in the first place. He would walk away from me muttering, "That's no excuse at all."

So from the white-bearded standpoint of eighty years of age, let me remind the reader:

In 1947 when I wrote "Generation of Noah," the Federation of Atomic Scientists kept trying to tell everyone how much they apologized for having helped to develop our nuclear weaponry. And a lot of them got investigated as un-American for making such noises. (After all, the military kept saying, the atomic bomb was a weapon just like any other weapon. A bigger bang for the buck, some general shrugged.)

By 1957, six years after the story was published, we knew full well that the Soviet Union not only had nuclear weapons too, but might even have better means of delivering them than we. Everyone had heard of the atomic bomb drills in the schools where the children learned that at a given signal they were to jump off their benches and lie down under their desks with their hands locked behind their heads to protect vital parts. I knew people—I swear this!—who said that in the event of an atomic attack one should above all close the windows and pull down the window shades. That would reduce the amount of radiation reaching you.

And, of course, this was the tail-end of the period where every new home built had a bomb shelter in the basement, a tiny room surrounded by well-plastered walls and maybe, if the contractor was an especially responsible type, by some walls of brick. You go now into homes built in this period and you find that those bomb shelters are being used as fruit cellars or wine vaults or, most likely, extra storage space.

Well, the bipolar Cold War has given way to the sunshine of monopolar power, and all that is behind us now.

Like hell.

John Campbell wrote a number of editorials in *Astounding Science Fiction* of the 1940s that were remarkably strong and good and gave him a free pass to be forgotten as the chief publicist of Dianetics and the Hieronymus Machine. I remember one where he talked of the atomic bomb as The Great Equalizer.

He pointed out that when the Colt six-gun reached the West, it had a tremendous effect on the relationships between small, weak men and the big, strong men who formerly had been able to bully them at will. Billy the Kid and others now had their equalizer. And from Los Alamos on, Campbell said, small countries that were unable to afford big navies and big artilleries and big air forces now could have weapons that would equalize the difference between them and the great powers of the Earth. All they had to do was find the right messenger with a suitcase to deliver them.

War is by no means gone from our planet, as a glance at almost any continent will unmistakably show. And if war ever comes our way again…

There is Lenin's dictum as enunciated in *State and Revolution:* "No ruling class in history ever laid down power of its own free will." Which makes me think of Hitler, 1945, in that last bunker in the ruins of Berlin. An aide comes to him and says, "*Mein Führer,* we have just now perfected a weapon that will vaporize the enemy, city by city, patch of countryside by patch of countryside. But—"

"But *what?*" yells red-eyed Hitler.

"If we use it, we just may set off a reaction that will destroy the entire planet. What should we do?"

And Hitler, hearing the Russian guns going off in one direction, and knowing that the Americans, British, and French are scant miles off in the other direction—what do you think Adolf Hitler would say to do?

No, until we as a species grow a couple of moral inches, or until we have daughter colonies on planets outside Earth, until then—

I will keep my Greek chorus ending.

WRITTEN 1947———PUBLISHED 1951

꩜

Down Among the Dead Men

I stood in front of the junkyard's outer gate and felt my stomach turn over slowly, grindingly, the way it had when I saw a whole terrestrial subfleet—close to 20,000 men—blown to bits in the Second Battle of Saturn more than eleven years ago. But then there had been shattered fragments of ships in my visiplate and imagined screams of men in my mind; there had been the expanding images of the Eoti's box-like craft surging through the awful, drifting wreckage they had created, to account for the icy sweat that wound itself like a flat serpent around my forehead and my neck.

Now there was nothing but a large, plain building, very much like the hundreds of other factories in the busy suburbs of Old Chicago, a manufacturing establishment surrounded by a locked gate and spacious proving grounds—the Junkyard. Yet the sweat on my skin was colder and the heave of my bowels more spastic than it had ever been in any of those countless, ruinous battles that had created this place.

All of which was very understandable, I told myself. What I was feeling was the great-grandmother hag of all fears, the most basic rejection and reluctance of which my flesh was capable. It was understandable, but that didn't help any. I still couldn't walk up to the sentry at the gate.

I'd been almost all right until I'd seen the huge square can against the fence, the can with the slight stink coming out of it and the big colorful sign on top:

> DON'T *WASTE* WASTE
> PLACE *ALL* WASTE HERE
> remember —
> WHATEVER IS WORN CAN BE SHORN
> WHATEVER IS MAIMED CAN BE RECLAIMED
> WHATEVER IS USED CAN BE REUSED
> PLACE *ALL* WASTE HERE
> —*Conservation Police*

I'd seen those square, compartmented cans and those signs in every barracks, every hospital, every recreation center, between here and the asteroids. But seeing them, now, in this place, gave them a different meaning. I wondered if they had those other posters inside, the shorter ones. You know: "We need all our resources to defeat the enemy—and GARBAGE IS OUR BIGGEST NATURAL RESOURCE."

329

Decorating the walls of this particular building with those posters would be downright ingenious.

Whatever is maimed can be reclaimed... I flexed my right arm inside my blue jumper sleeve. It felt like a part of me, always would feel like a part of me. And in a couple of years, assuming that I lived that long, the thin white scar that circled the elbow joint would be completely invisible. Sure. Whatever is maimed can be reclaimed. All except one thing. The most important thing.

And I felt less like going in than ever.

And then I saw this kid. The one from Arizona Base.

He was standing right in front of the sentry box, paralyzed just like me. In the center of his uniform cap was a brand-new, gold-shiny Y with a dot in the center: the insignia of a sling-shot commander. He hadn't been wearing it the day before at the briefing; that could only mean the commission had just come through. He looked real young and real scared.

I remembered him from the briefing session. He was the one whose hand had gone up timidly during the question period, the one who, when he was recognized, had half risen, worked his mouth a couple of times and finally blurted out: "Excuse me, sir, but they don't—they don't smell at all bad, do they?"

There had been a cyclone of laughter, the yelping laughter of men who've felt themselves close to the torn edge of hysteria all afternoon and who are damn glad that someone has at last said something that they can make believe is funny.

And the white-haired briefing officer, who hadn't so much as smiled, waited for the hysteria to work itself out, before saying gravely: "No, they don't smell bad at all. Unless, that is, they don't bathe. The same as you gentlemen."

That shut us up. Even the kid, blushing his way back into his seat, set his jaw stiffly at the reminder. And it wasn't until twenty minutes later, when we'd been dismissed, that I began to feel the ache in my own face from the unrelaxed muscles there.

The same as you gentlemen...

I shook myself hard and walked over to the kid. "Hello, Commander," I said. "Been here long?"

He managed a grin. "Over an hour, Commander. I caught the eight-fifteen out of Arizona Base. Most of the other fellows were still sleeping off last night's party, I'd gone to bed early; I wanted to give myself as much time to get the feel of this thing as I could. Only it doesn't seem to do much good."

"I know. Some things you can't get used to. Some things you're not *supposed* to get used to."

He looked at my chest. "I guess this isn't your first sling-shot command?"

My first? More like my twenty-first, son! But then I remembered that everyone tells me I look young for my medals, and what the hell, the kid looked so pale—"No, not exactly my first. But I've never had a blob crew before. This is exactly as new to me as it is to you. Hey, listen, Commander: I'm having a hard time, too. What say we bust through that gate together? Then the worst'll be over."

The kid nodded violently. We linked arms and marched up to the sentry. We showed him our orders. He opened the gate and said: "Straight ahead. Any elevator on your left to the fifteenth floor."

So, still arm in arm, we walked into the main entrance of the large building, up a long flight of steps and under the sign that said in red and black:

HUMAN PROTOPLASM RECLAMATION CENTER
THIRD DISTRICT FINISHING PLANT

There were some old-looking but very erect men walking along the main lobby and a lot of uniformed, fairly pretty girls. I was pleased to note that most of the girls were pregnant. The first pleasing sight I had seen in almost a week.

We turned into an elevator and told the girl, "Fifteen." She punched a button and waited for it to fill up. She didn't seem to be pregnant. I wondered what was the matter with her.

I'd managed to get a good grip on my heaving imagination, when I got a look at the shoulder patches the other passengers were wearing. That almost did for me right there. It was a circular red patch with the black letters TAF superimposed on a white G-4. TAF for Terrestrial Armed Forces, of course: the letters were the basic insignia of all rear-echelon outfits. But why didn't they use G-1, which represented Personnel? G-4 stood for the Supply Division. *Supply!*

You can always trust the TAF. Thousands of morale specialists in all kinds of ranks, working their educated heads off to keep up the spirits of the men in the fighting perimeters—but every damn time, when it comes down to scratch, the good old dependable TAF will pick the ugliest name, the one in the worst possible taste.

Oh, sure, I told myself, you can't fight a shattering, no-quarter interstellar war for twenty-five years and keep every pretty thought dewy-damp and intact, But not *Supply,* gentlemen. Not this place—not the Junkyard. Let's at least try to keep up appearances.

Then we began going up and the elevator girl began announcing floors and I had lots of other things to think about.

"Third floor—Corpse Reception and Classification," the operator sang out.

"Fifth floor—Preliminary Organ Processing."

"Seventh floor—Brain Reconstitution and Neural Alignment."

"Ninth floor—Cosmetics, Elementary Reflexes, and Muscular Control."

At this point, I forced myself to stop listening, the way you do when you're on a heavy cruiser, say, and the rear engine room gets flicked by a bolt from an Eoti scrambler. After you've been around a couple of times when it's happened, you learn to sort of close your ears and say to yourself, "I don't know anybody in that damned engine room, not anybody, and in a few minutes everything will be nice and quiet again." And in a few minutes it is. Only trouble is that then, like as not, you'll be part of the detail that's ordered into the steaming place to scrape the guck off the walls and get the jets firing again.

Same way now. Just as soon as I had that girl's voice blocked out, there we were on the fifteenth floor ("Final Interviews and Shipping") and the kid and I had to get out.

He was real green. A definite sag around the knees, shoulders sloping forward like his clavicle had curled. Again I was grateful to him. Nothing like having somebody to take care of.

"Come on, Commander," I whispered. "Up and at 'em. Look at it this way: for characters like us, this is practically a family reunion."

It was the wrong thing to say. He looked at me as if I'd punched his face. "No thanks to you for the reminder, Mister," he said. "Even if we are in the same boat." Then he walked stiffly up to the receptionist.

I could have bitten my tongue off. I hurried after him. "I'm sorry, kid," I told him earnestly. "The words just slid out of my big mouth. But don't get sore at me; hell, I had to listen to myself say it too."

He stopped, thought about it, and nodded. Then he gave me a smile. "OK. No hard feelings. It's a rough war, isn't it?"

I smiled back. "Rough? Why, if you're not careful, they tell me, you can get killed in it."

The receptionist was a soft little blonde with two wedding rings on one hand, and one wedding ring on the other. From what I knew of current planet-side customs, that meant she'd been widowed twice.

She took our orders and read jauntily into her desk mike: "Attention Final Conditioning. Attention Final Conditioning. Alert for immediate shipment the following serial numbers: 70623152, 70623109, 70623166, and 70623123. Also 70538966, 70538923, 70538980, and 70538937. Please route through the correct numbered sections and check all data on TAF AGO forms 362 as per TAF Regulation 7896, of 15 June, 2145. Advise when available for Final Interviews."

I was impressed. Almost exactly the same procedure as when you go to Ordnance for a replacement set of stern exhaust tubes.

She looked up and favored us with a lovely smile. "Your crews will be ready in a moment. Would you have a seat, gentlemen?"

We had a seat gentlemen.

After a while, she got up to take something out of a file cabinet set in the wall. As she came back to her desk, I noticed she was pregnant—only about the third or fourth month—and, naturally, I gave a little, satisfied nod. Out of the corner of my eye, I saw the kid make the same kind of nod. We looked at each other and chuckled. "It's a rough, rough war," he said.

"Where are you from anyway?" I asked. "That doesn't sound like a Third District accent to me."

"It isn't. I was born in Scandinavia—Eleventh Military District. My home town is Goteborg, Sweden. But after I got my—my promotion, naturally I didn't care to see the folks any more. So I requested a transfer to the Third, and from now on, until I hit a scrambler, this is where I'll be spending my furloughs and Earth-side hospitalizations."

I'd heard that a lot of the younger sling-shotters felt that way. Personally, I never had a chance to find out how I'd feel about visiting the old folks at home. My father was knocked off in the suicidal attempt to retake Neptune way back when I was still in high school learning elementary combat, and my mother was Admiral Raguzzi's staff secretary when the flagship *Thermopylae* took a direct hit two years later in the famous defense of Ganymede. That was before the Breeding Regulations, of course, and women were still serving in administrative positions on the fighting perimeters.

On the other hand, I realized, at least two of my brothers might still be alive. But I'd made no attempt to contact them since getting my dotted Y. So I guessed I felt the same way as the kid—which was hardly surprising.

"Are you from Sweden?" the blonde girl was asking. "My second husband was born in Sweden. Maybe you knew him—Sven Nossen? He had a lot of relatives in Stockholm."

The kid screwed up his eyes as if he was thinking real hard. You know, running down a list of all the Swedes in Stockholm. Finally, he shook his head. "No, can't say that I do. But I wasn't out of Goteborg very much before I was called up."

She clucked sympathetically at his provincialism. The baby-faced blonde of classic anecdote. A real dumb kid. And yet—there were lots of very clever, high-pressure cuties around the inner planets these days who had to content themselves with a one-fifth interest in some abysmal slob who boasted the barest modicum of maleness. Or a certificate from the local sperm bank. Blondie here was on her third full husband.

Maybe, I thought, if I were looking for a wife myself, this is what I'd pick to take the stink of scrambler rays out of my nose and the yammer-yammer-yammer of Irvingles out of my ears. Maybe I'd want somebody nice and simple to come home to from one of those complicated skirmishes with the Eoti where you spend most of your conscious thoughts trying to figure out just what battle rhythm the filthy insects are using this time. Maybe, if I were going to get married, I'd find a pretty fluffhead like this more generally desirable than—oh, well. Maybe. Considered as a problem in psychology it was interesting.

I noticed she was talking to me. "You've never had a crew of this type before either, have you, Commander?"

"Zombies, you mean? No, not yet, I'm happy to say."

She made a disapproving pout with her mouth. It was fully as cute as her approving pouts. "We do not like that word."

"All right, blobs then."

"We don't like bl—that word either. You are talking about human beings like yourself, Commander. Very much like yourself."

I began to get sore fast, just the way the kid had out in the hall. Then I realized she didn't mean anything by it. She didn't know. What the hell—it wasn't on our orders. I relaxed. "You tell me. What do you call them here?"

The blonde sat up stiffly. "*We* refer to them as soldier surrogates. The epithet 'zombie' was used to describe the obsolete Model 21 which went out of production over five years ago. You will be supplied with individuals based on Models 705 and 706, which are practically perfect. In fact, in some respects—"

"No bluish skin? No slow-motion sleepwalking?"

She shook her head violently, Her eyes were lit up. Evidently she'd digested all the promotional literature. Not such a fluffhead, after all; no great mind, but her husbands had evidently had someone to talk to in between times. She rattled on enthusiastically: "The cyanosis was the result of bad blood oxygenation; blood was our second most difficult tissue reconstruction problem, The nervous system was the hardest. Even though the blood cells are usually in the poorest shape of all by the time the bodies arrive, we can now turn out a very serviceable rebuilt heart. But, let there be the teeniest battle damage to the brain or spine and you have to start right from scratch. And then the troubles in reconstitution! My cousin Lorna works in Neural Alignment and she tells me all you need to make is just one wrong connection—you know how it is, Commander, at the end of the day your eyes are tired and you're kind of watching the clock—just one wrong connection, and the reflexes in the finished individual turn out to be so bad that they just have to send him down to the third floor and begin all over again. But you don't have to worry about that. Since Model 663, we've been using the two-team inspection system in Neural Alignment. And the 700 series—oh, they've just been *wonderful*."

"That good, eh? Better than the old-fashioned mother's son type?"

"Well-l-l," she considered. "You'd really be amazed, Commander, if you could see the very latest performance charts. Of course, there is always that big deficiency, the one activity we've never been able to—"

"One thing *I* can't understand," the kid broke in, "why do they have to use corpses! A body's lived its life, fought its war—why not leave it alone? I know the Eoti can outbreed us merely by increasing the number of queens in their flagships; I know that manpower is the biggest single TAF problem—but we've been synthesizing protoplasm for a long, long time now. Why not synthesize the whole damn body, from toenails to frontal lobe, and turn out real, honest-to-God androids that don't wallop you with the stink of death when you meet them?"

The little blonde got mad. "Our product *does not stink!* Cosmetics can now guarantee that the new models have even less of a body odor than you, young man! And we do not reactivate or revitalize corpses, I'll have you know; what we do is *reclaim* human protoplasm, we reuse worn-out and damaged human cellular material in the area where the greatest shortages currently occur, military personnel. You wouldn't talk about corpses, I assure you, if you saw the condition that some of those bodies are in when they arrive. Why, sometimes in a whole baling package—a baling package contains twenty casualties—we don't find enough to make one good, whole kidney. Then we have to take a little intestinal tissue here and a bit of spleen there, alter them, unite them carefully, activa—"

"That's what I mean. If you go to all that trouble, why not start with real raw material?"

"Like what, for example?" she asked him.

The kid gestured with his black-gloved hands. "Basic elements like carbon, hydrogen, oxygen and so on. It would make the whole process a lot cleaner."

"Basic elements have to come from somewhere," I pointed out gently. "You might take your hydrogen and oxygen from air and water. But where would you get your carbon from?"

"From the same place where the other synthetics manufacturers get it—coal, oil, cellulose."

The receptionist sat back and relaxed, "Those are organic substances," she reminded him. "If you're going to use raw material that was once alive, why not use the kind that comes as close as possible to the end-product you have in mind? It's simple industrial economics, Commander, believe me. The best and cheapest raw material for the manufacture of soldier surrogates is soldier bodies."

"Sure," the kid said. "Makes sense. There's no other use for dead, old, beaten-up soldier bodies. Better'n shoving them in the ground where they'd be just waste, pure waste."

Our little blonde chum started to smile in agreement, then shot him an intense look and changed her mind. She looked very uncertain all of a sudden. When the communicator on her desk buzzed, she bent over it eagerly.

I watched her with approval. Definitely no fluffhead. Just feminine. I sighed. You see, I figure lots of civilian things out the wrong way, but only with women is my wrongness an all-the-time proposition. Proving again that a hell of a lot of peculiar things turn out to have happened for the best.

"Commander," she was saying to the kid. "Would you go to Room 1591? Your crew will be there in a moment." She turned to me. "And Room 1524 for you, Commander, if you please."

The kid nodded and walked off, very stiff and erect. I waited until the door had closed behind him, then I leaned over the receptionist. "Wish they'd change the Breeding Regulations again," I told her. "You'd make a damn fine rear-echelon orientation officer. Got more of the feel of the Junkyard from you than in ten briefing sessions."

She examined my face anxiously, "I hope you mean that, Commander. You see, we're all very deeply involved in this project. We're extremely proud of the progress the Third District Finishing Plant has made. We talk about the new developments all the time, everywhere—even in the cafeteria. It didn't occur to me until too late that you gentlemen might—" she blushed deep, rich red, the way only a blonde can blush "—might take what I said personally. I'm sorry if I—"

"Nothing to be sorry about," I assured her. "All you did was talk what they call shop. Like when I was in the hospital last month and heard two surgeons discussing how to repair a man's arm and making it sound as if they were going to nail a new arm on an expensive chair. Real interesting, and I learned a lot."

I left her looking grateful, which is absolutely the only way to leave a woman, and barged on to Room 1524.

It was evidently used as a classroom when reconverted human junk wasn't being picked up. A bunch of chairs, a long blackboard, a couple of charts. One of the charts was on the Eoti, the basic information list, that contains all the limited information we have been able to assemble on the bugs in the bloody quarter-century since they came busting in past Pluto to take over the solar system. It hadn't been changed much since the one I had to memorize in high school: the only difference was a slightly longer section on intelligence and motivation. Just theory, of course, but more carefully thought-out theory than the stuff I'd learned. The big brains had now concluded that the reason all attempts at communicating with them had failed was not because they were a conquest-crazy species, but because they suffered from the same extreme xenophobia as their smaller, less intelligent communal insect cousins here on Earth. That is, an ant wanders up to a strange anthill—*zok!* No discussion, he's chopped down at the entrance. And the sentry ants react even faster if it's a creature of another genus. So despite the Eoti science, which in too many respects was more advanced than ours, they were psychologically incapable of the kind of mental projection, or empathy, necessary if one is to realize that a completely alien-looking individual has intelligence, feelings—and rights!—to substantially the same extent as oneself.

Well, it might be so. Meanwhile, we were locked in a murderous stalemate with them on a perimeter of never-ending battle that sometimes expanded as far as Saturn and occasionally contracted as close as Jupiter. Barring the invention of a new weapon of such unimaginable power that we could wreck their fleet before they could duplicate the weapon, as they'd been managing to up to now, our only hope was to discover somehow the stellar system from which they came, somehow build ourselves not one starship but a fleet of them—and somehow wreck their home base or throw enough of a scare into it so that they'd pull back their expedition for defensive purposes. A lot of somehows.

But if we wanted to maintain our present position until the *somehows* started to roll, our birth announcements had to take longer to read than the casualty lists. For the last decade, this hadn't been so, despite the more and more stringent Breeding Regulations which were steadily pulverizing every one of our moral codes and sociological advances. Then there was the day that someone in the Conservation Police noticed that almost half our ships of the line had been fabricated from the metallic junk of previous battles. Where was the personnel that had manned those salvage derelicts, he wondered…

And thus what Blondie outside and her co-workers were pleased to call soldier surrogates.

I'd been a computer's mate, second class, on the old *Jenghiz Khan* when the first batch had come aboard as battle replacements. Let me tell you, friends, we had real good reason for calling them zombies! Most of them were as blue as the uniforms they wore, their breathing was so noisy it made you think of asthmatics with built-in public address systems, their eyes shone with all the intelligence of petroleum jelly— *and the way they walked!*

My friend Johnny Cruro, the first man to get knocked off in the Great Breakthrough of 2143, used to say that they were trying to pick their way down a steep hill at the bottom of which was a large, open, family-size grave. Body held strained and tense. Legs and arms moving slow, slow, until suddenly they'd finish with a jerk. Creepy as hell.

They weren't good for anything but the drabbest fatigue detail. And even then—if you told them to polish a gun mounting, you had to remember to come back in an hour and turn them off or they might scrub their way clear through into empty space. Of course, they weren't all that bad. Johnny Cruro used to say that he'd met one or two who could achieve imbecility when they were feeling right.

Combat was what finished them as far as the TAF was concerned. Not that they broke under battle conditions—just the reverse. The old ship would be rocking and screaming as it changed course every few seconds; every Irvingle, scrambler, and nucleonic howitzer along the firing corridor turning bright golden yellow from the heat it was generating; a hoarse yelping voice from the bulkhead loudspeakers pouring out orders faster than human muscles could move, the shock troops—their faces ugly with urgency—running crazily from one emergency station to another; everyone around you working like a blur and cursing and wondering out loud why the Eoti were taking so long to tag a target as big and as slow as the *Khan*... and suddenly you'd see a zombie clutching a broom in his rubbery hands and sweeping the deck in the slack-jawed, moronic, and horribly earnest way they had...

I remember whole gun crews going amuck and slamming into the zombies with long crowbars and metal-gloved fists; once, even an officer, sprinting back to the control room, stopped, flipped out his side-arm and pumped bolt after bolt of jagged thunder at a blue-skin who'd been peacefully wiping a porthole while the bow of the ship was being burned away. And as the zombie sagged uncomprehendingly and uncomplainingly to the floor plates, the young officer stood over him and chanted soothingly, the way you do to a boisterous dog: "Down, boy, down, *down, down, damn you, down!*"

That was the reason the zombies were eventually pulled back, not their own efficiency: the incidence of battle psycho around them just shot up too high. Maybe if it hadn't been for that, we'd have got used to them eventually—God knows you get used to everything else in combat. But the zombies belonged to something beyond mere war.

They were so terribly, terribly unstirred by the prospect of dying again!

Well, everyone said the new-model zombies were a big improvement. They'd better be. A sling-shot might be one thin notch below an outright suicide patrol, but you need peak performance from every man aboard if it's going to complete its crazy mission, let alone get back. And it's an awful small ship and the men have to kind of get along with each other in very close quarters...

I heard feet, several pairs of them, rapping along the corridor. They stopped outside the door.

They waited. I waited. My skin began to prickle. And then I heard that uncertain shuffling sound. They were nervous about meeting me!

I walked over to the window and stared down at the drill field where old veterans whose minds and bodies were too worn out to be repaired taught fatigue-uniformed zombies how to use their newly conditioned reflexes in close-order drill. It made me remember a high-school athletic field years and years ago. The ancient barking commands drifted tinily up to me: *"Hup,* two, three, four. *Hup,* two, three, four." Only they weren't using *hup!,* but a newer, different word I couldn't quite catch.

And then, when the hands I'd clasped behind me had almost squeezed their blood back into my wrists, I heard the door open and four pairs of feet clatter into the room. The door closed and the four pairs of feet clicked to attention.

I turned around.

They were saluting me. Well, what the hell, I told myself, they were supposed to be saluting me, I was their commanding officer. I returned the salute, and four arms whipped down smartly.

I said, "At ease." They snapped their legs apart, arms behind them. I thought about it. I said, "Rest." They relaxed their bodies slightly. I thought about it again. I said, "Hell, men, sit down and let's meet each other."

They sprawled into chairs and I hitched myself up on the instructor's desk. We stared back and forth. Their faces were rigid, watchful; they weren't giving anything away.

I wondered what my face looked like. In spite of all the orientation lectures, in spite of all the preparation, I must admit that my first glimpse of them had hit me hard. They were glowing with health, normality, and hard purpose. But that wasn't it.

That wasn't it at all.

What was making me want to run out of the door, out of the building, was something I'd been schooling myself to expect since that last briefing session in Arizona Base. Four dead men were staring at me. Four very famous dead men.

The big man, lounging all over his chair, was Roger Grey, who had been killed over a year ago when he rammed his tiny scout ship up the forward jets of an Eoti flagship. The flagship had been split neatly in two. Almost every medal imaginable and the Solar Corona. Grey was to be my co-pilot.

The thin, alert man with the tight shock of black hair was Wang Hsi. He had been killed covering the retreat to the asteroids after the Great Breakthrough of 2143. According to the fantastic story the observers told, his ship had still been firing after it had been scrambled fully three times. Almost every medal imaginable and the Solar Corona. Wang was to be my engineer.

The darkish little fellow was Yussuf Lamehd. He'd been killed in a very minor skirmish off Titan, but when he died he was the most decorated man in the entire TAF. A *double* Solar Corona. Lamehd was to be my gunner.

The heavy one was Stanley Weinstein, the only prisoner of war ever to escape from the Eoti. There wasn't much left of him by the time he arrived on Mars, but the ship he came in was the first enemy craft that humanity could study intact. There was no Solar Corona in his day for him to receive even posthumously, but they're still naming military academies after that man. Weinstein was to be my astrogator.

Then I shook myself back to reality. These weren't the original heroes, probably didn't have even a particle of Roger Grey's blood or Wang Hsi's flesh upon their reconstructed bones. They were just excellent and very faithful copies, made to minute physical specifications that had been in the TAF medical files since Wang had been a cadet and Grey a mere recruit.

There were anywhere from a hundred to a thousand Yussuf Lamehds and Stanley Weinsteins, I had to remind myself—and they had all come off an assembly line a few floors down. "Only the brave deserve the future," was the Junkyard's motto, and it was currently trying to assure that future for them by duplicating in quantity any TAF man who went out with especial heroism. As I happened to know, there were one or two other categories who could expect similar honors, but the basic reasons behind the hero-models had little to do with morale.

First, there was that little gimmick of industrial efficiency again. If you're using mass-production methods, and the Junkyard was doing just that, it's plain common sense to turn out a few standardized models, rather than have everyone different—like the stuff an individual creative craftsman might come up with. Well, if you're using standardized models, why not use those that have positive and relatively pleasant associations bound up with their appearance rather than anonymous characters from the designers' drawing boards?

The second reason was almost more important and harder to define. According to the briefing officer, yesterday, there was a peculiar feeling—a superstitious feeling, you might almost say—that if you copied a hero's features, musculature, metabolism, and even his cortex wrinkles carefully enough, well, you might build yourself another hero. Of course, the original personality would never reappear—that had been produced by long years of a specific environment and dozens of other very slippery factors—but it was distinctly possible, the biotechs felt, that a modicum of clever courage resided in the body structure alone...

Well, at least these zombies didn't *look* like zombies!

On an impulse, I plucked the rolled sheaf of papers containing our travel orders out of my pocket, pretended to study it and let it slip suddenly through my fingers. As the outspread sheaf spiraled to the floor in front of me, Roger Grey reached out and caught it. He handed it back to me with the same kind of easy yet snappy grace. I took it, feeling good. It was the way he moved. I like to see a co-pilot move that way.

"Thanks," I said.

He just nodded.

I studied Yussuf Lamehd next. Yes, he had it too. Whatever it is that makes a first-class gunner, he had it. It's almost impossible to describe, but you walk into a bar in some rest area on Eros, say, and out of the five sling-shotters hunched over the blow-top table, you know right off which is the gunner. It's a sort of carefully bottled nervousness or a dead calm with a hair-trigger attachment. Whatever it is, it's what you need sitting over a firing button when you've completed the dodge, curve, and twist that's a sling-shot's attacking dash and you're barely within range of the target, already beginning your dodge, curve, and twist back to safety. Lamehd had it so strong that I'd have put money on him against any other gunner in the TAF I'd ever seen in action.

Astrogators and engineers are different. You've just got to see them work under pressure before you can rate them. But, even so, I liked the calm and confident manner with which Wang Hsi and Weinstein sat under my examination. And I liked them.

Right there I felt a hundred pounds slide off my chest. I felt relaxed for the first time in days. I really liked my crew, zombies or no. We'd make it.

I decided to tell them. "Men," I said, "I think we'll really get along. I think we've got the makings of a sweet, smooth sling-shot. You'll find me—"

And I stopped. That cold, slightly mocking look in their eyes. They way they had glanced at each other when I told them I thought we'd get along, glanced at each other and blown slightly through distended nostrils. I realized that none of them had said anything since they'd come in; they'd just been watching me, and their eyes weren't exactly warm.

I stopped and let myself take a long, deep breath. For the first time, it was occurring to me that I'd been worrying about just one end of the problem, and maybe the least important end. I'd been worrying about how I'd react to them and how much I'd be able to accept them as shipmates. They were zombies, after all. It had never occurred to me to wonder how they'd feel about me.

And there was evidently something very wrong in how they felt about me.

"What is it, men?" I asked. They all looked at me inquiringly. "What's on your minds?"

They kept looking at me. Weinstein pursed his lips and tilted his chair back and forth. It creaked. Nobody said anything.

I got off the desk and walked up and down in front of the classroom. They kept following me with their eyes.

"Grey," I said. "You look as if you've got a great big knot inside you. Want to tell me about it?"

"No, Commander," he said deliberately. "I don't want to tell you about it."

I grimaced. "If anyone wants to say anything—anything at all—it'll be off the record and completely off the record. Also for the moment we'll forget about such matters as rank and TAF regulations." I waited. "Wang? Lamehd? How about you, Weinstein?" They stared at me quietly. Weinstein's chair creaked back and forth.

It had me baffled. What kind of gripe could they have against me? They'd never met me before. But I knew one thing: I wasn't going to haul a crew nursing a subsurface grudge as unanimous as this aboard a sling-shot. I wasn't going to chop space with those eyes at my back. It would be more efficient for me to shove my head against an Irvingle lens and push the button.

"Listen," I told them. "I meant what I said about forgetting rank and TAF regulations. I want to run a happy ship and I have to know what's up. We'll be living, the five of us, in the tightest, most cramped conditions the mind of man has yet been able to devise; we'll be operating a tiny ship whose only purpose is to dodge at tremendous speed through the fire-power and screening devices of the larger enemy craft and deliver a single, crippling blast from a single oversize Irvingle. We've got to get along whether we like each other or not. If we don't get along, if there's any unspoken hostility getting in our way, the ship won't operate at maximum efficiency. And that way, we're through before we—"

"Commander," Weinstein said suddenly, his chair coming down upon the floor with a solid whack, "I'd like to ask you a question."

"Sure," I said and let out a gust of relief that was the size of a small hurricane. "Ask me anything."

"When you think about us, Commander, or when you talk about us, which word do you use?"

I looked at him and shook my head. "Eh?"

"When you talk about us, Commander, or when you think about us, do you call us zombies? Or do you call us blobs? That's what I'd like to know, Commander."

He'd spoken in such a polite, even tone that I was a long time in getting the full significance of it.

"Personally," said Roger Grey in a voice that was just a little less polite, a little less even, "personally, I think the Commander is the kind who refers to us as canned meat. Right, Commander?"

Yussuf Lamehd folded his arms across his chest and seemed to consider the issue very thoughtfully. "I think you're right, Rog. He's the canned-meat type. Definitely the canned-meat type."

"No," said Wang Hsi. "He doesn't use that kind of language. Zombies, yes; canned meat, no. You can observe from the way he talks that he wouldn't ever get mad enough to tell us to get back in the can. And I don't think he'd call us blobs very often. He's the kind of guy who'd buttonhole another sling-shot commander and tell him, 'Man, have I got the sweetest zombie crew you ever saw!' That's the way I figure him. Zombies."

And then they were sitting quietly staring at me again. And it wasn't mockery in their eyes. It was hatred.

I went back to the desk and sat down. The room was very still. From the yard, fifteen floors down, the marching commands drifted up. Where did they latch on to this, zombie-blob-canned meat stuff? They were none of them more than six months old; none of them had been outside the precincts of the Junkyard yet. Their conditioning, while mechanical and intensive, was supposed to be absolutely foolproof, producing hard, resilient, and entirely human minds, highly skilled in their various specialties and as far from any kind of imbalance as the latest psychiatric knowledge could push them. I knew they wouldn't have got it in their conditioning. Then *where*—

And then I heard it clearly for a moment. The word. The word that was being used down in the drill field instead of *Hup!* That strange, new word I hadn't been able to make out. Whoever was calling the cadence downstairs wasn't saying, "*Hup,* two, three, four."

He was saying, "*Blob,* two, three, four. *Blob,* two, three, four."

Wasn't that just like the TAF? I asked myself. For that matter, like any army anywhere anytime? Expending fortunes and the best minds producing a highly necessary product to exact specifications, and then, on the very first level of military use, doing something that might invalidate it completely. I was certain that the same officials who had been responsible for the attitude of the receptionist outside could have had nothing to do with the old, superannuated TAF drill-hacks putting their squads through their paces down below. I could imagine those narrow, nasty minds, as jealously proud of their prejudices as of their limited and painfully acquired military knowledge, giving these youngsters before me their first taste of barracks life, their first glimpse of the "outside." It was so stupid!

But was it? There was another way of looking at it, beyond the fact that only soldiers too old physically and too ossified mentally for any other duty could be spared for this place. And that was the simple pragmatism of army thinking. The fighting perimeters were places of abiding horror and agony, the forward combat zones in which sling-shots operated were even worse. If men or materiel were going to collapse out there, it could be very costly. Let the collapses occur as close to the rear echelons as possible.

Maybe it made sense, I thought. Maybe it was logical to make live men out of dead men's flesh (God knows humanity had reached the point where we had to have reinforcements from *somewhere!*) at enormous expense and with the kind of care usually associated with things like cotton wool and the most delicate watchmakers' tools; and then to turn around and subject them to the coarsest, ugliest environment possible, an environment that perverted their carefully instilled loyalty into hatred and their finely balanced psychological adjustment into neurotic sensitivity.

I didn't know if it was basically smart or dumb, or even if the problem had ever been really weighed as such by the upper, policy-making brass. All I could see was my own problem, and it looked awfully big to me. I thought of my attitude toward these men before getting them, and I felt pretty sick. But the memory gave me an idea.

"Hey, tell me something," I suggested. "What would you call me?"

They looked puzzled.

"You want to know what I call you," I explained. "Tell me first what you call people like me, people who are—who are *born*. You must have your own epithets."

Lamehd grinned so that his teeth showed a bright, mirthless white against his dark skin. "Realos," he said. "We call you people realos. Sometimes, realo trulos."

Then the rest spoke up. There were other names, lots of other names. They wanted me to hear them all. They interrupted each other; they spat the words out as if they were so many missiles; they glared at my face, as they spat them out, to see how much impact they had. Some of the nicknames were funny, some of them were rather nasty. I was particularly charmed by utie and wombat.

"All right," I said after a while. "Feel better?"

They were all breathing hard, but they felt better. I could tell it, and they knew it. The air in the room felt softer now.

"First off," I said, "I want you to notice that you are all big boys and as such, can take care of yourselves. From here on out, if we walk into a bar or a rec camp together and someone of approximately your rank says something that sounds like zombie to your acute ears, you are at liberty to walk up to him and start taking him apart—if you can. If he's of approximately my rank, in all probability, *I'll* do the taking apart, simply because I'm a very sensitive commander and don't like having my men deprecated. And any time you feel that I'm not treating you as human beings, one hundred percent, full solar citizenship and all that, I give you permission to come up to me and say, 'Now look *here*, you dirty utie, sir—'"

The four of them grinned. Warm grins. Then the grins faded away, very slowly, and the eyes grew cold again. They were looking at a man who was, after all, an outsider. I cursed.

"It's not as simple as that, Commander," Wang Hsi said, "unfortunately. You can call us hundred-percent human beings, but we're not. And anyone who wants to call us blobs or canned meat has a certain amount of right. Because we're not as good as—as you mother's sons, and we know it. And we'll never be that good. Never."

"I don't know about that," I blustered. "Why, some of your performance charts—"

"Performance charts, Commander," Wang Hsi said softly, "do not a human being make."

On his right, Weinstein gave a nod, thought a bit, and added: "Nor groups of men a race."

I knew where we were going now. And I wanted to smash my way out of that room, down the elevator, and out of the building before anybody said another word. *This is it,* I told myself: *here we are, boy, here we are.* I found myself squirming from corner to corner of the desk; I gave up, got off it, and began walking again.

Wang Hsi wouldn't let go. I should have known he wouldn't. "Soldier surrogates," he went on, squinting as if he were taking a close look at the phrase for the first time. "Soldier surrogates, but not soldiers. We're not soldiers, because soldiers are men. And we, Commander, are not men."

There was silence for a moment, then a tremendous blast of sound boiled out of my mouth. "And what makes you think that you're *not* men?"

Wang Hsi was looking at me with astonishment, but his reply was still soft and calm. "You know why. You've seen our specifications, Commander. We're not men, real men, because we can't reproduce ourselves."

I forced myself to sit down again and carefully placed my shaking hands over my knees.

"We're as sterile," I heard Yussuf Lamehd say, "as boiling water."

"There have been lots of men," I began, "who have been—"

"This isn't a matter of lots of men," Weinstein broke in. "This is a matter of all— all of *us.*"

"Blobs thou art," Wang Hsi murmured. "And to blobs returneth. They might have given at least a few of us a chance. The kids mightn't have turned out so bad."

Roger Grey slammed his huge hand down on the arm of his chair. "That's just the point, Wang," he said savagely. "The kids might have turned out good—too good. Our kids might have turned out to be better than their kids—and where would that leave the proud and cocky, the goddam name-calling, the realo trulo human race?"

I sat staring at them once more, but now I was seeing a different picture. I wasn't seeing conveyor belts moving along slowly covered with human tissues and organs on which earnest biotechs performed their individual tasks. I wasn't seeing a room filled with dozens of adult male bodies suspended in nutrient solution, each body connected to a conditioning machine which day and night clacked out whatever minimum information was necessary for the body to take the place of a man in the bloodiest part of the fighting perimeter.

This time, I saw a barracks filled with heroes, many of them in duplicate and trip-licate. And they were sitting around griping, as men will in any barracks on any planet, whether they look like heroes or no. But their gripes concerned humiliations deeper than any soldiers had hitherto known—humiliations as basic as the fabric of human personality.

"You believe, then," and despite the sweat on my face, my voice was gentle, "that the reproductive power was deliberately withheld?"

Weinstein scowled. "Now, Commander. Please. No bedtime stories."

"Doesn't it occur to you at all that the whole problem of our species at the mo-ment is reproduction? Believe me, men, that's all you hear about on the outside. Grammar-school debating teams kick current reproductive issues back and forth in the district medal competitions; every month scholars in archaeology and the botany of fungi come out with books about it from their own special angle. Everyone knows that if we don't lick the reproduction problem, the Eoti are going to lick us. Do you seriously think under such circumstances, the reproductive powers of *anyone* would be intentionally impaired?"

"What do a few male blobs matter, more or less?" Grey demanded. "According to the latest news bulletins, sperm bank deposits are at their highest point in five years. They don't need us."

"Commander," Wang Hsi pointed his triangular chin at me. "Let me ask you a few questions in your turn. Do you honestly expect us to believe that a science capable of reconstructing a living, highly effective human body with a complex digestive sys-tem and a most delicate nervous system, all this out of dead and decaying bits of protoplasm, is incapable of reconstructing the germ plasm in one single, solitary case?"

"You have to believe it," I told him. "Because it's so."

Wang sat back, and so did the other three. They stopped looking at me.

"Haven't you ever heard it said," I pleaded with them, "that the germ plasm is more essentially the individual than any other part of him? That some whimsical biolo-gists take the attitude that our human bodies and all bodies are merely vehicles, or hosts, by means of which our germ plasm reproduces itself? It's the most complex biotechnical riddle we have! Believe me, men," I added passionately, "when I say that biology has not yet solved the germ-plasm problem, I'm telling the truth. I know."

That got them.

"Look," I said. "We have one thing in common with the Eoti whom we're fighting. Insects and warm-blooded animals differ prodigiously. But only among the com-munity-building insects and the community-building men are there individuals who, while taking no part personally in the reproductive chain, are of fundamental importance to their species. For example, you might have a female nursery school teacher who is barren but who is of unquestionable value in shaping the personali-ties and even physiques of children in her care."

"Fourth Orientation Lecture for Soldier Surrogates," Weinstein said in a dry voice. "He got it right out of the book."

"I've been wounded," I said, "I've been seriously wounded fifteen times." I stood before them and began rolling up my right sleeve. It was soaked with my perspiration.

"We can tell you've been wounded, Commander," Lamehd pointed out uncertainly. "We can tell from your medals. You don't have to—"

"And every time I was wounded, they repaired me good as new. Better. Look at that arm." I flexed it for them. "Before it was burned off in a small razzle six years ago, I could never build up a muscle that big. It's a better arm they built on the stump, and, believe me, my reflexes never had it so good."

"What did you mean," Wang Hsi started to ask me, "when you said before—"

"Fifteen times I was wounded," my voice drowned him out, "and fourteen times the wound was repaired. The fifteenth time— *The fifteenth time*— Well, the fifteenth time it wasn't a wound they could repair. They couldn't help me one little bit the fifteenth time."

Roger Grey opened his mouth,

"Fortunately," I whispered, "it wasn't a wound that showed."

Weinstein started to ask me something, decided against it and sat back. But I told him what he wanted to know.

"A nucleonic howitzer. The way it was figured later, it had been a defective shell. Bad enough to kill half the men on our second-class cruiser. I wasn't killed, but I was in range of the back-blast."

"That back-blast," Lamehd was figuring it out quickly in his mind. "That back-blast will sterilize anybody for two hundred feet. Unless you're wearing—"

"And I wasn't." I had stopped sweating. It was over. My crazy little precious secret was out. I took a deep breath. "So you see—well, anyway, I *know* they haven't solved that problem yet."

Roger Grey stood up and said, "Hey." He held out his hand. I shook it. It felt like any normal guy's hand. Stronger maybe.

"Sling-shot personnel," I went on, "are all volunteers. Except for two categories: the commanders and soldier surrogates."

"Figuring, I guess," Weinstein asked, "that the human race can spare them most easily?"

"Right," I said. "Figuring that the human race can spare them most easily." He nodded.

"Well, I'll be damned," Yussuf Lamehd laughed as he got up and shook my hand, too. "Welcome to our city."

"Thanks," I said. "*Son.*"

He seemed puzzled at the emphasis.

"That's the rest of it," I explained. "Never got married and was too busy getting drunk and tearing up the pavement on my leaves to visit a sperm bank."

"Oho," Weinstein said, and gestured at the walls with a thick thumb. "So this is it."

"That's right: this is it. The Family. The only one I'll ever have. I've got almost enough of these—" I tapped my medals "—to rate replacement. As a sling-shot commander, I'm sure of it."

"All you don't know yet," Lamehd pointed out, "is how high a percentage of re-placement will be apportioned to your memory. That depends on how many more of these chest decorations you collect before you become an—ah, should I say *raw material?*"

"Yeah," I said, feeling crazily light and easy and relaxed. I'd got it all out and I didn't feel whipped any more by a billion years of reproduction and evolution. And I'd been going to do a morale job on them! "*Say* raw material, Lamehd."

"Well, boys," he went on, "it seems to me we want the commander to get a lot more fruit salad. He's a nice guy and there should be more of him in the club."

They were all standing around me now, Weinstein, Lamehd, Grey, Wang Hsi. They looked real friendly and real capable. I began to feel we were going to have one of the best sling-shots in— What did I mean *one* of the best? *The* best, mister, *the* best.

"Okay," said Grey. "Wherever and whenever you want to, you start leading us—*Pop.*"

AFTERWORD

There's not much I have to say about "Down Among the Dead Men." Horace L. Gold said he needed a novelette almost immediately for *Galaxy,* and most of all he wanted a space opera.

"You've never written a space opera, a real bangety-bang space opera," he said. "Why not?"

"I don't like them," I told him. "I don't like to read them, and I don't like to write them. Science-fiction westerns: they're kill-'em-on-Mercury-instead-of-Montana."

Well, he explained, if—in spite of my bullshit fastidiousness—I managed to write one in the next week, he would give me a large bonus on the word rate and voucher the check through immediately.

As always, in those days, I could very much use the money; so I agreed to think about it. To my surprise, by the time I got home, I had an idea. I began writing.

It went fast. I completed the piece in a weekend.

Horace loved it, bought it. "It's a real space opera," he marveled, "but all the important action takes place completely offstage. A *tour de force!*"

I rarely agreed with Horace, but I told him I was thoroughly with him on his last sentence.

The point being that, despite its disreputable origin, I have grown to be very fond of this story. I'm almost astonished to say that now I would rank it among my best.

And it *is* a space opera. Of a kind, anyway.

WRITTEN 1954——PUBLISHED 1954

The Future

TIME IN ADVANCE

Twenty minutes after the convict ship landed at the New York Spaceport, reporters were allowed aboard. They came boiling up the main corridor, pushing against the heavily armed guards who were conducting them, the feature-story men and byline columnists in the lead, the TV people with their portable but still-heavy equipment cursing along behind.

As they went, they passed little groups of spacemen in the black-and-red uniform of the Interstellar Prison Service walking rapidly in the opposite direction, on their way to enjoy five days of planetside leave before the ship roared away once more with a new cargo of convicts.

The impatient journalists barely glanced at these drab personalities who were spending their lives in a continuous shuttle from one end of the galaxy to the other. After all, the life and adventures of an IPS man had been done thousands of times, done to death. The big story lay ahead.

In the very belly of the ship, the guards slid apart two enormous sliding doors—and quickly stepped aside to avoid being trampled. The reporters almost flung themselves against the iron bars that ran from floor to ceiling and completely shut off the great prison chamber. Their eager, darting stares were met with at most a few curious glances from the men in coarse gray suits who lay or sat in the tiers of bunks that rose in row after sternly functional row all the way down the cargo hold. Each man clutched—and some caressed—a small package neatly wrapped in plain brown paper.

The chief guard ambled up on the other side of the bars, picking the morning's breakfast out of his front teeth. "Hi, boys," he said. "Who're you looking for—as if I didn't know?"

One of the older, more famous columnists held the palm of his hand up warningly. "Look, Anderson: no games. The ship's been almost a half-hour late in landing and we were stalled for fifteen minutes at the gangplank. Now where the hell are they?"

Anderson watched the TV crews shoulder a place for themselves and their equipment right up to the barrier. He tugged a last bit of food out of one of his molars.

"Ghouls," he muttered. "A bunch of grave-happy, funeral-hungry ghouls." Then he hefted his club experimentally a couple of times and clattered it back and forth against the bars. "Crandall!" he bellowed. "Henck! Front and center!"

The cry was picked up by the guards strolling about, steadily, measuredly, clubtwirlingly, inside the prison pen. "Crandall! Henck! Front and center!" It went ricocheting authoritatively up and down the tremendous curved walls. "Crandall! Henck! Front and center!"

Nicholas Crandall sat up cross-legged in his bunk on the fifth tier and grimaced. He had been dozing and now he rubbed a hand across his eyes to erase the sleep. There were three parallel scars across the back of his hand, old and brown and straight scars such as an animal's claws might rake out. There was also a curious zigzag scar just above his eyes that had a more reddish novelty. And there was a tiny, perfectly round hole in the middle of his left ear which, after coming fully awake, he scratched in annoyance.

"Reception committee," he grumbled. "Might have known. Same old goddam Earth as ever."

He flipped over on his stomach and reached down to pat the face of the little man snoring on the bunk immediately under him. "Otto," he called. "Blotto Otto—up and at 'em! They want us."

Henck immediately sat up in the same cross-legged fashion, even before his eyes had opened. His right hand went to his throat where there was a little network of zigzag scars of the same color and size as the one Crandall had on his forehead. The hand was missing an index and forefinger.

"Henck here, sir," he said thickly, then shook his head and stared up at Crandall. "Oh—Nick. What's up?"

"We've arrived, Blotto Otto," the taller man said from the bunk above. "We're on Earth and they're getting our discharges ready. In about half an hour, you'll be able to wrap that tongue of yours around as much brandy, beer, vodka and rotgut whiskey as you can pay for. No more prison-brew, no more raisin-jack from a tin can under the bed, Blotto Otto."

Henck grunted and flopped down on his back again. "In half an hour, but not now, so why did you have to go and wake me up? What do you take me for, some dewy, post-crime, petty-larceny kid, sweating out my discharge with my eyes open and my gut wriggling? Hey, Nick, I was dreaming of a new way to get Elsa, a brand-new, really ugly way."

"The screws are in an uproar," Crandall told him, still in a low, patient voice. "Hear them? They want us, you and me."

Henck sat up again, listened a moment, and nodded. "Why is it," he asked, "that only space-screws have voices like that?"

"It's a requirement of the service," Crandall assured him. "You've got to be at least a minimum height, have a minimum education and with a minimum nasty voice of just the right ear-splitting quality before you can get to be a space-screw. Otherwise, no matter how vicious a personality you have, you are just plain out of luck and have to stay behind on Earth and go on getting your kicks by running down slowpoke copters driven by old ladies."

A guard stopped below, banged angrily at one of the metal posts that supported their tier of bunks. "Crandall! Henck! You're still convicts, don't you forget that! If you don't front-and-center in a double-time hurry, I'll climb up there and work you over once more for old-time's sake!"

"Yes, *sir!* Coming, *sir!*" they said in immediate, mumbling unison and began climbing down from bunk to bunk, each still clutching the brown-paper package that contained the clothes they had once worn as free men and would shortly be allowed to wear again.

"Listen, Otto." Crandall leaned down as they climbed and brought his lips close to the little man's ear in the rapid-fire, extremely low-pitched prison whisper. "They're taking us to meet the television and news boys. We're going to be asked a lot of questions. One thing you want to be sure to keep your lip buttoned about—"

"Television and news? Why us? What do they want with us?"

"Because we're celebrities, knockhead! We've seen it through for the big rap and come out on the other side. How many men do you think have made it? But *listen,* will you? If they ask you who it is you're after, you just shut up and smile. You don't answer that question. Got that? You don't tell them whose murder you were sentenced for, no matter what they say. They can't make you. That's the law."

Henck paused a moment, one and a half bunks from the floor. "But, Nick, *Elsa* knows! I told her that day, just before I turned myself in. She knows I wouldn't take a murder rap for anyone but her!"

"She knows, she knows, of *course* she knows!" Crandall swore briefly and almost inaudibly. "But she can't *prove* it, you goddam human blotter! Once you say so in public, though, she's entitled to arm herself and shoot you down on sight—pleading self-defense. And till you say so, she can't; she's still your poor wife whom you've promised to love, honor and cherish. As far as the world is concerned—"

The guard reached up with his club and jolted them both angrily across the back. They dropped to the floor and cringed as he snarled over them: "Did I say you could have a talk-party? *Did I?* If we have any time left before you get your discharge, I'm taking you cuties into the guard-room for one last big going-over. Now pick them up and put them down!"

They scuttled in front of him obediently, like a pair of chickens before a snapping collie. At the barred gate near the end of the prison hold, he saluted and said: "Pre-criminals Nicholas Crandall and Otto Henck, sir."

Chief Guard Anderson wiped the salute back at him carelessly. "These gentlemen want to ask you fellas a couple of questions. Won't hurt you to answer. That's all, O'Brien."

His voice was very jovial. He was wearing a big, gentle, half-moon smile. As the subordinate guard saluted and moved away, Crandall let his mind regurgitate memories of Anderson all through this month-long trip from Proxima Centauri. Anderson nodding thoughtfully as that poor Minelli—Steve Minelli, hadn't that been his name?—was made to run through a gauntlet of club-swinging guards for going to the toilet without permission. Anderson chuckling just a moment before he'd kicked a gray-headed convict in the groin for talking on the chow-line. Anderson—

Well, the guy had guts, anyway, knowing that his ship carried two pre-criminals who had served out a murder sentence. But he probably also knew that they wouldn't waste the murder on him, however viciously he acted. A man doesn't volunteer for a hitch in hell just so he can knock off one of the devils.

"Do we have to answer these questions, sir?" Crandall asked cautiously, tentatively.

The chief guard's smile lost the tiniest bit of its curvature. "I said it wouldn't hurt you, didn't I? But other things might. They *still* might, Crandall. I'd like to do these gentlemen from the press a favor, so you be nice and cooperative, eh?" He gestured with his chin, ever so slightly, in the direction of the guard-room and hefted his club a bit.

"Yes, sir," Crandall said, while Henck nodded violently. "We'll be cooperative, sir."

Dammit, he thought, *if only I didn't have such a use for that murder! Let's keep remembering Stephanson, boy, no one but Stephanson! Not Anderson, not O'Brien, not anybody else: the name under discussion is Frederick Stoddard Stephanson!*

While the television men on the other side of the bars were fussing their equipment into position, the two convicts answered the preliminary, inevitable questions of the feature writers:

"How does it feel to be back?"

"Fine, just fine."

"What's the first thing you're going to do when you get your discharge?"

"Eat a good meal." (From Crandall.)

"Get roaring drunk." (From Henck.)

"Careful you don't wind up right behind bars again as a post-criminal." (From one of the feature writers.) A good-natured laugh in which all of them, the newsmen, Chief Guard Anderson, and Crandall and Henck, participated.

"How were you treated while you were prisoners?"

"Oh, pretty good." (From both of them, concurrent with a thoughtful glance at Anderson's club.)

"Either of you care to tell us who you're going to murder?"

(Silence.)

"Either of you changed your mind and decided not to commit the murder?"

(Crandall looked thoughtfully up, while Henck looked thoughtfully down.) Another general laugh, a bit more uneasy this time, Crandall and Henck not participating.

"All right, we're set. Look this way, please," the television announcer broke in. "And smile, men—let's have a really *big* smile."

Crandall and Henck dutifully emitted big smiles, which made three smiles, for Anderson had moved into the cheerful little group.

The two cameras shot out of the grasp of their technicians, one hovering over them, one moving restlessly before their faces, both controlled, at a distance, by the little box of switches in the cameramen's hands. A red bulb in the nose of one of the cameras lit up.

"Here we are, ladies and gentlemen of the television audience," the announcer exuded in a lavish voice. "We are on board the convict ship *Jean Valjean*, which has just landed at the New York Spaceport. We are here to meet two men—two of the rare men who have managed to serve all of a voluntary sentence for murder and thus are legally entitled to commit one murder apiece.

"In just a few moments, they will be discharged after having served out seven full years on the convict planets—and they will be free to kill any man or woman in the Solar System with absolutely no fear of any kind of retribution. Take a good look at them, ladies and gentlemen of the television audience—it might be you they are after!"

After this cheering thought, the announcer let a moment or two elapse while the cameras let their lenses stare at the two men in prison gray. Then he stepped into range himself and addressed the smaller man.

"What is your name, sir?" he asked.

"Pre-criminal Otto Henck, 525514," Blotto Otto responded automatically, though not able to repress a bit of a start at the *sir*.

"How does it feel to be back?"

"Fine, just fine."

"What's the first thing you're going to do when you get your discharge?"

Henck hesitated, then said, "Eat a good meal," after a shy look at Crandall.

"How were you treated while you were a prisoner?"

"Oh, pretty good. As good as you could expect."

"As good as a criminal could expect, eh? Although you're not really a criminal yet, are you? You're a pre-criminal."

Henck smiled as if this were the first time he was hearing the term. "That's right, sir. I'm a pre-criminal."

"Want to tell the audience who the person is you're going to become a criminal for?"

Henck looked reproachfully at the announcer, who chuckled throatily—and alone.

"Or if you've changed your mind about him or her?" There was a pause. Then the announcer said a little nervously: "You've served seven years on danger-filled, alien planets, preparing them for human colonization. That's the maximum sentence the law allows, isn't it?"

"That's right, sir. With the pre-criminal discount for serving the sentence in advance, seven years is the most you can get for murder."

"Bet you're glad we're not back in the days of capital punishment, eh? That would make the whole thing impractical, wouldn't it? Now, Mr. Henck—or pre-criminal Henck, I guess I should still call you—suppose you tell the ladies and gentlemen of our television audience: What was the most horrifying experience you had while you were serving your sentence?"

"Well," Otto Henck considered carefully. "About the worst of the lot, I guess, was the time on Antares VIII, the second prison camp I was in, when the big wasps started to spawn. They got a wasp on Antares VIII, see, that's about a hundred times the size of—"

"Is that how you lost two fingers on your right hand?"

Henck brought his hand up and studied it for a moment. "No. The forefinger—I lost the forefinger on Rigel XII. We were building the first prison camp on the planet and I dug up a funny kind of red rock that had all sorts of little bumps on it. I poked it, kind of—you know, just to see how hard it was or something—and the tip of my finger disappeared. *Pow*—just like that. Later on, the whole finger got infected and the medics had to cut it off.

"It turned out I was lucky, though; some of the men—the convicts, I mean—ran into bigger rocks than the one I found. Those guys lost arms, legs—one guy even got swallowed whole. They weren't really rocks, see. They were alive—they were alive and hungry! Rigel XII was lousy with them. The middle finger—I lost the middle finger in a dumb kind of accident on board ship while we were being moved to—"

The announcer nodded intelligently, cleared his throat and said: "But those wasps, those giant wasps on Antares VIII—they were the worst?"

Blotto Otto blinked at him for a moment before he found the conversation again.

"Oh. They sure were! They were used to laying their eggs in a kind of monkey they have on Antares VIII, see? It was real rough on the monkey, but that's how the baby wasps got their food while they were growing up. Well, we get out there, and it turns out that the wasps can't see any difference between those Antares monkeys and human beings. First thing you know, guys start collapsing all over the place and when they're taken to the dispensary for an X-ray, the medics see that they're completely crammed—"

"Thank you very much, Mr. Henck, but Herkimer's Wasp has already been seen by and described to our audience at least three times in the past on the Interstellar Travelogue, which is carried by this network, as you ladies and gentlemen no doubt remember, on Wednesday evening from seven to seven-thirty PM terrestrial standard time. And now, Mr. Crandall, let me ask you, sir: How does it feel to be back?"

Crandall stepped up and was put through almost exactly the same verbal paces as his fellow prisoner.

There was one major difference. The announcer asked him if he expected to find Earth much changed. Crandall started to shrug, then abruptly relaxed and grinned. He was careful to make the grin an extremely wide one, exposing a maximum of tooth and a minimum of mirth.

"There's one big change I can see already," he said. "The way those cameras float around and are controlled from a little switch-box in the cameraman's hand. That gimmick wasn't around the day I left. Whoever invented it must have been pretty clever."

"Oh, yes?" The announcer glanced briefly backward. "You mean the Stephanson Remote Control Switch? It was invented by Frederick Stoddard Stephanson about five years ago— Was it five years, Don?"

"Six years," said the cameraman. "Went on the market five years ago."

"It was *invented* six years ago," the announcer translated. "It went on the market *five* years ago."

Crandall nodded. "Well, this Frederick Stoddard Stephanson must be a clever man, a very clever man." And he grinned again into the cameras. *Look at my teeth,* he thought to himself. *I know you're watching, Freddy. Look at my teeth and shiver.*

The announcer seemed a bit disconcerted. "Yes," he said. "Exactly. Now, Mr. Crandall, what would you describe as the most horrifying experience in your entire…"

After the TV men had rolled up their equipment and departed, the two pre-criminals were subjected to a final barrage of questions from the feature writers and columnists in search of odd shreds of color.

"What about the women in your life?" "What books, what hobbies, what amusements filled your time?" "Did you find out that there are no atheists on convict planets?" "If you had the whole thing to do over again—"

As he answered, drably, courteously, Nicholas Crandall was thinking about Frederick Stoddard Stephanson seated in front of his luxurious wall-size television set.

Would Stephanson have clicked it off by now? Would he be sitting there, staring at the blank screen, pondering the plans of the man who had outlived odds estimated at ten thousand to one and returned after seven full, unbelievable years in the prison camps of four insane planets?

Would Stephanson be examining his blaster with sucked-in lips—the blaster that he might use only in an open-and-shut situation of self-defense? Otherwise, he would incur the full post-criminal sentence for murder, which, without the fifty percent discount for punishment voluntarily undergone in advance of the crime, was as much as fourteen years in the many-pronged hell from which Crandall had just returned.

Or would Stephanson be sitting, slumped in an expensive bubblechair, glumly watching a still-active screen, frightened out of his wits but still unable to tear himself away from the well-organized program the network had no doubt built around the return of two—count 'em: two!—homicidal pre-criminals?

At the moment, in all probability, the screen was showing an interview with some Earthside official of the Interstellar Prison Service, an expansive public relations character who had learned to talk in sociology.

"Tell me, Mr. Public Relations," the announcer would ask (a different announcer, more serious, more intellectual), "how often do pre-criminals serve out a sentence for murder and return?"

"According to statistics"—a rustle of papers at this point and a penetrating glance downward—"according to statistics, we may expect a man who has served a full sentence for murder, with the fifty percent pre-criminal discount, to return only once in 11.7 years on the average."

"You would say, then, wouldn't you, Mr. Public Relations, that the return of two such men on the same day is a rather unusual situation?"

"*Highly* unusual, or you television fellows wouldn't be in such a fuss over it." A thick chuckle here, which the announcer dutifully echoes.

"And what, Mr. Public Relations, happens to the others who don't return?"

A large, well-fed hand gestures urbanely. "They get killed. Or they give up. Those are the only two alternatives. Seven years is a long time to spend on those convict planets. The work schedule isn't for sissies and neither are the life-forms they encounter—the big man-eating ones as well as the small virus-sized types.

"That's why prison guards get such high salaries and such long leaves. In a sense, you know, we haven't really abolished capital punishment; we've substituted a socially useful form of Russian Roulette for it. Any man who commits or pre-commits one of a group of particularly reprehensible crimes is sent off to a planet where his services will benefit humanity and where he's forced to take his chances on coming back in one piece, if at all. The more serious the crime, the longer the sentence and, therefore, the more remote the chances."

"I see. Now, Mr. Public Relations, you say they either get killed or they give up. Would you explain to the audience, if you please, just how they give up and what happens if they do?"

Here a sitting-back in the chair, a locking of pudgy fingers over paunch. "You see, any pre-criminal may apply to his warden for immediate abrogation of sentence. It is just a matter of filling out the necessary forms. He's pulled off work detail right then and he is sent home on the very next ship out of the place. The catch is this: Every bit of time he's served up to that point is canceled—he gets nothing for it.

"If he commits an actual crime after being freed, he has to serve the full sentence. If he wants to be committed as a pre-criminal again, he has to start serving the sentence, with the discount, from the beginning. Three out of every four pre-criminals apply for abrogation of sentence in their very first year. You get a bellyful fast in those places."

"I guess you certainly do," agrees the announcer. "What about the discount, Mr. Public Relations? Aren't there people who feel that's offering the pre-criminal too much inducement?"

The barest grimace of anger flows across the sleek face, to be succeeded by a warm, contemptuous smile. "Those are people, I'm afraid, who, however well-intentioned, are not well versed in the facts of modern criminology and penology. We don't want to discourage pre-criminals; we want to *encourage* them to turn themselves in.

"Remember what I said about three out of four applying for abrogation of sentence in their very first year? Now these are individuals who were sensible enough to try to get a discount on their sentence. Are they likely to be foolish enough to risk twice as much when they have found out conclusively they can't stand a bare twelve months of it? Not to mention what they have discovered about the value of human life, the necessity for social cooperation, and the general desirability of civilized processes on those worlds where simple survival is practically a matter of a sweepstakes ticket.

"The man who doesn't apply for abrogation of sentence? Well, he has that much more time to let the desire to commit the crime go cold—and that much greater likelihood of getting killed with nothing to show for it. Therefore, so few pre-criminals in *any* of the categories return to tell the tale and do the deed that the social profit is absolutely enormous! Let me give you a few figures.

"Using the Lazarus Scale, it has been estimated that the decline in premeditated homicides alone, since the institution of the pre-criminal discount, has been forty-one percent on Earth, thirty-three and a third percent on Venus, twenty-seven percent—"

Cold comfort, chillingly cold comfort, that would be to Stephanson, Nicholas Crandall reflected pleasurably, those forty-one percents and thirty-three and a third percents. Crandall's was the balancing statistic: the man who wanted to murder, and for good and sufficient cause, one Frederick Stoddard Stephanson. He was a leftover fraction on a page of reductions and cancellations—he had returned, astonishingly, unbelievably, after seven years to collect the merchandise for which he had paid in advance.

He and Henck. Two ridiculously long long-shots. Henck's wife Elsa—was she, too, sitting in a kind of bird-hypnotized-by-a-snake fashion before her television set, hoping dimly and desperately that some comment of the Interstellar Prison Service official would show her how to evade her fate, how to get out from under the ridiculously rare disaster that was about to happen to her?

Well, Elsa was Blotto Otto's affair. Let him enjoy it in his own way; he'd paid enough for the privilege. But Stephanson was Crandall's.

Oh, let the arrogant bean-pole sweat, he prayed. *Let me take my time and let him sweat!*

The newsman kept squeezing them for story angles until a loudspeaker in the overhead suddenly cleared its diaphragm and announced:

"Prisoners, prepare for discharge! You will proceed to the ship warden's office in groups of ten, as your name is called. Convict ship discipline will be maintained throughout. Arthur, Augluk, Crandall, Ferrara, Fu-Yen, Garfinkel, Gomez, Graham, Henck—"

A half hour later, they were walking down the main corridor of the ship in their civilian clothes. They showed their discharges to the guard at the gangplank, smiled still cringingly back at Anderson, who called from a porthole, "Hey, fellas, come back soon!" and trotted down the incline to the surface of a planet they had not seen for seven agonizing and horror-crowded years.

There were a few reporters and photographers still waiting for them, and one TV crew which had been left behind to let the world see how they looked at the moment of freedom.

Questions, more questions to answer, which they could afford to be brusque about, although brusqueness to any but fellow prisoners still came hard.

Fortunately, the newsmen got interested in another pre-criminal who was with them. Fu-Yen had completed the discounted sentence of two years for aggravated assault and battery. He had also lost both arms and one leg to a corrosive moss on Procyon III just before the end of his term and came limping down the gangplank on one real and one artificial leg, unable to grasp the hand rails.

As he was being asked, with a good deal of interest, just how he intended to commit simple assault and battery, let alone the serious kind, with his present limited resources, Crandall nudged Henck and they climbed quickly into one of the many hovering gyrocabs. They told the driver to take them to a bar—any quiet bar—in the city.

Blotto Otto almost went to pieces under the impact of actual free choice. "I can't do it," he whispered. "Nick, there's just too damn much to drink!"

Crandall settled it by ordering for him. "Two double scotches," he told the waitress. "Nothing else."

When the scotch came, Blotto Otto stared at it with the kind of affectionate and wistful astonishment a man might show toward an adolescent son whom he saw last as a babe in arms. He put out a gingerly trembling hand.

"Here's death to our enemies," Crandall said, and tossed his down. He watched Otto sip slowly and carefully, tasting each individual drop.

"You'd better take it easy," he warned. "Elsa might have no more trouble from you than bringing flowers every visiting day to the alcoholic ward."

"No fear," Blotto Otto growled into his empty glass. "I was weaned on this stuff. And, anyway, it's the last drink I have until I dump her. That's the way I've been figuring it, Nick: one drink to celebrate, then Elsa. I didn't go through those seven years to mess myself up at the payoff."

He set the glass down. "Seven years in one steaming hell after another. And before that, twelve years with Elsa. Twelve years with her pulling every dirty trick in the book on me, laughing in my face, telling me she was my wife and had me legally where she wanted me, that I was gonna support her the way she wanted to be supported and I was gonna like it. And if I dared to get off my knees and stand on my hind legs, *pow*, she found a way to get me arrested.

"The weeks I spent in the cooler, in the workhouse, until Elsa would tell the judge maybe I'd learned my lesson, she was willing to give me one more chance! And me begging for a divorce on my knees—hell, on my belly!—no children, she's able-bodied, she's young, and her laughing in my face. When she wanted me in the cooler, see, then she's crying in front of the judge; but when we're alone, she's always laughing her head off to see me squirm.

"I supported her, Nick. Honest, I gave her almost every cent I made, but that wasn't enough. She liked to see me squirm; she *told* me she did. Well, who's squirming now?" He grunted deep in his throat. "Marriage—it's for chumps!"

Crandall looked out of the open window he was sitting against, down through the dizzy, busy levels of Metropolitan New York.

"Maybe it is," he said thoughtfully. "I wouldn't know. My marriage was good while it lasted, five years of it. Then, all of a sudden, it wasn't good any more, just so much rancid butter."

"At least she gave you a divorce," said Henck. "She didn't take you."

"Oh, Polly wasn't the kind of girl to take anyone. A little mixed up, but maybe no more than I was. Pretty Polly, I called her; Big Nick, she called me. The starlight faded and so did I, I guess. I was still knocking myself out then trying to make a go out of the wholesale electronics business with Irv. Anyone could tell I wasn't cut out to be a millionaire. Maybe that was it. Anyway, Polly wanted out and I gave it to her. We parted friends. I wonder, every once in a while, what she's—"

There was a slight splashy noise, like a seal's flipper making a gesture in the water. Crandall's eyes came back to the table a moment after the green, melonlike ball had hit it. And, at the same instant, Henck's hand had swept the ball up and hurled it through the window. The long, green threads streamed out of the ball, but by then it was falling down the side of the enormous building and the threads found no living flesh to take root in.

From the corner of his eye, Crandall had seen a man bolt out of the bar. By the way people kept looking back and forth fearfully from their table to the open doorway, he deduced that the man had thrown it. Evidently Stephanson had thought it worthwhile to have Crandall followed and neutralized.

Blotto Otto saw no point in preening over his reflexes. The two of them had learned to move fast a long time ago—over a lot of dead bodies. "A Venusian dandelion bomb," he observed. "Well, at least the guy doesn't want to kill you, Nick. He just wants to cripple you."

"That would be Stephanson's style," Crandall agreed, as they paid their check and walked past the faces which were just now beginning to turn white. "He'd never do it himself. He'd hire a bully-boy. And he'd do the hiring through an intermediary just in case the bully-boy ever got caught and blabbed. But that still wouldn't be safe enough: he wouldn't want to risk a post-criminal murder charge.

"A dose of Venusian dandelion, he'd figure, and he wouldn't have to worry about me for the rest of my life. He might even come to visit me in the home for incurables— like the way he sent me a card every Christmas of my sentence. Always the same message: 'Still mad? Love, Freddy.'"

"Quite a guy, this Stephanson," Blotto Otto said, peering around the entrance carefully before stepping out of the bar and onto the fifteenth-level walkway.

"Yeah, quite a guy. He's got the world by the tail and every once in a while, just for fun, he twists the tail. I learned how he operated when we were roommates way back in college, but do you think that did me any good? I ran into him just when that wholesale electronics business with Irv was really falling apart, about two years after I broke up with Polly.

"I was feeling blue and I wanted to talk to someone, so I told him all about how my partner was a penny-watcher and I was a big dreamer, and how between us we were turning a possible nice small business into a definite big bankruptcy. And then I got onto this remote-control switch I'd been fooling around with and how I wished I had time to develop it."

Blotto Otto kept glancing around uneasily, not from dread of another assassin, but out of the unexpected sensation of doing so much walking of his own free will. Several passersby turned around to have another stare at their out-of-fashion knee-length tunics.

"So there I was," Crandall went on. "I was a fool, I know, but take my word, Otto, you have no idea how persuasive and friendly a guy like Freddy Stephanson can be. He tells me he has this house in the country he isn't using right now and there's a complete electronics lab in the basement. It's all mine, if I want it, as long as I want it, starting next week; all I have to worry about is feeding myself. And he doesn't want any rent or anything—it's for old time's sake and because he wants to see me do something really big in the world.

"How smart could I be with a con artist like that? It wasn't till two years later that I realized he must have had the electronics lab installed the same week I was asking Irv to buy me out of the business for a couple of hundred credits. After all, what would Stephanson, the owner of a brokerage firm, be doing with an electronics lab of his own? But who figures such things when an old roommate's so warm and friendly and interested in you?"

Otto sighed. "So he comes up to see you every few weeks. And then, about a month after you've got it all finished and working, he locks you out of the place and moves all your papers and stuff to another joint. And he tells you he'll have it patented long before you can get it all down on paper again, and anyhow it was his place—he can always claim he was subsidizing you. Then he laughs in your face, just like Elsa. Huh, Nick?"

Crandall bit his lip as he realized how thoroughly Otto Henck must have memorized the material. How many times had they gone over each other's planned revenge and the situations which had motivated it? How many times had they told and retold the same bitter stories to each other, elicited the same responses from each other, the same questions, the same agreements and even the very same disagreements?

Suddenly, he wanted to get away from the little man and enjoy the luxury of loneliness. He saw the sparkling roof of a hotel two levels down.

"Think I'll move into that. Ought to be thinking about a place to sleep tonight."

Otto nodded at his mood rather than at his statement. "Sure. I know just how you feel. But that's pretty plush, Nick: The Capricorn-Ritz. At least twelve credits a day."

"So what? I can live high for a week, if I want to. And with my background, I can always pick up a fast job as soon as I get low. I want something plush for tonight, Blotto Otto."

"Okay, okay. You got my address, huh, Nick? I'll be at my cousin's place."

"I have it, all right. Luck with Elsa, Otto."

"Thanks. Luck with Freddy. Uh—so long." The little man turned abruptly and entered a main street elevator. When the doors slid shut, Crandall found that he was feeling very uncomfortable. Henck had meant more to him than his own brother. Well, after all, he'd been with Henck day and night for a long time now. And he hadn't seen Dan for—how long was it?—almost nine years.

He reflected on how little he was attached to the world, if you excluded the rather negative desire of removing Stephanson from it. One thing he should get soon was a girl—almost any girl.

But, come to think of it, there was something he needed even more.

He walked swiftly to the nearest drugstore. It was a large one, part of a chain. And there, featured prominently in the window, was exactly what he wanted.

At the cigar counter, he said to the clerk: "It's pretty cheap. Do they work all right?"

The clerk drew himself up. "Before we put an item on sale, sir, it is tested thoroughly. We are the largest retail outlet in the Solar System—*that's* why it's so cheap."

"All right. Give me the medium-sized one. And two boxes of cartridges."

With the blaster in his possession, he felt much more secure. He had a good deal of confidence—based on years of escaping creatures with hair-trigger nervous systems—in his ability to duck and wriggle and jump to one side. But it would be nice to be able to fight back. And how did he know how soon Stephanson would try again?

He registered under a false name, a ruse he thought of at the last moment. That it wasn't worth much, as ruses went, he found out when the bellhop, after being tipped, said: "Thank you, Mr. Crandall. I hope you get your victim, sir."

So he was a celebrity. Probably everyone in the world knew exactly what he looked like. All of which might make it a bit more difficult to get at Stephanson.

While he was taking a bath, he asked the television set to check through Information's file on the man. Stephanson had been rich and moderately important seven years ago; with the Stephanson Switch—how do you like that, the *Stephanson Switch!*—he must be even richer now and much more important.

He was. The television set informed Crandall that in the last calendar month, there were sixteen news items relating to Frederick Stoddard Stephanson. Crandall considered, then asked for the most recent.

That was datelined today. "Frederick Stephanson, the president of the Stephanson Investment Trust and Stephanson Electronics Corporation, left early this morning for his hunting lodge in Central Tibet. He expects to remain there for at least—"

"That's enough!" Crandall called through the bathroom door.

Stephanson was scared! The arrogant bean-pole was frightened silly! That was something; in fact, it was a large part of the return on those seven years. Let him seethe in his own sweat for a while, until he found the actual killing, when it did come at last, almost welcome.

Crandall asked the set for the fresh news and was immediately treated to a bulletin about himself and how he had registered at the Capricorn-Ritz under the name of Alexander Smathers. "But neither is the correct name, ladies and gentlemen," the playback rolled out unctuously. "Neither Nicholas Crandall nor Alexander Smathers is the right name for this man. There is only one name for that man—and that name is Death! Yes, the grim reaper has taken up residence at the Ritz-Capricorn Hotel tonight, and only he knows which one of us will not see another sunrise. That man, that grim reaper, that deputy of death, is the only one among us who knows—"

"Shut up!" Crandall yelled, exasperated. He had almost forgotten the kind of punishment a free man was forced to endure.

The private phone circuit on the television screen lit up. He dried himself, hurried into clothes and asked, "Who's calling?"

"Mrs. Nicholas Crandall," said the operator's voice.

He stared at the blank screen for a moment, absolutely thunderstruck. Polly! Where in the world had she come from? And how did she know where he was? No, the last part was easy—he was a celebrity.

"Put her on," he said at last.

Polly's face filled the screen. Crandall studied her quizzically. She'd aged a bit, but possibly it wasn't obvious at anything but this magnification.

As if she realized it herself, Polly adjusted the controls on her set and her face dwindled to life-size, the rest of her body as well as her surroundings coming into the picture. She was evidently in the living room of her home; it looked like a low-to-middle-income-range furnished apartment. But she looked good—awfully good. There were such warm memories....

"Hi, Polly. What's this all about? You're the last person I expected to call me."

"Hello, Nick." She lifted her hand to her mouth and stared over its knuckles for some time at him. Then: "Nick. Please. Please don't play games with me."

He dropped into a chair. "Huh?"

She began to cry. "Oh, Nick! *Don't!* Don't be that cruel! I know why you served that sentence—those seven years. The moment I heard your name today, I knew why you did it. But, Nick, it was only one man—just one man, Nick!"

"Just one man *what?*"

"It was just that one man I was unfaithful with. And I thought he loved me, Nick. I wouldn't have divorced you if I'd known what he was really like. But you know, Nick, don't you? You know how much he made me suffer. I've been punished enough. Don't kill me, Nick! Please don't kill me!"

"Listen, Polly," he began, completely confused. "Polly girl, for heaven's sake—"

"Nick!" she gulped hysterically. "Nick, it was over eleven years ago—ten, at least. Don't kill me for that, please, Nick! Nick, truly, I wasn't unfaithful to you for more than a year, two years at the most. Truly, Nick! And, Nick, it was only that one affair—the others didn't count. They were just—just casual things. They didn't matter at all, Nick! But don't kill me! Don't kill me!" She held both hands to her face and began rocking back and forth, moaning uncontrollably.

Crandall stared at her for a moment and moistened his lips. Then he said, "Whew!" and turned the set off. He leaned back in his chair. Again he said, "Whew!" and this time it hissed through his teeth.

Polly! Polly had been unfaithful during their marriage. For a year—no, two years! And—what had she said?—the others, the *others* had just been casual things!

The woman he had loved, the woman he suspected he had always loved, the woman he had given up with infinite regret and a deep sense of guilt when she had come to him and said that the business had taken the best part of him away from her, but that since it wasn't fair to ask him to give up something that obviously meant so much to him—

Pretty Polly. Polly girl. He'd never thought of another woman in all their time together. And if anyone, anyone at all, had ever suggested—had so much as *hinted*—he'd have used a monkey wrench on the meddler's face. He'd given her the divorce only because she'd asked for it, but he'd hoped that when the business got on its feet and Irv's bookkeeping end covered a wider stretch of it, they might get back together again. Then, of course, business grew worse, Irv's wife got sick and he put even less time in at the office and—

"I feel," he said to himself numbly, "as if I've just found out for certain that there is no Santa Claus. Not Polly, not all those good years! One affair! And the others were just casual things!"

The telephone circuit went off again. "Who is it?" he snarled.

"Mr. Edward Ballaskia."

"What's he want?" Not *Polly, not Pretty Polly!*

An extremely fat man came on the screen. He looked to right and left cautiously. "I must ask you, Mr. Crandall, if you are positive that this line isn't tapped."

"What the hell do you want?" Crandall found himself wishing that the fat man were here in person. He'd love to sail into somebody right now.

Mr. Edward Ballaskia shook his head disapprovingly, his jowls jiggling slowly behind the rest of his face. "Well, then, sir, if you won't give me your assurances, I am forced to take a chance. I am calling, Mr. Crandall, to ask you to forgive your enemies, to turn the other cheek. I am asking you to remember faith, hope and charity—and that the greatest of these is charity. In other words, sir, open your heart to him or her you intended to kill, understand the weaknesses which caused them to give offenses—and forgive them."

"Why should I?" Crandall demanded.

"Because it is to your profit to do so, sir. Not merely morally profitable—although let us not overlook the life of the spirit—but financially profitable. *Financially* profitable, Mr. Crandall."

"Would you kindly tell me what you are talking about?"

The fat man leaned forward and smiled confidentially. "If you can forgive the person who caused you to go off and suffer seven long, seven *miserable* years of acute discomfort, Mr. Crandall, I am prepared to make you a most attractive offer. You are entitled to commit one murder. I desire to have one murder committed. I am very wealthy. You, I judge—and please take no umbrage, sir—are very poor.

"I can make you comfortable for the rest of your life, extremely comfortable, Mr. Crandall, if only you will put aside your thoughts, your unworthy thoughts, of anger and personal vengeance. I have a business competitor, you see, who has been—"

Crandall turned him off. "Go serve your own seven years," he venomously told the blank screen. Then, suddenly, it was funny. He lay back in the chair and laughed his head off.

That butter-faced old slob! Quoting religious texts at him!

But the call had served a purpose. Somehow it put the scene with Polly in the perspective of ridicule. To think of the woman sitting in her frowzy little apartment, trembling over her dingy affairs of more than ten years ago! To think she was afraid he had bled and battled for seven years because of that!

He thought about it for a moment, then shrugged. "Well, anyway, I bet it did her good."

And now he was hungry.

He thought of having a meal sent up, just to avoid a possible rendezvous with another of Stephanson's ball-throwers, but decided against it. If Stephanson was really hunting him seriously, it would not be much of a job to have something put into the food he was sent. He'd be much safer eating in a restaurant chosen at random.

Besides, a few bright lights, a little gaiety, would be really welcome. This was his first night of freedom—and he had to wash that Polly taste out of his mouth.

He checked the corridor carefully before going out. There was nothing, but the action reminded him of a tiny planet near Vega where you made exactly the same precautionary gesture every time you emerged from one of the tunnels formed by the long, parallel lines of moist, carboniferous ferns.

Because if you didn't—well, there was an enormous leech-like mollusk that might be waiting there, a creature which could flip chunks of shell with prodigious force. The shell merely stunned its prey, but stunned it long enough for the leech to get in close.

And that leech could empty a man in ten minutes flat.

Once he'd been hit by a fragment of shell, and while he'd been lying there, Henck— Good old Blotto Otto! Crandall smiled. Was it possible that the two of them would look back on those hideous adventures, one day, with actual nostalgia, the kind of beery, pleasant memories that soldiers develop after even the ugliest of wars? Well, and if they did, they hadn't gone through them for the sake of fat cats like Mr. Edward Ballaskia and his sanctified dreams of evil.

Nor, when you came right down to it, for dismal little frightened trollops like Polly. *Frederick Stoddard Stephanson. Frederick Stoddard—*

Somebody put an arm on his shoulder and he came to, realizing that he was half-way through the lobby.

"Nick," said a rather familiar voice.

Crandall squinted at the face at the end of the arm. That slight, pointed beard—he didn't know anyone with a beard like that, but the eyes looked so terribly familiar....

"Nick," said the man with the beard. "I couldn't do it."

Those eyes—of course, it was his younger brother!

"Dan!" he shouted.

"It's me all right. Here." Something clattered to the floor. Crandall looked down and saw a blaster lying on the rug, a larger and much more expensive blaster than the one he was carrying. *Why was Dan toting a blaster? Who was after Dan?*

With the thought, there came half-understanding. And there was fear—fear of the words that might come pouring out of the mouth of a brother whom he had not seen for all these years...

"I could have killed you from the moment you walked into the lobby," Dan was saying. "You weren't out of the sights for a second. But I want you to know, Nick, that the post-criminal sentence wasn't the reason I froze on the firing button."

"No?" Crandall asked in a breath that was exhaled slowly through a retroactive lifetime.

"I just couldn't stand adding any more guilt about you. Ever since that business with Polly—"

"With Polly. Yes, of course, with Polly." Something seemed to hang like a weight from the point of his jaw; it pulled his head down and his mouth open. "With Polly. That business with Polly."

Dan punched his fist into an open palm twice. "I knew you'd come looking for me sooner or later. I almost went crazy waiting—and I did go nearly crazy with guilt. But I never figured you'd do it this way, Nick. Seven years to wait for you to come back!"

"That's why you never wrote to me, Dan?"

"What did I have to say? What *is* there to say? I thought I loved her, but I found out what I meant to her as soon as she was divorced. I guess I always wanted what was yours because you were my older brother, Nick. That's the only excuse I can offer and I know exactly what it's worth. Because I know what you and Polly had together, what I broke up as a kind of big practical joke. But one thing, Nick: I won't kill you and I won't defend myself. I'm too tired. I'm too guilty. You know where to find me. Anytime, Nick."

He turned and strode rapidly through the lobby, the metal spangles that were this year's high masculine fashion glittering on his calves. He didn't look back, even when he was walking past the other side of the clear plastic that enclosed the lobby.

Crandall watched him go, then said "Hm" to himself in a lonely kind of way. He reached down, retrieved the other blaster and went out to find a restaurant.

As he sat, poking around in the spiced Venusian food that wasn't one-tenth as good as he had remembered it, he kept thinking about Polly and Dan. The incidents—he could remember incidents galore, now that he had a couple of pegs on which to hang them. To think he'd never suspected—but who could suspect Polly, who could suspect Dan?

He pulled the prison discharge out of his pocket and studied it. *Having duly served a maximum penal sentence of seven years, discounted from fourteen years, Nicholas Crandall is herewith discharged in a pre-criminal status—*

—to murder his ex-wife, Polly Crandall?

—to murder his younger brother, Daniel Crandall?

Ridiculous!

But they hadn't found it so ridiculous. Both of them, so blissfully secure in their guilt, so egotistically certain that they and they alone were the objects of a hatred intense enough to endure the worst that the galaxy had to offer in order to attain vengeance—why, they had both been so positive that their normal and already demonstrated cunning had deserted them and they had completely misread the warmth in his eyes! Either one could have switched confessions in mid-explanation. If they had only not been so preoccupied with self and had noted his astonishment in time, either or both of them could still be deceiving him!

Out of the corner of his eye, he saw that a woman was standing near his table. She had been reading his discharge over his shoulder. He leaned back and took her in while she stood and smiled at him.

She was fantastically beautiful. That is, she had everything a woman needs for great beauty—figure, facial structure, complexion, carriage, eyes, hair, all these to perfection—but she had those other final touches that, as in all kinds of art, make the difference between a merely great work and an all-time masterpiece. Those final touches included such things as sufficient wealth to create the ultimate setting in coiffure and gown, as well as the single Saturnian *paeaea* stone glowing in priceless black splendor between her breasts. Those final touches included the substantial feminine intelligence that beat in her steady eyes; and the somewhat overbred, over-indulged, overspoiled quality mixed in with it was the very last piquant fillip of a positively brilliant composition in the human medium.

"May I sit with you, Mr. Crandall?" she asked in a voice of which no more could be said than that it fitted the rest of her.

Rather amused, but more exhilarated than amused, he slid over on the restaurant couch. She sat down like an empress taking her throne before the eyes of a hundred tributary kings.

Crandall knew, within approximate limits, who she was and what she wanted. She was either a reigning post-debutante from the highest social circles in the System, or a theatrical star newly arrived and still in a state of nova.

And he, as a just-discharged convict, with the power of life and death in his hands, represented a taste she had not yet been able to indulge but was determined to enjoy.

Well, in a sense it wasn't flattering, but a woman like this could only fall to the lot of an ordinary man in very exceptional circumstances; he might as well take advantage of his status. He would satisfy her whim, while she, on his first night of freedom —

"That's your discharge, isn't it?" she asked and looked at it again. There was a moistness about her upper lip as she studied it—what a strange, sense-weary patina for one so splendidly young!

"Tell me, Mr. Crandall," she asked at last, turning to him with the wet pinpoints on her lip more brilliant than ever. "You've served a pre-criminal sentence for murder. It is true, is it not, that the punishment for murder and the most brutal, degraded rape imaginable are exactly the same?"

After a long silence, Crandall called for his check and walked out of the restaurant.

He had subsided enough when he reached the hotel to stroll with care around the transparent lobby housing. No one who looked like a Stephanson trigger man was in sight, although Stephanson was a cautious gambler. One attempt having failed, he'd be unlikely to try another for some time.

But that girl! And Edward Ballaskia!

There was a message in his box. Someone had called, leaving only a number to be called back.

Now what? he wondered as he went back up to his room. Stephanson making overtures? Or some unhappy mother wanting him to murder her incurable child?

He gave the number to the set and sat down to watch the screen with a good deal of curiosity.

It flickered—a face took shape on it. Crandall barely restrained a cry of delight. He did have a friend in this city from pre-convict days. Good old dependable, plodding, realistic Irv. His old partner.

And then, just as he was about to shout an enthusiastic greeting, he locked it inside his mouth. Too many things had happened today. And there was something about the expression on Irv's face...

"Listen, Nick," Irv said heavily at last. "I just want to ask you one question."

"What's that, Irv?" Crandall kept himself rock-steady.

"How long have you known? When did you find out?"

Crandall ran through several possible answers in his mind, finally selecting one. "A long time now, Irv. I just wasn't in a position to do anything about it."

Irv nodded. "That's what I thought. Well, listen. I'm not going to plead with you. I know that after seven years of what you've gone through, pleading isn't going to do me any good. But, believe me or not, I didn't start dipping into the till very much until my wife got sick. My personal funds were exhausted. I couldn't borrow any more, and you were too busy with your own domestic troubles to be bothered. Then, when business started to get better, I wanted to prevent a sudden large discrepancy on the books.

"So I continued milking the business, not for hospital expenses any more and not to deceive you, Nick—really!—but just so you wouldn't find out how much I'd taken from it before. When you came to me and said you were completely discouraged and wanted out—well, there I'll admit I was a louse. I should have told you. But after all, we hadn't been doing too well as partners and I saw a chance to get the whole business in my name and on its feet, so I—I—"

"So you bought me out for three hundred and twenty credits," Crandall finished for him. "How much is the firm worth now, Irv?"

The other man averted his eyes. "Close to a million. But listen, Nick, business has been terrific this past year in the wholesale line. I didn't cheat you out of all that! Listen, Nick—"

Crandall blew a snort of grim amusement through his nostrils. "What is it, Irv?"

Irv drew out a clean tissue and wiped his forehead. "Nick," he said, leaning forward and trying hard to smile winningly. "Listen to me, Nick! You forget about it, you stop hunting me down, and I've got a proposition for you. I need a man with your technical know-how in top management. I'll give you a twenty percent interest in the business, Nick—no, make it twenty-five percent. Look, I'll go as high as thirty percent—thirty-*five* percent—"

"Do you think that would make up for those seven years?"

Irv waved trembling, conciliatory hands. "No, of course not, Nick. Nothing would. But listen, Nick. I'll make it forty-five per—"

Crandall shut him off. He sat for a while, then got up and walked around the room. He stopped and examined his blasters, the one he'd purchased earlier and the one he'd gotten from Dan. He took out his prison discharge and read it through carefully. Then he shoved it back into the tunic pocket.

He notified the switchboard that he wanted a long-distance Earthside call put through.

"Yes, sir. But there's a gentleman to see you, sir. A Mr. Otto Henck."

"Send him up. And put the call in on my screen as soon as it goes through, please, Miss."

A few moments later, Blotto Otto entered his room. He was drunk, but carried it, as he always did, remarkably well.

"What do you think, Nick? What the hell do you—"

"Sh-h-h," Crandall warned him. "My call's coming in."

The Tibetan operator said, "Go ahead, New York," and Frederick Stoddard Stephanson appeared on the screen. The man had aged more than any of the others Crandall had seen tonight. Although you never could tell with Stephanson: he always looked older when he was working out a complex deal.

Stephanson didn't say anything; he merely pursed his lips at Crandall and waited. Behind him and around him was a TV spectacular's idea of a hunting lodge.

"All right, Freddy," Crandall said. "What I have to say won't take long. You might as well call off your dogs and stop taking chances trying to kill and/or injure me. As of this moment, I don't even have a grudge against you."

"You don't even have a grudge—" Stephanson regained his rigid self-control. "Why not?"

"Because—oh, because a lot of things. Because killing you just wouldn't be seven hellish years of satisfaction, now that I'm face to face with it. And because you didn't do any more to me than practically everybody else has done—from the cradle, for all I know. Because I've decided I'm a natural-born sucker: that's just the way I'm constructed. All you did was take your kind of advantage of my kind of construction."

Stephanson leaned forward, peered intently, then relaxed and crossed his arms. "You're actually telling the truth!"

"Of course I'm telling the truth! You see these?" He held up the two blasters. "I'm getting rid of these tonight. From now on, I'll be unarmed. I don't want to have the least thing to do with weighing human life in the balance."

The other man ran an index nail under a thumb nail thoughtfully a couple of times. "I'll tell you what," he said. "If you mean what you say—and I think you do—maybe we can work out something. An arrangement, say, to pay you a bit— We'll see."

"When you don't have to?" Crandall was astonished. "But why didn't you make me an offer before this?"

"Because I don't like to be forced to do anything. Up to now, I was fighting force with more force."

Crandall considered the point. "I don't get it. But maybe that's the way you're constructed. Well, we'll see, as you said."

When he rose to face Henck, the little man was still shaking his head slowly, dazedly, intent only on his own problem. "What do you think, Nick? Elsa went on a sightseeing jaunt to the Moon last month. The line to her oxygen helmet got clogged, see, and she died of suffocation before they could do anything about it. Isn't that a *hell* of thing, Nick? One month before I finish my sentence—she couldn't wait one lousy little month! I bet she died laughing at me!"

Crandall put his arm around him. "Let's go out for a walk, Blotto Otto. We both need the exercise."

Funny how the capacity for murder affected people, he thought. There was Polly's way—and Dan's. There was old Irv bargaining frantically but still shrewdly for his life. Mr. Edward Ballaskia—and that girl in the restaurant. And there was Freddy Stephanson, the only intended victim—and the only one who wouldn't beg.

He wouldn't beg, but he might be willing to hand out largess. Could Crandall accept what amounted to charity from Stephanson? He shrugged. Who knew what he or anyone else could or could not do?

"What do we do now, Nick?" Blotto Otto was demanding petulantly once they got outside the hotel. "That's what I want to know—what do we do?"

"Well, I'm going to do this," Crandall told him, taking a blaster in each hand. "Just this." He threw the gleaming weapons, right hand, left hand, at the transparent window walls that ran around the luxurious lobby of the Ritz-Capricorn. They struck *thunk* and then *thunk* again. The windows crashed down in long, pointed daggers. The people in the lobby swung around with their mouths open.

A policeman ran up, his badge jingling against his metallic uniform. He seized Crandall.

"I saw you! I saw you do that! You'll get thirty days for it!"

"Hm," said Crandall. "Thirty days?" He pulled his prison discharge out of his pocket and handed it to the policeman. "I tell you what we'll do, officer— Just punch the proper number of holes in this document or tear off what seems to you a proportionately sized coupon. Either or both. Handle it any way you like."

AFTERWORD

My friend, Calder Willingham, was attacked by two muggers one night, as he walked in Greenwich Village from his apartment on Perry Street to mine on Jane Street. They ran up to him as he turned a corner and one of them seized the left sleeve of his overcoat and, as Calder put it, "began reeling me in like a goddam fish." He broke away, still wearing the overcoat, but leaving the ripped-off sleeve in the hands of the mugger. At this point, a car came down the street, with its headlights on and its horn blaring. The muggers stopped pursuing and ran off in the other direction.

Calder rang my bell and came upstairs, understandably very much upset. He and I examined the coat with the tear where the sleeve had been amputated. Calder said that while the overcoat had been an expensive one, what bothered him most was that henceforth he would not feel easy about walking through the Village any more.

"It kind of breaks your nerve," he said. "That's the worst thing about these rotten criminals—not what they do to you at the moment, but what they do to you in the future, when they're not even around. And they don't even have any real point or complicated motive. They just want to get their hands on your money or valuables or whatever. There's nothing more to them than that."

After our chess game, I offered to walk him home, but he said no. "I don't want these bastards to change my life," he said, and left.

Really, it was as simple as that. I sat down at the typewriter and, with nothing else in my mind, immediately began typing "Time in Advance" as if I'd been plotting the story for days. I typed it with all the sociological overtones, all the moral issues, speech by speech, character by character, in one sitting, one draft, until I typed "the end" early the next morning.

Then I took it to Horace Gold in his home-office in Stuyvesant Town (an apartment complex off Manhattan's East Fourteenth Street). His wife, Evelyn, gave me a cup of coffee and chatted with me while Horace read the story. He bought it then and there with (for once!) absolutely no changes, and I went home to sleep.

Sometimes a writer walks the floor and pounds his fist into his palm for hours, for days, while trying to have a story make sense to himself. Sometimes you rewrite this and cross out that and dig furrows in your scalp with your fingernails.

And sometimes a story like "Time in Advance" spills itself out in front of you, perfectly formed and finished, with nothing to be subtracted and nothing to be added and nothing to be changed.

All right. But even happy endings don't have happy endings. "Time in Advance" is my first and only movie sale as of this date. Universal bought it twelve years ago, and they haven't been able to film it yet. They keep telling me that it's coming along, "But it *is* a difficult piece, you know." I tell them I don't think so, and then they stop talking to me for a while.

WRITTEN 1956——PUBLISHED 1956

THE SICKNESS

For the record, it was a Russian, Nicolai Belov, who found it and brought it back to the ship. He found it in the course of a routine geological survey he was making some six miles from the ship the day after they landed. For what it might be worth, he was driving a caterpillar jeep at the time, a caterpillar jeep that had been made in Detroit, U.S.A.

He radioed the ship almost immediately. Preston O'Brien, the navigator, was in the control room at the time, as usual, checking his electronic computers against a dummy return course he had set up. He took the call. Belov, of course, spoke in English; O'Brien in Russian.

"O'Brien," Belov said excitedly, once identification had been established. "Guess what I've found? Martians! A whole city!"

O'Brien snapped the computer relays shut, leaned back in the bucket seat, and ran his fingers through his crew-cut red hair. They'd had no right to, of course—but somehow they'd all taken it for granted that they were alone on the chilly, dusty, waterless planet. Finding it wasn't so gave him a sudden acute attack of claustrophobia. It was like looking up from his thesis work in an airy, silent college library to find it had filled with talkative freshmen just released from a class in English composition. Or that disagreeable moment at the beginning of the expedition, back in Benares, when he'd come out of a nightmare in which he'd been drifting helplessly by himself in a starless black vacuum to find Kolevitch's powerful right arm hanging down from the bunk above him and the air filled with sounds of thick Slavic snores. It wasn't just that he was jumpy, he'd assured himself; after all, everyone was jumpy...these days.

He'd never liked being crowded. Or being taken by surprise. He rubbed his hands together irritably over the equations he'd scribbled a moment before. Of course, come to think of it, if anyone was being crowded, it was the Martians. There was *that*.

O'Brien cleared his throat and asked:

"*Live* Martians?"

"No, of course not. How could you have live Martians in the cupful of atmosphere this planet has left? The only things alive in the place are the usual lichens and maybe a desert flatworm or two, the same as those we found near the ship. The last of the Martians must have died at least a million years ago. But the city's intact, O'Brien, intact and almost untouched!"

For all his ignorance of geology, the navigator was incredulous. "Intact? You mean it hasn't been weathered down to sand in a million years?"

371

"Not a bit," Belov chortled. "You see, it's underground. I saw this big sloping hole and couldn't figure it: it didn't go with the terrain. Also there was a steady breeze blowing out of the hole, keeping the sand from piling up inside. So I nosed the jeep in, rode downhill for about fifty, sixty yards—and there it was, a spacious, empty Martian city, looking like Moscow a thousand, ten thousand years from now. It's beautiful, O'Brien, beautiful!"

"Don't touch anything," O'Brien warned. Moscow! Like Moscow yet!

"You think I'm crazy? I'm just taking a couple of shots with my Rollei. Whatever machinery is operating that blower system is keeping the lights on; it's almost as bright as daylight down here. But what a place! Boulevards like colored spider webs. Houses like—like—talk about the Valley of the Kings, talk about Harappa! They're nothing, nothing at all to this find. You didn't know I was an amateur archaeologist, did you, O'Brien? Well, I am. And let me tell you, Schliemann would have given his eyes—his eyes!—for this discovery! It's magnificent!"

O'Brien grinned at his enthusiasm. At moments like this you couldn't help feeling that the Russkies were all right, that it would all work out—somehow. "Congratulations," he said. "Take your pictures and get back fast. I'll tell Captain Ghose."

"But listen, O'Brien, that's not all. These people—these Martians—they were like us! They were human!"

"Human? Did you say *human*? Like *us?*"

Belov's delighted laugh irradiated the earphones. "That's exactly the way I felt. Amazing, isn't it? They were human, like us. If anything, even more so. There's a pair of nude statues in the middle of a square that the entrance opens into. Phidias or Praxiteles or Michelangelo wouldn't have been ashamed of those statues, let me tell you. And they were made back in the Pleistocene or Pliocene, when saber-tooth tigers were still prowling the Earth!"

O'Brien grunted and switched off. He strolled to the control-room porthole, one of the two that the ship boasted, and stared out at the red desert that humped and hillocked itself endlessly, repetitiously, until, at the furthest extremes of vision, it disappeared in a sifting, sandy mist.

This was Mars. A dead planet. Dead, that is, except for the most primitive forms of vegetable and animal life, forms which could survive on the minute rations of water and air that their bitterly hostile world allotted them. But once there had been men here, men like himself and Nicolai Belov. They had had art and science as well as, no doubt, differing philosophies. They had been here once, these men of Mars, and were here no longer. Had they too been set a problem in coexistence—and had they failed to solve it?

Two spacesuited figures clumped into sight from under the ship. O'Brien recognized them through their helmet bubbles. The shorter man was Fyodor Guranin, Chief Engineer; the other was Tom Smathers, his First Assistant. They had evidently been going over the rear jets, examining them carefully for any damage incurred on the outward journey. In eight days, the first Terrestrial Expedition to Mars would start home: every bit of equipment had to be functioning at optimum long before that.

Smathers saw O'Brien through the porthole and waved. The navigator waved back. Guranin glanced upwards curiously, hesitated a moment, then waved too. Now O'Brien hesitated. Hell, this was silly! Why not? He waved at Guranin, a long, friendly, rotund wave.

Then he smiled to himself. Ghose should only see them now! The tall captain would be grinning like a lunatic out of his aristocratic, coffee-colored face. Poor guy! He was living on emotional crumbs like these.

And that reminded him. He left the control room and looked in at the galley where Semyon Kolevitch, the Assistant Navigator and Chief Cook, was opening cans in preparation for their lunch. "Any idea where the captain is?" he inquired in Russian.

The man glanced at him coolly, finished the can he was working on, tossed the round flat top into the wall disposer-hole, and then replied with a succinct English "No."

Out in the corridor again, he met Dr. Alvin Schneider on the way to the galley to work out his turn at K.P. "Have you seen Captain Ghose, Doc?"

"He's waiting down in the engine room, waiting to have a conference with Guranin," the chubby little ship's doctor told him. Both men spoke in Russian.

O'Brien nodded and kept going. A few minutes later, he pushed open the engine-room door and came upon Captain Subodh Ghose, late of the Benares Polytechnic Institute, Benares, India, examining a large wall chart of the ship's jet system. Despite his youth—like every other man on the ship, Ghose was under twenty-five—the fantastic responsibilities he was carrying had ground two black holes into the flesh under the captain's eyes. They made him look perpetually strained. Which he was, O'Brien reflected, and no two ways about it.

He gave the captain Belov's message.

"Hm," Ghose said, frowning. "I hope he has enough sense not to—" He broke off sharply as he realized he had spoken in English. "I'm terribly sorry, O'Brien!" he said in Russian, his eyes looking darker than ever. "I've been standing here thinking about Guranin; I must have thought I was talking to him. Excuse me."

"Think nothing of it," O'Brien murmured. "It was my pleasure."

Ghose smiled, then turned it off abruptly. "I better not let it happen again. As I was saying, I hope Belov has enough sense to control his curiosity and not touch anything."

"He said he wouldn't. Don't worry, Captain, Belov is a bright boy. He's like the rest of us; we're all bright boys."

"An operating city like that," the tall Indian brooded. "There might be life there still—he might set off an alarm and start up something unimaginable. For all we know, there might be automatic armament in the place, bombs, anything. Belov could get himself blown up, and us, too. There might be enough in that one city to blow up all of Mars."

"Oh, I don't know about that," O'Brien suggested. "I think that's going a little too far. I think you have bombs on the brain, Captain."

Ghose stared at him soberly. "I have, Mr. O'Brien. That's a fact."

O'Brien felt himself blushing. To change the subject, he said: "I'd like to borrow

Smathers for a couple of hours. The computers seem to be working fine, but I want to spot-check a couple of circuits, just for the hell of it."

"I'll ask Guranin if he can spare him. You can't use your assistant?"

The navigator grimaced. "Kolevitch isn't half the electronics man that Smathers is. He's a damn good mathematician, but not much more."

Ghose studied him, as if trying to decide whether or not that was the only obstacle. "I suppose so. But that reminds me. I'm going to have to ask you to remain in the ship until we lift for Earth."

"Oh, no, Captain! I'd like to stretch my legs. And I've as much right as anyone to—to walk the surface of another world." His phraseology made O'Brien a bit self-conscious, but dammit, he reflected, he hadn't come forty million miles just to look at the place through portholes.

"You can stretch your legs inside the ship. You know and I know that walking around in a spacesuit is no particularly pleasant exercise. And as for being on the surface of another world, you've already done that, O'Brien, yesterday, in the ceremony where we laid down the marker."

O'Brien glanced past him to the engine room porthole. Through it, he could see the small white pyramid they had planted outside. On each of its three sides was the same message in a different language: English, Russian, Hindustani. *First Terrestrial Expedition to Mars. In the Name of Human Life.*

Cute touch, that. And typically Indian. But pathetic. Like everything else about this expedition, plain pathetic.

"You're too valuable to risk, O'Brien," Ghose was explaining. "We found that out on the way here. No human brain can extemporize suddenly necessary course changes with the speed and accuracy of those computers. And, since you helped design them, no one can handle those computers as well as you. So my order stands."

"Oh, come now, it's not that bad: you'd always have Kolevitch."

"As *you* remarked just a moment ago, Semyon Kolevitch isn't enough of an electronic technician. If anything went wrong with the computers, we'd have to call in Smathers and use the two of them in tandem—not the most efficient working arrangement there is. And I suspect that Smathers plus Kolevitch still would not quite equal Preston O'Brien. No, I'm sorry, but I'm afraid we can't take chances: you're too close to being indispensable."

"All right," O'Brien said softly. "The order stands. But allow me a small disagreement, Captain. You know and I know that there's only one indispensable man aboard this ship. And it isn't me."

Ghose grunted and turned away. Guranin and Smathers came in, having shed their spacesuits in the airlock at the belly of the craft. The captain and the chief engineer had a brief English colloquy, at the end of which, with only the barest resistance, Guranin agreed to lend Smathers to O'Brien.

"But I'll need him back by three at the latest."

"You'll have him," O'Brien promised in Russian and led Smathers out. Behind him, Guranin began to discuss engine-repair problems with the captain.

"I'm surprised he didn't make you fill out a requisition for me," Smathers commented. "What the hell does he think I am anyway, a Siberian slave laborer?"

"He's got his own departmental worries, Tom. And for God's sake, talk Russian. Suppose the captain or one of the Ivans overheard you? You want to start trouble at this late date?"

"I wasn't being fancy, Pres. I just forgot."

It was easy to forget, O'Brien knew. Why in the world hadn't the Indian government been willing to let all seven Americans and seven Russians learn Hindustani so that the expedition could operate under a mutual language, the language of their captain? Although, come to think of it, Ghose's native language was Bengali....

He knew why, though, the Indians had insisted on adding these specific languages to the already difficult curriculum of the expedition's training program. The idea was that if the Russians spoke English to each other and to the Americans, while the Americans spoke and replied in Russian, the whole affair might achieve something useful in the ship's microcosm even if it failed in its macrocosmic political objectives. And then, having returned to Earth and left the ship, each of them would continue to spread in his own country the ideas of amity and cooperation for survival acquired on the journey.

Along that line, anyway. It was pretty—and pathetic. But was it any more pathetic than the state of the world at the moment? Something had to be done, and done fast. At least the Indians were trying. They didn't just sit up nights with the magic figure *six* dancing horrendous patterns before their eyes: *six, six bombs, six of the latest cobalt bombs and absolutely no more life on Earth.*

It was public knowledge that America had at least nine such bombs stockpiled, that Russia had seven, Britain four, China two, that there were at least five more individual bombs in existence in the armories of five proud and sovereign states. What these bombs could do had been demonstrated conclusively in the new proving grounds that America and Russia used on the dark side of the moon.

Six. Only six bombs could do for the entire planet. Everyone knew that, and knew that if there were a war, these bombs would be used, sooner or later, by the side that was going down to defeat, by the side that was looking forward grimly to occupation by the enemy, to war crimes trials for their leader.

And everyone knew that there was going to be a war.

Decade after decade it had held off, but decade after decade it had crept irresistibly closer. It was like a persistent, lingering disease that the patient battles with ever-diminishing strength, staring at his thermometer with despair, hearing his own labored breathing with growing horror, until it finally overwhelms him and kills him. Every crisis was surmounted somehow—and was followed by a slight change for the worse. International conferences followed by new alliances followed by more international conferences, and ever war came closer, closer.

It was almost here now. It had almost come three years ago, over Madagascar, of all places, but a miracle had staved it off. It had almost come last year, over territorial rights to the dark side of the moon, but a super-miracle, in the form of last-minute arbitration by the government of India, had again prevented it. But now the world was definitely on the verge. Two months, six months, a year—it would come. Everyone knew it. Everyone waited for extinction, wondering jerkily, when they had time, why they did no more than wait, why it had to be. But they knew it had to be.

In the midst of this, with both the Soviet Union and the United States of America going ahead full-blast with rocket research and space travel techniques—to the end that when the time came for the bombs to be delivered, they would be delivered with the maximum efficiency and dispatch—in the midst of this, India made her proposal public. Let the two opposing giants cooperate in a venture which both were projecting, and in which each could use the other's knowledge. One had a slight edge in already-achieved space travel, the other was known to have developed a slightly better atomic-powered rocket. Let them pool their resources for an expedition to Mars, under an Indian captain and under Indian auspices, in the name of humanity as a whole. And let the world find out once and for all which side refused to cooperate.

It was impossible to refuse, given the nature of the proposition and the peculiarly perfect timing. So here they were, O'Brien decided; they had made it to Mars and would probably make it back. But, while they might have proven much, they had prevented nothing. The spastic political situation was still the same; the world would still be at war within the year. The men on this ship knew that as well, or better, than anybody.

As they passed the airlock, on the way to the control room, they saw Belov squeezing his way out of his spacesuit. He hurried over clumsily, hopping out of the lower section as he came. "What a discovery, eh?" he boomed. "The second day and in the middle of the desert. Wait till you see my pictures!"

"I'll look forward to it," O'Brien told him. "Meanwhile you better run down to the engine room and report to the captain. He's afraid that you might have pressed a button that closed a circuit that started up a machine that will blow up all of Mars right out from under us."

The Russian gave them a wide, slightly gap-toothed smile. "Ghose and his planetary explosions." He patted the top of his head lightly and shook it uneasily from side to side.

"What's the matter?" O'Brien asked.

"A little headache. It started a few seconds ago. I must have spent too much time in that spacesuit."

"I just spent twice as much time in a spacesuit as you did," Smathers said, poking around abstractedly at the gear that Belov had dropped, "and I don't have a headache. Maybe we make better heads in America."

"Tom!" O'Brien yelped. "For God's sake!"

Belov's lips had come together in whitening union. Then he shrugged. "Chess, O'Brien? After lunch?"

"Sure. And, if you're interested, I'm willing to walk right into a fried liver. I still insist that black can hold and win."

"It's your funeral," Belov chuckled and went on to the engine room gently massaging his head.

When they were alone in the control room and Smathers had begun to dismantle the computer bank, O'Brien shut the door and said angrily: "That was a damned dangerous, un-called-for crack you made, Tom! And it was about as funny as a declaration of war!"

"I know. But Belov gets under my skin."

"*Belov?* He's the most decent Russky on board."

The second assistant engineer unscrewed a side panel and squatted down beside it. "To you maybe. But he's always taking a cut at me."

"How?"

"Oh, all sorts of ways. Take this chess business. Whenever I ask him for a game, he says he won't play me unless I accept odds of a queen. And then he laughs—you know, that slimy laugh of his."

"Check that connection at the top," the navigator warned. "Well, look, Tom, Belov is pretty good. He placed seventh in the last Moscow District tournament, playing against a hatful of masters and grandmasters. That's good going in a country where they feel about chess the way we do about baseball and football combined."

"Oh, I know he's good. But I'm not that bad. Not queen odds. A *queen!*"

"Are you sure it isn't something else? You seem to dislike him an awful lot, considering your motivations."

Smathers paused for a moment to examine a tube. "And you," he said without looking up. "You seem to *like* him an awful lot, considering *your* motivations."

On the verge of anger, O'Brien suddenly remembered something and shut up. After all, it could be anyone. It could be Smathers.

Just before they'd left the United States to join the Russians in Benares, they'd had a last, ultra-secret briefing session with Military Intelligence. There had been a review of the delicacy of the situation they were entering and its dangerous potentialities. On the one hand, it was necessary that the United States not be at all backward about the Indian suggestion, that before the eyes of the world it enter upon this joint scientific expedition with at least as much enthusiasm and cooperativeness as the Russians. On the other, it was equally important, possibly even more important, that the future enemy should not use this pooling of knowledge and skills to gain an advantage that might prove conclusive, like taking over the ship, say, on the return trip, and landing it in Baku instead of Benares.

Therefore, they were told, one among them had received training and a commission in the Military Intelligence Corps of the U.S. Army. His identity would remain a secret until such time as he decided that the Russians were about to pull something. Then he would announce himself with a special code sentence and from that time on all Americans on board were to act under his orders and not Ghose's. Failure to do so would be adjudged *prima facie* evidence of treason.

And the code sentence? Preston O'Brien had to grin as he remembered it. It was: "Fort Sumter has been fired upon."

But what happened after one of them stood up and uttered that sentence would not be at all funny....

He was certain that the Russians had such a man, too. As certain as that Ghose suspected both groups of relying on this kind of insurance, to the serious detriment of the captain's already-difficult sleep.

What kind of a code sentence would the Russians use? "Fort Kronstadt has been fired upon?" No, more likely, "Workers of the world unite!" Yes, no doubt about it, it could get very jolly, if someone made a real wrong move.

The American MI officer could be Smathers. Especially after that last crack of his. O'Brien decided he'd be far better off not replying to it. These days, everyone had to be very careful; and the men in this ship were in a special category.

Although he knew what was eating Smathers. The same thing, in a general sense, that made Belov so eager to play chess with the navigator, a player of a caliber that, back on Earth, wouldn't have been considered worthy to enter the same tournament with him.

O'Brien had the highest I.Q. on the ship. Nothing special, not one spectacularly above anyone else's. It was just that in a shipful of brilliant young men chosen from the thick cream of their respective nation's scientific *élite,* someone had to have an I.Q. higher than the rest. And that man happened to be Preston O'Brien.

But O'Brien was an American. And everything relative to the preparation for this trip had been worked out in high-level conferences with a degree of diplomatic finagling and behind-the-scenes maneuvering usually associated with the drawing of boundary lines of the greatest strategical significance. So the lowest I.Q. on the ship also had to be an American.

And that was Tom Smathers, second assistant engineer.

Again, nothing very bad, only a point or two below that of the next highest man. And really quite a thumpingly high I.Q. in itself.

But they had all lived together for a long time before the ship lifted from Benares. They had learned a lot about each other, both from personal contact and official records, for how did anyone know what piece of information about a shipmate would ward off disaster in the kind of incredible, unforeseeable crises they might be plunging into?

So Nicolai Belov, who had a talent for chess as natural and as massive as the one Sarah Bernhardt had for the theater, got a special and ever-renewing pleasure out of beating a man who had barely made the college team. And Tom Smathers nursed a constant feeling of inferiority that was ready to grow into adult, belligerent status on any pretext it could find.

It was ridiculous, O'Brien felt. But then, he couldn't know: he had the long end of the stick. It was easy, for *him.*

Ridiculous? As ridiculous as six cobalt bombs. *One, two, three, four, five, six*—and *boom!*

Maybe, he thought, maybe the answer was that they were a ridiculous species. Well. They would soon be gone, gone with the dinosaurs.

And the Martians.

"I can't wait to get a look at those pictures Belov took," he told Smathers, trying to change the subject to a neutral, nonargumentative level. "Imagine human beings walking around on this blob of desert, building cities, making love, investigating scientific phenomena—a million years ago!"

The second assistant engineer, wrist deep in a tangle of wiring, merely grunted as a sign that he refused to let his imagination get into the bad company that he considered all matters connected with Belov.

O'Brien persisted. "Where did they go—the Martians, I mean? If they were that advanced, that long ago, they must have developed space travel and found some more desirable real estate to live on. Do you think they visited Earth, Tom?"

"Yeah. And they're all buried in Red Square."

You couldn't do anything against that much bad temper, O'Brien decided; he might as well drop it. Smathers was still smarting over Belov's eagerness to play the navigator on even terms.

But all the same, he kept looking forward to the photographs. And when they went down to lunch, in the big room at the center of the ship, that served as combination dormitory, mess hall, recreation room, and storage area, the first man he looked for was Belov.

Belov wasn't there.

"He's up in the hospital room with the doctor," Layatinsky, his table-mate, said heavily, gravely. "He doesn't feel well. Schneider's examining him."

"That headache get worse?"

Layatinsky nodded. "A lot worse—and fast. And then he got pains in his joints. Feverish, too. Guranin says it sounds like meningitis."

"Ouch!" Living as closely together as they did, something like meningitis would spread through their ranks like ink through a blotter. But Guranin was an engineer, not a doctor. What did he know about it, where did he come off making a diagnosis?

And then O'Brien noticed it. The mess hall was unusually quiet, the men eating with their eyes on their plates as Kolevitch dished out the food—a little sullenly, true, but that was probably because after preparing the meal, he was annoyed at having to serve it, too, since the K.P. for lunch, Dr. Alvin Schneider, had abruptly been called to more pressing business.

But whereas the Americans were merely quiet, the Russians were funereal. Their faces were as set and strained as if they were waiting to be shot. They were all breathing heavily, the kind of slow, snorting breaths that go with great worry over extremely difficult problems.

Of course. If Belov were really sick, if Belov went out of action, that put them at a serious disadvantage relative to the Americans. It cut their strength almost fifteen percent. In case of a real razzle between the two groups...

Therefore, Guranin's amateur diagnosis should be read as a determined attempt at optimism. Yes, optimism! If it was meningitis and thus highly contagious, others were likely to pick it up, and those others could just as well be Americans as Russians. That way, the imbalance could be redressed.

O'Brien shivered. What kind of lunacy—

But then, he realized, if it had been an American, instead of a Russian, who had been taken real sick and was up there in the hospital at the moment, his mind would have been running along the same track as Guranin's. Meningitis would have seemed like something to hope for desperately.

Captain Ghose climbed down into the mess hall. His eyes seemed darker and smaller than ever.

"Listen, men. As soon as you've finished eating, report up to the control room which, until further notice, will serve as an annex to the hospital."

"What for, Captain?" someone asked. "What do we report for?"

"Precautionary injections."

There was a silence. Ghose started out of the place. Then the chief engineer cleared his throat.

"How is Belov?"

The captain paused for a moment, without turning around. "We don't know yet. And if you're going to ask me what's the matter with him, we don't know that yet either."

They waited in a long, silent, thoughtful line outside the control room, entering and leaving it one by one. O'Brien's turn came.

He walked in, baring his right arm, as he had been ordered. At the far end, Ghose was staring out of the porthole as if he were waiting for a relief expedition to arrive. The navigation desk was covered with cotton swabs, beakers filled with alcohol, and small bottles of cloudy fluid.

"What's this stuff, Doc?" O'Brien asked when the injection had been completed and he was allowed to roll down his sleeve.

"Duoplexin. The new antibiotic that the Australians developed last year. Its therapeutic value hasn't been completely validated, but it's the closest thing to a general cure-all that medicine's come up with. I hate to use anything so questionable, but before we lifted from Benares, I was told to shoot you fellows full of it if any off-beat symptoms showed up."

"Guranin says it sounds like meningitis," the navigator suggested.

"It isn't meningitis."

O'Brien waited a moment, but the doctor was filling a new hypodermic and seemed indisposed to comment further. He addressed Ghose's back. "How about those pictures that Belov took? They been developed yet? I'd like to see them."

The captain turned away from the porthole and walked around the control room with his hands clasped behind his back. "All of Belov's gear," he said in a low voice, "is under quarantine in the hospital along with Belov. Those are the doctor's orders."

"Oh. Too bad." O'Brien felt he should leave, but curiosity kept him talking. There was something these men were worried about that was bigger even than the fear niggling the Russians. "He told me over the radio that the Martians had been distinctly humanoid. Amazing, isn't it? Talk about parallel evolution!"

Schneider set the hypodermic down carefully. "Parallel evolution," he muttered.

"Parallel evolution and parallel pathology. Although it doesn't seem to act quite like any terrestrial bug. Parallel susceptibility, though. That you could say definitely."

"You mean you think Belov has picked up a *Martian* disease?" O'Brien let the concept careen through his mind. "But that city was so old. No germ could survive anywhere near that long!"

The little doctor thumped his small paunch decisively. "We have no reason to believe it couldn't. Some germs we know of on Earth might be able to. As spores—in any one of a number of ways."

"But if Belov—"

"That's enough," the captain said. "Doctor, you shouldn't think out loud. Keep your mouth shut about this, O'Brien, until we decide to make a general announcement. Next man!" he called.

Tom Smathers came in. "Hey, Doc," he said, "I don't know if this is important, but I've begun to generate the lousiest headache of my entire life."

The other three men stared at each other. Then Schneider plucked a thermometer out of his breast-pocket and put it into Smathers's mouth, whispering an indistinct curse as he did so. O'Brien took a deep breath and left.

They were all told to assemble in the mess-hall dormitory that night. Schneider, looking tired, mounted a table, wiped his hands on his jumper and said:

"Here it is, men. Nicolai Belov and Tom Smathers are down sick, Belov seriously. The symptoms seem to begin with a mild headache and temperature which rapidly grow worse and, as they do, are accompanied by severe pains in the back and joints. That's the first stage. Smathers is in that right now. Belov—"

Nobody said anything. They sat around in various relaxed positions watching the doctor. Guranin and Layatinsky were looking up from their chess board as if some relatively unimportant comments were being made that, perforce, just had to be treated, for the sake of courtesy, as of more significance than the royal game. But when Guranin shifted his elbow and knocked his king over, neither of them bothered to pick it up.

"Belov," Dr. Alvin Schneider went on after a bit, "Belov is in the second stage. This is characterized by a weirdly fluctuating temperature, delirium, and a substantial loss of coordination—pointing, of course, to an attack on the nervous system. The loss of coordination is so acute as to affect even peristalsis, making intravenous feeding necessary. One of the things we will do tonight is go through a demonstration-lecture of intravenous feeding, so that any of you will be able to take care of the patients. Just in case."

Across the room, O'Brien saw Hopkins, the radio and communications man, make the silent mouth-movement of "Wow!"

"Now as to what they're suffering from. I don't know, and that about sums it up. I'm fairly certain though that it isn't a terrestrial disease, if only because it seems to have one of the shortest incubation periods I've ever encountered as well as a fantastically rapid development. I think it's something that Belov caught in that Martian city and brought back to the ship. I have no idea if it's fatal and to what degree, although it's sound procedure in such a case to expect the worst. The only hope I can hold out at the moment is that the two men who are down with it exhibited symptoms before I had a chance to fill them full of duoplexin. Everyone else on the ship —including me—has now had a precautionary injection. That's all. Are there any questions?"

There were no questions.

"All right," Dr. Schneider said. "I want to warn you, though I hardly think it's necessary under the circumstances, that any man who experiences any kind of a headache—*any* kind of a headache—is to report immediately for hospitalization and quarantine. We're obviously dealing with something highly infectious. Now if you'll all move in a little closer, I'll demonstrate intravenous feeding on Captain Ghose. Captain, if you please."

When the demonstration was over and they had proved their proficiency, to his satisfaction, on each other, he put together all the things that smelled pungently of antiseptic and said: "Well, now that's taken care of. We're covered, in case of emergency. Get a good night's sleep."

Then he started out. And stopped. He turned around and looked carefully from man to man. "O'Brien," he said at last. "You come up with me."

Well, at least, the navigator thought, as he followed, at least it's even now. One Russian and one American. If only it stayed that way!

Schneider glanced in at the hospital and nodded to himself. "Smathers," he commented. "He's reached the second stage. Fastest-acting damn bug ever. Probably finds us excellent hosts."

"Any idea what it's like?" O'Brien asked, finding, to his surprise, that he was having trouble catching up to the little doctor.

"Uh-uh. I spent two hours with the microscope this afternoon. Not a sign. I prepared a lot of slides, blood, spinal fluid, sputum, and I've got a shelf of specimen jars all filled up. They'll come in handy for Earthside doctors if ever we— Oh, well. You see, it could be a filterable virus, it could be a bacillus requiring some special stain to make it visible, anything. But the most I was hoping for was to detect it—we'd never have the time to develop a remedy."

He entered the control room, still well ahead of the taller man, stood to one side, and, once the other had come in, locked the door. O'Brien found his actions puzzling.

"I can't see why you're feeling so hopeless, Doc. We have those white mice down below that were intended for testing purposes if Mars turned out to have half an atmosphere after all. Couldn't you use them as experimental animals and try to work up a vaccine?"

The doctor chuckled without turning his lips up into a smile. "In twenty-four hours. Like in the movies. No, and even if I intended to take a whirl at it, which I did, it's out of the question now."

"What do you mean—*now?*"

Schneider sat down carefully and put his medical equipment on the desk beside him. Then he grinned. "Got an aspirin, Pres?"

Automatically, O'Brien's hand went into the pocket of his jumper. "No, but I think that—" Then he understood. A wet towel unrolled in his abdomen. "When did it start?" he inquired softly.

"It must have started near the end of the lecture, but I was too busy to notice it. I first felt it just as I was leaving the mess hall. A real ear-splitter at the moment. No, keep away!" he shouted, as O'Brien started forward sympathetically. "This probably won't do any good, but at least keep your distance. Maybe it will give you a little extra time."

"Should I get the captain?"

"If I needed him, I'd have asked him along. I'll be turning myself into the hospital in a few minutes. I'd just wanted to transfer my authority to you."

"Your *authority?* Are you the—the—"

Doctor Alvin Schneider nodded. He went on—in English. "I'm the American Military Intelligence officer. Was, I should say. From now on, you are. Look, Pres, I don't have much time. All I can tell you is this. Assuming that we're not all dead within a week, and assuming that it is decided to attempt a return to Earth with the consequent risk of infecting the entire planet (something which, by the way, I personally would not recommend from where I sit), you are to keep your status as secret as I kept mine, and in the event it becomes necessary to tangle with the Russians, you are to reveal yourself with the code sentence you already know."

"Fort Sumter has been fired upon," O'Brien said slowly. He was still assimilating the fact that Schneider had been the MI officer. Of course, he had known all along that it could have been any one of the seven Americans. But Schneider!

"Right. If you then get control of the ship, you are to try to land her at White Sands, New Mexico, where we all got our preliminary training. You will explain to the authorities how I came to transfer authority to you. That's about all, except for two things. If you get sick, you'll have to use your own judgment about who to pass the scepter to—I prefer not to go any further than you at the moment. And—I could very easily be wrong—but it's my personal opinion, for whatever it may be worth, that my opposite number among the Russians is Fyodor Guranin."

"Check." And then full realization came to O'Brien. "But, Doc, you said you gave yourself a shot of duoplexin. Doesn't that mean—"

Schneider rose and rubbed his forehead with his fist. "I'm afraid it does. That's why this whole ceremony is more than a little meaningless. But I had the responsibility to discharge. I've discharged it. Now, if you will excuse me, I think I'd better lie down. Good luck."

On his way to report Schneider's illness to the captain, O'Brien came to realize how the Russians had felt earlier that day. There were now five Americans to six Russians. That could be bad. And the responsibility was his.

But with his hand on the door to the captain's room, he shrugged. Fat lot of difference it made! As the plump little man had said: *"Assuming that we're not all dead within a week...."*

The fact was that the political setup on Earth, with all of its implications for two billion people, no longer had very many implications for them. They couldn't risk spreading the disease on Earth, and unless they got back there, they had very little chance of finding a cure for it. They were chained to an alien planet, waiting to be knocked off, one by one, by a sickness which had claimed its last victims a thousand thousand years ago.

Still— He didn't like being a member of a minority.

By morning, he wasn't. During the night, two more Russians had come down with what they were all now referring to as Belov's Disease. That left five Americans to four Russians—except that by that time, they had ceased to count heads in national terms.

Ghose suggested that they change the room serving as mess hall and dormitory into a hospital and that all the healthy men bunk out in the engine room. He also had Guranin rig up a radiation chamber just in front of the engine room.

"All men serving as attendants in the hospital will wear spacesuits," he ordered. "Before they re-enter the engine room, they will subject the spacesuit to a radiation bath of maximum intensity. Then and only then will they join the rest of us and re-move the suit. It's not much, and I think any germ as virulent as this one seems to be won't be stopped by such precautions, but at least we're still making fighting motions."

"Captain," O'Brien inquired. "What about trying to get in touch with Earth some way or other? At least to tell them what's hitting us, for the guidance of future expe-ditions. I know we don't have a radio transmitter powerful enough to operate at such a distance, but couldn't we work out a rocket device that would carry a message and might have a chance of being picked up?"

"I've thought of that. It would be very difficult, but granted that we could do it, do you have any way of insuring that we wouldn't send the contagion along with the message? And, given the conditions on Earth at the moment, I don't think we have to worry about the possibility of another expedition if we don't get back. You know as well as I that within eight or nine months at the most—" The captain broke off. "I seem to have a slight headache," he said mildly.

Even the men who had been working hard in the hospital and were now lying down got to their feet at this.

"Are you sure?" Guranin asked him desperately. "Couldn't it just be a—"

"I'm sure. Well, it had to happen, sooner or later. I think you all know your duties in this situation and will work together well enough. And you're each one capable of running the show. So. In case the matter comes up, in case of any issue that involves a command decision, the captain will be that one among you whose last name starts with the lowest letter alphabetically. Try to live in peace—for as much time as you may have left. Goodbye."

He turned and walked out of the engine room and into the hospital, a thin, dark-skinned man on whose head weariness sat like a crown.

By suppertime, that evening, only two men had still not hospitalized themselves: Preston O'Brien and Semyon Kolevitch. They went through the minutiae of intravenous feeding, of cleaning the patients and keeping them comfortable, with dullness and apathy.

It was just a matter of time. And when they were gone, there would be no one to take care of them.

All the same, they performed their work diligently, and carefully irradiated their spacesuits before returning to the engine room. When Belov and Smathers entered Stage Three, complete coma, the navigator made a descriptive note of it in Dr. Schneider's medical log, under the column of temperature readings that looked like stock market quotations on a very uncertain day in Wall Street.

They ate supper together in silence. They had never liked each other and being limited to each other's company seemed to deepen that dislike.

After supper, O'Brien watched the Martian moons, Deimos and Phobos, rise and set in the black sky through the engine room porthole. Behind him, Kolevitch read Pushkin until he fell asleep.

The next morning, O'Brien found Kolevitch occupying a bed in the hospital. The assistant navigator was already delirious.

"And then there was one," Preston O'Brien said to himself. "Where do we go from here, boys, where do we go from here?"

As he went about his tasks as orderly, he began talking to himself a lot. What the hell, it was better than nothing. It enabled him to forget that he was the only conscious intellect at large on this red dust-storm of a world. It enabled him to forget that he would shortly be dead. It enabled him, in a rather lunatic way, to stay sane.

Because this was it. This was really it. The ship had been planned for a crew of fifteen men. In an emergency, it could be operated by as few as five. Conceivably, two or three men, running about like crazy and being incredibly ingenious, could take it back to Earth and crash-land it somehow. But one man...

Even if his luck held out and he didn't come down with Belov's Disease, he was on Mars for keeps. He was on Mars until his food ran out and his air ran out and the spaceship became a rusting coffin around him. And if he did develop a headache, well, the inevitable end would come so much the faster.

This was it. And there was nothing he could do about it.

He wandered about the ship, suddenly enormous and empty. He had grown up on a ranch in northern Montana, Preston O'Brien had, and he'd never liked being crowded. The back-to-back conditions that space travel made necessary had always irritated him like a pebble in the shoe, but he found this kind of immense, ultimate loneliness almost overpowering. When he took a nap, he found himself dreaming of crowded stands at a World Series baseball game, of the sweating, soggy mob during a subway rush-hour in New York. When he awoke, the loneliness hit him again.

Just to keep himself from going crazy, he set himself little tasks. He wrote a brief history of their expedition for some wholly hypothetical popular magazine; he worked out a dozen or so return courses with the computers in the control room; he went through the Russians' personal belongings to find out—just for curiosity's sake, since it could no longer be of any conceivable importance—who the Soviet MI man had been.

It had been Belov. That surprised him. He had liked Belov very much. Although, he remembered, he had also liked Schneider very much. So it made some sense, on a high-order planning level, after all.

He found himself, much to his surprise, regretting Kolevitch. Damn it, he should have made some more serious attempt to get close to the man before the end!

They had felt a strong antipathy toward each other from the beginning. On Kolevitch's side, it no doubt had something to do with O'Brien's being chief navigator when the Russian had good reason to consider himself by far the better mathematician. And O'Brien had found his assistant singularly without humor, exhibiting a kind of sub-surface truculence that somehow never managed to achieve outright insubordination.

Once, when Ghose had reprimanded him for his obvious attitude toward the man, he had exclaimed: "Well, you're right, and I suppose I should be sorry. But I don't feel that way about any of the other Russians. I get along fine with the rest of them. It's only Kolevitch that I'd like to swat and that, I'll admit, is all the time."

The captain had sighed. "Don't you see what that dislike adds up to? You find the Russian crew members to be pretty decent fellows, fairly easy to get along with, and that can't be: you know the Russians are beasts—they should be exterminated to the last man. So all the fears, all the angers and frustrations, you feel you should logically entertain about them, are channeled into a single direction. You make one man the psychological scapegoat for a whole nation, and you pour out on Semyon Kolevitch all the hatred which you would wish to direct against the other Russians, but can't, because, being an intelligent, perceptive person, you find them too likable.

"Everybody hates somebody on this ship. And they all feel they have good reasons. Hopkins hates Layatinsky because he claims he's always snooping around the communications room. Guranin hates Doctor Schneider, why, I'll never know."

"I can't buy that. Kolevitch has gone out of his way to annoy me. I know that for a fact. And what about Smathers? He hates all the Russians. Hates 'em to a man."

"Smathers is a special case. I'm afraid he lacked emotional security to begin with, and his peculiar position on this expedition—low man on the I.Q. pole—hasn't done his ego any good. You could help him, if you made a particular friend of him. I know he'd like that."

"A-ah," O'Brien had shrugged uncomfortably. "I'm no psychological social worker. I get along all right with him, but I can take Tom Smathers only in very small doses."

And that was another thing he regretted. He'd never been ostentatious about being absolutely indispensable as navigator and the smartest man on board; he'd even been positive he rarely thought about it. But he realized now, against the background glare of his approaching extinction, that almost daily he had smugly plumped out this fact, like a pillow, in the back of his mind. It had been there: it had been nice to stroke. And he had stroked it frequently.

A sort of sickness. Like the sickness of Hopkins-Layatinsky, Guranin-Schneider, Smathers-everyone else. Like the sickness on Earth at the moment, when two of the largest nations on the planet and as such having no need to covet each other's territory, were about ready, reluctantly and unhappily, to go to war with each other, a war which would destroy them both and all other nations besides, allies as well as neutral states, a war which could so easily be avoided and yet was so thoroughly unavoidable.

Maybe, O'Brien thought then, they hadn't caught any sickness on Mars; maybe they'd just brought a sickness—call it the Human Disease—to a nice, clean, sandy planet and it was killing them, because here it had nothing else on which to feed.

O'Brien shook himself.

He'd better watch out. This way madness lay. "Better start talking to myself again. How are you, boy? Feeling all right? No headaches? No aches, no pains, no feelings of fatigue? Then you must be dead, boy!"

When he went through the hospital that afternoon, he noticed that Belov had reached what could be described as Stage Four. Beside Smathers and Ghose, who were still in the coma of Stage Three, the geologist looked wide awake. His head rolled restlessly from side to side and there was a terrible, absolutely horrifying look in his eyes.

"How are you feeling, Nicolai?" O'Brien asked tentatively.

There was no reply. Instead the head turned slowly and Belov stared directly at him. O'Brien shuddered. That look was enough to freeze your blood, he decided, as he went into the engine room and got out of his spacesuit.

Maybe it wouldn't go any further than this. Maybe you didn't die of Belov's Disease. Schneider had said it attacked the nervous system: so maybe the end-product was just insanity.

"Big deal," O'Brien muttered. "Big, big deal."

He had lunch and strolled over to the engine room porthole. The pyramidal marker they had planted on the first day caught his eye: it was the only thing worth looking at in this swirling, hilly landscape. *First Terrestrial Expedition to Mars. In the Name of Human Life.*

If only Ghose hadn't been in such a hurry to get the marker down. The inscription needed rewriting. *Last Terrestrial Expedition to Mars. In the Memory of Human Life—Here and on Earth.* That would be more apt.

He knew what would happen when the expedition didn't return—and no message arrived from it. The Russians would be positive that the Americans had seized the ship and were using the data obtained on the journey to perfect their bomb-delivery technique. The Americans would be likewise positive that the Russians...

They would be the incident.

"Ghose would sure appreciate that," O'Brien said to himself wryly.

There was a clatter behind him. He turned.

The cup and plate from which he'd had lunch were floating in the air!

O'Brien shut his eyes, then opened them slowly. Yes, no doubt about it, they were floating! They seemed to be performing a slow, lazy dance about each other. Once in a while, they touched gently, as if kissing, then pulled apart. Suddenly, they sank to the table and came to rest like a pair of balloons with a last delicate bounce or two.

Had he got Belov's Disease without knowing it, he wondered? Could you progress right to the last stage—hallucinations—without having headaches or fever?

He heard a series of strange noises in the hospital and ran out of the engine room without bothering to get into his spacesuit.

Several blankets were dancing about, just like the cup and saucer. They swirled through the air, as if caught in a strong wind. As he watched, almost sick with astonishment, a few other objects joined them—a thermometer, a packing case, a pair of pants.

But the crew lay silently in their bunks. Smathers had evidently reached Stage Four too. There was the same restless head motion, the same terrible look whenever his eyes met O'Brien's.

And then, as he turned to Belov's bunk, he saw that it was empty! Had the man gotten up in his delirium and wandered off? Was he feeling better? Where had he gone?

O'Brien began to search the ship methodically, calling the Russian by name. Section by section, compartment by compartment, he came at last to the control room. It too was empty. Then where could Belov be?

As he wandered distractedly around the little place, he happened to glance through the porthole. And there, outside, he saw Belov. Without a spacesuit!

It was impossible—no man could survive for a moment unprotected on the raw, almost airless surface of Mars—yet there was Nicolai Belov, walking as unconcernedly as if the sand beneath his feet were the Nevsky Prospekt! And then he shimmered a little around the edges, as if he'd been turned partially into glass—and disappeared.

"Belov!" O'Brien found himself yelping. "For God's sake! Belov! *Belov!*"

"He's gone to inspect the Martian city," a voice said behind him. "He'll be back shortly."

The navigator spun around. There was nobody in the room. He *must* be going completely crazy.

"No, you're not," the voice said. And Tom Smathers rose slowly through the solid floor.

"What's happening to you people?" O'Brien gasped. "What *is* all this?"

"Stage Five of Belov's Disease. The last one. So far, only Belov and I are in it, but the others are entering it now."

O'Brien found his way to a chair and sat down. He worked his mouth a couple of times but couldn't make the words come out.

"You're thinking that Belov's Disease is making magicians out of us," Smathers told him. "No. First, it isn't a disease at all."

For the first time, Smathers looked directly at him and O'Brien had to avert his eyes. It wasn't just that horrifying look he'd had lying on the bed in the hospital. It was—it was as if Smathers were no longer Smathers. He'd become something else.

"Well, it's caused by a bacillus, but not a parasitic one. A symbiotic one."

"Symbi—"

"Like the intestinal flora, it performs a useful function. A highly useful function."

O'Brien had the impression that Smathers was having a hard time finding the right words, that he was choosing very carefully, as if—as if—as if he were talking to a small child!

"That's correct," Smathers told him. "But I believe I can make you understand. The bacillus of Belov's Disease inhabited the nervous system of the ancient Martians as our stomach bacteria live in human digestive systems. Both are symbiotic, both enable the systems they inhabit to function with far greater effectiveness. The Belov bacillus operates within us as a kind of neural transformer, multiplying the mental output almost a thousand times."

"You mean you're a thousand times as intelligent as before?"

Smathers frowned. "This is very difficult. Yes, roughly a thousand times as intelligent, if you must put it that way. Actually, there's a thousandfold increase in mental powers. Intelligence is merely one of those powers. There are many others, such as telepathy and telekinesis, which previously existed in such a minuscule state as to be barely observable. I am in constant communication with Belov, for example, wherever he is. Belov is in almost complete control of his physical environment and its effect on his body. The movable objects which alarmed you so were the results of the first clumsy experiments we made with our new minds. There is still a good deal we have to learn and get used to."

"But—but—" O'Brien searched through his erupting brain and at last found a coherent thought. "But you were so sick!"

"The symbiosis was not established without difficulty," Smathers admitted. "And we are not identical with the Martians physiologically. However, it's all over now. We will return to Earth, spread Belov's Disease—if you want to keep calling it that—and begin our exploration of space and time. Eventually, we'd like to get in touch with the Martians in the—the *place* where they have gone."

"And we'll have bigger wars than we ever dreamed of!"

The thing that had once been Tom Smathers, second assistant engineer, shook its head. "There will be no more wars. Among the mental powers enlarged a thousand times is one that has to do with what you might call moral concepts. Those of us on the ship could and would stop any presently threatening war; but when the population of the world has made neural connection with Belov's bacillus, all danger will be past. No, there will be no more wars."

A silence. O'Brien tried to pull himself together. "Well," he said. "We really found something on Mars, didn't we? And if we're going to start back for Earth, I might as well prepare a course based on present planetary positions."

Again that look in Smathers' eyes, stronger than ever. "That won't be necessary, O'Brien. We won't go back in the same manner as we came. Our way will be—well, *faster.*"

"Good enough," O'Brien said shakily and got to his feet. "And while you're working out the details, I'll climb into a spacesuit and hustle down to that Martian city. I want to get me a good strong dose of Belov's Disease."

The thing that had been Tom Smathers grunted. O'Brien stopped. Suddenly he understood the meaning of that frightening look he had had first from Belov and now from Smathers.

It was a look of enormous pity.

"That's right," said Smathers with infinite gentleness. "You can't ever get Belov's Disease. You are naturally immune."

AFTERWORD

The year before I wrote this story I had met a man, a professor at a small university, who told me a moral tale out of his life that I found I couldn't ever forget. He had always been very proud of his I.Q., which was at genius level, and had been determined since adolescence to marry a woman with at least as high an I.Q., so that he would be the father of utterly brilliant children.

He had found such a woman, not anyone he considered particularly attractive, but someone who was several points farther along on the Wechsler-Bellevue Scale than he— and had immediately suggested marriage. His wife seemed to feel pretty much the same as he did about the matter of physical attraction, but—what was crucial—she most of all agreed with him on the importance of combining and passing along their very special genes.

They had a child within a year of their marriage. And the child was not brilliant. The child was not even of normal intelligence. The child was badly retarded—in I.Q. terms, somewhere down near moron level.

His wife divorced him and got a job far away, leaving him with the child.

"We sinned," he told me. "We sinned against the laws of sex. It was as if we had mated for money, instead of for love. And we had a child who was born not out of mutual love, but out of genetic greed. We deserved what we got."

All right. That was the first part of what made this story. The rest…

Well, two years before Sputnik and ten years after Los Alamos, I wrote "The Sickness," out of a desperate hope and a telling fear. Unlike Eisenhower, the president (who remarked plaintively, after Sputnik, "But nobody ever told me anything about these things"), I felt we had some time ago reached the capability of space travel, and I wanted to see it done— in my lifetime—and I didn't particularly care *who* or *what* finally did it. I wanted to see my fellow humans, in the words of the first science-fiction story I ever read, "at last put their feet on the soil of another world."

That was the desperate hope. The fear— We were then in the midst of the Cold War, which I felt in 1955 and still feel in 2001 (despite our present lordly bestriding of a monopolar political world) to be the most damnable question we face and the most damnable answer we fruitlessly pursue. So what: so we and the Soviet Union are not now at irreconcilable odds, and we and the Soviet Union are not at the moment feverishly piling up nuclear weapons against each other in preparation for a nuclear Ragnarok. The reason? There is no longer a Soviet Union.

There remain nations and sects and individuals (India, for example, is no longer seen as an all-around good guy) who know us as one or another version of the Great Satan—and we do them at least a similar bloody honor. Ragnarok is still a tiny, but definite, glow on the horizon of our time. It may yet reach meridian. This story was written as a crazy, loopy, hysterically pathetic suggestion of a way to prevent the meridian.

And with that, I tug off the hair shirt and return the upward-pointing forefinger to my sweaty palm. A last anecdote re "The Sickness":

After the story appeared in print, my friend, the college professor with the high I.Q., telephoned me. He recognized his role in precipitating the piece, and he wanted to tell me where he stood now with regard to his child.

"It's changed my life, redirected all my research," he said. "I used to be interested only in gifted children—their education, their socialization, their problems. Now, since my son was born, I've been working only with the issues of rearing backward kids, kids who badly need help with everything. And I've been doing very useful and much-needed work."

"You might say God pointed you in a new way," I told him.

"Yes, you might," he said. "And to hell with God."

WRITTEN 1955———PUBLISHED 1955

ஃ

The Servant Problem

This was the day of complete control...

Garomma, the Servant of All, the World's Drudge, the Slavey of Civilization, placed delicately scented fingertips to his face, closed his eyes and allowed himself to luxuriate in the sensation of ultimate power, absolute power, power such as no human being had even dared to dream of before this day.

Complete control. Complete...

Except for one man. One single ambitious maverick of a man. One very *useful* man. Should he be strangled at his desk this afternoon, that was the question, or should he be allowed a few more days, a few more weeks, of heavily supervised usefulness? His treason, his plots, were unquestionably coming to a head. Well, Garomma would decide that later. At leisure.

Meanwhile, in all other respects, with everyone else there was control. Control not only of men's minds but of their glands as well. And those of their children.

And, if Moddo's estimates were correct, of their children's children.

"Yea," Garomma muttered to himself, suddenly remembering a fragment of the oral text his peasant father had taught him years ago, "yea, unto the seventh generation."

What ancient book, burned in some long-ago educational fire, had that text come from, he wondered? His father would not be able to tell him, nor would any of his father's friends and neighbors; they had all been wiped out after the Sixth District Peasant Uprising thirty years ago.

An uprising of a type that could never possibly occur again. Not with complete control.

Someone touched his knee gently, and his mind ceased its aimless foraging. Moddo. The Servant of Education, seated below him in the depths of the vehicle, gestured obsequiously at the transparent, missile-proof cupola that surrounded his leader down to the waist.

"The people," he stated in his peculiar half-stammer. "There. Outside."

Yes. They were rolling through the gates of the Hovel of Service and into the city proper. On both sides of the street and far into the furthest distance were shrieking crowds as black and dense and exuberant as ants on a piece of gray earthworm. Garomma, the Servant of All, could not be too obviously busy with his own thoughts; he was about to be viewed by those he served so mightily.

He crossed his arms upon his chest and bowed to right and left in the little dome that rose like a tower from the squat black conveyance. Bow right, bow left, and do it humbly. Right, left—and humbly, humbly. Remember, you are the Servant of All.

As the shrieks rose in volume, he caught a glimpse of Moddo nodding approval from beneath. Good old Moddo. This was his day of triumph as well. The achievement of complete control was most thoroughly and peculiarly the achievement of the Servant of Education. Yet Moddo sat in heavy-shadowed anonymity behind the driver with Garomma's personal bodyguards; sat and tasted his triumph only with his leader's tongue—as he had for more than twenty-five years now.

Fortunately for Moddo, such a taste was rich enough for his system. Unfortunately, there were others—one other at least—who required more…

Garomma bowed to right and left and, as he bowed, looked curiously through the streaming webs of black-uniformed motorcycle police that surrounded his car. He looked at the people of Capital City, *his* people, his as everything and everyone on Earth was his. Jamming madly together on the sidewalks, they threw their arms wide as his car came abreast of them.

"Serve us, Garomma," they chanted. "Serve us! Serve us!"

He observed their contorted faces, the foam that appeared at the mouth-corners of many, the half-shut eyes and ecstatic expressions, the swaying men, the writhing women, the occasional individual who collapsed in an unnoticed climax of happiness. And he bowed. With his arms crossed upon his chest, he bowed. Right and left. Humbly.

Last week, when Moddo had requested his views on problems of ceremony and protocol relative to today's parade, the Servant of Education had commented smugly on the unusually high incidence of mob hysteria expected when his chief's face was seen. And Garomma had voiced a curiosity he'd been feeling for a long time.

"What goes on in their minds when they see me, Moddo? I know they worship and get exhilarated and all that. But what precisely do you fellows call the emotion when you talk about it in the labs and places such as the Education Center?"

The tall man slid his hand across his forehead in the gesture that long years had made thoroughly familiar to Garomnma.

"They are experiencing a trigger release," he said slowly, staring over Garomma's shoulder as if he were working out the answer from the electronically pinpointed world map on the back wall. "All the tensions these people accumulate in their daily round of niggling little prohibitions and steady coercions, all the frustrations of 'don't do this and don't do this, do *that*' have been organized by the Service of Education to be released explosively the moment they see your picture or hear your voice."

"Trigger release. Hm! I've never thought of it quite *that* way."

Moddo held up a hand in rigid earnestness. "After all, you're the one man whose life is supposedly spent in an abject obedience beyond anything they've ever known. The man who holds the—the intricate strands of the world's coordination in his patient, unwearying fingers; the ultimate and hardest-worked employee; the—the scapegoat of the multitudes!"

Garomma had grinned at Moddo's scholarly eloquence. Now, however, as he observed his screaming folk from under submissive eyelids, he decided that the Servant of Education had been completely right.

On the Great Seal of the World State was it not written: *All Men Must Serve Somebody, But Only Garomma Is the Servant of All?*

Without him, they knew, and knew irrevocably, oceans would break through dikes and flood the land, infections would appear in men's bodies and grow rapidly into pestilences that could decimate whole districts, essential services would break down so that an entire city could die of thirst in a week, and local officials would oppress the people and engage in lunatic wars of massacre with each other. Without him, without Garomma working day and night to keep everything running smoothly, to keep the titanic forces of nature and civilization under control. They knew, because these things happened whenever "Garomma was tired of serving."

What were the unpleasant interludes of their lives to the implacable dreary—but, oh, so essential!—toil of his? Here, in this slight, serious-looking man bowing humbly right and left, right and left, was not only the divinity that made it possible for Man to exist comfortably on Earth, but also the crystallization of all the sub-races that ever enabled an exploited people to feel that things could be worse, that relative to the societal muck beneath them, they were, in spite of their sufferings, as lords and monarchs in comparison.

No wonder they stretched their arms frantically to him, the Servant of All, the World's Drudge, the Slavey of Civilization, and screamed their triumphant demand with one breath, their fearful plea with the next: "Serve us, Garomma! Serve us, serve us, serve us!"

Didn't the docile sheep he had herded as a boy in the Sixth District mainland to the northwest, didn't the sheep also feel that he was their servant as he led them and drove them to better pastures and cooler streams, as he protected them from enemies and removed pebbles from their feet, all to the end that their smoking flesh would taste better on his father's table? But these so much more useful herds of two-legged, well-brained sheep were as thoroughly domesticated. And on the simple principle they'd absorbed that government was the servant of the people and the highest power in the government was the most abysmal servant.

His sheep. He smiled at them paternally, possessively, as his special vehicle rolled along the howling, face-filled mile between the Hovel of Service and the Educational Center. His sheep. And these policemen on motorcycles, these policemen on foot whose arms were locked against the straining crowds every step of the way, these were his sheepdogs. Another kind of domesticated animal.

That's all *he* had been, thirty-three years ago, when he'd landed on this island fresh from a rural Service of Security training school to take his first government job as a policeman in Capital City. A clumsy, overexcited sheepdog. One of the least important sheepdogs of the previous regime's Servant of All.

But three years later, the peasant revolt in his own district had given him his chance. With his special knowledge of the issues involved as well as the identity of the real leaders, he'd been able to play an important role in crushing the rebellion. And then, his new and important place in the Service of Security had enabled him to meet promising youngsters in the other services—Moddo, particularly, the first and most useful human he had personally domesticated.

With Moddo's excellent administrative mind at his disposal, he had become an expert at the gracious art of political throat-cutting, so that when his superior made his bid for the highest office in the world, Garomma had been in the best possible position to sell him out and become the new Servant of Security. And from that point, with Moddo puffing along in his wake and working out the minutiae of strategy, it had been a matter of a few years before he had been able to celebrate his own successful bid in the sizzling wreckage of the preceding administration's Hovel of Service.

But the lesson he had taught the occupants of that blasted, projectile-ridden place he had determined never to forget himself. He couldn't know how many Servants of Security before him had used their office to reach the mighty wooden stool of the Servant of All: after all, the history books, and all other books, were rewritten thoroughly at the beginning of every new regime; and the Oral Tradition, usually a good guide to the past if you could sift the facts out properly, was silent on this subject. It was obvious, however, that what he had done, another could do—that the Servant of Security was the logical, self-made heir to the Servant of All.

And the trouble was you couldn't do anything about the danger but be watchful.

He remembered when his father had called him away from childhood games and led him out to the hills to tend the sheep. How he had hated the lonesome, tiresome work! The old man had realized it and, for once, had softened sufficiently to attempt an explanation.

"You see, son, sheep are what they call domestic animals. So are dogs. Well, we can domesticate sheep and we can domesticate dogs to guard the sheep, but for a smart, wide-awake shepherd who'll know what to do when something real unusual comes up and will be able to tell us about it, well, for that we need a man."

"Gee, Pa," he had said, kicking disconsolately at the enormous shepherd's crook they'd given him, "then why don't you—whatdoyoucallit—*domesticate* a man?"

His father had chuckled and then stared out heavily over the shaggy brow of the hill. "Well, there are people trying to do that, too, and they're getting better at it all the time. The only trouble, once you've got him domesticated, he isn't worth beans as a shepherd. He isn't sharp and excited once he's tamed. He isn't interested enough to be any use at all."

That was the problem in a nutshell, Garomma reflected. The Servant of Security, by the very nature of his duties, could not be a domesticated animal.

He had tried using sheepdogs at the head of Security; over and over again he had tried them. But they were always inadequate and had to be replaced by men. And— one year, three years, five years in office—men sooner or later struck for supreme power and had to be regretfully destroyed.

As the current Servant of Security was about to be destroyed. The only trouble— the man was so damned useful! You had to time these things perfectly to get the maximum length of service from the rare, imaginative individual who filled the post to perfection and yet cut him down the moment the danger outweighed the value. And since, with the right man, the danger existed from the very start, you had to watch the scale carefully, unremittingly…

Garomma sighed. This problem was the only annoyance in a world that had been virtually machined to give him pleasure. But it was, inevitably, a problem that was with him always, even in his dreams. Last night had been positively awful.

Moddo touched his knee again to remind him that he was on exhibition. He shook himself and smiled his gratitude. One had to remember that dreams were only dreams.

They had the crowds behind them now. Ahead, the great metal gate of the Educational Center swung slowly open and his car rumbled inside. As the motorcycle policemen swung off their two-wheelers with a smart sidewise flourish, the armed guards of the Service of Education in their crisp white tunics came to attention. Garomma, helped nervously by Moddo, clambered out of the car just as the Center Band, backed by the Center Choir, swung into the roaring, thrilling credo of *Humanity's Hymn:*

> *Garomma works day and night,*
> *Garomma's tasks are never light;*
> *Garomma lives in drudgery,*
> *For the sake of me, for the sake of thee…*

After five verses, protocol having been satisfied, the band began *The Song of Education* and the Assistant Servant of Education, a poised, well-bred young man, came down the steps of the building. His arm-spread and "Serve us, Garomma," while perfunctory, was thoroughly correct. He stood to one side so that Garomma and Moddo could start up the steps and then swung in, straight-backed, behind them. The choirmaster held the song on a high, worshipping note.

They walked through the great archway with its carved motto, *All Must Learn from the Servant of All,* and down the great central corridor of the immense building. The gray rags that Garomma and Moddo wore flapped about them. The walls were lined with minor employees chanting, "Serve us, Garomma. Serve us! Serve us! Serve us!"

Not quite the insane fervor of the street mobs, Garomma reflected, but entirely satisfactory paroxysms nonetheless. He bowed and stole a glance at Moddo beside him. He barely restrained a smile. The Servant of Education looked as nervous, as uncertain as ever. Poor Moddo! He was just not meant for such a high position. He carried his tall, husky body with all the *élan* of a tired berry-picker. He looked like anything but the most important official in the establishment.

And that was one of the things that made him indispensable. Moddo was just bright enough to know his own inadequacy. Without Garomma, he'd still be checking statistical abstracts for interesting discrepancies in some minor department of the Service of Education. He *knew* he wasn't strong enough to stand by himself. Nor was he sufficiently outgoing to make useful alliances. And so Moddo, alone of all the Servants in the Cabinet, could be trusted completely.

In response to Moddo's diffident touch on his shoulder, he walked into the large room that had been so extravagantly prepared for him and climbed the little cloth-of-gold platform at one end. He sat down on the rough wooden stool at the top; a moment later, Moddo took the chair that was one step down, and the Assistant Servant of Education took the chair a further step below. The chief executives of the Educational Center, dressed in white tunics of the richest, most flowing cut, filed in slowly and stood before them. Garomma's personal bodyguards lined up in front of the platform.

And the ceremonies began. The ceremonies attendant upon complete control.

First, the oldest official in the Service of Education recited the appropriate passages from the Oral Tradition. How every year, in every regime, far back almost to prehistoric democratic times, a psychometric sampling had been taken of elementary school graduating classes all over the world to determine exactly how successful the children's political conditioning had been.

How every year there had been an overwhelming majority disclosed which believed the current ruler was the very pivot of human welfare, the mainspring of daily life, and a small minority—five percent, seven percent, three percent—which had successfully resisted indoctrination and which, as adults, were to be carefully watched as potential sources of disaffection.

How with the ascension of Garomma and his Servant of Education, Moddo, twenty-five years ago, a new era of intensive mass-conditioning, based on much more ambitious goals, had begun.

The old man finished, bowed and moved back into the crowd. The Assistant Servant of Education rose and turned gracefully to face Garomma. He described these new goals which might be summed up in the phrase "complete control," as opposed to previous administrations' outdated satisfaction with 97 percent or 95 percent control, and discussed the new extensive fear mechanisms and stepped-up psychometric spot-checks in the earlier grades—by which they were to be achieved. These techniques had all been worked out by Moddo—"under the never-failing inspiration and constant guidance of Garomma, the Servant of All"—and had, in a few years, resulted in a sampling which showed the number of independent juvenile minds to be less than one percent. All others worshipped Garomma with every breath they took.

Thereafter, progress had been slower. They had absorbed the most brilliant children with the new conditioning process, but had hit the hard bedrock of the essential deviates, the psychological misfits whose personal maladjustments made it impossible for them to accept the prevailing attitudes of their social milieu, *whatever* these attitudes should happen to be. Over the years, techniques of conditioning had been painfully worked out which enabled even misfits to fit into society in the one respect of Garomma-worship and, over the years, the samplings indicated the negative doctrinal responses to be receding in the direction of zero: .016 percent, .007 percent, .0002 percent.

And *this* year. Well! The Assistant Servant of Education paused and took a deep breath. Five weeks ago, the Uniform Educational System of Earth had graduated a new crop of youngsters from the elementary schools. The customary planet-wide sampling had been taken on graduation day; collation and verification had just been completed. The results: negative response was zero to the very last decimal place! Control was complete.

Spontaneous applause broke out in the room, applause in which even Garomma joined. Then he leaned forward and placed his hand paternally, possessively on Moddo's head of unruly brown hair. At this unusual honor to their chief, the officials in the room cheered.

Under the noise, Garomma took the opportunity to ask Moddo, "What does the population in general know about this? What exactly are you telling them?"

Moddo turned his nervous, large-jawed face around. "Mostly just that it's a holiday. A lot of obscure stuff about you achieving complete control of the human environment all to the end of human betterment. Barely enough so that they can know it's something you like and can rejoice with you."

"In their own slavery. I like that." Garomma tasted the sweet flavor of unlimited rulership for a long moment. Then the taste went sour and he remembered. "Moddo, I want to take care of the Servant of Security matter this afternoon. We'll go over it as soon as we start back."

The Servant of Education nodded. "I have a few thoughts. It's not so simple, you know. There's the problem of the successor."

"Yes. There's always that. Well, maybe in a few more years, if we can sustain this sampling and spread the techniques to the maladjusted elements in the older adult population, we'll be able to start dispensing with Security altogether."

"Maybe. Strongly set attitudes are much harder to adjust, though. And you'll always need a security system in the top ranks of officialdom. But I'll do the best—I'll do the best I can."

Garomma nodded and sat back, satisfied. Moddo would always do his best. And on a purely routine level, that was pretty good. He raised a hand negligently. The cheering and the applause stopped. Another Education executive came forward to describe the sampling method in detail. The ceremony went on.

This was the day of complete control...

Moddo, the Servant of Education, the Ragged Teacher of Mankind, rubbed his aching forehead with huge, well-manicured fingers and allowed himself to luxuriate in the sensation of ultimate power, absolute power, power such as no human being had even dared to dream of before this day.

Complete control. Complete...

There was the one remaining problem of the successor to the Servant of Security. Garomma would want a decision from him as soon as they started back to the Hovel of Service; and he was nowhere near a decision. Either one of the two Assistant Servants of Security would be able to fill the job admirably, but that wasn't the question.

The question was which one of the two men would be most likely to maintain at high pitch in Garomma the fears that Moddo had conditioned him to feel over a period of thirty years?

That, so far as Moddo was concerned, was the whole function of the Servant of Security; to serve as primary punching bag for the Servant of All's fear-ridden subconscious until such time as the mental conflicts reached a periodic crisis. Then, by removing the man around whom they had been trained to revolve, the pressure would be temporarily eased.

It was a little like fishing, Moddo decided. You fed the fish extra line by killing off the Servant of Security, and then you reeled it in quietly, steadily, in the next few years by surreptitiously dropping hints about the manifest ambitions of his successor. Only you never wanted to land the fish. You merely wanted to keep it hooked and constantly under your control.

The Servant of Education smiled an inch or two behind his face as he had trained himself to smile since early boyhood. Landing the fish? That would be the equivalent of becoming Servant of All himself. And what intelligent man could satisfy his lust for power with such an idiotic goal?

No, leave that to his colleagues, the ragged high officials in the Hovel of Service, forever scheming and plotting, making alliances and counter-alliances. The Servant of Industry, the Servant of Agriculture, the Servant of Science and the rest of those highly important fools.

To be the Servant of All meant being the target of plots, the very bull's eye of attention. An able man in this society must inevitably recognize that power—no matter how veiled or disguised—was the only valid aim in life. And the Servant of All— veiled and disguised though he might be in a hundred humbling ways—was power incarnate.

No. Far better to be known as the nervous, uncertain underling whose knees shook beneath the weight of responsibilities far beyond his abilities. Hadn't he heard their contemptuous voices behind his back?

"…Garomma's administrative toy…"

"…Garomma's fool of a spiritual valet…"

"…nothing but a footstool, a very ubiquitous footstool, mind you, but a footstool nonetheless on which rests Garomma's mighty heel…"

"…poor, colorless, jittery slob…"

"…when Garomma sneezes, Moddo sniffles…"

But from that menial, despised position, to be the real source of all policy, the maker and breaker of men, the *de facto* dictator of the human race…

He brought his hand up once more and smoothed at his forehead. The headache was getting worse. And the official celebration of complete control was likely to take another hour yet. He should be able to steal away for twenty or thirty minutes with Loob the Healer, without getting Garomma too upset. The Servant of All had to be handled with special care at these crisis points. The jitters that had been induced in him were likely to become so overpowering that he might try to make a frantic decision for himself. And that possibility, while fantastically dim, must not be given a chance to develop. It was too dangerous.

For a moment, Moddo listened to the young man in front of them rattle on about modes and means, skew curves and correlation coefficients, all the statistical jargon that concealed the brilliance of the psychological revolution that he, Moddo, had wrought. Yes, they would be there another hour yet.

Thirty-five years ago, while doing his thesis in the Central Service of Education Post-Graduate Training School, he had found a magnificent nugget in the accumulated slag of several centuries of mass-conditioning statistics; the concept of *individual* application.

For a long while, he had found the concept incredibly difficult to close with: when all your training has been directed toward the efficient handling of human attitudes in terms of millions, the consideration of one man's attitudes and emotions is as slippery a proposition as an eel, freshly caught and moribundly energetic.

But after his thesis had been completed and accepted—the thesis on suggested techniques for the achievement of complete control which the previous administration had filed and forgotten—he had turned once more to the problem of individual conditioning.

And in the next few years, while working at his dull job in the Applied Statistics Bureau of the Service of Education, he had addressed himself to the task of refining the individual from the group, or reducing the major to the minor.

One thing became apparent. The younger your material, the easier your task—exactly as in mass-conditioning. But if you started with a child, it would be years before he would be able to operate effectively in the world on your behalf. And with a child you were faced with the constant counter-barrage of political conditioning which filled the early school years.

What was needed was a young man who already had a place of sorts in the government, but who, for some reason or other, had a good deal of unrealized—and *unconditioned*—potential. Preferably, also, somebody whose background had created a personality with fears and desires of a type which could serve as adequate steering handles.

Moddo began to work nights, going over the records of his office in search of that man. He had found two or three who looked good. That brilliant fellow in the Service of Transport, he reminisced, had seemed awfully interesting for a time. Then he had come across Garomma's papers.

And Garomma had been perfect. From the first. He was a directorial type, he was likable, he was clever—and he was very receptive.

"I could learn an awful lot from you," he had told Moddo shyly at their first meeting. "This is such a big complicated place—Capital Island. So much going on all the time. I get confused just thinking about it. But you were born here. You really seem to know your way around all the swamps and bogs and snakepits."

Due to sloppy work on the part of the Sixth District Conditioning Commissioner, Garomma's home neighborhood had developed a surprising number of quasi-independent minds on all levels of intelligence. Most of them tended to revolution, especially after a decade of near-famine crops and exorbitant taxation. But Garomma had been ambitious; he had turned against his peasant background and entered the lower echelons of the Service of Security.

This meant that when the Sixth District Peasant Uprising occurred, his usefulness in its immediate suppression had earned him a much higher place. More important, it had given him freedom from the surveillance and extra adult conditioning which a man of his suspicious family associations might normally have expected.

It also meant that, once Moddo had maneuvered an introduction and created a friendship, he had at his disposal not only a rising star but a personality that was superb in its plasticity.

A personality upon which he could laboriously create the impress of his own image.

First, there had been that wonderful business of Garomma's guilt about disobeying his father that had eventually led to his leaving the farm altogether—and later to his becoming an informer against his own family and neighbors. This guilt, which had resulted in fear and therefore hatred for everything associated with its original objects, was easy to redirect to the person of his superior, the Servant of Security, and make that the new father-image.

Later, when Garomma had become Servant of All, he still retained—under Moddo's tireless ministrations—the same guilt and the same omnipresent fear of punishment toward whoever was the reigning Head of Security. Which was necessary if he was not to realize that his real master was the large man who sat at his right hand, constantly looking nervous and uncertain...

Then there had been education. And re-education. From the beginning, Moddo had realized the necessity of feeding Garomma's petty peasant arrogance and had abased himself before it. He gave the other man the impression that the subversive thoughts he was now acquiring were of his own creation, even leading him to believe that he was domesticating Moddo—curious how the fellow never escaped from his agricultural origins even in his metaphors!—instead of the other way around.

Because Moddo was now laying plans for a tremendous future, and he didn't want them upset some day by the cumulative resentment one may develop toward a master and teacher; on the contrary, he wanted the plans reinforced by the affection one feels toward a pet dog whose nuzzling dependence constantly feeds the ego and creates a more ferocious counter-dependence than the owner ever suspects.

The shock that Garomma had exhibited when he began to realize that the Servant of All was actually the Dictator of All! Moddo almost smiled with his lips at the memory. Well, after all, when his own parents had suggested the idea years ago in the course of a private sailing trip they took together pursuant to his father's duties as a minor official in the Service of Fisheries and Marine—hadn't he been so upset that he'd let go of the tiller and vomited over the side? Losing your religion is a hard thing at any age, but it gets much harder as you get older.

On the other hand, Moddo had lost not only his religion at the age of six, but also his parents. They had done too much loose talking to too many people under the incorrect assumption that the then Servant of Security was going to be lax forever.

He rubbed his knuckles into the side of his head. This headache was one of the worst he'd had in days! He needed fifteen minutes at least—surely he could get away for fifteen minutes—with Loob. The Healer would set him up for the rest of the day, which, on all appearances, was going to be a tiring one. And he had to get away from Garomma, anyway, long enough to come to a clear-headed, personal decision on who was to be the next Servant of Security.

Moddo, the Servant of Education, the Ragged Teacher of Mankind, took advantage of a pause between speakers to lean back and say to Garomma: "I have a few administrative matters to check here before we start back. May I be excused? It—it won't take more than about twenty or twenty-five minutes."

Garomma scowled imperiously straight ahead. "Can't they wait? This is your day as much as mine. I'd like to have you near me."

"I know that, Garomma, and I'm grateful for the need. But"—and now he touched the Servant of All's knee in supplication—"I beg of you to let me attend to them. They are very pressing. One of them has to do—it has to do indirectly with the Servant of Security and may help you decide whether you want to dispense with him at this particular time."

Garomma's face immediately lost its bleakness. "In that case, by all means. But get back before the ceremony is over. I want us to leave together."

The tall man nodded and rose. He turned to face his leader. "Serve us, Garomma," he said with outstretched arms. "Serve us, serve us, serve us." He backed out of the room, always facing the Servant of All.

Out in the corridor, he strode rapidly through the saluting Center of Education guards and into his private elevator. He pressed the third-floor button. And then, as the door swept shut and the car began to rise, he permitted himself a single, gentle, mouth-curling smile.

The trouble he had taken to pound that one concept into Garomma's thick head: the basic principle in modern scientific government is to keep the government so unobtrusive as to appear nonexistent, to use the illusion of freedom as a kind of lubricant for slipping on invisible shackles—above all, to rule in the name of anything but rulership!

Garomma himself had phrased it in his own laborious fashion one day when, shortly after their great coup, they stood together—both still uncomfortable in the rags of greatness—and watched the construction of the new Hovel of Service in the charred place where the old one had stood for almost half a century. A huge, colorful, revolving sign on top of the unfinished building told the populace that FROM HERE WILL YOUR EVERY WANT AND NEED BE ATTENDED TO, FROM HERE WILL YOU BE SERVED MORE EFFICIENTLY AND PLEASANTLY THAN EVER BEFORE. Garomma had stared at the sign which was being flashed on the video receivers of the world—in the homes as well as in factories, offices, schools and compulsory communal gatherings—every hour on the hour.

"It's like my father used to say," he told Moddo at last with the peculiar heavy chuckle he used to identify a thought he felt was entirely original; "the right kind of salesman, if he talks long enough and hard enough, can convince a man that the thickest thorns feel as soft as roses. All he has to do is keep calling them roses, hey, Moddo?"

Moddo had nodded slowly, pretending to be overcome by the brilliance of the analysis and savoring its complexities for a few moments. Then, as always, merely appearing to be conducting an examination of the various latent possibilities in Garomma's ideas, he had proceeded to give the new Servant of All a further lesson.

He had underlined the necessity of avoiding all outward show of pomp and luxury, something the so-recently dead officials of the previous administration had tended to forget in the years before their fall. He had pointed out that Servants of Mankind must constantly appear to be just that—the humble instruments of the larger mass will. Then anyone who acted contrary to Garomma's whim would be punished, not for disobeying his ruler, but for acting against the overwhelming majority of the human race.

And he had suggested an innovation that had been in his mind for a long time; the occasional creation of disasters in regions that had been uninterruptedly loyal and obedient. This would accentuate the fact that the Servant of All was very human indeed, that his tasks were overwhelming and that he occasionally grew tired.

This would intensify the impression that the job of coordinating the world's goods and services had almost grown too complex to be handled successfully. It would spur the various Districts on to uncalled-for prodigies of frantic loyalty and self-regimentation, so that they at least would have the Servant of All's maximum attention.

"Of course," Garomma had agreed. "That's what I said. The whole point is not to let them know that you're running their lives and that they're helping you do it. You're getting the idea."

He was getting the idea! He, Moddo, who ever since his adolescence had been studying a concept that had originated centuries ago when mankind had begun to emerge from the primitive chaos of self-rule and personal decision into the organized social universe of modern times...*he* was getting the idea!

He had smirked gratefully. But he had continued applying to Garomma himself the techniques that he was teaching Garomma to apply to the mass of men as a whole. Year in, year out, seemingly absorbed in the immensities of the project he had undertaken on behalf of the Service of Education, he had actually left its planning in the hands of subordinates while he concentrated on Garomma.

And today, while superficially acquiring complete control over the minds of an entire generation of human beings, he had tasted for the first time complete control over Garomma. For the past five years, he had been attempting to crystallize his ascendancy in a form that was simpler to use than complicated need-mechanisms and statement-patterns.

Today, for the first time, the weary hours of delicate, stealthy conditioning had begun to work out perfectly. The hand-signal, the touch-stimulus that he had organized Garomma's mind to respond to, had resulted in the desired responses every single time!

As he walked down the third-floor corridor to Loob's modest office, he searched for an adequate expression. It was like, he decided, being able to turn a whole vast liner by one touch on the wheel. The wheel activated the steering engine, the steering engine pushed against the enormous weight of rudder, and the rudder's movements eventually forced the great ship to swing about and change its course.

No, he reflected, let Garomma have his glorious moments and open adulation, his secret palaces and multitudes of concubines. He, Moddo, would settle for the single, occasional touch…and complete control.

The anteroom to Loob's office was empty. He stood there impatiently for a moment, then called out: "Loob! Isn't anyone taking care of this place? I'm in a hurry!"

A plump little man with a tiny pointed beard on his chin came scurrying out of the other room. "My secretary—everyone had to go downstairs when the Servant of All entered—things are so disrupted—she hasn't returned yet. But I was careful," he went on, catching up to his own breath, "to cancel all my appointments with other patients while you were in the building. Please come in."

Moddo stretched himself out on the couch in the Healer's office. "I can only spare about—about fifteen minutes. I have a very important decision to make, and I have a headache that's gouging out my—my brains."

Loob's fingers circled Moddo's neck and began massaging the back of his head with a serene purposefulness. "I'll do what I can. Now try to relax. Relax. That's right. *Relax.* Doesn't this help?"

"A lot," Moddo sighed. He must find some way of working Loob into his personal entourage, to be with him whenever he had to travel with Garomma. The man was *invaluable.* It would be wonderful to have him always available in person. Just a matter of conditioning Garomma to the thought. And now *that* could be handled with the same suggestion. "Do you mind if I just talk?" he inquired. "I don't feel very much—very much like free association."

Loob sat down in the heavily upholstered chair behind the desk. "Do whatever you want. If you care to, go into what's troubling you at the moment. All we can hope to do in fifteen minutes is help you relax."

Moddo began to talk.

This was the day of complete control…

Loob, the Healer of Minds, the Assistant to the Third Assistant Servant of Education, threaded his fingers through the small, triangular beard that was his professional badge and allowed himself to luxuriate in the sensation of ultimate power, absolute power, power such as no human being had even dared to dream of before this day.

Complete control. Complete…

It would have been extremely satisfying to have handled the Servant of Security matter directly, but such pleasures would come in time. His technicians in the Bureau of Healing Research had almost solved the problem he had set them. Meanwhile he still had revenge and the enjoyment of unlimited dominion.

He listened to Moddo talking of his difficulties in a carefully guarded, nonspecific fashion and held up a round fat hand to cover his grin. The man actually believed that after seven years of close therapeutic relationship, he could conceal such details from Loob!

But of course. He had to believe it. Loob had spent the first two years restructuring his entire psyche upon that belief, and then—and only then—had begun to effect transference on a total basis. While the emotions Moddo felt toward his parents in childhood were being duplicated relative to the Healer, Loob had begun to probe in the now unsuspicious mind. At first he hadn't believed what the evidence suggested. Then, as he got to know the patient much better he became completely convinced and almost breathless at the scope of his windfall.

For more than twenty-five years, Garomma, as the Servant of All, had ruled the human race, and for longer than that, Moddo, as a sort of glorified personal secretary, had controlled Garomma in every important respect.

So, for the past five years, he, Loob, as psychotherapist and indispensable crutch to an uncertain, broken ego, had guided Moddo and thus reigned over the world, undisputed, unchallenged—and thoroughly unsuspected.

The man behind the man behind the throne. What could be safer than that?

Of course, it would be more efficient to fasten his therapeutic grip directly on Garomma. But that would bring him out in the open far too much. Being the Servant of All's personal mental physician would make him the object of jealous scrutiny by every scheming high-echelon cabal.

No, it was better to be the one who had custody of the custodian, especially when the custodian appeared to be the most insignificant man in all the Hovel of Service officialdom.

And then, some day, when his technicians had come up with the answer he required, he might dispose of the Servant of Education and control Garomna at firsthand, with the new method.

He listened with amusement to Moddo discussing the Servant of Security matter in terms of a hypothetical individual in his own department who was about to be replaced. The question was: which one of two extremely able subordinates should be given his job?

Loob wondered if the patient had any idea how transparent his subterfuges were. No, they rarely did. This was a man whose upset mind had been so manipulated that its continued sanity depended on two factors: the overpowering need to consult Loob whenever anything even mildly delicate came up, and the belief that he could be consulted without revealing the actual data of the situation.

When the voice on the couch had come to the end of its ragged, wandering summation, Loob took over. Smoothly, quietly, almost tonelessly, he reviewed what Moddo had said. On the surface he was merely restating the concepts of his patient in a more coherent way. Actually, he was reformulating them so that, considering his personal problems and basic attitudes, the Servant of Education would have no alternative. He would have to select the younger of the two candidates, the one whose background had included the least opposition to the Healers Guild.

Not that it made very much difference. The important thing was the proof of complete control. That was implicit in having made Moddo convince Garomma of the necessity of getting rid of a Servant of Security at a time when the Servant of All faced no particular mental crisis. When, in fact, his euphoria was at its height.

But there was, admittedly, the additional pleasure in finally destroying the man who, years ago as Chief of the Forty-seventh District's Security, had been responsible for the execution of Loob's only brother. The double achievement was as delicious as one of those two-flavor tarts for which the Healer's birthplace was famous. He sighed reminiscently.

Moddo sat up on the couch. He pressed his large, spreading hands into the fabric on either side and stretched. "You'd be amazed how much help this one short session has been, Loob. The—the headache's gone, the—the confusion's gone. Just talking about it seems to clarify everything. I know exactly what I have to do now."

"Good," drawled Loob the Healer in a gentle, carefully detached voice.

"I'll try to get back tomorrow for a full hour. And I've been thinking of having you transferred to my personal staff, so that you can straighten out—straighten out the kinks at the time they occur. I haven't reached a decision on it yet, though."

Loob shrugged and escorted his patient to the door. "That's entirely up to you. However you feel I can help you most."

He watched the tall, husky man walking down the corridor to the elevator. "*I haven't reached a decision on it yet, though.*" Well, he wouldn't—not until Loob did. Loob had put the idea into his mind six months ago, but had deferred having him take action on it. He wasn't sure that it would be a good idea to get even that close to the Servant of All as yet. And there was that wonderful little project in the Bureau of Healing Research which he still wanted to give maximum daily attention.

His secretary came in and went right to work at her typewriter. Loob decided to go downstairs and check on what had been done today. With all the fanfare attendant upon the Servant of All's arrival to celebrate complete control, the researchers' routine had no doubt been seriously interrupted. Still, the solution might come at any time. And he liked to examine their lines of investigation for potential fruitfulness: these technicians were blunderingly unimaginative!

As he walked down to the main floor, he wondered if Moddo, anywhere in the secret depths of his psyche, had any idea of how much he had come to depend on the Healer, how thoroughly he needed him. The fellow was such a tangle of anxiety and uncertainty—losing his parents as a child, the way he had, of course had not helped too much, but his many repressions had been in existence even then. He had never even remotely suspected that the reason he wanted Garomma to be the ostensible leader was because he was afraid of taking personal responsibility for anything. That the fake personality he was proud of presenting to the world was his real personality, the difference being that he had learned to use his fears and timidity in a positive fashion. But only up to a point. Seven years ago, when he had looked up Loob ("a fast bit of psychotherapy for some minor problems I've been having"), he'd been on the point of complete collapse. Loob had repaired the vast flapping structure on a temporary basis and given it slightly different functions. Functions for Loob.

He couldn't help wondering further if the ancients would have been able to do anything basic for Moddo. The ancients, according to the Oral Tradition at least, had developed, just before the beginning of the modern era, a psychotherapy that accomplished wonders of change and personal reorganization for the individual.

But to what end? No serious attempt to use the method for its obvious purpose, for the only purpose of any method...*power*. Loob shook his head. Those ancients had been so incredibly naive! And so much of their useful knowledge had been lost. Concepts like superego merely existed in the Oral Tradition of the Healers Guild as words; there was no clue as to their original meaning. They might be very useful to-day, properly applied.

On the other hand, were most of the members of his own modern Healers Guild, across the wide sea, any less naive, including his father and the uncle who was now its reigning head? From the day when he had passed the Guild's final examinations and begun to grow the triangular beard of master status, Loob had seen that the ambitions of his fellow-members were ridiculously limited. Here, in this very city, where, according to legend, the Guild of the Healers of Minds had originated, each member asked no more of life than to use his laboriously learned skill at transference to acquire power over the lives of ten or fifteen wealthy patients.

Loob had laughed at these sparse objectives. He had seen the obvious goal which his colleagues had been overlooking for years. The more powerful the individual whom you subjected to transference and in whom you created a complete dependence, the more power you, as his healer, enjoyed. The world's power center was on Capital Island across the great ocean to the west. And it was there that Loob determined to go.

It hadn't been easy. The strict rules of custom against changing your residence except on official business had stood in his way for a decade. But once the wife of the Forty-seventh District's Communications Commissioner had become his patient, it got easier. When the commissioner had been called to Capital Island for promotion to the Second Assistant Servantship of Communication, Loob had gone with the family; he was now indispensable. Though them he had secured a minor job in the Service of Education. Through that job, practicing his profession on the side, he had achieved enough notice to come to the august attention of the Servant of Education himself.

He hadn't really expected to go this far. But a little luck, a great deal of skill and constant, unwinking alertness had made an irresistible combination. Forty-five minutes after Moddo had first stretched out on his couch, Loob had realized that he, with all of his smallness and plumpness and lack of distinction, was destined to rule the world.

Now the only question was what to do with that rule. With wealth and power unlimited.

Well, for one thing there was his little research project. That was very interesting, and it would serve, once it came to fruition, chiefly to consolidate and insure his power. There were dozens of little pleasures and properties that were now his, but their enjoyment tended to wear off with their acquisition. And finally there was knowledge.

Knowledge. Especially forbidden knowledge. He could now enjoy it with impunity. He could collate the various Oral Traditions into one intelligible whole and be the only man in the world who knew what had really happened in the past. He had already discovered, through the several teams of workers he had set at the task, such tidbits as the original name of his birthplace, lost years ago in a numbering system that had been created to destroy patriotic associations inimical to the world state. Long before it had been the Fifth City of the Forty-seventh District, he had learned, it had been Austria, the glorious capital of the proud Viennese Empire. And this island on which he stood had been Havanacuba, no doubt once a great empire in its own right which had established hegemony over all other empires somewhere in the dim war-filled beginnings of modern times.

Well, these were highly personal satisfactions. He doubted very much if Garomma, for example, would be interested to know that he hailed, not from the Twentieth Agricultural Region of the Sixth District, but from a place called Canada, one of the forty-eight constituent republics of the ancient Northern United States of America. But he, Loob, was interested. Every additional bit of knowledge gave you additional power over your fellowmen, that some day, some way, would be usable.

Why, if Moddo had had any real knowledge of the transference techniques taught in the upper lodges of the Guild of the Healers of Minds, he might still be running the world himself! But no. It was inevitable that a Garomma should actually be no more than a creature, a thing, of Moddo. It was inevitable that a Moddo, given the peculiar forces that had informed him, should inexorably have had to come to Loob and pass under his control. It was also inevitable that Loob, with his specialized knowledge of what could be done with the human mind, should be the only independent man on Earth today. It was also very pleasant.

He wriggled a little bit, very satisfied with himself, gave his beard a final finger-comb, and pushed into the Bureau of Healing Research.

The chief of the bureau came up rapidly and bowed. "Nothing new to report today." He gestured at the tiny cubicles in which the technicians sat at old books or performed experiments on animals and criminally convicted humans. "It took them a while to get back to work, after the Servant of All arrived. Everyone was ordered out into the main corridor for regulation empathizing with Garomma."

"I know," Loob told him. "I don't expect much progress on a day like this. Just so you keep them at it. It's a big problem."

The other man shrugged enormously. "A problem which, as far as we can tell, has never been solved before. The ancient manuscripts we've discovered are all in terrible shape, of course. But those that mention hypnotism all agree that it can't occur under any of the three conditions you want: against the individual's will, contrary to his personal desires and best judgment, and maintaining him over a long period of time in the original state of subjection without need for new applications. I'm not saying it's impossible, but—"

"But it's very difficult. Well, you've had three and a half years to work on it, and you'll have as much more time as you need. *And* equipment. *And* personnel. Just ask. Meanwhile, I'll wander around and see how your men are doing. You needn't come with me. I like to ask my own questions."

The bureau chief bowed again and turned back to his desk in the rear of the room. Loob, the Healer of Minds, the Assistant to the Third Assistant Servant of Education, walked slowly from cubicle to cubicle, watching the work, asking questions, but mostly noting the personal quality of the psychological technician in each cubicle.

He was convinced that the right man could solve the problem. And it was just a matter of finding the right man and giving him maximum facilities. The right man would be clever enough and persistent enough to follow up the right lines of research, but too unimaginative to be appalled by a goal which had eluded the best minds for ages.

And once the problem was solved—then in one short interview with Garomma, he could place the Servant of All under his direct, personal control for the rest of his life and dispense with the complications of long therapeutic sessions with Moddo where he constantly had to suggest, and suggest in roundabout fashion, rather than give simple, clear and unambiguous orders. Once the problem was solved—

He came to the last cubicle. The pimply-faced young man who sat at the plain brown table studying a ripped and damp-rotted volume didn't hear him come in. Loob studied him for a moment.

What frustrated, bleak lives these young technicians must lead! You could see it in the tightly set lines of their all-too-similar faces. Growing up in one of the most rigidly organized versions of the world state that a ruler had yet contrived, they didn't have a thought that was in any way their own, could not dream of tasting a joy that had not been officially allotted to them.

And yet this fellow was the brightest of the lot. If anyone in the Bureau of Healing Research could develop the kind of perfect hypnotic technique Loob required, he could. Loob had been watching him with growing hope for a long time now.

"How is it coming, Sidothi?" he asked.

Sidothi looked up from his book.

"Shut the door," he said.

Loob shut the door.

This was the day of complete control...

Sidothi, the Laboratory Assistant, Psychological Technician Fifth Class, snapped his fingers in Loob's face and allowed himself to luxuriate in the sensation of ultimate power, absolute power, power such as no human being had even dared to dream of before this day.

Complete control. Complete...

Still sitting, he snapped his fingers again.

He said: "Report."

The familiar glazed look came into Loob's eyes. His body stiffened. His arms hung limply at his sides. In a steady, toneless voice he began to deliver his report.

Magnificent. The Servant of Security would be dead in a few hours and the man Sidothi liked would take his place. For an experiment in complete control, it had worked out to perfection. That was all it had been; an attempt to find out if—by creating a feeling of vengefulness in Loob for the sake of a nonexistent brother—he could force the Healer to act on a level he always wanted to avoid; making Moddo do something that the Servant of Education had no interest at all in doing. That was to prod Garomma into an action against the Servant of Security at a time when Garomma was in no particular mental crisis.

The experiment had worked perfectly. He'd pushed a little domino named Loob three days ago, and a whole series of other little dominoes had begun to fall one right after the other. Today, when the Servant of Security was strangled at his desk, the last one would have fallen.

Yes, control was absolutely complete.

Of course, there had been another, minor reason why he had elected to conduct this experiment in terms of the Servant of Security's life. He didn't like the man. He'd seen him drink a liqueur in public four years ago. Sidothi didn't believe the Servants of Mankind should do such things. They should lead clean, simple, abstemious lives; they should be an example to the rest of the human race.

He'd never seen the Assistant Servant of Security whom he had ordered Loob to have promoted, but he had heard that the fellow lived very narrowly, without luxury even in private. Sidothi liked that. That was the way it should be.

Loob came to the end of his report and stood waiting. Sidothi wondered whether he should order him to give up this bad, boastful idea of controlling Garomma directly. No, that wouldn't do: that attitude led into the mechanism of coming down to the Bureau of Healing Research every day to check on progress. While a simple order to come in daily would suffice, still Sidothi felt that until he had examined all aspects of his power and become thoroughly familiar with its use, it was wise to leave original personality mechanisms in place, so long as they didn't get in the way of anything important.

And that reminded him. There *was* an interest of Loob's which was sheer time-wasting. Now, when he was certain of absolute control, was a good time to get rid of it.

"You will drop this research into historical facts," he ordered. "You will use the time thus freed for further detailed examination of Moddo's psychic weaknesses. And you will find that more interesting than studying the past. That is all."

He snapped his fingers in Loob's face, waited a moment, then snapped them again. The Healer of Minds took a deep breath, straightened and smiled.

"Well, keep at it," he said, encouragingly.

"Thank you, sir. I will," Sidothi assured him.

Loob opened the door of the cubicle and walked out, pompously, serenely. Sidothi stared after him. The idiotic assurance of the man—that once the process of complete control by hypnotic technique was discovered it would be given to Loob!

Sidothi had begun to reach the answer three years ago. He had immediately covered up, letting his work take a superficially different line. Then, when he had the technique perfected, he'd used it on Loob himself. Naturally.

At first he'd been shocked, almost sickened, when he found out how Loob controlled Moddo, how Moddo controlled Garomma, the Servant of All. But after a while, he'd adjusted to the situation well enough. After all, ever since the primary grades, the only reality he and his contemporaries had accepted completely was the reality of power. Power in each class, in each club, in each and every gathering of human beings, was the only thing worth fighting for. And you chose an occupation not only because you were most fitted for it, but because it gave the greatest promise of power to a person of your particular interests and aptitude.

But he'd never dreamed of, never imagined, this much power! Well, he had it. That was reality, and reality was to be respected above all else. Now the problem was what to do with his power.

And that was a very hard question to answer. But the answer would come in time. Meanwhile, there was the wonderful chance to make certain that everyone did his job right, that bad people were punished. He intended to stay in his menial job until the proper time came for promotion. There was no need at the moment to have a big title. If Garomma could rule as the Servant of All, he could rule Garomma at third or fourth hand as a simple Psychological Technician Fifth Class.

But in what way exactly did he want to rule Garomma? What important things did he want to make Garomma do?

A bell rang. A voice called out of a loudspeaker set high in the wall. "Attention! Attention, all personnel! The Servant of All will be leaving the Center in a few minutes. Everyone to the main corridor to beg for his continued service to mankind. Everyone—"

Sidothi joined the mob of technicians pouring out of the huge laboratory room. People were coming out of offices on both sides of them. He was swept up with a crowd constantly enlarging from the elevators and stairways to the main corridor where the Service of Education guards prodded them and jammed them against the walls.

He smiled. If they only knew whom they were pushing! Their ruler, who could have any one of them executed. The only man in the world who could do anything he wanted to do. *Anything.*

There was sudden swirling movement and a cheer at the far distant end of the corridor. Everyone began to shuffle about nervously, everyone tried to stand on tiptoe in order to see better. Even the guards began to breathe faster.

The Servant of All was coming.

The cries grew more numerous, more loud. People in front of them were heaving about madly. And suddenly Sidothi saw him!

His arms went up and out in a flashing paroxysm of muscles. Something tremendous and delighted seemed to press on his chest and his voice screamed, "Serve us, Garomma! Serve us! Serve us! Serve us!" He was suffused with heaving waves of love, love such as he never knew anywhere else, love for Garomma, love for Garomma's parents, love for Garomma's children, love for anything and everything connected with Garomma. His body writhed, almost without coordination, delicious flames licked up his thighs and out from his armpits, he twisted and turned, danced and hopped, his very stomach seeming to strain against his diaphragm in an attempt to express its devotion. None of which was very strange, considering that these phenomena had been conditioned in him since early childhood...

"Serve us, Garomma!" he shrieked, bubbles of saliva growing out of the corner of his mouth. "Serve us! Serve us! Serve us!"

He fell forward, between two guards, and his outstretched fingertips touched a rustling flapping rag just as the Servant of All strode by. His mind abruptly roared off into the furthest, most hidden places of ecstasy. He fainted, still babbling. "*Serve* us, O Garomma."

When it was all over, his fellow-technicians helped him back to the Bureau of Healing Research. They looked at him with awe. It wasn't every day you managed to touch one of Garomma's rags. What it must do to a person!

It took Sidothi almost half an hour to recover.

THIS WAS THE DAY OF COMPLETE CONTROL.

AFTERWORD

I have long referred to this as "my good gray story": not a single mote of sunlight dances in it anywhere. Horace Gold bought it for *Galaxy* only because, he was most careful to tell me, he happened to have a novelette-sized slot open in that particular issue.

What was on my mind when I wrote it? Two novels, chiefly—Zamiatin's *We* and Orwell's *Nineteen Eighty-Four*. There was a third, actually, but Huxley's *Brave New World* was less concerned with the issue of power in a future society than the other two. (Interestingly enough, to the best of my knowledge Huxley never admitted to the debt he owed Zamiatin, while Orwell not only did it for himself but proclaimed it also for *Brave New World*.)

I kept asking myself, as I reread each novel, what would the human relations be like on the upper levels of power in these relatively stable, utterly totalitarian and controlled worlds, where education, the media, even psychotherapy were completely at the service of the state? What form would ambition take for different individuals on the ruling level who had grown up in these societies and fully understood how they worked? Stalin's Russia, Mao's China, and Hitler's Germany offered clues, but little more than sheer clues because these were all relatively young states and had not had time to become mature political cultures that could forever reproduce themselves.

I tried to go beyond clues in "The Servant Problem," and I wound up horrifying myself. I also wound up, inevitably, with a perfectly circular plot.

And finally…despite its unrelieved grayness, this is a very important story to me as a writer in a very special genre. Only in science fiction could such a fictional investigation be attempted, because only science fiction provides the theater where the character of a society rather than that of an individual can be elaborated.

WRITTEN 1954——PUBLISHED 1955

☙

A Man of Family

Stewart Raley found his seat in the Commuter's Special—the stratojet that carried him every day from the Metropolitan New York Business Area to his suburban home in northern New Hampshire—with legs that literally felt not and eyes that really and truly saw not.

It was pure habit, years and years of the same repetitive act, that enabled him to find his accustomed place at the window beside Ed Greene; it was habit that pushed his forefinger at the button imbedded in the seat back immediately ahead of him; and it was habit that then kept him staring at the late-afternoon news telecast in the tiny seat-back screen, even though none of his senses registered a single one of the rapid-fire, excitedly announced bulletins.

He did hear, dimly, the scream of the jet's takeoff, but it was habit again that kept his feet firm on the floor and that tensed his abdominal muscles against the encircling safety belt. And that meant, he realized, that he was getting closer to a situation where habit would be of no help at all—where nothing would be of any help. Not against about the worst possible thing that could happen to a man in 2080 AD.

"Had a rough day, Stew?" Ed Greene asked him with beery loudness. "You look tired as hell."

Raley felt his lips move, but it was a while before sound came out of his throat. "Yes," he said finally. "I had a rough day."

"Well, and who asked you to work for Solar Minerals?" Ed asked, as if he were replying to a sharply phrased argument. "These interplanetary corporations are all the same: pressure, pressure, pressure. You got to get the invoices ready right now, this minute, this second, because the Neptunian supply ship is leaving and there won't be another one for six months; you got to get the Mercury correspondence all dictated because— Don't I know? I worked for Outer Planet Pharmaceuticals fifteen years ago and I had a goddam bellyful. Give me the real-estate racket and accounts in the Metropolitan New York Business Area. Quiet. Solid. Calm."

Raley nodded heavily and rubbed at his forehead. He didn't have a headache, but he wished he had one. He wished he had anything that would make it impossible for him to think.

"Course, there's not much money in it," Ed went on, boomingly viewing the other side of the question. "There's not much money, but there's no ulcers either. I'll probably be stuck in a two-child bracket all my life—but it'll be a long life. We take things slow and easy in my office. We know little old New York's been here a long time, and it'll be here a long time to come."

"Yes," Raley said, still staring straight ahead of him. "It will be. New York will be here for a long time to come."

"Well, don't say it in such a miserable tone of voice, man! Ganymede will be here for a long time, too! No one's going to run away with Ganymede!"

Frank Tyler leaned forward from behind them. "How about a little seven-card stud, fellas?" he inquired. "We've got a half-hour to kill."

Raley didn't feel at all like playing cards, but he felt too grateful to Frank to refuse. His fellow-employee at Solar Minerals had been listening to Greene—as, inevitably, had everyone else on the plane—and he alone knew what anguish the real-estate man had been unconsciously creating. He'd probably become more and more uncomfortable and had decided to provide a distraction, any distraction.

Nice of him, Raley thought, as he and Ed spun their seats around so that they faced the other way. After all, he'd been promoted to the Ganymede desk over Frank's head; another man in Frank's position might have enjoyed hearing Ed sock it to him. Not Frank, he was no ghoul.

It was the usual game, with the usual four players. Bruce Robertson, the book illustrator, who sat on Frank Tyler's left, brought his huge portfolio up off the floor and placed it tablewise on their knees. Frank opened a fresh deck and they cut for deal. Ed Greene won.

"Usual stakes?" he asked, as he shuffled the cards. "Ten, twenty, thirty?"

They nodded, and Ed began to lay out a hand. He didn't stop talking though.

"I was telling Stew," he explained in a voice that must have carried clear to the pilot in his sealed-off cabin, "that real estate is good for the blood pressure, if not much else. My wife is all the time telling me to move into a more hotshot field. 'I feel so ashamed,' she says, 'a woman of my age with only two children. Stewart Raley is ten years younger than you and already Marian has had her fourth baby. If you were half a man, you'd be ashamed, too. If you were half a man, you'd *do* something about it.' You know what I tell her? 'Sheila,' I say, 'the trouble with you is you're 36A-happy.' "

Bruce Robertson looked up, puzzled. "36A?"

Ed Greene guffawed. "Oh, you lucky bachelor, you! Wait'll you get married! You'll find out what 36A is all right. You'll eat, sleep and drink 36A."

"Form 36A," Frank Tyler explained to Bruce quietly as he raked in the pot, "is what you fill out when you make application to the FPB for permission to have another child."

"Oh. Of course. I just didn't know the number. But wait a minute, Ed. Economic status is only one of the factors. The Family Planning Bureau also considers health of the parents, heredity, home environment—"

"What did I tell you?" Ed crowed. "A bachelor! A wet-behind-the-ears, no-child bachelor!"

Bruce Robertson turned white. "I'll be getting married one of these days, Ed Greene," he said through tightly set teeth. "And when I do, I'll have more children than you ever—"

"You're right about economic status being only one of the factors," Frank Tyler broke in hurriedly, peaceably. "But it's the most important single factor, and if there already are a couple of children in the family, and they seem to be in pretty good shape, it's the factor that the FPB considers to the exclusion of almost everything else in handing down its decision."

"Right!" Ed brought his hand down positively and the cards danced about on the portfolio-table. "Take my brother-in-law, Paul. Day and night, my wife is going *Paul this, Paul that;* it's no wonder I know more about him than I do myself. Paul owns half of Mars-Earth Freighting Syndicate, so he's in an eighteen-child bracket. His wife's sort of lazy, she doesn't care much for appearances, so they only have ten children, but—"

"Do they live in New Hampshire?" Frank asked. A moment before, Stewart Raley had noticed Frank glancing at him with real concern: he was evidently trying to change the subject, feeling that the direction the conversation had taken could only make Raley more miserable. It probably showed on his face.

He'd have to do something about his face: he'd be meeting Marian in a few minutes. If he wasn't careful, she'd guess immediately.

"New Hampshire?" Ed demanded contemptuously. "My brother-in-law, Paul? With *his* money? No, sir! No backyard suburb for him! He lives in the *real* country, west of Hudson Bay, up in Canada. But, like I was saying, he and his wife don't get along so good, the home life for the kids isn't the best in the world, if you know what I mean. You think they have trouble getting a 36A okayed? Not on your life! They fill it out and it's back the next morning with a big blue *approved* all over it. The way the FPB figures, what the hell, with their money they can afford to hire first-class nurse-maids and child psychologists, and if the kids still have trouble when they grow up, they'll get the best mental therapy that money can buy."

Bruce Robertson shook his head. "That doesn't sound right to me. After all, prospective parents are being turned down every day for negative heredity."

"Heredity is one thing," Ed pointed out. "Environment's another. One can't be changed—the other can. And let me tell you, mister, the thing that makes the biggest change in the environment is money. M-O-N-E-Y: money, cash, gelt, moolah, wampum, the old spondulix. Enough money, and the FPB figures your kid *has* to have a good start in life—especially with it supervising the early years. Your deal, Stew. Hey, Stew! You in mourning for that last pot? You haven't said a word for the past fifteen minutes. Anything wrong? You didn't get fired today, did you?"

Raley tried to pull himself together. He picked up the cards. "No," he said thickly. "I didn't get fired."

Marian was waiting with the family jetabout at the landing field. Fortunately, she was too full of gossip to be very observant. She looked oddly at him only once, when he kissed her.

"That was a poor, tired thing," she said. "You used to do a lot better than that."

He dug his fingernails into his palms and tried to be whimsical. "That was before I was a poor, tired thing. Had a real hard day at the office. Be sweet and gentle with me, honey, and don't expect too much."

She nodded sympathetically and they climbed into the small craft. Lisa, twelve years old and their first child, was in the back seat with Mike, the latest. Lisa kissed her father resoundingly and then held up the baby for a similar ceremony.

He found he had to force himself to kiss the baby.

They shot up into the air. All around them, the jetabouts radiated away from the landing field. Stewart Raley stared at the suburban roofs rushing by below and tried to decide when he was going to tell her. After supper, that would be a good time. No, better wait until the children were all in bed. Then, when he and Marian were alone in the living room—

He felt his stomach go solid and cold, just as it had that afternoon after lunch. Would he be able to bring himself to tell her at all, he wondered?

He had to. That was all there was to it. He had to—and tonight.

"—if I ever believed a word Sheila said in the first place," Marian was saying. "I told her: 'Connie Tyler is not that sort of woman, and that's enough for me.' You remember, darling, last month when Connie came to visit me in the hospital? Well, of course, I knew what she was thinking. She was looking at Mike and saying to herself that if Frank had only become head of the Ganymede department and had a two-thousand territ raise instead of you, *she'd* be having her fourth child now and I'd be visiting *her*. I knew what she was thinking, because in her place I'd be thinking exactly the same thing. But when she said it was the cutest, healthiest baby she'd ever seen, she was sincere. And when she wished me a fifth child for next year, she wasn't just being polite: she really meant it!"

A *fifth* child, Stewart Raley thought bitterly. A *fifth!*

"—so I leave it up to you. What should I do about Sheila if she comes around tomorrow and starts in all over again?"

"Sheila?" he asked stupidly. "Sheila?"

Marian shook her head impatiently over the controls. "Sheila Greene. Ed's wife, remember? Stewart, haven't you heard a word I said?"

"Sure, honey. About—uh, the hospital and Connie. And Mike. I heard everything you said. But where does Sheila come in?"

She turned around now and stared at him. The large green cat's-eyes, that had once pulled him across a dance floor to the side of a girl he didn't know, were very intent. Then she flipped a switch, letting the automatic pilot take over to keep them on course. "Something's wrong, Stewart. And it's not just a hard day at the office. Something's really wrong. What is it?"

"Later," he said. "I'll tell you later."

"No, now. Tell me now. I couldn't go through another second with you looking like that."

He blew out a chestful of breath and kept his eyes on the house-after-house-after-house beneath him.

"Jovian Chemicals bought the Keohula Mine today."

"So. What is that to you?"

"The Keohula Mine," he explained painfully, "is the only mine on Ganymede in full operation."

"I still—I'm afraid I still don't understand. Stewart, please tell me in words of one syllable, but tell me fast. What *is* it?"

He looked up, noticing how terrified she was. She had no idea what he was talking about, but she had always had remarkable instincts. Almost telepathic.

"With the Keohula Mine sold, and for a good price, Solar Minerals feels it is uneconomic to maintain an installation on Ganymede. They are therefore shutting it down, effective immediately."

Marian raised her hands to her mouth in horror. "And that means—that means—"

"That means they no longer need a Ganymede Department. Or a Ganymede Department Chief."

"But they won't send you back to your old job!" she cried. "That would be too cruel! They couldn't demote you, Stewart, not after you've gone and had another child on the strength of your raise! There must be another department, there must be—"

"There isn't," he told her with a tongue that felt like cardboard. "They're shutting down operations on all the Jovian satellites. I'm not the only one affected. There's Cartwright of the Europa desk and McKenzie of Io—they both have seniority over me. From now on, Solar Minerals is going to lean heavily on its holdings on Uranus, Neptune, and Pluto, and light everywhere else."

"Well, what about *those* planets? They'll need department heads at Solar Minerals, won't they?"

Raley sighed helplessly. "They have them. *And* assistant department heads. Good men who know their work, who've handled it for years. And as far as your next question goes, honey, I've spoken to Jovian Chemicals about a transfer. No go. They already have a Ganymede Department and the man handling it is very satisfactory. All day I kept trying one angle after another. But tomorrow, I'll be back in Ore Shipments."

"At your old salary?" she whispered. "Seven thousand territs a year?"

"Yes. Two thousand less than I'm getting now. Two thousand less than the minimum for four children."

Marian's hands crept up to her eyes, which filled, abruptly, with tears. "I'm not going to do it!" she sobbed. "I'm not! I'm not!"

"Honey," he said. "Honey-baby, it's the law. What can we do?"

"I absolutely—I absolutely refuse to decide which—which one of my children I'm going to—to give up!"

"I'll get promoted again. I'll be making nine thousand territs in no time. More, even. You'll see."

She stopped crying and stared at him dully. "But once a child is put up for adoption, the parents can't reclaim it. Even if their income increases. You know that, Stewart, as well as I. They can have other children, but they can't ever have the superfluous child back."

Of course he knew that. That regulation had been framed by the FPB to protect the foster-parents and encourage adoption into higher-bracket families. "We should have waited," he said. "Damn it, we should have waited!"

"We did," she reminded him. "We waited six months, to make certain your job was secure. Don't you remember the night that we had Mr. Halsey to dinner and he told us that you were working out very well and were definitely on your way up in the organization? 'You'll have ten children yet, Mrs. Raley,' he said, 'and my advice is to get started on them as soon as possible.' Those were his exact words."

"Poor Halsey. He couldn't meet my eyes all through the executive conference this afternoon. Just before I left the office, he came up and told me how sorry he was, how he'd look out for me in the very next promotion list. But he pointed out that practically everybody's retrenching these days; it's been a bad year for extraterrestrial products. And when I move back into my old job in Ore Shipments, I bump back the man who took my place. He moves down and bumps back somebody else. It's hell all around."

Marian dried her eyes with determined waves of the dashboard breezespout. "*Our* problem's enough for me, Stewart. I'm not interested in anybody else right now. What can we do?"

He leaned back and grimaced. "The best I could think of—I called my lawyer. Cleve said he'd be down this evening after dinner to go over the whole matter with us. If there's an out, Cleve will find it. He's handled a lot of FPB appeals."

She inclined her head in recognition of this effort. "That's a beginning. How much time do we have?"

"Well, I have to file a Notice of Superfluity form tomorrow morning. We have two weeks to decide which—which child."

Marian nodded again. They sat there, letting the automatic pilot throb the jetabout to its destination. After a while, Stewart Raley reached across the seat and took his wife's hand. Her fingers curled about his fingers spasmodically.

"I know which child," said a voice from behind them.

They both turned around sharply. "Lisa!" Marian gasped. "I forgot you were here! You've been listening!"

Lisa's round cheeks were glistening with wetness. "I've been listening," she admitted. "And I know which child it has to be. Me. I'm the oldest. I'm the one who should be put up for adoption. Not Penny or Susie or Mike, but me."

"Now you shush up, Lisa Raley. Your father and I will decide what to do. It's more than possible that nothing will happen. Nothing at all."

"I'm the oldest, so I should be put up for adoption. That's what my teacher says is supposed to happen. My teacher says that the young children are af-affected more than older children. And my teacher says that it's a very good thing, because you're sure to be adopted by a very rich family and you get more toys and better schools and—and all sorts of things. My teacher says that maybe you're a little s-sad at first, but you have so many good things happening to you, that—that you get to be very ha-happy. And anyway, my teacher says, that's the way it has to be, 'cause that's the law."

Stewart Raley hit the seat hard. "That's enough! Your mother said she and I will decide."

"And besides," Lisa went on defiantly, wiping her face with one hand, "besides, I don't *want* to be a member of a three-child family. All my friends are four-child family girls. I'd have to go back to those poky old friends I used to have, and I—"

"Lisa!" Raley roared. "I'm still your father! Do you want me to prove it to you?"

Silence. Marian switched back to manual for the landing. She took the baby from the twelve-year-old and they all got out of the jetabout without looking at each other.

Raley took a moment before entering the house to adjust the handi-robot from "Gardening" to "Waiting on Tables." Then he followed the whirring metal figure through the door.

The trouble was that Lisa was right. All other things being equal, the oldest child was the usual choice for outside adoption. For her, it was a much less traumatic experience. And the Family Planning Bureau would select the new parents carefully, from among the horde of applicants, and see to it that the transfer was made as smoothly and happily as possible. Child psychologists would make twice-weekly visits for the first few years, insuring the maximum adjustment to the new situation.

Who would the new parents be? Probably someone like Ed Greene's brother-in-law, Paul, someone whose income had far outstripped the permissible family. That could be due to a variety of reasons: a lazy, unconventional wife, latent sterility in either partner to the marriage, a suddenly necessary hysterectomy. In any case, something that left them without the means of achieving the only kind of prestige that mattered.

You could have a real flossy jetabout—but you might have bought it on credit and still owe ten years' worth of salary on it. You might have an enormous home in expensive, estate-filled Manitoba, where the top executives of the New York Business Area lived side by side with their opposite numbers from the Chicago and Los Angeles Business Areas, a home whose walls were paneled in rare Martian woods and which was replete with every kind of specialized robot—but, for all anyone knew, you might be doing it by carrying a mortgage which was slowly but surely choking you into financial submission.

Children, now, children were definite. You couldn't have a child on credit, you didn't have a child because you were expecting business to get better. You only had a child when the FPB, having accepted you and your wife heredity-wise and environment-wise, decided your income was large enough to give that child all the advantages it deserved. Every child a family had represented a license that the FPB issued only after the most searching investigation. And *that* was status.

That was why you didn't have to give job data or references when you were buying something on time if you could pull out a six-child license. The clerk just took down your name and address and the serial number on the license—and that was that. You walked out of the store with the merchandise.

All through supper, Raley thought about that. He couldn't help feeling doubly guilty over his demotion in Solar Minerals when he remembered what his first thought was on the morning the license to have Mike arrived. It was a jubilant *now we get into the country club, now they'll invite us to join.* He'd been happy about the permission to have another baby, of course—he and Marian both loved kids, and in quantity—but he'd already had three by then; it was the fourth child which was the big jump.

"Well," he said to himself, "and which father wouldn't have felt the same way? Even Marian, the day after Mike's birth, began calling him 'our country-club son.'"

Those were happy, pride-filled days. They'd walked the Earth, Marian and he, like young monarchs on their way to coronation. Now—

Cleveland Boettiger, Raley's lawyer, arrived just as Marian was scolding Lisa into bed. The two men went into the living room and had the handi-robot mix them a drink.

"I won't sugar-coat it, Stew," the lawyer said, spreading the contents of his briefcase on the antique coffee-table that Marian had cleverly converted from an early twenti-eth-century army foot-locker. "It doesn't look good. I've been going over the latest FPB rulings and, in terms of your situation, it doesn't look good."

"Isn't there any chance? Any angle?"

"Well, that's what we'll try to find tonight."

Marian came in and curled up on the sofa next to her husband. "That Lisa!" she exclaimed. "I almost had to spank her. She's already beginning to look on me as a stranger with no authority over her. It's maddening."

"Lisa insists that she's the one who should be put up for adoption," Raley explained. "She heard us talking about it."

Boettiger picked up a sheet covered with notes and shook it out. "Lisa's right, of course. She's the oldest. Now, let's review the situation. You two married on a salary of three thousand territs a year, the minimum for one child. That's Lisa. Three years later, accumulated raises brought your income up two thousand. That's Penelope. Another year and a half, another two thousand. Susan. Last year, in February, you took over the Ganymede desk at nine thousand a year. Mike. Today, you were de-moted and went back to seven thousand, which is a maximum three-child bracket. Does that cover it?"

"That covers it," his host told him. *The story of my adult life,* he thought: *in a couple of sentences. It doesn't cover the miscarriage Marian almost had with Penny or the time the handi-robot short-circuited near the playpen and we had to take six stitches in Susie's head. It doesn't cover the time—*

"All right, then, Stew, let's hit the income possibilities first. Do either of you have any hope of a sizable amount of money coming in soon, a legacy, say, or some piece of property that may substantially increase in value?"

They looked at each other. "Both Stewart's family and mine," Marian answered slowly, "are three- or four-child-bracket people. There won't be much of an estate. And all we own, besides the house and the furniture and the jetabout, are some gov-ernment bonds and a little Solar Minerals stock that won't be worth much more than we paid for it for a long, long time."

"That takes care of income. Let me ask you people this, then—"

"Wait a minute," Raley burst out. "Why does it take care of income? Suppose I get a part-time job, working week-ends or evenings here in New Hampshire?"

"Because the license to have a child is predicated on the income from a normal thirty-hour week," the lawyer pointed out patiently. "If the father has to work additional time in order to reach or maintain that income, his child sees that much less of him and, in the legal phrase, 'is denied the normal prerogatives of a normal infancy.' Remember, the rights of the child are absolutely paramount in present-day law. There's no way around it."

Stewart Raley stared at the opposite wall. "We could emigrate," he said in a low voice. "There are no birth-control regulations on Venus or any of the other colonies."

"You're thirty-eight, Marian is thirty-two. They like 'em young, real young, on Mars and Venus—not to mention the fact that you're an office worker, not a technician or a mechanic or farmer. I doubt very much that you could get a permanent extraterrestrial visa. No, the income possibilities are out. That leaves Special Hardship. Is there any claim you could think of under that heading?"

Marian saw a straw and clutched at it. "There might be something. I had to have a Caesarean when Mike was born."

"Um." Cleveland Boettiger reached for another document and studied it. "According to your medical data sheet, that was because of the child's position in the womb at birth. It is not expected to interfere in any way with future child-bearing. Anything else? Any negative psychological reports on Lisa, for example, that would make it inadvisable for her to transfer to another set of parents at this time? Think."

They thought. They sighed. There was nothing.

"Pretty much as I thought, then, Stew. It definitely doesn't look good. Well, suppose you sign this and hand it in with the Notice of Superfluity tomorrow. I've filled it out."

"What is it?" Marian asked, peering anxiously at the paper he had handed them.

"A Request for a Delay in Execution. The grounds I've given are that you were eminently satisfactory in your job and that therefore the demotion may be only temporary. It won't stand up once the FPB sends an investigator to your main office, but that will take time. You'll get an extra month to decide which child and—who knows?—maybe something will turn up by then. A better job with another outfit, another promotion."

"I couldn't get a better job with another outfit these days," Raley said miserably. "I'm lucky to have the one I do, the way things are. And a promotion is out for at least a year."

There was a screech outside as a jetabout landed on their lawn.

"Company?" Marian wondered. "We weren't expecting anyone."

Her husband shook his head. *"Company!* The last thing in the world we want tonight is company. See who it is, Marian, and tell them please to go away."

She left the living room, waving to the handi-robot, as she went, to refill Boettiger's empty glass. Her face was stiff with pain.

"I don't see," Stewart Raley exclaimed, "why the FPB has to be that rigid and meticulous in interpreting the birth-control statutes! Can't they give a guy a little leeway?"

"They do," the lawyer reminded him as he put the papers carefully back in the briefcase. "They certainly do. After the child has been approved and conceived, you're allowed a drop in income up to nine hundred territs—a concession to the unexpected. But two thousand, a whole two thousand…"

"It's unfair, though, it's damned unfair! After you have a child and raise it, for it to be taken away by a minor bureau of the world government is—"

"Now, Raley, don't be an ass!" Boettiger said sharply. "I'm your lawyer and I'll help you to the limits of my professional competence, but I won't sit here listening to you make noises that I know you don't believe yourself. Either family planning on a worldwide basis makes sense, or it doesn't. Either we make sure that each and every child is a wanted child, a valued child, with a solid chance for a decent, happy, fulfilled life, or we go back to the irresponsible, catch-as-catch-can childbearing methods of the previous centuries. We both know that intelligent family planning has made the world a far better place. Well, Form 36A is the symbol of family planning—and the Notice of Superfluity is just the reverse side of the coin. You cannot reasonably have one without the other."

Raley bowed his head and spread his hands. "I don't argue with that, Cleve. It's just—it's just—"

"It's just that the shoe happens to pinch you right now. I'm sorry for that, deeply sorry. But the way I feel is this: If a client comes to me and tells me he absent-mindedly flew his jetabout over a restricted area, I'll use all my legal education and every inch of my dirty mind to get him off with as low a fine as possible. When he goes further, though, and starts telling me that the traffic regulations are no good—then I get impatient and tell him to shut up. And that's all the birth-control statutes are: a series of regulations to make the reproductive traffic of the human race flow more efficiently."

The voices from the entrance hall stopped abruptly. They heard Marian make a peculiar noise, halfway between a squeal and a scream. Both men leaped to their feet and ran through the archway to her.

She was in the foyer, standing beside Bruce Robertson. Her eyes were shut and she had one hand on the wall as if it alone kept her from falling.

"I'm sorry I upset her, Stew," the book illustrator said rapidly. His face was very pale. "You see, I want to adopt Lisa. Frank Tyler told me what happened today."

"*You?* You want to— But you're a bachelor!"

"Yes, but I'm in a five-child income bracket. I can adopt Lisa if I can prove that I can give her as good a home as a married couple might. Well, I can. All I want is for her last name to be changed legally to Robertson—I don't care what name she uses in school or with her friends—and she'll go on staying here, with me providing for her maintenance. The FPB would consider that the best possible home."

Raley stared at Boettiger. The lawyer nodded. "It would. Besides that, if the natural parents express any wishes for a feasible adoptive situation, the weight of administrative action tends to be thrown in that direction. But what would you be getting out of that, young man?"

"I'd be getting a child—officially," Robertson told him. "I'd be getting a kid I could talk about, boast about, when other men boast about theirs. I'm sick and tired of being a no-child bachelor. I want to be *somebody*."

"But you might want to get married one day," Raley said, putting his arm about his wife, who had let a long breath out and turned to him. "You might want to get married and have children of your own."

"No, I wouldn't," Bruce Robertson said in a low voice. "Please don't pass this on, but there's amaurotic idiocy in my hereditary background. The only woman who'd ever marry me would be a sterile one. I doubt that I'll ever get married, but I certainly won't ever have kids. This—this is my only chance."

"Oh, darling," Marian sobbed happily in Raley's arms. "It will work. It really will work!"

"All I ask," the book illustrator went on uncertainly, "is the privilege of coming here once in a while, to kind of see Lisa and see what's going on with her."

"Once in a while!" Raley roared. "You can come every night. After all, you'll be like a member of the family. *Like* a member of the family? You'll *be* a member of the family; man, you'll *be* the family!"

AFTERWORD

I wish someone would tell me why I don't like this story. It is competently written. It is social science fiction. It does have all sorts of fine touches about the future, really valid touches.

And, dammit, it *is* competently written.

WRITTEN 1954———PUBLISHED 1956

჻

THE JESTER

History can be as dangerous as a traffic accident: it can happen to people. And cause even more damage. One fine day—about the year 2208, say—a bright, cheerful and maybe too-smart-for-his-own-good young man wakes up to find he's tripped over his cleverest idea and crashed into a brand-new age.

Away back when—early in the nineteen hundreds—people began listening to record players instead of trudging off to a vaudeville theater through the cold and wet. Later, in the radio era, most top-level executives were finding dictaphones more efficient than human stenographers and mechanical sorters better than an army of file clerks. And, at the peak of the television boom, every bride dreamed of owning a vocalex kitchen someday that would exactly obey her most casual command to heat a roast for such and such a time and baste it at such and such intervals.

With the deluxe models, of course, came a set of flavor-fix rheostats which, among other talents, could mix salads according to the recipe of a famous chef slightly better than the chef could himself. Then along came All-Purpose Radar Broadcast power; television went three-dimensional and became teledar, inexpensive enough so that every Eskimo could own a set and, incidentally, the only industry where an actor might make a living.

As teledar took over entertainment, household devices began to move around in the form of robots powered by APRB, rocket ships piloted only by automatics made time-table flights to every planet in the system, and everyone agreed that man could hardly ask for more control over his environment.

So one fine day—oh, about the year 2208—

The doorscreen above the valuable antique radiator in Lester's living room fluoresced for a moment, then crackled into a picture of the husky man waiting outside the apartment. He wore the visored helmet of a service mechanic. An enormous yellow box beside him filled most of the doorscreen.

"Lester the Jester? Rholg's Robot Reorganizers. I have your butler-valet combo here all fitted with the special custom-built adjustments you ordered. You have to sign a danger-and-damage release before I can leave him."

"Uhm." The red-haired young man nodded and wiped the sleep from his eyes so that the worry could shine through. He rose from the couch, stretched jerkily, "I'd sign a life-and-liberty waiver to get what I need out of that robot. Hey, door," he called, "Twenty-three, there—twenty-three."

Swiftly the door slid up into its sandwiched recess. The mechanic flipped a switch on his beamlock and the huge crate floated delicately into the apartment, bumped gently to rest against a wall. Lester rubbed his hands nervously. "I hope…"

"You know, Mr. Lester, I never thought a guy like me would ever get to see you in person. In my line I meet all kinds of celebrities—like yesterday, when I returned two receptionist-robots to the police commissioner. We'd equipped them with lie-detectors and flat feet. But wait till I tell my wife I met the biggest comedian in teledar! She always says, Mr. Lester—"

"Not Mr. Lester. Lester—Lester the Jester."

The mechanic grinned widely and appreciatively. "Like on the program, huh?" He pointed his beamlock at the crate, moving the switch from *carry* to *disrupt.* "And when one of the boys at the shop figured you were going to use this robot like a gagwriter, I asked him would he like his head broken. I told him your jokes were strictly off the cuff—I heard. Right?"

"*Right!*" A very loud, vastly amused laugh. "Lester the Jester using a gagwriter! What kind of rumors—imagine that! Me, the glib sahib of ad-lib—as my fans like to call me—working from someone else's boffolas. *Such a thing!* Just because I thought it would be snappy for the hemisphere's top comedian to have a robot valet who can give with gags on demand. *Hah!* Well, let me see him."

A rattling whirr as directive force tore out of the beamlock, dissolving the yellow crate into quickly scattered dust. When it had settled they were looking at five feet of purple metal man.

"You changed his shape!" Lester yelped accusingly. "I sent you a smooth-lined twenty-two hundred and seven model with the new cylindrical trunk. You bring back a pear-shaped piece of machinery looking squeezed down—as if it had a paunch all the way around. And bow-legged!"

"Look, sir, the techs just had to expand his midsection. Even on microwire that file of jokes took up an awful lot of space. And your order said for him to be able to work out twists on the gags in the file—so they rassled up a new gimmick, what they call a variable modifier. More space, more weight. But let me turn him on."

The man in the visored helmet inserted a convoluted length of iridium—an Official Robot Master Key—into the back of the robot's neck. Two full clicking turns and machinery purred. Metal arms crossed upon a metal chest in the accepted gesture of servility. Eyebrow ridges clinked upward. Multilinked lips pursed questioningly.

"*Migosh!*" the mechanic marveled. "I never seen such a snooty expression on any face before."

"My fiancée, Josephine Lissy—she's the singer on my program—designed it," Lester told him proudly. "Her idea of what a butler-valet combo should look like—sort of in the ancient English tradition. She also thought up his name. Hey, Rupert, tell me a joke."

Rupert's mouth opened. His voice clacked out, rising and falling like a sine wave. "On what subject, sir?"

"Oh, anything. A vacation trip. A small belly-laugh joke."

"Ginsberg was making his first voyage to Mars," Rupert began. "He was shown to a small table in the salon and told that his tablemate would be a Frenchman. Since the other had not yet—"

The Rholg's mechanic leaned across his flat purple chest. "That's another gimmick—a meson filter. You said you wanted him able to distinguish between laughpower in different gags so he could fit them to the audience. And price was no object. That's all you have to tell a tech. They knocked themselves out developing a gadget to do the job just right."

"If it does, a couple of writers I know are going to be sorry pigeons. We'll see who's the comedian around here," Lester muttered. "Lester the Jester or Green and Anderson. Greedy little paper-spoilers!"

"—the Frenchman, noticing Ginsberg already at his meal, stopped. He clicked his heels and bowed from the waist. '*Bon appétit*,' he said. Ginsberg, not to be outdone, rose to *his*—"

"A meson filter is what they call it, eh? Well, even that bill in galactic figures your outfit sent me will be worth it if I can get what I want out of Rupert. But I wish you hadn't spoiled his looks!"

"—this succinct dialogue was repeated. Until, the day before the end of the voyage, Ginsberg sought the steward and asked him to explain the meaning of—"

"We'd have found some way of packaging all the stuff or at least distributing it better if you hadn't been in such a hurry. You wanted him back by Wednesday, no matter what."

"Yes, of course. I go on the waves tonight. I needed the—ah, stimulation Rupert would give me." Lester ran nervous fingers through his red hair. "He seems to be okay."

"—approached the Frenchman, who was already at table. He clicked his heels and bowed from the waist. '*Bon appétit*,' Ginsberg told him. Joyfully, the Frenchman leaped to his feet and—"

"Then you won't mind signing this. Regular release form. You take all responsibility for the actions of Rupert. I can't leave him here till I get it."

"Sure." Lester signed. "Anything else?"

"—'Ginsberg,' the Frenchman said!" Rupert had finished.

"Not bad. But I can't use it quite that way. We need a— Holy options, what's that?" Lester teetered backward.

The robot, standing perfectly immobile, was clacking wildly, grinding his gears and *pinging* wires as if he were coming apart.

"Oh, *that*." The man from Rholg's gestured. "That's another bug the techs didn't have time to clean up. Comes from the meson filter. Near as we can figure out, it's what they call an after-effect of his capacity to distinguish between gags that are partly funny and gags that are very funny. Electronic differentiation of the grotesque, it says in the specifications—in a man, a sense of humor. 'Course, in a robot it only means there's a kink in the exhaust."

"Yeah. I hope he doesn't blow that at me when I have a hangover. A robot that laughs at his own jokes! *Whooee*, what a sound!" Lester shivered. "Rupert, go mix me one of those Three-Ply Lunar Landings."

The mass of purple metal turned and waddled off to the kitchen. Both men chuckled at his bow-legged teetering gait.

"Here's a couple of bucks for your trouble. Sorry I don't have more change on me. Like a carton of Star-Gazers? My sponsor keeps me stocked to the curls on them. Licorice, maple-walnut?"

"I sorta like my cigarettes flavored with crab-apple. The missus too—gee, thanks. Hope everything goes all right."

The service mechanic stuffed his beamlock into his tunic and left. Lester called, "Three-and-twenty," after him. The door slid down into place.

Rupert tottered back with an intricate spiral of transparent tubing filled with a yellow-and-white liquid. The comedian sucked the drink out rapidly and exhaled.

"Right! That was delicious in its own foul way. Whoever built that master bartender unit into you really knew his electronics. Now look, I don't know just how to order you in this deal—though you're able to read now, come to think of it. Here's the script for tonight's teledar show, the straight part.

"Type a companion script for me based on each speech in the original that I've underlined, a gag variation on the statement. That's what I memorize to give the famous ad-lib effect—but you don't have to know that. Start typing."

Without a word, the robot flipped through the sheaf of papers handed to him, instantly "memorizing" on his microwire files every word in them.

Then he dropped the script on the floor again and walked over to the electric typewriter. He pushed the chair in front of it aside. His torso slid down his metallic legs until he was just at the right height for typing. He went to work. Paper boiled up out of the machine.

Lester watched admiringly. "If only his ideas are half as funny as they are fast—hello!" He picked the sheaf of typescript off the floor and set it on a table. "Never did that before. Used to be the neatest piece of machinery on the planet, always picking up after me. But—well, genius has the right to be temperamental!" The phone buzzed almost affirmatively.

He grinned and caught the phone as it bounded into his hands. "Radio Central," said the mouthpiece. "Miss Josephine Lissy calling. Will you take it on your scrambler or on hers?"

"Mine. LY—one hundred thirty-four—YJ. Check."

"Yes sir. Here's your party."

The radio phone sputtered as it adjusted to Lester's personal scrambling system that meant privacy for a conversation on a wavelength shared by millions. A girl with hair as brightly carrotty as Lester's appeared in the tiny screen above the mouthpiece.

"Hi, Red," she smiled. "Know something? Jo loves Lester."

"Smart girl—smart. Wait a minute while I get you transferred. Looking at you on this thing strains my eyes—besides, there isn't enough of you."

He twirled a dial, translated the phone's vibrations into the frequency of the door-screen. Then, while the instrument whizzed back into place on the ceiling, he made a similar adjustment on the doorscreen manual dials, setting it for interior reception.

Josephine Lissy's image appeared above the antique radiator as he sighed down into the couch.

"Look, funnyman, this is no love-call. I'll get right down to the most recent mess. Green and Anderson have blabbed to Haskell."

"What!" He leaped to his feet. "I'll sue them! I can, too—the mutual release they signed specified that my use of gagwriters was not to be made public."

She shrugged. "A lot that'll help you. Besides, they didn't publicize it—just told it to Haskell. You couldn't even prove *that.* All I got was grapevine to the effect that Haskell is screaming over to see you.

"Green and Anderson have convinced him that without memorizing their gag copy on the straight part of the show you won't even be able to ad-lib a burp. And Haskell is just scared that the first program under his sponsorship will be a flop."

Lester grinned, "Don't worry, Jo. With any luck—"

"My sacred aunt's favorite space-opera!" she squealed. "What's that?"

That was an ear-splitting series of clanks, bumps, singing metal and siren-like shrieks. Lester whirled.

Rupert had finished typing. He held the long sheet of completed copy between purple fingers and shook over it. *Whirr,* he went. *Glongety-glonk. Pingle, pingle, pingle. Ka-zam!* He sounded like a cement mixer inside a cement mixer.

"Oh, that's Rupert. He's got a kink in his exhaust—makes like a mindless sense of humor. Of course he isn't human but does he seem to go for his own stuff! Come here, Rupert!"

The robot stopped clattering and slid up his legs to his full height. He walked to the doorscreen.

"When did they bring him back?" Jo asked. "Did they put all the stuff in him that you—why, they've *ruined* him! He looks like a case of dropsy—as if he has an abdominal ruff! And that beautiful expression on his face I designed—it's all gone! He doesn't look superior anymore, just sad—very sad. Poor Rupert!"

"Your imagination," Lester told her. "Rupert can't change his expression even if he wanted to. It's all automatic, built in at the factory. Just because we call him by a name instead of the number cues we use on the rest of the household machinery doesn't mean he has feelings. Outside of his duties as a valet, which he performs as imaginatively as a watch tells time, he's just a glorified filing system with a wadjacallit—a variable modifier to select—"

"Oh, that isn't so. Rupert has feelings, don't you, Rupert?" she cooed at him in a small voice. "You remember me, Rupert? Jo. How are you, Rupert?" The robot stared silently at the screen.

"Of all the unquaint feminine conceits—"

There was a definite *clang* as Rupert's heels smote together. He bowed stiffly from the hips. "Gins—" he began to say. His head went down majestically, kept on going down. It hit the floor with a terrific *zok.*

Jo became almost hysterical. Lester flapped his arms against his sides. Rupert, the back of his paunch peak-high in the air, rested stolidly respectful, his body making a right-angled triangle with the floor.

"—berg," Rupert finished from where his face angled against the floor. He made no move to rise. He *whurgled* softly, reminiscently.

"Well?" Lester glowered at him. "Are you going to lie there and look silly all day? Get up!"

"H-he c-*can't*," Jo shrieked. "Th-they've shifted h-his center of gra-gravity and he can't get up. If you ever do anything as funny as that bow over the teledar you'll kill two hundred million innocent people!"

Lester the Jester grimaced and bent over his robot. He caught it round the shoulders and tugged. Very slowly, very reluctantly, Rupert straightened. He pointed at Jo's image on the screen.

"That ain't no lady," he enunciated metallically. "That's gonna be your wife. *Or*— it may not be Hades but brother it's gonna be life! *Or*—she's not shady, she's only—"

"*Can* it!" Lester yelled. "And I do mean *can* it!"

He brooded while the robot went into another gear-clashing paroxysm. "My fine tile floor! The best mid-twentieth-century floor in the whole tower and look at it! A dent the size of…"

Jo clucked at him. "I've told you a dozen times that they only used tiled floors in *bathrooms* in the nineteen forties and fifties. Mostly in bathrooms, anyway. And that nineteen-forties radiator and rolltop desk are from two widely separated periods— you just don't have a sense of the antique, Lester lad. Wait till we've signed a marriage contract with each other—I'll show you what a Roosevelt-era home really looks like. How are Rupert's gags—on paper, I mean?"

"Don't know yet. He's just finished the script." The screen fluoresced along an edge. "Better get off, Jo. Someone's at the door. Call for me before the 'cast at the usual time. Bye."

At a signal from his master, the robot scuttled to the door and *twenty-three'd* at it. Two things happened simultaneously—the service mechanic from Rholg's Custom-Built Robots walked in and Rupert's head *zokked* against the floor.

Lester sighed and pulled Rupert straight again. "I hope he isn't going to repeat that courtly gesture anytime someone comes here. I'll have shellholes all over the living room."

"Has he done that before? That's not good. Remember, all of his basic control units are in his head and a lot of them have just started meshing the new service patterns. He's liable to fracture a bearing and go choo-choo. Like me to take him back to the plant for recalibration?"

"No, I don't have time. I start 'casting in two hours. That reminds me—did your techs build that word-scanner into his forehead?"

The mechanic nodded. "Sure. See that narrow green plate over his eyes? Just flip that to one side or have him do it whenever you want silent written transmission. The words will flow across like on a regular news sign. I came back for the key. Left it stuck in his neck and I'd be in one sweet fix if I got back to the factory without it."

"Take it. I thought you were somebody else." Lester turned to face the dumpy little man in a striped tunic who had just barged in through the open door. "Hello, Mr. Haskell. Would you have a seat? I'll be with you in a moment."

"Give me the key," the mechanic commanded. Rupert pulled the Official Robot Master Key out of the back of his neck and held it out. The mechanic reached for it. Rupert dropped it.

"Well, I'll be—" the man from Rholg's started. "If I didn't know better, I'd swear he did it on purpose." He bent down to retrieve the key.

As his fingers closed over it, Rupert's right hand flicked forward slightly. The man jumped to his feet and sprang backwards through the doorway.

"No you don't!" he snarled. "Did you see what he was trying to do? Why—"

"Three-and-twenty," said Rupert. The door slid shut, cutting off the service mechanic's last statement. The robot came back into the apartment, *clacking* ever so slightly. His facial expression seemed even sadder than before—somehow disappointed.

"Two of those Lunar Landing specials," his master told him. He waddled off to prepare them.

"Now look here, Lester," John Haskell boomed in a voice surprising for his size. "I'll come right to the point. I didn't know you were using writers until Green and Anderson told me you'd fired them because they wouldn't take a cut in salary. I go with them when they say they've made you the highest paid comedian in United Americas. Now this show tonight is only an option of a possible contract."

"Wait up, sir. I wrote my own stuff before they came to work for me and they operated entirely from my personal gag files. I fired them because they demanded a higher percentage of my earnings than I got. I can still ad-lib faster than any standup man in the business."

"I don't care whether you ad-lib or whether the stuff comes to you in a dream! I just want laughs on my program to get people in a proper frame of mind to hear my commercials. No, that's not what I mean—oh!" He reached out and grabbed one of the convoluted masses that Rupert had brought in and drained it rapidly. His face didn't even change color. "Not strong enough. Tasteless. Needs stuff."

The robot held the returned and empty receptacle for a moment and studied it. Then he bow-legged it back to the kitchen.

Lester decided that he didn't agree with the president of Star-Gazers, Inc. This drink had *wowie* in every alcoholic drop. But the drinks at the Planetmasters Club where Haskell lived were reputedly powerful.

"All I care about is this," Haskell was saying. "Can you work up a funny program tonight without Green and Anderson or can't you? You may have a high comic rating but they're spreading the word: people hear what they say in the industry. If Star-Gazers fail to pick up your thirteen-week option tonight after the trial 'cast, you'll have to go back to daytime soap operas."

"Sure, Mr. Haskell, sure. But take a look at this script and *then* make your comments." Lester plucked the long sheet of copy out of the electric typewriter and handed it to the little man.

Dangerous, that. It might stink seven ways from Monday. But he hadn't had time to read it himself. Rupert had better be good!

He was, to judge from Haskell's reaction. The president of Star-Gazers had roared himself into the antique swivel-chair and sat there shaking. "Wonderful!" he wiped the tears from his eyes. "*Terrific!* Almost, but not quite, colossal! I apologize, Lester. You don't need any gagwriters, you really do write comedy. Think you can memorize this before the program?"

"Shouldn't be any trouble. I always have to use a little infra-scopolamine for a rush job anyway. And in case I need an ad-lib suddenly, I've got my robot."

"Robot? You mean him?" Mr. Haskell gestured to where Rupert stood *whirring* over his shoulder as he stared at the script. He pulled a dark spiral of tubing out of the purple hand, sucked at it.

"Yes, he has a gag file in his mid-section. He'll stand out of camera range and anytime I need a gag I just look at him and the words are spelled out on the forehead scanner. Had it all inserted in my butler-valet combo by the Rholg— Mr. Haskell! What's the matter?"

Haskell had dropped the tube. It lay on the floor, a thin wisp of black smoke steaming out of the open end. "Th-the drink," Haskell said hoarsely. His face, after experimenting with red, green and lavender for a while, compromised and settled on all three in a sort of alternated mottled arrangement. "Where's your—your—"

"In there! Second door to the left!"

The little man scurried off, his body low. He seemed to have lost all of his bones.

"Now what can—" Lester sniffed at the spiral drinking tube. My God! He was abruptly aware that Rupert was going *whirretty-whirretty-klonk.* "Rupert, what did you put in that drink?"

"He asked for something stronger, more tasty—"

"*What did you put in that drink?*"

The robot considered. "Five parts—*(whizz-clang)*—castor oil to three parts—*(bing-bong)*—Worcestershire sauce to—*(tinkle-tinkle-burr-r-r)*—four parts essence of red pepper—*(g-r-rang)*—to one part Cro—"

Lester whistled and the phone leaped into his hand. "Radio Central? Hospital emergency and I mean emerge! Lester the Jester, Artist's Tower, apartment one thousand and six. Hurry!" He ran down the hall to help his guest sit on his stomach.

When the intern saw the brightly colored mess Haskell was becoming, he shook his head. "Let's get him in the stretcher and out!"

Rupert stood in the corner of the living room as the stretcher, secure in the grip of the intern's beamlock, floated through the door. "Musta been something he et," he clacked.

The intern glared back. "A comedian!"

Lester hurriedly drank three Lunar Landings. He mixed them himself. He had just finished memorizing the robot's ad-lib script with the aid of a heavy dose of infra-scopolamine when Jo breezed in. Rupert opened the door for her. *Clang. Zok.*

"You know, he's been doing this all day," Lester told her as he tugged the robot upright again. "And not only is he adding an original design to my floor but I suspect that he's not helping his bedamned mental processes any. Of course, he's obeyed me completely so far and all of his practical jokes have been aimed at others…"

Rupert rolled something around in his mouth. Then he pursed his lips. Multi-linked wrinkles appeared in his cheeks. He spat.

A brass hexagonal nut bounced against the floor. The three of them stared at it. Finally, Jo raised her head.

"*What* practical jokes?"

Lester told her.

"*Whew!* You're lucky your contract has a personal immunity clause. Otherwise Haskell could sue you from Patagonia to Nome. But he still won't feel any affection for you, any *real* affection. He'll probably live, though. Get into your costume."

As Lester hustled into his spangled red suit in the next room, he called at her, "What're you singing tonight?"

"Why don't you come to a rehearsal sometime and find out?"

"Have to keep up my impromptu reputation. What is it?"

"Oh, 'Subjective Me, Objective You' from Googy Garcia's latest hit—*Love Among the Asteroids.* This robot of yours may write good comedy but he sure is a bust as a butler. The junk he leaves scattered around. Paper, cigarettes, drink-tubes! When I enter your life on a permanent basis, young feller…" Her voice died as she bent and began picking up the litter from the floor of the living room. Behind her Rupert meditated at her back. "*Whirr?*" he went.

His right hand flashed up. He came at her fast. He reached her.

"*Yeeee-eeee!*" Jo screamed as she climbed halfway up the opposite wall. She turned as she came down. Her eyes literally crackled.

"Who—what—" she began menacingly. Then she noticed Rupert standing, his hand still out, all of his machinery going *whistle-clong-ka-bankle* all at once.

"Why, he's laughing at me! Think it funny do you, you mechanical pervert?" She sped at him in fury, her right hand going far back for a terrific slap.

Lester had torn out of the kitchen when she screamed. Now he saw her hand whistling around in a great arc, almost at Rupert's face.

"*Jo!*" he yelled. "Not in the head!"

Moing-g-g-g-g!

"Think you'll be all right, Miss Lissy," the doctor said. "Just keep your hand in this cast for two weeks. Then we'll X-ray again."

"Let's get started for the studio, Jo," Lester said nervously. "We'll be late. Shame this had to happen."

"Isn't it, though? But before I let you accompany me anywhere I want to get one thing straight. You get rid of Rupert."

"But, Jo darling, honey, sweet, do you know what a writer he is?"

"I don't care. I wouldn't think of bringing children up in a home that he infested. According to the Robot Laws you have to keep him at home. I frankly think he's gone dotty in a humorous way. But I don't like it. So—you'll have to choose between me and that gear-happy gagman." She smoothed the cast on her arm as she waited for his reply.

Now Rupert, in his present condition—for all of his eccentricities—meant that Lester's career as a comedian was assured, that never again would he have to worry about material, that he was set for life. On the other hand, he doubted he'd ever meet a woman who was as close to what he wanted in a wife as Jo. She was—well, Lester's ideal—she alone among the girls he knew met his requirements for a successful marriage.

It was a clear choice between money and the woman he loved.

"Well," Lester told Jo at last. "We can still be good friends?"

Jo was finishing her song by the time he arrived at the studio. She didn't even glower at him as she walked away from the camera-mikes. The commercial began.

Lester stationed Rupert against the wall of the control booth where no camera could pick up a view of his purple body. Then he joined the other actors under the dead camera who were waiting for the end of the commercial before starting their combination drama and comedy.

The announcer came to the end of the last rolling syllable of admiration. The five Gloppus sisters came up for the finale:

> *S—G—F, F, C!*
> *Star-Gazer's Fifteen Flavored Cigarettes!*
> *Stay away from tastes like hay!*
> *Days are gay with nasal play,*
> *Star-Gazer's Fifteen Flavored Way!*
> *S—G—F, F, C! From choc-o-late—to chereeee!*

The camera above Lester sparked colors as he and the actors took over. A simple playlet—romance in a fueling station on Phobos. Lester was extraneous to the plot—he merely came in with gags from time to time, gags based on some action or line in the straight story.

Good gags tonight—even the program manager was laughing. Well, not laughing—but he *smiled* now and then. And, buddy, if a program manager smiles, then people all over the western hemisphere have collapsed into a cataleptic hysteria. This is a fact as demonstrably certain and changeless as that the third vice-president of a teledar corporation shall always be the butt of the very worst jokes or, as it is known sociologically, the Throttlebottom Effect.

From time to time Lester glanced at his robot. The creature was not staring at him always—that was annoying. He had turned to examine the interior of the control booth through the transparent door which shut it off from the rest of the studio. Lester had removed the narrow green plate from above Rupert's eyes in case an ad-lib were necessary.

One was suddenly necessary. The second ingenue worked her way into a line beginning, "So when Harold said he had come to Mars to get away from militarism and regimentation"—and expired into a frantic "I told him—I told him—um, I had to tell him that—that—" She gaped, snapped her fingers spasmodically as she tried to remember.

Out of camera range, the prompter's fingers flew over the keys of the silent typewriter which projected the entire line on a screen above their heads. Meanwhile there was dead air. Everyone waited for Lester to make a crack that would fill the horrible space.

He spun to his robot. Thankfully he noticed that Rupert was staring at him. Good! Now if he could only meson-filter an ad-lib!

Words flowed across the screen on Rupert's forehead. Lester read them off as fast as they appeared. "Say, Barbara, why don't you tell the station manager to switch from atomics to petroleum?"

"I don't know," she said, feeding the line back like a good straight-man while she remembered the passage she had forgotten. "Why should I tell him to switch from atomics to petroleum?"

From the corner, Rupert roared, "Because there's no fuel like an oil fuel!"

The studio guffawed. Rupert guffawed. Only he sounded as if he were coming apart. All over United Americas, people grabbed at their teledar sets and tried to hold them together as the electronic apparatus *klunked, pingled* and *whirrety-whirred.*

Even Lester laughed. Beautiful! A lot more sophisticated than the crud he'd been getting from Green and Anderson, yet mixed with the pure old Iowa corn on which all belly-laughter is based. The robot was—

Hey! Rupert hadn't fed him that line—he'd used it himself. People weren't laughing at Lester the Jester—they were laughing at Rupert, even if they couldn't see him. *Hey-y-y!*

When the playlet ended the camera-mikes shifted to Josephine Lissy and the orchestra.

Lester took advantage of the break to charge up to Rupert. He pointed imperiously at the control booth.

"Get inside, you topper-copper, and don't come out until I'm ready to leave. Save the punch-line for yourself, will you? Bite the hand that oils you? Git, damn you, git!"

Rupert moved back a pace, almost crushing a property man. *"Bing-bing?"* he chuckled inquiringly. *"Honk-beeper-bloogle?"*

"No, I'm not kidding," Lester told him. "Get inside that control booth and stay there!"

With a dragging step that cut a thin groove in the plastic floor, Rupert went off to St. Helena.

Going on with the show, Lester watched him take his place behind the technicians, his shoulders slumped in a dejection the smoothlined 2207 model was never designed to register. From time to time he noticed the robot stride jerkily about the tiny booth, the word-scanner in his forehead making such abortive efforts as "Why is hyperspace like a paperweight?" and "When is a mutant not a mutant?" Lester indignantly ignored these attempts to make amends.

The mid-program commercial—"Have you ever asked yourself," the announcer put it to them, "why among the star-blazers it's Star-Gazers one thousand to one? Impartial tests show that these adventurous seekers in empty space always prefer—*what in*—"

Rupert slammed the door shut behind the last of three angry control technicians. Then he began pulling switches. He turned dials.

"He just up and threw us out!"

"That robot's gone psycho! Listen, he can shift the control to the inside of the booth. It's very simple. Is he a talking robot—no, please God!"

"Yeah! He can broadcast himself! Can he talk?"

"*Can* he!" Lester groaned. "Better blast him out fast!"

"Blast him?" An engineer laughed painfully. "He's locked the door. And do you know what the doors and walls of that booth are made of? He can stay in there until we get clearance from the IPCC. Which—"

"You know why they call them Star-Gazers, don't you?" Rupert's voice boomed over the teledar speaker which carried through the studio and incidentally all through the western hemisphere. "One puff and you're flat on your back! *Wongle-wangle-ding-ding!* Yes sir, you see stars all right—all colors. You smoke 'em and novas go off in your head. *Gr-r-rung! Ka-bam-ka-blooie!* Fifteen flavors and all of them just worth a raspberry! *Zingam-bong*—"

The walls of the control booth shivered with huge scraping laughter. And not only the walls were shivering.

Jo soothed Lester as best she could. "He can't go on forever, darling. He's got to stop!"

"Not with that file he has—and that variable modifier—and that meson-filter. I'm through. I'll never 'cast again—they'll never let me in anywhere. And I don't know how to do anything else. No other skills, no other experience. I'm through for life, Jo!"

The engineers finally had to shut off all power in Teledar City. That meant all 'casting stopped, including messages to space-ships and emergency calls to craft on the ground. It meant that elevators in the building stopped between floors, that lights went out in government offices all over the tower. Then they were able to open the doors with an auxiliary remote control unit and drag the inert robot out.

When the radiant power was shut off, so was he.

So Lester married Jo. But he didn't live happily ever after. He was barred from teledar for life.

He didn't starve, though. He wished he had from time to time. Because the 'cast that ruined him made Rupert. People wrote in demanding to hear more of this terrific robot who kidded the crass off sponsors. And Star-Gazers tripled their sales. Which, after all, is the ultimate test...

Lester manages Rupert the Rollicking Robot—("The screwiest piece of machinery since the invention of the nut"). He lives with him too, has to by Robot Law. He can't sell him—who'd want to get rid of their only source of bread and marmalade? And he can't hire anyone to take care of Rupert—anyone in his right mind, that is. But worst of all, Lester has to *live* with Rupert. He finds it difficult.

Once a week he visits Jo and his children. He looks very haggard then. Rupert's practical jokes get more complicated all the time.

AFTERWORD

All right, so it's not one of Asimov's positronic robots, nor is it Brian Aldiss's "Who Can Replace a Man?" It's just a little old robot story I wrote—the only one I ever did. It's full to overflowing with what, in another context, I called temporal provincialisms: the cigarettes that were still being smoked in the twenty-third century; the material typed on an electric typewriter, rather than on a computer; the 1940s-type broadcasting commercials; etc., *and* etc.

So isn't a science-fiction writer entitled to be a bit time-bound once in a while?

For what it's worth— The Ginsberg joke was given to me by Cyril Kornbluth. It was his favorite. The concluding "oil fuel" joke was contributed by Theodore Sturgeon. It was definitely not his favorite.

WRITTEN 1948———*PUBLISHED 1951*

Project Hush

Secret? We were about as secret as you could be and still exist. Listen, do you know the name of our official listing in Army documents?

Project Hush.

You can imagine. Or, come to think of it, you really can't. Of course, everyone remembers the terrific espionage fever that gripped this county in the late nineteen-sixties, how every official named Tom had another official named Dick checking up on him, how Dick had someone named Harry checking up on *him*—and how Harry didn't have the slightest idea of the work Tom was doing because there was a limit as to how far you could trust even counter-intelligence men...

But you had to be in a top-secret Army project to really get it. Where a couple of times a week you reported to Psycho for DD and HA (Dream Detailing and Hypno-Analysis to you carefree civilians). Where even the commanding general of the heavily fortified research post to which you were assigned could not ask what the hell you were doing, under penalty of court-martial—and was supposed to shut his imagination off like a faucet every time he heard an explosion. Where your project didn't even appear in the military budget by name but under the classification *Miscellaneous X Research*—a heading that picked up a bigger appropriation every year like a runaway snowball. Where—

Oh, well, maybe you can still remember it. And, as I said, we were called Project *Hush*.

The goal of our project was not just to reach the Moon and set up a permanent station there with an original complement of two men. That we had just done on that slightly historic day of 24 June 1967. More important, in those wild, weapon-seeking times when fear of the H-bomb had churned the nation into a viscid mass of hysteria, was getting to the Moon before anybody else and without anybody else knowing about it.

We'd landed at the northern tip of Mare Nubium, just off Regiomontanus, and, after planting a flag with appropriate throat-catching ceremony, had swung into the realities of the tasks we had practiced as so many dry runs back on Earth.

Major Monroe Gridley prepared the big rocket, with its tiny cubicle of living space, for the return journey to Earth which he alone would make.

Lieutenant Colonel Thomas Hawthorne painstakingly examined our provisions and portable quarters for any damage that might have been incurred in landing.

And I, Colonel Benjamin Rice, first commanding officer of Army Base No. 1 on the Moon, dragged crate after enormous crate out of the ship on my aching academic back, and piled them in the spot two hundred feet away where the plastic dome would be built.

We all finished at just about the same time, as per schedule, and went into Phase Two.

Monroe and I started work on building the dome. It was a simple pre-fab affair, but big enough to require an awful lot of assembling. Then, after it was built, we faced the real problem—getting all the complex internal machinery in place and in operating order.

Meanwhile, Tom Hawthorne took his plump self off in the single-seater rocket which, up to then, had doubled as a lifeboat.

The schedule called for him to make a rough three-hour scouting survey in an ever-widening spiral from our dome. This had been regarded as a probable waste of time, rocket fuel and manpower—but a necessary precaution. He was supposed to watch for such things as bug-eyed monsters out for a stroll on the Lunar landscape. Basically, however, Tom's survey was intended to supply extra geological and astronomical meat for the report which Monroe was to carry back to Army HQ on Earth.

Tom was back in forty minutes. His round face, inside its transparent bubble helmet, was fishbelly white. And so were ours, once he told us what he'd seen.

He had seen another dome.

"The other side of Mare Nubium—in the Riphaean Mountains," he babbled excitedly. "It's a little bigger than ours, and it's a little flatter on top. And it's not translucent, either, with splotches of different colors here and there—it's a dull, dark, heavy gray. But that's all there is to see."

"No markings on the dome?" I asked worriedly. "No signs of anyone—or anything—around it?"

"Neither, Colonel." I noticed he was calling me by my rank for the first time since the trip started, which meant he was saying in effect, "Man, have *you* got a decision to make!"

"Hey, Tom," Monroe put in. "Couldn't be just a regularly shaped bump in the ground, could it?"

"I'm a geologist, Monroe, I can distinguish artificial from natural topography. Besides—" He looked up— "I just remembered something I left out. There's a brand-new tiny crater near the dome—the kind usually left by a rocket exhaust."

"Rocket exhaust?" I seized on that. "*Rockets,* eh?"

Tom grinned a little sympathetically. "Spaceship exhaust, I should have said. You can't tell from the crater what kind of propulsive device these characters are using. It's not the same kind of crater our rear-jets leave, if that helps any."

Of course it didn't. So we went into our ship and had a council of war. And I do mean war. Both Tom and Monroe were calling me Colonel in every other sentence. I used their first names every chance I got.

Still, no one but me could reach a decision. About what to do, I mean.

"Look," I said at last, "here are the possibilities. They know we are here—either from watching us land a couple of hours ago or from observing Tom's scoutship—or they do not know we are here. They are either humans from Earth—in which case they are in all probability enemy nationals—or they are alien creatures from another planet—in which case they may be friends, enemies or what-have-you. I think common sense and standard military procedure demand that we consider them hostile until we have evidence to the contrary. Meanwhile, we proceed with extreme caution, so as not to precipitate an interplanetary war with potentially friendly Martians, or whatever they are.

"All right. It's vitally important that Army Headquarters be informed of this immediately. But since Moon-to-Earth radio is still on the drawing boards, the only way we can get through is to send Monroe back with the ship. If we do, we run the risk of having our garrison force, Tom and me, captured while he's making the return trip. In that case, their side winds up in possession of important information concerning our personnel and equipment, while our side has only the bare knowledge that somebody or something else has a base on the Moon. So our primary need is more information.

"Therefore, I suggest that I sit in the dome on one end of a telephone hookup with Tom, who will sit in the ship, his hand over the firing button, ready to blast off for Earth the moment he gets the order from me. Monroe will take the single-seater down to the Riphaen Mountains, landing as close to the other dome as he thinks safe. He will then proceed the rest of the way on foot, doing the best scouting job he can in a spacesuit.

"He will not use his radio, except for agreed-upon nonsense syllables to designate landing the single-seater, coming upon the dome by foot, and warning me to tell Tom to take off. If he's captured, remembering that the first purpose of a scout is acquiring and transmitting knowledge of the enemy, he will snap his suit radio on full volume and pass on as much data as time and the enemy's reflexes permit. How does that sound to you?"

They both nodded. As far as they were concerned, the command decision had been made. But I was sitting under two inches of sweat.

"One question," Torn said. "Why did you pick Monroe for the scout?"

"I was afraid you'd ask that," I told him. "We're three extremely unathletic Ph.D.s who have been in the Army since we finished our schooling. There isn't too much choice. But I remembered that Monroe is half Indian—Arapaho, isn't it, Monroe?— and I'm hoping blood will tell."

"Only trouble, Colonel," Monroe said slowly as he rose, "is that I'm one-*fourth* Indian and even that... Didn't I ever tell you that my great-grandfather was the only Arapaho scout who was with Custer at the Little Big Horn? He'd been positive Sitting Bull was miles away. However, I'll do my best. And if I heroically don't came back, would you please persuade the Security Officer of our section to clear my name for use in the history books? Under the circumstances, I think it's the least he could do."

I promised to do my best, of course.

After he took off, I sat in the dome over the telephone connection to Tom and hated myself for picking Monroe to do the job. But I'd have hated myself just as much for picking Tom. And if anything happened and I had to tell Tom to blast off, I'd probably be sitting here in the dome all by myself after that, waiting...

"*Broz neggle!*" came over the radio in Monroe's resonant voice. He had landed the single-seater.

I didn't dare use the telephone to chat with Tom in the ship, for fear I might miss an important word or phrase from our scout. So I sat and sat and strained my ears. After a while, I heard "*Mishgashu!*" which told me that Monroe was in the neighborhood of the other dome and was creeping toward it under cover of whatever boulders were around.

And then, abruptly, I heard Monroe yell my name and there was a terrific clattering in my headphones. Radio interference! He'd been caught, and whoever had caught him had simultaneously jammed his suit transmitter with a larger transmitter from the alien dome.

Then there was silence.

After a while, I told Tom what had happened. He just said, "Poor Monroe." I had a good idea of what his expression was like.

"Look, Tom," I said, "if you take off now, you still won't have anything important to tell. After capturing Monroe, whatever's in that other dome will come looking for us, I think. I'll let them get close enough for us to learn something of their appearance—at least if they're human or nonhuman. Any bit of information about them is important. I'll shout it up to you and you'll still be able to take off in plenty of time. All right?"

"You're the boss, Colonel," he said in a mournful voice. "Lots of luck."

And then there was nothing to do but wait. There was no oxygen system in the dome yet, so I had to squeeze up a sandwich from the food compartment in my suit. I sat there, thinking about the expedition. Nine years, and all that careful secrecy, all that expenditure of money and mind-cracking research—and it had come to this. Waiting to be wiped out, in a blast from some unimaginable weapon. I understood Monroe's last request. We often felt we were so secret that our immediate superiors didn't even want *us* to know what we were working on. Scientists are people—they wish for recognition, too. I was hoping the whole expedition would be written up in the history books, but it looked unpromising.

Two hours later, the scout ship landed near the dome. The lock opened and, from where I stood in the open door of our dome, I saw Monroe come out and walk toward me.

I alerted Tom and told him to listen carefully. "It may be a trick—he might be drugged..."

He didn't act drugged, though—not exactly. He pushed his way past me and sat down on a box to one side of the dome. He put his booted feet up on another, smaller box.

"How are you, Ben?" he asked. "How's every little thing?"

I grunted. "*Well?*" I know my voice skittered a bit.

He pretended puzzlement. "Well *what?* Oh, I see what you mean. The other dome—you want to know who's in it. You have a right to be curious, Ben. Certainly. The leader of a top-secret expedition like this—Project Hush they call us, huh, Ben—finds another dome on the Moon. He thinks he's been the first to land on it, so naturally he wants to—"

"Major Monroe Gridley!" I rapped out. "You will come to attention and deliver your report. Now!" Honestly, I felt my neck swelling up inside my helmet.

Monroe just leaned back against the side of the dome. "That's the *Army* way of doing things," he commented admiringly. "Like the recruits say, there's a right way, a wrong way and an Army way. Only there are other ways, too." He chuckled. "Lots of other ways."

"He's off," I heard Tom whisper over the telephone. "Ben, Monroe has gone and blown his stack."

"They aren't extraterrestrials in the other dome, Ben," Monroe volunteered in a sudden burst of sanity. "No, they're humans, all right, and from Earth. Guess *where.*"

"I'll kill you," I warned him. "I swear I'll kill you, Monroe. Where are they from—Russia, China, Argentina?"

He grimaced. "What's so secret about those places? Go on!—guess again."

I stared at him long and hard. "The only place else—"

"Sure," he said. "You got it, Colonel. The other dome is owned and operated by the Navy. The goddamn United States Navy!"

AFTERWORD

This was written in the early part of the security-mad, spy-hunting nineteen fifties (thus its title and many of its ruminations) and took for granted an even madder decade to follow. Instead, of course, the nineteen-sixties began with the assassination of John, and proceeded with that of Bobby and Martin—ending with the Woodstock Festival. (Go ahead. *You* define "mad.")

And lest the predictive proclivities of science fiction be ignored, the author wishes to point to the date of the first manned landing on the Moon, as imagined in early 1953: June 24, 1967. Pretty close—considering that the prediction was made before the space race had even begun, before Sputnik, even!

Not that the story was seen as prediction by the readership of its time, although its satiric motifs were definitely appreciated in some of the more improbable places. It was, I have been told, read aloud with great glee at the War College.

For what it's worth, Major Monroe Gridley was meant to stand for a good buddy of mine with whom I went overseas to the European Theater of Operations in World War II. He was a full-blooded Arapaho Indian who taught me much, much about Custer.

But I was never a colonel; like Adolf, I stopped at corporal.

WRITTEN 1953————*PUBLISHED 1954*

Winthrop Was Stubborn

That was the trouble right there. That summed it up.

Winthrop was stubborn.

Mrs. Brucks stared at her three fellow-visitors from the twentieth century. "But he can't!" she exclaimed. "He's not the only one—he's got to think of us! He can't leave us stranded in this crazy world!"

Dave Pollock shrugged his shoulders inside the conservative gray suit that clashed so mightily with the décor of the twenty-fifth-century room in which they sat. He was a thin, nervous young man whose hands had a tendency to perspire. Right now, they were extremely wet.

"He says we should be grateful. But whether we are or aren't grateful isn't important to him. He's staying."

"That means *we* have to stay," Mrs. Brucks pleaded. "Doesn't he understand that?"

Pollock spread his moist palms helplessly. "What difference does it make? He's absolutely set on staying. He *likes* the twenty-fifth century. I argued with him for two hours; I've never seen anyone so stubborn. I can't budge him, and that's all I know."

"Why don't you talk to him, Mrs. Brucks?" Mary Ann Carthington suggested. "He's been nice to you. Maybe you could make him act sensible."

"Hm." Mrs. Brucks patted her hairdo, which after two weeks in the future, was beginning to get straggly. "You think so? Mr. Mead, you think it's a good idea?"

The fourth person in the oval room, a stoutish middle-aged man whose face bore an emphatically respectable expression considered the matter for a moment, and nodded. "Can't do any harm. Might work. And we've got to do *something*."

"All right. So I'll try."

Mrs. Brucks sniffled deep inside her grandmotherly soul. She knew what the others were thinking, weren't quite saying. To them, Winthrop and she were the "old folks"—both over fifty. Therefore, they should have something in common; they should be able to communicate sympathetically.

The fact that Winthrop was ten years her senior meant little to Mr. Mead's forty-six years, less to Dave Pollock's thirty-four, and in all probability was completely meaningless to Mary Ann Carthington's even twenty. One of the "old folks" should be able to talk sense to the other, they would feel.

What could they see, from the bubbling distance of youth, of the chasms that separated Winthrop from Mrs. Brucks even more finally than the others? It was unimportant to them that he was a tight and unemotional old bachelor, while she was the warm and gossipy mother of six children, the grandmother of two, with her silver wedding anniversary proudly behind her. She and Winthrop had barely exchanged a dozen sentences with each other since they'd arrived in the future: they had disliked each other deeply from the moment they had met in Washington at the time-travel finals.

But—Winthrop was stubborn. That fact remained. Mr. Mead had roared his best executive-type roars at him. Mary Ann Carthington had tried to jog his senility with her lush, lithe figure and most fluttery voice. Even Dave Pollock, an educated man, a high-school science teacher with a master's degree in something or other, Dave Pollock had talked his heart out to him and been unable to make him budge.

So it was up to her. Someone had to change Winthrop's mind. Or they'd all be stuck in the future, here in this horrible twenty-fifth century. No matter if she hated it more than anything she'd had to face in a lifetime of troubles—it was up to her.

She rose and shook out the wrinkles in the expensive black dress her proud husband had purchased in Lord & Taylor's the day before the group had left. Try to tell Sam that it was purely luck that she had been chosen, just a matter of fitting the physical specifications in the message from the future! Sam wouldn't listen: he probably boasted all over the shop, to each and every one of the other cutters with whom he worked, about his wife—one of five people selected in the whole United States of America to make a trip five hundred years into the future. Would Sam still be boasting when the six o'clock deadline passed that night and she didn't return?

This time the sniffle worked its way through the cushions of her bosom and exploded tinily at her nose.

Mary Ann Carthington crooned back sympathetically. "Shall I ring for the jumper, Mrs. Brucks?"

"I'm crazy?" Mrs. Brucks shot back at her angrily. "A little walk down the hall, I need that headache-maker? A little walk I can walk."

She started for the door rapidly before the girl could summon the upsetting device which exploded you from one place to another and left you with your head swimming and your stomach splashing. But she paused for a moment and took a last wistful look at the room before leaving it. While it was by no means a cozy five-room apartment in the Bronx, she'd spent almost every minute of her two weeks in the future here, and for all of its peculiar furniture and oddly colored walls, she hated to leave it. At least here nothing rippled along the floor, nothing reached out from the walls; here was as much sanity as you could find in the twenty-fifth century.

Then she swallowed hard, said "Ah-h!" with regretful finality and closed the door behind her. She walked rapidly along the corridor, being careful to stay in the exact middle, the greatest distance possible from the bumpy writhing walls on either side.

At a point in the corridor where one purple wall flowed restlessly around a stable yellow square, she stopped. She put her mouth, fixed in a scowl of distaste, to the square. "Mr. Winthrop?" she inquired tentatively.

"Well, well, if it isn't Mrs. Brucks!" the square boomed back at her. "Long time no see. Come right in, Mrs. Brucks."

The patch of yellow showed a tiny hole in the center which dilated rapidly into a doorway. She stepped through gingerly, as if there might be a drop of several stories on the other side.

The room was shaped like a long, narrow isosceles triangle. There was no furniture in it, and no other exits, except for what an occasional yellow square suggested. Streaks of color chased themselves fluently along the walls and ceilings and floors, shifting the predominant hue of the interior up and down the spectrum, from pinkish gray to a thick, dark ultramarine. And odors came with the colors, odors came and filled the room for a brief spell, some of them unpleasant, some of them intriguing, but all of them touched with the unfamiliar and alien. From somewhere behind the walls and above the ceiling, there was music, its tones softly echoing, gently reinforcing the colors and the odors. The music too was strange to twentieth-century ears: strings of dissonances would be followed by a long or short silence in the midst of which an almost inaudible melody might be heard like a harmonic island in an ocean of sonic strangeness.

At the far end of the room, at the sharp apex of the triangle, an aged little man lay on a raised portion of the floor. Periodically, this raised portion would raise a bit of itself still further or lower a section, very much like a cow trying to find a comfortable position on the grass.

The single garment that Winthrop wore similarly kept adjusting itself upon him. At one moment it would be a striped red and white tunic, covering everything from his shoulders to his thighs; then it would slowly elongate into a green gown that trickled over his outstretched toes; and, abruptly, it would contract into a pair of light brown shorts decorated with a complex pattern of brilliant blue seashells.

Mrs. Brucks observed all this with an almost religious disapproval. A man was meant, she felt dimly, to be dressed approximately the same way from one moment to the next, not to swoop wildly from one garment to another like a montage sequence in the movies.

The shorts she didn't mind, though her modest soul considered them a bit too skimpy for receiving lady callers. The green gown, well, she didn't think it went with Winthrop's sex—as *she'd* been brought up—but she could go along with it; after all, if he wanted to wear what was essentially a dress, it was his business. Even the red and white tunic which reminded her strongly and nostalgically of her grand-daughter Debbie's sunsuit was something she was willing to be generous about. But at least stick to *one* of them, show some will-power, some concentration!

Winthrop put the enormous egg he was holding on the floor. "Have a seat, Mrs. Brucks. Take the load off your feet," he suggested jovially.

Shuddering at the hillock of floor which came into being at her host's gesture, Mrs. Brucks finally bent her knees and sat, her tentative rear making little more than a tangent to it.

"How—how are you, Mr. Winthrop?"

"Fine, just fine! Couldn't be better, Mrs. Brucks. Say, have you seen my new teeth? Just got them this morning. Look."

He opened his jaws and pulled his lips back with his fingers.

Mrs. Brucks leaned forward, really interested, and inspected the mouthful of white, shining enamel. "A good job," she pronounced at last, nodding. "The dentists here made them for you so fast?"

"Dentists!" He spread his bony arms wide in a vast and merry gesture. "They don't have *dentists* in 2458 AD. They *grew* these teeth for me, Mrs. Brucks."

"*Grew*? How *grew*?"

"How should I know how they did it? They're smart, that's all. A lot smarter than us, every way. I just heard about the regeneration clinic. It's a place where you lose an arm, you go down there, they grow it right back on the stump. Free, like everything else. I went down there, I said 'I want new teeth' to the machine that they've got. The machine tells me to take a seat, it goes one, two, three—and bingo! there I am, throwing my plates away. You want to try it?"

She shifted uncomfortably on her hillock. "Maybe—but I better wait until it's perfected."

Winthrop laughed again. "You're scared," he announced. "You're like the others, scared of the twenty-fifth century. Anything new, anything different, you want to run for a hole like a rabbit. Only me, only Winthrop, I'm the only one that's got guts. I'm the oldest, but that doesn't make any difference—I'm the only one with guts."

Mrs. Brucks smiled tremulously at him. "But Mr. Winthrop, you're also the only one without no one to go back to. I got a family, Mr. Mead has a family, Mr. Pollock's just married, a newly-wed, and Miss Carthington is engaged. We'd all like to go back, Mr. Winthrop."

"Mary Ann is engaged?" A lewd chuckle. "I'd never have guessed it from the way she was squirming round that temporal supervisor fellow. That little blondie is on the make for any guy she can get."

"Still and all, Mr. Winthrop, she's engaged. To a bookkeeper in her office she's engaged. A fine, hard-working boy. And she wants to go back to him."

The old man pulled up his back and the floor-couch hunched up between his shoulder blades and scratched him gently. "Let her go back, then. Who gives a damn?"

"But, Mr. Winthrop—" Mrs. Brucks wet her lips and clasped her hands in front of her. "*She* can't go back, *we* can't go back—unless we all go back together. Remember what they told us when we arrived, those temporal supervisors? We *all* have to be sitting in our chairs in the time machine building at six o'clock on the dot, when they're going to make what they call the transfer. If we aren't *all* there on time, they can't make the transfer, they said. So, if one of us, if you, for instance, doesn't show up—"

"Don't tell me your troubles," Winthrop cut her off savagely. His face was deeply flushed and his lips came back and exposed the brand-new teeth. There was a sharp acrid smell in the room and blotches of crimson on its walls as the place adjusted to its owner's mood. All around them the music changed to a staccato, vicious rumble. "Everybody wants Winthrop to do a favor for them. What did they ever do for Winthrop?"

"Umh?" Mrs. Brucks inquired. "I don't understand you."

"You're damn tooting you don't understand me. When I was a kid, my old man used to come home drunk every night and beat the hell out of me. I was a small kid, so every other kid on the block took turns beating the hell out of me, too. When I grew up, I got a lousy job and a lousy life. Remember the Depression and those pictures of the breadlines? Well, who do you think it was on those breadlines, on every damn breadline in the whole damn country? Me, that's who. And then, when the good times came back, I was too old for a decent job. Night-watchman, berry-picker, dishwasher, that's me. Cheap flophouses, cheap furnished rooms. Everybody gets the gravy, Winthrop got the garbage."

He picked up the large egg-shaped object he had been examining when she entered and studied it moodily. In the red glow of the room, his face seemed to have flushed to a deeper color. A large vein in his scrawny neck buzzed bitterly.

"Yeah. And like you said, everybody has someone to go back to, everybody but me. You're damn tooting I don't have anyone to go back to. *Damn* tooting. I never had a friend, never had a wife, never even had a girl that stayed around longer than it took her to use up the loose change in my pocket. So why should I go back? I'm happy here, I get everything I want and I don't have to pay for it. You people want to go back because you feel different—uncomfortable, out of place. *I* don't. I'm used to being out of place: I'm right at home. I'm having a good time. I'm *staying*."

"Listen, Mr. Winthrop," Mrs. Brucks leaned forward anxiously, then jumped as the seat under her slunk forward. She rose and stood, deciding that on her feet she might enjoy at least minimal control of her immediate environment. "Listen, Mr. Winthrop, everybody has troubles in their life. With my daughter, Annie, I had a time that I wouldn't wish on my worst enemy. And with my Julius— But because I have troubles, you think I should take it out on other people? I should prevent them from going home when they're sick and tired of jumper machines and food machines and— I don't know—*machine* machines and—"

"Speaking of food machines," Winthrop perked up, "have you seen my new food phonograph? The latest model. I heard about it last night, I said I wanted one, and sure enough, first thing this morning a brand new one is delivered to my door. No fuss, no bother, no money. What a world!"

"But it's not your world, Mr. Winthrop. You didn't make anything in it, you don't work in it. Even if everything is free, you're not entitled. You got to *belong*, to be entitled."

"There's nothing in their laws about that," he commented absent-mindedly as he opened the huge egg and peered inside at the collection of dials and switches and spigots. "See, Mrs. Brucks, *double* volume controls, *double* intensity controls, *triple* vitamin controls. What a set! With this one, you can raise the oil texture of a meal, say, while reducing its sweetness with that doohickey there—and if you press that switch, you can compress the whole meal so it's no bigger than a mouthful and you're still hungry enough to try a couple of other compositions. Want to try it? I got it set for the latest number by Unni Oehele, that new Aldebaranian composer: *Memories of a Martian Soufflé*."

She shook her head emphatically. "No, by me, a meal is served in plates. I don't want to try it. Thank you very much."

"You're missing something. Believe me, lady, you're missing something. The first course is a kind of light, fast movement, all herbs from Aldebaran IV mixed with a spicy vinegar from Aldebaran IX. The second course, *Consomme Grand,* is a lot slower and kind of majestic. Oehele bases it all on a broth made from the white *chund,* a native rabbity animal they have on Aldebaran IV. See, he uses only native Aldebaranian foods to *suggest* a Martian dish. Get it? The same thing Kratzmeier did in *A Long, Long Dessert on Deimos and Phobos,* only it's a lot better. More modern-like, if you know what I mean. Now in the *third* course, Oehele really takes off. He—"

"Please, Mr. Winthrop!" Mrs. Brucks begged. "Enough! Too much! I don't want to hear any more." She glared at him, trying to restrain her lips from curling in contempt. She'd had far too much of this sort of thing from her son, Julius, years ago, when he'd been running around with a crazy art crowd from City College and been spouting hours of incomprehensible trash at her that he'd picked up from the daily newspaper's musical reviews and the printed notes in record albums. One thing she'd learned the hard way was how to recognize an aesthetic phony.

Winthrop shrugged. "Okay, okay. But you'd think you'd at least want to try it. The others at least tried it. They took a bite of classical Kratzmeier or Gura-Hok, they didn't like it, they spat it out—fine. But you've been living on nothing but that damn twentieth-century grub since we arrived. After the first day, you haven't set foot outside your room. And the way you asked the room to decorate itself—Keerist! It's so old-fashioned, it makes me sick. You're living in the twenty-fifth century, lady; wake up!"

"Mr. Winthrop," she said sternly. "Yes or no? You're going to be nice or not?"

"You're in your fifties," he pointed out. "*Fifties,* Mrs. Brucks. In our time, you can expect to live what? Ten or fifteen more years. Tops. Here, you might see another fifty, maybe sixty. Me, I figure I'm good for at least another forty. With the medical machines they got, they can do wonders. And no wars to worry about, no epidemics, no depressions, nothing. Everything free, lots of exciting things to do, Mars, Venus, the stars. Why in hell are you so crazy to go back?"

Mrs. Brucks's already half-dissolved self-control gave way completely. "Because it's my home," she sobbed. "Because it's what I understand. Because I want to be with my husband, my children, my grandchildren. And because I don't *like* it here, Mr. Winthrop, I don't *like* it here!"

"So go back!" Winthrop yelled. The room which for the last few moments had settled into a pale golden-yellow, turned rose-color again in sympathy. "Go the hell back! There's not one of you with the guts of a cockroach. Even that young fellow, what's-his-name, Dave Pollock, I thought he had guts. He went out with me for the first week and he tried everything once. But he got scared too, and went back to his little old comfy room. It's too *dec-a-dent,* he says, too *dec-a-dent.* So take him with you—and go back, all of you!"

"But we *can't* go back without you, Mr. Winthrop. Remember they said the transfer has to be complete on both sides? One stays behind, all stay. We can't go back without you."

Winthrop smiled and stroked the throbbing vein on his neck. "You're damn tooting you can't go back without me. And I'm staying. This is one time that old Winthrop calls the tune."

"Please, Mr. Winthrop, don't be stubborn. Be nice. Don't make us force you."

"You can't force me," he told her with a triumphant leer. "I know my rights. According to the law of twenty-fifth-century America, no human being can be forced to do anything. Fact. I looked it up. You try to gang up on me, carry me out of here, all I do is set up a holler that I'm being forced and *one! two! three!* a flock of government machines show up and turn me loose. That's the way it works. Put that in your old calabash and smoke it!"

"Listen," she said, as she turned to leave. "At six o'clock, we'll all be in the time machine building. Maybe you'll change your mind, Mr. Winthrop."

"I won't," he shot after her. "That's one thing you can be sure of—I won't change my mind."

So Mrs. Brucks went back to her room and told the others that Winthrop was stubborn as ever.

Oliver T. Mead, vice-president in charge of public relations for Sweetbottom Septic Tanks, Inc., of Gary, Indiana, drummed impatiently on the arm of the red leather easy chair that Mrs. Brucks's room had created especially for him. "Ridiculous!" he exclaimed. "Ridiculous and absolutely nonsensical. That a derelict, a vagrant, should be able to keep people from going about their business…do you know that there's going to be a nationwide sales conference of Sweetbottom retail outlets in a few days? I've *got* to be there. I absolutely must return tonight to our time as scheduled, no ifs, no ands, no buts. There's going to be one unholy mess, I can tell you, if the responsible individuals in this period don't see to that."

"I bet there will be," Mary Ann Carthington said from behind round, respectful and well-mascaraed eyes. "A big firm like that can really give them what for, Mr. Mead."

Dave Pollock grimaced at her wearily. "A firm five hundred years out of existence? Who're they going to complain to—the history books?"

As the portly man stiffened and swung around angrily, Mrs. Brucks held up her hands and said, "Don't get upset, don't fight. Let's talk, let's think it out, only don't fight. You think it's the truth we can't force him to go back?"

Mr. Mead leaned back and stared out of a non-existent window. "Could be. Then again, it might not. I'm willing to believe anything—anything!—of 2458 AD by now, but this smacks of criminal irresponsibility. That they should invite us to visit their time and then not make every possible effort to see that we return safe and sound at the end of two weeks as scheduled—besides, what about their people visiting in *our* time, the five with whom we transferred? If we're stuck here, they'll be stuck in 1958. Forever. Any government worthy of the name owes protection to its citizens traveling abroad. Without it, it's less than worthless: a tax-grabbing, boondoggling, inept bureaucracy that's—that's positively criminal!"

Mary Ann Carthington's pert little face had been nodding in time to his fist beating on the red leather armchair. "That's what I say. Only the government seems to be all machines. How can you argue with machines? The only government *man* we've seen since we arrived was that Mr. Storku who welcomed us officially to the United States of America of 2458. And he didn't seem very interested in us. At least, he didn't *show* any interest."

"The Chief of Protocol for the State Department, you mean?" Dave Pollock asked. "The one who yawned when you told him how distinguished he looked?"

The girl made a slight, slapping gesture at him, accompanied by a reproachful smile. "Oh, *you.*"

"Well, then, here's what we have to do. One," Mr. Mead rose and proceeded to open the fingers of his right hand one at a time. "We have to go on the basis of the only human being in the government we've met personally, this Mr. Storku. Two, we have to select a qualified representative from among us. Three, this qualified representative has to approach Mr. Storku in his official capacity and lay the facts before him. The facts, complete and unequivocal. How his government managed somehow to communicate with our government the fact that time travel was possible, but only if certain physical laws were taken into consideration, most particularly the law of— the law of— What *is* that law, Pollock?"

"The law of the conservation of energy and mass. Matter, or its equivalent in energy, can neither be created nor destroyed. If you want to transfer five people from the cosmos of 2458 AD to the cosmos of 1958 AD, you have to replace them simultaneously in their own time with five people of exactly the same structure and mass from the time they're going to. Otherwise, you'd have a gap in the mass of one space-time continuum and a corresponding surplus in the other. It's like a chemical equation—"

"That's all I wanted to know, Pollock. I'm not a student in one of your classes. You don't have to impress *me*, Pollock," Mr. Mead pointed out.

The thin young man grunted. "Who was trying to impress you?" he demanded belligerently. "What can you do for me—get me a job in your septic tank empire? I just tried to clear up something you seemed to have a lot of trouble understanding. That's at the bottom of our problem: the law of the conservation of energy and mass. And the way the machine's been set for all five of us and all five of them, nobody can do anything about transferring back unless all of us and all of them are present at both ends of the connection at the very same moment."

Mr. Mead nodded slowly and sarcastically. "All right," he said. "All right! Thank you very much for your lesson, but now, if you don't mind, I'd like to go on, please. Some of us aren't civil service workers: our time is valuable."

"Listen to the tycoon, will you?" Dave Pollock suggested with amusement. "*His* time is valuable. Look, Ollie, my friend, as long as Winthrop goes on being stubborn, we're all stuck here together. And as long as we're stuck here, we're all greenhorns together in 2458 AD, savages from the savage past. For your information, right now, your time is my time, and vice versa."

"Sh-h-h!" Mrs. Brucks commanded. "Be nice. Go on talking, Mr. Mead. It's very interesting. Isn't it interesting, Miss Carthington?"

The blonde girl nodded. "It sure is. They don't make people executives for nothing. You put things so—so *right,* Mr. Mead."

Oliver T. Mead, somewhat mollified, smiled a slender thanks at her. "Three, then. We lay the facts before this Mr. Storku. We tell him how we came in good faith, after we were selected by a nationwide contest to find the exact opposite numbers of the five people from his time. How we did it partly out of a natural and understandable curiosity to see what the future looks like, and partly out of patriotism. Yes, patriotism! For is not this America of 2458 AD our America? Is it not still our native land, however strange and inexplicable the changes in it? As patriots we could follow no other course, as patriots we—"

"Oh, for God's sake!" the high school teacher exploded. "Oliver T. Mead pledges allegiance to the flag! We know you'd die for your country under a barrage of stock market quotations. You're no subversive, all right? What's your idea, what's your idea?"

There was a long silence in the room while the stout middle-aged man went through a pantomime of fighting for control. The pantomime over, he slapped his hands against the sides of his hand-tailored dark business suit and said: "Pollock, if you don't want to hear what I have to say, you can always take a breather in the hall. *As I was saying,* having explained the background facts to Mr. Storku, we come to the present impasse. We come to point four, the fact that Winthrop refuses to return with us. And we demand, do you hear me?—we *demand* that the American government of this time take the appropriate steps to insure our safe return to our own time even if it involves, well—*martial law* relative to Winthrop. We put this flatly, definitely, unequivocally to Storku."

"Is that your idea?" Dave Pollock asked derisively. "What if Storku says *no?*"

"He can't say no, if it's put right. Authority, I think that's the keynote. It should be put to him with authority. We are citizens—in temporal extension—of America. We demand our rights. On the other hand, if he refuses to recognize our citizenship, we demand to be sent back where we came from. That's the right of any foreigner in America. He can't refuse. We explain the risks his government runs: loss of good will, irreparable damage to future contacts between the two times, his government standing convicted of a breach of good faith, that sort of thing. In these things, it's just a matter of finding the right words and making them good and strong."

Mrs. Brucks nodded agreement. "I believe. You can do it, Mr. Mead."

The stout man seemed to deflate. "*I?*"

"Of course," Mary Ann Carthington said enthusiastically. "You're the only one who can do it, Mr. Mead. You're the only one who can put things so—so *right.* Just like you said, it has to be said good and strong. That's the way *you* can say it."

"I'd, well—I'd rather not. I don't think I'm the best one for the job. Mr. Storku and I don't get along too well. Somebody else, I think, one of you, would be—"

Dave Pollock laughed. "Now, don't be modest, Ollie. You get along with Storku as well as any of us. You're elected. Besides, isn't this public-relations work? You're a big man in public relations."

Mr. Mead tried to pour all the hatred in the universe at him in one long look. Then he shot his cuffs and straightened his shoulders. "Very well. If none of you feel up to the job, I'll take it on myself. Be back soon."

"Jumper, Ollie?" Pollock asked as he was leaving the room. "Why not take the jumper? It's faster."

"No, thank you," Mr. Mead said curtly. "I'll walk. I need the exercise."

He hurried through the corridor and toward the staircase. Though he went down them at a springy, executive trot, the stairs seemed to feel he wasn't going fast enough. An escalator motion began, growing more and more rapid, until he stumbled and almost fell.

"Stop, dammit!" he yelled. "I can do this myself!"

The stairs stopped flowing downward immediately. He wiped his face with a large white handkerchief and started down again. After a few moments, the stairs turned into an escalator once more.

Again and again, he had to order them to stop; again and again, they obeyed him, and then sneakily tried to help him along. He was reminded of a large, affectionate St. Bernard he had once had who persisted in bringing dead sparrows and field mice into the house as gifts from an overflowing heart. When the grisly objects were thrown out, the dog would bring them back in five minutes and lay them on the rug with a gesture that said: "No, I really want you to have it. Don't worry about the expense and hard work involved. Look on it as a slight expression of my esteem and gratitude. Take it, go on, take it and be happy."

He gave up forbidding the stairs to move finally, and when he reached ground level, he was moving so fast that he shot out of the empty lobby of the building and onto the sidewalk at a tremendous speed. He might have broken a leg or dislocated his back.

Fortunately, the sidewalk began moving under him. As he tottered from right to left, the sidewalk did so too, gently but expertly keeping him balanced. He finally got his footing and took a couple of deep breaths.

Under him, the sidewalk trembled slightly, waiting for him to choose a direction so that it could help.

Mr. Mead looked around desperately. There was no one in sight along the broad avenue in either direction.

"What a world!" he moaned. "What a loony-bin of a world! You'd think there'd be a cop—somebody!"

Suddenly there was somebody. There was the *pop-pop* of a jumper mechanism in operation slightly overhead and a man appeared some twelve feet in the air. Behind him, there was an orange hedge-like affair, covered with eyes.

A portion of the sidewalk shot up into a mound right under the two creatures. It lowered them gently to surface level.

"Listen!" Mr. Mead yelled. "Am I glad I ran into you! I'm trying to get to the State Department and I'm having trouble. I'd appreciate a little help."

"Sorry," the other man said. "Klap-Lillth and I will have to be back on Ganymede in a half-hour. We're late for an appointment as is. Why don't you call a government machine?"

"Who is he?" the orange hedge inquired as they began to move swiftly to the entrance of a building, the sidewalk under them flowing like a happy river. "He doesn't *narga* to me like one of you."

"Time traveler," his companion explained. "From the past. One of the exchange tourists who came in two weeks ago."

"Aha!" said the hedge. "From the *past*. No wonder I couldn't *narga* him. It's just as well. You know, on Ganymede we don't believe in time travel. It's against our religion."

The Earthman chuckled and dug the hedge in the twigs. "You and your religion! You're as much an atheist as I am, Klap-Lillth. When was the last time you attended a *shkoot-seem* ceremony?"

"Not since the last syzygy of Jupiter and the Sun," the hedge admitted. "But that's not the point. I'm still in good standing. What all you humans fail to understand about the Ganymedan religion..."

His voice trailed off as they disappeared inside the building. Mead almost spat after them. Then he recollected himself. They didn't have much time to fool around—and, besides, he was in a strange world with customs insanely different from his own. Who knew what the penalties were for spitting?

"Government machine," he said resignedly to the empty air. "I want a government machine."

He felt a little foolish, but that was what they had been told to do in any emergency. And, sure enough, a gleaming affair of wires and coils and multicolored plates appeared from nothingness beside him.

"Yes?" a toneless voice inquired. "Service needed?"

"I'm on my way to see Mr. Storku at your Department of State," Mr. Mead explained, staring suspiciously at the largest coil nearest him. "And I'm having trouble walking on the sidewalk. I'm liable to fall and kill myself if it doesn't stop moving under me."

"Sorry, sir, but no one has fallen on a sidewalk for at least two hundred years, and that was a highly neurotic sidewalk whose difficulties had unfortunately escaped our attention in the weekly psychological checkup. May I suggest you take a jumper? I'll call one for you."

"I don't *want* to take a jumper. I want to walk. All you have to do is tell this damn sidewalk to relax and be quiet."

"Sorry, sir," the machine replied, "but the sidewalk has its job to do. Besides, Mr. Storku is not at his office. He is taking some spiritual exercise at either Shriek Field or Panic Stadium."

"Oh, no," Mr. Mead moaned. His worst fears had been realized. He didn't want to go to those places again.

"Sorry, sir, but he is. Just a moment, while I check." There were bright blue flashes amongst the coils. "Mr. Storku is doing a shriek today. He feels he has been over-aggressive recently. He invites you to join him."

Mr. Mead considered. He was not the slightest bit interested in going to one of those places where sane people became madmen for a couple of hours; on the other hand, time *was* short, Winthrop *was* still stubborn.

"All right," he said unhappily. "I'll join him."

"Shall I call a jumper, sir?"

The portly man stepped back. "No! I'll—I'll walk."

"Sorry, sir, but you would never get there before the shriek has begun."

Sweetbottom's vice-president in charge of public relations put the moist palms of his hands against his face and gently massaged it, to calm himself. He must remember that this was no bellhop you could complain to the management about, no stupid policeman you could write to the newspapers about, no bungling secretary you could fire or nervous wife you could tell off—this was just a machine into whose circuits a given set of vocal reactions had been built. If he had an apoplectic fit in front of it, it would not be the slightest bit concerned: it would merely summon another machine, a medical one. All you could do was give it information or receive information from it.

"I-don't-like-jumpers," he said between his teeth.

"Sorry, sir, but you expressed a desire to see Mr. Storku. If you are willing to wait until the shriek is over, there is no problem, except that you would be well advised to start for the Odor Festival on Venus where he is going next. If you wish to see him immediately, however, you must take a jumper. There are no other possibilities, sir, unless you feel that my memory circuits are inadequate or you'd like to add a new factor to the discussion."

"I'd like to add a— Oh, I give up." Mr. Mead sagged where he stood. "Call a jumper, call a jumper."

"Yes, sir. Here you are, sir." The empty cylinder that suddenly materialized immediately over Mr. Mead's head caused him to start, but while he was opening his mouth to say, "Hey! I changed—" it slid down over him.

There was darkness. He felt as if his stomach were being gently but insistently pulled out through his mouth. His liver, spleen and lungs seemed to follow suit. Then the bones of his body all fell inward to the center of his now-empty abdomen and dwindled in size until they disappeared. He collapsed upon himself.

Suddenly he was whole and solid again, and standing in a large green meadow, with dozens of people around him. His stomach returned to its proper place and squirmed back into position.

"—changed my mind. I'll walk after all," he said, and threw up.

Mr. Storku, a tall, genial, yellow-haired young man, was standing in front of him when the spasms had subsided and the tears ceased to leak from his eyes. "It's such a simple thing, really, Mr. Mead. Just a matter of being intently placid during the jump."

"Easy—easy to say," Mr. Mead gasped, wiping his mouth with his handkerchief. What was the reason Storku always exuded such patronizing contempt toward him? "Why don't you people—why don't you people find another way to travel? In my time, comfort in transportation is the keystone, the very *keystone* of the industry. Any busline, any airline, which doesn't see to it that their passengers enjoy the maximum comfort en route to their destination is out of business before you can bat an eye. Either that, or they have a new board of directors."

"Isn't he *intriguing?*" a girl near him commented to her escort. "He talks just like one of those historical romances."

Mr. Mead glanced at her sourly. He gulped. She was nude. For that matter, so was everyone else around him, including Mr. Storku. Who knew what went on at these Shriek Field affairs, he wondered nervously? After all, he had only seen them before from a distance in the grandstand. And now he was right in the middle of these deliberate lunatics.

"Surely you're being a bit unjust," Mr. Storku suggested. "After all, if an Elizabethan or a man from the Classic Greek period were to go for a ride in one of your horseless carriages or iron horses—to use your vernacular—he would be extremely uncomfortable and exhibit much more physical strain than you have. It's purely a matter of adjustment to the unfamiliar. Some adjust, like your contemporary, Winthrop; some don't, like yourself."

"Speaking of Winthrop—" Mr. Mead began hurriedly, glad both of the opening and the chance to change the subject.

"Everybody here?" an athletic young man inquired as he bounded up. "I'm your leader for this Shriek. On your feet, everybody, come on, let's get those kinks out of our muscles. We're going to have a real fine shriek."

"Take your clothes off," the government man told Mr. Mead. "You can't run a shriek dressed. Especially dressed like that."

Mr. Mead shrank back. "I'm not going to— I just came here to talk to you. I'll watch."

A rich, roaring laugh. "You can't watch from the middle of Shriek Field! And besides, the moment you joined us, you were automatically registered for the shriek. If you withdraw now, you'll throw everything off."

"I will?"

Storku nodded. "Of course. A different quantity of stimuli has to be applied to any different quantity of people, if you want to develop the desired shriek-intensity in each one of them. Take your clothes off, man, and get into the thing. A little exercise of this sort will tone up your psyche magnificently."

Mr. Mead thought it over, then began to undress. He was embarrassed, miserable and more than a little frightened at the prospect, but he had an urgent job of public relations to do on the yellow-haired young man.

In his time, he had gurgled pleasurably over rope-like cigars given him by politicians, gotten drunk in incredible little stinking bars with important newspapermen and suffered the slings and the arrows of outrageous television quiz shows—all in the interests of Sweetbottom Septic Tanks, Inc. The motto of the Public Relations Man was strictly *When in Rome...*

And obviously the crowd he had made this trip with from 1958 was composed of barely-employables and bunglers. They'd never get themselves and him back to their own time, back to a world where there was a supply-and-demand distributive system that made sense instead of something that seemed absolutely unholy in the few areas where it was visible and understandable. A world where an important business executive was treated like *somebody* instead of like a willful two-year-old. A world where inanimate objects stayed inanimate, where the walls didn't ripple around you, the furniture didn't adjust constantly under you, where the very clothes on a person's back didn't change from moment to moment as if it were being revolved in a kaleidoscope.

No, it was up to him to get everybody back to that world, and his only channel of effective operation lay through Storku. Therefore, Storku had to be placated and made to feel that Oliver T. Mead was one of the boys.

Besides, it occurred to him as he began slipping out of his clothes, some of these girls looked real cute. They reminded him of the Septic Tank Convention at Des Moines back in July. If only they didn't shave their heads!

"All together, now," the shriek leader sang out. "Let's bunch up. All together in a tight little group, all bunched up and milling around."

Mr. Mead was pushed and jostled into the crowd. It surged forward, back, right, left, being maneuvered into a smaller and smaller group under the instructions and shoving of the shriek leader. Music sprang up around them, more noise than music, actually, since it had no discernible harmonic relationships, and grew louder and louder until it was almost deafening.

Someone striving for balance in the mass of naked bodies hit Mr. Mead in the stomach with an outflung arm. He said "Oof!" and then "Oof!" again as someone behind him tripped and piled into his back. "Watch *out!*" a girl near him moaned as he trod on her foot. "Sorry," he told her, "I just couldn't—" and then an elbow hit him in the eye and he went tottering away a few steps, until, the group changing its direction again, he was pushed forward.

Round and round he went on the grass, being pushed and pushing, the horrible noise almost tearing his ear-drums apart. From what seemed a greater and greater distance he could hear the shriek leader chanting: "Come on, this way, hurry up! No, that way, around that tree. Back into the bunch, you: everybody together. Stay *together*. Now, backwards, that's right, *backwards. Faster, faster.*"

They went backwards, a great mass of people pushing on Mead, jamming him into the great mass of people immediately behind him. Then, abruptly, they went forwards again, a dozen little cross-currents of humanity at work against each other in the crowd, so that as well as moving forward, he was also being hurled a few feet to the right and then turned around and being sucked back diagonally to his left. Once or twice, he was shot to the outskirts of the group, but, much to his surprise when he considered it later, all he did was claw his way back into the jam-packed surging middle.

It was as if he belonged nowhere else by this time, but in this mob of hurrying madmen. A shaved female head crashing into his chest as the only hint that the group had changed its direction was what he had come to expect. He threw himself backwards and disregarded the grunts and yelps he helped create. He was part of this—

this—whatever it was. He was hysterical, bruised and slippery with sweat, but he no longer thought about anything but staying on his feet in the mob.

He was part of it, and that was all he knew.

Suddenly, somewhere outside the maelstrom of running, jostling naked bodies, there was a yell. It was a long yell, in a powerful male voice, and it went on and on, almost drowning out the noise-music. A woman in front of Mr. Mead picked it up in a head-rattling scream. The man who had been yelling stopped, and, after a while, so did the woman.

Then Mr. Mead heard the yell again, heard the woman join in, and was not even remotely surprised to hear his own voice add to the din. He threw all the frustration of the past two weeks into that yell, all the pounding, shoving and bruises of the past few minutes, all the frustrations and hatreds of his lifetime. Again and again the yell started up, and each time Mr. Mead joined it. All around him others were joining it, too, until at last there was a steady, unanimous shriek from the tight mob that slipped and fell and chased itself all over the enormous meadow. Mr. Mead, in the back of his mind, experienced a child-like satisfaction in getting on to the rhythm they were working out—and in being part of working it out.

It went pulse-beat, pulse-beat, *shriek-k-k-k,* pulse-beat, pulse-beat, *shriek-k-k-k,* pulse-beat, pulse-beat, *shriek-k-k-k.*

All together. All around him, all together. It was good!

He was never able to figure out later how long they had been running and yelling, when he noticed that he was no longer in the middle of a tight group. They had thinned out somehow and were spread out over the meadow in a long, wavering, yelling line.

He felt a little confused. Without losing a beat in the shriek-rhythm, he made an effort to get closer to a man and woman on his right.

The yells stopped abruptly. The noise-music stopped abruptly. He stared straight ahead where everybody else was staring. He saw it.

A brown, furry animal about the size of a sheep. It had turned its head and thrown one obviously startled, obviously frightened look at them, then it had bent its legs and begun running madly away across the meadow.

"Let's get it!" the shriek leader's voice sounded from what seemed all about them. "Let's get it! All of us, together! Let's get it!"

Somebody moved forward, and Mr. Mead followed. The shriek started again, a continuous, unceasing shriek, and he joined in. Then he was running across the meadow after the furry brown animal, screaming his head off, dimly and proudly conscious of fellow human beings doing the same on both sides of him.

Let's get it! his mind howled. *Let's get it, let's get it!*

Almost caught up with, the animal doubled on its tracks abruptly, and dodged back through the line of people. Mr. Mead flung himself at it and made a grab. He got a handful of fur and fell painfully to his knees as the animal galloped away.

He was on his feet without abating a single note of the shriek, and after it in a moment. Everyone else had turned around and was running with him.

Let's get it! Let's get it! Let's get it!

Back and forth across the meadow, the animal ran and they pursued. It dodged and twisted and jerked itself free from converging groups.

Mr. Mead ran with them, ran in the very forefront. Shrieking.

No matter how the furry brown animal turned, they turned too. They kept getting closer and closer to it.

Finally, they caught it.

The entire mob trapped it in a great, uneven circle and closed in. Mr. Mead was the first one to reach it. He smashed his fist into it and knocked it down with a single blow. A girl leaped onto the prostrate figure, her face contorted, and began tearing at it with her fingernails. Just before everyone piled on, Mr. Mead managed to close his hand on a furry brown leg. He gave the leg a tremendous yank and it came off in his hand. He was remotely astonished at the loose wires and gear mechanisms that trailed out of the torn-off leg.

"We got it!" he mumbled, staring at the leg. *We got it,* his mind danced madly. *We got it, we got it!*

He was suddenly very tired, almost faint. He dragged himself away from the crowd and sat down heavily on the grass. He continued to stare at the loose wires that came out of the leg.

Mr. Storku came up to him, breathing hard. "Well," said Mr. Storku. "Did you have a nice shriek?"

Mr. Mead held up the furry brown leg. "We got it," he said bewilderedly.

The yellow-haired young man laughed. "You need a good shower and a good sedative. Come on." He helped Mr. Mead to his feet and, holding on to his arm, crossed the meadow to a dilated yellow square under the grandstand. All around them the other participants in the shriek chattered gaily to each other as they cleansed themselves and readjusted their metabolism.

After his turn inside one of the many booths which filled the interior of the grandstand, Mr. Mead felt more like himself. Which was not to say he felt better.

Something had come out of him in those last few moments as he tore at the mechanical quarry, something he wished infinitely had stayed at the dank bottom of his soul. He'd rather never have known it existed.

He felt vaguely, dismally, like a man who, flipping the pages of a textbook of sexual aberrations, comes upon a particularly ugly case history which parallels his life history in every respect, and understands—in a single, horrified flash—exactly what all those seemingly innocent quirks and nuances of his personality mean.

He tried to remind himself that he was still Oliver T. Mead, a good husband and father, a respected business executive, a substantial pillar of the community and the local church—but it was no good. Now, and for the rest of his life, he was also…this other thing.

He had to get into some clothes. Fast.

Mr. Storku nodded when the driving need was explained. "You probably had a lot saved up. About time you began discharging it. I wouldn't worry: you're as sane as anyone in your period. But your clothes have been cleaned off the field along with all the rubbish of our shriek; the officials are already preparing for the next one."

"What do I do?" Mr. Mead wailed. "I can't go home like this."

"No?" the government man inquired with a good deal of curiosity. "You really can't? Hm, fascinating! Well, just step under that outfitter there. I suppose you'd like twentieth-century costume?"

Mr. Mead nodded and placed himself doubtfully under the indicated mechanism as a newly-clad citizen of the twenty-fifth century America walked away from it briskly. "Ye-es. Please make it something sane, something I can wear."

He watched as his host adjusted some dials rapidly. There was a slight hum from the machine overhead: a complete set of formal, black-and-white evening wear sprang into being on the stout man's body. In a moment, it had changed into another outfit: the shoes grew upwards and became hip-length rubber boots, the dinner jacket lengthened itself into a sou'wester. Mr. Mead was perfectly dressed for the bridge of any whaling ship.

"Stop it!" he begged distractedly as the raincoat began showing distinctive sports shirt symptoms. "Keep it down to one thing."

"You could do it yourself," Mr. Storku pointed out, "if your subconscious didn't heave about so much." Nonetheless, he good-naturedly poked at the machine again, and Mr. Mead's clothes subsided into the tweed jacket and golf knickers that had been so popular in the 1920s. They held fast at that.

"Better?"

"I—I guess so." Mr. Mead frowned as he looked down at himself. It certainly was a queer outfit for the vice-president of Sweetbottom Septic Tanks, Inc., to return to his own time in, but at least it was *one* outfit. And as soon as he got home —

"Now, look here, Storku," he said, rubbing his hands together briskly and putting aside the recent obscene memories of himself with as much determination as he could call up. "We're having trouble with this Winthrop fella. He won't go back with us."

They walked outside and paused on the edge of the meadow. In the distance, a new shriek was being organized.

"That so?" Mr. Storku asked with no very great interest. He pointed at the ragged mob of nude figures just beginning to jostle each other into a tight bunch. "You know, two or three more sessions out there and your psyche would be in fine shape. Although, from the looks of you. I'd say Panic Stadium would be even better. Why don't you do that? Why don't you go right over to Panic Stadium? One first-rate, screaming, headlong panic and you'd be absolutely—"

"Thank you, but no! I've had enough of this, quite enough, already. My psyche is my own affair."

The yellow-haired young man nodded seriously. "Of course. *The adult individual's psyche is under no other jurisdiction than that of the adult individual concerned.*—The Covenant of 2314, adopted by unanimous consent of the entire population of the United States of America. Later, of course, broadened by the international plebiscite of 2337 to include the entire world. But I was just making a personal, friendly suggestion."

Mr. Mead forced himself to smile. He was distressed to find that when he smiled, the lapels of his jacket stood up and caressed the sides of his chin affectionately. "No offense, no offense. As I've said, it's just that I've had all I want of this nonsense. But what are you going to do about Winthrop?"

"Do? Why nothing, of course. What can we do?"

"You can force him to go back! You represent the government, don't you? The government invited us here, the government is responsible for our safety."

Mr. Storku looked puzzled. "Aren't you safe?"

"You know what I mean, Storku. Our safe return. The government is responsible for it."

"Not if that responsibility is extended to interference with the desires and activities of an adult individual. I just quoted the Covenant of 2314 to you, my friend. The whole philosophy of government derived from that covenant is based on the creation and maintenance of the individual's perfect sovereignty over himself. Force may never be applied to a mature citizen and even official persuasion may be resorted to only in certain rare and carefully specified instances. This is certainly not one of them. By the time a child has gone through our educational system, he or she is a well-balanced member of society who can be trusted to do whatever is socially necessary. From that point on, government ceases to take an active role in the individual's life."

"Yeah, a real neon-lit Utopia," Mr. Mead sneered. "No cops to safeguard life and property, to ask direction of even— Oh, well, it's your world and you're welcome to it. But that's not the point. Don't you see—I'm certain you can see, if you just put your mind to it—that Winthrop isn't a citizen of your world, Storku? He didn't go through your educational system, he didn't have these psychological things, these readjustment courses, every couple of years, he didn't—"

"But he came here as our invited guest," Mr. Storku pointed out. "And, as such, he's entitled to the full protection of our laws."

"And we aren't, I suppose," Mr. Mead shouted. "He can do whatever he wants to us and get away with it. Do you call that law? Do you call that justice? I don't. I call it bureaucracy, that's what I call it. Red-tape and bureaucracy, that's all it is!"

The yellow-haired young man put his hand on Mr. Mead's shoulder. "Listen, my friend," he said gently, "and try to understand. If Winthrop tried to *do* anything to you, it would be stopped. Not by interfering with Winthrop directly, but by removing you from his neighborhood. In order for us to take even such limited action, he'd have to *do*. That would be commission of an act interfering with your rights as an individual: what Winthrop is accused of, however, is *omission* of an act. He refuses to go back with you. Well, now. He has a right to refuse to do anything with his own body and mind. The Covenant of 2314 covers that area in so many words. Would you like me to quote the relevant passage to you?"

"No, I would not like you to quote the relevant passage to me. So you're trying to say that nobody can do anything, is that it? Winthrop can keep all of us from getting back to our own time, but you can't do anything about it and we can't do anything about it. One hell of a note."

"An interesting phrase, that," Mr. Storku commented. "If there had only been an etymologist or linguist in your group, I would be interested in discussing it with him. However, your conclusion, at least in regard to this particular situation, is substantially correct. There is only one thing you can do: you can try to *persuade* Winthrop. Up to the last moment of the scheduled transfer, that, of course, always exists as a possible solution."

Mr. Mead brushed down his overly emotional jacket lapels. "And if we don't, we're out of luck? We can't take him by the scruff of the neck and—and—"

"I'm afraid you can't. A government machine or manufactured government official would appear on the scene and liberate him. Without any damage to your persons, you understand."

"Sure. No damage," Mr. Mead brooded. "Just leaving us stuck in this asylum for the rest of our lives, no ifs, no ands, no buts."

Mr. Storku looked hurt. "Oh, come now, my friend: I'm certain it's not that bad! It may be very different from your own culture in many ways, it may be uncomfortably alien in its artifacts and underlying philosophy, but surely, surely, there are compensations. For the loss of the old in terms of family, associates and experiences, there must be a gain in the new and exciting. Your Winthrop has found it so—he's at Panic Stadium or Shriek Field almost every day, I've run into him at seminars and salons at least three times in the past ten days, and I hear from the Bureau of Home Appliances of the Department of Internal Economics that he's a steady, enthusiastic, and thoroughly dedicated consumer. What he can bring himself to do—"

"Sure he gets all those gadgets," Mr. Mead sneered. "He doesn't have to pay for them. A lazy relief jack like him couldn't ask for anything better. What a world—*gahhh!*"

"My only point," Mr. Storku continued equably, "is that being, well, 'stuck in this asylum,' as you rather vividly picture it, has its positive aspects. And since there seems to be a distinct possibility of this, it would seem logical for you people to begin investigating these positive aspects somewhat more wholeheartedly than you have instead of retreating to the security of each other's company and such twentieth-century anachronisms as you are able to recreate."

"We have—all we want to. What we want now, all of us, is to go home and to keep on living the lives we were born into. So what it comes down to is that nobody and nothing can help us with Winthrop, eh?"

Mr. Storku called for a jumper and held up a hand to arrest the huge cylinder in the air as soon as it appeared. "Well, now. That's rather a broad statement. I wouldn't quite want to go as far as that without conducting a thorough personal investigation of the matter. It's entirely possible that someone, something, in the universe could help you if the problem were brought to its attention and if it were sufficiently interested. It's rather a large, well-populated universe, you know. All I can say definitely is that the Department of State can't help you."

Mr. Mead pushed his fingernails deep into his palms and ground his teeth together until he felt the top enamel coming off in flakes and grit. "You couldn't possibly," he asked at last, very, very slowly, "be just a little more specific in telling us where to go for help next? We have less than two hours left—and we won't be able to cover very much of the galaxy in that time."

"A good point," Mr. Storku said approvingly. "A very well-taken point. I'm glad to see that you have calmed down and are at last thinking clearly and resourcefully. Now, who—in this immediate neighborhood—might be able to work out the solution of an insoluble problem? Well, first there's the Temporal Embassy, which handled the exchange and brought you people here in the first place. They have all kinds of connections, the Temporal Embassy people do; they can, if they feel like it, tap the total ingenuity of the human race for the next five thousand years. The trouble is, they take too much of the long view for my taste. Then there are the Oracle Machines, which will give you the answer to any question that *can* be answered. The problem there, of course, is interpreting the answer correctly. Then, on Pluto, there's a convention this week of vector psychologists. If anyone could figure out a way of persuading Winthrop to change his mind, *they* can. Unfortunately, the dominant field of interest in vector psychology at the moment is fetal education: I'm afraid they'd find your Winthrop far too mature a specimen. Then, out around Rigel, there's a race of remarkably prescient fungi whom I can recommend out of my own personal experience. They have a most unbelievable talent for—"

The portly man waggled a frantic hand at him. "That's enough! That's enough to go on for a while! We only have two hours—remember?"

"I certainly do. And since it's very unlikely that you can do anything about it in so short a time, may I suggest that you drop the whole matter and take this jumper with me to Venus? There won't be another Odor Festival there for sixty-six years: it's an experience, my friend, that should just not be missed. Venus always does these things right: the greatest odor-emitters in the universe will be there. And I'll be very happy to explain all the fine points to you. Coming?"

Mr. Mead dodged out of the way of the jumper which Mr. Storku was gesturing down invitingly. "No, *thank* you! Why is it," he complained when he had retreated to a safe distance, "that you people are always taking vacations, you're always going off somewhere to relax and enjoy yourselves? How the hell does any work ever get done in this world?"

"Oh, it gets done," the yellow-haired young man laughed as the cylinder began to slide down over him. "Whenever there's a piece of work that only a human being can do, one of us—the nearest responsible individual with the applicable training—takes care of it. But our personality goals are different from yours. In the words of the proverb: All play and no work makes Jack a dull boy."

And he was gone.

So Mr. Mead went back to Mrs. Brucks's room and told the others that the Department of State, as personified by Mr. Storku, couldn't help them with Winthrop's stubbornness.

Mary Ann Carthington tightened the curl of her blonde hair with a business-like forefinger while she considered the matter. "You told him all that you told us, and he still wouldn't do anything, Mr. Mead? Are you sure he knows who you are?"

Mr. Mead didn't bother to answer her. He had other things on his mind. Not only was his spirit badly bruised and scratched by his recent experiences, but his golf knickers had just woken into sentiency. And whereas the jacket merely had attempted to express its great affection for his person by trying to cuddle under his chin, the knickers went in more for a kind of patrolling action. Up and down on his thighs they rippled; back and forth across his buttocks they marched. Only by concentrating hard and pressing them tight against his body with his hands was he able to keep away the feeling of having been swallowed by an anaconda.

"Sure he knows who he is," Dave Pollock told her. "Ollie waved his vice-presidency in his face, but Storku heard that Sweetbottom Septic Tanks Preferred fell to the bottom of the stock market just four hundred years ago today, so he wasn't having any. Hey, Ollie?"

"I don't think that's funny, Dave Pollock," Mary Ann Carthington said and shook her head at him once in a "so, there!" manner. She knew that old beanpole of a schoolteacher was just jealous of Mr. Mead, but she wasn't sure whether it was because he didn't make as much money or because he wasn't nearly as distinguished looking. The only thing, if a big executive like Mr. Mead couldn't get them out of this jam, then nobody could. And that would be awful, positively and absolutely awful.

She would never get back to Edgar Rapp. And while Edgar might not be everything a girl like Mary Ann wanted, she was quite willing to settle for him at this point. He worked hard and made a good living. His compliments were pale, pedestrian things, true, but at least he could be counted on not to say anything that tore a person into little, worthless bits right before their very eyes. Not like somebody she knew. And the sooner she could leave the twenty-fifth century and be forever away from that somebody, the better.

"Now, Mr. Mead," she cooed insistently. "I'm sure he told you *something* we could do. He didn't just tell you to give up hope completely and absolutely, did he?"

The executive caught the strap end of his knickers as it came unbuckled and started rolling exultantly up his leg. He glared at her out of eyes that had seen just too damn much, that felt things had gone just too damn far.

"He told me something we could do," he said with careful viciousness. "He said the Temporal Embassy could help us, if we only had the right kind of pull there. All we need is somebody with pull in the Temporal Embassy."

Mary Ann Carthington almost bit the end off the lipstick she was applying at that moment. Without looking up, she knew that Mrs. Brucks and Dave Pollock had both turned to stare at her. And she knew, deep down to the bottom of her dismayed intestines, just exactly what they were thinking.

"Well, I certainly don't—"

"Now, don't be modest, Mary Ann," Dave Pollock interrupted. "This is your big chance—and right now it looks like our only chance. We've got about an hour and a half left. Get yourself into a jumper, skedaddle out there, and girlie, turn on the charm!"

Mrs. Brucks sat down beside her and gave her shoulders the benefit of a heavy maternal arm. "Listen, Miss Carthington, sometimes we have to do things, is not so easy. But what else? Stuck here is better? *That* you like? So—" she spread her hands "— a touch here with the powder puff, a touch there with the lipstick, a this, a that, and, believe me, he won't know what to do first for you. Crazy about you he is already—you mean to say a little favor he wouldn't do, if you asked him?" She shrugged her massive contempt for such a sleeveless thought.

"You really think so? Well—maybe—" The girl began a preen that started at her delicately firm bottom and ended in a couple of self-satisfied wriggles somewhere around her chest.

"No maybes," Mrs. Brucks informed her after considering the matter with great care. "A sure, yes. A certainly, yes. But maybes, no. A pretty girl like you, a man like him, nothing to maybe about. It's the way, let me tell you. Miss Carthington, it's always the way. What a man like Mr. Mead can't accomplish, a woman has to do all the time. And a pretty girl like you can do it without lifting her little finger."

Mary Ann Carthington gave a nod of agreement to this rather female view of history and stood up with determination. Dave Pollock immediately called for a jumper. She stepped back as the great cylinder materialized in the room.

"Do I *have* to?" she asked, biting her lip. "Those awful things, they're so *upsetting*."

He took her arm and began working her under the jumper with a series of gentle, urging tugs. "You can't walk: we don't have the time anymore. Believe me, Mary Ann, this is *D*-day and *H*-hour. So be a good girl and get under there and— Hey, listen. A good angle with the temporal supervisor might be about how his people will be stuck in our period if Winthrop goes on being stubborn. If anyone around here is responsible for them, he is. So, as soon as you get there—"

"I don't need you to tell me how to handle the temporal supervisor, Dave Pollock!" she said haughtily, flouncing under the jumper. "After all, he happens to be a friend of mine, not of yours—a very *good* friend of mine!"

"Sure," Pollock groaned, "but you still have to convince the man. And all I'm suggesting—" He broke off as the cylinder slid the final distance down to the floor and disappeared with the girl inside.

He turned back to the others who had been watching anxiously. "Well, that's it," he announced, flapping his arms with a broad, hopeless gesture. "That's our very last hope. A Mary Ann Carthington!"

Mary Ann Carthington felt exactly like a Last Hope as she materialized in the Temporal Embassy.

She fought down the swimming nausea which always seemed to accompany jumper transportation and, shaking her head rapidly, managed to draw a deep breath.

As a means of getting places, the jumper certainly beat Edgar Rapp's gurgling old Buick—if only it didn't make you feel like a chocolate malted. That was the trouble with this time: every halfway nice thing in it had such unpleasant after-effects!

The ceiling undulated over her head in the great rotunda where she was now standing and bulged a huge purplish lump down at her. It still looked, she decided nervously, like a movie house chandelier about to fall.

"Yes?" inquired the purplish lump politely. "Whom did you wish to see?"

She licked at her lipstick, then squared her shoulders. She'd been through all this before. You had to carry these things off with a certain amount of poise: it just did not do to show nervousness before a ceiling.

"I came to see Gygyo—I mean, is Mr. Gygyo Rablin in?"

"Mr. Rablin is not at size at the moment. He will return in fifteen minutes. Would you like to wait in his office? He has another visitor there."

Mary Ann Carthington thought swiftly. She didn't entirely like the idea of another visitor, but maybe it would be for the best. The presence of a third party would be a restraining influence for both of them and would take a little of the inevitable edge off her coming back to Gygyo as a suppliant after what had happened between them.

But what was this about his not being "at size"? These twenty-fifth-century people did so many positively weird things with themselves....

"Yes, I'll wait in his office," she told the ceiling. "Oh, you needn't bother," she said to the floor as it began to ripple under her feet. "I know the way."

"No bother at all, Miss," the floor replied cheerfully and continued to carry her across the rotunda to Rablin's private office. "It's a pleasure."

Mary Ann sighed and shook her head. Some of these houses were so opinionated! She relaxed and let herself be carried along, taking out her compact on the way for a last quick check of her hair and face.

But the glance at herself in the mirror evoked the memory again. She flushed and almost called for a jumper to take her back to Mrs. Brucks's room. No, she couldn't—this was their last chance to get out of this world and back to their own. But damn Gygyo Rablin, anyway—damn and damn him!

A yellow square in the wall having dilated sufficiently, the floor carried her into Rablin's private office and subsided to flatness again. She looked around, nodding slightly at the familiar surroundings.

There was Gygyo's desk, if you could call that odd, purring thing a desk. There was that peculiar squirmy couch that—

She caught her breath. A young woman was lying on the couch, one of those horrible bald-headed women that they had here.

"Excuse me," Mary Ann said in one fast breath. "I had no idea— I didn't mean to—"

"That's perfectly all right," the young woman said, still staring up at the ceiling. "You're not intruding. I just dropped in on Gygyo myself. Have a seat."

As if taking a pointed hint, the floor shot up a section of itself under Mary Ann's bottom and, when she was securely cradled in it, lowered itself slowly to sitting height.

"You must be that twentieth-century—" the young woman paused, then amended rapidly: "the *visitor* whom Gygyo has been seeing lately. My name's Flureet. I'm just an old childhood friend—way back from Responsibility Group Three."

Mary Ann nodded primly. "How nice, I'm sure. My name is Mary Ann Carthington. And really, if in any way I'm— I mean I just dropped in to—"

"I told you it's all right. Gygyo and I don't mean a thing to each other. This Temporal Embassy work has kind of dulled his taste for the everyday female: they've either got to be atavisms or precursors. Some kind of anachronism, anyway. And I'm awaiting transformation—*major* transformation—so you couldn't expect very strong feelings from my side right now. Satisfied? I hope so. Hello to you, Mary Ann."

Flureet flexed her arm at the elbow several times in what Mary Ann recognized disdainfully as the standard greeting gesture. Such women! It made them look like a man showing off his muscle. And not so much as a polite glance in the direction of a guest!

"The ceiling said," she began uncertainly, "that Gyg—Mr. Rablin isn't at size at the moment. Is that like what we call not being at home?"

The bald girl nodded. "In a sense. He's in this room, but he's hardly large enough to talk to. Gygy's size right now is—let me think, what did he say he was setting it for?—Oh, yes, thirty-five microns. He's inside a drop of water in the field of that microscope to your left."

Mary Ann swung around and considered the spherical black object resting on a table against the wall. Outside of the two eyepieces set flush with the surface, it had little in common with pictures of microscopes she had seen in magazines.

"In—in there? What's he doing in there?"

"He's on a micro-hunt. You should know your Gygyo by now. An absolutely incurable romantic. Who goes on micro-hunts anymore? And in a culture of intestinal amebae, of all things. Killing the beasties by hand instead of by routine psycho- or even chemotherapy appeals to his dashing soul. Grow up, Gygyo, I said to him: these games are for children and for Responsibility Group Four children at that. Well, that hurt his pride and he said he was going in with a fifteen-minute lock. A fifteen-minute *lock!* When I heard that, I decided to come here and watch the battle, just in case."

"Why—is a fifteen-minute lock dangerous?" Mary Ann asked. Her face was tightly set however; she was still thinking of that 'you should know your Gygyo' remark. That was another thing about this world she didn't like: with all their talk of privacy and the sacred rights of the individual, men like Gygyo didn't think twice of telling the most intimate matters about people to—to other people.

"Figure it out for yourself. Gygyo's set himself for thirty-five microns. Thirty-five microns is about twice the size of most of the intestinal parasites he'll have to fight— amebae like *Endolimax nana, Iodamoeba butschlii* and *Dientamoeba fragilis.* But suppose he runs into a crowd of *Endamoeba coli,* to say nothing of our tropical dysentery friend, *Endamoeba hystolytica?* What then?"

"What then?" the blonde girl echoed. She had not the slightest idea. One did not face problems like this in San Francisco.

"Trouble, that's what. Serious trouble. The *coli* might be as large as he is, and *hystolyticae* run even bigger. Thirty-six, thirty-seven microns, sometimes more. Now, the most important factor on a micro-hunt, as you know, is size. Especially if you're fool enough to limit your arsenal to a sword and won't be seen carrying an automatic weapon even as insurance. Well, under those circumstances, you lock yourself down to smallness, so that you can't get out and nobody can take you out for a full fifteen minutes, and you're just asking for trouble. And trouble is just what our boy is having!"

"He is? I mean, is it bad?"

Flureet gestured at the microscope. "Have a look. I've adjusted my retinas to the magnification, but you people aren't up to that yet, I believe. You need mechanical devices for everything. Go ahead, have a look. That's *Dietamoeba fragilis* he's fighting now. Small, but fast. And very, very vicious."

Mary Ann hurried to the spherically shaped microscope and stared intently through the eyepieces.

There, in the very center of the field, was Gygyo. A transparent bubble helmet covered his head and he was wearing some sort of thick but flexible one-piece garment over the rest of his body. About a dozen amebae the size of dogs swarmed about him, reaching for his body with blunt, glassy pseudopods. He hacked away at them with a great, two-handed sword in tremendous sweeps that cut in two the most venturesome and persistent of the creatures. But Mary Ann could see from his frantic breathing that he was getting tired. Every once in a while he glanced rapidly over his left shoulder as if keeping watch on something in the distance.

"Where does he get air from?" she asked.

"The suit always contains enough oxygen for the duration of the lock," Flureet's voice explained behind her, somewhat surprised at the question. "He has about five minutes to go, and I think he'll make it. I think he'll be shaken up enough though, to— Did you see *that?*"

Mary Ann gasped. An elongated, spindle-shaped creature ending in a thrashing whip-like streak had just darted across the field, well over Gygyo's head. It was about one and a half times his size. He had gone into a crouch as it passed and the amebae surrounding him had also leaped away. They were back at the attack in a moment, however, once the danger had passed. Very wearily now, he continued to chop at them.

"What was it?"

"A trypanosome. It went by too fast for me to identify it, but it looked like either *Trypanosoma gambiense* or *rhodisiense*—the African sleeping sickness protozoans. It was a bit too big to be either of them, now that I remember. It could have been— Oh, the fool, the fool!"

Mary Ann turned to her, genuinely frightened. "Why—what did he do?"

"He neglected to get a pure culture, that's what he did. Taking on several different kinds of intestinal amebae is wild enough, but if there are trypanosomes in there with him, then there might be anything! And him down to thirty-five microns!"

Remembering the frightened glances that Gygyo had thrown over his shoulder, Mary Ann swung back to the microscope. The man was still fighting desperately, but the strokes of the sword came much more slowly. Suddenly, another ameba, different from those attacking Gygyo, swam leisurely into the field. It was almost transparent and about half his size.

"That's a new one," she told Flureet. "Is it dangerous?"

"No, *Iodamoeba butschlii* is just a sluggish, friendly lump. But what in the world is Gygyo afraid of to his left? He keeps turning his head as if— *Oh.*"

The last exclamation came out almost as a simple comment, so completely was it weighted with despair. An oval monster—its length three times and its width fully twice Gygyo's height—shot into the field from the left boundary as if making a stage entrance in reply to her question. The tiny, hair-like appendages with which it was covered seemed to give it fantastic speed.

Gygyo's sword slashed at it, but it swerved aside and out of the field. It was back in a moment, coming down like a dive bomber. Gygyo leaped away, but one of the amebae which had been attacking him was a little too slow. It disappeared, struggling madly, down the funnel-shaped mouth which indented the forward end of the egg-shaped monster.

"*Balantidium coli,*" Flureet explained before Mary Ann could force her trembling lips to frame the question. "One hundred microns long, sixty-five microns wide. Fast and deadly and terribly hungry. I was afraid he'd hit something like this sooner or later. Well, that's the end of our micro-hunting friend. He'll never be able to avoid it long enough to get out. And he can't kill a bug that size."

Mary Ann held quivering hands out to her. "Can't you *do* something?"

The bald woman brought her eyes down from the ceiling at last. Making what seemed an intense effort, she focused them on the girl. They were lit with bright astonishment.

"What can I do? He's locked inside that culture for another four minutes at least; an absolutely unbreakable lock. Do you expect me to—to go in there and *rescue* him?"

"If you can—of course!"

"But that would be interfering with his sovereign rights as an individual! My dear girl! Even if his wish to destroy himself is unconscious, it is still a wish originating in an essential part of his personality and must be respected. The whole thing is covered by the subsidiary-rights covenant of—"

"How do you *know* he wants to destroy himself?" Mary Ann wept. "I never heard of such a thing! He's supposed to be a—a friend of yours! Maybe he just accidentally got himself into more trouble than he expected, and he can't get out. I'm positive that's what happened. Oh—poor Gygyo, while we're standing here talking, he's getting killed!"

Flureet considered. "You may have something there. He is a romantic, and associating with you has given him all sorts of swaggering adventuresome notions. He'd never have done anything as risky as this before. But tell me: do you think it's worth taking a chance of interfering with someone's sovereign individual rights, just to save the life of an old and dear friend?"

"I don't *understand* you," Mary Ann said helplessly. "Of *course!* Why don't you let me—just do whatever you have to and send me in there after him. Please!"

The other woman rose and shook her head. "No, I think I'd be more effective. I must say, this romanticism is catching. And," she laughed to herself, "just a little intriguing. You people in the twentieth century led such lives!"

Before Mary Ann's eyes, she shrank down rapidly. Just as she disappeared, there was a whispering movement, like a flame curving from a candle, and her body seemed to streak toward the microscope.

Gygyo was down on one knee, now, trying to present as small an area to the oval monster as possible. The amebae with which he had been surrounded had now either all fled or been swallowed. He was swinging the sword back and forth rapidly over his head as the *Balantidium coli* swooped down first on one side, then on the other, but he looked very tired. His lips were clenched together, his eyes squinted with desperation.

And then the huge creature came straight down, feinted with its body, and, as he lunged at it with the sword, swerved slightly and hit him from the rear. Gygyo fell, losing his weapon.

Hairy appendages churning, the monster spun around fluently so that its funnel-shaped mouth was in front, and came back rapidly for the kill.

An enormous hand, a hand the size of Gygyo's whole body, swung into view and knocked it to one side. Gygyo scrambled to his feet, regained the sword, and looked up unbelievingly. He exhaled with relief and then smiled. Flureet had evidently stopped her shrinkage at a size several times larger than a hundred microns. Her body was not visible in the field of the microscope to Mary Ann, but it was obviously far too visible to the *Balantidium coli,* which turned end over end and scudded away.

And for the remaining minutes of the lock, there was not a creature which seemed even vaguely inclined to wander into Gygyo's neighborhood.

To Mary Ann's astonishment, Flureet's first words to Gygyo when they reappeared beside her at their full height were an apology: "I'm truly sorry, but your fire-eating friend here got me all excited about your safety, Gygyo. If you want to bring me up on charges of violating the Covenant and interfering with an individual's carefully prepared plans for self-destruction—"

Gygyo waved her to silence. "Forget it. In the words of the poet: Covenant, Shmovenant. You saved my life, and, as far as I know, I wanted it saved. If I instituted proceedings against you for interfering with my unconscious, in all fairness we'd have to subpoena my conscious mind as a witness in your defense. The case could drag on for months, and I'm far too busy."

The woman nodded. "You're right. There's nothing like a schizoid lawsuit when it comes to complications and verbal quibbling. But all the same I'm grateful to you— I didn't *have* to go and save your life. I don't know quite what got into me."

"That's what got into you." Gygyo gestured at Mary Ann. "The century of regimentation, of total war, of massive eavesdropping. I know: it's contagious."

Mary Ann exploded. "Well, really! I never in my life—really I—I—I just can't believe it! First, she doesn't want to save your life, because it would be interfering with your unconscious—your *unconscious!* Then, when she finally does something about it, she apologizes to you—she *apologizes!* And you, instead of thanking her, you talk as if you're excusing her for—for committing assault and battery! And then you start insulting *me*—and—and—"

"I'm sorry," Gygyo said. "I didn't intend to insult you, Mary Ann, neither you nor your century. After all, we must remember that it was the first century of modern times, it was the crisis-sickness from which recovery began. And it was in very many ways a truly great and adventuresome period, in which Man, for the last time, dared many things which he has never since attempted."

"Well. In that case." Mary Ann swallowed and began to feel better. And at that moment, she saw Gygyo and Flureet exchange the barest hint of a smile. She stopped feeling better. Damn these people! Who did they think they were?

Flureet moved to the yellow square exit. "I'll have to be going," she said. "I just stopped in to say goodbye before my transformation. Wish me luck, Gygyo."

"Your transformation? So soon? Well, all the best of course. It's been good knowing you, Flureet."

When the woman had left, Mary Ann looked at Gygyo's deeply concerned face and asked hesitantly: "What does she mean—'transformation'? And she said it was a *major* transformation. I haven't heard of that so far."

The dark-haired young man studied the wall for a moment. "I'd better not," he said at last, mostly to himself. "That's one of the concepts you'd find upsetting, like our active food for instance. And speaking of food—I'm hungry. Hungry, do you hear? *Hungry!*"

A section of the wall shook violently as his voice rose. It protruded an arm of itself at him. A tray was balanced on the end of the arm. Still standing, Gygyo began to eat from the tray.

He didn't offer Mary Ann any, which, as far as she was concerned, was just as well. She had seen at a glance that it was the purple spaghetti-like stuff of which he was so terribly fond.

Maybe it tasted good. Maybe it didn't. She'd never know. She only knew that she could never bring herself to eat anything which squirmed upwards toward one's mouth and wriggled about cozily once it was inside.

That was another thing about this world. The things these people *ate!*

Gygyo glanced up and saw her face. "I wish you'd try it just once, Mary Ann," he said wistfully. "It would add a whole new dimension to food for you. In addition to flavor, texture and aroma, you'd experience *motility.* Think of it: food not just lying there limp and lifeless in your mouth, but food expressing eloquently its desire to be eaten. Even your friend, Winthrop, culinary aesthete that he is, admitted to me the other day that Centaurian *libalilil* has it all over his favorite food symphonies in many ways. You see, they're mildly telepathic and can adjust their flavor to the dietary wishes of the person consuming them. That way, you get—"

"Thank you, but *please!* It makes me absolutely and completely sick even to think of it."

"All right." He finished eating, nodded at the wall. The wall withdrew the arm and sucked the tray back into itself. "I give up. All I wanted was to have you sample the stuff before you left. Just a taste."

"Speaking of leaving, that's what I came to see you about. We're having trouble."

"Oh, Mary Ann! I was hoping you'd come to see me for myself alone," he said with a disconsolate droop of his head.

She couldn't tell whether he was being funny or serious; she got angry as the easiest way of handling the situation. "See here, Gygyo Rablin, you are the very last man on Earth—past, present, or future—that I ever want to see again. And you know why! Any man who—who says things to a girl like you said to m-me, and at s-such a t-time…"

Against her will, and to her extreme annoyance, her voice broke. Tears burst from her eyelids and itched their way down her face. She set her lips determinedly and tried to shake them away.

Gygyo looked really uncomfortable now. He sat down on a corner of the desk which squirmed under him more erratically than ever.

"I am sorry, Mary Ann. Truly, terribly, sincerely sorry. I should never have made love to you in the first place. Even without our substantial temporal and cultural differences, I'm certain that you know, as well as I do, we have precious little in common. But I found you—well, enormously attractive, overpoweringly attractive. I found you exciting like no woman in my own time, or any woman that I've ever encountered in a visit to the future. I just couldn't resist the attraction. The one thing I didn't anticipate was the depressing effect your peculiar cosmetics would have upon me. The actual tactile sensations were extremely upsetting."

"That's not what you said. And the way you said it! You rubbed your finger on my face and lips, and you went: '*Grea-sy! Grea-sy!*' " Thoroughly in control of herself now, she mimicked him viciously.

Gygyo shrugged. "I said I'm sorry, and I meant it. But, Mary Ann, if you only know how that stuff feels to a highly educated tactile sense! That smeary red lipstick—and oh that finely-grated nonsense on your cheeks! There's no excuse for me, that I'll grant, but I'm just trying to make you understand why I erupted so stupidly."

"I suppose you think I'd be a lot nicer if I shaved my head like some of these women—like that horrible Flureet!"

He smiled and shook his head. "No, Mary Ann, you couldn't be like them, and they couldn't be like you. There are entirely different concepts of womanhood and beauty involved. In your period, the greatest emphasis is on a kind of physical similarity, the use of various artificial props which will make the woman most nearly approach a universally-agreed-upon ideal, and an ideal which consists of such items as redness of lips, smoothness of complexion and specific bodily shape. Whereas we place the accent on difference, but most particularly on *emotional* difference. The more emotions a woman can exhibit, and the more complex they are—the more striking is she considered. That's the point of the shaved heads: to show suddenly-appearing subtle wrinkles that might be missed if the area were covered with hair. And that's why we call Woman's bald head her frowning glory."

Mary Ann's shoulders slumped and she stared down at the floor which started to raise a section of itself questioningly but sank back down again as it realized that nothing was required of it. "I don't understand, and I guess I won't ever understand.

All I know is that I just can't stay in the same world with you, Gygyo Rablin—the very thought of it makes me feel kind of all wrong and sick inside."

"I understand," he nodded seriously. "And whatever comfort it may be—you have the same effect on me. I'd never have done anything as supremely idiotic as going on a locked micro-hunt in an impure culture before I met you. But those exciting stories of your adventuresome friend Edgar Rapp finally crept under my skin. I found I had to prove myself a man, in *your* terms, Mary Ann, in *your* terms!"

"Edgar *Rapp?*" she raised her eyes and looked at him incredulously. "Adventuresome? Exciting? *Edgar?* The only time *he* ever gets close to sport is when he sits on his behind all night playing poker with the boys in the payroll department!"

Gygyo rose and ambled about the room aimlessly, shaking his head. "The way you say it, the casual, half-contemptuous way you say it! The constant psychic risks run, the inevitably recurring clashes of personality—subliminal and overt—as hand after hand is played, as hour after hour goes by, with not two, not three, but as many as five, six, or even seven different and highly aggressive human beings involved— The bluffs, the raises, the outwitting, the fantastic contest of it! And to you these things are almost nothing, they're no more than what you'd expect of a masculine man! I couldn't face it; in fact, there is not a man in my entire world who'd be able to stand up to fifteen minutes of such complex psychological punishment."

Her gaze was very soft and tender as she watched him knock unhappily about the room. "And that's why you went into that awful microscope, Gygyo? To prove that you could be as good a man as Edgar is when he's playing poker?"

"It's not just the poker, Mary Ann. That's hair-raising enough, I grant you. It's so many things. Take this used car he has, that he drives you around in. Any man who'd drive one of those clumsy, unpredictable power-plants through the kind of traffic and the kind of accident statistics that your world boasts— *And every day, as a matter of course!* I knew the micro-hunt was a pathetic, artificial affair, but it was the only thing available to me that even came close!"

"You don't have to prove anything to me, Gygyo."

"Maybe I don't," he brooded. "But I had reached the point where I had to prove it to myself. Which is quite silly when you come to think of it, but that doesn't make it any less real. And I proved something after all. That two people with entirely different standards for male and female, standards that have been postulated and recapitulated for them since infancy, don't have a chance, no matter how attractive they find each other. I can't live with my knowledge of your innate standards, and you—well, you certainly have found mine upsetting. We don't mesh, we don't resonate, we don't go. As you said before, we shouldn't be in the same world. That's doubly true ever since—well, ever since we found out how strongly we tend to come together."

Mary Ann nodded. "I know. The way you stopped making love to me, and—and said—that horrid word, the way you kind of shuddered when you wiped your lips— Gygyo, you looked at me as if I stank, as if I *stank!* It tore me absolutely and completely to bits. I knew right then I had to get out of your time and out of your universe forever. But with Winthrop acting the way he is—I don't know what to do!"

"Tell me about it." He seemed to make an effort to pull himself together as he sat beside her on a section of upraised floor.

By the time she had finished, his recovery was complete. The prodigious leveling effect of mutual emotional involvement was no longer operative. Dismayed, Mary Ann watched him becoming once more a highly urbane, extremely intelligent and slightly supercilious young man of the twenty-fifth century, and felt in her very bone marrow her own awkwardness increase, her garish, none-too-bright primitiveness come thickly to the surface.

"I can't do a thing for you," he said. "I wish I could."

"Not even," she asked desperately, "with the problems we have? Not even considering how terrible it'll be if I stay here, if I don't leave on time?"

"Not even considering all that. I doubt that I could make it clear to you, however much I tried, Mary Ann, but I can't force Winthrop to go, I can't in all conscience give you any advice on how to force him—and I can't think of a thing that would make him change his mind. You see, there's a whole social fabric involved which is far more significant than our personal little agonies, however important they may be to us. In my world, as Storku pointed out, one just doesn't do such things. And that, my sweet, is that."

Mary Ann sat back. She hadn't needed the slightly mocking hauteur of Gygyo's last words to tell her that he was now completely in control of himself, that once more he was looking upon her as an intriguing but—culturally speaking—extremely distant specimen.

She knew only too well what was happening: she'd been on the other end of this kind of situation once or twice herself. Just two months ago, a brilliantly smooth salesman, who handled the Nevada territory for her company, had taken her out on a date and almost swept her off her feet.

Just as she'd reached the point where the wine in her brain was filled with bubbles of starlight, she'd taken out a cigarette and dreamily, helplessly, asked him for a light. The salesman had clicked a lighter at her in an assured and lordly gesture, but the lighter had failed to work. He had cursed, clicked it futilely a few more times, then had begun picking at the mechanism madly with his fingernails. In the next few moments as he continued to claw at the lighter, it had seemed to Mary Ann that the glossy surface of his personality developed an enormous fissure along its entire length and all the underlying desperation that was essentially him leaked out. He was no longer a glamorous, successful and warmly persuasive young man, but a pathetically driven creature who was overpoweringly uncertain, afraid that if one item in his carefully prepared presentation missed its place in the schedule, the sale would not take place.

And it didn't. When he'd looked at her again, he saw the cool comprehension in her eyes; his lips sagged. And no matter how wittily he tried to recapture the situation, how cleverly he talked, how many oceans of sparkling urgency he washed over her, she was his master now. She had seen through his magic to the unhooded yellow light bulbs and the twisted, corroded wires which made it work. She remembered feeling somewhat sorry for him as she'd asked him to take her home—not sorry for someone with whom she'd almost fallen in love, but slight sorrow for a handicapped child (someone else's handicapped child) who had tried to do something utterly beyond his powers.

Was that what Gygyo was feeling for her now? With brimming anger and despair, Mary Ann felt she had to reach him again, reach him very personally. She had to wipe that smile off his eyelids.

"Of course," she said, selecting the first arrow that came to hand, "it won't do you any good if Winthrop doesn't go back with us."

He looked at her questioningly. "Me?"

"Well, if Winthrop doesn't go back, we'll be stuck here. And if we're stuck here, the people from your time who are visiting ours will be stuck in the twentieth century. You're the temporal supervisor—you're responsible, aren't you? You might lose your job."

"My dear little Mary Ann! I can't lose my job. It's mine till I don't want it any more. Getting fired—what a concept! Next you'll be telling me I'm liable to have my ears cropped!"

To her chagrin, he chuckled all over his shoulders. Well, at least she had put him in a good mood; no one could say that she hadn't contributed to this hilarity. And *My dear little Mary Ann*. That stung!

"Don't you even *feel* responsible? Don't you feel anything?"

"Well, whatever I feel, it certainly isn't responsible. The five people from this century who volunteered to make the trip back to yours were well educated, extremely alert, highly responsible human beings. They knew they were running certain inevitable risks."

She rose agitatedly. "But how were they to know that Winthrop was going to be stubborn? And how could we, Gygyo, how could we know that?"

"Even assuming that the possibility entered nobody's mind," he pointed out, tugging at her arm gently until she sat down beside him again, "one has to, in all reason, admit that transferring to a period five centuries distant from one's own must be accompanied by certain dangers. Not being able to return is one of them. Then, one has to further admit that, this being so, one or more of the people making the transfer recognized this danger—at least unconsciously—and wished to subject themselves to its consequences. If this is at all the situation, interference would be a major crime, not only against Winthrop's conscious desires, but against such people's unconscious motivations as well—and both have almost equal weight in the ethics of our period. There! That's about as simple as I can make it, Mary Ann. Do you understand, now?"

"A—a little," she confessed. "You mean it's like Flureet not wanting to save you when you were almost being killed in that micro-hunt, because maybe, unconsciously, you *wanted* to get yourself killed?"

"Right! And believe me, Flureet wouldn't have lifted a finger, old friend or no old friend, your romantic twentieth-century dither notwithstanding, if she hadn't been on the verge of major transformation with the concurrent psychological remove from all normal standards and present-day human frames of reference."

"What *is* this major transformation business?"

Gygyo shook his head emphatically. "Don't ask me that. You wouldn't understand it, you wouldn't like it—and it's not at all important for you to know. It's a concept and a practice as peculiar to our time as, oh say, tabloid journalism and election-night excitement is to yours. What you want to appreciate is this other thing—the way we protect and nurture the individual eccentric impulse, even if it should be suicidal. Let me put it this way: The French Revolution tried to sum itself up in the slogan, *Liberté, Egalité, Fraternité;* the American Revolution used the phrase, Life, Liberty and the Pursuit of Happiness. We feel that the entire concept of our civilization is contained in these words: The Utter Sacredness of the Individual and the Individual Eccentric Impulse. The last part is the most important, because without it our society would have as much right to interfere with the individual as yours did; a man wouldn't even have the elementary freedom of doing away with himself without getting the proper papers filled out by the proper government official. A person who wanted to—"

Mary Ann stood up with determination. "All right! I'm not the least little bit interested in this nonsense. You won't help us in any way, you don't care if we're stuck here for the rest of our natural lives, and that's that! I might as well go."

"In the name of the Covenant, girl, what did you *expect* me to tell you? I'm no Oracle Machine. I'm just a man."

"A man?" she cried scornfully. "A man? You call yourself a man? Why, a man would—a man would—a real man would just— Oh, let me get out of here!"

The dark-haired young man shrugged and rose, too. He called for a jumper. When it materialized beside them, he gestured toward it courteously. Mary Ann started for it, paused, and held out a hand to him.

"Gygyo," she said, "whether we stay or leave on time, I'm never going to see you again. I've made up my mind on that. But there's one thing I want you to know."

As if knowing what she was going to say, he had dropped his eyes. His head was bent over the hand he had taken.

Seeing this, Mary Ann's voice grew gentler and more tender. "It's just—just that— oh, Gygyo, it's that you're the only man I've ever loved. Ever really truly, absolutely and completely loved. I want you to know that, Gygyo."

He didn't reply. He was still holding her fingers tightly, and she couldn't see his eyes.

"Gygyo," she said her voice breaking. "Gygyo! You're feeling the same, aren't—"

At last Gygyo looked up. There was an expression of puzzlement on his face. He pointed to the fingers he had been holding. The nail of each one was colored with a bright lacquer.

"Why in the world," he asked, "do you limit it to the fingernail? Most primitive peoples who went in for this sort of thing did it on other and larger parts of the body. One would expect that at least you would tattoo the whole hand— Mary Ann! Did I say anything wrong again?"

Sobbing bitterly, the girl darted past him and into the jumper.

She went back to Mrs. Brucks's room, and, when she had been calmed sufficiently, explained why Gygyo Rablin, the temporal supervisor, either could not or would not help them with Winthrop's stubbornness.

Dave Pollock glared around the oval room. "So we give up? Is that what it comes down to? Not one person in all this brilliant, gimmicky, gadgety future will lift a finger to help us get back to our own time and our own families—and we can't help ourselves. A brave new world, all right. Real achievement. Real progress."

"I don't see what call you have to shoot your mouth off, young man," Mr. Mead muttered from where he was sitting at the far end of the room. Periodically, his necktie curled upwards and tried to nuzzle against his lips; wearily, petulantly, he slapped it down again. "At least we tried to do something about it. That's more than you can say."

"Ollie, old boy, you just tell me something I can do, and I'll do it. I may not pay a whopping income tax, but I've been trained to use my mind. I'd like nothing better than to find out what a thoroughly rational approach to this problem could do for us. One thing I know: it can't possibly come up with less than all this hysteria and emotional hoopla, this flag-waving and executive-type strutting have managed to date."

"Listen, a difference it makes?" Mrs. Brucks held her wrist out and pointed to the tiny, gold-plated watch strapped around it. "Only forty-five minutes left before six o'clock. So what can we do in forty-five minutes? A miracle maybe we can manufacture on short notice? Magic we can turn out to order? Go fight City Hall. My Barney I know I won't see again."

The thin young man turned on her angrily. "I'm not talking of magic and miracles. I'm talking of logic. Logic and the proper evaluation of data. These people not only have a historical record available to them that extends back to and includes our own time, but they are in regular touch with the future—their future. That means there are also available to them historical records that extend back to and include *their* time."

Mrs. Brucks cheered up perceptibly. She liked listening to education. She nodded. "So?"

"Isn't it obvious? Those people who exchanged with us—our five opposite numbers—they must have known in advance that Winthrop was going to be stubborn. Historical records to that effect existed in the future. They wouldn't have done it—it stands to reason they wouldn't want to spend the rest of their lives in what is for them a pretty raw and uncivilized environment—unless they had known of a way out, a way that the situation could be handled. It's up to us to find that way."

"Maybe," Mary Ann Carthington suggested, bravely biting the end off a sniffle, "maybe the next future kept it a secret from them. Or maybe all five of them were suffering from what they call here a bad case of individual eccentric impulse."

"That's not how the concept of individual eccentric impulse works, Mary Ann," Dave Pollock told her with a contemptuous grimace. "I don't want to go into it now, but *believe me,* that's not how it works! And I don't think the temporal embassies keep this kind of secret from the people in the period to which they're accredited. No, I tell you the solution is right here if we can only see it."

Oliver T. Mead had been sitting with an intent expression on his face, as if he were trying to locate a fact hidden at the other end of a long tunnel of unhappiness. He straightened up suddenly and said: "Storku mentioned that! The Temporal Embassy. But he didn't think it was a good idea to approach them—they were too involved with long-range historical problems to be of any use to us. But something else he said— something else we could do. What was it, now?"

They all looked at him and waited anxiously while he thought. Dave Pollock had just begun a remark about "high surtax memories" when the rotund executive clapped his hands together resoundingly.

"I remember! The Oracle Machine! He said we could ask the Oracle Machine. We might have some difficulty interpreting the answer, according to him, but at this point that's the least of our worries. We're in a desperate emergency, and beggars can't be choosers. If we get any kind of answer, any kind of an answer at all…"

Mary Ann Carthington looked away from the tiny cosmetics laboratory she was using to repair the shiny damage caused by tears. "Now that you bring it up, Mr. Mead, the temporal supervisor made some such remark to me, too. About the Oracle Machine, I mean."

"He did? Good! That firms it up nicely. We may still have a chance, ladies and gentlemen, we may still have a chance. Well then, as to who shall do it. I am certain I don't have to draw a diagram when it comes to selecting the one of us most capable of dealing with a complex piece of futuristic machinery."

They all stared at Dave Pollock who swallowed hard and inquired hoarsely, "You mean me?"

"Certainly I mean you, young man," Mr. Mead said sternly. "You're the long-haired scientific expert around here. You're the chemistry and physics professor."

"I'm a teacher, that's all, a high-school science *teacher*. And you know how I feel about having anything to do with the Oracle Machine. Even the thought of getting close to it makes my stomach turn over. As far as I'm concerned it's the one aspect of this civilization that's most horrible, most decadent. Why, I'd rather—"

"My stomach didn't turn over when I had to go in and have an argument with that crazy Mr. Winthrop?" Mrs. Brucks broke in. "Till then, out of this room I hadn't taken a step, with all the everything I had positively nothing to do—you think I liked watching one minute a pair of rompers, the next minute, I don't know what, an evening gown he starts wearing? And that crazy talk he talks—smell this from a Mars, taste this from a Venus—you think maybe, Mr. Pollock, I enjoyed myself? But somebody had to do, so I did. All we're asking you is a try. A try you can make?"

"And I can assure you," Mary Ann Carthington came on in swiftly, "that Gygyo Rablin is absolutely and completely the last person on Earth I would go to for a favor. It's a personal matter, and I'd rather not discuss it now, if you don't mind, but I would die, positively die, rather than go through that again. I did it though, because there was the teeniest chance it would help us all get home again. I don't think we're asking too much of you, I don't think so one little bit."

Mr. Mead nodded. "I agree with you, young lady. Storku is a man I haven't seen eye to eye with since we've arrived, and I've gone out of my way to avoid him, but to have to get involved in that unholy Shriek Field madness in the bargain—" He brooded for a while over some indigestible mental fragment, then, as his cleated golf shoes began squirming lovingly about on his feet, shook himself determinedly and went on: "It's about time you stopped shooting off your mouth, Pollock, and got down to humdrum, specific brass tacks. Einstein's theory of relativity isn't going to get us back to good old 1958, and neither is your Ph.D. or M.A. or whatever. What we need now is action, action with a capital *A* and no ifs, no ands, no buts."

"All right, all right. I'll do it."

"And another thing." Mr. Mead rolled a wicked little thought pleasurably to and fro in his mind for a moment or two before letting it out. "You take the jumper. You said yourself we don't have the time to do any walking, and that's doubly true right now, doubly true, when we're right up against the dead, dead deadline. I don't want to hear any whining and any whimpering about it making you sick. If Miss Carthington and I could take the jumper, so can you."

In the midst of his misery, Dave Pollock rallied. "You think I won't?" he asked scornfully. "I've done most of my traveling here by jumper. I'm not afraid of mechanical progress—just so long as it's genuine *progress*. Of course I'll take the jumper."

He signaled for one with a tiny return of his old swagger. When it appeared, he walked under it with squared shoulders. Let them all watch how a rational, scientifically-minded man goes about things, he thought. And anyway, using the jumper wasn't nearly as upsetting to him as it seemed to be to the others. He could take jumpers in stride.

Which was infinitely more than he could say for the Oracle Machine.

For that reason, he had himself materialized outside the building which housed the machine. A bit of a walk and he might be able to get his thoughts in order.

The only trouble was, the sidewalk had other ideas. Silently, obsequiously, but nonetheless firmly, it began to move under his feet as he started walking around the squat, slightly quivering structure. It rippled him ahead at a pace somewhat faster than the one he set, changing direction as soon as he changed his.

Dave Pollock looked around at the empty streets and smiled with resignation. The sentient, eager-to-serve sidewalks didn't bother him, either. He had expected something like that in the future, that and the enormously alert servitor houses, the clothes which changed their color and cut at the wearers' caprice—all more or less, in one form or another, to be anticipated, by a knowledgeable man, of human progress. Even the developments in food—from the wriggling, telepathic, please-eat-me-and-enjoy-me stuff all the way up to the more complex culinary compositions on which an interstellarly famous chef might have worked for a year or more—was logical, if you considered how bizarre to an early American colonist, would be the fantastic, cosmopolitan variety of potables and packaged meals available in any twentieth-century supermarket.

These things, the impediments of daily life, all change and modify in time. But certain things, *certain* things, should not.

When the telegram had arrived in Houston, Texas, informing him that—of all the people in the United States of America—he was most similar in physical composition and characteristics to one of the prospective visitors from 2458 AD, he had gone almost mad with joy. The celebrity he suddenly enjoyed in the faculty lunchroom was unimportant, as were the Page One stories in local newspapers under the heading: LONE STAR SON GALLOPING FUTUREWARDS.

First and foremost, it was reprieve. It was reprieve and another chance. Family responsibilities, a dying father, a sick younger sister, had prevented him from getting the advanced academic degrees necessary for a university teaching position with all of its accompanying prestige, higher income, and opportunities for research. Then, when they had come to an end and he had gone back to school, a sudden infatuation and too-hasty marriage had thrown him back onto the same treadmill. He had just begun to realize—despite the undergraduate promise he had shown and none-too-minute achievement—how thoroughly he was trapped by the pleasant residential neighborhood and cleanly modern high school between which he shuttled daily, when the telegram arrived, announcing his selection as one of the group to be sent five hundred years ahead. How it was going to help him, what, precisely, he would do with the chance, he did not know—but it had lifted him out of the ruck of anonymity; somehow, some way, it would enable him to become a striking individual at last.

Dave Pollock had not realized the extent of his good fortune until he met the other four in Washington, D.C. He had heard, of course, how the finest minds in the country had bitterly jostled and elbowed each other in a frenzied attempt to get into the group and find out what was going to develop in *their* speciality half a millennium hence. But not until he had talked with his prospective fellow-tourists—an itinerant worker, a Bronx housewife, a pompous midwestern business executive, a pretty but otherwise very ordinary San Francisco stenographer—did it come to him that he was the only one with any degree of scientific training.

He would be the only one capable of evaluating the amount of major technological advance! He would be the only one to correlate all the bewildering mass of minor changes into something resembling coherence! And thus, above all, he would be the only one to appreciate the essential quality of the future, the basic threads that would run through it from its underlying social fabric to its star-leaping fringes!

He, who had wanted to devote his life to knowledge-seeking, would exist for two weeks, unique and intellectually alone, in a five-century-long extrapolation of every laboratory and library in his age!

At first, it had been like that. Everywhere there was glory and excitement and discovery. Then, little, disagreeable things began to creep in, like the first stages of a cold. The food, the clothing, the houses—well, you either ignored it or made other arrangements. These people were extremely hospitable and quite ingenious: they didn't at all mind providing you with more familiar meals when your intestines had revolted a couple of times. The women, with their glossy baldness and strange attitudes toward relations between the sexes—well, you had a brand-new wife at home and didn't have to get involved with the women.

But Shriek Field, Panic Stadium, that was another matter. Dave Pollock was proud of being a thoroughly rational person. He had been proud of the future, when he first arrived, taking it almost as a personal vindication that the people in it should be so thoroughly, universally rational, too. His first acquaintance with Shriek Field had almost nauseated him. That the superb intellects he had come to know should *willingly* transform themselves into a frothing, hysterical pack of screaming animals, and at regular, almost medically-prescribed intervals...

They had explained to him painfully, elaborately, that they could not be such superb intellects, so thoroughly rational, unless they periodically released themselves in this fashion. It made sense, but—still—*watching* them do it was absolutely horrifying. He knew he would never be able to stand the sight of it.

Still, this one could make acceptable in some corner of the brain. But the chess business?

Since his college days, Dave Pollock had fancied himself as a chess player. He was just good enough to be able to tell himself that if ever he had the time to really concentrate on the game, to learn the openings, say, as they should be learned, he'd be good enough to play in tournaments. He'd even subscribed to a chess magazine and followed all the championship matches with great attention. He'd wondered what chess would be like in the future—surely the royal game having survived for so many centuries would survive another five? What would it be like: a version of three-dimensional chess, or possibly another, even more complex evolution?

The worst of it was the game was almost identical with the one played in the twentieth century.

Almost every human being in 2458 played it; almost every human being in 2458 enjoyed it. But there were no human champions. There were no human opponents.

There were only the chess machines. And they could beat anybody.

"What's the sense," he had wailed, "of playing with a machine which has millions of 'best moves and counter-moves' built into its memory circuits? That has a selector mechanism able to examine and choose from every chess game ever recorded? A machine which has been *designed* never to be beaten? What's the sense—where's the excitement?"

"We don't play to win," they had explained wonderingly. "We play to play. It's the same with all our games: aggressions are gotten rid of in a Shriek or a Panic; games are just for mental or physical exercise. And so, when we play, we want to play against the best. Besides, every once in a while, an outstandingly good player, once or twice in his lifetime, is able to hold the machine to a draw. Now, *that* is an achievement. *That* merits excitement."

You had to love chess as much as he did, Dave Pollock supposed, to realize what an obscenity the existence of these machines made of it. Even the other three in his group, who had become much more restive than he at twenty-fifth-century mechanisms and mores, only stared at him blankly when he raged over it. No, if you didn't love something, you weren't bothered overmuch when it was degraded. But surely they could see the abdication of human intellect, of human reason, that the chess machines implied?

Of course, that was nothing compared to the way human reason had abdicated before the Oracle Machine. That was the last, disgusting straw to a rational person.

The Oracle Machine. He glanced at his watch. Only twenty-five minutes left. Better hurry. He took one last, self-encouraging breath and climbed the cooperative steps of the building.

"My name is Stilia," a bald-headed, rather pleasant-faced young woman said as she came toward him in the spacious anteroom. "I'm the attendant of the machine for today. Can I help you?"

"I suppose so." He looked uncomfortably at a distant, throbbing wall. Behind the yellow square on that well, he knew, was the inner brain of the Oracle Machine. How he'd love to kick a hole in that brain!

Instead, he sat down on an upraised hummock of floor and wiped his perspiring hands carefully. He told her about their approaching deadline, about Winthrop's stubbornness, about the decision to consult the Oracle Machine.

"Oh, Winthrop, yes! He's that delightful old man. I met him at a dream dispensary a week ago. What wonderful awareness he has! Such a total immersion in our culture! We're very proud of Winthrop. We'd like to help him every way we possibly can."

"If you don't mind, lady," Dave Pollock said morosely, "we're the ones who need help. We've *got* to get back."

Stilia laughed. "Of course. We'd like to help everybody. Only Winthrop is—*special.* He's trying hardest. Now, if you'll just wait here, I'll go in and put your problem before the Oracle Machine. I know how to do it so that it will activate the relevant memory circuits with the least loss of time."

She flexed her right arm at him and walked toward the yellow square. Pollock watched it expand in front of her, then, as she went through the opening it made, contract behind her. In a few minutes she returned.

"I'll tell you when to go in, Mr. Pollock. The machine is working on your problem. The answer you get will be the very best that can be made, given the facts available."

"Thanks." He thought for a while. "Tell me something. Doesn't it seem to take something out of life—out of your thinking life—to know that you can take absolutely any problem, personal problem, scientific problem, or working problem, to the Oracle Machine and it will solve it much better than you could?"

Stilia looked puzzled. "Not at all. To begin with, problem-solving is a very small part of today's thinking life. It would be as logical to say that it took something vital out of life to make a hole with an electric drill instead of a hand drill. In your time, no doubt, there are people who feel just that way; they have the obvious privilege of not using electric drills. Those who use electric drills, however, have their physical energy freed for tasks they regard as more important. The Oracle Machine is the major tool of our culture; it has been designed toward just one end—computing all the factors of a given problem and relating them to the totality of pertinent data that is in the possession of the human race. But even if people consult the Oracle Machine, they may not be able to understand and apply the answer. And, if they do understand it, they may not choose to act on it."

"They may not choose to act on it? Does that make sense? You said yourself the answers are the very best that can be made, given the facts available."

"Human activities don't necessarily have to make sense. That is the prevailing and rather comfortable modern view, Mr. Pollock. There is always the individual eccentric impulse."

"Yeah, there's always that," he growled. "Resign your private, distinct personality by running with a howling mob at Shriek Field, lose all of yourself in an insane crowd—but don't forget your individual eccentric impulse. Never, *never* forget your individual eccentric impulse!"

She nodded soberly. "That really sums it up, I must say, in spite of your rather unmistakable sarcasm. Why do you find it so hard to accept? Man is both a herd animal and a highly individualistic animal—what we call a self-realizable animal. The herd instincts must be satisfied at whatever cost, and have been in the past through such mechanisms as warfare, religion, nationalism, partyism, and various forms of group chauvinism. The need to resign one's personality and immerse in something larger than self has been recognized since earliest times: Shriek Fields and Panic Stadiums everywhere on the planet provide for this need and expend it harmlessly."

"I wouldn't say it was so harmless from the look of that mechanical rabbit, or whatever it was."

"I understand that human beings who took the place of the mechanical rabbit in the past looked much worse when a herd of men was through with them," she suggested, locking eyes with him. "Yes, Mr. Pollock, I think you know what I mean. The self-realizable instincts, on the other hand, must be satisfied, too. Usually, they can be satisfied in terms of one's daily life and work, as the herd instincts can be fulfilled by normal group relationships and identification with humanity. But occasionally, the self-realizable instincts must be expressed at abnormal strengths, and then we have to have a kind of private Shriek Field—the concept of individual eccentric impulse. The two are opposite poles of exactly the same thing. All we require is that another human being will not be actively interfered with."

"And so long as that doesn't happen, *anything* goes!"

"Exactly. Anything goes. Absolutely anything a person may want to do out of his own individual eccentric impulse is permitted. Encouraged, actually. It's not only that we consider that some of humanity's greatest achievements have come out of individual eccentric impulses, but that we feel the greatest glory of our civilization is the homage we pay to such intrinsically personal expression."

Dave Pollock stared at her with reluctant respect. She was bright. This was the kind of girl he might have married if he'd gone on to his doctorate, instead of Susie. Although Susie— He wondered if he'd ever see Susie again. He was astonished at how bitterly homesick he felt.

"It sounds good," he admitted. "But living with it is another thing entirely. I guess I'm too much a product of my own culture to ever swallow it down all the way. I can't get over how much difference there is between our civilizations. We talk the same language, but we sure as hell don't think the same thoughts."

Stilia smiled warmly and sat back. "One of the reasons your period was invited to exchange visitors with us is because it was the first in which most speech patterns became constant and language shifts came to an end. Your newly invented speech recording devices were responsible for that. But technological progress continued, and sociological progress actually accelerated. Neither was solidified to any great extent until the invention in the latter part of the twenty-third century—"

A hum began in the distant wall. Stilia broke off and stood up. "The Oracle Machine is ready to give you the answer to your problem. Just go inside, sit down and repeat your question in its simplest form. I wish you well."

I wish me well, too, Dave Pollock thought, as he went through the dilated yellow square and into the tiny cube of a room. For all of Stilia's explication, he was supremely uncomfortable in this world of simply satisfied herd instincts and individual eccentric impulses. He was no misfit; he was no Winthrop: he very much wanted out and to return to what was smoothly familiar.

Above all, he didn't want to stay any longer in a world where almost any question he might think of would be answered best by the bluish, narrow, throbbing walls which surrounded him.

But— He did have a problem he couldn't solve. And this machine could.

He sat down. "What do we do about Winthrop's stubbornness?" he asked, idiotically feeling like a savage interrogating a handful of sacred bones.

A deep voice, neither masculine nor feminine in quality, rumbled from the four walls, from the ceiling, from the floor.

"You will go to the time travel bureau in the Temporal Embassy at the proper time."

He waited. Nothing more was forthcoming. The walls were still.

The Oracle Machine evidently had not understood.

"It won't do us any good to be there," he pointed out. "Winthrop is stubborn, he won't go back with us. And, unless all five of us go back together, none of us can go. That's the way the transferring device is set. So, what I want to know is, how do we persuade Winthrop without—"

Again the enormous voice.

"You will go to the time travel bureau in the Temporal Embassy at the proper time."

And that seemed to be that.

Dave Pollock trudged out and told Stilia what had happened. "It seems to me," he commented just a little nastily, "that the machine found the problem was just a bit too much for it and was trying hard to change the subject."

"Just the same, I would do what it advised. Unless, of course, you find another, subtler interpretation of the answer."

"Or unless my individual eccentric impulse gets in the way?"

This time the sarcasm was lost on her. She opened her eyes wide. "That would be best of all! Imagine if you should at last learn to exercise it!"

So Dave Pollock went back to Mrs. Brucks's room and, thoroughly exasperated, told the others of the ridiculous answer the Oracle Machine had given him on the problem of Winthrop's stubbornness.

At a few minutes to six, however, all four of them—Mrs. Brucks, Oliver T. Mead, Mary Ann Carthington, Dave Pollock—were in the time-travel bureau of the Temporal Embassy, having arrived in varying stages of upset by way of jumper. They didn't have any particular hopes: there just wasn't anything else to do.

They sat dispiritedly in their transfer seats and stared at their watches.

At precisely one minute to six, a large group of twenty-fifth-century citizens came into the transfer room. Gygyo Rablin, the temporal supervisor, was among them, as was Stilia the attendant of the Oracle Machine, Flureet, wearing the drawn look of one awaiting major transformation, Mr. Storku, returned temporarily from the Odor Festival on Venus—and many, many others. They carried Winthrop to his proper seat and stood back with reverent expressions on their faces. They looked like people who had seen the fulfillment of a religious ceremony—and they had.

The transfer began.

Winthrop was an old man, sixty-four, to be exact. He had, in the past two weeks, undergone much excitement. He had been on micro-hunts, undersea hunts, teleported jaunts to incredibly distant planets, excursions, numerous and fantastic. He had had remarkable things done to his body, spectacular things done to his mind. He had pounded in pursuit at Shriek Field, scuttled fearfully at Panic Stadium. And, above all, he had eaten plentifully and repeatedly of foods grown in distant stellar systems, of dishes prepared by completely alien entities, of meals whose composition had been totally unsuspected by his metabolism in the period of its maturing. He had not grown up with these things, with this food, as had the people of the twenty-fifth century: it had all been shatteringly new to his system.

No wonder they had observed with such pleased astonishment his individual eccentric impulse assert itself. No wonder they had guarded its unfolding so lovingly.

Winthrop was no longer stubborn. Winthrop was dead.

AFTERWORD

I had more trouble writing "Winthrop" than any other story, with the possible exception of "Alexander the Bait," my first published piece. At least with "Alexander," I didn't know what I was doing. Not really. I floundered here and floundered there and finally came up with something barely deserving to be printed.

But I knew only too well what I was doing when I wrote "Winthrop Was Stubborn." I had planned a piece with a specific theme: how fundamentally unpleasant time travel to the future had to be. And almost everything in the story had to be there because it was underlining that theme.

When I was young and had just begun to read science fiction, I loved time-travel stories. I recall just one thing from the first such story I ever read—bald-headed men a hundred years from 1932 rented out their shiny scalps to be tattooed for advertising purposes. At the age of twelve, I considered such a description of minor social change a brilliant flash of creativity. And I had long, complicated daydreams, as I sat in school, of futures in which interplanetary and interstellar travel were the very least of the wonders in which I would participate when I stepped out of my time machine a century or a millennium hence. The daydreams continued through my twenties, and I bled them into fiction and got paid for them. Then, as I moved into my thirties, something happened.

What happened? Well, for one thing, Greenwich Village, the neighborhood I loved most in New York City, began to change as its special qualities were noted by real estate entrepreneurs. Pretty brownstones where Ford Madox Ford and John Reed and Eugene O'Neill had once lived were pulled down to be replaced by multilevel buildings. Clubby, charming residences like the Rhinelander Gardens with its New-Orleans-style wrought-iron balconies disappeared; where they had been there were now virtual skyscraper apartment houses in which people lived who asked each other, "Where is that picturesque Village we used to hear about?"

Upper Sixth Avenue, where my artist and photographer friends had once had their studios, now became a place where enormous corporation and bank structures squeezed against each other block after block after dismal block. I kept finding that the new, the innovative was frequently tasteless—or at least not to my specific taste. And I began realizing that you paid for change, frequently with beauty, often at least with grace. I began realizing that a trip to the future might well leave me a stranger and afraid in a cruel new place, a world I had not only never made but one that was without all the sweetly recognizable things I valued because they had been with me since first awareness.

Consider. If we could reach back in time and transport Shakespeare to our era, would he be at all a happy man? Oh, he would no doubt find our television and movies fascinating—if a little too simple and a little too cheap—but how about the important things, the ones that really make up a life? How would he feel about the impossibility of determining anyone's rank, of being able to do no more than frown when some ugly fellow jostled him or spoke to him with careful discourtesy? And how in the world to tell an honest woman from a whore, when the neighborhoods they lived in were no clue and the clothes they wore were pretty much all blatantly seductive? And the food—oh, the food! You go into an inexpensive eating establishment and, instead of a slice off the joint and a mug of brown ale, they offer you things like vegetable plates and spaghetti with red sauce and—abomination of abominations!—chicken *croquettes*.

In other words, if the important small familiars of life are gone, who gives a damn for the whiz-bangs?

What I had set myself to do in "Winthrop," then, was to create a future I once would have found fascinating—and now find terrifying and a little disgusting. It went incredibly slowly, my younger self and my older self arguing with each other, getting in each other's way, constantly tripping each other up.

But I had incentives, too. For one, Horace L. Gold of *Galaxy* had seen a very rough draft of the story and had told me he would pay a hefty bonus word-rate for it no matter how long it was. For another—well, it was to be my marriage story.

I had shown as much as was done of it to Fruma and had told her that as soon as it was completed I would sell it to Horace, and we would get married and go on our honeymoon with the money from the sale.

But the weeks went by and the months went by, and Winthrop continued to be stubborn. The story got longer and longer. Horace got suspicious and begged me not to play at an auction and try to sell it to John Campbell of *Astounding* at a higher rate. Fruma had a serious talk with me: telling me she was willing to let me off the hook as far as the marriage was concerned.

"*Then* will you be able to finish the thing?" she said. "I want to read it!"

And I wrote and wrote, and rewrote and rewrote. Finally, finally, the piece was done. Gagging with lack of sleep, I brought it to Horace. He read it then and there and called the office to voucher a check for me.

"What took so long?" he asked. "It reads smooth and easy."

"That's what took so long," I said.

WRITTEN 1957——PUBLISHED 1957

Out There

The Dark Star

So it's here again, is it? Another year and it's here again. The Day. Only this time it's the fiftieth anniversary. Your editors and program directors will be really spreading themselves tomorrow. Celebrations in every major city on Earth, a holiday on every planet of the Solar System, and on the Moon—*well!* Noisemakers for the school children, speeches in the parks, fireworks, drinking, dancing, parades—and you boys will have to cover it all. *The* Day.

Go ahead, sit down and make yourselves comfortable. I've been expecting you. I don't have very much that's new, I'm afraid. It will be just about the same old story everyone's heard for the past forty-nine years, but they never seen to get tired of it, do they?

Human interest, your editors call it. The story behind the news, the color behind the historical event. The strictly human side of today's holiday—that's all I am.

Those of you who want any refreshment, please help yourselves. I particularly recommend that Martian brandy; they're turning out some highly drinkable stuff in New Quebec these days. No, thank you, young fellow, I'm afraid I can't join you—a man's lining gets real soft at my time of life. But I still like to watch, so drink up, all of you, drink up and drink hearty.

The fiftieth anniversary. The years, the years! There I was, young and practically bubbling with high-test fuel like all of you, and here I am now, full of doddering, aimless talk. And in between, a full volume of history, but such history as the human race has not written for itself since it began climbing down from the trees.

And I was there on the very first page of that volume!

I was there, and Caldicott, Bresh, McGuire and Stefano. Just the five of us, five desperate and determined competitors, all that was left of an even hundred determined and brilliant young men that the best universities in the country had sent. We'd been examined mentally and examined physically, tested on our math and tested on our nerve, eliminated for this reason and for that reason, too tall, too slow, too heavy, too talkative—until only the pleased, happy, and shakingly tense five of us were left.

Then the finals began.

Picture it, five young men on a plane bound for the Arizona Research Station, looking at each other, wondering who it was going to be, who was going to end up the winner, the pilot of the first ship to land on the Moon. Each one of us wanting to be the man, the Columbus who would open up not a mere hemisphere but the incredible, infinite universe itself. Each of us wanting to be that man so bad that we had terrible little aches running up and down our insides.

Try to picture the world we'd grown up in. The first radio-controlled rocket to burst outside the Earth's atmosphere, the first piloted ship to go halfway to the Moon and back, the first robot craft to circle the Moon—interplanetary travel, *space* travel, getting closer all the time. The newspapers full of it, the television full of it, our very grammar-school textbooks chock-full of it.

And now, just as we'd graduated, the question was no longer exciting but remote news. It was as personal as a new neighbor moving next door. Who was he going to be, what would be his name—that first explorer—that hero of all-time heroes?

There were exactly five possibilities: Caldicott, Bresh, McGuire, Stefano—and myself. The Moon ship had been built and was waiting for its pilot. One of us would be the modern Columbus.

I remember glancing around from face to face in that plane and thinking to myself that we could have been brothers. Cousins, anyway.

The ship had been built to exact specifications with regard to lift and mass, and there was only just so much room for the pilot. He had to fit into his cubicle like a machined part, which meant a maximum height and a maximum weight, but still nothing sacrificed in the way of strength and reflexes.

So we were all, all five of us, small, stern-bodied men with almost identical scholastic training behind us and almost identical psychological mechanisms inside us. The way we moved, the way we noticed things, even the way we talked—everything was remarkably, eerily similar. Especially considering that we'd each come from a different part of the country.

Any one of us would have been adequate. But the Moon ship had cost millions of dollars and nine years of painstaking construction. For that, they didn't want adequacy; they wanted the best that could be found.

We began talking to each other guardedly then, just before we landed at the Arizona Research Station. Not to make friends—hell, no!—but to get a line on relative weaknesses and strengths. Believe me, the differences were almost microscopic.

Stefano, for example. He had one more math course to his credit than I. Theory of Equations, I think it was—and how I bit my lip over skipping it for the sake of the Glee Club Tuesday afternoons! But it was on the record that he'd sprained his back in a high-school football game. Of course, the sprain was ancient history and long over with; still, it was on his record. How would *you* figure it?

And how would you figure, we wondered as we landed at the hot, dusty Station and were led right into our first testing complex, how would you weigh the balances of sexual involvement? McGuire was married, a newlywed, Caldicott and I were more or less engaged, while Stefano and Bresh were carefree characters who took what they could where they could.

One way, engagement, marriage, pointed to an adjusted emotional life—and adjustment rated high. And someone to return to might provide that extra bit of incentive where the chances of return were considered no higher than two out of three.

On the other hand, McGuire's wife, my Irene and Caldicott's Edna might be looked upon by the powers-that-were as so much psychological dead weight, so much extra responsibility and worry that the men involved had to carry. Stefano and Bresh, I could just hear some jowl-heavy individual in a white smock argue, had nothing to concentrate on but themselves and the ship.

I tell you, I began to get awfully moody and regretful about Irene. Fine, I'd say to myself, I love the girl. But did I have to go and get engaged?

Yet there was no way to figure. You didn't know how they'd rate it.

Once we got into the routine at the Station, though, there was very little time to worry. Morning after morning, we'd be dragged out of bed and, pushing our yawns in front of us, made to go through a round of tests. Afternoon after afternoon, we'd get particularized instruction in the handling and maintenance of the Moon ship and made to go through the motions in a dummy model. Evening after evening, there'd be a light supper followed by a dessert of more tests, checkup tests, validation tests, and recapitulation tests.

Over and over again, they tested us where they had tested us before, mentally, physically, psychologically, always probing for a hair's-breadth of difference, for a third decimal place of advantage.

And then, when we had reached the point where our reflexes had become edgy, where our dreams were eight hours' worth of raising, flying and landing the ship, where we chewed bread in the mess-hall with the certain feeling that somewhere a stopwatch must be recording, the pressure came off abruptly.

And the results were announced.

I was first, by a millimicron. Bresh was second, by the same distance. Then came McGuire, Caldicott and Stefano.

I was first!

I would pilot the first ship to the Moon! *I* would be the new Columbus! *I* would start the era of space travel!

We didn't know who had invented the first crude tool, who had taken the first bareback ride on a horse, but as long as human history endured, the name of the first man to leave Earth and land on another world would be celebrated. And it would be *my* name—Emanuel Mengild.

I felt like the ten-year-old kid who is suddenly told, all right, tomorrow he can go out West and become a cowboy—like the man lying on a flophouse bed who opens a telegram informing him he's just inherited a million dollars—like the cracklefingered, red-eyed seamstress who's invited to go out to Hollywood and become a film star. But much more than all of those, for someone of my generation and background, I would pilot the first Moon ship!

There were consolation prizes given out, too. If I dropped dead in the next week, or went crazy and refused to go, Bresh would be up. After him, of course, McGuire, Caldicott and Stefano, in that order. The way they looked at me!

When I got the order to report to Colonel Graves, the Commandant of the Station, I swaggered all the way into his office. I wasn't throwing any weight around. I just felt exactly that way.

Any time up to today that his eye fell on me, I'd pulled my shoulders back a little further, put a little extra snap into my step. As Commandant, he was a member of the testing board, and, for all I knew, the decisive one. There was always the possibility that he might notice me yawning a bit longer after breakfast than the others, that he might put that one extra question mark beside my name that would just make a vital difference.

But now! Now he was simply George Johnstown Graves, a superannuated rocket pilot from the old days when men had thought it exciting to climb high enough to see the Earth as a curving horizon beneath. He was courageous enough and smart enough and fast enough, but he'd been born a mite too early. For all his rank, he was just a Portuguese fisherman, while I—well, as I said, I was Columbus.

He was middle height, a bit taller than I, and he was leaning back in his swivel chair with his collar open, his sleeves rolled up and a funny, faraway look in his eyes which I interpreted as envy.

I sat down alertly in the chair he nodded at.

He said "Um" at the opposite wall, as if he were agreeing with it. Then he looked at me.

"Mengild," he said, "you're engaged, aren't you? A Miss Rass?"

"Yes, sir," I told him snappily. The five of us were all civilians, but we'd gotten in the habit of saying "sir" to everyone, even the people who made up our beds. How did you know who would be contributing to the final, crucial decision?

He glanced flittingly across his desktop. The desktop held a single folderful of papers, but closed. I had the impression that he'd memorized everything in the folder. "You've requested permission to have her enter the Station tonight on a four-hour civilian pass?"

I got a bit uncomfortable. "That's right, sir. When the results were posted, we were told we'd have a thirty-six-hour vacation from classes. We were told we could invite any one outsider to join us for this evening. I got in touch with Irene—Miss Rass— and she's flying down from Des Moines. I hope there's nothing wrong with—"

Colonel Graves shook his head sharply. "Nothing. Nothing wrong, Mengild. You don't expect to marry the lady before you take off, do you?"

"No-o-o. We'd pretty much set it up the other way, sir. That is, if I were picked and I got back in one piece, we'd do it the day I landed back on Earth. She sort of wanted to get married first, but I talked her out of it."

"She knows your chances of return in one piece are only slightly better than fifty percent?"

I felt relieved. I thought I understood what he was driving at. "Yes, sir. But she still wants me to go. She knows how I've grown up with the idea. Irene wouldn't want it any differently."

The colonel folded his hands under his chin and stared straight at me. "Miss Rass is a domestic type, isn't she? Wants the usual things—a home, babies, so on?"

"I guess so. She's a pretty normal girl."

"You want them, too?"

I looked off to one side and thought for a moment. "Well, sir, I've wanted one thing since I was a kid and another for the past three years—space flight and Irene. And whatever Irene wants in the way of a home, once I'm back, once I've made it, I guess I want that as well."

He examined the opposite wall again. When he got its opinion, he started talking at it in a low, soft voice. Didn't sound military at all.

"All right, I'll put it to you very briefly, Mengild. As you know, your engines are atomics and they have to be shielded. They are. Out in space, cosmic rays stream into the ship and it has to be shielded from them. It is. Thus far, except for a few unfortunate and preventable accidents, we've had no trouble on this matter. The shielding we've devised is good and it works. But this will be the longest trip that a man has taken under these conditions and the very latest poop from the lab is that the shielding, in all likelihood, will not be effective for its duration."

My lips suddenly weren't working too well. "Does this mean, sir, that—"

"It means that the pilot of the first Earth-Moon ship will probably be completely sterilized somewhere on the return journey. We could improve the shielding and no doubt will—in the future. To do it now would mean a long delay at best. At worst, it might mean completely redesigning and rebuilding the ship, which, as you know, has been figured for pretty close tolerances in terms of the equipment it can carry and the fuel it must carry. Our decision is therefore not to delay, but to put it up to the individual most concerned."

I thought it out for just a moment, for one emotion-churning moment. "I can give you my answer right now, sir. I've spent too much of my life dreaming of—"

He said "Um" to the wall once more. "Suppose you take twenty-four hours. We can wait till then. Talk it over with your girl, try to find out exactly how you feel."

"I *know* exactly how I feel, sir. There's nothing more important to me than this trip. And Irene will agree with me. If she doesn't—well, as I said, there's nothing more important than this trip. Why, do you think—do you think, sir, that after having come all this way, I'd let any risk, any risk at all, get in the way of my being the first man to make it to the Moon and back?"

You can imagine that I was pretty excited. But Colonel Graves knotted his tie and rolled down his sleeves and said firmly to the wall: "Suppose you take twenty-four hours, Mengild."

The moment I got out of his office, I understood what he meant. Irene was due tonight. I wasn't set to take off for close to three weeks. Plenty of time to get married, the way Irene had wanted to in the first place, and get a baby started.

Of course. That's what Colonel Graves had meant.

Bresh and McGuire were standing outside the administration building when I came down. They looked at me with carefully controlled eagerness.

"No," I told them, "it hasn't been suddenly discovered that my grandfather took sick on his first airplane ride. I still go."

Bresh socked his forehead with a thumb-knuckle, just under his spiky red hair. "Well," he grinned, "can you feel a heart murmur developing? Headaches? Vertigo?"

I pushed between the death watch with both hands, on my way to my quarters to shower and shave. I had to go through the same routine there with Caldicott and Stefano, although, being lower on the list, they were less grisly.

When Irene arrived at the gate in the sand-streaked taxi, I hauled her into my arms and let her soak there for a while. She looked so good, she felt so good!

We had a quickish snack at the recreation hall, while she filled me in on her mother's sciatica and her kid brother Lennie's art scholarship. Then she grabbed my hand and congratulated me on being selected for the Earth-Moon ship.

"Let me show you what it looks like," I suggested. "The next time you see it, it will be on the newscasts when I take off."

Irene glanced around as we left the rec hall. She pointed her little chin at the swarm of lab buildings rising in concrete squareness from the raw Arizona earth, at the guards pacing their intervals along the wire fence.

"Such a"—she thought for a moment—"such a *male* place."

I laughed. "What else should it be?"

She came in on the tail end of my laugh. "What else?" she repeated.

It was getting dark by the time we reached the ship. Irene gave a tiny and thoroughly feminine grunt of admiration. The ship stood on its tail, staring greedily, unswervingly at the enormous sky above. The lights from the station covered its sides with long thin glints and long thin shadows that seemed to be urging it to move, *move,* MOVE!

"The first one," she breathed. "And you're going to pilot it."

I figured it was exactly the right time. So I hoisted her up on the steps that led to the pilot's hatch, lit a cigarette for her—and started talking.

It took a surprisingly short time, even including the proposal. She had barely smoked one-third of the cigarette when I finished. But she kept on smoking the rest in quiet, long inhalations until it became a butt that burned her fingers and she had to throw it away.

I ground the butt into the sand and said, "Well?"

Her next words kind of astonished me. "Well what?"

"Well, we're going to get married, aren't we? Right away?"

"No, we're not," she said.

"Irene! But when I come back I may not be able to have children. You want to have children, don't you?"

A long pause. I wished it wasn't so dark: I couldn't see her face. "Yes, I want to have children. That's why we won't get married. Not before you go or after you come back."

I felt like saying *Oh, no!* I felt like grabbing her and squeezing her until she was my sensible, lovable, loving Irene again. Instead, I stepped back away from her. I gave up talking and thought for a while.

"Look," I said at last. "Correct me if I'm wrong. You knew the risks I was running when I volunteered for this flight and you were with me all the way. You knew what it meant to me. You were willing to take the chance that I might not come back, and that if I did, it would be in three separate paper bags. This business is just some more of the same."

"No, it isn't." I could tell from her voice that she was crying. "I wasn't happy about the risks, but I knew you had to do it. You've been preparing for this moment since you were a little boy. But this—this is different, Mannie."

"*How* is it different? *How?*"

She wiped the sniffles off her nose-tip. "It's different, that's all. Maybe a man just can't understand these things. But it's different, altogether different for a woman."

"Baby, darling," I said, trying to take her in my arms, but she made a little away movement and I stopped. "I *want* to have a child. I want to have a child with *you*. Will you please tell me why we can't get married tonight, tomorrow, as soon as we can, and start a baby?"

"Suppose I don't get pregnant before you leave? And if I do—suppose I have a miscarriage?"

"Listen, Irene," I told her desperately. "In my position, we could have the best doctors in the world taking care of you. And if anything went wrong, we could adopt a baby. I know it isn't the same, but for all we know, one of us might be sterile to begin with! Lots of couples adopt babies and they're happy."

"Oh, Mannie, it wouldn't be the same thing with us, not if we started out this way. Besides, miscarriages, that sort of thing, that's not the real reason."

I put my fists on my hips and shoved my face close to hers. "Well, will you kindly stop all this, woman, and *tell* me the real reason?"

She asked me for another cigarette. I lit it up and handed it to her.

"Mannie, I don't know if you can understand this, but I'll try. I wouldn't want to limit my childbearing powers in advance. And—I wouldn't want to marry a man who would deliberately give up his ability to become a father. He'd never be completely a man to me."

That took some absorption. "What would you think of a man," I asked slowly, "who gave up his ability to make the kind of trip I've been offered? Would *he* be completely a man?"

"I don't *know*," she said, crying again. "But I don't think they're the same thing. I don't—I don't—and that's all!"

"But that's what you're asking me to do, Irene," I pointed out. "You're asking me to give up a dream that I've had since I was a—"

"I'm not asking you to do a single thing, Emanuel Mengild! I'm only telling you what I can and can't do. *I*, not *you*. You—*you* can go straight up in a rocket!"

And that's where we left it. I walked her back, walked her around, and, when her time was up, I walked her to the gate. We didn't hug when she left; we didn't even blow kisses at each other. I just stared after the cab until it sand-clouded around a big boulder and disappeared.

Then I walked myself around.

One way to look at it: I was in one Earth-Moon trip and out one woman. Rack up Fame and Fortune, scratch Family.

One way to look at it.

Another way: I could get mad at Irene for failing me at a crucial moment, for leaving when the going got rough. I got mad.

Then I got over it.

After all, I could see her point. It *wasn't* the same for a man as for a woman. A man had his work, his achievement; a woman had children. A woman grew up with the dream of kids the way I'd grown up with the dream of the stars. It wasn't the same for a man.

But wasn't it? I began to realize, walking myself around and around in a plodding, sweaty circle, how much I had counted on Irene to come through for me. I wanted kids—only I'd never said to myself two kids, five kids. I'd settle for one.

But *no* kids? Ever?

I'd taken it for granted, I now understood, when Colonel Graves had hit me with the problem, that Irene loved me enough to marry me right away and cancel out the chance of having no family. That's why I'd been so sure. That had been the little nubbin of security nestling comfortably at the back of my mind.

This, now, was a different matter.

It had taken a couple of billion years to produce me. In that couple of billion years, I had millions upon millions of ancestors. Slime-like ancestors, jelly-like ancestors, water-breathing ancestors, air-breathing ancestors, ancestors that floated, that swam, that crawled, that ran, that climbed, that finally walked. And all those ancestors, no matter how different, had one thing in common.

They had survived long enough to have descendants. Other species didn't and their lines were extinct, bare bones in rock strata. But no matter how scarce food got, no matter what enemies they faced, what unprecedented natural upheavals they had to adjust to, *my* ancestors somehow managed to pull through and have offspring. That's how I happen to be here.

If I didn't carry on, all their effort would come to nothing: I would be a biological dead-end. They might just as well not have bothered.

But that was only part of it, I decided, coming to the gate for the tenth time and starting off again.

What was it all about, for example? What was I here for? What was good, what was bad, what was right, what was wrong? What in the world was I sure of, with all my studies, with all my aspirations, with all my attitudes? Very damn little.

But while life continued, there was a chance of finding out, of getting a little closer, all the time a little closer. And my kind of life—me—could only find out if it went on.

It was like, I decided, my entering this competition for the Moon ship. I'd entered it partly because I wanted to very badly, but also because I felt I was the right man. I possessed inside me, I believed, the values necessary to make that difficult attempt which would initiate the age of interplanetary travel. Well, relative to life, I felt I was the right man, too. Both were conceits, but they were *fundamental* conceits. If I felt I was good enough, of value enough, I could not withdraw my entry.

That got me to the Moon ship. Life wasn't just reproduction—not human life. Life was achievement, too. Mankind pushed its collective nose past barrier after barrier, because one of its component individuals just *had* to, whether or not he reproduced. And I lived in a time of a major barrier and it had fallen to my lot to do the pushing. Wasn't that more important than children?

On the other hand, I couldn't fool myself—any of the other four men who had come out to the Station with me could do the job as well as I. And if this ship didn't make it, another would. I wasn't that necessary.

But I *wanted* to be.

So there I was, back again. I waved to the guard at the gate and kept going. By now, I'd worn a path for myself.

My mouth felt as if it were full of big teardrops that had fallen out of my eyes when I reported to Colonel Graves the next morning. He stared at my face with a good deal of interest as I sat down.

"It wasn't so easy, was it, Mengild?"

"No, sir," I told him unhappily, "it wasn't. But I've made up my mind. And I'll stick to the decision."

He waited.

"I've decided—maybe I'll regret this for the rest of my life, but, as I said, I stick by it—I've decided not to go."

"Um. The sterilization business?"

"Yes, sir."

"I take it the young lady said no."

I wiped my face with my wet handkerchief and shrugged. "She said no, all right, but that wasn't it. I thought it over all night and this is my personal decision—I'd rather have children than have the Moon ship."

He rocked back and forth in his chair. "You know, Mengild, there's such a thing as artificial insemination. And you still could be the father by being a donor before the take-off."

"I can see myself," I muttered, "running around with a test tube in my hand, trying to get women to marry me."

"Well, when you put it that way, I'll admit it isn't too romantic. However, there *are* women who would. Remember, Mengild, you'd be a hero, one of the greatest heroes of all time."

"Suppose it worked," I challenged. "Suppose I got married—to one of those women who would—and she were artificially inseminated and I were the father—what then if there were miscarriages? Or abnormal births? The frozen spermatozoa don't remain viable more than a year or two. But that's only part of it, sir. The rest would be that I had voluntarily and forever risked the chance of never becoming an ancestor. I've decided I don't want to."

Colonel Graves stood up. "Your business. And your decision. Certainly. I made these suggestions because, frankly, we would rather have you pilot the ship. You're a shade better than anyone else who competed with you. That would mean a shade better chance for the ship to get to the Moon and return. We want very much to have it return."

They offered the job to the next man in line and he jumped at it. They told him the problem and he laughed. They told him to take twenty-four hours to think it over, and he did, and he came back and said he still wanted to go. Bresh, of course.

He took off three weeks later, landed on the Moon and returned safely to one of the greatest and most heroic receptions ever. That's why we celebrate Paul Bresh Day all over the Solar System. That's why you reporters are here today for some of the usual human-interest fill-in material.

And I can't tell you anything more than I've told you before.

No, that's not so. There's a new item.

As you know, I never married Irene. I married Frances, a year later, when I got the maintenance crew job. That's all I've ever done for interplanetary travel—keep the ships in good shape for the flight into space. I've made a good living, even made a name for myself as a ground-crew chief. Now, naturally, I'm retired.

I do regret that I never made a space flight when I was younger. Too old now, heart too weak, to be allowed even on one of those luxury passenger liners.

Not like Paul Bresh. Besides making the first flight to the Moon in history, he was a member of the Second Exploratory Party to Mars; the time he sort of wandered off into the desert and was never heard of again.

Me? All I have now is my son David and his wife in New Quebec on Mars, my daughter Ann and her family on Ganymede, my daughter Mildred and her family on Titan, and—oh, yes, the new item.

I got word last week that when the first starship lifted from Pluto on its way to Alpha Centauri, my grandson Aaron and his wife Phyllis were aboard. The trip will take thirty years, they tell me, so I'll probably have a great-grandson born on the way.

There it is, my side of the story. That's what I got out of it. Maybe I didn't become the new Columbus, but I'm an ancestor. Paul Bresh has his day. I have my millennia.

AFTERWORD

Among the stories I have written, this is one of my favorites—although it is a failure basically as a piece of science fiction.

That is, if science fiction is seen, as it is by most of the great unwashed and literary, as simply predictive, "The Dark Star" fails miserably. It's what you might call a story that's been *undated* or *dedated:* that is, now the events described in it can absolutely never happen. We've been to the moon ("one small step..." and all the rest of that P.R.-crafted crap), *and* returned, *and* decided not have a space age, after all, at least not in our lifetimes. No sterilized Columbus of space, and damn few of the glorious exploratory episodes that were supposed to occur after the Columbus of space had done his historical job.

Of course, if you are willing to be very charitable you might point to a few things. You might, for example, murmur that the moon landing in this story is actually to be understood as a Mars-ship landing or starship landing some time in the years yet to come—as H.G. Wells's 1898 *The War of the Worlds* is not to be jeered at today as an impossible attack from a Mars that could not exist, but rather a possible prophecy of an invasion yet to come from an ancient planet orbiting Alpha Centauri or Rigel or Sirius. And if you wanted to be very, very nice, you might even remember that *after* "The Dark Star" was published, those in charge of Projects Mercury and Gemini were quite careful to send out publicity releases emphasizing that all of the projected astronauts were already fathers.

(For that matter, Isaac Asimov once wrote a delightful essay, titled "The Lovely Lost Seas of Luna," about many good pieces of science fiction that the march of science and learning had now made impossible to read with a necessary suspension of disbelief...)

And, listen, if you didn't want to be either charitable or nice, you might just let me tell you that I enjoyed writing this story and even (this is rare for me) enjoyed reading it once it was published. Yet I am, after all these years, more than slightly startled at the amount of what we would now call "sexism" in this innocent little 1957 fable, and more than a little baffled at why I found it so important to include so many secret references to one of my siblings and even a sibling-in-law.

But it *is* a good story, damn it, with all of these problems, with all of these questions— and, for once, I'm not afraid to stick my chin out and say so. I feel excessively tender toward it.

WRITTEN 1957——PUBLISHED 1957

Consulate

I see by the papers where Professor Fronac says that interplanetary travel will have to go through what he calls a period of incubation. He says that after reaching the Moon, we now have hit so many new problems that we must sit down and puzzle out new theories to fit them before we can build a ship that will get us to Venus or Mars.

Of course, the Army and Navy are supervising all rocket experiments these days, and the professor's remarks are censored by them. That makes his speeches hard to understand.

But you know and I know what Professor Fronac is really saying,

The Second Martian Expedition was a complete flop. Just like the First Martian Expedition and the Venusian ones. The ships came back with all the machinery working fine and all the crews grinning with health.

But they hadn't been to Mars. They couldn't make it.

The professor goes on to say how wonderful it is that science is so wonderful, because no matter how great the obstacles, the good old scientific approach will eventually overcome them. This, he claims, is the drawing of unprejudiced conclusions from all the data available.

Well, if that's what Professor Fronac really believes, he sure didn't act like it last August when I went all the way to Arizona to tell him just what he'd been doing wrong in those latest rocket experiments. Let me tell you, even if I am only a small-town grocer and he's a big physics professor with a Nobel Prize under his belt, he had no call to threaten me with a jail sentence just because I slipped past the Army guards at the field and hid in his bedroom! I was there only because I wanted to tell him he was on the wrong track.

If it hadn't been for poor old Fatty Myers and that option on the Winthrop store which he's going to lose by Christmas, I'd have walked out on the whole business right then and kept my mouth shut. After all, it's no skin off my nose if we never go any further than the Moon. I'm happier right here on *terra firma,* and I do mean *firma.* But, if I convince scientists, maybe I'll convince Edna.

So, for the last time, Professor Fronac and anybody else who's interested—if you really want to go places in the Solar System, you have to come down here to Massachusetts. You have to take a boat out on Cassowary Cove at night, every night, and wait. I'll help if you act halfway decent—and I'm sure Fatty Myers will do what he can—but it'll still add up to a whole lot of patience. Shoin wasn't dreefed in a riz. So they say.

Fatty had just told his assistant to take charge of the gas station that evening in March and walked slowly past the Winthrop store up to my grocery window. He waited till my wife was busy with a customer; then he caught my eye and pointed at his watch.

I shucked off my apron and pulled the heavy black sweater over my head. I had my raincoat in one hand and my fishing tackle in the other, and was just tiptoeing out when Edna saw me.

She came boiling around the counter and blocked the door with her right arm. "And where do you think you're going and leaving me to do the work of two?" she asked in that special sin-chasing voice she saves for my tiptoeing moments.

"Aw, Edna!" I said, trying to work up a grin. "I told you. Fatty's bought a new thirty-foot sloop he wants me to make sure will be in shape for the tourist trade this summer. It's dangerous for one man to sail a new boat alone at night."

"It's twice as dangerous for him with you along." She glared the grin off my face. "For the past thirty years, ever since we graduated from school, one unfailing recipe for trouble has been Paul Garland and Fatty Myers doing anything together. I still haven't forgotten the time he came over to help you install the new gas heater in our basement. You were in the hospital for five weeks and the street still looks crooked."

"The flashlight went out, Edna, and Fatty just struck a match to—"

"And what about the time, Mr. Garland," Louisa Capek, the customer, hit me from behind, "that you and Mr. Myers volunteered to shingle the church roof and fell through it on top of the minister? For eight Sundays he had to deliver sermons with his back in a cast and every one of them 'answering a fool according to his folly'!"

"How were we to know the beams were rotten? We volunteered for the job."

"You're not going, and that's final," Edna came in fast with the finisher. "So you might as well get that sweater off and the apron back on and start uncrating those cans of sardines. The two of you out on Cassowary Cove at night in a sailboat might bring on anything, including a tidal wave."

I gave Fatty the high sign, and he opened the door and squeezed in just as we had agreed he'd do in case I had trouble getting away.

"Hello, Edna and Miss Capek," he said in that cheerful belly-voice of his. "Every time I see how beautiful you look, Edna, I could kick myself around town for letting Paul steal you away from me. Ready, Paul? Paul and I are going to do a spot of fishing tonight. Maybe we can bring a nice four-pound fish back to you. Do you think you could fit it into one of those pots I gave you last Christmas, hey?"

My wife cocked her head and studied him. "Well, I think I could. But you won't be out past midnight?"

"Have him back by eleven—word of honor," Fatty promised as he grabbed me and squeezed back through the doorway.

"Remember, Paul!" Edna called after me. "Eleven o'clock! And you needn't come home if you're ten minutes late!"

That's the kind of pal Fatty was. Any wonder that I knock myself out trying to get this story told where it'll do the most good? Of course, he and Edna had been kind of sweet on each other back in school and it had been nip and tuck between us which one she'd marry. No one knew till we both got drunk at Louisa Capek's birthday party that we'd settled the problem. Fatty and I, by each catching a frog out of the creek and jumping them. Mine jumped the furthest—nine and a half feet—so I got Edna. Fatty stayed single and got fatter.

While he was starting the car, Fatty asked me what I thought of the Winthrop store as a buy for nine thousand. The Winthrop store was a big radio and electrical gadget place between my grocery and Fatty's corner service station.

I told him I thought it was a good buy for nine thousand if anyone who had the money wanted such a place.

"Well, *I* want it, Paul. I just paid old man Winthrop five hundred dollars for an option until Christmas. Between what I have in the bank and a mortgage I think I can raise on my service station, I'll have the rest. It's the coming thing in the new age."

"What's the coming thing in what new age?"

"All those scientific gadgets. The Army has just announced it's established a base on the Moon and they're going to equip it with a radio transmitter. Think of it, Paul! In a little while, we'll be getting TV broadcasts from the Moon! Then, we'll be tuning in on the latest news from Mars and Venus, the latest exploration on Mercury, the latest discovery on Pluto. People will be crazy to buy the new sets they'll need to receive that distance, kids'll be fooling around with all the new gimmicks that'll be coming out because of the inventions interplanetary travel will develop."

I watched the countryside get dark as we bounced along toward the cove. "Meanwhile, we don't have interplanetary travel. All we have is the Moon, and it don't look as if we're going further. Did you read about the Second Venusian Expedition coming back after they got two million miles out? The same thing's happened to them before, and we can't seem to make Mars either."

Fatty slapped the wheel impatiently. His jalopy swerved off the road and almost hit a fence post. "So what? They keep trying, don't they? Don't forget, the Fronac Drive's only been around for two years, and all scientists agree that, with the Drive, we can eventually go anywhere in the Solar System—maybe even to the stars after a while. It's just a matter of perfecting it, of getting the kinks out. We'll reach the planets, and in our lifetimes too. How do you know what kind of crazy problems they run into two or three million miles from the Earth?"

Naturally, I had to admit I didn't know. All the newspapers had said was that both the First Martian and the two Venusian Expeditions had "experienced difficulties and been forced to return." I shut up and tried to think out another argument. That's all it was: the argument for me, and a business proposition for Fatty Myers. If you remember, back in March, the newspapers and magazines were still full of feature articles on "the expanding empire of man."

We reached the cove and Fatty locked his car. The sloop was all ready to go, as we'd fixed her up the night before. When we shoved off, she handled like a dream that Lipton might have had as a boy. She was gaff-rigged, but not too broad of beam so that we couldn't run a little if we wanted to. Fatty handled the tiller and I crewed. That way, we only needed ballast forward.

Neither of us were crazy about fishing. We'd made that up as an excuse for Edna. Sailing in the moonlight in the great, big loneliness of Cassowary Cove, with the smells of the Atlantic resting quietly around us—that was all the wallop we wanted.

"But suppose," I said, as soon as I'd trimmed sail, "suppose we got to Venus and there's a kind of animal there that finds us more appetizing than chili con carne. And suppose they're smarter than we are and have disintegrators and heat-rays like that fellow described in the story. And the minute they see us, they'll yell, 'Oh, boy—rations!' and come piling down on Earth.

"That'll do your business a lot of good, won't it? Why, when we get through driving them back off the planet, won't be a man or woman who'll be able to think of interplanetary travel without spitting. I go along with Reverend Pophurst: we shouldn't poke our noses into strange places where they were never meant to go or we'll get them bitten off."

Fatty thought a while and patted his stomach with his free hand like he always does when I score a good point. Most folks in town don't know it, but Fatty and I usually get so lathered up in arguments just before Election Day, that we always vote opposite tickets, no matter what.

"First place, if we hit animals smart enough to have disintegrators and such-like when we don't have them, *and* if they want this planet, they're going to take it away from us, and no movie hero in a tight jumper and riding boots is going to stop them at the last minute by discovering that the taste of pickled beets kills 'em dead. If they're smarter than we are and have more stuff, we'll be licked, that's all. We just won't be around any more, like the dinosaur. Second place, didn't you read Professor Fronac's article in last week's *Sunday Supplement*? He says there can't be any smarter animals— Say! What'd you call that? There, over to starboard?"

I turned and looked off to the right.

Where a streak of moonlight grinned on the water between the lips of the cove, something green and bulbous was coming in fast. It looked like the open top of an awfully big umbrella. I judged it to be thirty-five, forty feet across. It was floating straight for Mike's Casino on the southern lip where lights were blazing, music was banging, and people generally were having themselves a whale of a time.

"Seaweed," I guessed. "Bunch of seaweed all scrunched up in an ice-jam. Jam melted or broke up and it comes floating down here in one lump."

"Never saw that much seaweed in these parts." Fatty squinted at it. "Nor in that shape. And that bunch *came* into this cove; it didn't float in. The ocean's too quiet for it to have so much speed. Know what I think it is?"

"The first summer tourist?"

"No! A Portuguese man-of-war. They're jellyfish. They have a bladder, kind of, that floats on the surface, and long filaments underneath that trail into the water and catch fish. I've read about them but never expected to see one. Pretty rare around here. And that's a real big fellow. Want to take a look?"

"Not on your life! It may be dangerous. Besides, this is the first time in a month Edna's let me go out with you. She doesn't know exactly what's going to happen, but she's sure *something* is. I want to be home safe and sound by eleven. What were you saying about smarter animals, Fatty? On other planets?"

"It can't be dangerous," he muttered, still keeping his eyes on its track. "Only catches very small fish. But— Like I was saying, if there was something on Neptune, say, which is more advanced than we are, why then it'd be smart enough to have space travel and they'd be visiting us instead of us them. Look how we've explored our planet. We've gone down into the ground nine miles and more, across every sea and into every ocean, back and forth over every piece of land, and now up into the air. If there was another kind of intelligent life on this Earth, we'd know it by now. Aliens with space travel would do the same. So, like Professor Fronac says, we must conclude— Am I wrong, or is that man-of-war coming at us now?"

It was. The green mass had turned in a great, rippling circle and was headed for our sloop, but fast.

Fatty slammed the tiller hard to starboard and I leaped for the sails. They went slack.

"What a time for the wind to drop!" he moaned. "There's a pair of emergency oars in the— Too late, it's abreast! You'll find a hatchet in the cockpit. See if you can—"

"I thought you said it wasn't dangerous," I puffed, as I scrambled back with the hatchet.

Fatty had dropped the tiller and picked up a marlin-spike. He stood up next to me and stared at the floating mound alongside. Both it and our boat seemed to be perfectly still. We could see water rushing past us. Far off, in Mike's Casino, the band was playing "Did Your Mother Come from Ireland?" I stopped being sad and got sentimental. That song always makes me sentimental.

"It isn't dangerous," Fatty admitted. "But I just remembered that the Portuguese man-of-war has batteries of stingers that it uses to catch fish. They can hurt a man sometimes, too. And in anything this big— Of course, we're inside a boat and it can't get at us."

"You hope. Something tells me that I won't be home at eleven tonight. And if that's just supposed to be an air-filled bladder, what are those black things floating in it? Eyes?"

"They sure look like eyes. *Feel* like eyes." We watched the black dots flickering over the green surface and began to shuffle our feet. We felt as if a crowd of people were watching us undress in Courthouse Square. I know we both did, because we compared notes later. We had plenty of time—later.

"Know what?" Fatty said. "I don't think it's a Portuguese man-of-war, after all. It's too big and green, and I don't remember seeing anything like those black dots inside the air bladder in any of those pictures I saw. And it doesn't seem to have any filaments hanging from it. Besides, it moves too fast."

"Then what is it?"

Fatty patted his stomach and looked at it. He opened his mouth.

I forgot to ask him what he was going to say just then, and he never told me. He didn't say it anyway. He just went "Beep?" and sat down hard. I also sat down hard, only I went more like "Foof?"

The sloop had gone straight up in the air for about fifteen feet. As soon as I could, I jumped up and helped Fatty wheeze to a standing position.

We both gulped. The gulps seemed to get stuck going down.

Even though we were fifteen feet above the surface of the cove, the boat was still in the water. A little cup of water, that is, extending twenty feet out on both port and starboard and only about five feet on the bow and stern.

Beyond the water, there was a kind of gray haze that was transparent enough for me to see the lights of Mike's Casino where they were still playing "Did Your Mother Come from Ireland?" This gray haze went all the way around, covering the mast and the gaff tops.

When we rushed over to the side and looked down, we saw it came around under the keel too. Solid stuff, that gray haze—it contained us, the boat and enough water to float it.

Somebody had taken an awfully big bite out of Cassowary Cove, and we were included. We knew who that somebody was. We looked around for him.

The big slob was busy outside the gray haze. First, he was under the keel, fastening a little box to the bottom of the haze. Then he squirmed around to the top, directly over the mast, and stuck another doohickey up there. Those little black dots were still bubbling around inside his green body, but they didn't make me feel queer any more.

I had other things to feel queer about. "Do you think we might try yelling at him?" Fatty asked in the kind of whisper he uses in church. "Whatever he is, he looks intelligent."

"What could you yell?"

He scratched his head. "I dunno. How about, 'Friend. Me friend. No hurt. Peace.' Think he'd understand?"

"He'd think you were an Indian in the movies, that's what. Why should you think he understands English? Let's drop our weapons and raise both our hands. That gesture's universal, I read."

We kept our hands over our heads until they got tired. The lump of green jelly had moved from the box he had fixed over the mast to a position in line with the slant of the gaff. He boiled around for a few seconds until a section of the gray haze began to sparkle with color, a lot of colors, shifting in and out of each other. Then, as soon as the patch was coruscating nicely, he dropped off the side and hit the water fifteen feet below.

He hit the water without a splash.

He zoomed along the surface, faster than I could breathe my own initials, for about half a mile, paused just outside the cove—and dropped out of sight. There wasn't a ripple to show the path he'd been traveling, or where he'd sunk. All that was left was our floating gray bubble. With us inside.

"Hey!" Fatty began yammering. "You can't do this to me! Come back and let us out, d'ye hear? Hey, you in that green jelly, come back here!"

I got him quiet by pointing out that the animated shrimp cocktail was no longer with us. Also, there didn't seem much cause for worry. If he'd wanted to do us any harm, he could pretty much have done it while he was close up, considering the brand of parlor tricks he had already demonstrated. Let well enough alone, I argued; I was satisfied to be alive and unwell, while the bubble-blowing object did a Weismuller somewhere in the Atlantic.

"But we can't stay here all night," Fatty complained. "Suppose someone from town could see us—why, with our reputation, they'd laugh us clear into the comic strips. Whyn't you shinny up the mast and stick an arm into that stuff, Paul? Find out what it's made of, maybe make a hole and wriggle through?"

That sounded reasonable. We sure had to do something. He bent down and gave me a boost. I wrapped my legs around the mast, grabbed handfuls of sail and dragged myself to the top. The mast ended just under the box outside of the gray haze.

"There's a purring noise coming from the box," I called down to Fatty. "Nothing inside it but silver wheels going round and round like the one in an electric meter. Only they're not attached to anything. They're floating at all kinds of angles to each other and spinning at different speeds."

I heard Fatty curse uncertainly, and I punched up into the grayness. I hurt my fist. I pulled my arm back, massaged it as my feet slipped, scrambled on the mast and sail, and stabbed up with a forefinger. I hurt my forefinger.

"Gray stuff hard?" Fatty asked.

Unprintably unprintable it was hard. I told him.

"Come on down and get the hatchet. You might be able to chop a hole."

"I don't think so. This fog is almost transparent and I don't think it's made of any material we know. Fact is, I don't think it's made of any material."

Above my head, the purring got a little louder. There was a similar noise coming from the bottom of the bubble where the other box was located.

I took a chance and, holding myself by one arm and one leg, I swung out and peered at the spot of shifting color near the box. It looked like the spectrum you see in an oil puddle—you know, colors changing their position while you look at them. I pushed up against the gray near the colored patch. It didn't give either.

The nasty thing was I had the feeling that it wasn't like trying to push a hole through a sheet of steel; it was more as if I were trying to drive a nail into an argument, or break a sermon across my knee. Kind of a joke in a scary sort of way.

"Hand up the hatchet," I called. "I don't see how it'll do any good, but I'll try it anyway."

Fatty lifted the hatchet high and stood up on his toes. I started to slide down the mast. The purring from the box became a whine.

Just as my stretching fingers closed around the hatchet handle, the box on top and the box on the bottom of the boat began going *clinkety-clangety-clung*. It reached *clung* and I was no longer doing it to the mast. I was on top of Fatty and he was spread-eagled on the deck.

I had a glimpse of the hatchet sailing over the side.

"Wh-what f-for you wanted to d-do th-that," Fatty gasped as I rolled off him and we both groaned upright. "C-couldn't you tell me you w-wanted to get down fast? I'd have moved away, honest!"

"Wasn't my fault," I said. "I was pushed."

Fatty wasn't listening. He was staring at something else. And, when I noticed it, so was I.

A lot of sea-water had splashed into the cockpit. Some of it had wet us.

All of the water on deck rolled into a little lake abaft of the mast, the water on our bodies dripping down and joining it. Then, the entire puddle rolled to port and spilled off the deck. The boat was perfectly dry again. So were we.

"This I'm beginning not to like," Fatty commented hoarsely. I nodded my head, too. Under the circumstances I didn't feel easy in my mind.

Stepping very delicately, as if he were afraid he might fracture a commandment, Fatty moved over to the side and looked out. He shook his head and looked down.

"Paul," he said after a while in a low voice. "Paul, would you come here? Something I—" he choked.

I took a look. I gulped, one of those really long gulps that start down from your Adam's apple and wind up squishing out between your toes.

Below us, under the water and the gray haze, was a slew of darkness. Beyond that, at a respectable distance, I could see the Atlantic Ocean and the New England coastline with Cape Cod hooking out its small, bent finger. New England was moving away fast and became the eastern seaboard of the United States even as I watched.

The moonlight gave it a sort of unhealthy dimness, just enough to make out details and recognize the North and South American continents when they grew out of the eastern seaboard. The western coast was a little dark and blurry, but it made me homesick for the days when Fatty and Edna and I sat next to a map looking just like that in school.

Right then, I couldn't think of anything more absolutely enjoyable than standing near Edna in the grocery while she nagged the ears off me.

"That's what happened," Fatty was whimpering. "That's why we fell and the water jumped into the boat. We just shot up in a straight line suddenly and we're still traveling—us, the sloop, and enough water to float the whole business. We're inside a gray ball that isn't made of anything and which we can't break out of even if we still wanted to."

"Take it easy. Fatty, and we'll be all right," I told him with all the assurance of a bank robber trying to explain to the policeman who caught him that he was only trying to deposit his gun in the vault and the cashiers misunderstood him.

We sat down heavily in the cockpit and Fatty automatically grabbed the tiller. He sighed and shook his head.

"I feel just like a package being sent some place." He gestured up towards the spot of changing color. "And that's the label. Please do not open until Christmas."

"What is it, do you think? An invasion from another planet?"

"And we're the first battle? Don't be silly, Paul. Although it could be, at that. We could be a sample being sent back to headquarters to give them an idea of how tough a nut Earth might be. The careless, offhand way that green whatnot acted is what gripes me! It was as if he was going after Mike's Casino first and then decided to take us because we were closer, or because our disappearance would attract less notice than a night-club's. But either way it didn't matter much. He did it and went back home, or—"

"I can still hear Mike's Casino. At least I can hear the band playing 'Did Your Mother Come from Ireland?' "

Fatty slanted his big, loose face at the mast. "I hear it too. But it's coming from that box with the wheels up there. This whole thing is so crazy, Paul: I'm beginning to think that creature knew it was your favorite song and fixed the box to play it all the time. So you'd be more comfortable, kind of. Like the glow we have inside the bubble to provide us with light. He wants the package to arrive in good condition."

"A space-going jukebox," I muttered.

There was a longish bit of silence after that. We sat and watched the stars go by. I tried to make out the Big Dipper but it must have been lost in the shuffle, or maybe its position was different up here. The Moon was shrinking off to port, so I decided we weren't going there. Not that it made much difference. But at least there was an Army base on the Moon and I've seen enough western films to have great confidence in the United States Army—at least in the cavalry part. The sun wasn't a pleasant sight from empty space.

The funny thing is that neither of us were really frightened. It was partly the suddenness with which we'd been wrapped up and mailed, partly the care that was being taken of us. Inside the bubble there was a glow like broad daylight, strong enough to read by.

Fatty sat and worried about the option on the Winthrop store he'd lose if he didn't pick it up in time. I figured out explanations for Edna on why I didn't make it home by eleven. The box on top and the box on the bottom hummed and mumbled. The sloop maintained the position it had originally had in Cassowary Cove, perfectly steady in the water. Every once in a while, Fatty bit a fingernail and I tied a shoelace.

No, we weren't really frightened—there didn't seem to be anything solid enough to get frightened about, sitting in a sailboat out there with trillions of tiny lights burning all around. But we sure would have given our right arms clear up to our left hands for a sneak preview of the next act.

"One consolation, if you can call it that," Fatty said. "There's some sort of barrier two or three million miles from the Earth and this contraption may not be able to get past it. The papers don't say exactly what the spaceships hit out here, but I gathered it was something that stopped them cold, but didn't smash them and allowed them to turn and come back. Something like—like—"

"Like the stuff this gray bubble is made of," I suggested. We stared at each other for a few minutes, then Fatty found an unbitten nail on one of his fingers and took care of it, and I tied both my shoelaces.

We got hungry. There was nothing in our pockets that could be eaten. That made us hungrier.

Fatty lumbered over to the side and looked down into the water. "Just as I thought. Hey, Paul, break out your fishing tackle. There's a mackerel swimming around under the boat. Must have been caught up with us."

"Fishing'll take too long. I'll net it." I undressed, grabbed my landing net. "There's not much water and he won't have maneuvering space. But what about a fire? If we try to cook it, won't we use up the air?"

He shook his head, "Nope. We've been in long enough for the air to foul if it wasn't being changed. It's as fresh as ever. Whatever that machinery is up there, it's not only tooling us along at a smart clip and playing 'Did Your Mother Come from Ireland?' for your special benefit, but it's also pumping fresh air in and stale air out. And if you ask me where it gets oxygen and nitrogen in empty space—"

"I wouldn't dream of it," I assured him.

As soon as I spied the mackerel, a small one, less than a foot long, I stepped into the water and went for it with the net. I'm a pretty good underwater swimmer.

Pretty good, but the mackerel was better. More practice. I felt silly caroming off the keel and gray haze while the fish dodged all around me. After a while, he got positively insulting. He actually swam backward, facing me, just out of reach of the net.

I came to the surface, swallowed air, and climbed back aboard.

"He's too spry," I began. "I'll get my fishing gear and—"

I stopped. I was back in the gulping groove again.

Fatty was sitting in the cockpit, looking as if he had sat down suddenly. In front of him there was a flock of plates, six glasses and two snowy napkins on which rested assorted knives, forks and spoons.

There were two glasses of water, two glasses of milk and two glasses of beer. The plates were filled with food: grapefruit, soup, beefsteak, French fried potatoes, green peas, and—for dessert—ice cream. Enough for two. Our dream meal.

"It came from the box above," Fatty told me as I dressed with clumsy fingers. "I heard a click and looked up. There was this stuff floating down in single file. They distributed themselves evenly as they hit the deck."

"At least they feed you well."

Fatty grimaced at me. "You know where else you get served a meal with everything your heart desires."

Well, we unwrapped the cutlery and ate. What else could we do? The food was delicious, perfectly cooked. The drinks and the ice cream were cold, the grapefruit was chilled. When we finished, there was another click. First, three cigars that I remembered smoking at Louisa Capek's birthday party and liking more than any others I'd ever had, then, a plug of Fatty Myers's favorite chaw appeared. When the matches breezed down, we had stopped shrugging our shoulders. Fatty talked to himself a little, though.

I was halfway through the first cigar when Fatty heaved himself upright. "Got an idea."

He picked up a couple of plates and heaved them over the side. We both stood and watched them sink. Just before they got to the bottom—they disappeared. Like that. About two feet away from the lower box.

"So that's what happens to the waste."

"What?" I asked him.

He glared at me. "That."

We got rid of the rest of the service in the same way. On Fatty's suggestion we kept the knives. "We might need weapons when we arrive where—where we're going. Characters there might want to dissect us, or torture information out of us about Earth."

"If they can pull this kind of stuff, do you think we can stop them?" I wanted to know. "With knives that they made up for us out of empty emptiness?"

But we kept the knives.

We also kept the mackerel. For a pet. If we were going to be fed this as a steady diet, who wanted mackerel? There were only the three of us in that bubble and we felt we all had to stick together. The mackerel felt it too, for he began swimming up near the surface whenever we came close to the side. We became pretty good friends, and I fed him the bait I'd brought along—free.

About four hours later—it may have been five, because neither Fatty nor I had watches—the box clicked and the same meal wafted down with all the fixings. We ate some and threw the rest overboard.

"You know," Fatty said, "if it weren't for that 'Did Your Mother Come from Ireland?' playing over and over, I could almost be enjoying myself."

"Yeah. I'm getting tired of it myself. But would you rather be listening to 'I'm Forever Blowing Bubbles'?"

The Earth was just a shrinking, shining disk but neither of us could resist grabbing a fast look at it, now and then. It meant my grocery and Edna, Fatty's service station and his option on the Winthrop store. Home, 'mid planets and galaxies…

We got sleepy and pulled down the sails, which weren't being overwhelmingly useful at the time. We rolled them up into a sort of mattress and, together with some blankets Fatty had in the cockpit, made ourselves a fairish bed.

When we woke out of a mutual nightmare in which Fatty and I were being dissected by a couple of oyster stews, there were two complete steak dinners on deck. That is, two for me and two for Fatty. We had a grapefruit and a glass of milk apiece and got rid of the rest. We lounged around uncomfortably and cursed the composer of "Did Your Mother Come from Ireland?" I couldn't understand how I'd ever liked that song.

I didn't think too much of the sloop, either. It was one of the most idiotic boats I'd ever seen, narrow, hard, uninteresting lines. If I ever bought a boat it wouldn't be a sloop.

We shucked our clothes off and went for a swim around the edges. Fatty floated on his back, his immense belly rising above the surface, while I dived down and played tag with the mackerel.

Around us was nothing but the universe. Stars, stars and still more stars. I'd have given anything for a street light.

We climbed back in the boat to find another steak dinner waiting. The swim had made us hungry, so we ate about a quarter of it.

"Not very efficient," Fatty grumbled. "I mean that green monster. Some way or other—telepathy, maybe—he figured we liked certain things. Steak dinners, special tobacco, a song. He didn't bother to go into it any further and find out how *much* of those things we liked—and how often. Careless workmanship."

"Talk about carelessness," I shot at him. "You wanted to go out and take a look at him when he first came into the cove. You were at the tiller and couldn't even get us about in time. You didn't see he was chasing us until he was abreast!"

His little eyes boiled red. "I was at the tiller, but what were you doing right then? You were pretty unoccupied and you should have seen him coming! But did you?"

"Hah! You thought he was a Portuguese man-of-war. Like the time we were shingling the church roof and you thought that the black spot near the steeple was a sheet of metal when all the time it was only a hole. We wouldn't have fallen past the beam either, if you weren't such a big fat slob."

Fatty stood up and waved his stomach at me, "For a little hen-pecked squirt, you sure— Hey, Paul, don't let's get going this way. We don't know how long we may have to be together on this flea-bitten rowboat and we don't want to start arguing."

He was right. I apologized. "My fault, that church roof—"

"No, *my* fault," he insisted generously. "I *was* a little too heavy at that moment. Shake, old pal, and let's keep our heads. We'll be the only representatives of humanity wherever we're heading, and we have to stick together."

We shook, and had a glass of beer on it.

All the same, it did get tight as steak dinner followed steak dinner and "Did Your Mother Come from Ireland?" went through chorus after chorus. We carved a checkerboard out of some deck boards and tore up old newspapers to make checkers. We went for swims around the boat, and we made up little guessing games to try on each other. We tested the gray haze and thought up a thousand different ways that the boxes might be working, a thousand different explanations of the spot of color near the top, a thousand different reasons for our being bubbled and sent out into the wild black yonder.

But we were down to counting stars when the red planet began to grow large.

"Mars," Fatty said. "It looks like the picture of Mars in the article Professor Fronac had in the *Sunday Supplement*."

"I wish he was here instead of us. He wanted to go to Mars. We didn't."

There wasn't a cloud in the sky on Mars as we came down through the clearest air I've ever seen. We landed ever so gently in a flat desert of red sand. On all sides of the gray ball we could see acres on acres of sand.

Nothing else.

"Don't know if this is much of an improvement on what we've been through," I remarked morosely.

Fatty wasn't listening. He was standing on his toes and staring around eagerly.

"We're seeing what no man has ever seen before us," he said softly. "We're on Mars, do you understand, Paul? The sun—notice how much smaller it looks than on Earth? What wouldn't Professor Fronac give to be in our shoes!"

"He can have mine any time he shows up. And I'll throw in a new pair of soles and heels. Looking at a red desert isn't my idea of a really big time, if you know what I mean. Gives me no bang at all. And where are the Martians?"

"They'll show, Paul, they'll show. They didn't send us forty million miles just to decorate their desert. Hold your horses, feller."

But I didn't have to hold them long. Off at the edge of the horizon, two specks appeared, one in the air and coming fast, and one mooching along the ground.

The speck in the air grew into a green and bulbous mass about the size of the one in Cassowary Cove. It didn't have any wings or jets or any other way of pushing itself along that I could see. It just happened to be flying.

When it reached us, the one on the ground was still far away.

Our new buddy had eyes, too—if that's what they were. Only they weren't black dots floating inside it; they were dark knob-like affairs stuck on the outside. But they felt just the same as the other when it paused on top of our bubble—as if they could undress our minds.

Just a second of this. Then it moved to the box, fiddled with it a moment and the music stopped. The silence sounded wonderful.

When it slid round to the bottom, going down through the sand as if the desert was made of mirage, Fatty handed me a couple of the knives we'd saved and picked out three for himself.

"Stand by," he whispered. "It may come off any minute now."

I didn't make any sarcastic crack about the usefulness of such weapons because I was having trouble breathing. Besides, the knives gave me a little confidence. I couldn't see where we might go if we happened to have a battle with these things and won, but it was nice holding something that could conceivably do damage.

By this time, the guy on the ground had arrived. He was in a one-wheeled car that was filled with wires and gadgets and crackly stuff. We didn't get a good glimpse of him until he stepped out of the car and stood stiffly against it.

When we did, we didn't like it. This whole play was getting peculiar.

He wasn't green and he wasn't bulbous. He was about half our height, very thin, shaped like a flexible cylinder. He was blue, streaked with white, and about a dozen tentacles trailed out from the middle of the cylinder under a battery of holes and bumps that I figured were the opposite number of ears, noses and mouths.

He stood on a pedestal of a smaller cylinder that seemed to have a sucking bottom to grip the sand.

When our green friend had finished working on the underside, he came tearing up to Jo-Jo near the car. Jo-Jo stiffened even more for a second, then seemed to get all loose and flexible and bent over, his tentacles drooping on the sand.

It wasn't a bow. It reminded me more of the way a dog fawns.

"They *could* have two intelligent races here on Mars," Fatty suggested in a low voice.

Then, while the tentacled chap was still scraping desert, the blob of green lifted and skimmed away in the direction he'd come. It was exactly like the business back in Cassowary Cove, except this time it was flying away while back on Earth it had zoomed along the water and submerged. But both were done so quickly and carelessly as to be positively insulting. After all, I'm not exactly small potatoes in my part of the country: one of my ancestors would have come over on the *Mayflower* if he hadn't been in jail.

This cylinder character turned and watched until the jellyfish was out of sight. Very slowly, he turned back again and looked at us. We shuffled our feet.

Our visitor began piling equipment out of the car and on the sand. He fitted this in that, one doojigger into another doohickey. A crazy-angled, shiny machine took shape which was moved against our little gray home away from home. He climbed into it and twirled thingumajigs with his tentacles.

A small bubble formed around the machine, attached to the gray haze.

"Airlock," Fatty told me. "He's making an airlock so that he can come in without having our air belch into the desert. Mars has no atmosphere to speak of."

He was right. An opening appeared in the grayness and Kid Tentacles sucked through slightly above water level. He was suspended in the air like that for a while, considering us.

Without warning, he dropped down into the water—only he splashed—and out of sight. We hurried to the side and looked down.

He was resting on the bottom, all his tentacles extended out at the mackerel which was scrunched up hard against the wall of gray, its tail curved behind it. A bunch of bubbles dripped up to the surface from the cylinder's mid-section and burst.

I didn't get it. "Wonder what he wants of that poor mackerel. He's sure scaring it silly. It must think he's the Grim Angler."

The moment I'd opened my mouth, the blue and white fellow started rising. He came up over the side and hit our deck with a wet sound from the base of his pedestal.

A couple of tentacles uncoiled at us. We moved back. One of the holes in his midsection expanded, twisted like a mouth in the middle of a stutter. Then in a rumbling, terrifically deep bass: "You—ah—are the intelligent life from Earth? Ah, I did not expect two."

"English!" we both yelped.

"Correct language? Ah, I think so. You—ah, are New English, but English is correct language. This language has been dreefed into me—ah, dreefed is not right—so that I could adjust correctly. But excuse me. Ah, I only expected one and I didn't know whether you were marine or land form. Ah, I thought at first— Permit me: my name is Blizel-Ri-Ri-Bel."

"Mine's Myers," Fatty stepped forward and shook a tentacle, taking control of the situation as he always did. "This is my pal, Paul Garland. I guess you're here to give us the score?"

"To give you the score," Blizel echoed. "To adjust. To make the choice. To explain. To—"

Fatty raised a pudgy hand and headed him off. "What happened to the other Martian?"

Blizel coiled two of his tentacles into a braid. "No, ah, other Martian, that. I am Martian, ah, and representative of Martian Government. It-of-Shoin is Ambassador from Shoin."

"Shoin?"

"Shoin. Galactic nation, ah, of which our system is a province. Shoin is nation of this galaxy and other galaxies. Ah, it in turn is part of larger nation whose name we do not know. It-of-Shoin, the, ah, ambassador, has, ah, already decided which of you will be best but has not told me. Ah, I must make choice myself to prove partially our capabilities, ah, and our readiness to assume complete citizenship in Shoin. This is difficult as we, ah, are but five times as advanced as you, to round the numbers."

"You want to find out which of us is best? For what?"

"To stay as diplomatic functionary so that your people will be able to come here and there as they could now, but for the barrier of forces in balance which has been dreefed, ah, about your planet and satellite. This barrier has protected you from unwarranted intrusion, ah, as well as prevented you from unexpectedly, ah, appearing in a civilized part of Shoin to your detriment. It-of-Shoin on your planet has been more interested in observing the development of the intelligent life forms at the core of your planet than on its surface, no discredit, ah, intended. It-of-Shoin was unaware you had acquired space travel."

"It-of-Shoin on Earth," Fatty mused. "The one who sent us here. The Ambassador to Earth, hey?"

The Martian twisted his tentacles in genuine embarrassment. His white streaks got broader. "Ah, Earth does not require an ambassador as yet. It-of-Shoin is, ah, a—yes, a consul. To all the intelligent life forms of, ah, Earth. Ah, I will return."

He plopped backward into the smaller bubble which was his airlock and started collecting machinery.

Fatty and I compared notes.

All of our galaxy and several others were part of a federation called "Shoin." Mars was practically ready to join or be accepted into the federation, whose other members they considered pretty terrific operators. Earth was a backward planet and only rated a consul who was an "It-of-Shoin." He had a much higher regard for several other specimens of life he'd found on our planet than for man. Nevertheless, we'd surprised him by giving out with spaceships long before we should have. These ships hadn't been able to go anywhere else than the Moon because of something called "forces-in-balance" which acted as a barrier both within and without.

For some reason, a representative of Earth was needed on Mars. This consul had scooted up one night and grabbed us off. When we'd arrived on Mars, the Shoinian ambassador had inspected us and decided which he wanted. Did that mean that one of us could return? And what about the other?

Anyway, he was too all-fired superior to tell the Martians which was the lucky man. He'd taught some government official our language by "dreefing" and it was up to the

Martian from then on. The Martian, for all his humbleness, thought he was at least five times as good as we were. Finally, his English wasn't too good.

"Maybe he was only dreefed once," I suggested. "And it didn't take." I was nervous: we were still being treated too casually.

"What's with this dreefing?" Fatty asked Blizel when he plopped back on deck with a couple of tentacleloads of equipment.

"They-of-Shoin alone can dreef. We, ah, of Mars must use machinery still. Dreef is not the image but a construction of an, ah, of a transliteration for your delight. They-of-Shoin dreef by, ah, utilizing force-patterns of what you call *cosmos*. Thus any product can be realized into, ah, existence—whether material or otherwise. Now testing for you."

The Martian was presenting us with various gadgets on which colored lights flickered. We found that he wanted us to match switches with the colored lights in certain patterns but we couldn't seem to get any of them right.

While he was playing around with the toys, Fatty asked innocently what would happen if we refused to split up and leave one of us here. The Martian replied innocently: one of us *would* be left here, as we had no choice since we couldn't do a thing unless we were allowed to by them.

Fatty told him of the presence on Earth of very brilliant men who knew calculus and suchlike and would give both eyeteeth and maybe an eye or so for the chance to spend their lives on Mars. These men, he pointed out, would be much more interesting for the Martians to have around, maybe even for They-of-Shoin too, than a small-town grocer and gas-station owner who had both flunked elementary algebra.

"Ah, I think," Blizel delicately commented, "that you overestimate the gulf between their intellects and yours, in our views."

Fatty was elected. His experience with motors turned the trick. I congratulated him. He looked miserably at me.

Blizel withdrew, saying that he expected Fatty to go with him on a little trip to their "slimp"—which we decided was a city of sorts. He would bring Fatty back to "ah, organize farewell" if it turned out that Fatty was the right candidate. He was awfully nervous about the whole proposition himself.

Fatty shook his round head at the Martian, who was building a small bubble outside of ours for transportation purposes.

"You know, we can't really blame those guys. They have troubles of their own, after all. They're trying to get into a galactic federation on equal terms with some big shots and they want to prove themselves. They feel like rookies going into a game with a world-series pitcher to bat against. But I don't get the way they crawl and suck around these Shoiners. They need a little backbone. When you come right down to it, they're nothing but exploited natives, and everyone thinks we'll be the same, but on a lower level."

"Wait'll we get here. We'll stiffen these Martians, Fatty. We'll get the system free of galactic imperialists, with our atom bombs and all. Bet our scientists have this forces-in-balance thing licked in no time. And dreefing, too."

"Sure. Think of it—another life-form, maybe more than one, in the core of the

Earth with this It-of-Shoin leading them around by the noses or whatever. Golly! And these Martians here with their civilization, and no telling what other intelligent characters we have scattered between Mercury and Pluto. A whole empire, Paul, bigger than anything on Earth—all controlled by those green jellies!"

Blizel finished building the bubble and Fatty went into it through the airlock. It was darker than the one he left behind. I guessed Blizel wasn't as skilled as that fellow down in Cassowary Cove.

The Martian got back into his machine and started off. Fatty's bubble floated along above it.

I spent about ten or twelve hours on Mars alone. Night fell, and I watched two moons chase across the sky. Some sort of big snake wriggled up out of the sand, looked at me and went away on his own private big deal.

No more steak dinners came down, and I actually found myself missing the stuff. I was hungry!

When Fatty and Blizel returned, the Martian stayed outside and tinkered with the equipment. Fatty came back through the airlock slowly.

He was licking his lips and sighing in half-breaths. I got scared.

"Fatty, did they harm you? Did they do anything drastic?"

"No, Paul, they didn't," he said quietly. "I've just been through a—well, a *big* experience."

He patted the mast gently before continuing. "I've seen the slimp, and it's really not a city, not as we understand cities. It's as much like New York or Boston as New York or Boston is like an anthill or beehive. Just because Blizel spoke our language so very damn poorly, we had him pegged as a sort of ignorant foreigner. Paul, it's not that way at all. These Martians are so far above us, beyond us, that I'm amazed. They've had space travel for thousands of years. They've been to the stars and every planet in the system that isn't restricted. Uranus and Earth are restricted. Barriers.

"But they have colonies and scientists on all the others. They have atomic power and stuff after atomic power and stuff after that. And yet they look up to these fellows from Shoin so much that you can just begin to imagine. They're not exploited, just watched and helped. And these fellows from Shoin, they're part of a bigger federation which I don't quite understand, and they're watched and guarded and helped too— by other things. The universe is old, Paul, and we're newcomers, such terribly new newcomers! Think of what it will do to our pride when we find it out."

There was a dollop of quietness while Fatty slapped the mast and I frowned at him. They must have done something to the poor guy, his backbone had just slipped right out. Some devilish machine, they probably had. Once Fatty was back on Earth he'd be normal again—the same old cocky Fatty Myers.

"Are—are you acceptable?"

"Yeah, I'm acceptable. The ambassador—It-of-Shoin," he said with more respect in his voice than I'd ever heard before, "says I'm the one he picked. You should have seen the way Blizel and his crowd bucked up when they heard that! Now you have to get back to Earth. Blizel will fix the bubble so you'll have more variety in your meals and can let them know what's what. When humans start coming here regularly, they can appoint another man to handle affairs and, if he's acceptable to Shoin and Mars, I can go back."

"Fatty, what if I can't get anyone to believe me?"

He shrugged. "I don't know what happens in that case. Blizel tells me that if you can't operate successfully enough to get man through the barrier in a riz or two, they will conclude that he isn't enough of an intellect as yet to warrant their interest. You've just got to do it, Paul, because I don't know what happens to me if you don't, and from what I can see, nobody up here cares much."

"Meanwhile, you'll be all right?"

"I'll be preparing a sort of city for Earthmen to live in on Mars. If you send any folks in the right channels, I'm supposed to verify them and greet them when they arrive. I'll explain the setup as one human to another. Makes me out as an official greeter, doesn't it?"

After Blizel finished tinkering with the boxes, he applied another spot of color near the top and I shot away from Mars. The return trip was pretty boring, and the mackerel died on the way. There were a lot of different dishes served, and I was able to keep up my interest in food, but everything had a soapy taste.

Blizel just wasn't up to that guy in Cassowary Cove, no two ways about it.

I landed on the same spot from which we'd taken off—two months before, as I found.

The bubble dissolved as I hit the water. I didn't bother to sail the sloop in, but dived off the deck and swam ashore.

It felt good to be able to swim a distance in a straight line.

It seems that there were folks who wanted to hold a funeral for us, but Edna had put her foot down. She insisted that so long as no wreckage was found, she'd consider me alive.

I'd probably turn up in Europe one fine day with Fatty, she told them.

So when I walked into the grocery, being Edna, she merely turned to face me. She asked me where I'd been. Mars, I said. She hasn't spoken to me since.

A reporter from our local paper interviewed me that night and wrote up a crazy story about how I'd claimed I had established consulates all over the solar system. I hadn't; I'd just told him my friend Fatty Myers was the acting consul for Earth on Mars.

The story was reprinted in one of the Boston papers as a little back-page squib with a humorous illustration. That's all. I've been going crazy since, trying to get someone to believe me.

Remember, there's a time limit: one riz, two at the most.

For the last time, then, to anyone who's interested in space travel after all I've said: Stop knocking yourself out trying to break through a barrier of forces-in-balance that isn't meant to be broken through. You have to come down to Cassowary Cove and take a boat out and wait for It-of-Shoin to appear. I'll help, and you can be sure that when it gets to him, Fatty Myers will verify and do whatever else is necessary. But you won't be able to go to Venus or Mars any other way.

You need a visa.

AFTERWORD

This was the second story Ted Sturgeon agented for me. He liked it (at least he always said he liked it) and kept telling me it was a better story than I thought it was.

I don't know what went wrong with it in the writing. Well, for one thing, I may have been reaching for something that was a bit beyond my strength at the time—I mean all the It-of-Shoin stuff. For another, I think upon rereading it, I should have decided early on as between the comic and the cosmic; as it was, they kept getting in each other's way. Finally, I was experimenting with something—the idiomatic narrative—that I was to do a little more successfully later on with stories like "Bernie the Faust" and "On Venus Have We Got a Rabbi." When I wrote "Consulate," I was dealing with both an unfamiliar idiom and an unfamiliar culture. I was, after all, even much more than I am now, an intellectual Brooklyn Jew. New England was only something I had read about.

At least the editor of *Thrilling Wonder* thought it was a good story. And so, according to the letter columns of the magazine, did a good many of his readers.

As far as I'm concerned? An early stage in the learning process. (But I am fond of the alien-and-the-mackerel bit.)

WRITTEN 1947——PUBLISHED 1948

The Last Bounce

There wasn't much difference between Commissioner Breen's office and the office of any other memorandum baron in Sandstorm, the interstellar headquarters of the Patrol on Mars. If you've seen one, Vic Carlton decided, you'd seen them all; and, in twelve years of standing at attention during the wet-with-tradition ceremony known as the Kiss of Death, he had seen them all—every last uncompromising whitewashed cubicle. Rooms as friendly as a surgical table.

A few star maps speckling the glare from the walls; a bookcase filled with miscellaneous handbooks and manuals of space; one stiff, thin chair behind the stiff, square desk; and, over the desk, the Scout Roll of Honor—names of 563 men who had laid down their lives in the Service: 563 casualties out of a total all-time roster of 1,420.

Yet the Scouts were a volunteer service, and every year, all over the galaxy, young men broke their backs and overloaded their brains to get into it.

The speech was pretty much the same as usual. Perhaps even better in one way: Breen was new to the job and slightly—well, *embarrassed* by this aspect of it. He kept his talk short; made the Kiss of Death almost a peck.

He was tall and straight as they: he had no more than three years on Vic Carlton, the oldest of the three; and his blue uniform differed from theirs only in the badge of office, a gold star instead of a silver rocket, on his chest.

"Lutz and O'Leary, you are under the command of Victor Carlton—one of the very few men on active duty with over ten years' experience. Carlton, your two juniors have been certified as psychologically, physically, and educationally fit for this mission: no more can be said of any man. I must remind you that the Patrol has been called the glory of space and the Scouts the glory of the Patrol; but I need not remind you how jealously that glory should be guarded. Good scouting, good luck. That is all."

He exhaled a tiny gust of relief before shutting his mouth.

All? Vic Carlton thought, as they saluted and about-faced to the door. *This is only the beginning. You know that, Breen. The danger and the horror—death perhaps, agony without death perhaps—start officially when the commissioner's talk is finished. You should know: you decided you had a bellyfull six months ago and resigned from active duty for this sleek office job. When we walk out of your office, it's only the beginning.*

Then he thought: *Hey, those are dangerous ideas for a commander. Maybe Kay's right; maybe I'm getting old.*

And *then* he thought: *Breen's only thirty-five; I'm thirty-two. I remember when I thought all commissioners were shambling wrecks held together by will-power and a handful of regulations. Why, Breen's only thirty-five! I am getting old!*

They were out in the corridor, and a group of scouts being briefed for another set of missions swung down to the elevator with them. They clapped their helmets on, leaving the broad, flaring visors open.

"Attaboy, O'Leary, take it on the bounce!"

"You don't know how lucky you are, Lutz. Unkillable Carlton is my idea of a commander for a rookie's first mission."

"Look at Carlton, fellows. He's *bored!* What a man!"

"The first bounce is the hardest, O'Leary. Gee, I remember mine!"

"Hey, Lutz, what're you looking so green about? According to statistics, you have an even chance of coming back in one hunk!"

"On the bounce, O'Leary. On the bounce."

Carlton watched his men. O'Leary was the one to look out for at this point. Lutz was still riding the enthusiasm of graduation from the academy; he might be frightened at his baptismal mission, but he was even more exhilarated. He wouldn't be important until action started; and, even then, he'd probably have to be checked from daredevil stunts more than he would have to be encouraged to take a chance. But O'Leary was the one to watch.

It was tough making your first bounce. Vic remembered his—was it nine? No, eleven years ago. A commander who'd been so badly off that he'd requested disenrollment in preference to making a bounce, the other junior so psychologically smashed that he'd become a permanent resident of the tiny Patrol Mental Hospital on Ganymede. A kind of carnivorous moss had almost got them: pretty screaming awful. But Vic had been patched up and made his bounce on the very next mission out of Sandstorm. You had to bounce right back or your nerve would go.

Sure enough, O'Leary sounded off.

"We drew a creampuff. The planet's only three-tenths of a point off Earth-type."

The others hooted at that. "And it's out around the Hole in Cygnus! Where they found a nova acting like a third-magnitude star and a meteor stream traveling at the speed of light! The part of the galaxy that never heard of Newton! You can have it!"

"That region hasn't even been adequately mapped, O'Leary. It may be the place where time warped in on itself and exploded, where the universe got started. A creampuff, he calls it! You can have it: I'll be happy with a planet six full points off Earth-type, in a sane area like Virgo or Taurus or something."

"Sure, don't kid yourself, O'Leary. But on the bounce, boy, take it on the bounce!"

"Hey, Lutz, what're you looking so green about?"

Harry Lutz giggled weakly and wiped palm sweat off on his blue jumper. Carlton slapped him on the back, kneaded his shoulder blades. "Don't worry, you have two experienced men behind you. We'll take care of you, won't we, O'Leary?"

O'Leary looked up startled, then nodded seriously. "Sure; we'll show you the ropes, kid."

Good. Get O'Leary's mind off himself, get him to worrying about the rookie instead, and he'd have no time for a funk.

The elevator stopped on the main floor of the Scout Operations Building unimaginatively decorated in azure plastic. Through the open double doors. Vic Carlton could see the mob of civilian personnel who always left their jobs when a mission took off. Death-watch in Sandstorm, the Scouts called it. Oh, well, he shrugged, it must be exciting for civilians. Man's empire extends another couple of light-years into space—that was probably exciting to some people.

Someone started the song—

> Bell-bottomed helmet, suit of SP blue,
> He'll shoot the ether like his daddy used to do...

The three had linked arms when they began singing. Their feet beating the rhythm, they marched down to the slender little ship with the long blue stripe that lay waiting for them at the end of Sagittarius Runway. Behind them, their honor guard of Scouts bawled the chorus at the pink Martian sky. On either side, people cheered. Evidently, Vic reflected, this was something to cheer about.

"What about you," Kay had asked last night, after he had hummed the song, lying with his head on her lap and watching the two moons of Mars coruscating overhead. They'd walked in the Rosenbloom Desert for two hours, and when she'd sat down in the coarse red sand, he'd put his head on her lap and hummed the song because he felt so strangely tranquil. "What about you—don't you want a son? Don't you want him to—to shoot the ether like his daddy used to do?"

"Kay, please. Of course I want a son. As soon as we can get married—"

"But you can't. Not while you're on active duty with the Scouts. You can't have a son. The only children that active Scouts have are orphans. That's different, Vic. Orphans who never have seen their daddies."

He grimaced at her brown eyes, certain and serene under the perfect piles of blonde coiffure. "Look, I want to marry you, girl. I'm going to marry you. And I agree with you that we can't build a home life around Scout missions."

"Yes, Vic."

"You're right about my being no good to you—or any woman—until I decide on my own that one planet is good enough for me. You don't want me counting jet-trails wistfully; and you don't want me with all the fire gone out—you said so yourself. I've got to want to build a family as much as I want to scout."

"Yes, Vic."

He made an impatient gesture and cut it short as he watched her draw five parallel trails in the sand with her fingers. "So? So it's just a matter of patience on your part, just a matter of waiting until I'm ready to chuck the whole thing. After all, I've been a Scout for twelve years; the odds against that length of service are pretty high—most men who survive five years of it are ready to quit. You'll have me soon, Kay—and not as a shoulder-shrugging has-been, but a guy who's adventured enough in space and is ready to roost, I'm still young by ordinary standards—only thirty-two. Trip after next, three or four missions from now maybe, I'll be ready. Soon."

A pause. Then—"Yes, Vic." Her voice was low, agreeable.

Somehow, in retrospect, it seemed like the most final of quarrels.

Vic found himself looking for Kay past O'Leary's huge head. She worked in Administration; she'd be in the bunch near the great white dome. He wished he could kiss her before they took off; but tradition demanded that farewells be said the night before and nothing interrupt the march to the ship.

He caught sight of her just as they reached the part of the song that always made her wince. Vic grinned in anticipation.

> If it's a girl, dress her up in lace;
> If it's a boy, send the bastard off to space!

She winced so hard, screwing her eyes down and pulling her shoulders up, that they had marched past her and into the ship before she looked around again.

The two regular Patrolmen who were on duty saluted and said, "Ship in good order. Commander. Luck." They left.

The other Scouts gave them one more round of handshakes before climbing silently through the open locks.

Vic pressed the green hexagonal button that shut the airlocks, and, leaping to the portholes, they all took a last quick glimpse of Sandstorm's concrete buildings rising like so many bandaged thumbs out of the rosy Martian plain.

"Jets in good order, Commander," the voice of the ground-crew chief announced. "Awaiting take-off."

"Mission crew ready," Vic told him in the communaphone, as Lutz and O'Leary went to their stations. "Taking off."

His eyes swept around the pilot-room, focused on his juniors for a double-check, came to rest on the clicking gauges.

"Jets away," he said and cut the communaphone connection.

He counted to fifteen slowly, thinking of the immemorial cry of "Jets away! Jets away away, jets away!" that was being sung out on the ground below as the crowd scattered.

"Fifteen," he said, and O'Leary pulled the red switch the requisite two notches, while Lutz swung the tiny wheels of the balance control. They jerked slightly in the seats, then, as Vic adjusted acceleration helix, they relaxed comfortably. Mission begun.

Mission 1572 on the schedule of the Scouting Patrol; Number 29 in Vic's personal Service Record back in Sandstorm, the last page of which was headed "Circumstances of Death—Posthumous Citations—Provision for Dependents." Not many Service Records could count that high. When a man passed his twentieth mission, they began calling him "Lightning" Ching Lung or "Safety-First" Feuerbach or "Two-Blast" Bonislavski. You had to hang some such nickname on a man who, mission in, mission out, came back with three-fourths of his skin missing or some weird virus that made the medics dither and dream up whole new pathologies—but a man who *always* came back. Until, of course, there was that one time—

They called Vic "Unkillable" Carlton, and there were only two Scouts now shooting the ether who had longer active service. One of his very few ambitions was to be the Senior Scout of Space and wear the gold uniform that went with the rating. It meant that you never paid for anything anywhere, that you walked through Patrol cordons, that you were practically a one-man parade wherever you went. That would be nice, Vic thought; it was childish and garish, but it gave a man some sort of goal at this stage of his life. It meant that even in the Scouts who were the chosen of the Patrol, in turn the chosen of the galaxy's male population, you were still unique. It also meant that one day, you might cut your throat while shaving with a safety razor.

Cute idea, the Scouts. Economical. Instead of losing thirty or a hundred highly trained scientists at a clip, civilization, at most, would lose three men. True, the three would be rather unusual men with remarkable qualifications; but in a galaxy swarming with youths thirsty for a nice suicidal-type job in adventurous surroundings with a little glory, fair pay and *plenty* of room for advancement, the three would be replaced. And Honor-Rolled.

A Patrol cruiser happens to run across a previously uncharted star which is the one-in-a-thousand with a family of planets. Spectroscopic observations are made; and, if the cruiser has the time, robotjets are sent out to circle one or two of the more likely-looking worlds and make automatic observations on their atmospheres, ground conditions, evidences of intelligent life and the like. If there are no signs of an indigenous civilization anywhere, the cruiser goes on about its business and reports its findings to Sandstorm HQ at the earliest opportunity.

Sandstorm files the information along with a mass of deductions by physicists, chemists and biologists. Five years later, say, it becomes necessary to make a more detailed examination of one of the planets. Maybe the surface promises interesting mineral deposits; maybe it's a good spot for a fueling station or Patrol outpost or a colony; maybe it's just that someone important is curious.

Three available Scouts—one A, one B and one C Scout—are alerted. They are briefed for a month on all data handy, given the best ship and equipment that can be built, wished lots and lots of luck and sent off. If they aren't back in ninety days, Terran time, a heavy cruiser crowded to the stern jets with fancy weapons and brilliant minds goes after them to find out how they were knocked off. If any or all of them return in the prescribed time, their reports are examined and, on the basis of their experiences, an expedition is organized to do whatever job is necessary, from mapping the site of a colony to laying the foundations of an astronomical observatory.

The Scouts are sitting ducks. Oh, sure, their motto is "Take No Chances" and Scout Regulations 47 to 106 deal with safety measures to be observed. They are supposed to wander about the new planet with recording instruments, getting first-hand, on-the-spot data. That's all the books say they're supposed to do. And back in the academy—

"Back in the academy," Lutz confided to O'Leary as, outside the orbit of Pluto, they prepared to switch to the interstellar jets that would sweep them to their destination at several times the speed of light, "back in the academy, they told us three-fourths of all Scout casualties are caused by carelessness or disregard of the safety regulations. The commissioners said that as discipline improves and more men adhere closely to regulations, casualties will inevitably go down."

"They will, huh?" O'Leary glanced round at Carlton and sucked in his lower lip. "I'm right glad to hear that. It's nice to know that casualties are going down. I'll take a commissioner's word against nasty statistics any old time. *Down,* huh?"

Harry Lutz completed his sight and handed the instrument to O'Leary for checking. "Sure. We function simply as an advance-information crew. At the first hint of danger we're supposed to clear out. 'Better lose your bonus than lose your life.' "

"And outside that fat bonus for a full scouting period on a planet, what other compensations are there to this wacky job?" O'Leary nodded at Carlton. "Objective lined up, Vic. We can shoot. You try coming back from a mission with a scary story, boy; you'll find yourself demoted to watch-dog duty in the Patrol before you can say Aldebaran Betelgeuse Capricorn. Or take that last mission I was on. Nothing dangerous on the planet—nothing, that is, that *wanted* to do us harm. But there was a bird thing with funny wings which generated a high-frequency sound wave as it flew. Pure biological accident, but it happened to be on exactly the same frequency as our supersonic pistols. Yeah."

He breathed heavily and stared through the control levers. The other two men watched him closely. "First time we saw it was the day Jake Bertrand was making a geological survey outside the ship. It flew down and lit on a rock—it was curious, I guess—and Jake dropped dead. Hap MacPherson, the commander, ambled out to see why Jake had fainted. The bird thing got scared and flew away, so Hap dropped dead, too. I was inside the ship and noticed where the sound meters were pointing; I figured it out. After I had me a good round look at the horizon and made sure there was nothing flying anywhere, I dragged the two brain-curdled corpses in and went back to Base. I don't know whether they decided to wipe out the bird things, send a colony down with a new kind of head-shield or what. But they gave me my bonus."

Silence. Harry Lutz started to speak, looked at his companions and stopped. He wet his lips and leaned back in his seat, *"Gee,"* he said at last in a small, wondering voice.

"All right, O'Leary," Vic rapped out. "If you're through with your Horror Stories for Young Recruits we can move. Stations for interstellar shoot!"

"Station B manned," O'Leary said, grinning so that his teeth showed and the corners of his mouth didn't turn up.

Harry Lutz gulped and straightened his shoulders inside the blue jumper. "Sta—" he started and had to begin again. "Station A manned. Interstellar j-jets away."

Nope, you can't fool the Scouts. They know they're sitting ducks. All the same. Vic decided, Lutz and O'Leary were good for each other. When you made a bounce after a trip where Death had dug a humorous forefinger in your ribs and slapped your shivering back—about the best thing you could find on such a bounce was a younger man who knew less than you did, who needed guiding, whose fear was actually greater than yours because it was latent and had, as yet, hit nothing tangible to set it off.

O'Leary was coming out of himself, thinking less of his own problems and more of the younger man's. And Lutz wasn't being harmed either: if some stories could frighten him enough to make him an unreliable companion, the real thing was no place to discover it. Better find it out now, here, where steps could be taken to protect the other two. In twelve years of Scouting, Vic Carlton had concluded that the only man who didn't scare at what the missions encountered was either too phlegmatic to be useful or else a true lunatic: the normal man was afraid, but tried to handle the source of his fear. Let Lutz find out what they were likely to be up against: his survival chances would be the better for it.

"Oh, it's not such a bad life at that," Steve O'Leary admitted as, the interstellar shoot under way, they were relaxing in the spherical space which served as combination pilot house, living quarters and recreation room. "A month for briefing, two months—at maximum—for the round trip, a month on the planet of mission. If you're lucky, the whole duty period takes no more than four months, after which you get a full thirty days' leave—over and above any hospital time. Pay's good and the glamour-struck women are plentiful: what more can a man ask?"

"Besides," Lutz hunched forward eagerly, transparently glad of his colleague's change of mood. "Besides, there's the *real* glory—being the first humans to set foot on the soil of the planet, the first men to find out what each world is like, the first—"

"That part they can have," O'Leary told him curtly. "The first humans on each world—*hah!* The first *funerals!*"

Vic Carlton leaned back in his plastic chair and chuckled. "What's the matter, Steve—did the commissioner flog you into the ship? You didn't have to make the bounce; you could have disenrolled."

"When I'm only five months away from A Scout rating, double pay and retirement privileges? Not that I'll ever have sense enough to retire: the first O'Leary was a romantic bonehead and the male line has bred true. There was an O'Leary who got himself blown apart in the stratosphere back in the days when they were trying to ride to the moon on liquid oxygen; an O'Leary was navigation officer on the Second Venusian Expedition one hundred and fifty years ago—the expedition that fell into the sun. Science may come and Invention may go, but the O'Learys will go on sticking their heads into nooses forever. Amen."

They all laughed at his lugubrious nods, and Lutz said: "I only hope all my missions will be as dangerous as this one! The star is a yellow type G, just like our sun, and the planet—"

"The planet's only three-tenths of a point off Earth-type!" the B Scout broke in, his mood shifting again. "I know. That's what I told those jokers back in Sandstorm. But listen, boy, that planet and that star are around the Hole in Cygnus—do you know what that means? There hasn't been a single planet scouted in that area, let alone colonized. All anybody knows about the Hole in Cygnus are somebody else's theories. Ask any scientist why there are so few suns in the area, why matter behaves the way it does out there, what might have happened to that cartographic unit that got itself lost five or six years ago, and he'll tell you to please not bother him. One consolation, though; if we don't come back, there'll doubtless be a full-dress investigating expedition. Makes you feel good, doesn't it, Vic?"

Carlton shrugged, turned back to his book. He couldn't decide which was worse—Lutz with his callowness, his fumbling inexperience, or the older man whose wry humor flowered so easily into bitterness stemming from obvious fear. For such a mission, he thought, the Scouts might have reversed an ancient rule and allowed him, as commander, to choose his own men.

Although, on his own initiative, whom would he have chosen? A nice dependable B Scout like Barney Liverwright who had been knocked off around Virgo six months ago? An up-and-coming C Scout, full of blood and guts, like Hoagy Stanton who was even now dying on Ganymede in a room which the pathologist dared not enter for fear of a virus which might seep through any immunization procedure, any protective clothing?

No, you took what you got, what there was available—what there was still alive. Even on the mission to the Hole in Cygnus, the commander took the men assigned to him, and, Vic thought, watching them as the ship's chronometer told the passage of the weeks which only it could record out here in black space, he didn't have such a bad crew at that.

A tight comradeship developed that he had known before. The three men came closer and, despite their cramped quarters and the natural irritations arising from their log-book routine, felt the warmth of friendship.

Lutz in particular became more sure of himself as he was openly accepted by the other two. Vic watched him, his small dark head like a planet beside O'Leary's huge red sunburst as the two men beat out the measures of a sloppily sentimental ballad currently popular among the Scouts. He grinned at Harry Lutz's tearful tenor winding its melancholy around Steve O'Leary's stanchion-shaking bass.

> *No more to the stars will I go,*
> *No more a smooth jet will I know;*
> *Through spendthrift days, a maiden's praise*
> *Will hold me in thrall.*
>
> *I'll go my ways, and end my days*
> *On some mould'ring ball.*
> *No more to the stars will I go—O lads!*
> *No more to the stars will I go.*

It hardly applied to Kay, Vic decided, "A maiden's praise—" That was hardly what he got from her.

Kay was critical: Kay was strength seeking strength, not a limp flag of a female searching for a strong male staff. With her, for the first time, he had begun to examine the internal forces which had driven him into one of the most dangerous and least rewarding services ever organized by humanity.

That night when he'd come tardily to their date outside Sandstorm's swankiest restaurant and said casually, belligerently, "Just signed papers for Mission 1572. Adventure done got between us again, girl."

"There's nothing wrong with adventure," Kay had commented slowly, after turning aside, "Every young man must measure himself against obstacles too big for his fellows. That's how the race advances, that's how new governments are created. It gets to be a perpetuated adolescence when it leads to nothing fundamentally constructive; when it's pursued for its own sake."

"The Scouts don't pursue adventure for adventure's own sweet sake," Vic had growled. "The Scouts have initiated every colony in the galaxy—they've been responsible for every outpost in the stars."

She laughed. "The Scouts! Vic, you're talking of a service; I'm discussing the individuals in it. When a man of your age has nothing more to show for his life but a few scars and a dozen tarnished medals—I only know that as a woman, I want a strong, steady and reliable man. I don't want to marry a boy of thirty-two."

"You're saying," Vic went on doggedly, "that pioneers, revolutionaries and adventurers are not mature men. In essence, you feel that the race advances because of its cases of arrested development. Right, Kay? Isn't that what you really think, that adolescence is the period of experiment and excitement—and maturity, the period of settled stodgy dullness where you cultivate your ulcers instead of your mind?"

He remembered the way she had stared at him, then dropped her eyes as if caught in a fib. "I—I don't know how to answer *that*, Vic. It seems to me that you're talking like a little boy who wants to be a fireman and is secretly very much ashamed of his Dad who works for a fire insurance company, but I could be wrong. I know that with your ten years plus in the Scouts, you could get a commissioner's appointment by asking for it, and that it would be just as exciting to plan missions and prepare younger men for their dangers as rocketing out on them yourself. But I don't want you to give up active duty for me, or even for our possible family, if you haven't grown up enough to want it yourself."

"You mean grown *old* enough, Kay."

She gestured impatiently and turned to examine her hair in the mirror. "Let it go," she said, winding an intricate curl with complete concentration. "I never can see what there is about this discussion that upsets you so. Either you want to settle down and have a family—or you don't. When you decide, I'll be very much interested in hearing from you. Now let's see if Emile's Oasis has that band in from Earth yet."

He held the door open for her, irritably trying to decide why these conversations always left him with the feeling that he had committed some unpardonable social blunder which she had been gracious enough not to comment upon.

Looking back now, he found he still could not be critical. He found himself wondering what he was doing out here, sharing living space with two strangers named Harry Lutz and Steve O'Leary.

What was Mission 1572, what was the first scouting expedition to the Hole, as compared to Kay's soft presence and a youngster in whom they would both appear again? The urge that filled him—the hunger to found a family—was incredibly ancient, and every cell in his body had evolved to respond to it. Sitting watchful in the deep control chair, he plucked moodily at his stiff blue uniform.

And then a light in front of him flashed redly.

"Scouts to stations," Vic bawled. "On the double, there—on the double! Star of mission on the point! Stations for switch to planetary jets." He was calm again, and sure of himself: a mission chief.

"Station B manned," O'Leary rapped out, jolting into his seat and pulling a long bank of switches open.

"Station C manned," Lutz's voice was indistinct through the remains of a quiet supper he'd been enjoying in the galley. "Planetary jets away!"

Vic's eyes raked across them, considered the stellar map spread in front of him, noted the gauge needle palpitating in its circular prison, and checked the relay near his right hand for maximum gap.

And double checked.

"Planetary jets away," he called. "Planetary jets away, away. Jets away!"

They came into a system of eleven planets whose sun's spectroscopic reading was remarkably similar to that of Sol. Between the second and third planets there was one asteroid belt; between the eighth and ninth, there was another. Three of the planets were ringed—one both horizontally and vertically like a gyroscope—and only one world, the fifth from the sun, supported life.

"Could swear it was Earth if I didn't know better," Harry Lutz marveled as he looked up from an examination of the mission-planet.

O'Leary nodded. "Three-tenths of a point off Earth-type is pretty close. Slightly smaller diameter, oxygen and nitrogen balanced almost on the dot, only two degrees difference in the average equatorial temperatures. And *still* the exploring ship couldn't find any evidences of intelligent life. Hey Vic—according to Cockburn's Theory of Corresponding Environmental Evolution, shouldn't there be a creature down there who, at the least, approximates paleolithic man?"

The A Scout, wearily watching the transvisor click off the remaining million miles, moved his shoulders up expressively.

"I could give you a guess anywhere but in this gap in the wide open spaces. Sure, the biology of a planet that close to Earth physically should have produced an intelligent biped with the beginnings of a machine civilization—but who knows about the Hole in Cygnus? Take those white horrors out there."

They followed the direction of his arm pointing up at the planet-studded telescanner. Here and there in this system, between planets and upon them, floating free in empty space and clustered about the yellow primary, were seemingly tiny networks of white, dead-pale filaments extending for what were actually hundreds and thousands of miles. Like the broken webs of immense and ugly spiders they looked, uninterested in gravitation and resembling nothing in a logical cosmos.

"Don't try, Harry," Vic warned Lutz, who was feverishly leafing through an immense volume on the control desk. "You won't find them listed in Rosmarin's *Types of Celestial Bodies*. All that we know about those things is that they are there—everywhere in the Hole—and they're too dangerous for the best stuff we've been able to make up to now. Any ship that gets too snoopily close to them, goes out—pouf! It just isn't around any more. Our orders are: MAKE NO ATTEMPT REPEAT IN CAPITALS UNDERLINED MAKE NO ATTEMPT TO EXPLORE WHITE CLUSTERS AND ANY OTHER PHYSICAL MANIFESTATIONS PECULIAR TO HOLE IN CYGNUS."

O'Leary snorted. "That's just this trip. After we get back (*if* we do) someone at Base will scratch his head and wonder what those white clusters can possibly be made of. So they'll shake our hands, give us a couple of box lunches and a new ship, and say, 'Would you mind looking into this matter and seeing if it is really as dangerous as rumored—taking no unnecessary chances, of course? And it would be sort of nice if one of you could make it back in time for the Solarian Convention of Astrophysicists in January!' "

They guffawed, Lutz on a slightly higher note than the other two.

The planet was enough like Earth to bring on a severe case of homesickness. True, there were only four continents, and true, there was no dainty moon reigning over the warm nights; but the seas were sapphire enough for a man to lie on their white beaches with a bottle of whiskey and get drunk without opening the bottle, and the clouds pushed their curling bellies across a subtly tinted sky unaware of the glorious things poets could do with them. Here and there, a perfect island poised above the noiseless indigo waters, waiting for a painter to whom to give itself.

Tall trees boiled up the sides of mountains, lush grass waved on the uncombed prairies. Deserts sweltered their immense length of golden moistureless sand; and, in the north, a huge ice floe precipitated spring by plunging into the polar sea with a wild shriek of freedom.

But on all the land, and in all the seas, they saw no living thing move.

"Like the Garden of Eden," Harry Lutz breathed, "after the Fall."

O'Leary looked at him, bit his lip. "Or Hell, before it."

After they landed, Vic assigned investigative watches. Much easier than the nerve-wracking space watch, the investigative watch was, at this stage of their mission, much more crucial. Both Scout Regulations and their own appreciation of safety-first methods demanded that the most painstaking examination possible be made of the planet while they were still inside the ship. Not only did the ground have to be checked for such topographic capers as earthquakes, floods and volcanoes, not only did the possibility of dangerous submicroscopic life require careful consideration on so Earth-like a planet; but also—especially here in the Hole—they must be on the lookout for the completely alien, the peculiar deadliness without precedent—up to now.

Not until all these precautions had been taken and the log-book carried to the moment of landing did Vic realize he hadn't thought of Kay for ten—or was it fifteen?—hours. Kay Summersby was just one more blonde adventure that hadn't quite worked out, another backdrop in his memory—a little more important, a little more protracted than the rest. His only responsibility was the mission.

"Hey, Vic," Steve O'Leary frowned up from the telescanner. "Do you know there's a white tentacle thing on the other side of the planet?"

The mission commander grunted, moved to the side of the B Scout and scratched his chin at the instrument.

"Black Space!" he growled. "What would you call it? Doesn't seem to be alive, doesn't move, doesn't have any visible connection with the ground; just hangs there, hurting the eyes. Makes me think of an unhappy hour someone ripped up and threw away."

O'Leary pulled at his fingers. "Yeah. I don't like it, and I don't want to see it. According to regulations, we're supposed to stay at least a full jet-trail length from these babies—and here this thing is a stinking 7500 miles off in a straight line through the planet."

"That's just our own bad luck," Carlton told him. "It's on the planet of mission, and our mission orders always move ahead of Scout Regulations. Just remember to keep your distance on exploratory trips. Hear that, Lutz?"

The C Scout nodded. "When do we start the trips, Vic? If there's anything dangerous on this unearthly paradise, I'll eat my helmet from the antenna down. I'd like to feel some ground slapping at the soles of my feet."

His superior shook his head.

"Take it easy, boy, take it slow and easy. On a strange planet, all you get for hurrying is a sooner grave than your neighbor. And if there's anything dangerous on this world that you don't know about when you step out of the lock, why, you won't have to eat your helmet. Because it will eat you, helmet, radio phones and all. Now relax and get back to that telescanner. There must be *something* alive here besides trees, grass and potatoes."

But there wasn't. At least they couldn't find anything though they spelled each other at the telescanners, nudged the beam back and forth over the four continents and peered at the screens until their eyes writhed with fatigue. They found minute one-celled forms in the specimens of air, soil and water the ship's automatic dredges picked up; O'Leary's shout brought the other two tumbling out of their bunks the day he thought he saw a bird (it turned out to be only a leaf tortured by the wind); and a few large green balls they noticed scudding about excited their interest until the scouts decided from their aimlessness and lack of sensory apparatus that they were over-large spores of some plant.

They saw no herbivores cropping the rich vegetation, no carnivores slinking behind them for a spring. The seas held no fish, the woods no termites, the very earth itself no earthworms.

"I don't get it," Vic growled. "The botany of this planet is sufficiently close to Earth's to indicate a terrestrial zoology. Where is it? There's no creature out there large enough to have eaten all the others. So-o-o—"

"So?" Steve O'Leary prompted, watching his chief closely.

"Maybe it's something *small* enough to have done the job. A virus, say. A complex molecule halfway between the animal and mineral kingdom, something not quite alive but a million times more dangerous than anything that is."

"But Vic, wouldn't I have hit it with the electron microscope?" Harry Lutz spread his hands nervously. "And whatever I muffed—well, the robot eye is still classifying five thousand specimens a minute. If a virus did for the birds and beasts here, we'd have come across at least one culture by now."

"Would we? If it were a virus that couldn't adapt to plant life, it might not be very active—or very numerous—at the moment. Then again if we did turn up a specimen, how would we know?"

"The robot eye—"

Vic Carlton grimaced. "*The robot eye!* One way, Lutz, not to grow old in this service is to believe everything the manuals tell you about the equipment. Sure, the robot eye attached to the electron microscope makes a fine pathologist. But all the robot eye has behind it is a robot memory—a file of every microscopic and submicroscopic form of life which, in the parts of the galaxy explored up to this date, have been found inimical to man. If it sees something enough like one of the items in the file to close a ten-decimal relay, we're warned. And it's warned us of a dozen or so species on this planet which it turns out our stuff can handle. But there's never yet been anything like a robot imagination. Your little machine, Harry, can't scratch its mounting and say 'Now, I don't like the looks of that baby there, harmless though it may seem.' Whenever a robot eye hits something completely out of its memory file, you know what happens."

"Yeah." O'Leary chuckled and swung himself up to his bunk. "Three corpses in Scout uniforms and, after the investigative expedition, maybe another item for the eye's robot memory. That's the way we learn, Lutz, old soak: trial and error. Only, me brave young C Scout, we're the trials and—ever so often—we're the errors, too." He lay back on the bunk, and, as his huge red head disappeared from view, they could hear his deep voice caroling, "*Oh, I'm the bosun tight and the midshipmite—*"

Lutz looked unhappy as the other man slid into his morbid humor. The enforced seclusion aboard the little ship, from which he could see the gloriously free miles of acreage which surrounded them, had not done Steve O'Leary any particular good. He was too long in the service to question discipline, especially as regarded safety measures; but his subconscious could whisper irritably, and rumors of fear leaped irresistibly upwards in his mind.

More than ever, Vic felt himself drawn to the younger man. At least Lutz wasn't riding a recent scare: he had no idea, as yet, how cold his back could get.

"Look," the mission commander said kindly. "I'm not saying that there is a bug out there waiting to knock us off. I don't know. Maybe out here in the Hole, there's some radiation effect which inhibits the evolution of complex animal forms. Maybe. I'm just saying that we keep looking and keep guessing until we feel we've exhausted every possibility of danger. *Then*, when we finally take a stroll outside the ship, we wear spacesuits with both Grojen shielding and Mannheim baffles."

O'Leary's head came up out of his bunk again. "Hey!" he said disappointedly. "That much weight and we'll have to use electrical medullas to walk. I was looking forward to a hop, skip and jump under my own power. A little run across the ground would feel awful good."

He shut up and lay down under Vic's thoughtful glare. And it was the thought behind the glare that made Vic tell him the day they were ready to begin exploring the surface:

"I'm taking Lutz with me. We want the man in the ship to know what to do in case something pops. So you're elected, Steve."

The redhead watched them struggle into cumbersome, equipment-laden spacesuits. He kneaded huge hands into his hips. "That's not customary, Vic, and you know it. Man on a bounce is the first one through the lock."

"If the commander sees it that way," he was told curtly. "I don't. You'll get your exercise later. Meanwhile, I want you to sit over those jets like a runner in a hundred-yard dash. If we get into trouble and you can help us, fine; but if it looks at all tight or too unusual, remember the primary purpose of the mission is to gather information about the Hole. So you cut and run."

O'Leary turned his back and began working the airlock. "Thanks, pal," he muttered. "I can see myself back in Sandstorm swearing to the boys that you gave me exactly those orders. I can see myself."

They climbed down the ladder and started across the surface. Vic, in the lead, was being very cautious; behind him, Harry Lutz sweated, stumbled and cursed in the huge suit with which even a year's training had not thoroughly familiarized him.

The commander stopped in what looked like a grove of chest-high elm trees. "Take it easy, Lutz," he suggested. "You're carrying a lot of weight and you can't possibly move it all correctly. The trick in using an electrical medulla is not to let your right hand know what your left is doing. I know you had enough workouts in those things back at the academy to use the fingers on all the correct buttons. It'll be second nature if you give it a chance. Just relax and take in the scenery: concentrate on what you want to do, where you want to go—not how you want to do it. And once you stop thinking about them, your fingers will take care of the medulla-switches for you. They've been educated to do the job."

He heard the C Scout take a deep breath through the radio phones. Then, as Lutz looked about him and relaxed visibly, his pace became more regular, the movements of the suit—weighted down as it was with Grojen shielding, Mannheim baffles, and intricate operating apparatus—even and controlled. Lutz had managed to shift his thoughts from the motor to the conscious level; once that was done, he could be of maximum assistance while his fingers played over the proper switches inside their enormous metal mittens.

Good kid, Vic smiled to himself. Lots of rookies flopped about for days after they had occasion to use electrical medullas on actual mission work. Lutz had enough control to overcome the inevitable panic resulting from walking on a strange world for the first time in a garment that was essentially a robot. He caught on fast. He tried hard.

That's the way I'd like my son to—Vic shut the thought off. There was work to do. And a younger, more inexperienced man to watch. *Still*—

They picked their way through the miniature trees, Lutz now striding along easily, and up a slight rise in the ground. They stood at the top of the small hill finally and looked around while luxurious branches waved in the direction of their stomachs.

From the stern mountains in the distance to the stream dodging shrilly about rusty old rocks nearby, the land on which they stood yawned under a summer sun. Pink and blue grasses stretched and waved at each other. Mist rolled out of the huge lake a mile or so away.

Lutz chuckled inside his helmet. "Always did want to see what a vacation paradise looked like before the real estate boys moved in!"

"If they ever do. See anything moving here right now?"

"Well, that—and these." Harry Lutz indicated the towering bramble forest to their right and the dwarf trees around them.

"Plants. Trees and bushes bending with the wind, waving with the breeze. Nothing like a rabbit, say, breaking cover as we step over his burrow, or a bee skimming along and looking for an appetizing flower. No creatures like bugs working the soil, no birds flying overhead and considering the possibilities of bug-dinners."

"But we knew that already—from the telescanner."

"I know," the mission commander scraped a metallic mitten along his helmet. "But why? The plants aren't carnivorous: with minor alterations in chemistry and morphology, you might expect to find them on Earth. I tell you, I don't like it, Lutz. Why shouldn't this planet have a zoology?"

"Maybe all the animals went into the Hole," Lutz suggested brightly.

Carlton stared at him, "You know," he began, "you may really have something there. Of course, the Hole in Cygnus is an astronomical term," he went on hurriedly. "But there's a lot out here they never heard of on Mount Palomar or Sahara University either. Maybe all the animals went into the Hole. What about *that*—"

"Hey, Vic!" O'Leary's voice from the ship. "Green ball—one of those spore-things—rolling straight for us."

"From where?"

"You should be able to see it in a moment. Due north of that mountain range. There! See that speck coming through those twin peaks?"

The two Scouts outside the ship unsheathed supersonics and crouched as the speck grew into a dot and then into a ball of green hurtling at an almost unbelievable speed.

"Better go back?" Lutz asked nervously.

"We'd never make it—not with that baby traveling as fast as it is. Just keep still and keep down: I've an idea that the solution—"

"More of 'em," Steve O'Leary's voice cut in excitedly. "Two bowling up in a line from the southwest. I don't think they're spores at all; I think they're intelligent and mighty like animules. And they all—Hey-y-y! I just located the mother-lode with the telescanner. Guess where?"

"Let's play games another day," Vic told him.

"From that mess of white tentacles touching the planet on the opposite side. A whole flock of green balls just boiled out. Could those tentacles be alive, have sense-organs? Doesn't seem logical, though, when you consider a couple of them are floating in empty space—"

"Forget the tentacles, O'Leary, and concentrate on the green blobs for a while. I believe we started all this excitement—Lutz and I—by walking out of the ship. Stand by the jets for a scram—with or without us."

"Not on your rating. That's final, Vic! Either you boys fight your way back in or I come out to join you."

Carlton bit his lip. The green ball was almost overhead now, its smooth, completely featureless surface flickering most oddly. That was always the trouble with a man making a bounce. He fluctuated between abysmal fright and mountainous bravado, both nothing else than a simple fear of being afraid—and both always coming up at the wrong times. Right now, he wanted a subordinate who could understand the supreme importance of the first mission to the Hole, who could appreciate a situation where information might be a thousand times more important than the lives or opinions of others—and who would be rock-steady in an emergency instead of skittering about with a private neurosis.

"All right, O'Leary, Secondary attack precautions. Get into a spacesuit and man the bow gun. Robots on the others. Switch to full visiplate hookup. But keep those jets ready to blast!"

"Uh—commander," Lutz broke in. "Three of those balls overhead. More coming. But they're ignoring us: they just bang around the ship."

Vic Carlton stared upward. He'd never seen anything quite like these spheres. Their color might argue for chlorophyll, but they were far too animate, too purposeful, to have botanical origins. Vehicles in which sat sentient organisms? That might account for the lack of such things as eyes and locomotive appendages. But, then, where was the jet-trail or any other evidence of a propulsive device? And surely the way they expanded and contracted seemed to point to an intrinsic life of their own. That was really odd, now—

"Could they be breathing?" the C Scout wondered aloud.

"No. Too irregular for respiration, I'd say. Just keep still, Lutz, and wait it out. This is the hardest part of a mission, boy, but patience has saved more lives than all the Grojen shielding ever made."

They waited, inside their great suits, while the number of balls increased to twelve, all shooting about the ship in straight, determined lines. Evidently, Vic reflected, while they sat still, they went unnoticed.

Suddenly, one of the spheres paused outside the airlock.

"Seems to know its way around," O'Leary commented from the ship. He laughed twice, the second time after a few moments' pause. "I'm getting jumpy, Vic."

"Don't," he was advised. "They may be smart enough to know how we enter and leave the ship, but they can't have seen many spaceships if they get this close to a fully armed one. Sit on your nerves, Steve: once they thin out and we can get back, we might try communicating with them. Although they don't seem to be responsive. You're wearing side-arms, I hope?"

"Supersonics. And a heavy blaster across my lap. Blow a hole through the hull if I use it, but if I have to— Say! Is that baby doing what I see through the visiplate?"

It was. The ball had withdrawn a little distance from the ship and came rushing towards it rapidly. It bounced gently, soundlessly, off the hull, retired and repeated the process. The horizontal lines in which it moved and the insistent nature of its repetitious approach reminded the three Scouts of a fist knocking at a door.

Then—it disappeared!

They shook their heads and grimaced at the spot where it had last been in the midst of another rush at the airlock. It was gone, with no faintest emerald trace left behind on the lazy air. Around the ship, eleven balls shot back and forth, back and forth, in absolutely straight lines. But there had been twelve a moment ago!

"C-Commander, wh-what do you think h-happened?"

"Don't know, Lutz. But I definitely don't like it."

"Neither do I," O'Leary whispered in their radio phones. "This is one of those moments in a B Scout's life when he wonders what he ever saw in an A Scout rating to make him leave home and mama. I'd like to be back in— *No!* Vic, it's *impossible!* It couldn't— It—"

"What happened? Steve! What's going on?"

"The damn ball materialized inside the ship—just as I was reaching over to the— not five feet from me—made a rush at my head—almost got—" Steve O'Leary's voice came over in jerky snatches as if he were spitting out each fragment between jumps. "Chasing me all over the Control Room—*no, you don't*—caroming off the bulkheads like a billiard—wait, I think I have a sight—"

A tremendous roar. O'Leary had used the blaster. Echo after echo piled crazily upon their eardrums and a jagged hole flapped open near the nose of the ship as if it had been punched out.

"Missed! Could've sworn I had a clear sight—blast went practically head-on— don't know *how* I missed—now, maybe with a supersonic—well, what would you call *that?* Vic! It's disappeared again! Clean gone! I'm getting out of here!"

"Careful, Steve!" Carlton yelled. "You're panicky!"

There was no reply. Instead, the airlock swung open, and Steve O'Leary, spacesuited to almost twice his normal size, leaped out. He carried a supersonic in his left hand and a blaster in his right, and he came out shooting. Eleven green balls converged on him, riding imperturbably through his blasts.

The two Scouts on the hill had leaped to their feet. They shot bolt after bolt of high frequency sound, sound which could dissolve any conceivable organic structure into its component chemicals. They might have been using water-pistols for all the effect they had.

A twelfth ball appeared directly in O'Leary's path. It began the size of an apple, and, almost before their eyes could register the change, had coruscated glaucously to the diameter of a life boat. A little in advance of its fellows, it shot at the B Scout.

It touched him.

And he screamed.

His scream seemed to have begun years ago and continue into the unguessable future. And then, the entire spacesuit seemed to fly open and—not O'Leary, but his insides, came out. Where a metallic figure had been running, covered with a Grojen shield and lightly draped with Mannheim baffles, there was now only stomach and spleen, liver and intestine, stretched fantastically, unbelievably, into the shape of Steve O'Leary. The figure took another step, and the scream ululated out of human recognition. Then it stopped.

O'Leary was gone. And the green ball was gone.

The other balls had passed over the spot where Steve O'Leary had disappeared. Two of them disappeared in turn. Nine returned to the ship and continued their determined, whipping investigation.

Lutz was being violently sick inside his spacesuit. Vic fought for self-control. *Had he or had he not seen the emerald ball change to a deep olive and then to the color of pouring blood just before it went out?*

"Listen, kid," he said rapidly. "Keep still, keep absolutely, perfectly still—no matter what happens. Don't even roll your eyes. I think I know what those things are, and I don't think anything we have can stop them. Our only hope is to avoid attracting attention. So don't move until I give you the word. Got that?"

He heard Lutz's breathing become more regular. "Y-yes, commander. But don't they remember us shooting at them? And can't they see us standing here in plain sight?"

"Not if they're what I suspect. Relax, kid, relax as far back as you can. Remember, not a movement of any kind you can control. And no conversation for a while. Nothing. Just watch and wait."

They waited. They watched. They waited for hours, half-reclining in their immobile suits, while the green balls tore back and forth, appeared and disappeared silently, steadily, with unwavering purpose. They watched the blue line running the length of their precious ship—the line that proclaimed it a Scout vessel and able to outrun anything in space—they watched the blue line dissolve into the gray metal around it under the thick suds of twilight. And they made no movement, no, not even when a bloated sphere of green expanded in front of them suddenly and seemed to consider them under invisible optic organs before losing interest and scudding away.

That was the hardest part, after all, Vic decided: not moving even though the feeling that they were under surveillance increased with every second; not jerking suddenly, though most ancient instincts shouted that it was time to run, that this very moment they would be attacked by the unseeable.

He came to appreciate his companion's qualities in the course of the awful vigil: not many men could maintain that necessary exterior calm on the very knife-edge of extinction. *One good kid.*

They waited; they watched; they didn't move. And they thought about Steve O'Leary....

Finally, two of the balls rose and flew off to the north. An hour later, two more followed. The remaining five came to rest above the ship, forming the points of a rough pentagon.

"All right, Lutz," the A Scout murmured. "We can unbend—just a little! Six hours of daylight. We'll sleep two hours apiece, you first, one watching while the other takes a nap. That'll give us some rest before we make our play, and maybe in that time the five tumblebugs will decide to go home."

"What are they, commander? What in the name of intergalactic space can they be?"

"What are they? A leak in the Hole of Cygnus. They're where all the animals went."

"I—I don't understand."

Carlton almost gestured impatiently, stopped himself just in time. "There's much that's peculiar about the Hole. Not merely the absence of ordinary celestial phenomena, the rarity of stars and such-like, but loopholes in natural law which you find nowhere else. A minority of modern theories consider this general area the starting-place of our particular universe; whether they begin with space warping in on itself because it got tired of standing around in time, or with one version or another of the explosion of a primordial atom—whatever they begin with these days, they work in the Hole in Cygnus somehow as the place where it might have occurred."

"Yes. Ever since Boker came out here two hundred years ago and discovered the sectors of chronological gap."

"Right, kid. Now I don't claim to know how the universe started. But I'm willing to bet my next meal in Sandstorm against the dust on your right boot that this was where it did. And from the looks of things, the area around Cygnus never recovered. It remained a hole in space where all kinds of stuff that shouldn't be, is—and vice versa. That moment or millennium of creation tore it up plenty. And among the tears, among the cuts that were never healed, I classify those white tentacle thingumabobs all over this system."

"And the green balls came through the one on this planet from—from—"

"From some place outside. From another universe which we can't reach or even imagine."

Lutz thought about that for a moment. "On another plane, you mean, commander?"

"On another dimension. The fourth, to be specific."

"But way back in the twentieth century, they proved that the fourth dimension was time and *we* move through it!"

"I mean a fourth spatial dimension, Lutz. A universe where there's length, breadth, height—and, well, one *more* direction, besides. Time, too, but even a conceivable two-dimensional creature must have duration in order to exist. And that's the way to understand those babies: what they can do, what they can't, what happened to O'Leary, and what hope we have of covering those sixty yards to the ship and taking off. Analogy. Think of a two-dimensional man."

"You mean width and length, but no height? Gee—I don't know. I guess we'd see his skin as a thin line around his skeleton and internal organs. And—wait a minute—he'd be able to move and see only on an absolutely flat surface!"

Carlton silently thanked the academy officials for entrance examination that weeded out the least imaginative. "You're doing fine. Now suppose we stuck a finger into this two-dimensional world. The man in it would see the finger as a circle—just as we see these creatures as spheres. When the tip had gone through his world and the finger proper was visible, he would feel the circle had grown larger; when we pulled the finger out, he'd say it had disappeared. If we wanted to eat him, say, we could hover above him while he ran from the place where he'd last seen us. Then pounce down in front of him, and he'd think we'd suddenly materialized out of thin air. And, if we wanted to lift him into our world, our space—"

"We'd pick him up by the skin and his insides would momentarily be the only part of him visible in his world." Lutz shivered involuntarily. "Ugh. Then those balls are sections of fourth-dimensional fingers—or pseudopods?"

"I don't know. I suspect, though, that these creatures are only fourth-dimensional equivalents of our very simple forms—anything from bacteria to worms—but still dangerous as death itself. I don't think they're very complicated animals on their world because they seem to have pretty elementary sense-perceptions. They don't hear us, smell us or feel us; and they only chase us when we move. That all adds up to a fairly primitive organism, even in four dimensions. It would explain why there's no animal life on this planet, but plants of almost every kind: animals are motile, so they were chased and eaten; plants generally grow in one spot, so they were ignored."

"But, Vic, we have to move to get back in the ship!"

"We have to move, but not in straight lines. Not the way those balls move back and forth, not the way O'Leary moved. We'll run a purposely erratic course to the airlock, we'll stop unexpectedly, we'll zigzag, we'll turn around and double on our tracks. It'll take up extra time, but I'm betting that our green chums haven't the sensory or mental equipment to solve a random movement fast enough."

"Poor O'Leary! It'll seem all wrong going back without that big loud redhead."

"We aren't going, kid, until we get inside that ship and flush those jets behind us. Now grab some sleep before we run out of night."

As the C Scout closed his eyes obediently, Carlton risked a glance at him. Tired, scared as hell, but still swallowing orders with alacrity, still willing to take chances. *One good kid*, he repeated to himself. *Wonder if he's started shaving yet. Nope—with that jet-black hair and creamy complexion a beard would be very obvious, even a couple of hours growth.*

Wonder who he has waiting for him back home. Probably only his mother; doesn't act like the kind of kid who's played around much with girls. Probably only the girl, the one he took to the graduation ball at the academy.

Wonder what Kay would think of Lutz—would she understand him?

Wonder who's waiting for O'Leary…

The green spheres above the ship were perfectly still, their smooth bodies ignoring even the stern night wind that roared down from the mountains. Asleep, in their own peculiar way? Or waiting?

Lutz and O'Leary: two good guys, Kay. Adolescents? Spacewash!

Vic let Lutz sleep for almost three hours before awakening him. It would take two to do this job right, and he wanted the younger man's nerves to settle as much as possible.

"I lost track of *my* nerves about five years ago off Sirius," he explained.

"All the same. Vic, all the same, you can't punish yourself like that! Why you won't even have a full hour yourself."

"It'll do me fine. Now just stand guard and whistle once—loudly—if anything is on the verge of popping. And whistle at the end of the hour."

He fell asleep instantly and dreamlessly with the ease of the experienced Scout who has used his spacesuit as a flophouse many times. He woke a moment before the hour was up, when the alarm clock buried in his subconscious went off.

Lutz was singing under his breath to keep himself company. Almost without sound, just enough of the words came through over the radio phones to make the song clear. Carlton listened to Lutz sing with all the loneliness, the longing, of the last man alive:

> *...and end my days*
> *On some mould'ring ball.*
> *No more to the stars will I go—*
> *O lads!*
> *No more to the stars will I go!*

"First," the commander broke in cheerfully, "you need a maiden's praise, kid. To hold you in thrall. But you wouldn't understand that part."

"Sorry I woke you, Vic. I was just going to whistle. And when it comes to a maiden's praise, I do as well as the next guy. Had a tough time getting away for this mission, let me tell you!"

"Who—your sister? Or the girl next door?" This light banter would develop just the right mood for what they had to do.

"My *sister!*" Lutz laughed boyishly. "Hell, no. My wife."

Carlton was amazed, "Are *you* married?"

"Married? I sincerely hope for the sake of my children that I am!"

"Well, I'll be— How many do you have?"

"Two. Two girls. The youngest, Jeanette, is only three months old. She's a blonde, like her mother."

"Yes," Vic mused. "Kay's a blonde. Her daughter would probably—"

"Kay? Your wife, commander?"

"No. My fiancée," Vic told him stiffly. "Well, one good thing about marriage, Lutz; your dependents are well taken care of. The Scout finance department doesn't recognize engagement rings. I guess that's a comfort to a husband and father if he's knocked off somewhere in emptiness."

The C Scout looked down at the ship. "All five of them still there, commander. I'm ready to go any time you give the word."

There was a pause. "Look, Lutz," Carlton began awkwardly. "I'm sorry if—if—"

"No offense taken if none's given, Vic. Only thing, way back in my second year at the academy I decided that I wanted to get married, I wanted to have a family—*and* I wanted to be a Scout. All three. So you figure it out. Me, I find it hurts my head."

"All right, then; let's concentrate on what we have to do. When I yell, we leap sideways and come down upon the ship in two converging arcs. Using medulla-switches, we can run twice as fast as a horse. We don't run more than two steps in a straight line if we can remember it—and we've got to remember it! First man in kicks the jets over. If the other man isn't in by the time the ship takes off, he's left behind. No second chance, no waiting a moment longer, no looking back. I think if we do this right, we can confuse them enough to get away together, but if we don't—remember that we can't help each other and that our records and interpretation *must* make it to Sandstorm: Check?"

"Check. And good luck, Vic."

"Good luck, Harry. And good running."

The A Scout looked around one last time to judge the ground he would have to travel. His fingers crept over the switches in the mittens, ready to galvanize the suit into a breakneck speed. "Now!" he roared, leaping off to the left.

As he pounded down the slope, his speed and weight uprooting the tiny trees in his twisting path, he could see Lutz, far off to his right, zigzagging with him. They might make it. They might—

They got to twenty yards of the ship before the green balls noticed them. And streaked straight for them without hesitation.

Carlton stopped, leaped backward, sideward, and came around the stern of the ship in a great curve. Lutz was coming down the other side, his course resembling a drunk with rocket attachment. The airlock gaped open between them. Immense balls sped by hungrily, almost touching, almost— Only eleven yards. Double back and leap forward again. Nine yards. Jump away from the ship and cut in at a sharp angle. Seven.

"Look, commander. I'm in—I made it!" Only six yards from the airlock—only eighteen feet! Harry Lutz lost his head. He came up in a tremendous broad-jump powered by the motor of the heavy suit. He aimed at the open door of the airlock, evidently intending to catch it in mid-air and pull himself inside. But it was he who was caught in mid-air.

A green sphere materialized twelve feet from the lock and Lutz, unable to check himself, smashed into it. Almost before he began screaming, almost before he began to turn inside out, the remaining four balls had shot to the other side of the lock to observe or partake of the prey.

The way was clear for Carlton. He leaped inside, almost brushing the crimsoning ball—wondering whether he could have done it if they hadn't caught Harry Lutz.

"Poor little Jeanette," he wept as Lutz's scream bit and clawed at his eardrums. "Poor kid, she's only three months old!" he cried as he pulled the red switch on the control panel and jumped away for a moment just in case. "Poor little blonde Jeanette, she's only a baby! She can't remember anything," he screamed in sympathy to Lutz's continuing scream as he swung balance-control, adjusted acceleration-helix, felt the ship whip up and outward with him—and continued to zigzag about the control room because you never knew, you just never knew about those green balls.

But when he had switched to interstellar shoot, and found Lutz's scream still in his ears, still rising in insane volume, when he found himself unable to stop leaping backward, forward, sideward, about the control room—he attached the main oxygen tanks to his helmet and turned on the automatic alarm.

A patrol ship got to him three days later. There was no air in the little vessel because, while the lock had closed automatically upon takeoff, the hole in the nose had never been repaired. But Vic Carlton, completely exhausted and with eyes like diseased tomatoes, was alive in a spacesuit designed to *keep* a man alive under the most incredible conditions. He had disconnected his helmet phones and, when they hauled him out of his ship, he kept beating both mittened hands against his head in the region of his ears.

They gave him an anesthetic in the patrol ship hospital and set a fast course for Sol.

"Poor little Jeanette Lutz," he whispered painfully just before he fell asleep. "She's only three months old."

"Are you sure you can pull him through?" a perspiring commissioner asked in the hospital on Ganymede. "Because if there's any danger that you can't, let's use a hypnotic probe. The information he's carrying is worth the risk of permanent damage to his mind."

"We'll pull him through," the doctor said, making unhappy early-morning grimaces as he washed his mouth with his tongue. "We'll pull him through all right. According to his charts, he's survived concentrated therapy before. No point in blowing out his brains with a probe when he'll be able to tell you everything you want to know in a week or two."

"I told them everything," Vic informed Kay three weeks later when he met her on the main floor of the Scout Operations Building. "I told them off, too. How can you expect a man to take a bounce, I said, when the Service itself won't? That's what the Patrol big-brains decided—that the Hole is still too dangerous for anything mankind has. They're going to wait a while before sending another exploring party there. *Well,* I said—"

He stopped as the elevator doors slid open and the crowd of Scouts surrounding the three helmeted ones in the center moved toward the double doors chattering and chafing.

"Look at Spinelli, fellows! He's dead already!"

"Poor Spinelli, his first command! Hey, Spin, this is the bounce Carlton wouldn't take! He musta known something!"

"Hey, Tronck! What're you looking so green about!"

"Steady there, Spinelli. You're a commander now!"

Vic's hand crept to his chest as the men passed. He fingered the gold star which glowed from the spot where, an hour before, a silver rocket had poised.

Kay touched the star, too. Her back was to the men marching to the ship, but her eyes shone into Vic's. "Commissioner Carlton! It sounds as if it was always meant to be just that. Alliterative, too! Oh, Vic, this is the way we said it would be—this is the way we both wanted it. You, with the fire still in you, knowing that you're a grown man, knowing what you want—"

From the distance, they could hear the song:

> *If it's a girl, dress her up in lace;*
> *If it's a boy, send the bastard off to space.*

"Darling," she whispered, pressing his hand against her cheek. "We'll have lots of lace *and* lots of space. We'll have everything."

Vic didn't answer. He stood, ignoring her completely, as the three men sang themselves into the slender little ship with the long blue stripe. When the ground crew scattered with warning yells of "Jets away! Jets away away, jets away!" he took one resolute step forward, stopped—and put his hands in his pockets.

Then the sudden scream and clatter of flame, dying almost before it had been felt; then the silver pencil up in the sky that left a thin line of brightest scarlet behind it. The ship was gone, and a cloud waddled over its trail, but still Vic stared upward. Kay said nothing.

When, at last, he turned back to her, his eyes were full of middle age.

AFTERWORD

There are two points of origin for this story, two very different ones in terms of both quality and time. The first has to do with Abbott's *Flatland,* the mathematical fantasy I read and was entranced by at the age of thirteen. I immediately decided the suggestions of the narrator, A Square, about the fourth dimension deserved development and dramatization. How about, I wondered, a fourth-dimensional bacterium at loose in our universe? I thought about it often, but didn't know quite what to do with the idea.

I picked it up years later, when I was living with a woman I was preparing to marry, but who unfortunately was a very difficult person around whom to be a writer, at least for me. "You have such a good head, Phil," she would say. "Why do you write this garbage?" She was, of course, referring to science fiction. She would say yes to Chaucer and Donne, to Proust and Edith Sitwell, but definitely no to the likes of Clifford Simak, Olaf Stapledon, and Cordwainer Smith.

The trouble was I loved her mightily, and couldn't think of anyone else I'd rather sleep beside for the rest of my life. But the further trouble was that nothing ever got on paper for weeks after I'd spent the night with her.

So I stayed away from her for a long while and managed to write "The Last Bounce." She was very excited and more than a bit happy to learn that I was writing again. She demanded to see the story.

I showed it to her. She kept her head bowed for a long time after she read it. Then she looked up. "All right, little bird," she said in a low, low voice. "I hear you. Fly away. Fly away, little bird."

I flew away.

WRITTEN 1950———PUBLISHED 1950

ॐ

VENUS IS A MAN'S WORLD

I've always said that even if Sis is seven years older than me—and a girl besides—she don't always know what's best. Put me on a spaceship jam-packed with three hundred females just aching to get themselves husbands in the one place they're still to be had—the planet Venus—and you know I'll be in trouble.

Bad trouble. With the law, which is the worst a boy can get into.

Twenty minutes after we lifted from the Sahara Spaceport, I wriggled out of my acceleration hammock and started for the door of our cabin.

"Now you be careful, Ferdinand," Sis called after me as she opened a book called *Family Problems of the Frontier Woman.* "Remember you're a nice boy. Don't make me ashamed of you."

I tore down the corridor. Most of the cabins had purple lights on in front of the doors, showing that the girls were still inside their hammocks. That meant only the ship's crew was up and about. Ship's crews are men; women are too busy with important things like government to run ships. I felt free all over—and happy. Now was my chance to really see the *Eleanor Roosevelt!*

It was hard to believe I was traveling in space at last. Ahead and behind me, all the way up to where the companionway curved in out of sight, there was nothing but smooth black wall and smooth white doors—on and on and on. *Gee,* I thought excitedly, *this is one big ship!*

Of course, every once in a while I would run across a big scene of stars in the void set in the wall; but they were only pictures. Nothing that gave the feel of great empty space like I'd read about in *The Boy Rocketeers,* no portholes, no visiplates, nothing.

So when I came to the crossway, I stopped for a second, then turned left. To the right, see, there was Deck Four, then Deck Three, leading inward past the engine fo'c'sle to the main jets and the grav helix going *purr-purr-purrty-purr* in the comforting way big machinery has when it's happy and oiled. But to the left, the crossway led all the way to the outside level which ran just under the hull. There were portholes on the hull.

I'd studied all that out in our cabin, long before we'd lifted, on the transparent model of the ship hanging like a big cigar from the ceiling. Sis had studied it too, but she was looking for places like the dining salon and the library and Lifeboat 68 where we should go in case of emergency. I looked for the *important* things.

As I trotted along the crossway, I sort of wished that Sis hadn't decided to go after a husband on a luxury liner. On a cargo ship, now, I'd be climbing from deck to deck on a ladder instead of having gravity underfoot all the time just like I was home on the bottom of the Gulf of Mexico. But women always know what's right, and a boy can only make faces and do what they say, same as the men have to do.

Still, it was pretty exciting to press my nose against the slots in the wall and see the sliding panels that could come charging out and block the crossway into an airtight fit in case a meteor or something smashed into the ship. And all along there were glass cases with spacesuits standing in them, like those knights they used to have back in the Middle Ages.

"In the event of disaster affecting the oxygen content of companionway," they had the words etched into the glass, "break glass with hammer upon wall, remove spacesuit and proceed to don it in the following fashion."

I read the "following fashion" until I knew it by heart. *Boy,* I said to myself, *I hope we have that kind of disaster. I'd sure like to get into one of those! Bet it would be more fun than those diving suits back in Undersea!*

And all the time I was alone. That was the best part.

Then I passed Deck Twelve and there was a big sign. "Notice! Passengers not permitted past this point!" A big sign in red.

I peeked around the corner. I knew it—the next deck was the hull. I could see the portholes. Every twelve feet, they were, filled with the velvet of space and the dancing of more stars than I'd ever dreamed existed in the universe.

There wasn't anyone on the deck, as far as I could see. And this distance from the grav helix, the ship seemed mighty quiet and lonely. If I just took one quick look…

But I thought of what Sis would say and I turned around obediently. Then I saw the big red sign again. "Passengers not permitted—"

Well! Didn't I know from my civics class that only women could be Earth Citizens these days? Sure, ever since the Male Desuffrage Act. And didn't I know that you had to be a citizen of a planet in order to get an interplanetary passport? Sis had explained it all to me in the careful, patient way she always talks politics and things like that to men.

"Technically, Ferdinand, I'm the only passenger in our family. You can't be one, because, not being a citizen, you can't acquire an Earth Passport. However, you'll be going to Venus on the strength of this clause—'Miss Evelyn Sparling and all dependent male members of family, this number not to exceed the registered quota of subregulations pertaining'—and so on. I want you to understand these matters, so that you will grow into a man who takes an active interest in world affairs. No matter what you hear, women really like and appreciate such men."

Of course, I never pay much attention to Sis when she says such dumb things. I'm old enough, I guess, to know that it isn't what *women* like and appreciate that counts when it comes to people getting married. If it were, Sis and three hundred other pretty girls like her wouldn't be on their way to Venus to hook husbands.

Still, if I wasn't a passenger, the sign didn't have anything to do with me. I knew what Sis could say to *that,* but at least it was an argument I could use if it ever came up. So I broke the law.

I was glad I did. The stars were exciting enough, but away off to the left, about five times as big as I'd ever seen it, except in the movies, was the Moon, a great blob of gray and white pockmarks holding off the black of space. I was hoping to see the Earth, but I figured it must be on the other side of the ship or behind us. I pressed my nose against the port and saw the tiny flicker of a spaceliner taking off, Marsbound. I wished I was on that one!

Then I noticed, a little farther down the companionway, a stretch of blank wall where there should have been portholes. High up on the wall in glowing red letters were the words, "Lifeboat 47. Passengers: Thirty-two. Crew: Eleven. Unauthorized personnel keep away!"

Another one of those signs.

I crept up to the porthole nearest it and could just barely make out the stern jets where they were jammed against the hull. Then I walked under the sign and tried to figure the way you were supposed to get into it. There was a very thin line going around in a big circle that I knew must be the door. But I couldn't see any knobs or switches to open it with. Not even a button you could press.

That meant it was a sonic lock like the kind we had on the outer keeps back home in Undersea. But knock or voice? I tried the two knock combinations I knew, and nothing happened. I only remembered one voice key—might as well see if that's it, I figured.

"Twenty, Twenty-three. Open Sesame."

For a second, I thought I'd hit it just right out of all the million possible combinations— The door clicked inward toward a black hole, and a hairy hand as broad as my shoulders shot out of the hole. It closed around my throat and plucked me inside as if I'd been a baby sardine.

I bounced once on the hard lifeboat floor. Before I got my breath and sat up, the door had been shut again. When the light came on, I found myself staring up the muzzle of a highly polished blaster and into the cold blue eyes of the biggest man I'd ever seen.

He was wearing a one-piece suit made of some scaly green stuff that looked hard and soft at the same time.

His boots were made of it, too, and so was the hood hanging down his back.

And his face was brown. Not just ordinary tan, you understand, but the deep, dark, burned-all-the-way-in brown I'd seen on the life guards in New Orleans whenever we took a surface vacation—the kind of tan that comes from day after broiling day under a really hot sun. His hair looked as if it had once been blond, but now there were just long combed-out waves with a yellowish tinge that boiled all the way down to his shoulders.

I hadn't seen hair like that on a man except maybe in history books; every man I'd ever known had his hair cropped in the fashionable soup-bowl style. I was staring at his hair, almost forgetting about the blaster which I knew it was against the law for him to have at all, when I suddenly got scared right through.

His eyes.

They didn't blink and there seemed to be no expression around them. Just coldness. Maybe it was the kind of clothes he was wearing that did it, but all of a sudden I was reminded of a crocodile I'd seen in a surface zoo that had stared quietly at me for twenty minutes until it opened two long tooth-studded jaws.

"Green shatas!" he said suddenly. "Only a tadpole. I must be getting jumpy enough to splash."

Then he shoved the blaster away in a holster made of the same scaly leather, crossed his arms on his chest and began to study me. I grunted to my feet, feeling a lot better. The coldness had gone out of his eyes.

I held out my hand the way Sis had taught me. "My name is Ferdinand Sparling. I'm very pleased to meet you, Mr.—Mr.—"

"Hope for your sake," he said to me, "that you aren't what you seem—tadpole brother to one of them husbandless anura."

"*What?*"

"A 'nuran is a female looking to nest. Anura is a herd of same. Come from Flatfolk ways."

"Flatfolk are the Venusian natives, aren't they? Are you a Venusian? What part of Venus do you come from? Why did you say you hope—"

He chuckled and swung me up into one of the bunks that lined the lifeboat. "Questions you ask," he said in his soft voice. "Venus is a sharp enough place for a dryhorn, let alone a tadpole dryhorn with a boss-minded sister."

"I'm not a dryleg," I told him proudly. "*We're* from Undersea."

"Dry*horn*, I said, not dryleg. And what's Undersea?"

"Well, in Undersea we called foreigners and newcomers drylegs. Just like on Venus, I guess, you call them dryhorns." And then I told him how Undersea had been built on the bottom of the Gulf of Mexico, when the mineral resources of the land began to give out and engineers figured that a lot could still be reached from the sea bottoms.

He nodded. He'd heard about the sea-bottom mining cities that were bubbling under protective domes in every one of the Earth's oceans just about the same time settlements were springing up on the planets.

He looked impressed when I told him about Mom and Pop being one of the first couples to get married in Undersea. He looked thoughtful when I told him how Sis and I had been born there and spent half our childhood listening to the pressure pumps. He raised his eyebrows and looked disgusted when I told how Mom, as Undersea representative on the World Council, had been one of the framers of the Male Desuffrage Act after the Third Atomic War had resulted in the Maternal Revolution.

And then he punched my arm when I got to the time Mom and Pop were blown up in a surfacing boat.

"Well, after the funeral, there was a little money, so Sis decided we might as well use it to migrate. There was no future for her on Earth, she figured. You know, the three-out-of-four."

"How's that?"

"The three-out-of-four. No more than three women out of every four on Earth can expect to find husbands. Not enough men to go around. Way back in the twentieth century, it began to be felt, Sis says, what with the wars and all. Then the wars went on and a lot more men began to die or get no good from the radioactivity. Then the best men went to the planets, Sis says, until by now even if a woman can scrounge a personal husband, he's not much to boast about."

The stranger nodded violently. "Not on Earth, he isn't. Those busybody anura make sure of that. What a place! Suffering gridniks, I had a bellyful!"

He told me about it. Women were scarce on Venus, and he hadn't been able to find any who were willing to come out to his lonely little islands; he had decided to go to Earth, where there was supposed to be a surplus. Naturally, having been born and brought up on a very primitive planet, he didn't know "it's a woman's world," like the older boys in school used to say.

The moment he landed on Earth he was in trouble. He didn't know he had to register at a government-operated hotel for transient males; he threw a bartender through a thick plastic window for saying something nasty about the length of his hair; and *imagine!*—he not only resisted arrest, resulting in three hospitalized policemen, but he sassed the judge in open court!

"Told me a man wasn't supposed to say anything except through female attorneys. Told *her* that where *I* came from, a man spoke his piece when he'd a mind to, and his woman walked by his side."

"What happened?" I asked breathlessly.

"Oh, Guilty of This and Contempt of That. That blown-up brinosaur took my last munit for fines, then explained that she was remitting the rest because I was a foreigner and uneducated." His eyes grew dark for a moment. He chuckled again. "But I wasn't going to serve all those fancy little prison sentences. Forcible Citizenship Indoctrination, they call it? Shook the dead-dry dust of the misbegotten, God-forsaken mother world from my feet forever. The women on it deserve their men. My pockets were folded from the fines, and the paddlefeet were looking for me so close I didn't dare radio for more munit. So I stowed away."

For a moment, I didn't understand him. When I did, I was almost ill. "Y-you mean," I choked, "th-that you're b-breaking the law right now? And I'm with you while you're doing it?"

He leaned over the edge of the bunk and stared at me very seriously. "What breed of tadpole are they turning out these days? Besides, what business do *you* have this close to the hull?"

After a moment of sober reflection, I nodded. "You're right. I've also become a male outside the law. We're in this together."

He guffawed. Then he sat up and began cleaning his blaster. I found myself drawn to the bright killer-tube with exactly the fascination Sis insists such things have always had for men.

"Ferdinand your label? That's not right for a sprouting tadpole. I'll call you Ford. My name's Butt. Butt Lee Brown."

I liked the sound of Ford. "Is Butt a nickname, too?"

"Yeah. Short for Alberta, but I haven't found a man who can draw a blaster fast enough to call me that. You see, Pop came over in the eighties—the big wave of immigrants when they evacuated Ontario. Named all us boys after Canadian provinces. I was the youngest, so I got the name they were saving for a girl."

"You had a lot of brothers, Mr. Butt?"

He grinned with a mighty set of teeth. "Oh, a nestful. Of course, they were all killed in the Blue Chicago Rising by the MacGregor boys—all except me and Saskatchewan. Then Sas and me hunted the MacGregors down. Took a heap of time; we didn't float Jock MacGregor's ugly face down the Tuscany till both of us were pretty near grown up."

I walked up close to where I could see the tiny bright copper coils of the blaster above the firing button. "Have you killed a lot of men with that, Mr. Butt?"

"Butt. Just plain Butt to you, Ford." He frowned and sighted at the light globe. "No more'n twelve—not counting five government paddlefeet, of course. I'm a peaceable planter. Way I figure it, violence never accomplishes much that's important. My brother Sas, now—"

He had just begun to work into this wonderful story about his brother when the dinner gong rang. Butt told me to scat. He said I was a growing tadpole and needed my vitamins. And he mentioned, very off-hand, that he wouldn't at all object if I brought him some fresh fruit. It seemed there was nothing but processed foods in the lifeboat and Butt was used to a farmer's diet.

Trouble was, he was a special kind of farmer. Ordinary fruit would have been pretty easy to sneak into my pockets at meals. I even found a way to handle the kelp and giant watercress Mr. Brown liked, but things like seaweed salt and Venusian mudgrapes just had too strong a smell. Twice, the mechanical hamper refused to accept my jacket for laundering and I had to wash it myself. But I learned so many wonderful things about Venus every time I visited that stowaway...

I learned three wild-wave songs of the Flatfolk and what it is that the native Venusians hate so much; I learned how you tell the difference between a lousy government paddlefoot from New Kalamazoo and the slaptoe slinker who is the planter's friend. After a lot of begging, Butt Lee Brown explained the workings of his blaster, explained it so carefully that I could name every part and tell what it did from the tiny round electrodes to the long spirals of transformer. But no matter what, he would never let me hold it.

"Sorry, Ford, old tad," he would drawl, spinning around and around in the control swivel-chair at the nose of the lifeboat. "But way I look at it, a man who lets somebody else handle his blaster is like the giant whose heart was in an egg that an enemy found. When you've grown enough so's your pop feels you ought to have a weapon, why, then's the time to learn it and you might's well learn fast. Before then, you're plain too young to be even near it."

"I don't have a father to give me one when I come of age. I don't even have an older brother as head of my family like your brother Labrador. All I have is Sis. And *she*—"

"She'll marry some fancy dryhorn who's never been farther south than the Polar Coast. And she'll stay head of the family, if I know her breed of green shata. *Bossy, opinionated.* By the way, Fordie," he said, rising and stretching so the fish-leather bounced and rippled off his biceps, "that sister. She ever…"

And he'd be off again, cross-examining me about Evelyn. I sat in the swivel chair he'd vacated and tried to answer his questions. But there was a lot of stuff I didn't know. Evelyn was a healthy girl, for instance; how healthy, exactly, I had no way of finding out. Yes, I'd tell him, my aunts on both sides of my family had each had more than the average number of children. No, we'd never done any farming to speak of, back in Undersea, but—yes, I'd guess Evelyn knew about as much as any girl there when it came to diving equipment and pressure pump regulation.

How would I know that stuff would lead to trouble for me?

Sis had insisted I come along to the geography lecture. Most of the other girls who were going to Venus for husbands talked to each other during the lecture, but not *my* sister! She hung on every word, took notes even, and asked enough questions to make the perspiring purser really work in those orientation periods.

"I am very sorry, Miss Sparling," he said with pretty heavy sarcasm, "but I cannot remember any of the agricultural products of the Macro Continent. Since the human population is well below one per thousand square miles, it can readily be understood that the quantity of tilled soil, land or sub-surface, is so small that— Wait, I remember something. The Macro Continent exports a fruit though not exactly an edible one. The wild *dunging* drug is harvested there by criminal speculators. Contrary to belief on Earth, the traffic has been growing in recent years. In fact—"

"Pardon me, sir," I broke in, "but doesn't *dunging* come only from Leif Erickson Island off the Moscow Peninsula of the Macro Continent? You remember, purser— Wang Li's third exploration, where he proved the island and the peninsula didn't meet for most of the year?"

The purser nodded slowly. "I forgot," he admitted. "Sorry, ladies, but the boy's right. Please make the correction in your notes."

But Sis was the only one who took notes, and she didn't take that one. She stared at me for a moment, biting her lower lip thoughtfully, while I got sicker and sicker. Then she shut her pad with the final gesture of the right hand that Mom used to use just before challenging the opposition to come right down on the Council floor and debate it out with her.

"Ferdinand," Sis said, "let's go back to our cabin."

The moment she sat me down and walked slowly around me, I knew I was in for it. "I've been reading up on Venusian geography in the ship's library," I told her in a hurry.

"No doubt," she said dryly. She shook her night-black hair out. "But you aren't going to tell me that you read about *dunging* in the ship's library. The books there have been censored by a government agent of Earth against the possibility that they might be read by susceptible young male minds like yours. She would not have allowed—this Terran Agent—"

"Paddlefoot," I sneered.

Sis sat down hard in our zoom-air chair. "Now that's a term," she said carefully, "that is used only by Venusian riffraff."

"They're not!"

"Not what?"

"Riffraff," I had to answer, knowing I was getting in deeper all the time and not being able to help it. I mustn't give Mr. Brown away! "They're trappers and farmers, pioneers and explorers, who're building Venus. And it takes a real man to build on a hot, hungry hell like Venus."

"Does it now?" she said, looking at me as if I were beginning to grow a second pair of ears. "Tell me more."

"You can't have meek, law-abiding, women-ruled men when you start civilization on a new planet. You've got to have men who aren't afraid to make their own law if necessary—with their own guns. That's where law begins; the books get written up later."

"You're going to *tell*, Ferdinand, what evil, criminal male is speaking through your mouth!"

"Nobody!" I insisted. "They're my own ideas!"

"They are remarkably well organized for a young boy's ideas. A boy who, I might add, has previously shown a ridiculous but nonetheless entirely masculine boredom with political philosophy. I plan to have a government career on that new planet you talk about, Ferdinand—after I have found a good, steady husband, of course—and I don't look forward to a masculinist radical in the family. Now, who has been filling your head with all this nonsense?"

I was sweating. Sis has that deadly bulldog approach when she feels someone is lying. I began to pull my handkerchief from my pocket to wipe my face. Something rattled to the floor.

"What is this picture of me doing in your pocket, Ferdinand?"

A trap seemed to be banging noisily into place. "One of the passengers wanted to see how you looked in a bathing suit."

"The passengers on this ship are all female. I can't imagine any of them that curious about my appearance. Ferdinand, it's a man who has been giving you these antisocial ideas, isn't it? A war-mongering masculinist like all the frustrated men who want to engage in government and don't have the vaguest idea of how. Except, of course, in their ancient, bloody ways. Ferdinand, who has been perverting that sunny and carefree soul of yours?"

"Nobody! *Nobody!*"

"Ferdinand, there's no point in lying! I demand—"

"I told you, Sis. I told you! And don't call me Ferdinand. Call me Ford."

"Ford? *Ford?* Now, you listen to me, Ferdinand..."

After that it was all over but the confession. That came in a few moments. I couldn't fool Sis. She just knew me too well, I decided miserably. Besides, she was a girl.

All the same, I wouldn't get Mr. Butt Lee Brown into trouble if I could help it. I made Sis promise she wouldn't turn him in if I took her to him. And the quick, nodding way she said she would made me feel just a little better.

The door opened on the signal, "Sesame." When Butt saw somebody was with me, he jumped and the ten-inch blaster barrel grew out of his fingers. Then he recognized Sis from the pictures.

He stepped to one side and, with the same sweeping gesture, holstered his blaster and pushed his green hood off. It was Sis's turn to jump when she saw the wild mass of hair rolling down his back.

"An honor, Miss Sparling," he said in that rumbly voice. "Please come right in. There's a hurry-up draft."

So Sis went in and I followed right after her. Mr. Brown closed the door. I tried to catch his eye so I could give him some kind of hint or explanation, but he had taken a couple of his big strides and was in the forward section with Sis. She didn't give ground, though; I'll say that for her. She only came to his chest, but she had her arms crossed sternly.

"First, Mr. Brown," she began, like talking to a cluck of a kid in class, "you realize that you are not only committing the political crime of traveling without a visa, and the clear felony of stowing away without paying your fare, but the moral delinquency of consuming stores intended for the personnel of this ship solely in emergency?"

He opened his mouth to its maximum width and raised an enormous hand. Then he let the air out and dropped his arm.

"I take it you either have no defense or care to make none," Sis added caustically.

Butt laughed slowly and carefully as if he were going over each word. "Wonder if all the anura talk like that. And *you* want to foul up Venus."

"We haven't done so badly on Earth, after the mess you men made of politics. It needed a revolution of the mothers before—"

"Needed nothing. Everyone wanted peace. Earth is a weary old world."

"It's a world of strong moral fiber compared to yours, Mr. Alberta Lee Brown." Hearing his rightful name made him move suddenly and tower over her. Sis said with a certain amount of hurry and change of tone, "What *do* you have to say about stowing away and using up lifeboat stores?"

He cocked his head and considered a moment. "Look," he said finally, "I have more than enough munit to pay for round-trip tickets, but I couldn't get a return visa because of that brinosaur judge and all the charges she hung on me. Had to stow away. Picked the *Eleanor Roosevelt* because a couple of the boys in the crew are friends of mine and they were willing to help. But this lifeboat—don't you know that every passenger ship carries four times as many lifeboats as it needs? Not to mention the food I didn't eat because it stuck in my throat?"

"Yes," she said bitterly. "You had this boy steal fresh fruit for you. I suppose you didn't know that under space regulations that makes him equally guilty?"

"No, Sis, he didn't," I was beginning to argue. "All he wanted—"

"Sure I knew. Also know that if I'm picked up as a stowaway, I'll be sent back to Earth to serve out those fancy little sentences."

"Well, you're guilty of them, aren't you?"

He waved his hands at her impatiently. "I'm not talking law, female; I'm talking sense. Listen! I'm in trouble because I went to Earth to look for a wife. You're standing here right now because you're on your way to Venus for a husband. So let's."

Sis actually staggered back. "Let's? Let's *what?* Are—are you daring to suggest that—that—"

"Now, Miss Sparling, no hoopla. I'm saying let's get married, and you know it. You figured out from what the boy told you that I was chewing on you for a wife. You're healthy and strong, got good heredity, you know how to operate sub-surface machinery, you've lived underwater, and your disposition's no worse than most of the anura I've seen. Prolific stock, too."

I was so excited I just had to yell: "Gee, Sis, say *yes!*"

My sister's voice was steaming with scorn. "And what makes you think that I'd consider you a desirable husband?"

He spread his hands genially. "Figure if you wanted a poodle, you're pretty enough to pick one up on Earth. Figure if you charge off to Venus, you don't want a poodle, you want a man. I'm one. I own three islands in the Galertan Archipelago that'll be good oozing mudgrape land when they're cleared. Not to mention the rich berzeliot beds offshore. I got no bad habits outside of having my own way. I'm also passable good-looking for a slaptoe planter. Besides, if you marry me you'll be the first mated on this ship—and that's a splash most nesting females like to make."

There was a longish stretch of quiet. Sis stepped back and measured him slowly with her eyes; there was a lot to look at. He waited patiently while she covered the distance from his peculiar green boots to that head of hair. I was so excited I was gulping instead of breathing. Imagine having Butt for a brother-in-law and living on a wet-plantation in Flatfolk country!

But then I remembered Sis's level head and I didn't have much hope any more.

"You know," she began, "there's more to marriage than just—"

"So there is," he cut in. "Well, we can try each other for taste." And he pulled her in, both of his great hands practically covering her slim, straight back.

Neither of them said anything for a bit after he let go. Butt spoke up first.

"Now, me," he said, "I'd vote yes."

Sis ran the tip of her tongue kind of delicately from side to side of her mouth. Then she moved back thinking and looked at him as if she were figuring out how many feet high he was. She kept on moving backward, tapping her chin, while Butt and I got more and more impatient. When she touched the lifeboat door, she pushed it open and jumped out.

Butt ran over and looked down the crossway. After a while, he shut the door and came back beside me. "Well," he said, swinging to a bunk, "that's sort of it."

"You're better off, Butt," I burst out. "You shouldn't have a woman like Sis for a wife. She looks small and helpless, but don't forget she was trained to run an underwater city!"

"Wasn't worrying about that," he grinned. "*I* grew up in the fifteen long years of the

Blue Chicago Rising. Nope." He turned over on his back and clicked his teeth at the ceiling. "Think we'd have nested out nicely."

I hitched myself up to him and we sat on the bunk, glooming away at each other. Then we heard the tramp of feet in the crossway.

Butt swung down and headed for the control compartment in the nose of the lifeboat. He had his blaster out and was cursing very interestingly. I started after him, but he picked me up by the seat of my jumper and tossed me toward the door. The Captain came in and tripped over me.

I got all tangled up in his gold braid and million-mile space buttons. When we finally got to our feet and sorted out right, he was breathing very hard. The Captain was a round little man with a plump, golden face and a very scared look on it. He *humphed* at me, just the way Sis does, and lifted me by the scruff of my neck. The Chief Mate picked me up and passed me to the Second Assistant Engineer.

Sis was there, being held by the purser on one side and the Chief Computer's Mate on the other. Behind them, I could see a flock of wide-eyed female passengers.

"You cowards!" Sis was raging. "Letting your Captain face a dangerous outlaw all by himself!"

"I dunno. Miss Sparling," the Computer's Mate said, scratching the miniature slide-rule insignia on his visor with his free hand. "The Old Man would've been willing to let it go with a log entry, figuring the spaceport paddlefeet could pry out the stowaway when we landed. But you had to quote the Mother Anita Law at him, and he's in there doing his duty. He figures the rest of us are family men, too, and there's no sense making orphans."

"You promised, Sis," I told her through my teeth. "You promised you wouldn't get Butt into trouble!"

She tossed her spiral curls at me and ground a heel into the purser's instep. He screwed up his face and howled, but he didn't let go of her arm.

"*Shush,* Ferdinand, this is serious!"

It was. I heard the Captain say, "I'm not carrying a weapon, Brown."

"Then *get* one," Butt's low, lazy voice floated out.

"No, thanks. You're as handy with that thing as I am with a rocketboard." The Captain's words got a little fainter as he walked forward. Butt growled like a gusher about to blow.

"I'm counting on your being a good guy, Brown." The Captain's voice quavered just a bit. "I'm banking on what I heard about the blast-happy Browns every time I lifted gravs in New Kalamazoo; they have a code, they don't burn unarmed men."

Just about this time, events in the lifeboat went down to a mumble. The top of my head got wet and I looked up. There was sweat rolling down the Second Assistant's forehead; it converged at his nose and bounced off the tip in a thin little stream. I twisted out of the way.

"What's happening?" Sis gritted, straining toward the lock.

"Butt's trying to decide whether he wants him fried or scrambled," the Computer's

Mate said, pulling her back. "Hey, purse, remember when the whole family with their pop at the head went into Heatwave to argue with Colonel Leclerc?"

"Eleven dead, sixty-four injured," the purser answered mechanically. "And no more army stationed south of Icebox." His right ear twitched irritably. "But what're they saying?"

Suddenly we heard. "By authority vested in me under the Pomona College Treaty," the Captain was saying very loudly, "I arrest you for violation of Articles Sixteen to Twenty-one inclusive of the Space Transport Code, and order your person and belongings impounded for the duration of this voyage as set forth in Sections Forty-one and Forty-five—"

"Forty-three and Forty-five," Sis groaned. "Sections Forty-three and Forty-five, I told him. I even made him repeat it after me!"

"—of the Mother Anita Law, SC 2136, Emergency Interplanetary Directives."

We all waited breathlessly for Butt's reply. The seconds ambled on and there was no clatter of electrostatic discharge, no smell of burning flesh.

Then we heard some feet walking. A big man in a green suit swung out into the crossway. That was Butt. Behind him came the Captain, holding the blaster gingerly with both hands. Butt had a funny, thoughtful look on his face.

The girls surged forward when they saw him, scattering the crew to one side. They were like a school of sharks that had just caught sight of a dying whale.

"M-m-m-m! Are all Venusians built like that?"

"Men like that are worth the mileage!"

"*I want him!*" "*I want him!*" "*I want him!*"

Sis had been let go. She grabbed my free hand and pulled me away. She was trying to look only annoyed, but her eyes had bright little bubbles of fury popping in them.

"The cheap extroverts! And they call themselves responsible women!"

I was angry, too. And I let her know, once we were in our cabin. "What about that promise, Sis? You said you wouldn't turn him in. You *promised!*"

She stopped walking around the room as if she had been expecting to get to Venus on foot. "I know I did, Ferdinand, but he forced me."

"My name is Ford, and I don't understand."

"Your name is Ferdinand, and stop trying to act forcefully like a girl. It doesn't become you. In just a few days, you'll forget all this and be your simple, carefree self again. I really truly meant to keep my word. From what you'd told me, Mr. Brown seemed to be a fundamentally decent chap despite his barbaric notions on equality between the sexes—or worse. I was positive I could shame him into a more rational social behavior and make him give himself up. Then he—he—"

She pressed her fingernails into her palms and let out a long, glaring sigh at the door. "Then he kissed me! Oh, it was a good enough kiss—Mr. Brown has evidently had a varied and colorful background—but the galling idiocy of the man, trying that! I was just getting over the colossal impudence involved in *his* proposing marriage—as if *he* had to bear the children!—and was considering the offer seriously, on its merits, as one should consider *all* suggestions, when he deliberately dropped the pretense of reason. He appealed to me as most of the savage ancients appealed to their women, as an emotional machine. Throw the correct sexual switches, says this theory, and the female surrenders herself ecstatically to the doubtful and bloody murk of masculine plans."

There was a double knock on the door and the Captain walked in without waiting for an invitation. He was still holding Butt's blaster. He pointed it at me. "Get your hands up, Ferdinand Sparling," he said.

I did.

"I hereby order your detention for the duration of this voyage, for aiding and abetting a stowaway, as set forth in Sections Forty-one and Forty-five—"

"Forty-three and Forty-five," Sis interrupted him, her eyes getting larger and rounder. "But you gave me your word of honor that no charges would be lodged against the boy!"

"Forty-one and Forty-five," he corrected her courteously, still staring fiercely at me. "I looked it up. Of the Anita Mason Law, Emergency Interplanetary Directives. That was the usual promise one makes to an informer, but I made it before I knew it was Butt Lee Brown you were talking about. I didn't want to arrest Butt Lee Brown. You forced me. So I'm breaking my promise to you, just as, I understand, you broke your promise to your brother. They'll both be picked up at New Kalamazoo Spaceport and sent Terraward for trial."

"But I used all of our money to buy passage," Sis wailed.

"And now you'll have to return with the boy. I'm sorry, Miss Sparling. But as you explained to me, a man who has been honored with an important official position should stay close to the letter of the law for the sake of other men who are trying to break down terrestrial anti-male prejudice. Of course, there's a way out."

"There is? Tell me, please?"

"Can I lower my hands a minute?" I asked.

"No, you can't, son—not according to the armed surveillance provisions of the Mother Anita Law. Miss Sparling, if you'd marry Brown—now, now, don't look at me like that!—we could let the whole matter drop. A shipboard wedding and he goes on your passport as a 'dependent male member of family,' which means, so far as the law is concerned, that he had a regulation passport from the beginning of this voyage. And once we touch Venusian soil he can contact his bank and pay for passage. On the record, no crime was ever committed. He's free, the boy's free, and you—"

"—Are married to an uncombed desperado who doesn't know enough to sit back and let a woman run things. Oh, you should be ashamed!"

The Captain shrugged and spread his arms wide.

"Perhaps I should be, but that's what comes of putting men into responsible positions, as you would say. See here, Miss Sparling, I didn't want to arrest Brown, and, if it's at all possible, I'd still prefer not to. The crew, officers and men, all go along with me. We may be legal residents of Earth, but our work requires us to be on Venus several times a year. We don't want to be disliked by any members of the highly irritable Brown clan or its collateral branches. Butt Lee Brown himself, for all of his savage appearance in your civilized eyes, is a man of much influence on the Polar Continent. In his own bailiwick, the Galertan Archipelago, he makes, breaks, and occasionally readjusts officials. Then there's his brother Saskatchewan, who considers Butt a helpless, put-upon youngster—"

"Much influence, you say? Mr. Brown has?" Sis was suddenly thoughtful.

"*Power,* actually. The kind a strong man usually holds in a newly settled community. Besides, Miss Sparling, you're going to Venus for a husband because the male-female ratio on Earth is reversed. Well, not only is Butt Lee Brown a first-class catch, but you can't afford to be too particular in any case. While you're fairly pretty, you don't bring any wealth into a marriage and your high degree of opinionation is not likely to be well-received on a backward, masculinist world. Then, too, the woman-hunger is not so great any more, what with the *Marie Curie* and the *Fatima* having already deposited their cargoes, the *Mme. Sun Yat-sen* due to arrive next month…"

Sis nodded to herself, waved the door open, and walked out.

"Let's hope," the Captain said. "Like my father used to say, a man who knows how to handle women, how to get around them without their knowing it, doesn't need to know anything else in this life. I'm plain wasted in space. You can lower your hands now, son."

We sat down and I explained the blaster to him. He was very interested. He said all Butt had told him—in the lifeboat when they decided to use my arrest as a club over Sis—was to keep the safety catch all the way up against his thumb. I could see he really had been excited about carrying a lethal weapon around. He told me that back in the old days, captains—sea captains, that is—actually had the right to keep guns in their cabins all the time to put down mutinies and other things our ancestors did.

The telewall flickered, and we turned it on. Sis smiled down. "Everything's all right. Captain. Come up and marry us, please."

"What did you stick him for?" he asked. "What was the price?"

Sis's full lips went thin and hard, the way Mom's used to. Then she thought better of it and laughed. "Mr. Brown is going to see that I'm elected sheriff of the Galertan Archipelago."

"And I thought she'd settle for a county clerkship!" the Captain muttered as we spun up to the brig.

The doors were open and girls were chattering in every corner. Sis came up to the Captain to discuss arrangements. I slipped away and found Butt sitting with folded arms in a corner of the brig. He grinned at me. "Hi, tadpole. Like the splash?"

I shook my head unhappily. "Butt, why did you do it? I'd sure love to be your brother-in-law, but, gosh, you didn't have to marry Sis." I pointed at some of the bustling females. Sis was going to have three hundred bridesmaids. "Any one of them would have jumped at the chance to be your wife. And once on any woman's passport, you'd be free. Why Sis?"

"That's what the Captain said in the lifeboat. Told him same thing I'm telling you. I'm stubborn. What I like at first, I keep on liking. What I want at first, I keep on wanting until I get."

"Yes, but making Sis sheriff! And you'll have to back her up with your blaster. What'll happen to that man's world?"

"Wait'll after we nest and go out to my islands." He raised a calloused hand, palm upwards, and sighted along the top of it at Sis's back. "She'll be the sheriff, she will. But you know, tadpole, there are two kinds of law." The big hand went up and down. "Her law. And my law."

AFTERWORD

Three short comments about this story:

1. Pretty much all we knew about Venus in 1951 was that it was surrounded by clouds. So why not a warm, wet, swampy world? Please don't laugh. Almost every other science-fiction writer thought that way.

2. Horace Gold was worried about publishing this one. He said it was a bit too much of a feminist story. He was not sure that feminist stories belonged in science fiction. As I said, it *was* 1951.

3. As far as I know, the three appearances of "masculinist" in these pages were the first usage anywhere of that word. Later, of course, I wrote a whole novelette around the word.

WRITTEN 1951———PUBLISHED 1951

Alexander the Bait

You aren't likely to get a quick punch in the face these days by professing admiration for Alexander Parks. Time has softened even the families of the crews who rode the GA fleet into nowhere, and uncomfortable understanding of the great thing the man did has increased with the years.

Still, he is penalized by a hidebound agency in a manner that, to him at any rate, is especially horrible. I refer to the FLC. I hope they read this.

We wandered into each other a couple of years after the war to end isolationism. I had just landed a Toledo accordion on a freight runway and was now headed for a bar. There are some pilots who know just how much rye they need after towing an accordion; me, I just keep pouring it down until my heart floats back into place.

A cab came up to the flight building and a well-built man with a surprisingly small head got out. As I ran up to hail the cab, the man turned and stared at me. Something familiar about that narrow little skull made me stop.

"Were you in the Army Air Forces?" he asked.

"Yeah," I answered slowly. "The so-called Swasticker Squadron. Forty… Alex Parks! The voice with a dial!"

He grinned. "That's right, Dave. For a minute I thought you were only talking to ex-flying officers. Ground-control people carry a lot of inferiority complex around with them. You're looking well."

He looked better. The clothes he was wearing had been designed by a tailor with the salary of a movie executive. I remembered something from the newspapers. "Didn't you sell some invention or other to some corporation or other?"

"It was the Radar Corporation of America. Just been capitalized. I sold them my multilevel negative beam radar."

"Get much?"

He pursed his lips and let his eyes twinkle. "Oh, a million five-hundred thousand dollars."

I opened my lips and let my eyes bug. "A lot of dough. What're you going to do with it?"

"A couple of unholy scientific projects I've always dreamed about. I might be able to use you." He motioned to the cab. "Can we go somewhere and talk?"

"I'm on my way to a bar," I told him as the cab got under way. "Just came in with an accordion."

"Accordion? Is that what you freight pilots call these glider trains?"

"Yeah. And if you want to know why, just think of what happens when you hit an air pocket. Or a sudden headwind. Or a motor stall." I grunted. "We make music—heavenly music."

We sat in a back booth of the Matched Penny Café, Alex smiling admiringly as I consumed half the amber output of a good-sized distillery. "You'll have to cut down on that guzzling if you come with me," he said.

I finished the glass, licked my teeth, my lips, and sighed. "Where?"

"A mesa in Nevada I've purchased. Have to have someone I can trust to fly equipment in and help around the place with some moderately heavy construction. Someone I can trust to keep his mouth shut. A heavy drinker keeps his open too much to suit me."

"I'll do that," I assured him. "I'd drink nothing but curdled yak milk to get out of this aerial moving-van business. Making an occasional trip will be nothing compared to my daily routine with collapsible coffins. It's the combination of monotonous grind with the angel of death that's making me bottle-happy."

He nodded. "And the lack of any long-range useful goal. You flew on almost as rigid a schedule during the war, but—well, that was war. If there were something fine for which you were risking your life, instead of the transportation of electrical harmonicas—"

"Like interplanetary travel? That was one of your bugs. Going to do some experimenting along that line?"

Alex slid his forefinger along the green marble tabletop. "I'd need much more money than that. It's a nice thought—the human race finds itself at the point today where a little research, a little refinement of existing techniques, would send it to the stars. But the people who could do it, the big manufacturing corporations, can't see enough incentive; the people who would do it, the universities and research foundations, can't see enough money. We sit on this planet like a shipwrecked sailor on a desert island who sees a pair of oars in one spot and a boat in another and can't quite make up his mind to bring the two together.

"No, not interplanetary travel. Not yet. But something along that line. That beam I discovered gave me the reputation of the world's greatest radar expert. I intend to build the largest installation ever on that mesa—and make a long-distance radar survey."

This wasn't the Alexander Parks I'd known. This idea, I decided, showed nothing of what I'd always thought he'd do if he had the money to indulge his sardonically soaring mind, his genius for subtlety. "A radar survey?" I asked weakly.

His little head grew wide with laughter. "A map, my dear Dave—a topographical map of the Moon!"

Nevada was nice. Plenty of landing space. Plenty of working space. Practically no one to ask questions. Sharp, fragrant air on the top of Big Bluff Mesa that affected me almost as strongly as hooch used to. Alex claimed atmospheric conditions here were perfect for maximum equipment efficiency.

The equipment was odd. Of course, I knew radar had developed enormously since the days of primitive gadgetry in the early forties. Parks's own MLN Beam had successfully fused communication and noncommunication radio into a fantastic setup that required no transmitter and made it possible to tune in on any outdoor event in the world. (It was still in production then.)

Alex and I got the shacks built ourselves, but we ran into trouble with the huge horizontal antenna and the gyroscopically stabilized dipoles. In the end he hired a man named Judson from Las Vegas. Judson did odd jobs around the place and supplied an extra pair of hands in construction jobs. Mrs. Judson cooked our meals. Alex admitted the necessity for Judson, but seemed to regret it nonetheless. I suspected he sent me on sleeveless errands now and then, as if to keep me from having a coherent knowledge of his methods. I shrugged at that idea. If he thought I knew enough about modern radar, I was highly complimented.

When I flew in with a rattling glider train of impossible coils and surrealist tubes, he often insisted I stay put while he made some infinitesimal adjustment in the lab shack. I could climb out of the plane then, but only if I went directly to the hut which was our living quarters.

Emmanuel Corliss, of the Radar Corporation of America, begged a ride from me once. All the way to Nevada he sang Alex's praises; he told me of the statue of Alex in the foyer of the corporation's skyscraper in Manhattan; he even had a copy of an unauthorized biography titled *Alexander Parks—Father of Global Communication*. He said he wanted Alex to come back as chief research consultant. I thought Atomhead would enjoy having his ego caressed.

I was wrong.

Fifty miles from Big Bluff, a deep voice rattled the reception panel. "Who's that you're talking to, Dave?"

Corliss piped up. "Thought I'd look in on you, boy. We might be able to use whatever you're working on now."

"Well, you can't. The moment you land, Dave, unhitch the gliders and fly Mr. Corliss back to the nearest airport. Got enough fuel?"

"Yep." I was embarrassed. Felt like a neighbor overhearing a newlywed couple's first quarrel.

"But, Parks," the executive wailed, "you don't know what an important figure you've become. The world wants to know what you're doing. Radar Corporation of America wants to know what you're doing."

Parks chuckled. "Not just yet. Don't get out of that plane, Corliss, or you'll get a load of buckshot in the most sensitive part of your upholstery. Remember, I can call you a trespasser."

Corliss sputtered angrily. "Now you listen to me—"

"No, you listen to me. *Don't get out of that plane* as you love your swivel chair. Believe it or not, old man, I'm doing you a favor."

That was sort of that. After I'd deposited the red-faced corporation president, I bumped down to the mesa pretty thoughtfully. Alex was waiting for me; he looked thoughtful, too.

"Don't do that again," he told me. "Nobody comes out here until I'm ready for, well, for publication. I don't want strangers, especially scientific strangers, poking around in my layout."

"Afraid they'd copy it?"

My question tickled him. "That's it…almost too exactly."

"Afraid I'll copy it?"

He threw a quick, shrewd glance at me. "Let's have supper and do some talking, Dave." He put his arm around my shoulders.

While Mrs. Judson dealt out the plain food very plainly prepared, Alex studied me in the hard, unwinking fashion he had. I thought again that he resembled nothing more than a miniature camera set on a massive, unwieldy tripod. Grease-stained blue jeans had long ago replaced the soft, sartorial perfections in which I'd first seen him. The father of global communication!

He looked covertly at Judson, saw that the hired man was interested in nothing but his stew, and said in a low voice: "If you feel I distrust you, Dave, I'm sorry. There is a good reason for all this secrecy, believe me."

"That's your business," I told him shortly. "You don't pay me for asking questions. But I honestly wouldn't know an oscillator screen from an indicator rack. And if I did, I wouldn't tell anyone."

He shifted on the hard wooden bench and leaned against the unpainted metal wall behind him. "You know what I'm trying to do. I send a high-frequency beam at the Moon. Some of it is absorbed in the ionosphere, most of it gets through and bounces off the Moon's surface. I catch the reflection, amplify it, record the strength and minutest change in direction on a photographic plate, and send another, slightly different beam out immediately. On the basis of multiple beams, I build up a fairly detailed and accurate picture of the Moon from very close range. My multilevel negative radar provides a somewhat stronger beam than science has had at its disposal before, but essentially the principle is basic radar. It could have been done, with a little difficulty, ten years ago. Why wasn't it?"

Stew congealed into an unsavory jelly in my plate. I was interested in spite of myself.

"It wasn't done," he continued, "for the same reason we don't have interplanetary travel, suboceanic mining, grafting of complete limbs from corpses on amputation cases. Nobody can see any profit in it, any *immediate,* certain profit. Therefore, the small amount of research that is necessary to close the gap between the knowledge we already have and the knowledge we almost have goes unfinanced."

"But work goes on in those fields," I pointed out.

"Work goes on, all right. But at what a slow pace, under what heartbreaking conditions! Have you ever heard the legend of how my namesake, Alexander the Great, circled the world astride a giant bird? He hung a piece of meat from a long pole and dangled it in front of the bird's beak. A strong gust of wind blew the meat close enough for the creature to snatch, and the redoubtable Alexander immediately cut a piece of flesh from his side and attached it to the pole. Thus, he was able to complete his trip with the bird futilely trying to reach the meat by increasing its speed.

"The story occurs in several folklores with different heroes, but it shows how fundamental was the ancients' understanding of human motives. Incidentally, it is also a beautiful illustration of the laws of compensation. In every age, a man must offer himself up as bait so that progress will not be limited to the back pages of the dictionary. We can't be said to be moving forward if we touch none of our newer potentialities."

I stirred the stew with a heavy spoon, then pushed it away and reached for the coffee. "I see what you mean. But why tell me all this?"

Alex rose, stretched, and moved towards the door. I smiled apologetically at my coffee and Mrs. Judson and followed him.

The cool Nevada night hung heavily as we walked outside. A myriad stars blazed pinpoint mysteries. Was this black, inviting space man's natural medium, a domain waiting for the flashing tread of a master? Could it be that my puny species was the appointed ruler of these vastnesses? I wondered how it would feel to bank suddenly out there, to level out for a landing. My hands itched for an unmade, still nonexistent throttle.

"These are the maps I've made to date," my employer observed. We were standing in the lab shack with banked transformers, nightmares in spun glass and twisted wire weaving in and out of the huge display tubes around us.

I glanced carelessly at the maps; I was no astronomer. Then I glanced very carefully indeed at the maps.

The point is they weren't maps. They were pictures—over a thousand aerial photographs—taken from a uniform height of about five hundred feet. They had sharper detail than any aerial photographs I've ever seen. You could count the rocks on the surface; you could note pits and the narrowest fissures.

"They are pretty good," Alex said. He stroked one of the glossy sheets lovingly. "A section of the Tycho Brahë Crater."

"Why the Samuel Aloysius Hill don't you publish?"

"Couldn't till now." He seemed to be in the throes of a hard decision. "I had to check something first. And now I've got to trust you with my life's work by asking you to play a particularly dirty trick on yourself. I still can't afford to explain; my conversation tonight was sort of a song and dance to go with the request. But some day it will all fit."

"Go ahead. I'm a loyal employee; I love the firm."

The pinhead seemed to swell. "One week from today I want you to take a trip up to the Canadian North Woods with a couple of packages. You'll have a map with X's scattered over it; the coordinates of each X will be marked in the margin. Latitude and longitude in terms of degrees, minutes and seconds. Bury each package about two feet underground at X-designated spots, making certain that it is at the exact intersecting point of the coordinates. Then go away."

"Huh?"

"Go away and forget you ever saw those packages. Don't even dream about them. Don't see me except socially for at least three years. Forget you ever worked for me. You can keep the plane and I'll add a sizable check as a parting gift. Will you do it?"

I let my mind chew on it for a while. It didn't make sense, but I knew he'd told me all he intended to. "OK, Alex, I'll take the high road and I'll take the dough road. I'll make out."

He seemed tremendously relieved. "You will make out—much better than you think. Just wait a few months. When the united savants of the world start flocking in here, there will be lectures and juicy magazine articles thrown at anyone who ever worked for me. Don't touch them with a transmitting antenna."

That made me laugh. "I wouldn't anyway. I don't play those games."

Alex shut off the light and we returned to the Judsons feeling pretty good about each other. That was the way a sweet guy called Alexander Parks climbed up on the altar of history. When I think of the fundamental ambition that drove him to that conversation, the action of the FLC seems cruel and even petty.

A week later I was flitting about the north woods laying little tarp-covered eggs here and there by means of a chart so explicit as to be understandable by grade-school lads.

Newspapers caught my eye when I landed in Seattle. Full front-page spreads of the pictures Alex had showed me, smaller shots of Alex's small head surrounded by big-browed, white-maned profs from Oxford, Irkutsk, and points east.

"Radar Genius Maps Moon," they screamed. "Sage of Nevada reveals work of two years. Scientists flock to mesa, claim telescopes now obsolete except as check. Alexander Parks announces he will make mineralogical survey of lunar surface."

So he had announced it. Good. I spent a portion of my last pay check investigating any new developments in the gentle art of making whiskey. The liquor, I found, hadn't changed; unfortunately, *I* had. Laboring under a diminished capacity, I gamboled from binge to hangover, from bar to hotel room, until I woke up in a hospital surrounded by a straitjacket.

After the doctor had chased the six-headed snakes away, I sat up and chirruped at the nurses. One luscious little redhead took to reading me the newspapers in a pathetic attempt at self-defense. I was getting the news in jerky flashes, what with her dodging around night tables and behind screens, when I heard something that made me reach out and grab the newspaper. The girl, who had been preparing for a last, all-out effort, looked a little dazed.

I still have a hazy memory of that nurse standing in a corner and shaking her head while I got clearance. The doc didn't feel I was cured, but I had important friends.

Bascomb Rockets was the nearest, and I was there a half hour after a starchy clerk had given me my clothes, money and a little white certificate, suitable for framing. I'd gone through every newspaper in reach by the time I arrived; so I was prepared for what I saw.

A two-by-three experimental house which had been operating on a frayed shoe-string of a budget was expanding like a galaxy of stars all going supernova. Far off into the distance, I could see shops and hangars going up, stock piles being built, equipment arriving by the cubic ton.

Tim Bascomb was checking blueprints in front of the half-finished Parthenon that was to be the company's main building. I'd met him at an ex-pilot's convention a year after the war, but I thought I might as well reintroduce myself—some insensitive people manage to forget me.

The moment he heard my voice, he dropped the blueprints and grabbed my hand. "Dave! You haven't signed any contracts yet?" he finished anxiously.

"Nary a clause," I told him. "Can you use a former B-29er and accordion player?"

"Can we use you? Mr. Hennessey—Mr. Hennessey, get me contractual form 16, no, better make that 18. You were in on the early jet and rocket jobs," he explained. "That puts you into an advanced category."

"Hiring a lot of the boys?"

"Are we? Every backyard gadgeteer in the country is forming a corporation these days and we're keeping up with the best of them. They say the airlines are using hostesses as copilots and candy butchers as radiomen. You'll find Steve Yancy and Lou Brock of the Canada-Mexico Line in that shack, over there; they'd like to see you."

Mr. Hennessey and a stenographer served as witnesses. I started scribbling my name on that contract as soon as I saw the numbers after the dollar sign under "salary." Bascomb laughed.

"I'll back our payroll against any in the world. Not that at least fifty other companies don't do as well. We've got the backing of Radioactive Metals and the Ginnette Mining Corporation as well as a government subsidy of five million."

I wiped some blue-black ink off my fingers. "Since when is the government interested?"

He chuckled, "Since when?" We began walking to a huge structure labeled "Bascomb Rockets Experimental Pilots—No Admittance to Unauthorized Personnel." "Look, Dave boy, when Parks took those radar snapshots of the Moon, the astronomers were interested. When he worked out a spectroscopic table and found there were healthy hunks of gold under the surface, the banks and mines began to sit up. But when that Caltech prof turned Parks's gimmick along eighty miles of the Moon's Alpine Valley and found alternate layers of radium and uranium, the nations of this planet looked up from atom bomb experiments long enough to harness everybody who knows the Moon is a quarter of a million miles from Earth. It's no longer a matter of the first extraterrestrial explorer becoming a trillionaire overnight, but of folks cooking atom bombs in their kitchens."

I looked at the tractors backing and filling around me, at the cement-sloppy wheelbarrows being trundled by an army of construction workers, at the bare scaffolding of shops rising on every bare foot of ground. This scene was being duplicated everywhere in every state, probably in every nation. Slap some sort of a ship together, solve the problems with any kind of jerry-built apparatus—*but get to the Moon first!*

"It isn't only a matter of national defense, either," Tim was explaining. "We almost have atomic power, in fact, we already have it but not in a commercial form. With the uranium that can be dredged out of the Moon, the old *Sunday Supplement* dream of crossing the Atlantic with a teaspoonful of sand for fuel will come true. General Atomics is devoting half their budget to spaceship research. They may not be the first outfit to set a job down on Tycho, but they sure will bust a gut trying."

He led me into the pilots' shack, where a lecture on astrogation was in progress. And that day the only rockets on the Bascomb lot were still on drawing boards!

"The Mad Scramble"—isn't that the name of the definitive history of the period? It *was* mad. People still remember the first casualties to hit the front pages: Gunnar and Thorgersen getting blown to bits a half-mile up; those six Russian scientists flaming into an incandescence that registered on every astronomical camera pointed at the Moon. Then that wave of reaction sweeping the world toward the end of the decade and laws clamping down on irresponsible corporations and wildcat experimenters.

Even then, Steve Yancy and his kid brother got knocked off on a simple experimental flight outside Earth's atmosphere. No fundamental principle overlooked, we were just building carelessly.

When Parks finally dropped in on us on his way from the Leroy Propulsion Project, we seemed to be getting nowhere fast. That was the Black April, the month of the GA Fleet. Bascomb had discovered I knew Parks personally and begged me to bring him into the firm. "He's just hopping about giving advice to anyone who wants it from him. With his reputation, if he ever went to work for one organization, he could name his own price. Try to get him to name it for us."

"I'll try," I promised.

"Of course, I know his basic interest is in radar research. If his machine had stopped with mapping the Moon, every hick college would probably have had an appropriation for a radar telescope or whatever they call it. But since he found uranium in them thar craters, kids are being jerked into research projects as fast as they finish elementary physics. That guy from Caltech—what *was* his name?—who first detected radioactive stuff with Parks's equipment, they say he has to go up to the mesa every time he wants to survey some more moon. He can't get the university even vaguely interested in building a toy for him, and Alex P. won't let anyone near the layout unless he's on the scene holding their leash."

"Yeah." I grinned wryly, remembering the way Emmanuel Corliss had been sent back to his dictaphone. Even when some scientific journals had attacked the tight control he maintained over the world's only lunar-surveying radar, he had retorted angrily that the entire apparatus had been developed and built out of his own brain, time and funds, and if anyone didn't like it they could build themselves another. Of course, with every research penny eventually finding its way into spaceship design, he had the only game in town.

Parks laughed when I gave him Bascomb's message. He clambered out of the new-smelling black-and-silver job that I was to take on a shakedown in a week and sat on the curving metal runway.

"No, Dave, I like this being advisory expert to big business in rocket research. I get to travel and see all the different things we're trying. Did you know Garfinkel of Illinois is working on a Cosmoplane—sort of a sailboat sensitive to cosmic rays? I'd rather not get stuck in a job in one corner of this business. After all, anyone may hit it."

"But that isn't like you, Alex," I argued. "You were always the kind of guy who wanted to do things himself. This work isn't right up your alley, it *is* your alley. You're the one man Bascomb Rockets needs, not as a part-time unpaid specialist who hits us once a month on his look-see circuit, but as the director, the coordinator of our research. I'm just a stumblebum who can make with a joystick, but you are the guy who'll get us there."

"Ever mention our working together?"

"No." I sighed. He evidently didn't want in. I helped him change the subject. "Nasty—this GA business."

He was staring at the ground. He nodded slowly, then looked up. There were ridges of anguish on his face. "That was Corliss," he said in a low, earnest voice. "He became president of General Atomics six months ago. The idea of the Fleet probably seemed like a good publicity trick."

I disagreed with him. "After all," I pointed out, "the logic was good. Ten ships setting off for the Moon together. When one of them hit a snag, the others could come up and help. In case of an impending blowup, the crews of the threatened ship could be transferred to safety. It was just plain unfortunate that Fouquelles didn't discover the deep-space Jura rays until a week after they left. From now on everything we build will be insulated against the stuff."

"Five hundred men," Alex brooded. "Five hundred men and women lost without a trace. Nothing in the papers today about a radio signal, about some debris coming down somewhere?"

"No. They probably got out of control and drifted into the sun. Or maybe the ships—those that are left—are scudding aimlessly out of the system."

He was himself again when I left him at the gate. "Maybe I'll have cracked it the next time I see you," I said. "We're moving pretty slowly, though."

"That doesn't mean anything." He shook my hand warmly. "Man has his heart set on getting off this planet. He'll do it—perhaps sooner than he thinks."

Two months later. Captain Ulrich Gall landed the Canadian *Flutterer III* in Plato Crater, using the double-flow drive. It's high-school history now how Gall lined his space-suited crew behind him and prepared to move through the airlock. How he caught his foot on the ramp, and how his Polynesian "boy," Charles Wau-Neil, hurrying to extricate him, tripped on the lock and shot out onto the lunar surface—thus being the first human to touch another world.

I was copilot of the fifth ship to reach the Moon—*The Ambassador of Albuquerque.* I was also the first man to set insulated foot on the lunar Apennines. So I'll have a place in some six-volume detailed history of lunar exploration: "An interesting discovery is credited to a minor adventurer named—"

Well, you know what happened. Toehold, the colony Gall left on the Moon, continued the feverish examination of mineralogical samples. No go. In six months Toehold scientists radioed a complete confirmation of Gall's early suspicions.

There was no uranium on the Moon. No radium. And there was just enough gold to be detectable in the most delicate analyses.

Of course, they did find some nice beds of iron ore. And someone discovered rocks beneath the surface from which oxygen and the lighter elements could be extracted with ease, making possible Toehold's present indigenousness. But no uranium!

I was on Earth when the storm of public opinion broke. Financed and encouraged by hysterical corporations, it broke first around the head of a certain California professor of astronomy and buried him. He, it was, who had first announced the presence of radioactive minerals on the Moon as a result of experiments with Parks's radar. Then it turned on Parks.

Remember the headlines that day? "Parks Admits Fraud" in letters as big as the end of the world. "Alexander Parks, Nevada charlatan, explained to the F.B.I. today how he planted transmitters near pitchblende and gold deposits in Canada, coordinating his infernal machine with them to make it appear that the impulses were arriving from a given portion of the Moon. 'I never allowed anyone to investigate the machine too closely,' Parks leered, 'and this, with my international reputation as a radar expert, prevented discovery.' "

I scooted for his mesa. There were state police coming out of the woodwork, F.B.I. men being trampled underfoot and what looked like a full infantry regiment marching back and forth. After I'd satisfied everybody that I was a reputable citizen, I was allowed to see Alex. He was evidently a *de facto* prisoner.

Alex was sitting at the plain table, his hands clasped easily in front of him. He turned and smiled with pleasure as I walked in. The man walking puffily up and down the small room turned too. With some difficulty I recognized the face above the purple neck as belonging to Emmanuel Corliss. He tore up to me and peering out of red-rimmed eyes began to grunt. After a while, I interpreted the grunts as, "*You* ask him why. Ask him why he did it, why he ruined me!"

"I've told you that at least a dozen times," Parks said mildly. "There was nothing against you personally, nothing against anybody. I simply felt it was time we had interplanetary travel and that greed was a good incentive. I was right."

"Right!" Corliss screeched. "Right! Do you call it right to flimflam me out of three million dollars? I personally invested three million dollars to get what? Iron ore? If I want iron ore, isn't what we have on this planet good enough?"

"Your consolation, Mr. Corliss, in your financial bereavement, is that you have helped humanity to take a major historical step. You will recall that I went as far as using a shotgun in an attempt to keep you from getting involved in my…my plans. Beyond suggesting that you record it in your income tax under bad investments, I'm afraid I can't help you."

"Well, I can help you!" The president of General Atomics and the Radar Corporation of America shook a pudgy, quivering finger under Parks's nose. "I can help you into jail. I'll spend the rest of my life trying!" He slammed the door behind him so hard that the shack seemed to move three feet.

"Can he do anything, Alex?" I asked.

He shrugged. The pinhead looked tired. I suspected there had been a lot of this lately. "Not so far as I know. All the development on my lunar radar was out of my own funds. While I gave advice freely to those who wanted it, I never accepted a penny from any corporation or individual. I benefited in no material way from the fraud. My lawyers tell me it may be a tight squeeze, but there isn't anything that can be done in the way of punishment. I'm in the clear. Are…are you angry at me?"

"No!" I put my hand on his shoulder. "You've made life worth living for hundreds of us. Listen, Alex," I said softly, "I don't know what history will say, but there are a lot of sky-jockeys who will never forget you."

He grinned up. "Thanks pal. I did try to keep you out of the mess. Name a precipice after me."

We can't go any further than the Moon right now, but I have a dandy little two-man ferrying job—secondhand of course—and as soon as I can scrounge up enough cash, I'm going to fit it with that new triple-flow drive. They say Venus should be in an early geological stage, and that means a lot of whole radium and uranium will be lying about. The first man to get there and stake out a claim would be kinda well-to-do the rest of his life. Yeah, that talk may be just some more sucker bait, but, just think, if it *is* so—

Whatever its original impulses, interplanetary transportation is here to stay. But what of the man responsible?

The Federal Lunar Commission (FLC) has issued a permanent injunction to all its offices against granting Alexander Parks terrestrial clearance. And unless he stows away on some supply ship, or time heals that particular wound, I'm afraid he'll be a wistful Earthlubber to his dying day.

AFTERWORD

I find writing the afterword to "Alexander the Bait," my first purchased and published story, to be very, very difficult. I look upon the story now as an utter dog. It's full of the kind of dialogue and descriptive language that Raymond Chandler, among others, bequeathed to the pulps with his tough, indigent detectives. And science fiction in the nineteen forties, after all, was very much a pulp-fiction field.

Yet I cannot forget what it was like to come out of the subway on my way home from work in November, 1945, and see my brother, Morton, who had been waiting for me and was now waving his arms at me across the street from the subway exit. He held a long white envelope in his left hand and a long green check in the other.

I stopped in the exit doorway and took a heavy, terribly deep breath. "Is it from *Astounding?*" I called across the street. "Is it from Campbell?"

"It's from *Astounding,*" he called back. "It's from Campbell. It's ninety-six dollars and fifty cents. He *bought* 'Alexander the Bait.'"

And then I breathed another deep breath and strolled across the street, a full professional writer. I got the envelope and the check from Mort and we walked home together. As soon as we arrived, I took the carbon copy of the story to the privacy of the bathroom and read it through. I remember thinking it was quite good, remarkably good. But anyway, I remember thinking, it was good enough to be published.

In college, before the Second World War, I had briefly begun a course in Chemical Engineering, then transferred to Pre-Med. But three and a half years later, I came out of the army, having scribbled my way through four army posts and a large part of western Europe, knowing that all I really wanted to be was a writer.

My father had died a month before my discharge, and my mother and fifteen-year-old sister had almost no means of support, especially after my army allotment checks had stopped. So I got a job as Technical Editor in the Army Air Force Radar and Radio Laboratory in Red Bank, New Jersey. The commute from my home in Brooklyn was a little more than two and a half hours each way: I remember calculating that if I didn't waste too much time with my meals and in the bathroom, I could get a full eight hours sleep every night.

In the beginning, I used the commute to read. Then I began to take along a large clipboard and write. I wrote a little poetry (I still saw myself as chiefly a poet), but as I began to get more and more irritated at the length of the commute and the pointlessness of my job, I started to experiment with commercial fiction and nonfiction. I would write these going to work on the sequence of subway train, railroad train, and bus ride, revise them on the reverse sequence while going home, and type them for an hour in the evening and all weekend.

I wrote general articles, technical articles, love stories, western stories, detective stories, and science-fiction stories, everything the *Writer's Digest* assured me professional writers made their livings out of. I knew O. Henry and Mark Twain were the pen names of commercial writers who also wrote a lot of memorable prose, so I sent out my work with a different pen name on each piece.

On one commute, I wrote a story titled "Alexander the Bait," typed it when I got home, and sent it, under the pen name of William Tenn, to John W. Campbell, Jr., the editor of *Astounding Science Fiction.*

I had been an avid, earnest reader of—among many, many other kinds of fiction—Campbell's *Astounding,* but had stopped about the time I went into the army. I had never read it for the simple pulpy jazz effects, but for the same reason I read Thomas Mann and André Malraux then, and Jorge Luis Borges and Olaf Stapledon later: it opened up large imaginative vistas and raised questions about where my species was going after it concluded the twentieth century.

Now I felt, as I returned to Campbell's *Astounding,* that with my job at the radar and radio lab, I had something I lacked before—technical background of a sort and, what might be even more important, technical language. (Please remember that this was before the days of Ward Moore and Ursula K. Le Guin and even George Orwell's *1984:* the young writer aspiring to science fiction felt that, before he could begin to explore the social and moral issues peculiar to the field, he must talk of—as Sturgeon later contemptuously described it to me—"heterodynes and welded bus-bars and electron howitzers.")

I had not known a thing about radar before I got the job at Watson Labs. As technical editor, I had learned a lot, so much so, in fact, that I had begun to play with the potentialities of the equipment. Would it not be possible, I asked the research personnel, to aim a radar beam at the moon (something, by the way, that was done at the adjoining Belmar Labs a couple of months after I sold "Alexander the Bait"!) and use it to create a topographic map of the surface? Engineers scratched their heads and said that, yes, it might be possible—but who would want to do such a thing?

Behind my question, of course, there was something else.

Interplanetary travel. It is impossible, in these days of the maximally boring space shuttle, these days, after the Public Relations crap of "One small step" and the golf shot on the Moon and the planted metallic flag with the breeze swirl carefully constructed in—it is impossible these days to recapture the dreams of the space romantics who exhaled and shook themselves as they read Willy Ley's articles on how we might get to the Moon or Mars, or as they studied Goddard's experiments, or as they read science-fiction stories describing the life-forms and civilizations we might encounter on the moons of Jupiter or Saturn. But me in 1945, I was a technical editor, and I was a young Marxist, and I was a budding writer. I was also a thoroughgoing space romantic.

I didn't believe those stories in which space travel was achieved in what might be called the Wilbur and Orville Wright method: One or two scientists put the interplanetary vessel together in the equivalent of a backyard garage (as, for example, to take the most literary cases, in H.G. Wells's fine *First Men in the Moon* or C.S. Lewis's even finer *Out of the Silent Planet*). I believed in the power of economics, and I believed in greed.

I was convinced that space travel would be developed not by individuals but by institutions; inventions and exploration would be by the future equivalent of General Electric's research laboratory or the mariners of something like the Dutch East India Company. A group of people, working together, under budgetary restraints, hoping to make a lot of money.

Looking back now, I was close. It was to be by a group of people, working together, under budgetary restraints, hoping to make an awful lot of war.

Well, so I wrote it and sent it off and sold it and began my career as a writer. It's not a great story, perhaps not even a good one, but it is my firstborn. As such, it will always look just a *little* pretty to me. Even as a dog.

Now a last note, a rather odd one. There was a period, while I was trying to write science fiction, that I seemed to be on the lag end of a telepathic hook-up with Robert Heinlein. Every time I got a good idea, he would have a story published with that idea about a week after I thought of it. That, perhaps, was why I wrote "Alexander the Bait" so fast and typed it in one night. Well, a long time after the story was published, I met Heinlein and he told me that he hadn't sent "The Man Who Sold the Moon" to an editor until years after he had written it—because, he said, when he read "Alexander the Bait," he felt he had been pre-empted. I'd always admired his work, and was completely confounded when he told me that.

I had to say—in all honesty—that I thought his story was a lot better than mine. Then he confounded me again by telling me that I was being generous.

He was a very, very generous man.

WRITTEN 1945——PUBLISHED 1946

THE CUSTODIAN

MAY 9, 2190—Well, I did it! It was close, but fortunately I have a very suspicious nature. My triumph, my fulfillment, was almost stolen from me, but I was too clever for them. As a result, I am happy to note in this, my will and testament, I now begin my last year of life.

No, let me be accurate. This last year of life, the year that I will spend in an open tomb, really began at noon today. Then, in the second sub-basement of the Museum of Modern Astronautics, I charged a dial for the third successive time and got a completely negative response.

That meant that I, Fiyatil, was the only human being alive on Earth. What a struggle I have had to achieve that distinction!

Well, it's all over now, I'm fairly certain. Just to be on the safe side, I'll come down and check the anthropometer every day or so for the next week, but I don't think there's a chance in the universe that I'll get a positive reading. I've had my last, absolutely my final and ultimate battle with the forces of righteousness—and I've won. Left in secure, undisputed possession of my coffin, there's nothing for me to do now but enjoy myself.

And that shouldn't be too hard. After all, I've been planning the pleasures for years!

Still, as I tugged off my suit of berrillit blue and climbed upstairs into the sunlight, I couldn't help thinking of the others. Gruzeman, Prejaut, and possibly even Mo-Diki. They'd have been here with me now if only they'd had a shade less academic fervor, a touch more of intelligent realism.

Too bad in a way. And yet it makes my vigil more solemn, more glorious. As I sat down on the marble bench between Rozinski's heroic statues of the Spaceman and Spacewoman, I shrugged and dismissed the memories of Gruzeman, Prejaut, and Mo-Diki.

They had failed. I hadn't.

I leaned back, relaxing for the first time in more than a month. My eyes swept over the immense bronze figures towering above me, two pieces of sculpture yearning agonizingly for the stars, and I burst into a chuckle. The absolute incongruity of my hiding place hit me for the first time—imagine, the Museum of Modem Astronautics! Multiplied by the incredible nervous tension, the knuckle-biting fear of the past five days, the chuckle bounced up and down in my throat and became a giggle, then a splutter, and finally a reverberating, chest-heaving laugh that I couldn't stop. It brought all the deer out of the museum park to stand in front of the marble bench where Fiyatil, the last man on Earth, choked and coughed and wheezed and cackled at his senile accomplishment.

I don't know how long the fit might have held me, but a cloud, merely in the course of its regular duties as a summer cloud, happened to slide in front of the sun. That did it. I stopped laughing, as if a connection had been cut, and glanced upward.

The cloud went on, and the sunlight poured down as warmly as ever, but I shivered a bit.

Two pregnant young does came a little closer and stood watching as I massaged my neck. Laughter had given it a crick.

"Well, my dears," I said, tossing them a quotation from one of my favorite religions, "it would seem that in the midst of life, we are at last truly in death."

They munched at me impassively.

MAY 11, 2190—I have spent the last two days putting myself and my supplies in order and making plans for the immediate future. Spending a lifetime in sober preparation for the duties of custodianship is one thing. Finding suddenly that you have become *the* custodian, the last of your sect as well as your race—and yet, peculiarly, the fulfillment of them both—that is quite another thing. I find myself burning with an insane pride. And a moment later, I turn cold with the incredible, the majestic, responsibility that I face.

Food will be no problem. In the commissary of this one institution, there are enough packaged meals to keep a man like myself well fed for ten years, let alone twelve months. And wherever I go on the planet, from the Museum of Buddhist Antiquities in Tibet to the Panorama of Political History in Sevastopol, I will find a similar plenty.

Of course, packaged meals are packaged meals: somebody else's idea of what my menu should be. Now that the last Affirmer has gone, taking with him his confounded austerity, there is no longer any need for me to be a hypocrite. I can at last indulge my taste for luxury and bathe my tongue in gustatory baubles. Unfortunately, I grew to manhood under Affirmer domination, and the hypocrisies I learned to practice in sixty cringing years have merged with the essential substance of my character. I doubt, therefore, that I will be preparing any meals of fresh food from the ancient recipes.

And then, too, meals of fresh food would involve the death of creatures that are currently alive and enjoying themselves. This seems a bit silly under the circumstances....

Nor did I need to put any of the automatic laundries into operation. Yet I have. Why clean my clothes, I asked myself, when I can discard a tunic the moment it becomes slightly soiled and step into a newly manufactured garment, still stiff in memory of the machine matrix whence it came?

Habit told me why I couldn't. Custodian concepts make it impossible for me to do what an Affirmer in my position would find easiest: shrug out of the tunic on a clear patch of ground and leave it lying behind me like a huge, brightly colored dropping. On the other hand, much Affirmer teaching that my conscious mind has been steadfastly rejecting for decades, I find to my great annoyance, has seeped into the unconscious osmotically. The idea of deliberately destroying anything as functional, if relatively unesthetic, as a dirty Tunic, Male, Warm-Season, Affirmer Ship-Classification No. 2352558.3, appalls me—even against my will.

Over and over again, I tell myself that Affirmer Ship-Classification Numbers now mean nothing to me. Less than nothing. They are as meaningless as cargo symbols on the Ark to the stevedores who loaded it, the day after Noah sailed.

Yet I step into a one-seater flyball for a relaxing tour of the museum grounds and something in my mind says: *No. 58184.72.* I close my teeth upon a forkful of well-seasoned Luncheon Protein Component and note that I am chewing Ship-Classification Numbers *15762.94 through 15763.01.* I even remind myself that it is a category to be brought aboard among the last, and only when the shipboard representative of the Ministry of Survival and Preservation has surrendered his command to the shipboard representative of the Ministry of The Journey.

Not a single Affirmer walks the Earth at the moment. Together with their confounded multiplicity of government bureaus—including the one in which all people professing Custodianism had to be registered, the Ministry of Antiquities and Useless Relics—they are now scattered among a hundred or so planetary systems in the galaxy. But all this seems to matter not a bit to my idiotically retentive mind, which goes on quoting texts memorized decades ago for Survival Placement Examinations long since superseded and forgotten by those in authority.

They are so efficient, the Affirmers, so horribly, successfully efficient! As a youngster, I confided to my unfortunately loquacious comrade, Ru-Sat, that I had begun creative painting on canvas in my leisure hours. Immediately, my parents, in collaboration with my recreational adviser, had me volunteered into the local Children's *Extra Work for Extra Survival Group,* where I was assigned to painting numbers and symbols on packing cases. "Not pleasure but persistence, persistence, persistence will preserve the race of Man," I had to repeat from the Affirmer catechism before I was allowed to sit down to any meal from that time on.

Later, of course, I was old enough to register as a conscientious Custodian. "Please," my father choked at me when I told him, "don't come around any more. Don't bother us. I'm speaking for the entire family, Fiyatil, including your uncles on your mother's side. You've decided to become a dead man: that's your business now. Just forget you ever had parents and relatives—and let us forget we had a son."

This meant I could free myself from Survival chores by undertaking twice as much work with the microfilm teams that traveled from museum to museum and archaeological site to skyscraper city. But still there were the periodic Survival Placement Exams, which everyone agreed didn't apply to Custodians but insisted we take as a gesture of good will to the society which was allowing us to follow our consciences. Exams which necessitated putting aside a volume entitled *Religious Design and Decoration in Temples of the Upper Nile* for the dreary, dingy, well-thumbed *Ship-Classification Manual and Uniform Cargo Stowage Guide.* I had given up the hope of being an artist myself, but those ugly little decimals took up time that I wished to spend contemplating the work of men who had lived in less fanatic and less frenzied centuries.

They still do! So powerful is habit that, now that I have no questions on dehydration to answer ever again, I still find myself doing the logarithmic work necessary to find out where a substance is packed once its water is removed. It is horribly frustrating to be mired after all in an educational system from which I turned completely away!

Of course, the studies I am involved in at the moment probably don't help very much. Yet it is very important for me to pick up enough information from the elementary educatories in this museum, for example, to insure my not having to worry about the possibility of a flyball breakdown over a jungle area. I'm no technician, no trouble-shooter. I have to learn instead how to choose equipment in good working order and how to start operating it without doing any damage to delicate components.

This technological involvement irritates me. Outside, the abandoned art of 70,000 years beckons—and here I sit, memorizing dull facts about the power plants of worker robots, scrutinizing blueprints of the flyballs' antigrav-screws, and acting for all the world like an Affirmer captain trying to win a commendation from the Ministry of The Journey before he blasts off.

Yet it is precisely this attitude that is responsible for my being here now, instead of sitting disconsolately aboard the Affirmer scout ship with Mo-Diki, Gruzeman, and Prejaut. While they exulted in their freedom and charged about the planet like creaky old colts, I made for the Museum of Modern Astronautics and learned how to operate and read an anthropometer and how to activate the berrillit blue. I hated to waste the time, but I couldn't forget how significant to an Affirmer, especially a modern one, is the concept of the sacredness of human life. They had betrayed us once; they were bound to come back to make certain that the betrayal left no loose ends in the form of Custodians enjoying fulfillment. I was right then, and I know I am right now—but I get so bored with the merely useful!

Speaking of the anthropometer, I had a nasty shock two hours ago. The alarm went off—and stopped. I scurried downstairs to it, shaking out the berrillit blue suit as I ran and hoping desperately that I wouldn't blow myself up in the course of using it a second time.

By the time I got to the machine, it had stopped caterwauling. I charged the all-directional dial over ten times and got no response. Therefore, according to the anthropometer manual, nothing human was moving about anywhere in the entire solar system. I had keyed the machine to myself electrocephalographically so that I wouldn't set off the alarm. Yet the alarm *had* gone off, indisputably recording the presence of humanity other than myself, however temporary its existence had been. It was very puzzling.

My conclusion is that some atmospheric disturbance or faulty connection inside the anthropometer set the machine off. Or possibly, in my great joy over being left behind a few days ago, I carelessly damaged the apparatus.

I heard the Affirmer scout ship radio the news of the capture of my colleagues to a mother vessel waiting beyond Pluto: I *know* I'm the sole survivor on Earth.

Besides, if it had been skulking Affirmers who set the alarm off, their own anthropometer would have detected me at the same time, since I had been walking about unprotected by the insulating effect of berrillit blue. The museum would have been surrounded by flyball crews and I'd have been caught almost immediately.

No, I cannot believe I have anything more to fear from Affirmers. They have satisfied themselves with their last-moment return of two days ago, I am positive. Their doctrine would forbid any further returns, since they would be risking their own lives. After all, there are only 363 days left—at most—before the sun goes nova.

MAY 15, 2190—I am deeply disturbed. In fact, I am frightened. And the worst of it is, I do not know of what. All I can do now is wait.

Yesterday, I left the Museum of Modern Astronautics for a preliminary tour of the world. I planned to spend two or three weeks hopping about in my flyball before I made any decision about where I would stay for the bulk of my year.

My first error was the choice of a first destination. Italy. It is very possible that, if my little problem had not come up, I would have spent eleven months there before going on with my preliminary survey. The Mediterranean is a dangerous and sticky body of water to anyone who has decided that, his own talents being inadequate or aborted, he may most fittingly spend his life cherishing the masterpieces presented to humanity by other, much more fortunate individuals.

I went to Ferrara first, since the marshy, reclaimed plain outside the city was a major Affirmer launching site. I lingered a little while at one of my favorite buildings, the *Palazzo di Diamanti,* shaking my head as helplessly as ever at the heavy building stones of which it is constructed and which are cut and faceted like so many enormous jewels. To my mind, the city itself is a jewel, now somewhat dulled, that sparkled madly in the days of the Este court. One little city, one tiny, arrogant court— I would so happily have traded them for the two billion steadfastly boorish Affirmers. Over sixty years of almost unchallenged political control, and did an entire planetful of them produce a single competitor for a Tasso or an Ariosto? And then I realized that at least one native Ferraran would have felt at ease in the world that has just departed from me, its last romantic. I remembered that Savonarola had been born in Ferrara....

The plain outside Ferrara also reminded me of the dour Dominican. The launching field, stretching away for quite a few flat miles, was strewn with enough possessions discarded at the last moment, to make a truly towering Bonfire of Vanities.

But what pathetic vanities! Here, a slide rule that some ship's commander had ordered thrown out before takeoff because the last inspection had revealed it to be in excess of what the *Ship-Classification Manual* listed as the maximum number of slide rules necessary for a vessel of that size. There, a mimeographed collection of tally sheets that had been dropped out of the closing air lock after every last item had been checked off as per regulations—one check *before* the item by the Ministry of Survival and Preservation, and one check *after* the item by the Ministry of The Journey. Soiled clothing, somewhat worn implements, empty fuel and food drums lay about on the moist ground. Highly functional articles all, that had somehow come in the course of time to sin against function—and had fallen swiftly from use. And, surprisingly, an occasional doll, not looking very much like a doll, to be sure, but not looking like anything that had an objective purpose either. Staring about me at the squalid debris dotted so rarely with sentiment, I wondered how many parents had writhed with shame when, despite their carefully repeated admonitions and advance warnings, the last search had discovered something in the recesses of a juvenile tunic that could only be called an old toy—or, worse yet, a keepsake.

I remembered what my recreational adviser had said on that subject, long years ago. "It's not that we believe that children shouldn't have toys, Fiyatil; we just don't want them to become attached to any particular toy. Our race is going to leave this planet that's been its home from the beginning. We'll be able to take with us only such creatures and objects as are usable to make other creatures and objects which we'll need for sustenance wherever we come down. And because we can't carry more than so much weight in each ship, we'll have to select from among the usable objects those which are essential.

"We won't take anything along because it's pretty, or because a lot of people swear by it, or because a lot of people *think* they need it. We'll take it along only because nothing else will do an important job so well. That's why I come to your home every month or so to inspect your room, to make certain that your bureau drawers contain only new things, that you're not falling into dangerous habits of sentimentality that can lead only to Custodianism. You've got far too nice a set of folks to turn into *that* kind of person."

Nonetheless, I chuckled to myself, I had turned into that kind of person. Old Tobletej had been right: the first step on the road to ruin had been bureau drawers crammed with odds and ends of memory. The twig on which had sat the first butterfly I'd ever caught, the net with which I'd caught him, and the first butterfly himself. The wad of paper that a certain twelve-year-old lady had thrown at me. A tattered copy of a real printed book—no facsimile broadcast, this, but something that had once known the kiss of type instead of the hot breath of electrons. The small wooden model of Captain Karma's starship, *Man's Hope*, which an old spacehand at Lunar Line launching field had given me along with much misinformation....

Those paunchy bureau drawers! How my parents and teachers had tried to teach me neatness and a hatred of possessions! And here was I, now grown into man's estate, smug over my possession of a quantity of artistic masterpieces the like of which no Holy Roman Emperor, no Grand Khan, would have dared to dream about.

I chuckled once more and started looking for the launching site robots. They were scattered about, almost invisible in the unimportant garbage of the spaceship field. After loading the ship, they had simply wandered about until they had run down. I activated them once more and set them to cleaning the field.

This is something I will do in every one of the two hundred or so launching sites on Earth, and this is the chief reason I have been studying robotics. I want Earth to look as pretty as possible when she dies. I never could be an Affirmer, I am afraid; I form strong attachments.

Feeling as I did, I just couldn't continue on my trip without taking the quickest, the most cursory glance at Florence. Naturally.

But as I should have expected, I got drunk on oils and marble and metalwork. Florence was empty of Florentines, but the glorious galleries were still there. I walked across the fine Ponte Vecchio, the only one of the famous Arno bridges to have escaped destruction in the Second World War. I came to Giotto's campanile and the baptistery doors by Ghiberti and I began to feel despair, desperation. I ran to the Church of Santa Croce to see Giotto's frescoes and the Convent of St. Mark's for Fra Angelico. What good was one year, what could I see of even a single city like this in a bare twelve months? I could view, I could gallop by, but what would I have time to *see?* I was in the Boboli gardens trying frantically to decide whether to look up Michelangelo's *David* which I'd seen once before, or some Donatello which I hadn't, when the alarms went off.

Both of them.

The day before I'd left, I'd put together a small anthropometer that had originally been developed for locating lost colonists in the Venusian swamps. It was based on an entirely different design than the big machine that I'd found in the Hall of Gadgets. Since the circuits were unlike, and they had been planned for use in entirely different atmospheres, I believed they would serve as excellent checks on each other. I'd set the alarms to the frequency of my flyball communicator and had left the museum fairly confident that the only thing that could make both anthropometers go off would be the presence of a man other than myself.

I flew back to the Museum, feeling very confused. Both pieces of equipment had responded the same way. The alarm had gone off, indicating the sudden materialization of Man on the planet. Then, when the stimulus had disappeared, both alarms had stopped. No matter how many times I charged the directional dials on each anthropometer, there was not the faintest suspicion of mankind within their extreme range, which is a little under one-half of a light-year.

The initial confusion has given way to a strong feeling of discomfort. Something is very wrong here on Earth, something other than the sun's getting ready to explode in a year. Possibly I have the nontechnician's blind faith in a piece of apparatus which I don't fully understand, but I don't believe that the anthropometers should be acting this way unless something really abnormal is occurring.

It has pleased me to look upon this planet as an ocean-going ship about to sink, and myself as the gallant captain determined to go down with her. Abruptly, I feel as if the ship were beginning to act like a whale.

I know what I must do. I'll move a supply of food down to the Hall of Gadgets and sleep right under the anthropometers. The alarm usually lasts for a minute or two. I can leap to my feet, charge the all-direction dials and get enough of a reading right then to know exactly where the stimulus is coming from. Then I will pop into my flyball and investigate. It's really very simple.

Only, I don't *like* it.

MAY 17, 2190—I feel thoroughly ashamed of myself, as only an old man who has been seeing ghosts in the graveyard should be ashamed. That, in fact, is the only excuse I can make to myself. I have, I suppose, been thinking too much about death recently. The coming extinction of Earth and the solar system; my death which is inevitably involved with it; the death of millions of creatures of uncounted species; the death of proud old cities that Man has reared and occupied for centuries.... Well, perhaps the association with ghosties and beasties and other strange phenomena is understandable. But I *was* getting frightened.

When the alarms went off again this morning, I got a directional reading. My destination was the Appalachian Mountain region in eastern North America.

The moment I got out of the flyball and took in the pale azure fog covering the cave mouth in front of me, I began to understand—and feel ashamed. Through the fog, which thinned in one place and thickened in others as I watched, I could see several bodies lying on the floor of the cave. Obviously, one of them had to be alive for the anthropometer to have reacted as soon as a patch of berrillit blue got meager enough to make the presence of a human mind detectable. I walked around to the back of the cave and found no exit.

I went back to the museum in the flyball and returned with the necessary equipment. I deactivated the berrillit blue fog at the entrance and walked inside cautiously.

The interior of the cave, which had evidently been furnished as a domestic and comfortable hideout, was completely wrecked. Somebody had managed to get an activator as well as a quantity of berrillit blue which had not yet been given any particular shape and which, therefore, was about as stable as hydrogen and oxygen—if it is permissible to use a metaphor from chemistry to illustrate negative force-field concepts. The berrillit blue had been activated as a sort of curtain across the mouth of the cave and had blown up immediately. But, since the activator was still operating and the entrance was fairly narrow, it continued to function as a curtain of insulating negative force, a curtain which had holes in it through which one could occasionally "peek" by means of the anthropometer at the people imprisoned inside.

There were three bodies near the entrance, two male and one female, rather youthful looking. From the quantity and type of statuary on the walls of the cave, it was easy to deduce that these people had belonged to one of the numerous religious Custodian groups, probably the *Fire in the Heavens* cult. When, in the last week of the exodus, the Affirmers had denounced the Crohiik Agreement and stated that the Affirmation of Life required that even those who didn't Affirm had to be protected against themselves, these people had evidently taken to the mountains. Evading the subsequent highly effective search, they had managed to stay hidden until the last great vessel left. Then, suspecting as I had that at least one scout ship would return for a final round-up, they had investigated the properties of the anthropometer and found out about the only insulator, berrillit blue. Unfortunately, they had not found out enough.

Deep in the rear of the cave, a body twisted brokenly to meet me. It was a young woman. My first reaction was absolute astonishment at the fact that she was still alive.

The explosion seemed to have smashed her thoroughly below the waist. She had crawled from the cave mouth to the interior, where the group had stored most of their food and water. As I teetered, momentarily undecided whether to leave her and get medication and blood plasma from a hospital in the region or to risk moving her immediately, she rolled over on her back.

She had been covering a year-old infant with her body, evidently uncertain when the berrillit might blow again. And somehow, in spite of what must have been tremendous agony, she had been feeding the child.

I bent down and examined the baby. He was quite dirty and covered with his mother's blood, but otherwise unharmed. I picked him up and, in answer to the question in the woman's eyes, I nodded.

"He'll be all right," I said.

She started what may have been a nod in reply and stopped halfway through to die. I examined her carefully and, I will admit, a shade frantically. There was no pulse—no heartbeat.

I took the child back to the Museum and constructed a sort of play pen for him out of empty telescope sections. Then I went back to the cave with three robots and had the people buried. I admit the gesture was superfluous, but it wasn't only a matter of neatness. However fundamental our differences, we were all of Custodian persuasion, generally speaking. It somehow made me feel as if I were snapping my fingers in the face of the entire smug Affirmation to respect *Fire-in-Heaven* eccentricities in this fashion.

After the robots had completed their work, I placed a piece of the religious statuary (it was remarkably badly done, by the way) at the head of each grave and even said a short prayer, or rather a sermon. I developed the thought that I had suggested approximately a week earlier to some deer—to wit, that in the midst of life we are in death. I did not joke about it, however, but spoke seriously on the subject for several minutes. The robots who were my audience seemed even less excited by the intelligence than the deer had been.

MAY 21, 2190—I am annoyed. I am very, very annoyed and my great problem at the moment is that I lack an object on which to expend my annoyance.

The child has been an incredible amount of trouble.

I took him to the largest medical museum in the northern hemisphere and had him thoroughly examined by the best pediatric diagnostic machinery. He seems to be in excellent health, which is fortunate for both of us. And his dietary requirements, while not the same as mine, are fairly simple. I got a full tape on the kind of food he needs and, after a few readjustments in the commissary of the Museum of Modern Astronautics, I have arranged for this food to be prepared and delivered to him daily. Unfortunately, he does not seem to regard this arrangement, which took up an inordinate amount of my time, as wholly satisfactory.

For one thing, he will not accept food from the regulation robot nursemaid which I have activated for him. This, I suspect, is because of his parents' odd beliefs: he probably has never encountered mechanical affection before. He will only eat when I feed him.

That situation alone is intolerable, but I have found it almost impossible to leave him guarded by the robot nursemaid. Though he does little more than crawl, he manages to do this at surprisingly fast pace and is always disappearing into dark corridors of the museum. Then an alarm is flashed to me and I have to break off my examination of the gigantic palace of the Dalai Lama, the Potala, and come scudding back from Lhasa halfway across the world to the Museum.

Even then it would take us hours to find him—and by "us" I mean every robot at my disposal—if I were not able to resort to the anthropometer. This admirable gadget points out his hiding place very swiftly, and so, pulling him out of the firing chamber of the Space Howitzer in the Hall of Weapons, I return him to his play pen. Then, if I dare, and if it is not time for him to be fed, I may return—briefly—to the Tibetan plateau.

I am at present engaged in constructing a sort of enormous cage for him, with automatic heating and toilet facilities and devices that will screen out undesirable animals, insects, and reptiles. Though this is taking up far too much of my time, it will be an excellent investment, I believe.

I don't know quite what to do about the feeding problem. The only solution I can find in any of the literature on the subject that offers promise is the one about letting him go hungry if he refuses food from normal sources. After a brief experiment, however, in which he seemed cheerfully resigned to starvation, I was forced to give in. I now handle every one of his meals.

The trouble is that I don't know whom to blame. Since I have been a Custodian from early manhood, I failed to see the need to reproduce. I have never been interested even slightly in children. I know very little about them and care less.

I have always felt that my attitude was admirably summed up by Socrates' comments in the *Symposium*: "Who, upon reflecting on Homer and Hesiod and other such great poets, would not rather have their children than ordinary human ones? Who would not like to emulate them in the creation of children such as theirs, which have preserved their memory and given them everlasting glory?... Many are the temples which have been raised in their honor for the sake of such children as they have had, which were never raised in honor of anyone for the sake of his mortal children."

Unfortunately, we are the only two humans alive on Earth, this child and I. We are going to our doom together; we ride the same round tumbril. And the treasures of the world, which were wholly mine less than a week ago, now belong at least partially to him. I wish we could discuss the matters at issue, not only to arrive at more equitable arrangements, but also for the sheer pleasure of the discussion. I have come to the conclusion that I began this journal out of unconscious terror when I discovered, after the Affirmers left, that I was completely alone.

I find myself getting very wistful for conversation, for ideas other than my own, for opinions against which mine might be measured. Yet according to the literature on the subject, while this child may begin talking any day now, we will be immersed in catastrophe long before he learns to argue with me. I find that sad, however inevitable.

How I wander! The fact is that once again I am being prevented from studying art as I would like. I am an old man and should have no responsibilities; I have all but laid down my life for the privilege of this study. It is extremely vexing.

And conversation. I can just imagine the kind of conversation I might be having with an Affirmer at the moment, were one to have been stranded here with me. What dullness, what single-minded biological idiocy! What crass refusal to look at, let alone admit, the beauty his species has been seventy millennia in the making! The most he might have learned if he is European, say, is a bit about the accepted artists of his culture. What would he know of Chinese paintings, for example, or cave art? Would he be able to understand that in each there were primitive periods followed by eras of lusty development, followed in turn by a consolidation of artistic gains and an increase in formalization, the whole to be rounded off by a decadent, inner-groping epoch which led almost invariably into another primitive and lusty period? That these have occurred again and again in the major cultures so that even the towering genius of a Michelangelo, a Shakespeare, a Beethoven will likely be repeated—in somewhat different terms—in another complete cycle? That there was a Michelangelo, Shakespeare, and Beethoven in each of several different flower periods in ancient Egyptian art?

How could an Affirmer understand such concepts when he lacks the basic information necessary to understanding? When their ships departed from the moribund solar system laden only with immediately usable artifacts? When they refused to let their offspring keep childhood treasures for fear of developing sentimentality, so that when they came to colonize Procyon XII there would be no tears for either the world that had died or the puppy that had been left behind?

And yet history plays such incredible jokes on Man! They who ran away from their museums, who kept nothing but a cold microfilm record of what lay in their investment houses of culture, will learn that Man's sentimentality is not to be frustrated. The bleak, efficient ships that brought them to these alien worlds will become museums of the past as they oxidize out of existence on the strange sands. Their cruelly functional lines will become the inspiration for temples and alcoholic tears.

What in the world is happening to me? How I run on! After all, I merely wanted to explain why I was annoyed.

MAY 29, 2190—I have made several decisions. I don't know if I will be able to implement the most important of them, but I will try. In order, however, to give myself what I need most at the moment—time—I will write much less in this journal, if I write any more at all. I will try very hard to be brief.

To begin with the least important decision: I have named the child Leonardo. Why I chose to name him after a man who, for all of his talents—in fact, because of his talents—I regard as the most spectacular failure in the history of art, I do not know. But Leonardo was a well-rounded man, something which the Affirmers are not—and something which I am beginning to admit I am not.

By the way, the child recognizes his name. He is not yet able to pronounce it, but it is positively miraculous the way he recognizes it. And he makes a sound which is very like mine. In fact, I might say—

Let me go on.

I have decided to attempt an escape from the Earth—with Leonardo. My reasons are many and complex, and I'm not certain that I understand them all, but one thing I do know: I have felt responsibility for a life other than my own and can no longer evade it.

This is not a tardy emergence into Affirmer doctrine, but in a very real sense my own ideas come to judgment. Since I believe in the reality of beauty, especially beauty made with the mind and hands of man, I can follow no other course.

I am an old man and will achieve little with the rest of my life. Leonardo is an infant: he represents raw potential; he might become anything. A song beyond Shakespeare's. A thought above Newton, above Einstein. Or an evil beyond Gilles de Rais, a horror past Hitler.

But the potential should be realized. I think, under my tutelage, it is less likely to be evil, and there *I* have a potential to be realized.

In any case, even if Leonardo represents a zero personally, he may *carry* the germ-plasm of a Buddha, of a Euripides, of a Freud. And *that* potential must be realized....

There is a ship. Its name is *Man's Hope* and it was the first ship to reach the stars, almost a century ago when it had just been discovered that our sun would explode and become a nova in a little less than a hundred years. It was the ship that discovered for Man the heart-quickening fact that other stars have planets and that many of those planets are habitable to him.

It was a long time ago that Captain Karma brought his starship back down on the soil of Earth with the news that escape was possible. That was long before I was born, long before humanity divided unequally into Custodian and Affirmer, and long, long before either group were the unwinking fanatics they had become five years ago.

The ship is in the Museum of Modern Astronautics. I know it has been kept in good condition. I also know that twenty years ago, before the Affirmers had developed the position that absolutely nothing might be taken physically from a museum, the ship was equipped with the latest Léugio Drive. The motive was that, if it were needed on Exodus Day, it might make the trip to a star in months instead of the years it had required originally.

The only thing that I do not know is whether I, Fiyatil, the Custodian of Custodians and art critic extraordinary, can learn to run it in the time that Leonardo and I have left. But as one of my favorite comic characters remarked about the possibility of a man chopping his own head off; a man can *try*....

There is something else on my mind, even more exciting in a way, but this comes first. I find myself looking at the Sun a good deal these days. And very searchingly, too. Very.

NOVEMBER 11, 2190—I can do it. With the help of two robots which I will modify for the purpose, I can do it. Leonardo and I could leave immediately. But I have my other project to complete.

And this is my other project. I am going to use all the empty space in the ship. It was built originally for different motors and a very large crew, and I am going to use that space as a bureau drawer. Into that bureau drawer I will stuff the keepsakes of humanity, the treasures of its childhood and adolescence—at least as many as I can get in.

For weeks I have been collecting treasures from all over the world. Incredible pottery, breath-taking friezes, glorious statuary, and oil paintings almost beyond counting litter the corridors of the museum. Brueghel is piled on Bosch, Bosch on Dürer. I am going to bring a little of everything to that star toward which I point my ship, a little to show what the real things were like. I am including things like the holograph manuscripts of Jane Austen's *Pride and Prejudice,* Beethoven's Ninth Symphony, Gogol's *Dead Souls,* Mark Twain's *Huckleberry Finn,* and holographs of Dickens's letters and Lincoln's speeches. There are many others, but I cannot take everything. Within responsible limits, I must please myself.

Therefore, I am not taking anything from the Sistine Chapel ceiling. I have carved out two bits of the *Last Judgment* instead. They are my favorites; the soul that suddenly realizes that it is condemned, and the flayed skin on which Michelangelo painted his own portrait.

The only trouble is that fresco weighs so much! Weight, weight, weight—it is almost all I think about now. Even Leonardo follows me about and says "Weight, weight, weight!" He pronounces nothing else so well.

Still, what should I take of Picasso? A handful of oils, yes, but I must take the *Guernica.* And there is more weight.

I have some wonderful Russian copper utensils and some Ming bronze bowls. I have a lime spatula from Eastern New Guinea made of oiled wood that has a delightfully carved handle (it was used in chewing betel nut and lime). I have a wonderful alabaster figure of a cow from ancient Sumer. I have an incredible silver Buddha from northern India. I have some Dahomean brass figures of a grace to shame Egypt and Greece. I have a carved ivory container from Benin, West Africa, showing a thoroughly fifteenth-century European Christ on the cross. I have the *Venus* of Willendorf, Austria, the figure that was carved in the Aurignacian epoch of the Paleolithic and which is part of the artistic tradition of the "Venus" art of prehistoric mankind.

I have miniatures by Hilliard and Holbein, satiric prints by Hogarth, a beautiful Kangra painting of the eighteenth century on paper that shows astonishingly little Mughal influence, Japanese prints by Takamaru and Hiroshigi—and where may I stop? How may I choose?

I have pages from the Book of Kells, which is an illuminated, hand-executed manuscript of almost unmatched beauty; and I have pages from the Gutenberg Bible, put together in the infancy of printing, which has illuminated pages to give the *effect* of a hand-copied manuscript, because the printers didn't want their invention discovered. I have a tughra of Sulaiman the Magnificent, a calligraphic emblem that formed headings for his imperial edicts; and I have a Hebrew Scroll of the Law whose calligraphy outshines the jewels which encrust the poles on which it is wound.

I have Coptic textiles of the sixth century and Alençon lace of the sixteenth. I have a magnificent red krater vase from one of Athens' maritime colonies and a wooden figurehead of a minister from a New England frigate. I have a Rubens nude and an Odalisque by Matisse.

In architecture—I am taking the Chinese *Compendium of Architecture,* which I think has never been equalled as a text, and a model of a Le Corbusier house built by him. I would love to take one building, the Taj Mahal, but I *am* taking the pearl that the Mogul gave to her for whom he built the ineffable tomb. It is a reddish pearl, shaped like a pear and about three and a half inches long; shortly after it was buried with her, it turned up in the possession of an Emperor of China, who set it on gold leaves and surrounded it with jade and emeralds. At the turn of the nineteenth century, it was sold somewhere in the Near East for a tiny, ridiculous sum and ended in the Louvre.

And a tool: a small stone fistaxe, the first thing known to have been made by human creatures.

All this I have collected near the ship. But I've sorted none of it. And I suddenly remember, I have collected as yet no furniture, no decorated weapons, no etched glass....

I must hurry, hurry!

NOVEMBER 2190—Shortly after I finished the last entry, I glanced upward. There were green specks on the sun and strange orange streamers seemed to plume out to all points of the compass. Evidently there was not to be a year. These were the symptoms of death that the astronomers had predicted.

So there was an end to my collecting—and my sorting was done in less than a day. The one thing I suddenly found I had to do, when it became obvious that my sections of Michelangelo would be too heavy, was to go to the Sistine Chapel ceiling after all. This time I cut out a relatively tiny thing—the finger of the Creation as it stabs life into Adam. And I decided to take Da Vinci's *La Gioconda,* even though his *Beatrice d'Este* is more to my taste: the Mona Lisa's smile belongs to the world.

All posters are represented by one Toulouse-Lautrec. I dropped the *Guernica:* Picasso is represented instead by an oil from his blue period and a single striking ceramic plate. I dropped Harold Paris's *The Eternal Judgment* because of its bulk; all I have of his now is the print *Buchenwald #2, "Where Are We Going?"* And somehow or other, in my last-minute haste, I seem to have selected a large number of Safavid bottles from Iran of the sixteenth and seventeenth centuries. Let future historians and psychologists puzzle out the reasons for my choices: they are now irrevocable.

We are proceeding toward Alpha Centauri and should arrive in five months. How will we and all our treasures be received, I wonder? I suddenly feel insanely cheerful. I don't think it has anything to do with my rather belated realization that I, who have so little talent and have failed so miserably in the arts, will achieve a place in the history of art like no other man—a kind of esthetic Noah.

No, it is the fact that I am carrying both the future and the past to a rendezvous where they still have a chance to come to terms. A moment ago, Leonardo bounced a ball against the visiplate and, looking at it, I observed that old Sol was expanding apoplectically. As I remarked to him then: "I find, to my astonishment, that in the midst of death, I am—at last, at last!—truly in life."

AFTERWORD

This is my personal flat-out favorite among all my stories. That's strictly a minority voice you hear, however: the story has only been anthologized once—and only in a collection where various science-fiction writers were asked to submit their favorite pieces—and no critic or reviewer, over the years, has so much as mentioned the poor little thing.

Still, do me something: it's my dearest, dearest baby.

I came damn close to starving while writing it. It took me over two years of wandering around in museums and art books and cultural histories to intellectually assemble the material that Fiyatil looked at as well as the stuff he finally took with him when he left Earth. I wrote little else in those two years, and the only editor who liked the piece enough to buy it was Larry Shaw (God bless him, and may he rest easy) of *If* magazine. He paid me his maximum—one hundred and twenty-five dollars, which went out immediately to all my friends to pay off loans.

One last note. If you're wondering where science-fiction writers get the crazy names they use for future characters, Fiyatil, for example.... All Jewish children of even moderately religious parents are given Hebrew or Yiddish names when they are born.

Mine, depending on the transliteration you like, is Fiet'l or Fitel or Feitil.

Or even Fiyatil.

WRITTEN 1951——PUBLISHED 1953

On Venus, Have We Got a Rabbi

So you're looking at me, Mr. Important Journalist, as if you're surprised to see a little, gray-haired, gray-bearded man. He meets you at the spaceport and he's driving a piece of machinery that on Earth you wouldn't even give to a dog's grandmother, she should take it with her to the cemetery and be buried in it. This is the man—you're saying to yourself—this nobody, this piece of nothing, who's supposed to tell you about the biggest, strangest development in Judaism since Yohannan Ben Zakkai sat down with the Sanhedrin in Yavne and said, "The meeting will please come to order."

Are you talking to the wrong man, you want to know? Did you come across space, fifty, sixty, I don't know, maybe seventy million miles just to see a schlemiel in a cracked helmet with a second-hand oxygen canister on his back? The answer is this: you are not talking to the wrong man. Poor as he is, shabby as he is, unlucky as he is, you are talking to the one man who can tell you all you want to know about those trouble-makers from the fourth planet of the star Rigel. You are talking to Milchik, the TV repairman. Himself. In person.

All we do is put your belongings in the back of the module and then we get in the front. You have to slam the door—a little harder, please—and then, if this is still working and that is still working, and the poor old module feels like making another trip, we'll be off. Luxury it definitely is not, a spaceport limousine you certainly could not call it, but—module, shmodule—it gets you there.

You like dust storms? That's a dust storm. If you don't like dust storms, you shouldn't come to Venus. It's all we got in the way of scenery. The beach at Tel Aviv we don't got. Grossinger's, from ancient times in the Catskills, we don't got. Dust storms we got.

But you're saying to yourself, I didn't come for dust storms, I didn't come for conversation. I came to find out what happened to the Jews of the galaxy when they all gathered on Venus. Why should this schmendrik, this Milchik the TV man, have anything special to tell me about such a big event? Is he a special wise man, is he a scholar, is he a prophet among his people?

So I'll tell you. No, I'm not a wise man, I'm not a scholar, I'm certainly not a prophet. A living I barely make, going from level to level in the Darjeeling Burrow with a tool box on my back, repairing the cheapest kind of closed-circuit sets. A scholar I'm not, but a human being I am. And that's the first thing you ought to know. Listen, I say to Sylvia, my wife, don't our Sages say that he who murders one man murders the entire human race? So doesn't it follow then that he who listens to one man listens to the whole human race? And that he who listens to one Jew on Venus is listening to all the Jews on Venus, all the Jews in the universe, even, from one end to the other?

But Sylvia—go talk to a woman!—says, "Enough already with your Sages! We have three sons to marry. Who's going to pay for their brides' transportation to Venus? You think for nothing a nice Jewish girl will come here, from another planetary system maybe—she'll come to this gehenna of a planet and go live in a hole in the ground, she'll raise children, they won't see the sun, they won't see the stars, they'll only see plastic walls and elevators and drunken cadmium miners coming in to spend their pay and have a *goyische* good time. You think just because a girl likes the stereo transcript of one of our sons and is willing to come here and marry him, we don't have to pay her fare and maybe something a little extra she should enjoy herself on the way? Where do the Sages say the money comes from? Do they say maybe we should nail up a new collection box in the *shul:* 'Help the Milchik boys find brides—their father is too busy with philosophy'?"

I don't have to remind you—you're a journalist, you're an educated man—what Solomon says in Proverbs about women: a good one, he says, has got to cost you a lot more in the end than pearls. And still, someone in the family has to think about money and the boys getting brides. That's the second point. The first point is that I'm a human being and a Jew, two different things maybe, and I've got the right to speak for all human beings and for all Jews.

On top of that, I'm a Jewish father with three full-grown sons here on Venus, and if you want to do an injury to your worst enemy, you say to him, "Listen. You're Jewish? You got three sons? Go to Venus."

And that's the third point. Why I, Milchik the TV man, am telling you this, and why you come all the way from Earth just to listen to me. Because I'm not only a Jewish father, but I'm also— Listen. Could I ask you a question? You won't be offended? You sure you won't be offended?

You're not Jewish, by any chance? I mean, do you have any Jewish ancestors, a grandfather, a great-grandmother maybe? Are you sure? Well, that's what I mean. Maybe one of your ancestors changed his name back in 2533—2533 by *your* calendar, of course. It's not exactly that you *look* Jewish or anything like that, it's just that you're such an intelligent man and you ask such intelligent questions. I couldn't help wondering—

You like Jewish food? In twenty, twenty-five minutes my poor old tired module will pull us out of this orange dust and into the Darjeeling air lock. Then you'll sit down to a Jewish meal, believe me, you'll kiss every one of your fingers. We get almost all of our Jewish food shipped here from Earth, special packaging and special arrangement. And, naturally, special cost. My wife Sylvia makes a dish, they come from all over our level just to taste: chopped reconstituted herring. It's an appetizer and we like appetizers in our family. So what I've been telling you. after all, is only an appetizer. I have to get you in exactly the right mood for the main dish, the big story you came for.

Sylvia makes all the food we eat in the *shul*—our synagogue. You know, the hamantashen, all that. She even prepares the formal Saturday morning breakfast, the bagels and lox and cream cheese that all the men must eat before they say their Sabbath prayers. We're all orthodox here and we practice the Levittown rite. Our rabbi, Joseph Smallman, is superorthodox Levittown: he wears a yarmulka, and on top of the yarmulka a black homburg which has been passed down from father to son in his family for I don't know how many centuries.

Oh, look how you're smiling! You know I've moved from the appetizer to the main dish. Rabbi Joseph Smallman. It's only Venus, and it's maybe the seventh or eighth Darjeeling Burrow listed on the map, but have we got ourselves a rabbi! To us he's an Akiba, a Rambam.

More than that. You know what we call him when we're alone, among ourselves? We call him the Great Rabbi of Venus.

Now you're laughing out loud. No, don't apologize: I heard a chuckle come out of you, like a belch, you should excuse the expression, after a big dinner.

This Milchik the TV man, you're saying to yourself, he and his neighbors in the burrow they come to maybe seventy or eighty Jewish families, they're making a living, with God's help, out of the holes in each other's pockets—and *their* rabbi is the Great Rabbi of Venus? The littlest hole in the ground claims the biggest fire?

It's impossible, maybe? Is anything impossible to the Most High, blessed be His Name? After all, as the Sages tell us, "The last shall be first." Just don't ask me, please, which Sages.

Why is he the Great Rabbi? Well, first of all, why shouldn't Rabbi Smallman be a Great Rabbi? He needs a certificate from the Great Rabbi Licensing Bureau? You have to graduate from the Great Rabbi Special Yeshiva to become a Great Rabbi? That's first of all: you're a Great Rabbi because you *act* like a Great Rabbi, you're *recognized* like a Great Rabbi, you make *decisions* like a Great Rabbi. And you must have heard something of how he acted and how he decided when all the Jews in the universe held a congress right here on Venus. If you hadn't heard, you wouldn't have come all the way from Earth for this interview.

Other people had heard, too. They'd heard of his piety, learning, and wisdom—of his modesty, of course, I say nothing—long before the First Interstellar Neozionist Conference on Venus. People heard and people talked, and they came from as far away as the Gus Grissom Burrow to ask him for rabbinical decisions.

You've got the time to listen to just one example? Sure you've got the time: you're driving through a heavy dust storm in a module that's coughing its guts out, a module that knows Milchik the TV man gives it the best of everything—charged-up power cells, a brand-new fan belt—even if it means that he can't afford to put food on his own table. For Milchik, the module will keep going no matter what, when by itself it would ask for nothing better than to lie down and die in comfort. And the module also likes to listen to Milchik expounding *Halacha,* the holy rules and laws.

About five years ago, something terrible happened on the eve of the Passover. There was an explosion aboard a cargo ship on its way to Venus. No one was hurt, but the cargo was damaged and the ship arrived very late, just a couple of hours before the first seder was to begin. Now on this ship was all the special Passover food that had been ordered from Earth by the twenty-four Jewish families of the Altoona Burrow, and the special food was in cans and airtight packages. When the delivery was made, the Altoona people noticed that the cans had been banged about and dented—but, worse than that, most of the cans had tiny holes all over them. Disaster! According to the Rabbinical Council of 2135 on Space Travel Kashruth, food which is in a punc-tured can is automatically unclean, unclean for daily use, unclean for Passover use. And here it is almost the seder and what can they do?

These are not rich people: they don't have reserves, they don't have alternatives, they don't even have their own rabbi. If it's a matter of life and death, all right, any-thing goes; but it isn't life and death, all it means is that they'll have to eat *humetz,* non-Passover food, they won't be able to celebrate the seder. And a Jew who can't celebrate the Deliverance from Egypt with matzo, with bitter herb, with charoseth, with Passover wine, such a Jew is like a bride without a wedding canopy, like a syna-gogue without a Torah scroll.

The Altoona Burrow is connected to the Darjeeling Burrow; it's a suburb of ours. That's what I said—a suburb. Listen, I know we're a small place, but where is it writ-ten that small places, no matter how small, are not entitled to suburbs? If Grissom can have fourteen suburbs, we can have two. So naturally the Altoona people, white-faced, worried, their mouths opening and closing with aggravation, brought the prob-lem to our Rabbi Joseph Smallman. Nothing was leaking from the cans, they said, but the result of the one test they had conducted was bad: as recommended by the Rabbinical Council of 2135, they had taken a hair from somebody's head and poked it into a hole in a can—and the hair had not visibly curled back out. Did that mean that all the expensive food shipped across space had to be condemned, no seders in the Altoona Burrow?

Well, of course that's what it meant—or would have meant to an ordinary rabbi. Rabbi Smallman looked at them and looked at them, and he scratched the pimple on the right side of his nose. He's a pretty good-looking man, Rabbi Smallman, strong and chunky with a face like a young Ben-Gurion, but he does always seem to have a big red pimple on the side of his nose. Then he got up and went to his bookcase and took out half a dozen volumes of Talmud and the last three volumes of the Proceed-ings of the Rabbinical Council on Space Travel. And he looked in each book at least once, and he sat and thought for a long time after each passage. Finally he asked a question: "Which hair did you use and from whose head?"

They showed him the hair, a fine, white hair from the head of the oldest great-grand-father in the Altoona Burrow, a hair as thin and as delicate as a baby's first sigh. "So this hair did not curl back," he said, "from a hole in that particular can. So much for your test with a hair of your selection. Now for my test with a hair of my selection." And he called over my oldest boy, Aaron David, and told him to pluck out a hair.

You're not blind, you can see my hair, even at my age, how heavy and coarse it is. And believe me, it's thinning out, it's nothing to what it was. My boy, Aaron David, he has the traditional hair of our family, each one twice, three times as thick as a normal hair, his head always going up into a black explosion. When he comes with me, as helper on a job, the customer usually says something like, "With a head of hair like that, what for do you need to carry around coaxial cable?" I say to them: "Bite your tongue. Maybe Haman or Hitler would have used his hair for coaxial cable, or that unholy pair, Sebastian Pombal and Juan Crevea, they also liked to take our heads as raw material in their terrible factories, but don't you talk like that in the year 2859 to a Jewish father about his Jewish son." The Eternal, blessed be He, may demand my son of me, but to nobody else will I be an Abraham who doesn't defend his Isaac. You know what I mean?

So when Rabbi Smallman picks up a dented can and pokes Aaron David's hair at a hole, the hair comes back right away like a piece of bent wire. What else? And when he tries it with another can, again the hair won't go in. So Rabbi Smallman points to the first can they brought him, the one they tested with the old man's hair, and he says, "I declare the food in this can unfit and unclean. But these others," and he waves his hand at the rest of the shipment, "are perfectly acceptable. Carry them home and enjoy your seder."

They crowd around him with tears in their eyes and they thank him and they thank him. Then they gather the cans together and they hurry back to their burrow—it's getting late and it's time to begin the search for the last bits of *humetz* that you have to do before you can turn to the Pesadikeh food. The Altoona people rush out, in a few minutes, I tell you, it was as it says in the Second Book of the Holocaust: "There was none left, not one."

You understand, I hope, wherein lies the greatness of this decision? Jews from all over Venus discussed it and everyone, everywhere, marveled. No. I'm sorry, you're wrong: the greatness did not lie merely in a decision that made it possible for some poor Jews to enjoy their own Passover seders in their own homes. That's based on a simple precept—that it's better to have a Jew without a beard than a beard without a Jew. Try again. No, that's not right either: using a thick hair from my son's head was not especially brilliant—under those particular circumstances, any really good rabbi would have done the same. For that you don't have to be a Hillel already; you just have to avoid being a literal-minded Shammai. The point still eludes you, right? *Goyische kop!*

My apologies. I didn't mean to speak in a language you don't know. What did I say? It was just a simple comment about, well, how some people are intended to be students of Talmud, and other people are *not* intended to be students of Talmud. It's kind of like an old saying amongst us.

Sure I'll explain. Why great? In the *first* place. Almost any decent rabbi would have seen the importance of that food being found fit and clean. And in the *second* place. A good rabbi, a first-class rabbi, would have found a way to do it, a hair from my son, a this, a that, anything. But, in the *third* place, only a truly great rabbi would have examined that many books and thought that long and hard about the matter before he announced his decision. How could they really enjoy the seder unless they had perfect confidence in his decision? And how could they have perfect confidence unless they had seen him wrestle with it through nine separate volumes? Now do you see why we called him the Great Rabbi of Venus, even five years before the Neozionist Congress and the great Bulba scandal?

Now I didn't go so far in Talmudic study myself—a man has a family to support, and closed-circuit TV repair on a planet like Venus doesn't exactly help your mind in clearing up the problems of *Gemara*. But whenever I think of what our congregation here has in Rabbi Smallman, I think of how the Sages begin their argument: "A man finds a treasure…"

You shouldn't get the impression, please, that a treasure is a treasure to everyone. Almost all the Jews on Venus are *Ashkenazim*—people whose ancestors emigrated from Eastern Europe to America before the Holocaust and who didn't return to Israel after the Ingathering—but there are at least three kinds of Ashkenazim, and only our kind, the Levittown Ashkenazim, call Rabbi Smallman the Great Rabbi of Venus. The Williamsburg Ashkenazim, and there are a lot more of them than there are of us, the black-gabardined Ashkenazim who shake and pray and shake and pray, they call Rabbi Smallman the lox-and-bagels rabbi. And on the other hand, the Miami Ashkenazim, the rich all-rightniks who live in the big IBM Burrow, to them a rabbi is a girl who hasn't yet gotten married and is trying to do something intellectual with herself. It's said that the Williamsburg Ashkenazim believe in miracle-working, that the Levittown Ashkenazim believe it's a miracle when they find work, and that the Miami Ashkenazim don't believe in miracles and don't believe in work, they only believe in the import-export business.

I can see you're remembering I said before that I was through with the appetizer and ready to serve the main dish, the story you came for. And where, in all that I've just been telling you, is the main dish, you want to know? Listen, relax a little. Figure it this way: first I gave you an appetizer, then, after that, for the last few minutes, you've been having a soup course. You're through with the soup? Fine. Now we bring out the main dish.

Only—just a second more. There's something else you have to have first. Call it a salad. Look, it's a very small piece of salad. You'll be finished with it in no time. Now please. You're not the cook; you're only a customer. You want a story that's like a sandwich? Go someplace else. Milchik serves only complete meals.

That night, after the seder, I'm sitting on a bench outside our apartment in the Darjeeling Burrow. To me, this is always the best time. It's quiet, most people have gone to bed, and the corridor doesn't smell from crowds. All through the corridors, the lights are being turned down to half their wattage. That's to let us know it's night on Earth. Exactly *where* it's night on Earth, what part of Earth, I have no idea. Darjeeling, maybe.

As I sit thinking, Aaron David comes out of the apartment and sits down near me on the bench. "Papa," he says after a while. "That was a great thing Rabbi Smallman did today." I nod, sure, certainly it was a great thing. Aaron David puts his hand up to the part of his head where he pulled the single hair out. He holds his hand tight against the spot and looks across the corridor. "Before this," he says, "I just wanted, but now I more than want. I'm going to be a rabbi."

"Congratulations," I say. "Me, I'm going to be the Viceroy of Venus."

"I'm serious, Papa. I'm really serious."

"I'm joking? I don't think there's a chance I'll one day be appointed by the Council of Eleven Nations Terrestrial, and the Presidents of Titan and Ganymede? I'd do a worse job than that hooligan we got right now, his heart should only explode inside his chest? All right," I say to him, "all right," because now he turns and looks at me, with his eyes that are Sylvia's eyes, and eyes like that, let me tell you, can look. "So you want to be a rabbi. What good is the wanting? Anything you want that I can give, I'll give. You know I have that little insulated screwdriver, the blue one, that was made in Israel over five hundred years ago, when Israel was still a Jewish state. That precious little screwdriver, it's like the bones of my right hand, that I'll give you if you ask for it. But I can't give you tuition money for a yeshiva, and more important, I can't even find the transportation money for a bride. A tradition, now, it's hundreds of years old, ever since the Jews began emigrating into space, that a Levittown bride must come from another planet—and it's not only you, it's also your two brothers. A rational creature, boychik, has to worry in an organized way. First the bride money, then we talk about yeshiva money."

Aaron David is close to crying. "If only—if—" He bites his lip.

"If—," I say. "If— You know what we say about if. If your grandmother would have had testicles, she'd have been your grandfather. Consider the problem: if you want to be a rabbi, especially a Levittown rabbi, you have to know three ancient languages even before you begin; you have to know Hebrew, you have to know Aramaic, you have to know Yiddish. So I'll tell you what. *If.* If you can learn enough beforehand, maybe *if* the miracle ever happens and we can send you to a yeshiva, you can go through faster than usual, rapid-advance, before the whole family goes bankrupt. *If* Rabbi Smallman, for example, gives you lessons."

"He'll do that," he says excitedly. "He's doing it already!"

"No, I'm not talking about just lessons. I'm talking about *lessons.* The kind you have to pay for. He'll teach you one day after supper, and I'll review with you the next day after supper. That way I'll learn too, I won't be such an ignoramus. You know what the Sages say about studying Talmud: 'Get thee a comrade…' You'll be my comrade, and I'll be your comrade, and Rabbi Smallman will be both our comrade. And we'll explain to your mother, when she screams at us, that we're getting a bargain, two for one, a special."

So that's what we did. To make the extra money, I started hauling cargo from the spaceport in my module—you notice it drives now as if it's got a hernia? And I got Aaron David a part-time job down on the eighteenth level, in the boiler room. I figured if Hillel could almost freeze to death on that roof in order to become a scholar, it's no tragedy if my son cooks himself a little bit for the same reason.

It works. My son learns and learns, he begins to have more the walk and talk of a scholar and less the walk and talk of a TV repairman. I learn too, not so much of course, but enough so that I can sweeten my conversation with lines from Ibn Ezra and Mendele Mocher Sforim. I'm not any richer, I'm still a *kasrilik*, a schlemiel, but at least now I'm a bit of an educated schlemiel. And it works also for Rabbi Smallman: he's able to send his family once a year on a vacation to Earth, where they can sit around a piece of lake and see what real water is like in the natural state. I'm happy for him, me and my herniated module. The only thing I'm not happy about is that I still can't see any hope for yeshiva tuition money. But, listen, learning is still learning. As Freud says, just to see from Warsaw to Minsk, even if you don't see right and you don't understand what you see, it's still a great thing.

But who, I ask you, can see from here to Rigel? And on the fourth planet, yet, they'll come here and create such a commotion?

From the Neozionist movement, of course, we had already heard a long time ago. Jews always hear when other Jews are getting together to make trouble for them. We'd heard about Dr. Glickman's book, we'd heard about his being killed by Vegan Dayanists, we'd heard about his followers organizing all over the galaxy—listen, we'd even had a collection box installed in our synagogue by some of his party people here on Venus: "In memory of the heroic Dr. Glickman, and to raise funds to buy back the Holy Land from the Vegan aliens."

With that I have no particular quarrel; I've even dropped a couple of coins myself in the *pushke* from time to time. After all, why shouldn't Milchik the TV man, out of his great wealth, help to buy back the Holy Land?

But the Neozionist movement is another matter. I'm not a coward, and show me a real emergency, I'm ready to die for my people. Outside of an *emergency*—well, we Jews on Venus have learned to keep the tips of our noses carefully under the surface of our burrows. It's not that there's anti-Semitism on Venus—who would ever dream of saying such a thing? When the Viceroy announces five times a week that the reason Venus has an unfavorable balance of trade with other planets is that the Jews are importing too much kosher food: that's not anti-Semitism, that's pure economic analysis. And when his Minister of the Interior sets up a quota for the number of Jews in each burrow and says you can only move from one place to another if you have special permission: that also is not anti-Semitism, obviously, it's efficient administration. What I say is, why upset a government so friendly to the Jews?

There's another thing I don't like about Neozionism; and it's hard to say it out loud, especially to a stranger. This business about going back to Israel. Where else does a Jew belong but in that particular land? Right? Well, I don't know, maybe. We started out there with Abraham, Isaac, and Jacob. No good. So the first time we came back was with Moses, and that lasted for a while—until the Babylonians threw us out. Then we came back under Zerubbabel, and we stayed there for five hundred years—until Titus burned the Temple and the Romans made us leave again. Two thousand years of wandering around the world with nothing more to show for it than Maimonides and Spinoza, Marx and Einstein, Freud and Chagall, and we said, enough is enough, back to Israel. So back we went with Ben-Gurion and Chaim Weizmann and the rest of them. For a couple of centuries we did all right, we only had to worry about forty million Arabs who wanted to kill us, but that's not enough excitement for what God Himself, Blessed be His Name, called on Mount Sinai a "stiff-necked people." We have to get into an argument—in the middle of the Interplanetary Crisis—with Brazil *and* Argentina.

My feeling, I don't know about the rest of the Jews, but I'm getting tired. If no, is no. If out, is out. If goodbye, is goodbye.

That's not the way the Neozionists see it. They feel we've had our rest. Time for another round. "Let the Third Exile end in our lifetimes. Let the Knesset be rebuilt in our age. Israel for the Jews!"

Good enough. Don't we still say, after all the wine, "Next year in Jerusalem"? Who can argue? Except for the one small thing they overlooked, as you know: Israel and Jerusalem these days aren't even for human beings. The Council of Eleven Nations Terrestrial wants no trouble with the Vegans over a sliver of land like Israel, not in these times with what's going on in the galaxy: if both sides in the Vegan Civil War are going to claim the place as holy territory because the men they call the founders of their religions once walked in it, let the bivalves have it, says the Council, let them fight it out between themselves.

And I, Milchik the TV man, I for one see nothing strange in a bunch of Vegan bivalves basing their religion on the life and legend of a particular Jew like Moshe Dayan and wanting to chop up any other Jews who try to return to the land of their ancestors. In the first place, it's happened to us before: to a Jew such an attitude should by now begin to make sense. Where is it written that a Dayanist should like Dayan's relatives? In the second place, how many Jews protested fifty years ago when the other side, the Vegan Omayyads, claimed all human Mohammedans were guilty of sacrilege and expelled them from Jerusalem? Not, I'll admit, that such a protest would have been as noticeable as a ripple in a saucer of tea…

Well, the First Interstellar Neozionist Conference is organized, and it's supposed to meet in Basel, Switzerland, so that, I suppose, history can have a chance to repeat itself. And right away the Dayanist Vegans hear about it and they protest to the Council. Are Vegans honored guests of Earth, or aren't they? Their religion is being mocked, they claim, and they even kill a few Jews to show how aggravated they are. Of course the Jews are accused of inciting a pogrom, and it's announced that in the interests of law and order, not to mention peace and security, no Jewish entrance visas will be honored in spaceports anywhere on Earth. Fair is fair.

Meanwhile delegates to the Conference are on their way from all over the galaxy. If they can't land on Earth, where do they go? And to what site should the Conference be transferred by the authorities?

Where else but to Venus? It's the perfect place for such a conference. The scenery is gorgeous—on the other side of the dust storms—and there's a Viceroy whose administration loves the Jewish people most dearly. Besides, there's a desperate housing shortage on Venus. That will create the kind of problem Jews love to solve: a game of musical burrows.

Listen, it could have been worse. As Esther said to Mordecai when he told her of

Haman's plans to massacre all the Jews of Persia—it could have been worse, but I don't for the moment see exactly how.

So the delegates begin arriving in the Solar System, they're shunted to Venus—and don't ask. Life becomes full of love and bounce for us all. First, a decree comes down. The delegates can't use hotel facilities on Venus, even if they've got the money: there are too many of them, they'll put a strain on the hotel system or something. Next, the Jews of Venus are responsible for their coreligionists. In other words, not only is a Jew naturally a brother to every other Jew, he's now also got to be either a boarder or a landlord.

Stop for a moment and reflect on how many are inflicted upon us. Each and every planet in the galaxy which has a human population has at least a breath, a kiss, of Jewish population. So from this planet comes two delegates, from that one fifteen delegates, from that other one—where there are plenty of Jews, they should live and be healthy, but they disagree with each other—comes a total of sixty-three delegates, organized in eight separate caucuses. It may not be nice to number Jews, even if they're delegates, but you can figure for yourself that by the time the last one has landed at a Venusian spaceport, we've got more than enough to go around.

We've got plenty. And on Venus, you don't go up on the surface and throw together a couple of shacks for the visitors.

The Williamsburg Ashkenazim object. To them, some of these Jews aren't even Jews; they won't let them into their burrows, let alone their homes. After all, Shomrim in khaki pants whose idea of a religious service is to stand around singing *Techezachna*, Reconstructionists who pray from a *siddur* that is rewritten every Monday and Wednesday, Japanese Hasidim who put on *tefillin* once a year at sunset in memory of the Great Conversion of 2112—these are *also* Jews, say the Williamsburg Ashkenazim?

Exactly, these are also Jews, say the government officials of Venus. Brothers and boarders they are, and you will kindly make room for them. And they send in police, and they send in troops. Heads are cracked, beards are torn, life, as I said, is full of love and bounce.

And if you don't object, you think it helps? Sure it helps—like a groan it helps. The Levittown Ashkenazim announce we'll cooperate with the government, we'll provide housing for the delegates to the limit—beyond the limit, even. So what happens? My brother and his family and all their neighbors get evicted from the Kwantung Burrow, it's needed for delegate headquarters says the government.

An Interstellar Neozionist Congress we had to have?

I look around and I remember the promise made to Abraham, Isaac, and Jacob—"I will multiply your seed as the stars of heaven"—and I think to myself, "A promise is a promise, but even a promise can go too far. The stars by themselves are more than enough, but when each star has maybe ten, twenty planets…"

By this time, me and my whole family, we're living in what used to be the kitchen of our apartment. My brother and his family, it's a big family, they should live and be well, they're living in the dining room. In what my wife, Sylvia, calls the parlor, there's the wonder-working rabbi from Procyon XII and his entire court—plus, in one corner of the parlor, there's the correspondent from the *Jewish Sentinel* of Melbourne, Australia, and his wife, and their dog, an Afghan. In the bedrooms—listen, why should I go on? In the bedrooms, there are crowds and arguments and cooking smells that I don't even want to know about.

Enough already? No, I am sorry to tell you, not enough.

One day I go into the bathroom. A man is entitled once in a while to go into the bathroom of his own apartment? It's nature, no? And there in the bathtub I see three creatures, each as long as my arm and as thick as my head. They look like three brown pillows, all wrinkled and twisted, with some big gray spots on this side and on that side, and out of each gray spot there is growing a short gray tentacle. I didn't know what they were, giant cockroaches maybe, or some kind of plant that the delegates living with us brought along as food, but when they moved I let out a yell.

My son, Aaron David, came running into the bathroom. "What's the matter, Papa?"

I pointed to the brown pillows. They had some sort of ladder arrangement set up in the bathtub with small shelves in different places, and they were climbing up and down, up and down. "What's the matter, you want to know, when I see things like that in my bathroom?"

"Oh, them. They're the Bulbas."

"Bulbas?"

"Three of the delegates from the fourth planet of the star Rigel. The other three delegates are down the corridor in the Guttenplans' bathroom."

"Delegates? You mean they're Jewish?" I stared at them. "They don't look Jewish."

Aaron David rolled his eyes up to the ceiling of the bathroom. "Papa, you're so old-fashioned! You yourself told me that the blue Jews from Aldebaran show how adaptable our people are."

"You should pardon me," I said. "You and your adaptable. A Jew can be blue—I don't say I like it, but who am I to argue with somebody else's color scheme?—and a Jew can be tall or short. He can even be deaf from birth like those Jews from Canopus, Sirius, wherever they come from. But a Jew has to have arms and legs. He has to have a face with eyes, a nose, a mouth. It seems to me that's not too much to ask."

"So their mouths are not exactly like our mouths," Aaron David said excitedly. "Is that a crime? Is that any reason to show prejudice?"

I left him and I went to the bathroom in the synagogue. Call me old-fashioned, all right, but there are still boundaries, there are certain places where I have to stop. Here, I have to say, Milchik cannot force himself to be modern.

Well. You know what happened. It turns out I'm not the only one.

I took the day off and went to the first session of the Conference. "Rich man," my Sylvia says to me. "My breadwinner. Family provider. From political conferences you're going to get brides for your three sons?"

"Sylvia," I say to her. "Once in a lifetime my customers can maybe not have clear reception of the news broadcasts and *Captain Iliad*. Once in a lifetime I can go see representatives from all of the Jews of the Galaxy holding a meeting and getting along with each other."

So I went. Only I can't say they got along so good. First there was the demonstration by the Association of Latter-Day Mea Shearim ("If the Messiah appears and starts going from star to star, only to find that all Jews are already on Earth and in Israel..."). When that was quieted down, there was the usual Bronsteinite Trotskyist resolution aimed at the Union of Soviet Uganda and Rhodesia, followed by the usual attempt to excommunicate retroactively the authors of the Simplified Babylonian Talmud that had been published in 2685. Then we had to sit through an hour of discussion about how the very existence of a six-story-high statue of Juan Crevea in Buenos Aires was an affront and an insult and an agony to every Jew, and how we should all boycott Argentinian products until the statue was pulled down. I agreed with what the chairman said when he managed to rule the discussion out of order: "We cannot allow ourselves to be distracted by such ancient agonies, such stale affronts. If we do, where do we begin and where do we stop? Let Argentina have its statue of Crevea, let Düsseldorf have its Adolf Hitler University, let Egypt and Libya continue to maintain the Torquemada Observatory on Pluto. This is not our business here today."

At last, finally, after all the traditional Jewish preliminaries, they got down to the real problems of the opening session: the accreditation of delegates. And there, in no time at all, they got stuck. They got stuck and all mixed up, like bits of lox in a lox omelette.

The Bulbas. The three from my bathroom, the three from Max Guttenplan's bathroom—the total delegation from Rigel IV.

No question about their credentials, said the Committee on Accreditation. Their credentials are in order, and they're certainly delegates. The only thing is, they can't be Jews.

And why can't we be Jews, the six Bulbas wanted to know? And here I had to stand up to get a good look, I could hardly believe my eyes. Because guess who their interpreter was? No one else but my son, my *kaddish*, my Aaron David. Mr. Show-No-Prejudice in person.

"Why can't you be Jews? Because," says the Committee Chairman, stuttering with wet lips and plucking at the air with his right hand, "because Jews can be this, can be that. They can be a lot of things. But, first of all, they have to be human."

"You will kindly point out to us," the Bulbas say through my son, the interpreter, "where it says and in which book that Jews have to be human. Name an authority, provide a quotation."

At this point the Deputy Chairman comes up and apologizes to the Chairman of the Committee. The Deputy Chairman is the kind who wins scholarships and fellowships. "You'll pardon me," he says, "but you're not making it clear. It's a very simple matter, really." He turns to the Bulbas. "No one can be a Jew," he explains to the six of them, "who is not the child of a Jewish mother. That's the most ancient, most fundamental definition of a Jew."

"Aha," say the Bulbas. "And from what do you get the impression that we are *not* the children of Jewish mothers? Will you settle for the copies of our birth certificates that we brought along with us?"

That's when the meeting falls apart. A bunch of delegates in khakis starts cheering and stamping their feet. Another bunch with fur hats and long earlocks begins screaming that this whole colloquy is an abomination. All over the hall arguments break out, little clusters of argument between two and three people, big clusters of argument between twenty and thirty people, arguments on biology, on history, on the *Baba M'tziya*. The man sitting next to me, a fat, squinty-eyed man to whom I haven't said a word, suddenly turns to me and pushes his forefinger into my chest and says: "But if you take that position, my dear fellow, how in the world can you make it compatible with the well-known decision, to mention just one example—" And up on the platform, Bronsteinite Trotskyists have seized control of the public-address system and are trying to reintroduce their resolution on Uganda and Rhodesia.

By the time some kind of order is restored, two blue Jews have been carried away to the hospital and a lawyer from Ganymede has been arrested for using a hearing aid as a deadly weapon.

Someone calls for a vote, by the entire Congress, on the accreditation of the Bulbas. Accreditation as what—someone else wants to know—as delegates or as Jews? They've been accepted as delegates, and who are we to pass upon them as Jews? I'll accept them as Jews in the religious sense, someone else stands up to point out, but not in the biological sense. What kind of biological sense, he's asked by a delegate from across the hall; you don't mean biology, you mean race, you racist. All right, all right, cries out a little man who's sitting in front of him, but would you want your sister to marry one?

It's obvious that there are as many opinions as there are delegates. And the chairman, up there on the platform, he's standing there and he doesn't know what to do.

Suddenly I notice one of the Bulbas is climbing up on the platform. These little tentacles, they use them for everything, for walking, for eating, for talking, for I don't know what. And this Bulba, he gets to the public-address system, and he vibrates one short tentacle for a while, and finally we hear what he says, faint and very soft. We hear that funny voice, like a piece of paper rustling, all through the hall:

"*Modeh ani l'fonecha.*"

The line, just translated by itself, may not mean so much—"Here I am standing before you" or "I present myself before you"—but what Jew, even with only a fingernail's worth of religious background, could not be moved by it, delivered in such a way and at such a time? *Modeh ani l'fonecha,* the Jew says in the prayer, when he is directly addressing God, blessed be His Name. And that's what we all of us now hear in the hall.

Don't talk to me about race, the Bulba is actually saying, don't talk to me about religion, don't talk to me about any legal or philosophical technicalities. I claim that I am a Jew, whatever a Jew is, essentially and spiritually. As Jews, do you accept me or reject me?

No one can answer.

Of course, all this is not getting the Congress any closer to Israel, to a return from the Third Exile. But it's obvious on the one hand that the matter can't be put on the table, and it's obvious on the other hand that it can't be taken off the table. This is not quite the kind of *pilpul* that our learned ancestors had to deal with. We have to find out: what is a Space Age Jew?

So, by general agreement it is decided that as Moses smote the rock to get water, we're going to smite a High Rabbinical Court to get wisdom.

A High Rabbinical Court is appointed by the Accreditation Committee. It has the kind of membership that will satisfy everybody at least a little bit, even if it means that the members of the Court won't want to talk to each other. You know, a kind of kosher smorgasbord. There's the rabbi his followers call the Gaon of Tau Ceti. There's the president of the Unitarian Jewish Theological Seminary. There's the Borneo Mystic Rabbi. There's a member of the chalutziot rabbinate, with his bare chest and rolled-up sleeves. And so on, and so on. There are two women rabbis, one to satisfy the majority Reconstructionist sect, and the other to keep the Miami Ashkenazim happy. And finally, because this is Venus, there's a rabbi from Venus: Rabbi Joseph Smallman.

You want to know something? It's not only because he's from Venus, no matter what the Committee Chairman says. The Bulbas have been insisting that they're entitled to a rabbi who in some way will represent them, and suddenly they want that to be Rabbi Smallman. I can tell what's going on from where I sit, I can see my son with his big mop of black hair going from one Bulba to another, arguing, explaining, urging. He's talking them into it, that Aaron David of mine. He's become the floor manager at the nominating convention of a political party.

"We did it!" he says to me that night in the apartment. His eyes are dancing like meteors. "We got Rabbi Smallman on the Rabbinical Court."

I try to calm him down. "That by itself is not yet the equivalent of crossing the Red Sea on dry land, or of the oil which renewed itself night after night. Just because Rabbi Smallman can push a black hair into a dent, you think he can push Jews into accepting six lumpy brown pillows as fellow Jews?"

"He can if anyone can."

"And if anyone can, why should he? Why should he even try to do such a thing?"

My son gave me the kind of look you give a doctor who tells you he wants to spray disease germs at the electric fan. "Why, Papa! For the sake of justice."

When a son makes a father feel ashamed of himself, the father has a right to feel proud too. I sat down in a corner of the kitchen while Aaron David went into the bathroom to hold a consultation with his brown Bulbas.

But let me tell you, I also felt sad. The wisdom of The Preacher I don't quite have, but one thing I've learned. Whenever someone uses the word "justice," sooner or later there's going to be a split head or a broken heart.

From that day on, every free second I had, I rushed off to Decatur Burrow to attend the sessions of the High Rabbinical Court. Sylvia found out about it and my life was not easy. "While you're studying this new trade, you and that son of yours," she said, "someone's got to work at the old one. You'll be a judge, he'll be a district attorney, so I'll have to be the TV man. Give me a pair of pliers and the Index to the Printed Circuits, and I'll go out and make a living."

"Woman," I told her, "I'm doing my work and my son's work, and I'm keeping food on the table. If the customers don't complain, why should you? I don't get drunk, I don't take drugs. I'm entitled to nourish my spirit at the feet of scholars and wise men."

Sylvia looked up at the ceiling and clasped her hands together. "He can't nourish first a couple of daughters-in-law into the house?" she asked the ceiling. "That's a procedure that is specifically forbidden by the holy books?"

No, my life was not easy. Why should I tell you otherwise?

But what was going on in the Decatur Burrow was so interesting I could hardly sit still while I listened to it. It was like a legend had come to life, it was like watching the golem taking a stroll one day in downtown Prague, it was like coming across the River Sabbathion and seeing it boil and bubble and throw up stones every day in the week but Saturday. Such history as the Bulbas told the Rabbinical Court!

They'd come to the fourth planet of the star Rigel maybe seven, eight hundred years ago in one of the first star ships. Originally, they had been a small orthodox community living in Paramus, New Jersey, and the whole community had been expelled to make way for a new approach to the George Washington Bridge. So they had to go somewhere, right? So why not Rigel? In those days a trip to another solar system took almost a whole lifetime, children were born on the way, people had to live, you know, close. The star ship foundations were advertising for people who already got along with each other, who were living in groups—political groups, religious groups, village groups. The Paramus, New Jersey, people weren't the only ones who went out in a star ship looking for a quiet place where they'd be left alone. That's how the galaxy came to be so full of Amish and Mennonites, Black Muslims and Bangladesh intellectuals, and these old-fashioned polygamous Mormons who spit three times when you mention Salt Lake City.

The only trouble was that the one halfway comfortable planet in the Rigel system already had an intelligent race living on it, a race of brown creatures with short gray tentacles who called themselves Bulbas. They were mostly peasants living off the land, and they'd just begun their industrial revolution. They had at most a small factory here, a mill or two, and a small smelting plant there. The Jews from Paramus, New Jersey, had been hoping for a planet all to themselves, but the Bulbas made them so welcome, the Bulbas wanted them so much to settle on their planet and bring in trade with the rest of the galaxy, that they looked at each other and they said, why not?

So the Jews settled there. They built a small commercial spaceport, and they built houses, and they fixed up a *shul* and a *heder* and a teenage recreation center. *Nu*, they called the place home.

At this point in the story, one of the rabbinical judges leaned forward and interrupted. "But while this was going on, you looked like Jews? I mean, the kind of Jews we're familiar with?"

"Well, more or less. What we looked like particularly, we understand, was Jews from New Jersey."

"That's close enough. Continue."

For a hundred, a hundred and fifty years, there was happiness and prosperity. The Jews thrived, the Bulbas thrived, and there was peace between them. But you know what Isaac Leib Peretz says about the town of Tzachnovka? "It hangs by nothing." Every Jewish community, everywhere, hangs by nothing. And, unfortunately, nothing is not so strong. Sooner or later it gives way.

With the Jews to help them, the Bulbas began to become important. They built more factories, more smelting plants, they built banks and computer centers and automobile junkyards. They began to have big wars, big depressions, big political dictatorships. And they began to wonder why they were having them.

Is there any other answer to such a question? There's only one answer. The Jews, naturally. Philosophers and rabble-rousers pointed out that before the Jews came there'd been no such trouble. The Jews were responsible for everything. So Rigel IV had its first pogrom.

And after the government had apologized, and helped the Jews to bury their dead, and even offered to pay for some repairs, twenty or thirty years later there was a second pogrom. And then there was a third pogrom, and a fourth pogrom. By this time, the government was no longer apologizing, and it was the Jews who were paying for repairs.

Now there came ghettos, there came barring from certain occupations, there even came, from time to time, concentration camps. Not that it was all terrible: there were pleasant interludes. A government of murderers would be followed by a halfway decent government, a government, say, of just maimers. The Jews sank into the position of the Jews who lived in Yemen and Morocco a thousand years ago, in the eighteenth and nineteenth centuries. They did the dirtiest, most poorly paid work of all. Everybody spit at them, and they spit at themselves.

But Jews they remained. They continued their religious studies, even though, on the whole planet by this time, there was not one set of the Talmud without missing books, there was not one Torah scroll without empty spaces. And the centuries went by, and they knew wars and tyrannies, devastations and exterminations. Until recently, when a new, enlightened government had come to power over all of Rigel IV. It had restored citizenship to the Jews and allowed them to send a delegation to the Neozionist Congress.

The only trouble was that by this time, after all they'd been through, they looked like just plain Bulbas. And they looked like the weakest, poorest Bulbas of all, Bulbas of the very lowest class.

But in the past couple of months they'd learned that this sort of thing had happened to other Jews, in other places. Jews tended to blend into their environment. After all, hadn't there been blonde Jews in Germany, redheaded Jews in Russia, black Jews—the Falashas—in Ethiopia, tall Mountain Jews in the Caucasus who had been as fine horsemen and marksmen as their neighbors? Hadn't there been Jews who had settled in China far back in the Han Dynasty and who were known in the land as the "T'ai Chin Chiao"? What about the blue Jews sitting in this very Congress? And for that matter—

Another interruption. "These are normal physiological changes that can be explained on a reasonable genetic basis."

If it's possible for a brown cushion with short gray tentacles to look shocked, this brown cushion with short gray tentacles looked shocked. "Are you suggesting that such Jews—the Chinese Jews, the Russian Jews—intermarried and were allowed to remain within the congregation?"

"No, but there are other possibilities. Rape, for example."

"So much rape? Again and again?"

The judges muttered to each other uncomfortably. Then:

"In other words, despite your appearance, you are asking us to believe that you are Jews, and not Bulbas?"

The brown cushion stretched forward with all of its tentacles. "No, we are asking you to believe that we are Bulbas. *Jewish* Bulbas."

And it explained about the genealogical charts it was offering in evidence. The most prized possession of every Jewish family on Rigel IV was its genealogical chart. These records had been preserved intact through fires and wars and pogroms, no matter what else had been destroyed. No Jewish wedding ever took place on Rigel IV unless both parties could produce thoroughly validated genealogical charts. Through them, each Jewish Bulba could trace his ancestry back to the very first settlers on the planet.

"I, for example," the speaker said proudly, "I, Yitzhak ben Pinchas, am the direct descendant of Melvin Cohen, the assistant manager of a supermarket in Paramus, New Jersey."

And the argument got thicker and thicker. How is it possible, the judges wanted to know, for such tremendous changes to take place? Isn't it more likely that at some time or another all the Jews on Rigel IV were wiped out and that then there was a mass conversion of some sort, similar to the one experienced among the Khazars of the eighth century and the Japanese later? No, said the Bulbas, if you knew what conditions have been like for Jews on Rigel IV you wouldn't talk about mass conversions to Judaism. That would have been mass insanity. All that happened is that we began as ordinary Jews, we had a lot of trouble, a lot of time went by, and when it was all over *this* is what we looked like.

"But that denies the experimental facts of biology!"

The Bulbas were very reproachful. "Who are you going to believe, the experimental facts of biology—or your fellow Jews?"

And that was just the first day. I got back to my apartment and I told my brother all about it. We began discussing the case. He took one side and I took the other. In a few minutes, I was waving my fist in his face and he was screaming that I was "an idiot, an animal!" From the next room we heard the wonder-working rabbi from Procyon XII trying to quiet down a similar argument among the members of his court.

"They want to be Jews," my brother yelled at me, "let them convert to Judaism. Then they'll be Jews. Not before."

"Murderer!" I said to him. "Dolt of dolts! How can they convert to Judaism when they're already Jews? Such a conversion would be a filthy, shameful mockery!"

"Without a conversion I absolutely refuse to go up on the *bima* and read a portion with one of them. Without a conversion they cannot join my *minyan,* even if no matter where I look I can't come up with more than nine men. Without a conversion, even if I'm celebrating a circumcision ceremony for a son—" He broke off, his eyes got suddenly calmer, more thoughtful. "How do they circumcise, do you suppose, Milchik? Where and *what* do they circumcise?"

"They cut off a very little bit from the tip of their shortest tentacle, Uncle Fleischik," said my Aaron David, who'd just walked in. "It's a fold of flesh that looks a lot like a foreskin. Besides, you know, only one drop of blood is required by the Covenant. Blood they got."

"A new speciality," said Sylvia as she put out the supper. "*Now,* God be praised and thanked, my son is a *mohel.*"

Aaron David kissed her. "Put my supper aside until later, Mamma. Me and the Bulbas are going to meet with Rabbi Smallman in his study."

Let me tell you, maybe my son was no longer the interpreter since the Bulbas had found voices, but he was still their floor manager. Every day I could see him jumping from one to the other while the case was being discussed. Something special has to be looked up? They need a copy of Rov Chaim Mordecai Brecher's *Commentary on the Book of Ruth?* Who goes running out of the hall to get it but my Aaron David?

After all, that turns out to be a very important issue. Ruth was a Moabite, and from her came eventually King David. And how about Ezra and the problem of the Jewish men who took Canaanite wives? And where do you fit the Samaritans in all this? Jewish women, you'll remember, were not allowed to marry Samaritans. And what does Maimonides have to say on the subject? Maimonides is always Maimonides.

I tell you, day after day, it was like the dream of my life to listen to all those masters and sages.

And then the Court comes through time to the formation of the Jewish State in the twentieth century. All those problem cases when the Ingathering began. The Bene-Israel Jews, for example, of Bombay. The other Indians called them *Shanwar Teles,* "Saturday oilmen," and they were supposed to have arrived in India as a result of the invasion of Palestine by Antiochus Epiphanes. Almost all they remembered of Judaism was the *Shema,* and there were two castes who didn't intermarry, one white, one black. Were they really Jewish? Were both castes Jewish? And how do you prove it?

And more up-to-date, more complicated discussions. The Japanese and the Conversion of 2112, and the results among Jews of the *Ryo-Ritsu* tractates. The Mars-Sirius controversy and the whole problem of the blue Jews. The attitude of the Lubavitchers toward Sebastian Pombal—let Pombal and Crevea, I say, lie deep, *deep* in the ground— and what that meant to Israel as an independent state.

It all comes down to: What is a Jew?

So one of the Bulbas can say, in that thin, rustling voice: "Do not put me in the position of the Wicked Son in the *Haggadah.* Do not put me in the state of *yotzei min haklal,* one who departs from the Congregation. I have said *we* to my people; I have not said *you.*" So he quotes from the Passover service, and all of us have a catch in our throat and tears on our face. But it still comes down to: What is a Jew? Wherefore is this people different from every other people?

And you know something? That's not an easy question to answer. Not with all the different kinds of Jews you've got around today.

So the Court can move into other, even more tangled-up places. It can weigh the definition of a human being that was worked out by the Council of Eleven Nations Terrestrial, during the Sagittarian War. It can look at Napoleon's questions on inter-marriage and the answers of the Paris Sanhedrin of 1807. It can turn at last to *Cabala,* even if three of its members don't want to, and ask about the problem of monster births that are brought on by cohabitation with the Children of Lilith. But in the end it has to decide what a Jew is, once and for all—or it has to find some kind of new way out.

Rabbi Smallman found some kind of new way out. On Venus, I'm telling you, have we got a rabbi!

Since this was a special court, set up under special circumstances, facing a question nobody had ever faced before, I expected more than one decision. I expected sweet and sour decisions, hot decisions and cold decisions, chopped decisions and marinated decisions. I was sure we'd see them "confound there their language, that they may not understand one another's speech." But no. Rabbi Smallman argued with each and all, and he brought them around to one point of view, and he wrote most of what was the final judgment. To bring a bunch of Jews—and learned Jews!—to a single decision, that, my friend, is an achievement that can stand.

All through the case, whenever an argument broke out between the judges, and it looked like we were going to spend a couple of weeks on whether it was a black thread or a white thread, you'd see Rabbi Smallman scratch the red pimple on the side of his nose and say that maybe we could all agree on the fact that at least it was a piece of thread? And I got the impression—I admit it's a father speaking—that he looked at my Aaron David, and that my Aaron David nodded. This was even before they came in with a judgment.

Of course, between us, they knew they had to come in with a *something.* The Congress was at a standstill, the delegates didn't know how many delegates there were, and they were arguing the matter out every day along with the Court. There were fights over the Bulbas, there were factions over the Bulbas, and a lot of people had gone home already saying they were sick and tired of the Bulbas.

So.

The decision reviewed all the evidence, all the commentaries, all the history, from Ezra and Nehemia on. It showed what was to be said for the conservative group in the Court, the group which began and ended with the traditional proposition that a Jew is someone who is provably the child of a Jewish mother. Then it went into what was to be said for the liberal-radical wing, the people who felt that a Jew is anyone who freely accepts the *ol,* the yoke, the burden, of Jewishness. And then the decision discussed a couple of positions in between, and it pointed out that there was no way to sew them all together.

But do they have to be sewn together? Is there any chance that a human being and a Bulba will mate? And what happens if we go deeper and deeper into space, to another galaxy even, and we find all kinds of strange creatures who want to become Jews? Suppose we find a thinking entity whose body is nothing but waves of energy, do we say, no, you're entirely unacceptable? Do we know for sure that it is?

Look at it another way. Among human beings there are Jews and there are *goyim*, gentiles. Between Jews there are a lot of different types, Reformed, blue, Levittown, Williamsburg, and they don't get along with each other so good, but measure them against *goyim* and they're all Jews. Between Jew and *goy* there are a lot of differences, but measure them against any alien and they're both human beings. The word *goy* does not apply to aliens. *Up to recently.*

We've all seen, in the last century or two, how some creatures from the star Vega have adopted an Earth-type religion, two different Earth-type religions, in fact. They won't let Jews into the land of Israel, they maneuver against us, they persecute us. Are these ordinary aliens, then? Certainly not! They may look nonhuman, like crazy giant oysters, but they definitely have to be put into the category of *goyische* aliens. Aliens may be aliens, but the Vegans are quite different as far as Jews are concerned: the Vegans are alien *goyim*.

Well, if there are alien *goyim*, why can't there be alien Jews? We don't expect human *goyim* to marry alien *goyim*, and we don't expect human Jews to marry alien Jews. But we can certainly face the fact that there are aliens who live as we do, who face problems as we do, and—if you won't mind—who worship as we do. There are aliens who know what a pogrom tastes like, and who also know the sweetness of our Sabbath. Let's put it this way: there are Jews—and there are Jews. The Bulbas belong in the second group.

These are not the exact words of the decision, you understand. It's a kind of free translation, provided for you with no extra charge by Milchik the TV man. But it gives you enough to gnaw on.

Not everyone went along with the decision. Some of the Bulbas complained. And a whole bunch of Williamsburgniks walked out of the Congress saying, Well, what could you expect? But the majority of the delegates were so happy to have the thing settled at last that they voted to let the decision stand and to accept the Bulbas. So the Bulbas were also happy: they were full Jewish delegates.

The only trouble was, just as they were finally getting down to the business of the Congress, an order came down from the Viceroy of Venus abolishing it. He said the Congress had gone on too long and it was stirring up bad feelings. All the delegates were sent packing.

Some excitement for a planet like this, no? Rabbi Smallman is still our rabbi, even though he's famous now. He's always going away on lecture tours, from one end of the galaxy to the other. But he always comes back to us, every year, for the High Holy Days. Well, not exactly, you know how it is, once in a while he can't make it. A celebrity, after all. The Great Rabbi of Venus. He's in demand.

And so's my Aaron David, in a way. He finally made it to a yeshiva. The Bulbas are paying for it, they sent him to one on the other side of Venus, in the Yoruba Burrow. Once in a while I get a letter from him. What he plans to do, it's the agreement he has with them, he's going to go to Rigel IV and be their rabbi.

But of a possible bride he says nothing. Listen, maybe I'll turn out to be the grandfather of a lumpy brown pillow with short gray tentacles? A grandchild, I guess, is still a grandchild.

I don't know. Let's talk about something cheerful. How many people would you say were killed in that earthquake on Callisto?

AFTERWORD

Some time in late 1973, I was introduced to Jack Dann and George Zebrowski at a science-fiction convention. They impressed me mightily: they were a new young breed of science-fiction writer whose interests were as heavily literary as they were scientific.

And it didn't hurt at all that they thought highly of me and my work.

They asked me why I wasn't still writing. Several reasons, I told them: First, that the teaching I was now doing at Penn State was the only experience that gave me as much fulfillment and satisfaction as the act of artistic creation. Second, before I met them and heard their praise, I had thought I was completely forgotten by the genre. Finally, there was not much market for the fiction I wanted to write these days, especially for a specific story whose title was all I had but which had been on my mind for many months.

"What title?" they asked.

I told them. Jack Dann immediately said he had been brooding about an anthology for a year or more into which a story with that title would fit beautifully.

"Sell that anthology," I said, "and I'll write the story for you."

Well, he did, and I did. Harper and Row decided to publish *Wandering Stars* and commissioned me (*commissioned!*, did you hear *that*, my pulp-writer colleagues from the forties and fifties—Ted Sturgeon, Lester del Rey, Fred Brown, Cyril Kornbluth—*commissioned*, requested specifically, and paid for in advance!, like a goddam oratorio by a goddam Handel) to write a story that went with the title, "On Venus, Have We Got a Rabbi."

In 1974, Gerald Walker, one of the editors at *The New York Times Magazine*, who was going to be out of town, offered me and Fruma something extraordinary: the use of his air-conditioned West Side of Manhattan apartment for the whole summer. Instead of sweltering through my non-teaching months in State College, Pennsylvania, what a time we would have, my wife and I told each other. What theaters we would go to, what museums we would ramble through, what New York old friends we would entertain!

What nonsense. I spent the summer behind Gerald Walker's typewriter desk, writing and rewriting, and *rewriting* the story. And Fruma spent the summer almost always at my side, reading, and rereading, and criticizing. And getting yelled at for being too critical.

The story turned out to be a small monument to Sholem Aleichem, the nineteenth-century writer who was known as the Yiddish Mark Twain (although the generous Twain always insisted that *he* was known as the American Sholem Aleichem). I asked myself what kind of science-fiction story might Sholem Aleichem have written if he were alive today? I used several of Sholem Aleichem's characters and stories as models, particularly his "Modern Children." My ending is really one of Sholem Aleichem's endings, only very slightly changed. And I mention the name of almost every single famous Yiddish writer in my story. Except, very noticeably, for one.

The only one I don't mention in "On Venus, Have We Got a Rabbi," is Sholem Aleichem. How could I? After all, it's his story as much as it is mine.

WRITTEN 1974——PUBLISHED 1974

ॐ

Colophon

This book was set entirely in typefaces from the Adobe Minion font. Minion is a 1990 Adobe Originals font designed by Robert Slimbach, inspired by the classical typefaces of the late Renaissance.

The text was entered and set on a Compaq Presario running Windows NT, using Microsoft Word 7.0 and Adobe PageMaker 6.5. The dust jacket was created on a Macintosh G3 running PageMaker 6.01 and PhotoShop 5.5. The book was printed and bound by Sheridan Books in Chelsea, Michigan.

The New England
Science Fiction Association (NESFA)
and NESFA Press

Recent books from NESFA Press:

- *The Complete Short SF of Fredric Brown* $29.00
- *Quartet* by George R. R. Martin $25.00
- *Major Ingredients* by Eric Frank Russell $29.00
- *Shards of Honor* by Lois McMaster Bujold $22.00
- *Moon Dogs* by Michael Swanwick $22.00
- *The Essential Hal Clement, Volume III* $25.00
- *The Compleat Boucher: The Complete SF of Anthony Boucher* $25.00
- *Frankensteins and Foreign Devils* by Walter Jon Williams $23.00
- *First Contacts: The Essential Murray Leinster* $27.00
- *His Share of Glory: The Complete Short SF of C. M. Kornbluth* $27.00
- *Ingathering: The Complete People Stories of Zenna Henderson* $25.00

Find details and many more books on our web page: www.nesfa.org/press

Books may be ordered by writing to:
NESFA Press
PO Box 809
Framingham, MA 01701

We accept checks, Visa, or MasterCard. Please add $2.50 postage and handling per order.

The New England Science Fiction Association:

NESFA is an all-volunteer, non-profit organization of science fiction and fantasy fans. Besides publishing, our activities include running Boskone (New England's oldest SF convention) in February each year, producing a semi-monthly newsletter, holding discussion groups relating to the field, and hosting a variety of social events. If you are interested in learning more about us, we'd like to hear from you. Write to our address above!